THE STATION HILL
BLANCHOT
READER

✦

THE STATION HILL
BLANCHOT
READER

✦

Fiction & Literary Essays

Maurice Blanchot

TRANSLATED BY Lydia Davis
Paul Auster and Robert Lamberton
FOREWORD BY Christopher Fynsk
AFTERWORD BY George Quasha & Charles Stein
EDITED BY George Quasha

STATION HILL
─────────────
BARRYTOWN. LTD.

Published under the Station Hill Arts imprint of Barrytown, Ltd. in conjunction with Station Hill Press, Inc., Barrytown, New York 12507, as a project of The Institute for Publishing Arts, Inc., a not-for-profit, federally tax exempt, educational organization.

Online catalogue and purchasing: http://www.stationhill.org
E-mail: Publishers@stationhill.org

Book design and typesetting by Chie Hasegawa with assistance from Susan Quasha
Cover design by Susan Quasha

Grateful acknowledgement is due to the National Endowment for the Arts, a Federal agency in Washington, DC, and to the New York State Council on the Arts for partial financial support of the publishing program of The Institute for Publishing Arts and of the individual books in this collection in their original Station Hill Press publication, as well as support of some of the translations.

Library of Congress Cataloging-in-Publication Data

Blanchot, Maurice.
      [Selections. English. 1998]
      The Station Hill Blanchot reader: fiction & literary essays / by Maurice Blanchot; edited by George Quasha; translated by Lydia Davis, Paul Auster, & Robert Lamberton; Foreword by Christopher Fynsk; publisher's afterword by George Quasha & Charles Stein.
        p. cm.
      ISBN 1-886449-17-1
      I. Quasha, George. II. Davis, Lydia. III. Auster, Paul, 1947-. IV. Lamberton, Robert. V. Title.
PQ2603.L3343A6 1998
843'.912—dc21
                                            99-26242
                                                CIP

Contents

ACKNOWLEDGEMENTS

Grateful acknowledgement is due to the following publishers for the right to translate and publish works of Maurice Blanchot in English:

EDITIONS GALLIMARD

Thomas l'obscur, copyright © 1941 by Editions Gallimard.
L'Arrêt de mort, copyright © 1948 by Editions Gallimard.
Au moment voulu, copyright © 1951 by Editions Gallimard.
Celui qui ne m'accompagnait pas, copyright © 1953 by Editions Gallimard.

The translations of the essays from *The Gaze of Orpheus* are based on the French editions copyright © 1943, 1949, 1955, 1959, 1969 by Editions Gallimard, as follows:

"De l'Angoisse au langage" from *Faux Pas* (1943); "Littérature et le droit à la mort" from *La Part du feu* (1949); "La Solitude essentielle," "Le Regard d'Orphée," "Lire," and "Les Deux Versions de l'imaginaire" from *L'Espace littéraire* (1955); "Le Chant des Sirènes" and "La Puissance et la gloire" from *Le Livre à venir* (1959); "La Voix narrative" and "L'Absence du livre" from *L'Entretien infini* (1969).

EDITIONS DE MINUIT

Le Ressassement éternel, copyright © 1951 and as *Après coup* © 1983 by Editions de Minuit.

EDITIONS FATA MORGANA

La Folie du jour, copyright © 1973 by Editions Fata Morgana.

Copyright for the English translations is as follows:

Thomas the Obscure, copyright © 1973, 1988, 1999 by Robert Lamberton, published by arrangement with David Lewis, Inc.
Vicious Circle: Two Fictions & "After the Fact," copyright © 1985, 1999 by Paul Auster.
Death Sentence, copyright © 1978, 1998, 1999 by Lydia Davis.
The Madness of the Day, copyright © 1981, 1999 by Lydia Davis.
When the Time Comes, copyright © 1985, 1999 by Lydia Davis.
The One Who Was Standing Apart From Me, copyright © 1993, 1999 by Lydia Davis.
The Gaze of Orpheus and Other Literary Essays, copyright © 1981, 1999 by Lydia Davis.

Quotations from Hegel are from A.V. Miller's translation, *Phenomenology of Spirit* (Oxford: Oxford University Press, 1977).

LIST OF TRANSLATIONS
BY TRANSLATOR

Paul Auster

Vicious Circles: Two Fictions & "After the Fact"
IDYLL
LAST WORD

After the Fact

Robert Lamberton

Thomas The Obscure

Lydia Davis

Death Sentence
The Madness of The Day
When the Time Comes
The One Who Was Standing Apart From Me

FROM *The Gaze of Orpheus and Other Literary Essays:*

"From Dread to Language"
"Literature and the Right to Death"
"The Essential Solitude"
"Two Versions of the Imaginary"
"Reading"
"The Gaze of Orpheus"
"The Song of the Sirens"
"The Power and the Glory"
"The Narrative Voice"
"The Absence of the Book"

Publisher's Preface

The Station Hill Blanchot Reader comprises most of the books by Maurice Blanchot that Station Hill has published, and for us it is an appropriate way of celebrating two decades of publishing. *Death Sentence* (1978) was, after all, the Press's first full-length book. This fact underscores the great significance Blanchot has had for us in the development of our publishing program, all the more so in light of the present collection. Editing this edition has given us the opportunity to reread and rethink an astonishing body of work. We have always expected that, among the hundreds of books published, a certain number would remain fresh; but we were frankly unprepared for how much the whole of Blanchot's work continuously reinvents itself according to one's own capacity for "further reading"—reading "beyond oneself." By the *whole* of his work we of course mean not only the books published at Station Hill, but also the impressive number of his books to come into English very soon after the first three—that is, after 1981. These three—*Death Sentence, The Madness of the Day,* and *The Gaze of Orpheus and Other Literary Essays*—were the first books of Blanchot in English to go into full trade distribution. Of these, the first two, along with *Vicious Circles: Two Fictions and "After the Fact"* (1985), *When the Time Comes* (1985), *Thomas the Obscure* (1988),[1] and *The One Who Was Standing Apart from Me* (1993), are fiction, essentially what Blanchot has called *récits* (translatable variously as tale, telling, narrative, story, even recital, but in any case distinguished from novel).[2]

Thus most of the present book is in fact literary fiction, comprising most of the works Blanchot directly characterized as *récits. The Gaze of Orpheus,* most of which is reprinted here, is entirely non-fiction, what, for convenience, we have called literary essays. The two sections of this book, Fiction and Literary Essays, are arranged chronologically according to date of first publication; the exception is the "two fictions" of *Vicious Circles,* written in his 1935-36, so placed at the beginning here (discussed by Blanchot in his 1983 essay, "After the Fact," the latest text in the present book, placed at the end).[3] Also somewhat exceptional is *The Madness of the Day,* generally read in the 1973 version included here (Editions Fata Morgana), but arranged now according to the date of its 1949 magazine publication under the title, *"Un récit?"*

Each piece in the book, fiction and non-fiction alike, stands alone as a literary work.[4] *The Station Hill Blanchot Reader* is not a "thesis" book except in our saying that these works deserve to be read each in its own right and as the literary instance of itself—each for its own particular power. Such reading—reading that stays, as it were, *in the open*, remaining unencumbered by interpretation or contextualization—protects the free "space of literature" (in Blanchot's phrase) necessary for this work to be what it really is—*work so truly itself that it goes beyond itself.* There are many genuine ways of reading and interpreting Blanchot and the questions raised by his thought—deconstructive, historical/political, and so forth, and indeed a number of excellent discussions are now available.[5] But to enter a work by Blanchot armed from the start with a critical perspective violates the free and inquiring nature of his self-revolutional text. The text is first of all a mystery. It wants to be *read* pure and simple—for which one can receive no wiser counsel than Blanchot's own essay "Reading."

At the same time, it is the right of (maybe even a necessity for) any true reader of Blanchot to develop a working "theory of reading" the text. Certainly we have come to read him in a somewhat special way, which we sometimes think of as a poet's way, by way of poetics and, most especially, of *metapoetics*, the self-transformative. We mention this here to signal again Blanchot's importance for us in the context of Station Hill's history and development, and also to point to our own statement laying out a metapoetic view—of the *axial* and the *liminal*—which we have confined to an Afterword, "Publishing Blanchot in America." We have no wish to put our own view before the work itself. The force of Blanchot's text in fact may be, to a truly extraordinary degree, its power to generate *readings*, the plural voice in one's head that alone gives reading an ontological role like none other.

We are very grateful for Christopher Fynsk's Foreword which so spaciously prepares the ground for what follows. Like his own *Language and Relation: ...that there is language,* it puts us in a mind of realizing the barely audible urgency of Blanchot's invitation to read. We are personally grateful for Christopher Fynsk's support and gentle guidance in the preparation of this book.

To thank Maurice Blanchot at this point strains the performative value of words, yet the impulse is too strong to ignore. His generosity—perhaps the quality most frequently mentioned among his translators and friends—has been for twenty years the background support of the project of publishing him.

In the same spirit we feel indebted to the three remarkable writer/ translators to whom our opportunity here to read Blanchot in English literally owes everything: Lydia Davis, Robert Lamberton, Paul Auster. In addition to graciously carrying out the notoriously hard work of translating Blanchot—with celebrated brilliant results—they have always been supportive of each other's work and of the difficulties of independent publishing.

Thanks are due to P. Adams Sitney for urging us in 1977 to publish Blanchot, for editing *The Gaze Orpheus and Other Literary Essays* and for reading and helping revise the translations therein. On that book, Robert Lamberton generously served as translation text editor, "the book's essential critic" according to Lydia Davis. Paul Auster offered consultation, and Michael Coffey brought his copyediting and proofreading skills to the type in that book.

Publishing at Station Hill has always been collaborative, as has editing our series of books by Maurice Blanchot.[6] Many hands have touched these books in their making—too many to acknowledge more than a few individually: Patricia Nedds bravely printed the first few Blanchot titles in our Open Studio Print Shop—at the beginning, when we thought that we had to do everything ourselves. Susan Quasha, copublisher from the beginning, co-designed most of the books. For the present collection, Chie Hasegawa did the typesetting; Merabi Uridia and Siu Yuen contributed to our collective proofreading of the book.

Charles Stein has been my partner in every aspect of bringing this project to fruition, and of course he is co-author of the Afterword. To thank a true dialogical companion is curiously confusing, risking separation in what is held in common.

There have been many grants of financial assistance along the way that made the preeminently non-commercial project of publishing Blanchot in America possible for a non-institutional, non-endowed, independent literary publisher. Some of Lydia Davis' translations received special translation grants from the New York State Council on the Arts. Her many months of work on *The Gaze of Orpheus* were funded under the Comprehensive Employment and Training Act of the Department of Labor—certainly an unusual event in the history of public funding. The production of all of the individual books was in some measure funded by grants from the New York State Council on the Arts and the National Endowment for the Arts. Our deeply felt acknowledgement goes to the administrators and panelists who have stood behind us on these projects. May the radiant presence of Blanchot's work in English be received as a credit to the responsible people and the responsive process behind public arts funding.

George Quasha
Barrytown, New York

---

[1] First published in a small hardback edition by David Lewis, Inc. in 1973.

[2] The defining instance is *Thomas the Obscure*, the first version of which Blanchot called a *roman*, the reduced (by two-thirds) version a *récit*—an *opening* of fictional form by *reduction*. Blanchot says the *récit* "is not the narration of an event, but that event itself, the approach to that event, the place where that event is made to happen"—narrative as *performative*, moving, as it were, toward the condition of poetry. (See "The Song of the Sirens.") Written in 1935-36, contemporaneously with the first version of *Thomas the Obscure* (1932-1940), the "two fictions" of *Vicious Circles* may seem problematic in relation to the distinction *récit,* which is the word used for them in "After the Fact" (though the distinction is not emphasized in our translation).

[3] Note that while the categories fiction and non-fiction/essays break down quite thoroughly as Blanchot's work develops, none of the problematic later works, significantly liminal to the two domains, is presented here.

[4] The one Station Hill Blanchot book not represented here is *The Unavowable Community* (1988). While immensely important as an inquiry into community and as a contribution to Blanchot's works in which thinking integrates historical/political/social/philosophical focus, it does not stand alone to the degree that the others included here do. Optimally it would be read in dialogue with the works it discusses of Georges Bataille, Jean-Luc Nancy and Marguerite Duras.

[5] For instance, Michael Holland's excellent collection, *The Blanchot Reader* (Blackwell Publishers, Ltd.: Oxford, 1995), seeks "to situate its author squarely in his time." He aims, admirably, to correct an imbalance in Blanchot reading that makes it appear "as if [the writing] took place outside time and took no account of history." This view, however, should stand in a dialogical relation with others, including the other end of the temporal spectrum—the infinite, from which, according to Blanchot, all must also be viewed.

[6] The designation "editor" of this Reader is not meant to overshadow the roles of the others mentioned here, some of whom gave enormously of their time and energy. Perhaps being editor means little more, in this case, than feeling responsible, during two decades, for whatever could or did go wrong. The translators of the fiction decided for themselves what they would translate. Sitney chose the essays for *The Gaze of Orpheus*. For my part, I have always felt more instructed than instructing, especially by the agonizing/exhilarating "editorial" reading of a translation against Blanchot's original (most memorably, *The One Who Was Standing Apart from Me*), or the process of "inventing" Blanchot's titles in English. The latter too was collaborative— illuminatingly. Staring at our list of dozens of possible translations of *"Le Ressassement éternel,"* Michael Coffey and I flashed on "Vicious Circles" at virtually the same instant. (Blanchot, happily, expressed pleasure in the discovery.) Robert Kelly ended the impasse of another long list for *"Au Moment voulu"* with "When the Time Comes."

FOREWORD

To begin to define Maurice Blanchot's place in modern French letters, one must consider, in addition to the literary works, a newly available body of journalism and a vast range of literary and philosophical meditations published over a period of sixty years—writings with an extensive, but often indirect influence. One must consider the importance of the friendships with Georges Bataille and Emmanuel Lévinas, among others, and take into account the effects of his complex participation in French public life (an always active participation, even in times of withdrawal). The critical task is daunting, and it grows daily as the lineaments of Blanchot's activities are drawn into the historian's light.

But however many elements are gathered for the dossier, an appreciation of Blanchot's insistence in modern letters requires attention to the strange force of his language. Indissociable from the fascinating power of any Blanchotian theme or critical motif (the author's Orphic quest, for example, or the death that is the impossibility of dying) is the haunting presence of a language that brings language itself into question as it searches the borders of what can be said in its time. This language offers itself everywhere in Blanchot's text. But when it is heard from the multiple space of resonance created by Blanchot's own literary research—a series of singularly arresting textual events—one can begin to appreciate the sway of Blanchot's presence in texts as marking for our epoch as those of Jacques Derrida, Michel Foucault or Jacques Lacan. Only from the ground of such a relation to his language, in fact, can we properly appreciate Blanchot's importance for a generation of French poets, for the literary and cinematographic works of a Marguerite Duras, or, to leave the French context (as Blanchot's renown did long ago), the thought of Hajime Tanabe, the literary criticism and theory of Paul de Man, or the contemporary video art of Gary Hill. We can begin then to understand how Jacques Derrida could ascribe to one of the voices in his *"Pas"* the assertion that Blanchot remains far ahead of us: "Waiting for us, still to come, to be read, to be reread by those who have done so ever since they have known how to read, and *thanks* to him."[1]

I believe it is fair to say that Station Hill Press—initially, and still to this day in part, an artistic project—began from an assumption like the one I have offered concerning the place of Blanchot's literary language when it undertook to sponsor, in conjunction with a critical collection edited by P. Adams Sitney (*The Gaze of Orpheus*), a series of admirable literary translations by Robert Lamberton (*Thomas the Obscure*), Lydia Davis (*Death Sentence, The Madness of the Day, When the Time Comes, and The One Who Was Standing Apart from Me*), and Paul Auster (*Vicious Circles*). The importance of this initiative cannot be overestimated for the reception of Blanchot in the English-speaking world. For while the latter reception has been somewhat isolated (a representation of post-war literature that takes its start from Sartre has dominated the American academy), it has been intense—shaped in an essential way by the fact that English-speaking readers have been able to approach Blanchot's critical and theoretical writings from the basis of an engagement with works of the order of *Thomas the Obscure* and *Death Sentence*. Thus, the publication of a collection of Station Hill's translations is not an indifferent event, and the question immediately arises: Will the present collection, enabled by the growing recognition of Blanchot's place in modern French thought, renew in some way Station Hill's contribution to the reception of Blanchot? What might we expect from this new publishing venture, this partial summary of Station Hill's past efforts? Will this remarkable compilation of literary, critical and "speculative" works by Blanchot serve the futurity to which Derrida has referred?

In these prefatory words, I would like to suggest why it may indeed answer to that futurity by helping to change the very manner of reading Blanchot in the English-speaking world. My hope, at least, is that its juxtapositions—startling, perhaps even unnerving for some who have lived with the individual volumes—will invite readers to entertain the relations between the works presented, and then prompt them to consider their disruptive relations to a multiple set of histories: literary, philosophical, political and biographical. Commentators have not failed to evoke such relations, but most have found it difficult to make steps between the fictional works, or between those works and their historical sites.[2] This is in part because works like *Death Sentence* and *The Madness of the Day* actively inhibit such steps. Their formal coherence (if it may be called that) defies any extant critical categories, while their language, both limpid and strange, turns aside constantly from the "day" of referential ties. To these grounds of a forbidding solitude we must add an occasionally overt defiance (the first version of *Death Sentence* ends with a veritable threat to the reader), and an ostensive silence regarding what has brought them forth or what they are (not) saying. In brief: Blanchot's literary writings have commanded a cautious respect that seems almost unmatched in modern criticism; the works have been left alone.

Does the present collection transgress in departing from this reserve? Certainly—but perhaps not in a regrettable way. For while it is not easy to imagine these texts under the same cover, there is no basis for supposing that their proximity in a single volume will mute their potential as singular events and efface their solitude. It could well serve, on the contrary, to underscore the distances that open between them by virtue of the literary movements they share: their "common" engagement of the interruptions proper to what Blanchot sometimes names a "speech," sometimes "saying," and, increasingly in his later work, "writing." It could help to draw forth from each of the works (from their resonance, their interrupted rhythms, their folds) their exposure of an "infinite" in language that both divides and relates them in their differences from one another and from themselves. Blanchot would call the field of this exposure a "relation without relation"; borrowing from Bataille, he would call it a "communication" (without common terms). If such a communication is furthered by this collection, it will reinforce not only the solitude of the texts, but also the questions that speak in them, questions whose philosophical, political and ethical import is in no way limited by the opacity of their origin.

My hypothesis, in other words, is that the alignment of texts will help to bring forth in each of them, and between them, a trace of the "research" to which they belong, namely Blanchot's unending, multiple engagement with what he terms the question of literature. This volume will do more than make Blanchot's work more easily available or represent a significant portion of his literary accomplishments. In fact, it will do something quite different from what is traditionally expected of a "collection"; it will reinforce, even multiply the strangeness of each of the singular events of writing it presents, drawing forth in this way the question of what is at stake in the fact that such texts exist—a question that cannot but lead far beyond the name "Blanchot."

The last question appears in a "Note" to *The Infinite Conversation* that develops it in a way that is pertinent to what I would like to suggest

here. Beginning with a kind of history of this question, Blanchot observes that,

> Since Mallarmé...there has come to light the experience of some-
> thing one continues to call, but with a renewed seriousness, and
> moreover, in quotation marks, "literature." Essays, novels, po-
> ems seem to be there and to be written only in order to allow the
> labor of literature...to accomplish itself, and through this labor to
> let the question come forth: "What is at stake in the fact that some-
> thing like art or literature should exist?"

The question, he suggests, has been obscured by a secular tradition
of aestheticism. Nevertheless, he continues,

> Literary work and research—let us retain this qualifying "liter-
> ary"—contribute to shake the principles and the truths sheltered
> by literature. This work, in correlation with certain possibilities
> offered by knowledge, by discourse and by political struggle, has
> brought forth, though not for the first time...the question of lan-
> guage, and then, through the question of language, the question
> that perhaps overturns it and comes together in the word, today
> openly and easily allowed...: writing, "this mad game of writ-
> ing."[3]

"Writing, the exigency of writing," devoted seemingly only to itself
in its slow emergence (so that it could be confused, we might add, with
the formalist celebrations of literariness that have received renewed favor in the academy), has brought out "entirely other possibilities": forms
of "being in relation" that carry into the incommensurability of their
movements, "first the idea of God, of the Self, of the Subject, then of
Truth and the One, then finally the idea of the Book and the Work."

Enough to get us all locked up (to recall *The Madness of the Day*). But
such is the arc of questioning we might envision, one arc among the
many that cannot be foreseen. And the spring for this movement of questioning, I would like to emphasize, may be the cumulative and multiple
force of the literary works gathered in this collection—a force that proves
decisive in breaking through the customary relation to "literature" and
prompting the reader to ask about the implications of the fact that such
texts exist. I do not believe one can hear literary language in the same
way once one has encountered this question in and through Blanchot's

fictional writings—once one has encountered it, that is to say, in the strangeness of their language: a force, at times, that one associates with sacred texts or forms of mythopoiesis, a clarity, at other moments, that carries a sovereign humor at grips with the impossible, throughout a haunting presence and an enigmatic grace. "The words spoke alone," the narrator remarks in *The Madness of the Day*. Once one has heard this speech and the silence that attends it, one cannot also help hearing a "literary" pull in essays like "Literature and the Right to Death," a theoretical and critical text that is also of the highest dialectical subtlety and rigor in its exploration of the "two versions of the imaginary." And one cannot then help hearing it elsewhere: in philosophy, or in any discourse that draws from what "speaks" in language. From *the fact of language* as it is presented by Blanchot, in other words, the question, "What is at stake in the fact that such texts exist?" leads into a general questioning about language itself, a questioning that cannot avoid the problematic of writing as authors such as Heidegger and Derrida have helped define it in their respective ways. From there, it is a small step to the fundamental questions enumerated in the passage from Blanchot's "Note," including that of "another way of being in relation."

Blanchot refers in his "Note," as we have seen, to "the exigency of writing"—the genitive both subjective and objective. He refers elsewhere, and with a more ethical inflection, to "the exigency of another relation,"[4] implying with the same ambiguity of the genitive and the same notion of writing that the relation in question both demands or "requires" and is required. What is this relation? The reader will discover its trace at the thematic level perhaps first in the arresting descriptions of an encounter with a radical alterity. Thomas, for example, knows an endless becoming-other in exposure to what Blanchot names near the end of *Thomas the Obscure* "the supreme relation." We witness this "knowledge" in scene after scene of this work: scenes of struggle, flight, or abandon, in each case involving the presence of an absence that Blanchot names in his more theoretical statements (and with Lévinas), the *il y a*.[5] But this knowledge is exhibited nowhere more poignantly, perhaps, than in the opening of the monologue that follows the account of Anne's agony, and in what Thomas does not fully bring to speech: his relation to Anne's gift of her dying. Is his own "death" in these pages not intimately bound to hers? The "knowledge" to which I have referred, in any case, is a *dying*, as Blanchot thematizes it most frequently, and it is known first and foremost, as he demonstrates already here and as he asserts increasingly in his later works, via the other, via a human exposure to an infinite alterity that is also an exposure of the human.

The latter assertion is precarious, but no less imperative for that fact. It is precarious because it lends itself all too easily to a humanistic pathos and its philosophical underpinnings. It risks substantializing the human share in the relationality I am describing by positing some essence outside the interruptive opening (of language) that constitutes the source of the imperative. "The human," as Blanchot helps us think this term, is not thinkable apart from this latter opening, though not reducible to it.[6] To put this philosophical challenge in the briefest of terms: Language would not bear material witness to its finitude, to difference (and this is in fact the condition of its "speaking") did it not say this in-finite exposure that Blanchot understands as a human dying. The question of the relation between language and something like "the human" emerges increasingly in Blanchot's work as an ethical concern and as a point of focus, but it is also a logical imperative for a thinking as rigorously at grips with the question of finitude. This is in part why the question of the other human being insists already in the first version of *Thomas the Obscure* (1941), as it does later in *Death Sentence* (which turns precisely around the possibility of engaging the other in its relation to the "impossible"—around the possibility of a touch). And while the question of the human is given thematic emphasis in theoretical writings only a couple of decades later, its place is already prepared in the reflections on literary language contained in "Literature and the Right to Death." The haunted character of literary language, as he describes it, does not merely reflect its "imaginary," "nocturnal" nature, if we understand these terms in their traditional connotations; rather, it is a mark of the fact that what Blanchot calls the "image" or the "imaginary" in that essay communicates a material exposure that is at the origin of any relation.

I do not want to fall into anachronism by overemphasizing topics that will only gradually emerge in Blanchot's work, and I do not want to suggest that the exposure to which I have referred (the poor but indestructible condition of the name of humankind) is the proper origin of the text, or its "truth." There are multiple dimensions to the event(s) that form the "origin" of these works, and where the exposure

I have described is concerned, one can only say that Blanchot has taken many different tacks in exploring the writing in which alone its imperative is drawn forth. The relation to the other assumes an important place in the works collected here, for example, but the reader will also discover the encounter with alterity to which I have referred through various allusions to the experience of the writer: evocations of an extraordinary density of affectability (irreducible to any "self"-consciousness) and an infinitely suspended advance in relation to what impels to writing or is engaged by it. The latter complications would almost be difficult to bear were it not for their implacable precision, their poise, and the strange justice of their insistence as a form of response. But the fact of the *response* is perhaps the crucial point. However far Blanchot goes in his experimentation, and whatever tack he pursues, his writing is always at grips with an address or what he names an "exigency"; at every step it answers to an interrupting relation at the limits of language that he eventually offers as the (non)grounds of responsible engagement (any ethical relation). If, as I suspect, his readers are now prepared to approach the text with a sensitivity to this character of his writing, then it is perhaps not abusive to emphasize what he gradually comes to think as the human share in what his language engages beyond the power of the negative: that "dying" that is the (non)ground of all communication, all community. Here is how Blanchot puts it in a passage from *The Unavowable Community* on Bataille that could never suffer too many citations:

> Now, "the basis of communication" is not necessarily speech, or even the silence that is its foundation and punctuation, but the exposure to death, no longer my own exposure, but someone else's, whose living and closest presence is already the eternal and unbearable absence, an absence that the travail of deepest mourning does not diminish. And it is in life itself that that absence of someone else has to be met. It is with that absence—its uncanny presence, always under the prior threat of a disappearance—that friendship is brought into play and lost at each moment, a relation without relation other than the incommensurable (concerning which there is no ground to ask oneself if one has to be *sincere* or not, truthful or not, faithful or not, given that it represents the always prior absence of links or the infiniteness of abandonment). Such is, such would be the friendship that discovers the unknown

we ourselves are, and the meeting of our own solitude which, precisely, we cannot be alone to experience ("incapable by myself alone, of going to the limits of the extreme").[7]

Once again, I suspect it is now possible, or newly possible, for such a statement to be read in all its force. Of course, one cannot predict confidently in matters of reception. But in risking an assessment of Blanchot's legibility at this point shortly before the close of the century, one would have to take account of the fact that a new historicizing and politicizing imperative has overtaken the movement that hastened the initial need for translation. This is not the place to review the fortunes of the French philosophies of difference. But I believe it is fair to say that the fundamental research Blanchot has undertaken into the grounds of the social relation (relations of desire, relations of power, relations of law) throughout his various modes of writing has not been superceded. Indeed, the imperative to which I have referred has been served, for the most part, abstractly—despite all the claims to concreteness of various historicisms and forms of cultural critique. The exigencies of the ethico-political, as the material ground of any political meaning, have accordingly only grown and deepened. Here we find one source of the remaining "translatability" of Blanchot's work, attested to powerfully by the recent impact of his meditations on friendship, on the everyday, on death, and on the horrific forms of violence that have marked this century. And despite the fact that difficult questions of textuality have fallen from fashion, it may well be that it is now possible to hope for a few consequent steps in the task of thinking the historical and social questions raised by Blanchot's text (community, desire, the other, the law) from the language of the text.

It is not a matter, here, of reversing the arc of questioning I have described—a movement that started from the question of language and proceeded to that of the social, the ethical, etc. Rather, it is one of holding to the question from which we started: "What is at stake in the fact that such texts should exist?" It is a matter, in other words, of staying with the question of literary language in exploring the legibility of the ethico-political dimension of Blanchot's writings. Such an enterprise inevitably provokes suspicion on the part of those who police the order of representation (for the claims of disciplined "reason," communicative transparency, historical responsibility, or political propriety). *The Madness of the Day* stages precisely this scene. But if the question of the ethico-political is to be asked of literature *at a level where it actually opens*, indeed if it is to be raised at all *as a question*, then such a form of inquiry cannot be avoided, however little it offers in the way of security or good conscience. It means asking, for example, what the language of *The Madness of the Day* communicates of a "madness" at the heart of the law. What is the nature of the "allegory" staged here, assuming that the narrating voice is not that of a possible subject, at least not a "sane" one? What language is this—or what, of language, is this speech that in its extreme of passivity *provokes the law* (not only its reaction, but its "desire," and even its genesis)? What does it communicate in saying its inability (or refusal) to recount? This voice, incarcerated and under an interrogation that is inextricably medical and juridical (and then there is our own critical examination), declares serenely and simply a kind of "releasement" (what Heidegger termed "*Gelassenheit*") that is almost unimaginable. Do these ecstatic words—ecstatic in their expression of transcendence vis-à-vis the order of meaning itself, the "world," and ecstatic in their anticipation of *another death*, perhaps a repetition of the one that lies at the heart of the story and from which the narrator speaks—do these words say accession to "a different relation" and tell us, from their context, something of its (im)possibility? Are they, in their expression of an *amor fati*, in some way comparable to the concluding assertions of the narrating voice in *Death Sentence*, and are the conditions of such an expression somehow comparable? Is the strangeness of their joy and limpidity comparable to the clarity or glory Blanchot himself attributes to the "little idol," that "*eidolon*" that is the saying of "The Idyll"? And how do we read these various figures of the narrative voice or the affirmations they pronounce in relation to Blanchot's statement in "After the Fact" of their necessary interruption by the events that bear the collective name "Auschwitz?" If there can be no narrative after Auschwitz, how do we assess the possibility of the speech of the texts I have cited, or their writing (including the refusal of *The Madness of the Day*: its last words, "A story? No. No stories, never again," and its own refusal to the present of narration in its infinite folding upon itself)? How do we think their relation to the testimony of the "the death suffered by humanity as a whole" at Auschwitz, and the obligation "never again to die only once." What is a responsible speech, or what is "literature" after the interruption marked by that obligation?

These are not questions that can be answered satisfactorily with any theoretical statement, even if it reaches the level of a speculative thought respectful of all the nuances and ambiguities of historical context. They require other pragmatics of language, and there can be no end to such practices of thought and writing. If the interrupted, errant course of Blanchot's meditations says anything at all, it is that the "exigency of a different relation" cannot be satisfied and will never allow a peaceful conclusion. In his later works, Blanchot appears to evoke the possibility of a kind of advance in "giving expression to intermittence." He even evokes an end.[8] But the latter, the extreme of Blanchot's research, can only be the opening of another kind of vigilance, and even advance is without the satisfactions of any kind of secure achievement. (Hence the vanity, as Blanchot remarks in *The Writing of the Disaster,* of citing a happy formulation as though it marked a past success. Every such gesture finds achieved meaning when what is at stake, if there is indeed "success," is the event of a speaking that cannot be reduced to any such meaning.) There can be no *oeuvre* in such research if by "*oeuvre*" we designate some organic relation between product and sustained endeavor. Teachers, or any of those striving in their own ways for what Blanchot terms "communication" or "community" know their own version of the *désoeuvrement*, the "unworking," that belongs to this task. But what keeps such endeavors going is precisely the exigency that has been underscored here, the fact of its intermittent occurrence in each act of thinking/writing that answers it, and the knowledge that proceeds from that experience: that there is language that "says" the material exposure of existence that is the unsettling condition of any "true" speech, that there is something like a history of this speaking that must be recalled (including an interruption in the very possibility of narrative), that "a voice still comes from the other shore" to arrest the order of meaning and require writing.

Christopher Fynsk
Brooklyn, 1997

---

[1] In *Parages* (Paris: Galilée, 1990), p.55.

[2] I should note an important recent exception to this observation: Michael Holland's daring and richly informed commentary in *The Blanchot Reader* (Cambridge: Blackwell, 1995). Holland's provocative effort to construct the writer's biography (in and as a relation to a political "world") is invaluable for the perspectives it provides on the political engagements that punctuate Blanchot's career. Holland recognizes and demonstrates that one must also read the texts, in all their "untimeliness," from their history. I am not pursuing such a project here, because the necessary claims, however cautious, would seem obtrusive in this collection. But *The Blanchot Reader* is a fine companion volume to this one.

Two other volumes deserve mention in this context: the recent and quite informative biography by Christophe Bident, *Maurice Blanchot: Partenaire invisible* (Paris: Champ Villon, 1998), and Leslie Hill's very impressive study, *Blanchot: Extreme Contemporary* (London: Routledge, 1997).

[3] Maurice Blanchot, *The Infinite Conversation*, trans. Susan Hanson (Minneapolis: U. of Minnesota Press, 1993), pp. vi-vii.

[4] *The Infinite Conversation*, p.192.

[5] We must underscore the "*with* Lévinas." If one turns to the pages of *De l'existence à l'existant* cited by Blanchot in "Literature and the Right to Death," one will find a reference to the first version of *Thomas the Obscure* (1941).

[6] Hence the necessity of the quotation marks, a necessity that is noted by Blanchot near the end of a long dialogical effort in *The Infinite Conversation* to sustain the place of "*autrui*," the place of the other human being in the limit experience from which emerges "the exigency of a different relation." Under the pressure bearing on all philosophical categories involving selfhood or subjectivity, one of the voices from the dialogue remarks, "Perhaps it is also time to withdraw this term '*autrui*,' even while retaining what it would say to us: that the Other is always what calls upon 'man' (if only to place him under parentheses or quotation marks), not other as God or other as nature, but as 'man' more Other than everything other" (*The Infinite Conversation*, p. 72). It is difficult, in translating into English, to avoid gendering a movement that is in no way determined by sexual difference, but that is also not beyond or before... (as *The Madness of the Day* and *Death Sentence* enigmatically indicate in their respective ways).

I should note that I have attempted to address the question of "the human" in several chapters devoted to Blanchot in *Language and Relation:... that there is language* (Stanford: Stanford University Press, 1996) and *Infant Figures* (Stanford University Press, 1999).

[7] *The Unavowable Community*, trans. Pierre Joris (Barrytown: Station Hill Press, 1988), p. 25.

[8] I refer to statements from the opening dialogue in *The Infinite Conversation*, and to echoes of these statements that punctuate the volume.

FICTION

Vicious Circles

THE IDYLL
THE LAST WORD

The Idyll

♦

The moment he entered the city, the stranger was led to the Home. His guard said to him on the way:

"You'll hold it against me, but it's the rule. No one escapes the spectacle of happiness."

"Indeed," said the stranger. "Then what's so terrible about this Home?"

"Nothing," answered the guard, suddenly cautious, "nothing at all."

They walked through an empty garden and then rang the doorbell of a large house.

"I'm going now," the guard said to him in a low voice. "But I urge you to follow my advice: don't trust appearances."

It was a young woman who opened the door. She had round cheeks and plump hands.

"Hello," she said to him. "Don't be afraid of anything. The house is open to you."

She led him into the reception room where a young man with square shoulders and an open, smiling face stood up to greet him.

"This is my husband," the young woman said, offering him a seat. "He's good; you'll like him, everyone does."

"You'll like all of us, of course," the young man added jovially. Then, looking him over and noticing his muddy clothes and dirty face: "May I ask where you come from?"

The stranger felt a lump in his throat and did not manage to give an answer.

"Later," said the young woman, "you'll tell us everything later."

She led him out of the room and up to the next floor, to a place with a vast row of showers. She handed him a comb, a brush, and a bar of soap.

"See you later," she said, giving him a little push, and then, confidingly: "wash well; we're very concerned about hygiene here."

But as soon as she had closed the door, the stranger felt his exhaustion and cried out: "I'm hungry." He sat down on the floor, and as the steaming water began to splash out from the ten nozzles on the ceiling, he was overcome with nausea and lost consciousness. He woke up on a bed. There was an orderly beside him, rubbing his face with a damp cloth.

"Take it easy," he said, nursing him amiably. "It's not a crime to be hungry."

But the stranger looked at him intensely and asked if he would soon be returned to community life.

"Community life?" asked the orderly. "Everyone lives all together here, but there's no community life."

"No," the stranger murmured, "I'm talking about a free life."

As he got up, he saw the young woman by the door, looking at him in a friendly way.

"Oh well," she said, you can bathe another time. As soon as you can walk, come to the cafeteria. I'll be waiting for you there."

The orderly helped him slip on his miserable sandals. Then he put the stranger's clothes in order, slicked down his hair, and removed some of the mud that was splattered on his suit. Just as he opened the door, he said in his ear:

"It would be better if you went to see your comrades first."

There were about twenty of them gathered in a shed, yawning, playing cards, and drinking.

"This is the newcomer," said the orderly, speaking more or less to everyone, but most directly to a rather old man who was lying on a pile of sacks. "They're waiting for him at the cafeteria. You'll get to know him in a little while."

The young woman served the meal herself, her eyes bright, her face shining, hovering around the stranger as he ate. But after he was finished, she took his hand and asked him: "What do you think of my husband?" The stranger was shocked by this question.

"Why ask me?" he said, trying to get away. "I'm only a vagabond. I don't have time to observe people."

He imagined that he knew the words she was burning to hear.

"Oh!" she said, squeezing him harder, "just wait a few days, and then you'll come to me to talk about him. Look at me one last time."

She had the most joyful face he had ever seen.

"Well, see you soon, Alexander Akim."

This strange name suited him as well as any other: he was no more than a kind of beggar here. Once back in the shed, he lay down on the ground. They were playing and singing around him. But he could not free himself from the memory of that face.

"Where are you from?" asked the old man, crouching down beside him.

"So, you're a spy, too," he answered unpleasantly. "What difference does it make what country I come from? I'm a stranger, that's all."

The old man looked at him with a resigned and tranquil expression.

"I was born in the neighboring region," he said, "in Samard. When you cross the bridge, you can see it near a small stand of chestnut trees, and if you climb the hill, you can even make out the river that flows through the area. I have ten brothers over there, and three of them have daughters ready to be married. If you like, you can meet them later."

"Thank you," said Alexander Akim, "I already have a wife."

His bad humor did not discourage the old man, who called to one of the men yawning on the floor.

"Isaiah Sirotk, come play with us."

The cards were shuffled, cut, and dealt out, but the stranger refused to take part in the game, and all the normal cheating took place as he looked on with disapproval.

"Listen," said the old man, breaking off from the cards, "as you can see, I'm the oldest one here. All passions have died out in a man my age. In a few days, I'll be leaving the Home and returning to my country, and I'll soon forget this horrible past. Trust me, then, and if something is troubling you, confide in me."

The stranger thanked him but said there was nothing troubling him and that he only wanted to sleep. So he was left in a corner, looking with heavy eyes at these rough, slovenly men in the light of a weak electric lamp. Eventually, he managed to fall into a deep sleep. When he woke up in the morning, he was expecting to be beaten with sticks, for that was the punishment he believed was doled out to strangers. But he was led to the director, who greeted him very cordially.

"Alexander Akim," he said, after inviting him to sit down beside him on a couch, "I'm not going to question you by the rules, I'm too young to stick to protocol. Where are you from? Why have you left your country? Have you stolen anything on the way? I'm sure these questions have their usefulness, but they don't happen to interest me. My thoughts are elsewhere. My family absorbs me too much." He mused for several moments over his words, and then, gently sliding his hand along Akim's arm, he asked softly: "Are you married? At a time when you're already beginning to worry about middle age, do you know what it means to find a young woman who has more life and freshness than all the others, a person who understands you totally, who never stops thinking about you, someone who looks for you, someone you look for yourself and who is right there beside you all the time? Have you experienced this? Do you have any idea of the upheaval this causes in your life? It drives you crazy."

He shuddered as he stood up and walked from one end of the room to the other, obviously distraught. Then he recovered his composure, took a photograph album from the table, and leafed through it calmly with his guest. These were snapshots that had been taken during his engagement. The pictures were conventional, but it was impossible not to feel the extraordinary impact created by these two radiant figures who were always turned toward each other, as though they were but two sides of a single face. This display finally irritated Alexander Akim, whose eyes no longer dared to look at the signs of such collusion. He was relieved when the director finally put an end to their meeting by saying:

"We welcome you. I hope you'll have nothing to complain about during your stay."

Right after that, he was led to the quarry to work with the other men. They were supervised by a giant, a very ugly but good-natured person who was always agitated and upset. The work consisted of taking the stones that were dug out of the mountain each day by the city laborers and carting them to a huge pit. In the heat of the sun this was an exhausting task, exhausting and useless. Why throw the stones into this pit when special trucks would be coming afterwards to haul them away? Couldn't these trucks have been loaded right after the stones were dug up, when they were sitting there in neat piles? But the vagabonds had to be given work, and vagabond work was never to any great purpose. Alexander Akim attached himself to the overseer, who secretly passed on brandy and canned goods to him. They did not go back to the Home at night; a cave hollowed out in the mountain served as their shelter, and they rested, slept, and ate there. There was hardly any camaraderie among the members of this small society. Brawls sometimes broke out; but these moments of violence did not last very long and would give way to a reserve mixed with coarse behavior. It was not against the rules to exchange a few words with the laborers from the city, who were dressed in grey and green striped clothes and worked at the bottom of the hills. These were generally good-looking men, sober and serious, and they only talked to the beggarly riff-raff to reproach them for their intemperance and laziness. One of them arranged a meeting with Alexander Akim one day in the tall grass where they spent the noon hour, and without even looking at him declared that when you broke the law you should be deprived of food and lodging and should not be allowed to live comfortably in one of the most beautiful buildings in the city. The stranger left without answering him, but later he was sorry he had not clobbered this arbiter of morality. The overseer helped him to understand what was required of him. There were no major obligations: a little discipline was demanded, but only on certain days (for example, walking in single file and not talking during work). With the old man not there, the others paid no attention to the newcomer, and he likewise shunned their company. Everything was so arid in this region, with the sun burning all day long and the nights ravaged by silence and cold, that the presence of other men was seen as if through a dream. At dawn, they had to go down through a mine shaft to a little sandy beach where there was a spring. Drinking was the only thing that interested the prisoners. During the rest of the day, they would pass an alcohol-soaked rag over their lips, and the most favored ones would drink a few drops—which burned them but gave them the illusion of a new life. After a week, Akim went back to the Home. Just as he was leaving, the overseer said to him:

"I was married once, too. But women don't like my job. People who live with vagabonds aren't liked."

Covered with dust, his face dried out, his hands torn, Akim was sent to the infirmary where he became seriously ill, in spite of the good treatment he received. Every afternoon, when the memory of the sun became strongest, he would feel as though he were entering a false night; instead of bringing him sleep and coolness, it was all flames and storms. They wrapped him in icy sheets, but to no avail; his body was burning him and he would call out for the water that had refreshed him earlier, yet he would never drink it. The director came to see him.

"What's wrong with you?" he asked. "Why this sudden indisposition? Everyone else always feels so well here. Are you subject to these kinds of attacks?"

The sick man gave him a hateful look.

"You've treated me brutally," he said in a low voice. "A dog, a swine has the right to more respect. I'll remember your hospitality."

"What's that?" murmured the director, startled by so much passion. "Your words disappoint me. I've done everything I can to make things easy for you. Have you been slighted somehow?"

"Yes, as a matter of fact, I've been slighted," he cried out, totally beside himself with anger, and then, forgetting where he was, he started to scream: "Get out, get out," so that the director left without saying another word.

He was put in a dark cell where he continued to receive the best care. Only a feeble light came through the air vent, and he felt as though he had been cut off from the world forever, so great was the silence. The orderly tried to encourage him.

"Naturally," he said, "it's hard to have your freedom taken away from you. But is anyone ever free? Can we do what we want? And there are so many other reasons for being unhappy."

"Thank you," said Akim, "but you won't console me with the thought of others' unhappiness. My suffering belongs to me."

The fever let up, and the stranger abandoned hope of leaving his prison through a dream that would be more lasting than his nightmares.

"When can I leave this cell?" he asked. "Have I done such a terrible thing? You're not responsible for what you do in delirium."

The orderly went to find out.

"I couldn't find the director," he said when he returned. And then he added with an air of irritation: "The atmosphere is stormy."

Nevertheless, he was finally let out, and Akim went back to his comrades. He was surprised by the animation that reigned among them, and even though calm returned as soon as they saw him, he noticed a kind of satisfaction or unpleasant interest on their faces.

"What is it now?" he asked peevishly. "What are you hiding from me?"

"Be quiet," the old man said to him. "It's not your job to tell us what we can and can't do. Everyone here has his own prison, but in that prison each person is free."

One of the men, the one called Isaiah Sirotk, insulted him crudely. "Spy," he shouted at him, "informer." The two men began to scuffle. Akim let himself be taken by the throat. He saw his adversary's face, the large protruding ears, the eyes without irises, the hideous features. The old man separated them and swore loudly, but he suddenly stopped talking because a manservant stuck his head through the window and invited the stranger to go to the director.

"Listen," the old man said, pushing him into a corner, "you've already noticed that the director and his wife hate each other. It's a silent hatred with no cause, a terrible feeling that disrupts the whole house. It doesn't even have to be violent to be felt. Calm and hypocrisy are enough. Still, sometimes there are scenes. You can hear the shouting through the walls. It's better to be shut up in a cell than to appear before them."

"Is that so?" said the stranger. "You're so spiteful that now you're trying to upset me with lies just when I need my composure. Why are you trying to ruin me? What have I done?"

He was taken into the large reception room where he had been the first day. There were flowers scattered over the floor. Others had been made into garlands on the table.

"Well, what is it?" the director asked him, his face pinched and apparently unwell. "I only have a little time."

"May I see your wife?" the stranger asked, after giving him a furtive look.

"Yes, yes, of course," the director answered with a distracted smile. "But today is her birthday, and it would be better to wait a little."

The stranger apologized and then remained silent.

"Is that all?" the director asked impatiently. "Don't you have any other questions to ask me? Tell me why you've bothered me like this."

"But I'm only here because you sent for me," the stranger said.

"That's true," said the director with confusion." Forgive me. I'm feeling out of sorts. I'd like to offer my apologies for the punishment you were given. It was painful for me to behave like that towards a sick man. Try to forget it—and come back to see me."

Akim was about to leave, but the director held him back, saying, "I'll go call Louise. She'll be happy to say a few words to you." They came back together, she leaning on his arm, he bending towards her. Akim was struck by the youthfulness that lit up their features when they were together. The director seemed completely recovered. He was smiling and moving impishly with small steps.

"Stay and have a drink with us," she said to him, extending her hand. "Did Pierre tell you it's my birthday?" Then, on the way out: "Come back tomorrow, we'll talk."

When he returned to the shed he lay down, determined to stay apart from his comrades. But they all gathered around him, and he had to hold his own against them, contradicting everything they said in a sharp voice.

"Get out of here," the old man shouted, dispersing the group. Then he crouched down in his usual way. "Forgive me, Alexander Akim. You've been sick. You've been separated from the others. I should have been a better companion. Are you willing to listen to me today?"

"Let me sleep."

"Yes, you're going to sleep. But listen to me first. I don't want to be a nuisance. This is a request, a very humble prayer. Maybe you think I'm trying to slander the director?"

"To hell with your thoughts! I'm sick, I need to be alone."

"That's it, you think I have something against him. But no, he's a good man. He's always been generous with me. He could have sent me away, and yet he keeps me on, old as I am. Is he responsible for his unhappiness? Is there anything shameful in being unhappy? And what unhappiness could be more terrible than hating instead of loving yourself?"

"Enough of this, or I'll call the overseer."

"One more word. In your opinion, which one of them is to blame? She's a loose woman, a spoiled child; but he's so somber, so severe, how can anyone live with him?"

Seeing that the stranger had turned over on his side and was no longer listening, he withdrew with a sigh. The next morning, Akim went to the infirmary, where the young woman was treating several indigent men from the city. She made a friendly sign to him but didn't say anything. He went on wandering about the halls of the Home, searching through the empty rooms for traces of a drama that continued to elude him. That day the whole house was open to him. He walked into the administrative offices where, among the files and shelves loaded with documents, there was a flower in a frame, a touching and useless object that stirred up the memory of a faultless love. He lingered beside half-closed drawers, as if the letters he dared not read were meant to prove to him that an affection still existed. He entered the director's apartment. The walls were bare; shells, engraved stones, and glasses tinted with friendly colors adorned the mantlepiece and furniture. It seemed as though a wild river had flowed through these rooms, leaving behind the debris of earth and uprooted weeds in images of glass. Green branches went up to the ceiling, and it was impossible to say if this profusion would wither by the next day or if the garden on the floor would soon be giving off flowers and new leaves. Before he had discovered how this juvenile ornamentation was put together, Akim was surprised by the return of Louise. She looked at him dreamily for several moments.

"My room is around the hall," she said. "But let's stay here."

They sat down ceremoniously—he on a chair, she on a bench.

"You really are a stranger," she remarked. "Perhaps you'll begin to fit in to the way we live and work here, but I'd be surprised if you ever forgot your country."

Akim didn't answer.

"What do you find so displeasing about your city? Its size? Its overly tall houses? Its narrow streets? Are you put off by the Home? Have you left someone behind that you miss? I'd like to help you."

"You can," said Akim, straightening up. A new and unexpected expression transformed his face. "I'm suffering because I'm not free. Let me become the man I was before."

"But that's easy," said the young woman. "Your quarantine is almost over. Tomorrow you can visit the city if you like and talk to the people who live there." Then she added: "I'd like to tell you my story."

He listened as she spoke in that childish but cold voice of hers. Predictably, it was the story of her engagement.

"I don't understand why you confide in me like this," he interrupted her. "I know you're happy, even though people say the opposite, but in my situation I can't get mixed up in the private lives of people who are above me."

He thanked her and went back to his comrades. His first walk through the city did not make much of an impression on him. The houses were majestic, but the streets were narrow and irregular, and they lacked air. He was recognized by his slow, provincial way of walking. Entering a bookstore, he was questioned good-naturedly by the owner.

"Are you satisfied with your stay at the Home? What luxury there, what comfort! The people of the city are happy to have it, since it allows them to welcome strangers in the best possible way. We don't like people to live in exile among us."

Akim listened with an air of irritation.

"And what a good director!" said the bookstore owner. "He's an educated and just man. His troubles only make you like him more."

"Thank you for your kindness," Akim said. "Do you happen to have a detailed map of the city and the surrounding area?"

"A map of the city, yes. But we're not very interested in other regions. On the other hand, here is an excellent book about the Home."

The work was illustrated with photographs and, as he expected, it was filled with praise for the penal methods that were such a source of pride to the State: the mixture of severity and gentleness, the combination of freedom and restraint—these were the fruit of long experience, and it was difficult to imagine a more just or reasonable system. When he returned to the Home, he found the director sprawled out on a bench in the garden, his face livid.

"Are you in pain?" he asked. "Do you want me to call for help?"

"Mind your own business," the director answered. "It's only a passing attack; I'd rather be alone."

The house was plunged in silence. Decorated with those wild flowers that are little more than colored grass, it seemed more than ever to be the place of a simple and happy dream.

"A sad house," the orderly said to him, walking in a distracted way through the halls, far from the room where he was supposed to be working. "How can two young people go at each other like that? Who's pushing them to torment each other? The only time they're not in silent despair is when they burst out in anger at each other. And that constant trembling, the suffering in their mouths, their eyes, their hands, whenever they have to see or touch each other."

In the shed, the overseer was whipping a young prisoner—the unfortunate Nicholas Pavlon. Overcome by a burning fever, he had walked through the city almost naked. Akim saw how inhuman the ordeal of flogging was. At the tenth stroke, the victim fainted; the torturer, exhausted by his own violence, began to shudder, as though some poison had suddenly chilled his blood. The old man said to Akim:

"Tomorrow my detention is over. But I've come to an age when you stop hoping for a new life. What illusions could I have after all this use-less suffering? Can I still get married? Do I still have enough faith to join myself to a woman and live in peace? No. Everything is finished for a man who gets out of prison."

"Why are you complaining today?" asked Akim. "Yesterday you were thanking the director for not getting rid of you because of your age. Is living in the Home a privilege or a curse?"

The old man made no response. He turned and gave some advice to the prisoners who were sprinkling water on the body of the unfortunate young man.

"If he doesn't wake up before sunset, he'll be lost," he said.

He didn't wake up. The blood had stopped flowing from his body, and the men covered him with the long blanket he had used to wrap himself in at night. Even though Akim had no real feeling for this naive and rough companion, he felt as though his heart had been torn apart, and he let the old man spend the evening with him—groaning, com-plaining, and rambling on.

"What makes them enemies?" he said. "The lack of family? Orphans can never find happiness. They don't have the gentle common instinct that lies at the heart of family life to prepare them for living with others. And they themselves have no child. They hate everything that could make life easier for them.

"They've made a fatal mistake," he went on. "They thought love was drawing them together, but they really detested each other. Certain signs led them to think they were tied to the same destiny, but it was really a desire to tear each other apart through disagreements and tor-ments. How long did they fool themselves? When they finally discov-ered the marks of their old intimacy on their bodies, it was too late; these marks did no more than prove to them the fury that has been holding them together. They must go on loving each other in order to go on hating each other.

"Has she deceived him?" he said. "No, she's been very careful; she's denied him the possibility of moving away from her a little, of breathing some other air, another life perhaps free of violent feelings. She doesn't leave him, and in that way she can overwhelm him with her solicitude. This makes him see all the hatred she has for him, all the detachment she inspires in him. She follows him around, as if her only reason for exist-ing were to represent the void his life has become. He's calmer than she is. But nothing ever distracts him from his despair. He's silent. He speaks without caring what he says. When he says nothing, his silence is made into something infinitely sad, humiliated, contemptible. Unhappy young people. Sad house."

"Shut up," said Akim, losing all patience as these disjointed words went on and on. But as he shook the old man, he saw that his eyes were empty and inflamed, just as they were whenever he drank the water with alcohol in it. He tucked him in roughly and then passed the night in the calm that surrounds the dead.

Nicholas Pavlon was given a magnificent funeral. A bier with innumerable flowers stacked around it was set out in the largest room of the Home. The men took turns watching over it, and the overseer, the unwilling instrument of misery, did not leave the dead man, sitting behind the monument in a low chair, sinking into a deep regret over his terrible violence. The procession passed slowly through the city. The stranger had time to study the tall buildings that seemed to merge together in the sky, the dark and narrow shops, the apartments that became more elegant and spacious once they reached the upper floors. He was told that the cemetery was located in the center of the city; it stretched up the side of a hill in a swampy region surrounded by walls that marked off an enclosure. The solemnity of the ceremony, the apparent sadness of the city dwellers weeping falsely for a dead stranger, and the crudeness of the prisoners dressed up in party clothes, inspired a disgust in Akim that would have made him leave the procession immediately if he had not been afraid of being punished. At the moment when the director threw some flowers on the coffin, which had been set beside the grave, and spoke some words befitting the occasion, Akim could not stop himself from shouting out: "What's going on here? Is this a farce, a mockery— the revenge of depraved men?" But he regretted these words, since the people around him thought he was overcome with grief. Still, he could not have done otherwise. Back at the Home, he had to attend another ceremony: the old man's departure. All the prisoners were gathered in the reception room, still warm with the smell of death. Flowers, no less brilliant than the ones on the bier, transformed this farewell ceremony into something that felt like an engagement party. The old man, filled with emotion and already drunk, believed that he had committed grave injustices against those who were there, asked forgiveness, kept walking around the chairs and tables.

"You have honored this institution," the director said, smiling. "You're going home completely adjusted. I'm sure your stay here has not always been agreeable; there are dark hours when everything becomes inexplicable, when you blame the ones who love you, when the punishments seem to be absurd cruelties. But in every life it is so. The essential thing is to leave prison one day."

Everyone applauded. Akim wanted to ask something, but he was ashamed to speak up in front of all these people, and he withdrew silently into a corner. After the reception, the director called for him:

"I sense that you're impatient, troubled. That's not good. It will make getting used to your new life even harder. In my opinion, you're wrong not to see things as they are: you're in a house where we have your best interests in mind; you should leave it to us and not worry about unpleasant things."

The director was standing beside the table. His wife was sitting behind him, and she smiled as she listened. "Is it possible that they hate each other?" Akim asked himself. "No, everything is a travesty in this city. They love each other. At the most, they have the usual quarrels of young married people."

"I'm not troubled," he answered. "I don't understand the customs of the house and I suffer from it, that's all. If I'm allowed to go back to my own country, I'll always remember your excellent hospitality."

"He's a stranger," Louise said joyfully. "I always thought so—he'll never really fit in here."

"How long are you going to keep me prisoner?" he asked.

"Prisoner?" answered the director, frowning. "Why do you say prisoner? The Home isn't a jail. You weren't allowed to go out for several days for reasons of hygiene, but now you're free to go wherever you like in the city."

"Excuse me," said Akim, "I meant to say: when can I leave the Home?"

"Later," said the director, annoyed, "later. And besides, Alexander Akim, that depends on you. When you no longer feel like a stranger, then there will be no problem in becoming a stranger again."

He laughed. Akim wanted to get back at him for this joke, but he was overcome by sadness.

"You wife explained it: I'll never be anything but a man from another city."

"Please, please, no discouragement. My wife says anything that pops into her head; you mustn't take it seriously."

He leaned over Louise and caressed her shoulders. Akim looked at them for a moment before returning to the shed.

The vagabonds, who had secretly carried off some provisions, were still carousing. They were drinking and singing sad songs of this sort:

Land of my birth,
Why did I leave you?
I've lost my youth
And live with woe,
Loveless now
And jailed forever,
Death alone is not my foe.

They greeted Akim warmly, but soon Isaiah and a prisoner named Gregory began quarrelling. One was reproaching the other for having borrowed money from him.

"Give me back my money," Gregory was saying. "I'm not angry that you took it from me, but today I need it. Come on, give it back to me."

"Shut up, you souse," Isaiah answered. "Where would you earn any money? You stole it, that's what you did."

"Stole it?" said Gregory, suddenly overwhelmed by the enormity of the accusation. "Stole it? If anyone's a thief, it's you. I earned that money by working. It's my money from my work."

"Listen," said Isaiah impatiently. "You're drunk and you talk too much. There's no salary here. If you really earned that money, it's because you were paid to spy on us. I'll teach you what happens to stool pigeons." And he jumped at his throat.

These accusations of spying were frequent, and perhaps they were justified. After all, why not betray men you did not like? There was no sense of teamwork, each man lived for himself, and it was even taken for granted that the heterogeneity of the group would give rise to secret enmities. The absence of the old man weighed heavily on Akim. The old man had been the only person he could talk to. That evening, he felt that he had to talk to someone; he would die of suffocation if he could not get out of his thoughts. The memory of the director and his wife tormented him so cruelly that he felt drunk, drunk with a passion whose true nature no one else could see. He detested them, since they were responsible for his exile; and yet a feeling of tenderness touched him whenever he thought about them, this charming couple who lived in the simplicity of the heart. Yes, sometimes he wished that despair would tear them apart, that they would be dragged through endless torments, that hatred would be the sole bond between them. For what else was waiting for him in the world but hatred and torment? And yet, can you close your eyes to the truth? It was enough for him to recall those two handsome faces, the looks they exchanged, the naturalness of their smiles, to feel that bitter peace that comes when the spectacle of happiness is too close to you. He tried to rouse the overseer. The man was sleeping, exhausted by the day's emotions.

"Why all these lies about the director?" he shouted at him.

Torn from the consolation of sleep—and plunged back into the remorse that would not stop tormenting him—the giant groaned and then uttered a string of irrational words.

"I'm not a donkey that can be woken up any which way. I need sleep. Just leave me alone."

Akim shook him a second time.

"Let me take a walk around the house. There's no air in here, I'm suffocating."

The overseer swore and covered his face with his arms.

"Have the good sense to let me go out," Akim said a last time.

He kicked the sleeping man in the ribs with his boots. The man rose slowly, distraught, his eyes expressionless; then he staggered, as if trying to find a middle path between sleeping and waking; suddenly, a look of anguish came over his face; Akim did not have time to get out of the way, and he saw the man grimace and begin to vomit. Outside, the wind shook the trees, and the dry noise of the leaves rubbing against each other reminded him of an arid stretch of sand. A bitter smell came in gusts, now exciting and agreeable, now fetid; the swamps turned the night into a kind of trap, and it was unwise to get caught in it. The stranger sat on the bench and imagined having a conversation with the overseer.

"Lies?" said the guard. "I've known about them too long to want to talk about them. Leave these stories alone."

"Ah," said Akim, "that's just what I need: someone who's known about them for a long time. This isn't like other stories, is it?"

"In any case, it's not a story to analyze and repeat. Is it important to you?"

21

"No, no, not at all," said Akim. "But answer my question: are they happy or unhappy?"

The overseer sniffed, and the stranger did not dare to repeat his question. He said:

"Have they been married long?"

"Two years."

"And when they were married, they acted the same as they do today?"

"Yes."

"You see," said Akim, "if nothing has changed, it means that they've always been happy. Happiness is not deceptive. I'm sure they're bound together by a great and profound attachment."

The overseer continued to sniff.

"Is that your opinion?"

"Don't ask for my opinion on this subject. I'm an overseer. I don't know anything except what I see."

"Precisely. Tell me what you've seen." Silence from the guard. "Well," said Akim, "you're afraid to talk. I'll find out everything myself."

"No, Alexander Akim, don't try to find out: what good will it do? I'm going to speak to you with an open heart. I would tell this to anyone. When they were married, I already had my job at the Home. I had a wife, too. For the first few days, they didn't leave their room. There was a strange silence in the house, a feeling of idleness. In spite of all the work, you didn't know what to do with yourself. After a week, some strangers came, and I had to go tell them. In the first room, I didn't find anyone. There was dust on the furniture, as if no one had lived there for several years. I was afraid, I called out. Then, I went into the little office. But no one was there either. Everything was in order, and yet I already knew that something dreadful had happened. I stood there for several moments waiting. I wanted to run away. I thought they were both dead. But finally I opened the door a crack and lifted the curtain. They were sitting apart, not looking at each other, not looking at anything at all. I couldn't read anything in their faces. The only thing was that air of emptiness, and it made me turn away. Yes, an air that explained this bleak, heavy silence that was indifferent to misery, without bitterness towards anyone. I felt that I couldn't stay there. I moved, and he looked at me and said: "Yes, yes, I'm coming.""

"Is that all?" asked Akim. "But what you're describing is tranquil happiness, something extraordinary—the feeling that's at the heart of every idyll, a true happiness without words."

"Really?" said the overseer. "Really? Is that what you would call it?"

The stranger again heard the noise of the leaves, and they made the wind seem dry and barren. The smell became suffocating. Around the house, a ditch was forming where all the swampy odors of the city were stagnating. He returned and found the overseer sleeping soundly on a pile of sacks. But the next morning the man told him viciously:

"No going out at night. You'll get five lashes for that."

Towards the beginning of the afternoon, just when he was planning to go to the city, the old man arrived with the members of his family: two young men with brown skin who said nothing, and three girls, all of them small and fat. The old man said to his comrades: "These are my brothers' children," and he introduced Akim to the youngest girl. She was wearing a white cotton dress. The girls, who were at first intimidated, got it into their heads to tour the famous establishment, which was off limits to the families of prisoners before the prisoners were released. They ran idiotically through the halls, into the rooms on the first floor where the showers were located, and down into the dark cells, which had been dug out beneath the cellar.

"I didn't recognize anyone in the village," the old man said. "I feel out of place among my own people. The memory of the homeland can't survive the passing of time."

Akim thought these words were meant to console him, but they pointlessly wounded his hope.

"I got a friendly welcome. But what does it matter if kindness comes from people who are no more than strangers? I'm too old."

The girls came back, out of breath, their eyes sparkling, their faces shining with sweat. They were ugly but agreeable.

"I'll be back," the old man said to Akim. "Look to the future."

Even though he had only a short time to visit the city, once again he plunged into the narrow streets and stopped in to see the bookseller.

"You really don't have any works on the surrounding countries?" he asked. "No postcards, no pictures?"

"I'd be surprised if I did," said the bookseller. "But I'll go look if it will make you happy."

As he climbed the ladder and rapidly threw the books he chose from the shelves into his apron, Akim asked him:

"Is it true that the director and his wife…"

"Is what true?" said the bookseller.

"Aren't they happy?"

"If you don t know, who would?" said the bookseller. "The prisoners are always very well informed. We learn many things from them."

"Well, I believe their marriage has been a true idyll. I've rarely seen such a perfect relationship."

"Well, well," said the bookseller, climbing down. "I think I've found what you want."

It was a very old book that gave the history of the entire region and even included a few pictures. Akim asked if there weren't any more recent works.

"This is very rare," said the bookseller, not understanding. "You can study it at your leisure, but I can't allow you to take it away. You can consult it at this desk."

Akim sat down on a high stool. Enjoying the calm that reigned in the shop, he learned more than he had expected from his reading.

"Louise was my pupil," the bookseller suddenly said. "She often played in this store, and she learned to read from my books."

"Right here?" asked Akim.

"Yes, here. She was a very lively child, but well-behaved. Pictures and beautifully engraved letters enchanted her. She was very good at imitating their shapes. Who wouldn't have wished to see her happy?"

"Look who's curious," said Akim. Then, after studying some of the illustrations, he asked if he might not also be able to copy the most beautiful parts. Permission was given to him, but as it was growing late, he abruptly left the store.

At the Home, a work party was waiting for him. A group of unpleasant looking men, haggard and exhausted, had been collected in the street and were now shut up in the enclosure that served as a courtyard for the prisoners. The strangers who had been in the house for a while had to take turns looking after the new arrivals—to make it easier for them to bear the anxieties of this unwonted seclusion. Akim said to one of these miserable creatures:

"You'll learn that in this house it's hard to be a stranger. You'll also learn that it's not easy to stop being one. If you miss your country, every day you'll find more reasons to miss it. But if you manage to forget it and begin to love your new place, you'll be sent home, and then, uprooted once more, you'll begin a new exile."

24

These words were reported to the director, who made it known to Akim that he would be punished if this happened again. Akim immediately asked for an audience. His request was turned down. The next day, he had to go to the quarries with the newcomers, even though he had been led to believe that he would never be exposed to such an ordeal again—because of his illness, because of everything he had been told, and because of his conduct, which had been that of a free man. He found himself in a landscape burned by heat, with scrawny mountains on which precise and disciplined workers scratched like insects, surrounded by vast ditches that were filled with stones and little by little emptied by the trucks—and he was flooded with exaltation, convinced that he would either perish from this terrible isolation or find the way to freedom. Scraps of reality came to him in his delirium, but no sooner did they come than he cursed them. He ran towards one of the workers, grabbed his pick, and then banged it savagely against a rock. It seemed to him that he could find new dignity in this work, which was more useful than the vagabond's work, and each blow of the pick made him feel as though he were striking another blow against the walls of his prison. At the same time, he tasted some unknown freshness under the sun, as if, in the midst of a tormenting despair, among all the jostlings of hatred, some pure and gracious feeling had remained. But then, torn from this delirium and shut up in the cave, he fell back into a despondency that made him indifferent to the passing of time, and soon he found himself with the prisoners in one of the convoys returning to the Home. It was the old man Piotl—he was not able to use his real name—who welcomed him, along with his youngest niece. This time she was wearing a dress with bright colors and had poppies in her hair.

"I've come to see you every day," he said to him. "I have a real fondness for you, and I want to do something to help you. You could marry my niece."

Akim knew from reading the little book that a prisoner who got married could leave the Home immediately to be with his wife. But he was horrified by such a practice and flatly refused.

"There's delicacy in your refusal," Piotl said. "It only makes me admire you more. But think about my offer and you'll be able to overcome the repugnance that prevents you from accepting."

That night following his return, he heard a terrible cry that sent shudders through him. Thrusting aside the guard, he rushed towards the house, where he found Louise running through the halls in a flimsy nightgown. Her face was white, and she held her hands before her as though pushing away the darkness.

"In the name of heaven, what's wrong? What's happened?"

"He's there," she said, pointing to the door of the reception room, "and he's going to kill me."

The door opened and Pierre appeared, a coat slung over his shoulders, his face even more pale than his wife's. She let out a second cry that resounded horribly through the house; and then she fell down in a faint. Pierre went towards the stranger and then, when he was close enough to touch him: "Is it an idyll?" he asked. "Is it really an idyll?" Then he turned to his wife, carried her with Akim's help into the room, and put her in a large chair. The lights were shining in the house. It looked like a celebration, as though the clusters of light were tossing open flowers around the room. Something pure had turned the silence into a ceremony for the consecration of young souls. Akim slowly left the room, but before closing the door he nevertheless said to Pierre:

"An idyll? Yes, why not?"

The next day, he left early for the bookstore to make sketches of the pictures that had interested him. The morning air in the city was clear, as though renewed by the night; and yet at night a kind of poison came out of the earth, heavier and more loaded with stench than the deepest swamps. The bookseller greeted him jovially.

"I have a new book for you," he said. "You'll find a large map in it with many details. It's very precious."

Akim made rough sketches of the less simple routes; the others he would be able to remember.

"I'm probably going to get married," he told the bookseller, who was following his work with curiosity.

"Ah, yes! Marriage!" said the bookseller. "It's the great hope of youth. To love, to live with the person you love, to enter a new world in which you are at home both with yourself and another, of course that's the dream."

"I'm getting married in order to leave the Home," said Akim, continuing with his work.

"Good idea. If that's your destiny, I can only approve. But perhaps you shouldn't decide so hastily. The Home has its advantages. To be housed and fed, to enjoy all the modern comforts, and to give only a few rare moments of work in exchange—it's not a bad life. The rest of us envy you."

"To be free, that's what counts," said Akim, getting up and carefully sliding the documents into his pocket.

"Of course," said the bookseller. "Who doesn't wish for freedom? In this heavy and monotonous life, we look in vain for something to hope for. Everything is dark, everything is spoiled. You're right, you should get married."

On the road back, Akim bought some flowers from a young woman who ran a store in the garret of a dilapidated house: her flowers seemed beautiful to him.

"I'm getting married," he told her. "Pick some flowers for me that will last until tomorrow."

He gave her a little money (he too had caught the habit of stealing) and before returning took a long walk through the city, carefully studying the streets, questioning passers-by, acting like a man whose days as a stranger would soon be over. In the early hours of the afternoon, the moment he saw Piotl—who was becoming more and more hunched over, older even than an old man—he said to him:

"Forget what I said to you yesterday. I'll gladly marry your niece. She might not always be happy with me, since I'm often moody and find it difficult to be away from my country, but I'll behave like a loyal and faithful husband."

The two men went to the director.

"A marriage?" he said, in that attentive and indulgent voice of his that made him the brother of every unfortunate person. "This is good news, Alexander Akim. I'll tell my wife right away, and she can get to work preparing the happy day with you."

Louise was of course delighted. She would have liked to wait several days, since there were so many things to take care of.

"No," said Akim, "it will be tomorrow."

"Yes, tomorrow," said old Piotl. "At my age, you don't put off days of happiness."

This was a lot to ask, for marriage was a solemn and important ceremony, and it called for many preparations. There were flowers to attend to; lights had to be lit throughout the house; every resident of a certain status was allowed to eat with the new citizen—and to take advantage of the occasion by visiting the famous but by no means well-known institution. On top of that, the hangings had to be changed twice during the day; in the morning there would be gray and black curtains to symbolize the sadness of a man in permanent exile from his country, and in the afternoon there would be bright, multicolored drapes covered with ornaments and delicate emblems. The stranger would die in the morning, and in the afternoon an old friend would take his place. There would be a young woman on his arm, and she would be surprised by the fact that she was accompanied by a man who was no longer unknown to her. The director took Akim off to the side and said:

"Once married, you can never go back home. You have to say goodbye to the past."

"I'm ready," Akim answered.

The fiancée arrived, surrounded by her sisters and brothers, an entire family who silently observed the man who had been announced as her bridegroom several days ago. They were coarse men, their faces scarred by blows; but a naive goodness came forth from their features, and Akim already loved them as the witnesses of his own transformation—a transformation they would help him to achieve, but without understanding it, and perhaps without even noticing it. The girl told him her name.

"Elise," he said to her, moved by her simplicity, "you're at an age when you still don't understand everything, but you can feel many things that other people know nothing about. I ask you to forgive me in advance for the pains I will cause you and the misfortunes that will sadden you. Perhaps it would have been better if someone else were holding you in his arms and making you promises of happiness. Why has fate chosen you? I'm sorry, and yet I'm also happy about it, for it's a sweet thing to leave a mark on an innocent soul, even at the price of much sadness."

"Until tomorrow," he said, and he kissed her thick red fingers.

Louise sent everyone away so that she would have nothing to think about except the party. She went over the formalities with Akim, told him how he was to behave, and informed him about the language that would be used: during the entire day, the director of the Home was supposed to be like his father; he would introduce him to a new world; he would protect him and help him. Akim took note of these oddities. Then, after thanking her and telling her that she and her husband had been the only people who had helped him to live through such a long period of unhappiness, he added as he left:

"If I'm getting married, it's because I believe in your happiness. The despair, the torments you inflict on each other, the hatred you have for each other, the apologies that take so much out of you—everyone can see these things. But I can only see your love, and I think that a life in which such an idyll can blossom must be a happy one."

He returned to the shed, where he had to spend one last night. The overseer, inspired by the day's exceptional events, wanted to tell him the story of his marriage, which had made him both happy and unhappy.

"To love, to be loved," he said, "that's not enough. The circumstances also have to be favorable. Could my wife stay married to a man who lived in such a disagreeable house, living beside such an unfortunate couple? She left me, and I don't even know where she is."

The evening seemed long to Akim, sitting beside this giant who did not sleep. The other prisoners, warmed by the hope of an extraordinary day, tried to get close to the man responsible for this pleasure. Several of them also thought of marriage; weren't there families in which the children waited and waited to get married? It seemed to them that chance alone had selected Akim for this happy fate, and they too were ready to claim the same privilege.

"How noisy you are!" Akim said. "If you're punished, no party tomorrow."

But when silence and sleep came, the night was no less long, and the stranger had to go out to put an end to it. Outside, even though there were no stars or moon, he found the door and started walking down the road. The air was somewhat tainted, but soft. The sleeping city, hidden in the fog, let him pass, and he had no trouble recognizing the streets. Soon, he came to the cemetery. The wall was impregnable; the doors resisted him. Still, he had to cross this area, for he didn't know how far the swamp extended, and the only sure path was among the graves. He managed to climb over the gate and then made his way through the mounds to the road that led to the most populous neighborhood in the city. Just as he was leaving the cemetery, he felt the strange effects of the corrupted air; he was choking, but he did not experience the painful sensation that goes with asphyxia; on the contrary, he felt overcome by a lovely drunkenness. Beyond the gate, he became lucid again and slowly tried to find his way among unfamiliar streets. The map he had made that morning was fresh in his mind, but the city had changed; the houses, built one on top of the other, and made even more jumbled by the darkness, opened awkwardly onto alleyways in which people glided by. It seemed that by entering these streets he was entering the houses themselves; courtyards were mixed up with public squares; bridges went from one building to another and ran above the houses like endless balconies; as soon as you found a little open space, it meant that you were shut up in a garden, and to discover a new exit you had to climb stairs and plunge on through constructions you had no way of knowing would ever lead you outside.

After wandering hopelessly, Akim came to a vast promenade lined with great motionless trees. Perhaps this was the end of the city, perhaps this was the beginning of a new life, but as he was crushed by fatigue, he fell down and almost immediately a guard led him back to the Home. Again numbed by fever, he appeared before the director, who acted in the role of judge.

"You are guilty of a disturbing act," he said sadly. "You have deceived a girl by proposing marriage to her, when all along you were only thinking about running away. You have deceived us by causing us to relax our surveillance—under the pretext of preparing this wedding. You have upset the order of the house. Do you see any way to escape punishment?"

Akim wanted only to listen without interrupting.

"Punishments are rare," the director went on, "but they are necessary. I don't know how justice works in your country; each place is different, and it's not easy to imagine someone else's customs. But whatever the difference might be from people to people, the guilty can never be spared, nor can great crimes call for anything but great punishments. Do you accept this principle?"

"I await your judgment."

"My judgment is based on what you did," said the director.

"You will receive ten lashes."

Akim looked at him without saying anything.

"I'm annoyed, Alexander Akim, as annoyed as I could possibly be," he went on, drawing closer to him. "Why have you made it necessary for me to take such a measure? Who advised you to run away like that? Weren't you going to be free? Think of that girl who's been waiting for you since yesterday."

Akim still had his eyes fixed on him.

"Well," continued the irritated director, "after the punishment we'll try to forget all about it. I wish you good luck. The overseer is coming."

As usual, the punishment took place in the shed. Akim drank a glass of alcohol and the overseer, according to custom, asked his forgiveness, but with a sincerity and sadness that were out of the ordinary. The other prisoners, frightened at being treated to an execution rather than a party, were mute and stunned. After the first blow, Akim lost consciousness; but, with the third he came back to his senses and suffered a mortal pain. Between each blow, he had to wait while the overseer recovered his strength; he didn't know if he would live long enough to be killed by another blow; he was torn apart, humiliated, menaced by the thought of staying alive while enduring an agony powerful enough to kill him. At the sixth blow he heard the trumpets at the head of the procession announcing the celebration. The prisoners, suddenly inspired by these rejoicings which they so desperately wanted, urged him to stick it out. The overseer hastened to finish the ordeal. Akim was still alive when he fell from the torturer's hands.

The director himself led Elise to her fiancé's bedside. She was not pretty and she was crying. Nevertheless, he gave her a sort of smile, but his swollen lips, his half-open eyes, and slashed cheeks turned it into a horribly cynical expression.

"Well, that's it, it's finished," the director said. "I'm glad to see that everything turned out for the best. There's really no reason to talk about it again."

The orderly was not allowed to take care of prisoners after punishments. They helped each other awkwardly, with a special repugnance for everything that had to do with wounds and sores.

"Does it hurt?" the director asked stupidly. He looked at the stranger's black eyes that were stubbornly fixed on him, the bloodied mouth, the hands clammy with sweat.

"Say something to him"—he leaned towards Elise and pushed her forward—"tell him you're not bitter about what he did."

But the sobbing girl drew back, frightened.

"Still, someone has to try to help him," he added, upset by those stubborn black eyes that did not stop looking at him. "Doesn't he want to talk?"

Piotl came in, followed by his family, even though this was against the rules.

"If he goes to sleep," he said, "that's the end."

"Perhaps there are death rites in his country," the director said. "It looks as though he's waiting. Didn't he ever talk to one of you about it?"

"Death is death," said the old man. "Leave him alone."

The footsteps of the guests could be heard around the shed. The people had been stirred up by the change in plans—but they were also upset, and they walked around without saying anything. Louise came in and took Elise by the arm.

"This is no place for a young girl," she said. "Come outside with me to wait for the news."

But the girl, her face blinded by tears, escaped from her and snuggled up beside the old man.

"What does he want, then?" asked the director, looking at those large brilliant eyes, those extraordinarily large and pure eyes that were still fixed on him.

"He wants to die," said Piotl. "Believe me, nothing more."

After the ordeal the overseer had fallen into a state of exhaustion akin to sleep; now he woke from his spell and began to groan.

"Please be quiet," the director said, glad to be able to turn his head away. "Someone keep that brute quiet."

"Watch," said the old man, "something's going to happen. He's moving."

Louise again took the girl by the arm.

"Come out with me," she said. "We'll come back in a moment."

The girl went off without protest.

"Do you want something?" the director asked. "Can I help you? Won't you let me know what you want?"

The eyes kept looking at him, but they were becoming cloudy: one of his hands rose slightly.

"How terrible!" sighed the director. "Can't we know what he wants?"

"Be quiet," the old man said gruffly. "Right now, he doesn't want anything at all. He's going to sleep."

The men began to make signs, to remove their hats, to wipe their faces.

"Yes," said director, "it's the end."

He waited several moments, examined the quivering face, and then, after staunching the wounds with his handerchief, gently closed the eyes that could no longer see.

"You're losing a good comrade," he said to the others. "I'm sorry, truly sorry."

A large bier was set up in the entryway, and the guests remained to attend the funeral. The sun was shining now with a lovely radiance. The flowers in the garden, still a little wet, opened up. Branches came through the windows and tossed gently in the rooms.

"My dear," Louise said to the girl, who was sobbing on the bench with her head in her hands, "don't cry like that, my dear."

She drummed her fingers mechanically on her knees. Then, looking at the superb and victorious sky, the sky that in spite of death and tears still bound her under the mirror of spring to the reflections of an unshakeable faith, she rose to attend to her duties as mistress of the house.

The Last Word

♦

The words I heard that day rang strangely in my ears. I hailed a stranger on the finest street in the city.

"Can you tell me what the watchword is?"

"I'd be happy to tell you," he answered, "but somehow I haven't managed to hear it yet today."

"Never mind," I said. "I'll go find Sophonie."

He gave me a dark look.

"I'm not too happy with your language. Are you sure of your words?"

"No," I said, shrugging my shoulders. "How can I be sure? That's the risk you run.

I walked towards the esplanade; on the way I passed a narrow lane and heard sounds coming from a loudspeaker. A woman came out onto a porch.

"You're not ugly," she said, after looking me over. "But just now I can't ask you in. Imagine, a day like this!" The esplanade was at the edge of the city. As always, the sun was bathing it in a true light. Some children were playing on a pile of sand, but as soon as they saw me they started squawking hideously. They threw stones at me to block my way.

"May I go to the library?" I asked the janitor, entering a majestic building guarded by two bronze lions.

"What?" asked the janitor, with a frightened expression. "Will you be the last one? Go up quickly, time's running out."

I went into an enormous room. The walls were covered with empty shelves.

"I've come late," I said to a dry little man who was pacing back and forth. "What should I do?"

"Be quiet," he answered harshly. "This is the hour of solitude," and then he pushed me into a cell and carefully closed the door.

There was a book lying open on the table, apparently put there for me. Thinking I was alone, I was about to take a look at it when an old woman sleeping on some blankets in the corner let out a cry.

"I didn't see you," I said. "Does my presence disturb you?"

"Not at all. But at my age, I'm not used to visitor."

I sat down beside her. Then, with my eyes closed, I began to go through the customary greetings: "I didn't know you. I sought in vain to approach your face. Everything that is beautiful about you lies in the foul depths whose image I was pursuing. I called out to you, and your name was the echo of my basest thoughts. Days of shame. Now it's too late. I stand before you to offer up the spectacle of my mistakes."

"Come close, then," said the old woman. "We'll spend these few moments together."

She took off her clothes. Her body was covered in long black tights. She went over to get the book and then tore out some pages. She handed me a few of them; we sat down side by side, each wrapped in a blanket.

"This is an excerpt from the discourse on the third State," I said to her, after looking at the pages. "Listen to what it says. 'There was a time when language no longer linked words according to simple relationships. It became such a delicate instrument that most people were forbidden to use it. But men naturally lack wisdom. The desire to be united through outlawed bonds never left them in peace, and they mocked this decree. In the face of such folly, reasonable people decided to stop speaking. Those who had not been forbidden to speak, who knew how to express themselves, resolved to stay silent from then on. They seemed to have learned words only to forget them. Associating them with what was most secret, they turned them away from their natural course.'"

"I have only a few lines to read," the woman said when her turn came. But after beginning to spell out the word shipwreck in a very clumsy way, she added: "Excuse me, I can't go on."

She quickly got dressed again. Rummaging through one of her pockets, she took out a picture of a child's head.

"Accept this token. I have nothing else to give you to make up for the wrong I've done you."

"What do you mean?" I muttered. "What are you doing?"

Once again she leaned over the page that she had let drop to the floor.

"These things are not for people my age," she declared. "I'm sorry to have caused trouble for you, but I can't fulfill my role."

"I'm sorry. It's late now, and I'm going to sleep."

I fell into a sound sleep, but I was soon woken up again. "This won't do," I said. I pounced on the book. I wanted to tear it apart, to bite it. "Why am I being humiliated like this? What should I do? What have I forgotten?" Once again, I fell asleep. As I slept, the walls of the cell became covered with a brownish color. A dry vegetation similar to lichen overran the floor. A bitch crawled under the table, followed by her puppies, and I knew that she was howling weakly, ferociously: nothing could have been more hideous.

"What a racket!" I muttered in my sleep.

The cell had a round window made of opaque glass that resembled a porthole. Someone was pushing on it from the outside. Heavy pieces of plaster, eaten away by dampness, fell on the floor, exposing crumbling bricks in the walls. A thick vapor entered through the window, as though some mouth were spewing it out in fitful gusts. The woman shook me: "We have to read again," she said in an anguished voice. I pressed my face against the ground and said with the stubborness of sleep:

"You can't see what I see."

"Well," said the old woman. "I'll make you a more comfortable bed." She pushed me into a corner and then threw several blankets there as well.

A black cloud with coppery reflections had gathered on the ceiling. A veil of darkness fell from this cloud, then a plume of sparks that swept the air. Excited by these lights, the dogs began to prowl through the room—and then they suddenly jumped at me. I hid under the covers, but they knew where I was, and one by one they took little bites out of my neck.

"What a bad night," I shouted, throwing off the blankets. I tried to get some rest, but to no avail. Then an idea occurred to me: Why was this book so different from the others?

At that moment the door opened. Shouting and singing came from the esplanade, all the noises of a crowd about to take part in an event.

"It's time to go," the old woman said. "The procession is waiting. We're the last ones." I got up quickly and walked through the library, where I went and knocked on a large glass door.

"I'm entitled to some explanation," I said to the librarian, who was arranging miniscule objects on a table. "Why wasn't I told the watchword?"

"Because there is no watchword anymore," he said, without looking up. Then he showed me some objects that appeared to have been carved from the finest ivory. They were the smallest figures I had ever seen. "What do you think of these curios?" They reminded me of the animals who had been harassing me in my sleep.

"You can't get rid of me like that," I shouted. "How am I supposed to live now? Who will I talk to?"

After speaking these words I had to leave the room and go out into the street. I saw the old woman in front of the large door.

She was looking at me with a malicious smile: "Have you heard the news? There's no more library. From now on, people can read any way they like." "I want to kill you," I said to her, grabbing hold of her arm.

I walked with her from street to street, right into the middle of a chaotic celebration, with torches burning in broad daylight. A tremendous din of shouting rose up in response to an underground command, and it carried the whole crowd as one, back and forth from east to west. At some intersections the earth trembled, and it seemed that the people were walking over the void, crossing it on a footbridge of cries. The great consecration of *until* took place around noon. Using only little scraps of words, as if all that remained of language were the forms of a long sentence crushed by the crowd's trampling feet, they sang the song of a single word that could still be made out, no matter how loud the shouting. This word was *until*. "Listen," said the one who had been chosen to give the speech, "I beg you to pay attention to your words. When you say, *I will love you until the day you are unfaithful to me*, listen carefully. What have you said? You must be like a boat that has a rudder and in spite of that never manages to reach the shore. Through the intermediary of *until*, time throws back the rocks and becomes its own wreckage."

The people went home. The loudspeaker on the main street said to the crowd: "Don't neglect your worries." "I live far away," I said to the old woman, "and you might be pressed for time. Don't feel obligated to go with me." But she stayed with me everywhere. When we came to my house, she opened the door and forced me to enter a long hallway that went down into the ground. Being in this cellar made me short of breath, and I begged her to take me back outside.

"Where are we going?" I asked her. "What am I going to find now? I'm no more than an intruder in my own house. Can you explain to me what all this is about?"

But the woman was still completely absorbed by the celebration. She could think only of reminding me of the sudden changes that had taken place.

"I don't understand what you're worried about," she said. "Didn't you feel how good life can still be here during the procession? As we were walking down the streets, I took off my shoes and let myself be carried along by the crowd. It was pressing all around me. The cries came from a very deep place, they went through my body and came out of my mouth. I spoke without having to say a word."

"Enough of your blathering," I shouted. "I need to be alone."

She took the elevator upstairs and left me with my face against the ground. "O city," I prayed, "since the time is coming when I will no longer be able to communicate with you in my own language, allow me to rejoice to the end in the things that words correspond to when they break apart." A joyful clapping of hands called me upstairs, where I found the table set.

"Make the introductions," the woman said to me. She pointed to a corner where a young woman was sitting with a thick bandage around her neck.

"I don't know anyone here," I said, sitting down at the table. "Don't ask me to do it."

Everyone ate heartily, but at the end of the meal the thing I had been dreading happened: the girl threw herself at my knees and sobbed: "I beg of you, please recognize me." I stood up. She put her hand to her throat and undid the bandage. Ah! What have I seen! "World of mud," I thought, "where even dreams deceive you."

I ran away. It was already dusk. The city was invaded by smoke and clouds. Only the doors of the houses were visible, barred with gigantic inscriptions. A cold dampness was shining on the cobblestones. When I went down the stairway beside the river, some large dogs appeared on the opposite bank. They were similar to mastiffs and their heads bristled with crowns of thorns. I knew that the justice department used these dogs from time to time and that they had been trained to be quite ferocious. But I belonged to the justice department as well. That was my shame: I was a judge. Who could condemn me? Instead of filling the night with their barking, the dogs silently let me pass, as though they had not seen me. It was only after I had walked some distance that they began to howl again: trembling, muffled howls, which at that hour of the day resounded like the echo of the words *there is*.

"Those are probably the last words," I thought, listening to them.

But the words *there is* were still able to reveal the things that were in this remote neighborhood. Before reaching the pavillion, I entered a real garden with trees, roots tangled along the ground, a whole forest of branches and plants. The youngest children in the city were shut up in this pavilion—the ones who could talk only with shouts and cries. As soon as I went in, I was addressed by a very disagreeable looking woman:

"You have insulted my sons. What do you have to say in your defense?"

This woman was closed in between two halves of a table and did not have the freedom to do anything but stand up.

"Where are they?" I asked, trying to get away.

"No funny business! And don't go upstairs. It's a holiday today."

Upstairs, the children were noisily playing ball in a wide-open classroom. When I entered, everyone became silent. Each child went to his place quietly, and, as the veil fell over the statue of the teacher, their heads lined up hypocritically on their desks. I stood in front of a small table beside the plaster statue and indicated that it was time for work to begin. Right away, they asked me the traditional question that is asked in schools: "Are you the teacher or God?" I looked at them sadly. There were so many ways to answer them, but first I had to bring order to the class.

"Listen," I said to them, "at this special hour, we can help each other. I, too, am a little child in a cradle, and I need to speak with cries and tears. Let's be friends."

A lively child, older than the others, was sent to me by a delegation. He had red hair.

"Be reasonable," I said, holding out my hand to him. "It's in both our interests to see if we speak the same language. But first, you have to learn the alphabet."

I wrote out several sentences on the blackboard. For example: *Fear is your only master. If you think you are no longer afraid of anything, reading is useless. But it is the lump of fear in your throat that will teach you how to speak.* Then I alluded to my own torments.

"What happens when you live inside books for too long? You forget the first word and the last word."

"One moment," the boy shouted to me. "What is your connection to the statue?"

"So you're logicians, like everyone else. But first you must take my sadness into account. It wasn't just anyone you threw those stones at on the esplanade. I'm more vulnerable than other people, since no one can condemn me."

"Okay," said the child. "Let's move on to the commentary."

He went over to the pedestal of the statue and took out a large, thickly bound book. He opened it to a page marked with a red line. This text obliged me to give them a serious warning:

"Since the watchword was done away with," I said, "reading is free. If you think I talk without knowing what I'm saying, you are within your rights. I'm only one voice among many."

I couldn't stop trembling. I read the sentences and broke up their meaning by replacing some of the words with gasps and sighs. After a few moments the clamoring of the pupils merged with my groans, and I wrote out the passage on the blackboard, so that everyone could become familiar with it. *When the census of the population was taken, it happened that an individual by the name of Thomas was not included in the general list. He therefore became superfluous, and others began treating him as if, in relation to humanity—which was itself insane—he had lost his mind.* Then, according to custom, I asked the youngest child to pronounce each word along with me as loudly as he could. This attempt showed the enormous difference between a mature man and a child. Another passage from the same work was juxtaposed with the first to demonstrate the analogies of meaning. It included the last lines of the fable about the beseiged one: *The storm ended at the moment when the enemies took the balloon of the only surviving inhabitant and sent it off into the air. How did he manage to get away? By what means did he trick the guards and leave a place that was hemmed in on all sides? No one could say and not even he knew how it was done.*

"What I suggest," I said, "is to cross out all these words and replace them with the word *not*. For this is my commentary: after his extraordinary escape, no sooner did the inhabitant of the city set foot on free ground than he discovered the walls of his enormous prison all around him. He is asked: how was he able to get over the ramparts and fly through the air? But he doesn't know, and he can only express what has happened to him by saying: nothing happened."

The children all stood up at a single bound. They gathered around the statue, the oldest ones touching the robe, striking it as if it were made of brass or bronze and could strike them back. But this ceremony soon wearied them. Abandoning their reserve, they threw themselves on their visitor, screaming and showering him with displays of affection; some climbed up on the table, others pulled the chair from behind and tried to make it tip over; still others struggled to pull off pieces of my clothing. All this, of course, took place without a word. Finally, a person the children themselves looked upon with dread— and whom they had been hiding behind them until now—emerged from under the benches and came face to face with the teacher. He was extremely handsome, but an abundant outpouring of saliva kept falling from his mouth and soaking his clothes. Through the river that was flowing down his chin, this young person began to reprimand the teacher who had spoken too much, attacking him in the name of some former ideal of language. But I saw that this watery mouth was also trying to make itself understood. In order to reduce it to silence, he abruptly had to give up centuries of pride and return it to a state of innocence that the quest for the first word would not disturb, and it occurred to me that this spittle was the prophecy of a universal unhappiness. I became afraid, stood up, and stepped back among all those children who were gathered around me. They began to hiss like vipers, to sway from side to side and back and forth in a regular motion. I grabbed a piece of chalk and on the blackboard drew the face of the young mute—emerging from the mouth of a volcano amidst a shower of stones, rays of light, and garbage of every kind.

"This is our judge," I cried out. "In the name of what will you judge us? Who will challenge you? Poor children. A wound like this is caused by language, and it imposes no restraints on you."

The hissing and whistling pierced the air and became so strident that the whole house was shaken and a sheet of ice fell between the teacher and his pupils. I saw them through this frozen water, and at each deeper level it reflected shadows that became more and more jumbled. I saw myself in these images, and they were taking me back to childhood. At the bottom of this ocean, the door opened and the mother began to scream: "Give me back my sons!" The only thing I could do was leave, but before going I made this statement:

"The pupil listens to the teacher with docility. He learns his lessons from him and loves him. He makes progress. But if one day he sees this teacher as God, then he ridicules him and no longer knows anything."

The sound of their jeering accompanied me to the garden. There, I fell down. The saddest rays of the evening were at that moment reaching the city: houses in ruin, black trees painted against the sky. The great eagle with red wings that was set loose at dusk to drive back the threat of night now mingled with the shadows he was supposed to chase away, and I could hear his anxious cry through the fog that seemed to have become an immense nocturnal bird. I stood up and ran along the road that went down to where the arenas had been carved out of the rock. It was a desert, and drunken women sometimes walked there. The sound of footsteps aroused unknown animals from the city, and you moved toward the end of the territory through a whirl of insects, flies, and half-blind beasts. At that hour of the night, the mountain was empty.

"Where are you going?" shouted a woman, who was lying on the slope.

"To the tower!"

But several steps later, I bumped against a body and stopped. The girl I had knocked into emerged slowly from sleep and looked at me without saying anything. Because she was drunk, she saw me as I was.

"Are you the judge, then?" she asked with an expression of great surprise.

"Yes," I said, "but I can only judge myself."

She threw herself at my knees and muttered: "Rescue me from this wine I've drunk"—"All right! Let's run together," and then, taking her by the arm, I dragged her along with me. At a crossroads, the path came to an end.

"There's nothing here," I said. "Do you want me to take off your coat?"

It was a heavy robe made of gold cloth and it was trailing along the ground. She folded it over her arm and looked at me provocatively. "You see," she said, "I'm naked." But this veiled nakedness was not the sort of nakedness that called for the axe.

"Even at the point of death," I said, "a judge can't marry a guilty person without some minimal ceremony."

"Yes," she murmured, "but the evening is so black."

It was true that the darkness seemed to be carrying flowers for a festival. At the top of the hills, the animals that had been looking for shelter were all cries and complaints. I opened the material she was wrapped up in and got inside with her. For a few moments I became a man from another city. After that, she made this confession to me: "Drunkenness doesn't help me at all."—"Take a look at yourself, then," I said to her. She opened her coat a little and saw red spots all over her body, like marks of fire.

"Let's run now. I've drunk too much wine also."

Before reaching the tower, we had to walk across a vast plain that was covered with rocks and large stones. The expanse was so empty that we hesitated as we tried to find our way, even though the huge structure was only a few steps in front of us.

"It's my turn to confide in you now. I've condemned myself, it's true. I can't bear to talk without knowing what I'm saying."

"Strange language. To hear you talk, you'd think you were already a new man."

"Your insults won't change anything. You were in my path, and now you have to stay with me until the end."

"Let's keep going. We'll continue walking together."

After skirting some enormous rocks, we came to an enclosure surrounded by a large wall. "Whose guest are you going to be?" she asked me, suddenly worried. I pointed to the top of the tower and dragged her inside. We climbed the staircase very slowly; it seemed to take up the whole width of the structure. Half-way to the top, a memory came back to me. "Poor mute girl," I thought. "Here is where my scruples come to an end." We kept climbing: through an opening I saw how high above the countryside we already were. The nakedness of the desert absorbed the stones that were piled up around it, and the holes dug in the sand opened surprising paths that showed how deep the ground was. Several steps from the top, I became dizzy, and images of the city we had left behind passed before my eyes.

"Stay here," I told her.

I entered a small room that turned the tower into a lookout post. From there, the view extended all the way to the esplanade, where you could see bodies laid out on stretchers; it was the hour closest to night; these unfortunate and tormented people were suffering from what they thought was a cure, and they were crushed by the shame that had thrown them into the arms of a savior. You could see through it to the outside, and at the same time it reflected the things within. Right away, I had a severe attack. What an attack! It seemed to me that I was holding a gigantic, sleeping body in my arms—its weight, smell, and warm dampness proved that it came from some foul place. I couldn't put it on the floor. But I could hardly let it decompose on my lap either. My body shook, and the images of the room I could still see broke into pieces. Everything burst, tore apart, came from the depths. I was choking. I felt that I was hanging from the top of a tower that had already fallen—only to be rebuilt by my hatred of mankind. I myself flew into fragments, and yet I was unhurt. I cried out. I called to the girl, "My body is burning up." She opened her coat a little and showed me the marks of fire. They seemed to be forming the first shapes of a vague language.

I opened my eyes on this white body and sent her away. By looking in the mirror I was better able to see how the rock piles had fallen into their present shapes—and how they preserved the memory of the past. Everywhere in front of me there had once been splendid structures, and the heavy stability of the stones recalled those buildings that had now collapsed. I took several steps in the room. The only things in it were a chair and a rope for ringing the bell at the top of the tower. Timidly, I opened the door a crack and looked out at the darkness.

"Let me in," said the girl, who was waiting. "It's completely dark out here."

But even though the room was also without light, a weak phosphorescence came in from the outside, and she screamed and covered her eyes.

"Yes," I said, "you see it too—this terrible sun that burns and casts no light."

And I fell back into my lugubrious storm. The distant constellations rose in the sky. Thanks to the patience of my inert, almost paralyzed gaze, I was able to follow them, slow as they were. I broke the window, my hands were cut, my blood flowed drop by drop through this hole into the sky. It seemed to me that my eyes were finally closed. They were burning me, I couldn't see a thing; they were consuming me, and this burning gave me the happiness of being blind. Death, I thought. But then, something terrible happened. At the core of my sightless eyes the sky opened up, and it saw everything, and the vestige of the smoke and tears that had obscured them rose up to infinity, where it dissipated in light and glory. I began to stammer.

"What do you mean?" the girl shouted. She slapped me in the face. "Why do you have to speak?"

"I must explain things clearly to you," I said. "Up to the last moment, I'm going to be tempted to add one word to what has been said. But why would one word be the last? The last word is no longer a word, and yet it is not the beginning of anything else. I ask you to remember this, so you'll understand what you're seeing: the last word cannot be a word, nor the absence of words, nor anything else but a word. If I break apart because I stammer, I'll have to pay for it in my sleep, I'll wake up and then everything will begin again."

"Why so many precautions?"

"You know very well—there's no more watchword. I have to take on everything myself."

"Farewell, then," and she held out her hand to me, then withdrew to the back of the room.

I reached into my pocket, took out a photograph of a child that had been given to me by a woman I had met, and put it on the wall at eye-level. The picture immediately burst apart; it scorched my eyes and tore out a section of the wall. But this hole, opening on the emptiness again, didn't show me anything: it closed off my view, and the freer the horizon appeared to be, the more this freedom became a power to see nothing the emptiness would give in to. No eye could be reborn from such an exchange—it was as slight as the beating of a butterfly's wings. I turned to stone. I was the monument and the hammer that breaks it. I collapsed to the ground. I was still lying there when I received a visit from the owner of the tower.

"What's this?" he said to me. "What games are you playing here? There are customs and rituals when people come to my house. And who is this woman?"

I struggled to my feet and said in a low voice: "You see, you don't know anything." But I was so weak that I had to sit down, and the man put the bell-rope around my neck.

"I'm going to tell you about this building—which you seem to have entered in order to amuse yourself. It is the last tower left. It must not fall into ruin like the others. Spend some time here, if you like, but give up the hope of seeing it collapse on top of you at the last moment."

I felt the chill that came from these words.

"You're the owner of the tower," I muttered. "It's natural for you to think it's indestructible and that it won't fall down. But I don't own anything."

"If you can hold out until the cock crows," he said, raising his voice, you will see that I am the All Powerful One."

I laughed at these words, but this laughter robbed me of my last strength. How could I be so weak and yet still be able to talk? What weakness! What weariness! I knew that I was already too weak to die, and I saw myself as I was—an unlucky man who has no life and yet who struggles to live. It was this weakness that the master of the place was trying to take advantage of. What did he want from me? He made fun of my dizziness, he appeared and disappeared, he shouted: "Look me in the face," and also: "Who can deny me?" and also, quite suddenly, with a strange voice, the softest, most soothing voice I had ever heard: "My accomplice." What a voice! "Is it possible?" I said to myself, standing up. And then, what happened? I loved him, too, and in loving him I defied him. I bowed down, I humbled myself before him as though before a sovereign; and because I treated him as master, I chained him to his sovereignty. And we were bound together in such a way that for him to become who he was again, he had to say to me: "I'm laughing at you because I'm no more than a beast," but with that confession my adoration became twice as great, and in the end there was nothing left but a sad animal, watched over by a servant who swatted away the flies. A ray of sunlight, erect like a stone, enclosed both of them in an illusion of eternity. They blissfully sank into repose.

The woman, beside herself with worry, came over to wake them.

"Get up," she cried. "The woods are on fire and the earth is shaking."

She got down on her knees and begged them to save her.

"A woman's illusion," said the owner. "Everything is peaceful. The night beats in vain against the walls of the city."

"Help," she cried again, shaking them both. "Water is flooding the countryside, there's a storm blowing in the desert."

But they both looked at her skeptically. At that moment, through the window with the broken pane, they could hear cries of distress from an enormous crowd.

"We're lost," the woman said. "The city is in darkness. Better to run away than to stay in this tottering old building."

"Make her be silent," the owner said to his companion. "Her shouting is spoiling my sleep."

She tried to open the door, but a horrible noise shook the tower. "The staircase is collapsing," she shouted. Irritated, the master of the house took her in his hands. "I've ruled over the world," he scolded, "it shouldn't be difficult for me to make you be quiet." During this time, flames began to light up the room. "Come, come, don't be so nervous: we'll have no trouble getting along with each other." As a wave of stone and sand struck the building, he held her tightly in his arms.

"Oh no," she said, "can't you feel that we're not standing on anything?"

But he reassured her with his calmness, and when the tower collapsed and threw them outside, all three of them fell without saying a word.

1935, 1936

Thomas the Obscure

There is, for every work, an infinity of possible variants. The present version adds nothing to the pages entitled Thomas the Obscure *begun in 1932, delivered to the publisher in May of 1940 and published in 1941, but as it substracts a good deal from them, it may be said to be another, and even an entirely new version but identical at the same time, if one is right in making no distinction between the figure and that which is, or believes itself to be, its center, whenever the complete figure itself expresses no more than the search for an imagined center.*

I

THOMAS SAT DOWN and looked at the sea. He remained motionless for a time, as if he had come there to follow the movements of the other swimmers and, although the fog prevented him from seeing very far, he stayed there, obstinately, his eyes fixed on the bodies floating with difficulty. Then, when a more powerful wave reached him, he went down onto the sloping sand and slipped among the currents, which quickly immersed him. The sea was calm, and Thomas was in the habit of swimming for long periods without tiring. But today he had chosen a new route. The fog hid the shore. A cloud had come down upon the sea and the surface was lost in a glow which seemed the only truly real thing. Currents shook him, though without giving him the feeling of being in the midst of the waves and of rolling in familiar elements. The conviction that there was, in fact, no water at all made even his effort to swim into a frivolous exercise from which he drew nothing but discouragement. Perhaps he should only have had to get control of himself to drive away such thoughts, but his eye found nothing to cling to, and it seemed to him that he was staring into the void with the intention of finding help there. It was then that the sea, driven by the wind, broke loose. The storm tossed it, scattered it into inaccessible regions; the squalls turned the sky upside down and, at the same time, there reigned a silence and a calm which gave the impression that everything was already destroyed. Thomas sought to free himself from the insipid flood which was invading him. A piercing cold paralyzed his arms. The water swirled in whirlpools. Was it actually water? One moment the foam leapt before his eyes in whitish flakes, the next the absence of water took hold of his body and drew it along violently. His breathing became slower; for a few moments he held in his mouth the liquid which the squalls drove against his head: a tepid sweetness, strange brew of a man deprived of the sense of taste. Then, whether from fatigue or for an unknown reason, his limbs gave him the same sense of foreignness as the water in which they were tossed. This feeling seemed almost pleasant at first. As he swam, he pursued a sort of revery in which he confused himself with the sea. The intoxication of leaving himself, of slipping into the void, of dispersing himself in the thought of water, made him forget every discomfort. And even when this ideal sea which he was becoming ever more intimately had in turn become the real sea, in which he was virtually drowned, he was not moved as he should have been: of course, there was something intolerable about swimming this way, aimlessly, with a body which was of no use to him beyond thinking that he was swimming, but he also experienced a sense of relief, as if he had finally discovered the key to the situation, and, as far as he was concerned, it all came down to continuing his endless journey, with an absence of organism in an absence of sea. The illusion did not last. He was forced to roll from one side to the other, like a boat adrift, in the water which gave him a body to swim. What escape was there? To struggle in order not to be carried away by the wave which was his arm? To go under? To drown himself bitterly in himself? That would surely have been the moment to stop, but a hope remained; he went on swimming as if, deep within the restored core of his being, he had discovered a new possibility. He swam, a monster without fins. Under the giant microscope, he turned himself into an enterprising mass of cilia and vibrations. The temptation took on an entirely bizarre character when he sought to slip from the drop of water into a region which was vague and yet infinitely precise, a sort of holy place, so perfectly suited to him that it was enough for him to be there, to be; it was like an imaginary hollow which he entered because, before he was there, his imprint was there already. And so he made a last effort to fit completely inside. It was easy; he encountered no obstacles; he rejoined himself; he blended with himself, entering into this place which no one else could penetrate.

At last he had to come back. He found his way easily and his feet touched bottom at a place which some of the swimmers used for diving. The fatigue was gone. He still had a humming in his ears and a burning in his eyes, as might be expected after staying too long in the salt water. He became conscious of this as, turning toward the infinite sheet of water reflecting the sun, he tried to tell in which direction he had gone. At that point, there was a real mist before his sight, and he could pick out absolutely anything in this murky void which his gaze penetrated feverishly. Peering out, he discovered a man who was swimming far off, nearly lost below the horizon. At such a distance, the swimmer was always escaping him. He would see him, then lose sight of him, though he had the feeling that he was following his every move: not only perceiving him clearly all the time, but being brought near him in a completely intimate way, such that no other sort of contact could have brought him closer. He stayed a long time, watching and waiting. There was in this contemplation something painful which resembled the manifestation of an excessive freedom, a freedom obtained by breaking every bond. His face clouded over and took on an unusual expression.

II

HE NEVERTHELESS DECIDED to turn his back to the sea and entered a small woods where he lay down after taking a few steps. The day was about to end; scarcely any light remained, but it was still possible to see certain details of the landscape fairly clearly, in particular the hill which limited the horizon and which was glowing, unconcerned and free. What was disturbing to Thomas was the fact that he was lying there in the grass with the desire to remain there for a long time, although this position was forbidden to him. As night was falling he tried to get up, and, pushing against the ground with both hands, got one knee under him while the other leg dangled; then he made a sudden lurch and succeeded in placing himself entirely erect. So he was standing. As a matter of fact, there was an indecision in his way of being which cast doubt on what he was doing. And so, although his eyes were shut, it did not seem that he had given up seeing in the darkness, rather the contrary. Likewise, when he began to walk, one might have thought that it was not his legs, but rather his desire not to walk which pushed him forward. He went down into a sort of vault which at first he had believed to be rather large, but which very soon seemed to him extremely cramped: in front, in back, overhead, wherever he put out his hands, he collided brutally with a surface as hard as a stone wall; on all sides his way was barred, an insurmountable wall all around, and this wall was not the greatest obstacle for he had also to reckon on his will which was fiercely determined to let him sleep there in a passivity exactly like death. This was insane; in his uncertainty, feeling out the limits of the vaulted pit, he placed his body right up against the wall and waited. What dominated him was the sense of being pushed forward by his refusal to advance. So he was not very surprised, so clearly did his anxiety allow him to see into the future, when, a little later, he saw himself carried a few steps further along. A few steps: it was unbelievable. His progress was undoubtedly more apparent than real, for this new spot was indistinguishable from the last, he encountered the same difficulties here, and it was in a sense the same place that he was moving away from out of terror of leaving it. At that moment, Thomas had the rashness to look around himself. The night was more somber and more painful than he could have expected. The darkness immersed everything; there was no hope of passing through its shadows, but one penetrated its reality in a relationship of overwhelming intimacy. His first observation was that he could still use his body, and particularly his eyes; it was not that he saw anything, but what he looked at eventually placed him in contact with a nocturnal mass which he vaguely perceived to be himself and in which he was bathed. Naturally, he formulated this remark only as a hypothesis, as a convenient point of view, but one to which he was obliged to have recourse only by the necessity of unraveling new circumstances. As he had no means of measuring time, he probably took some hours before accepting this way of looking at things, but, for him, it was as if fear had immediately conquered him, and it was with a sense of shame that he raised his head to accept the idea he had entertained: outside himself there was something identical to his own thought which his glance or his hand could touch. Repulsive fantasy. Soon the night seemed to him gloomier and more terrible than any night, as if it had in fact issued from a wound of thought which had ceased to think, of thought taken ironically as object by something other than thought. It was night itself. Images which constituted its darkness inundated him. He saw nothing, and, far from being distressed, he made this absence of vision the culmination of his sight. Useless for seeing, his eye took on extraordinary proportions, developed beyond measure, and, stretching out on the horizon, let the night penetrate its center in order to receive the day from it. And so, through this void, it was sight and the object of sight which mingled together. Not only did this eye which saw nothing apprehend something, it apprehended the cause of its vision. It saw as object that which prevented it from seeing. Its own glance entered into it as an image, just when this glance seemed the death of all image. New preoccupations came out of this for Thomas. His solitude no longer seemed so complete, and he even had the feeling that something real had knocked against him and was trying to slip inside. Perhaps he might have been able to interpret this feeling in some other way, but he always had to assume the worst. What excuses him is the fact that the impression was so clear and so painful that it was almost impossible not to give way to it. Even if he had questioned its truth, he would have had the greatest difficulty in not believing that something extreme and violent was happening, for from all evidence a foreign body had lodged itself in his pupil and was attempting to go further. It was strange, absolutely disturbing, all the more disturbing because it was not a small object, but whole trees, the whole woods still quivering and full of life. He felt this as a weakness which did him no credit. He no longer even paid attention to the details of events. Perhaps a man slipped in by the same opening, he could neither have affirmed nor denied it. It seemed to him that the waves were invading the sort of abyss which was himself. All this preoccupied him only slightly. He had no attention for anything but his hands, busy recognizing the beings mingled with himself, whose character they discerned by parts, a dog represented by an ear, a bird replacing the tree on which it sang. Thanks to these beings which indulged in acts which escaped all interpretation, edifices, whole cities were built, real cities made of emptiness and thousands of stones piled one on another, creatures rolling in blood and tearing arteries, playing the role of what Thomas had once called ideas and passions. And so fear took hold of him, and was in no way distinguishable from his corpse. Desire was this same corpse which opened its eyes and knowing itself to be dead climbed awkwardly back up into his mouth like an animal swallowed alive. Feelings occupied him, then devoured him. He was pressed in every part of his flesh by a thousand hands which were only his hand. A mortal anguish beat against his heart. Around his body, he knew that his thought, mingled with the night, kept watch. He knew with terrible certainty that it, too, was looking for a way to enter into him. Against his lips, in his mouth, it was forcing its way toward a monstrous union. Beneath his eyelids, it created a necessary sight. And at the same time it was furiously destroying the face it kissed. Prodigious cities, ruined fortresses disappeared. The stones were tossed outside. The trees were transplanted. Hands and corpses were taken away. Alone, the body of Thomas remained, deprived of its senses. And thought, having entered him again, exchanged contact with the void.

III

HE CAME BACK to the hotel for dinner. Of course, he could have taken his usual place at the main table, but he chose not to and kept to one side. Eating, at this point, was not without importance. On the one hand, it was tempting because he was demonstrating that he was still free to turn back; but on the other hand, it was bad because he risked recovering his freedom on too narrow a foundation. So he preferred to adopt a less frank attitude, and took a few steps forward to see how the others would accept his new manner. At first he listened; there was a confused, crude noise which one moment would become very loud and then lessen and become imperceptible. Yes, there was no mistake about it, it was the sound of conversation and, moreover, when the talking became quieter, he began to recognize some very simple words which seemed to be chosen so that he might understand them more easily. Still, unsatisfied by the words, he wanted to confront the people facing him, and made his way toward the table: once there, he remained silent, looking at these people who all seemed to him to have a certain importance. He was invited to sit down. He passed up the invitation. They encouraged him more strongly and an elderly woman turned to him asking if he had swum that afternoon. Thomas answered yes. There was a silence: a conversation was possible, then? Yet what he had said must not have been very satisfying, for the woman looked at him with a reproachful air and got up slowly, like someone who, not having been able to finish her task, has some sort of regret; however, this did not prevent her from giving the impression by her departure that she abandoned her role very willingly. Without thinking, Thomas took the free place, and once seated on a chair which seemed to him surprisingly low, but comfortable, he no longer dreamed of anything but being served the meal which he had just refused. Wasn't it too late? He would have liked to consult those present on this point. Obviously, they were not showing themselves openly hostile toward him, he could even count on their goodwill, without which he would have been incapable of remaining so much as a second in the room; but there was in their attitude also something underhanded which did not encourage confidence, nor even any sort of communication. As he observed his neighbor, Thomas was struck by her: a tall, blonde girl whose beauty awoke as he looked at her. She had seemed very pleased when he came to sit down beside her, but now she held herself with a sort of stiffness, with a childish wish to keep apart, all the stranger because he was moving closer to get some sign of encouragement from her. He nevertheless continued to stare at her, for, bathed in a superb light, her entire person drew him. Having heard someone call her *Anne* (in a very sharp tone), and seeing that she immediately raised her head, ready to answer, he decided to act and, with all his strength, struck the table. Tactical error, no doubt about it, unfortunate move: the result was immediate. Everyone, as if offended by a foolish action which could be tolerated only by ignoring it, closed themselves off in a reserve against which nothing could be done. Hours might pass now without rekindling the slightest hope, and the greatest proofs of docility were doomed to failure, as were all attempts at rebellion. And so it seemed the game was lost. It was then that, to precipitate matters, Thomas began to stare at each of them, even those who turned away, even those who, when their glance met his, looked at him now less than ever. No one would have been in a mood to put up for very long with this empty, demanding stare, asking for no one knew what, and wandering without control, but his neighbor took it particularly badly: she got up, arranged her hair, wiped her face and prepared to leave in silence. How tired her movements were! Just a moment ago, it was the light bathing her face, the highlights of her dress which made her presence so comforting, and now this brilliance was fading away. All that remained was a being whose fragility appeared in her faded beauty and who was even losing all reality, as if the contours of the body had been outlined not by the light, but by a diffuse phosphorescence emanating, one might believe, from the bones. No encouragement was to be hoped for any longer from her. Persevering indecently in this contemplation, one could only sink deeper and deeper into a feeling of loneliness where, however far one wished to go, one would only lose oneself and continue to lose oneself. Nevertheless, Thomas refused to let himself be convinced by simple impressions. He even turned back deliberately toward the girl (although he had really not taken his eyes off her). Around him, everyone was getting up from the table in a disagreeable disorder and confusion. He rose as well, and, in the room which was now plunged in deep shadow, measured with his eye the space he had to cross to get to the door. At this moment, everything lit up, the electric lights shone, illuminating the vestibule, shining outside where it seemed one must enter as if into a warm, soft thickness. At the same moment, the girl called him from outside in a determined tone, almost too loud, which had a domineering ring, though it was impossible to tell whether this impression came from the order given or only from the voice which took it too seriously. Thomas was very sensitive to this invitation and his first impulse was to obey, rushing into the empty space. Then, when the silence had absorbed the call, he was no longer sure of having really heard his name and he contented himself with listening in the hope that he would be called again. As he listened, he thought about the distance of all these people, their absolute dumbness, their indifference. It was sheer childishness to hope to see all these distances suppressed by a single call. It was even humiliating and dangerous. At that point, he raised his head and, having assured himself that everyone had departed, he in turn left the room.

IV

THOMAS STAYED in his room to read. He was sitting with his hands joined over his brow, his thumbs pressing against his hairline, so deep in concentration that he did not make a move when anyone opened the door. Those who came in thought he was pretending to read, seeing that the book was always open to the same page. He was reading. He was reading with unsurpassable meticulousness and attention. In relation to every symbol, he was in the position of the male praying mantis about to be devoured by the female. They looked at each other. The words, coming forth from the book which was taking on the power of life and death, exercised a gentle and peaceful attraction over the glance which played over them. Each of them, like a half-closed eye, admitted the excessively keen glance which in other circumstances it would not have tolerated. And so Thomas slipped toward these corridors, approaching them defenselessly until the moment he was perceived by the very quick of the word. Even this was not fearful, but rather an almost pleasant moment he would have wished to prolong. The reader contemplated this little spark of life joyfully, not doubting that he had awakened it. It was with pleasure that he saw himself in this eye looking at him. The pleasure in fact became very great. It became so great, so pitiless that he bore it with a sort of terror, and in the intolerable moment when he had stood forward without receiving from his interlocutor any sign of complicity, he perceived all the strangeness there was in being observed by a word as if by a living being, and not simply by one word, but by all the words that were in that word, by all those that went with it and in turn contained other words, like a procession of angels opening out into the infinite to the very eye of the absolute. Rather than withdraw from a text whose defenses were so strong, he pitted all his strength in the will to seize it, obstinately refusing to withdraw his glance and still thinking himself a profound reader, even when the words were already taking hold of him and beginning to read him. He was seized, kneaded by intelligible hands, bitten by a vital tooth; he entered with his living body into the anonymous shapes of words, giving his substance to them, establishing their relationships, offering his being to the word "be." For hours he remained motionless, with, from time to time, the word "eyes" in place of his eyes: he was inert, captivated and unveiled. And even later when, having abandoned himself and, contemplating his book, he recognized himself with disgust in the form of the text he was reading, he retained the thought that (while, perched upon his shoulders, the word *He* and the word *I* were beginning their carnage) there remained within his person which was already deprived of its senses obscure words, disembodied souls and angels of words, which were exploring him deeply.

The first time he perceived this presence, it was night. By a light which came down through the shutters and divided the bed in two, he saw that the room was totally empty, so incapable of containing a single object that it was painful to the eye. The book was rotting on the table. There was no one walking in the room. His solitude was complete. And yet, sure as he was that there was no one in the room and even in the world, he was just as sure that someone was there, occupying his slumber, approaching him intimately, all around him and within him. On a naive impulse he sat up and sought to penetrate the night, trying with his hand to make light. But he was like a blind man who, hearing a noise, might run to light his lamp: nothing could make it possible for him to seize this presence in any shape or form. He was locked in combat with something inaccessible, foreign, something of which he could say: That doesn't exist... and which nevertheless filled him with terror as he sensed it wandering about in the region of his solitude. Having stayed up all night and all day with this being, as he tried to rest he was suddenly made aware that a second had replaced the first, just as inaccessible and just as obscure, and yet different. It was a modulation of that which did not exist, a different mode of being absent, another void in which he was coming to life. Now it was definitely true, someone was coming near him, standing not nowhere and everywhere, but a few feet away, invisible and certain. By an impulse which nothing might stop, and which nothing might quicken, a power with which he could not accept contact was coming to meet him. He wanted to flee. He threw himself into the corridor. Gasping and almost beside himself, he had taken only a few steps when he recognized the inevitable progress of the being coming toward him. He went back into the room. He barricaded the door. He waited, his back to the wall. But neither minutes nor hours put an end to his waiting. He felt ever closer to an ever more monstrous absence which took an infinite time to meet. He felt it closer to him every instant and kept ahead of it by an infinitely small but irreducible splinter of duration. He saw it, a horrifying being which was already pressing against him in space and, existing outside time, remained infinitely distant. Such unbearable waiting and anguish that they separated him from himself. A sort of Thomas left his body and went before the lurking threat. His eyes tried to look not in space but in duration, and in a point in time which did not yet exist. His hands sought to touch an impalpable and unreal body. It was such a painful effort that this thing which was moving away from him and trying to draw him along as it went seemed the same to him as that which was approaching unspeakably. He fell to the ground. He felt he was covered with impurities. Each part of his body endured an agony. His head was forced to touch the evil, his lungs to breathe it in. There he was on the floor, writhing, reentering himself and then leaving again. He crawled sluggishly, hardly different from the serpent he would have wished to become in order to believe in the venom he felt in his mouth. He stuck his head under the bed, in a corner full of dust, resting among the rejectamenta as if in a refreshing place where he felt he belonged more properly than in himself. It was in this state that he felt himself bitten or struck, he could not tell which, by what seemed to him to be a word, but resembled rather a giant rat, an all-powerful beast with piercing eyes and pure teeth. Seeing it a few inches from his face, he could not escape the desire to devour it, to bring it into the deepest possible intimacy with himself. He threw himself on it and digging his fingernails into its entrails, sought to make it his own. The end of the night came. The light which shone through the shutters went out. But the struggle with the horrible beast, which had ultimately shown itself possessed of incomparable dignity and splendor, continued for an immeasurable time. This struggle was terrible for the being lying on the ground grinding his teeth, twisting his face, tearing out his eyes to force the beast inside; he would have seemed a madman, had he resembled a man at all. It was almost beautiful for this dark angel covered with red hair, whose eyes sparkled. One moment, the one thought he had triumphed and, with uncontainable nausea, saw the word "innocence," which soiled him, slipping down inside him. The next moment, the other was devouring him in turn, dragging him out of the hole he had come from, then tossing him back, a hard, emptied body. Each time, Thomas was thrust back into the depths of his being by the very words which had haunted him and which he was pursuing as his nightmare and the explanation of his nightmare. He found that he was ever more empty, ever heavier; he no longer moved without infinite fatigue. His body, after so many struggles, became entirely opaque, and to those who looked at it, it gave the peaceful impression of sleep, though it had not ceased to be awake.

V

TOWARD THE MIDDLE of the second night, Thomas got up and went silently downstairs. No one noticed him with the exception of a nearly blind cat who, seeing the night change shape, ran after this new night which he did not see. After slipping into a tunnel where he did not recognize a single smell, this cat began to meow, forcing out from deep in his chest the raucous cry by which cats make it understood that they are sacred animals. He filled his lungs and howled. He drew from the idol he was becoming the incomprehensible voice which addressed itself to the night and spoke.

"What is happening?" said this voice. "The spirits with which I am usually in communication, the spirit that tugs at my tail when the bowl is full, the spirit that gets me up in the morning and puts me to bed in a soft comforter, and the most beautiful spirit of all, the one that meows and purrs and resembles me so closely that it is like my own spirit: they have all disappeared. Where am I now? If I feel gently with my paw, I find nothing. There's nothing anywhere. I'm at the very end of a gutter from which I can only fall. And that wouldn't scare me, falling. But the truth is that I can't even fall; no fall is possible; I am surrounded by a special void which repels me and which I wouldn't know how to cross over. Where am I then? Poor me. Once, by suddenly becoming a beast which might be cast into the fire with impunity, I used to penetrate secrets of the first order. By the flash of light which divided me, by the stroke of my claw, I knew lies and crimes before they were committed. And now I am a dull-eyed creature. I hear a monstrous voice by means of which I say what I say without knowing a single word of it all. I think, and my thoughts are as useless to me as hair standing on end or touching ears would be to the alien species I

71

depend upon. Horror alone penetrates me. I turn round and round crying the cry of a terrible beast. I have a hideous affliction: my face feels as large as a spirit's face, with a smooth, insipid tongue, a blind man's tongue, a deformed nose incapable of prophecy, enormous eyes without that straight flame which permits us to see things in ourselves. My coat is splitting. That is doubtless the final operation. As soon as it is no longer possible even in this night, to draw a supernatural light from me by stroking my hair, it will be the end. I am already darker than the shadows. I am the night of night. Through the shadows from which I am distinguished because I am their shadow, I go to meet the overcat. There is no fear in me now. My body, which is just like the body of a man, the body of the blessed, has kept its dimensions, but my head is enormous. There is a sound, a sound I have never heard before. A glow which seems to come from my body, though it is damp and lifeless, makes a circle around me which is like another body which I cannot leave. I begin to see a landscape. As the darkness becomes more oppressive, a great pallid figure rises before me. I say 'me,' guided by a blind instinct, for ever since I lost the good, straight tail which was my rudder in this world, I am manifestly no longer myself. This head which will not stop growing, and rather than a head seems nothing but a glance, just what is it? I can't look at it without uneasiness. It's mov-ing. It's coming closer. It is turned directly toward me and, pure glance though it is, it gives me the terrible impression that it doesn't see me. This feeling is unbearable. If I still had any hair, I would feel it standing up all over my body. But in my condition I no longer have even the means to experience the fear I feel. I am dead, dead. This head, my head, no longer even sees me, because I am annihilated. For it is I looking at myself and not perceiving myself. Oh over-cat whom I have become for an instant to establish the fact of my decease, I shall now disappear for good. First of all, I cease being a man. I again become a cold, uninhabitable little cat stretched out on the earth. I howl one more time. I take a last look at this vale which is about to be closed up, and where I see a man, himself an over-cat as well. I hear him scratch-ing the ground, probably with his claws. What is called the beyond is finished for me."

On his knees, his back bent, Thomas was digging in the earth. Around him extended several ditches on the edges of which the day was packed down. For the seventh time, leaving the mark of his hands in the soil, he was slowly preparing a great hole, which he was enlarging to his size. And while he was digging it, the hole, as if it had been filled by dozens of hands, then by arms and finally by the whole body, offered a resistance to his work which soon became insurmountable. The tomb was full of a being whose absence it absorbed. An immovable corpse was lodged there, finding in this absence of shape the perfect shape of its presence. It was a drama the horror of which was felt by the village folk in their sleep. As soon as the grave was finished, when Thomas threw himself into it with a huge stone tied around his neck, he crashed into a body a thousand times harder than the soil, the very body of the gravedigger who had already entered the grave to dig it. This grave which was exactly his size, his shape, his thickness, was like his own corpse, and every time he tried to bury himself in it, he was like a ridiculous dead person trying to bury his body in his body. There was, then, henceforth, in all the sepulchers where he might have been able to take his place, in all the feelings which are also tombs for the dead, in this annihilation through which he was dying without permitting himself to be thought dead, there was another dead person who was there first, and who, identical with himself, drove the ambiguity of Thomas's life and death to the extreme limit. In this subterranean night into which he had descended with cats and the dreams of cats, a double wrapped in bands, its senses sealed with the seven seals, its spirit absent, occupied his place, and this double was the unique one with which no compromise was possible, since it was the same as himself, realized in the absolute void. He leaned over this glacial tomb. Just as the man who is hanging himself, after kicking away the stool on which he stood, the final shore, rather than feeling the leap which he is making into the void feels only the rope which holds him, held to the end, held more than ever, bound as he had never been before to the existence he would like to leave, even so Thomas felt himself, at the moment he knew himself to be dead, absent, completely absent from his death. Neither his body, which left in the depths of himself that coldness which comes from contact with a corpse and which is not coldness but absence of contact, nor the darkness, which seeped from all his pores and even when he was visible made it impossible to use any sense, intuition or thought to see him, nor the fact that by no right could he pass for living, sufficed to make him pass for dead. And it was not a misunderstanding. He was really dead and at the same time rejected from the reality of death. In death itself, he was deprived of death, a horribly destroyed man, stopped in the midst of nothingness by his own image, by this Thomas running before him, bearer of extinguished torches, who was like the existence of the very last death. Already, as he still leaned over this void where he saw his image in the total absence of images, seized by the most violent vertigo possible, a vertigo which did not make him fall but prevented him from falling and rendered impossible the fall it rendered inevitable, already the earth was shrinking around him and night, a night which no longer responded to anything, which he did not see and whose reality he sensed only because it was less real than himself, surrounded him. In every way, he was invaded by the feeling of being at the heart of things. Even on the surface of this earth which he could not penetrate, he was within this earth, whose insides touched him on all sides. On all sides, night closed him in. He saw, he heard the core of an infinity where he was bound by the very absence of limits. He felt as an oppressive existence the nonexistence of this valley of death. Little by little the emanations of an acrid and damp leaf-mold reached him. Like a man waking up alive in his coffin, terrified, he saw the impalpable earth where he floated transformed into an air without air, filled with smells of the earth, of rotten wood, of damp cloth. Now truly buried, he discovered himself, beneath accumulated layers of a material resembling plaster, in a hole where he was smothering. He was soaked in an icy medium among objects which were crushing him. If he still existed, it was to recognize the impossibility of living again, here in this room full of funereal flowers and spectral light. Suffocating, he managed to breathe again. He again discovered the possibility of walking, of seeing, of crying out, deep within a prison where he was confined in impenetrable silence and darkness. What a strange horror was his, as, passing the last barriers, he appeared at the narrow gate of his sepulcher, not risen but dead, and with the certainty of being snatched at once from death and from life. He walked, a painted mummy; he looked at the sun which was making an effort to put a smiling, lively expression on its indifferent face. He walked, the only true Lazarus, whose very death was resurrected. He went forward, passing beyond the last shadows of night without losing any of his glory, covered with grass and earth, walking at an even pace beneath the falling stars, the same pace which, for those men who are not wrapped in a winding-sheet, marks the ascent toward the most precious point in life.

VI

ANNE SAW HIM coming without surprise, this inevitable being in whom she recognized the one she might try in vain to escape, but would meet again every day. Each time, he came straight to her, following with an inflexible pace a path laid straight over the sea, the forests, even the sky. Each time, when the world was emptied of everything but the sun and this motionless being standing at her side, Anne, enveloped in his silent immobility, carried away by this profound insensitivity which revealed her, feeling all the calm of the universe condensing in her through him, just as the sparkling chaos of the ultimate noon was resounding, mingled with the silence, pressed by the greatest peace, not daring to make a move or to have a thought, seeing herself burned, dying, her eyes, her cheeks aflame, mouth half open exhaling, as a last breath, her obscure forms into the glare of the sun, perfectly transparent in death beside this opaque corpse which stood by, becoming ever more dense, and, more silent than silence, undermined the hours and deranged time. A just and sovereign death, inhuman and shameful moment which began anew each day, and from which she could not escape. Each day he returned at the same time to the same place. And it was precisely the same moment, the same garden as well. With the ingenuousness of Joshua stopping the sun to gain time, Ann believed that things were going on. But the terrible trees, dead in their green foliage which could not dry out, the birds which flew above her without, alas, deceiving anyone or succeeding in making themselves pass for living, stood solemn guard over the horizon and made her begin again eternally the scene she had lived the day before. Nevertheless, that day (as if a corpse borne from one bed to another were really changing place) she arose, walked before Thomas and drew him toward the little woods nearby, along a road on which those who came from the other direction saw him recede, or thought he was motionless. In fact, he was really walking and, with a body like the others, though three-quarters consumed, he penetrated a region where, if he himself disappeared, he immediately saw the others fall into another nothingness which placed them further from him than if they had continued to live. On this road, each man he met died. Each man, if Thomas turned away his eyes, died with him a death which was not announced by a single cry. He looked at them, and already he saw them lose all resemblance beneath his glance, with a tiny wound in the forehead through which their face escaped. They did not disappear, but they did not appear again. As far away as they became visible, they were shapeless and mute. Nearer, if he touched them, if he directed toward them not his glance, but the glance of this dazzling and invisible eye which he was, every moment, completely... and nearer yet, almost blending with them, taking them either for his shadow or for dead souls, breathing them, licking them, coating himself with their bodies, he received not the slightest sensation, not the slightest image, as empty of them as they were empty of him. Finally they passed by. They went away, definitively. They slipped down a vertiginous slope toward a country whence nothing was any longer visible, except perhaps, like a great trail of light, their last phosphorescent stare on the horizon. It was a terrible and mysterious blast. Behind him there were no more words, no silence, no backward and no forward. The space surrounding him was the opposite of space, infinite thought in which those who entered, their heads veiled, existed only for nothing.

In this abyss Anne alone resisted. Dead, dissolved in the closest thing to the void, she yet found there the debris of beings with whom she maintained, in the midst of the holocaust, a sort of familial resemblance in her features. If he came straight up to her, brutally, to surprise her, she always presented him a face. She changed without ceasing to be Anne. She was Anne, having no longer the slightest resemblance to Anne. In her face and in all her features, while she was completely identical to another, she remained the same, Anne, Anne complete and undeniable. On his path, he saw her coming like a spider which was identical to the girl and, among the vanished corpses, the emptied men, walked through the deserted world with a strange peace, last descendant of a fabulous race. She walked with eight enormous legs as if on two delicate ones. Her black body, her ferocious look which made one think she was about to bite when she was about to flee, were not different from the clothed body of Anne, from the delicate air she had when one tried to see her close up. She came forward jerkily, now devouring space in a few bounds, now lying down on the path, brooding it, drawing it from herself like an invisible thread. Without even drawing in her limbs, she entered the space surrounding Thomas. She approached irresistibly. She stopped before him. Then, that day, seized by this incredible bravery and perseverance, recognizing in her something carefree which could not disappear in the midst of trials and which resounded like a memory of freedom, seeing her get up on her long legs, hold herself at the level of his face to communicate with him, secreting a whirlwind of nuances, of odors and thoughts, he turned and looked bitterly behind him, like a traveler who, having taken a wrong turn, moves away, then draws within himself and finally disappears in the thought of his journey. Yes, this woods, he recognized it. And this declining sun, he recognized that, and these trees drying out and these green leaves turning black. He tried to shake the enormous weight of his body, a missing body whose illusion he bore like a borrowed body. He needed to feel the factitious warmth which radiated from himself as from an alien sun, to hear the breath flowing from a false source, to listen to the beating of a false heart. And her, did he recognize her, this dead person on guard behind a hideous resemblance, ready to appear as she was, in the atmosphere studded with little mirrors where every one of her features survived? "It's you?" he asked. Immediately he saw a flame in a pair of eyes, a sad, cold flame on a face. He shuddered in this unknown body while Anne, feeling a sad spirit entering into her, a funereal youthfulness she was sworn to love, believed she was again becoming herself.

VII

ANNE HAD A FEW DAYS of great happiness. And she had never even dreamed of a simpler happiness, a lovelier tenderness. For her, he was suddenly a being she possessed without danger. If she took hold of him, it was with the greatest freedom. As for his head, he abandoned it to her. His words, before they were spoken, might as well have been in one mouth as the other, so completely did he let her do as she wished. In this way in which Anne played with his entire person and in the absence of risk which permitted her to treat this strange body as if it belonged to her, there was a frivolousness so perilous that anyone would have been pained at it. But she saw in him only a futile mouth, empty glances, and, rather than feeling uneasy at the realization that a man she could not approach, whom she could not dream of making speak, consented to roll his head in her lap, she enjoyed it. It was, on her part, a way to act which was difficult to justify. From one moment to the next one might anticipate, between these bodies bound so intimately together by such fragile bonds, a contact which would reveal in a terrible way their lack of bonds. The more he withdrew within himself, the more she came frivolously forward. He attracted her, and she buried herself in the face whose contours she still thought she was caressing. Did she act so imprudently because she thought she was dealing with someone inaccessible, or, on the other hand, with someone too easy to approach? Her stare was fixed on him... was this an impudent game, or a desperate one? Her words became moist, even her weakest movements glued her against him, while within her swelled up the pocket of humors from which she would perhaps, at the proper moment, draw an extreme power of adhesion. She covered herself with suction-cups. Within and without, she was no more than wounds trying to heal, flesh being grafted. And, despite such a change, she continued to play and to laugh. As she held out her hand to him she said: "Really, who could you be?"

Properly speaking, there was no question in this remark. Distracted as she was, how could she have interrogated a being whose existence was a terrible question posed to herself? But she seemed to find it surprising and slightly shocking, yes, really shocking, not yet to be able, not to understand him (which in itself would have been extremely presumptuous), but (and this time the rashness went beyond all limits) to get information about him. And this boldness was not enough for her, for the regret she felt at not knowing him, rather than trying to justify itself in its bizarre form through the violence and madness of its expression, emerged rather as a relaxed and almost indifferent regret. It was, beneath the benign appearance all such operations have, an actual attempt to tempt God. She looked him right in the face: "But, what are you?"

Although she did not expect to hear him answer and even if she were sure that he would not answer she would not in fact have questioned him, there was such a presumption in her manner of assuming that he could give an answer (of course, he would not answer, she did not ask him to answer, but, by the question she had posed him personally and relating to his person, she acted as if she might interpret his silence as an accidental refusal to answer, as an attitude which might change one day or another), it was such a crude way to treat the impossible that Anne had suddenly revealed to her the terrible scene she was throwing herself into blindfolded, and in an instant, waking from her sleep, she perceived all the consequences of her act and the madness of her conduct. Her first thought was to prevent him from answering. For the great danger, now that by an inconsiderate and arbitrary act she had just treated him as a being one might question, was that he might in turn act like a being that might answer and make his answer understood. She felt this threat deposited in the depths of her self, in the place of the words she had spoken. He was already grasping the hand held out to him. He seized it cruelly, giving Anne to believe that he understood her reasons, and that after all there was in fact a possibility of contact between them. Now that she was sure that, pitilessly unrelenting as he was, if he spoke he would say everything there was to say without hiding anything from her, telling her everything so that when he stopped speaking his silence, the silence of a being that has nothing more to give and yet has given nothing, would be even more terrifying, now she was sure that he would speak. And this certainty was so great that he appeared to her as if he had already spoken. He surrounded her, like an abyss. He revolved about her. He entranced her. He was going to devour her by changing the most unexpected words into words she would no longer be able to expect.

"What I am...."

"Be quiet."

It was late, and knowing that hours and days no longer concerned anyone but her, she cried louder in the shadows. She came near and lay down before the window. Her face melted, and again closed itself. When the darkness was complete, leaning in her tattered way toward the one she now called, in her new language drawn from the depths, her friend, without worrying about her own state she wanted (like a drunkard with no legs explaining to himself by his drunkenness the fact that he can no longer walk), she wanted to see why her relations with this dead man no longer seemed to be advancing. As low as she had fallen, and probably because from that level she perceived that there was a difference between them and a huge difference, but not such that their relationship must always be doomed, she was suddenly suspicious of all the politenesses they had exchanged. In the folds where she hid herself, she told herself with a profoundly sophisticated air that she would not allow herself to be deceived by the appearance of this perfectly lovable young man, and it was with deep pain that she recalled his welcoming manner and the ease with which she approached him. If she did not go so far as to suspect him of hypocrisy (she might complain, she might cry miserably because he kept her twenty fathoms below the truth in brilliant and empty words; but it never came into her head, in spite of her sullen efforts to speak of herself and of him in the same words, that there might be, in what she called the character of Thomas, any duplicity), it was because, just by turning her head, in the silence in which he necessarily existed, she perceived him to be so impenetrable that she saw clearly how ridiculous it would have been to call him insincere. He did not deceive her, and yet she was deceived by him. Treachery revolved about them, so much the more terrible because it was she who was betraying *him,* and she was deceiving herself at the same time with no hope of putting an end to this aberration since, not knowing who he was, she always found someone else beside her. Even the night increased her error, even time which made her try again and again without reprieve the same things, which she undertook with a fierce and humiliated air. It was a story emptied of events, emptied to the point that every memory and all perspective were eliminated, and nevertheless drawing from this absence its inflexible direction which seemed to carry everything away in the irresistible movement toward an imminent catastrophe. What was going to happen? She did not know, but devoting her entire life to waiting, her impatience melted into the hope of participating in a general cataclysm in which, at the same time as the beings themselves, the distances which separate beings would be destroyed.

VIII

IT WAS IN THIS NEW STATE that, feeling herself becoming an enormous, immeasurable reality on which she fed her hopes, like a monster revealed to no one, not even to herself, she became still bolder and, keeping company with Thomas, came to attribute to more and more penetrable motives the difficulties of her relationship with him, thinking, for example, that what was abnormal was that nothing could be discovered about his life and that in every circumstance he remained anonymous and without a history. Once she had started in this direction, there was no chance of her stopping herself in time. It would have been just as well to say whatever came into one's head with no other intention than to put the words to the test. But, far from condescending to observe these precautions, she saw fit, in a language whose solemnity contrasted with her miserable condition, to rise to a height of profanation which hung on the apparent truth of her words. What she said to him took the form of direct speech. It was a cry full of pride which resounded in the sleepless night with the very character of dream.

"Yes," she said, "I would like to see you when you are alone. If ever I could be before you and completely absent from you, I would have a chance to meet you. Or rather I know that I would not meet you. The only possibility I would have to diminish the distance between us would be to remove myself to an infinite distance. But I am infinitely far away now, and can go no further. As soon as I touch you, Thomas.... "

Hardly out of her mouth, these words carried her away: she saw him, he was radiant. Her head thrown back, a soft noise rose from her throat which drove all memories away; there was no need, now, to cry out... her eyes closed, her spirit was intoxicated; her breathing became slow and deep, her hands came together: this should reasonably have continued forever. But, as if the silence were also an invitation to return (for it bound her to nothing), she let herself go, opened her eyes, recognized the room and, once again, everything had to be begun anew. This deception, the fact that she did not have the desired explanation, left her unmoved. She certainly could no longer think that he would reveal to her what was, to her, a sort of secret, and for him had in no way the quality of a secret. On the contrary, clinging to the idea that what she might say would endure, in spite of everything, she was determined to communicate to him the fact that, though she was not unaware of the extraordinary distance which separated them, she would obstinately maintain contact with him to the very end, for, if there was something shameless in her concern to say that what she was doing was insane, and that nevertheless she was doing it fully conscious of the situation, there was something very tempting in it as well. But could one even believe that, infantile as that might be, she could do it on her own? Speak, yes, she could start to speak, with the sense of guilt of an accomplice betraying his companion, not in admitting what he knows—he knows nothing—but in admitting what he does not know, for she did not have it within her means to say anything true or even apparently true; and nevertheless what she said, without allowing her to perceive the truth in any sense, without the compensation of throwing the slightest light on the enigma, chained her as heavily, perhaps more heavily, than if she had revealed the very heart of secrets. Far from being able to slip into the lost pathways where she would have had the hope of coming near to him, she only went astray in her travels and led forth an illusion which, even in her eyes, was only an illusion. Despite the dimming of her perspective she suspected that her project was puerile and that furthermore she was committing a great mistake with nothing to gain from it, although she also had this thought (and in fact this was just the mistake): that the moment she made a mistake because of him or relating to him, she created between them a link he would have to reckon with. But she nevertheless guessed how dangerous it was to see in him a being who had experienced events no doubt different from others, but fundamentally analogous to all the others, to plunge him into the same water which flowed over her. It was not, at any event, a small imprudence to mix time, her personal time, with that which detested time, and she knew that no good for her own childhood could emerge from the caricature— and if the image had been a perfect one it would have been worse—of childhood which would be given by one who could have no historical character. So the uneasiness rose in her, as if time had already been corrupted, as if all her past, again placed in question, had been offered up in a barren and inevitably guilty future. And she could not even console herself in the thought that, since everything she had to say was arbitrary, the risk itself was illusory. On the contrary she knew, she felt, with an anguish which seemed to threaten her very life but which was more precious than her life, that, though she might say nothing true no matter how she might speak, she was exposing herself (in retaining only one version among so many others) to the danger of rejecting seeds of truth which would be sacrificed. And she felt further, with an anxiety which threatened her purity but which brought her a new purity, that she was going to be forced (even if she tried to cut herself off behind the most arbitrary and most innocent evocation) to introduce something serious into her tale, an impenetrable and terrible reminiscence, so that, as this false figure emerged from the shadows, acquiring through a useless meticulousness a greater and greater precision and a more and more artificial one, she herself, the narrator, already condemned and delivered into the hands of the devils, would bind herself unpardonably to the true figure, of which she would know nothing.

"What you are... ," she said.... And as she spoke these words, she seemed to dance around him and, fleeing him at the same time, to push him into an imaginary wolf-trap. "What you are.... "

She could not speak, and yet she was speaking. Her tongue vibrated in such a way that she seemed to express the meanings of words without the words themselves. Then, suddenly, she let herself be carried away by a rush of words which she pronounced almost beneath her breath, with varied inflections, as if she wanted only to amuse herself with sounds and bursts of syllables. She gave the impression that, speaking a language whose infantile character prevented it from being taken for a language, she was making the meaningless words seem like incomprehensible ones. She said nothing, but to say nothing was for her an all too meaningful mode of expression, beneath which she succeeded in saying still less. She withdrew indefinitely from her babbling to enter into yet another, less serious babbling, which she nevertheless rejected as too serious, preparing herself by an endless retreat beyond all seriousness for repose in absolute puerility, until her vocabulary, through its nullity, took on the appearance of a sleep which was the very voice of seriousness. Then, as if in the depths she had suddenly felt herself under the surveillance of an implacable consciousness, she leaped back, cried out, opened terribly clairvoyant eyes and, halting her tale an instant: "No," she said, "it's not that. What you really are…"

She herself took on a puerile and frivolous appearance. From beneath the murky look which had veiled her face for a few moments came forth expressions which made her seem distracted. She presented such a delicate appearance that, looking at her, it was impossible to fix one's attention on her features, or on the whole of her person. It was that much more difficult to remember what she said and to attach any meaning to it. It was impossible even to know about whom she was talking. One moment she seemed to be talking to Thomas, but the very fact that she was talking to him made it impossible to perceive her actual interlocutor. The next moment she was talking to no one, and, vain as her lisping was at that point, there came a moment when, brought forward by this endless wandering before a reality without reason, she stopped suddenly, emerging from the depths of her frivolity with a hideous expression. The issue was still the same. It was vain for her to search out her route at the ends of the earth and lose herself in infinite digressions—and the voyage might last her entire life; she knew that she was coming closer every minute to the instant when it would be necessary not only to stop but to abolish her path, either having found what she should not have found, or eternally unable to find it. And it was impossible for her to give up her project. For how could she be silent, she whose language was several degrees below silence? By ceasing to be there, ceasing to live? These were just more ridiculous strategies, for through her death, closing off all the exits, she would only have precipitated the eternal race in the labyrinth, from which she retained the hope of escape as long as she had the perspective of time. And she no longer saw that she was coming imperceptibly closer to Thomas. She followed him, step by step, without realizing it, or if she realized it, then, wanting to leave him, to flee him, she had to make a greater effort. Her exhaustion became so overwhelming that she contented herself with mimicking her flight and stayed glued to him, her eyes flowing with tears, begging, imploring him to put an end to this situation, still trying, leaning over this mouth, to formulate words to continue her narrative at any cost, the same narrative she would have wished to devote her last measure of strength to interrupting and stifling.

It was in this state of abandonment that she allowed herself to be carried along by the feeling of duration. Gently, her fingers drew together, her steps left her and she slipped into a pure water where, from one instant to the next, crossing eternal currents, she seemed to pass from life to death, and worse, from death to life, in a tormented dream which was already absorbed in a peaceful dream. Then suddenly with the noise of a tempest she entered into a solitude made of the suppression of all space, and, torn violently by the call of the hours, she unveiled herself. It was as if she were in a green valley where, invited to be the personal rhythm, the impersonal cadence of all things, she was becoming with her age and her youth, the age, the old age, of others. First she climbed down into the depths of a day totally foreign to human days, and, full of seriousness, entering into the intimacy of pure things, then rising up toward sovereign time, drowned among the stars and the spheres, far from knowing the peace of the skies she began to tremble and to experience pain. It was during this night and this eternity that she prepared herself to become the time of men. Endlessly, she wandered along the empty corridors lit by the reflected light of a source which always hid itself and which she pursued without love, with the obstinacy of an already lost soul incapable of seizing again the sense of these metamorphoses and the goal of this silent walk. But, when she passed before a door which looked like Thomas's, recognizing that the tragic debate was still going on, she knew then that she was no longer arguing with him with words and thoughts, but with the very time she was espousing. Now, each second, each sigh—and it was herself, nothing other than herself—dumbly attacked the unconcerned life he held up to her. And in each of his reasonings, more mysterious still than his existence, he experienced the mortal presence of the adversary, of this time without which, eternally immobilized, unable to come from the depths of the future, he would have been condemned to see the light of life die out on his desolate peak, like the prophetic eagle of dreams. So he reasoned with the absolute contradictor at the heart of his argument, he thought with the enemy and the subject of all thought in the depths of his thought, his perfect antagonist, this *time*, Anne, and mysteriously receiving her within himself he found himself for the first time at grips with a serious conversation. It was in this situation that she penetrated as a vague shape into the existence of Thomas. Everything there appeared desolate and mournful. Deserted shores where deeper and deeper absences, abandoned by the eternally departed sea after a magnificent shipwreck, gradually de-composed. She passed through strange dead cities where, rather than petrified shapes, mummified circumstances, she found a necropolis of movements, silences, voids; she hurled herself against the extraordi-nary sonority of nothingness which is made of the reverse of sound, and before her spread forth wondrous falls, dreamless sleep, the fading away which buries the dead in a life of dream, the death by which every man, even the weakest spirit, becomes spirit itself. In this explo-ration which she had undertaken so naively, believing that she might find the last word on herself, she recognized herself passionately in search of the absence of Anne, of the most absolute nothingness of Anne. She thought she understood—oh cruel illusion—that the in-difference which flowed the length of Thomas like a lonely stream came from the infiltration, in regions she should never have penetrated, of the fatal absence which had succeeded in breaking all the dams, so that, wanting now to discover this naked absence, this pure negative, the equivalent of pure light and deep desire, she had, in order to reach it, to yoke herself to severe trials. For lives on end she had to polish her thought, to relieve it of all that which made of it a miserable bric-a-brac, the mirror which admires itself, the prism with its interior sun: she needed an I without its glassy solitude, without this eye so long stricken with strabism, this eye whose supreme beauty is to be as crosseyed as possible, the eye of the eye, the thought of thought. One might have thought of her as running into the sun and at every turn of the path tossing into an ever more voracious abyss an eternally poorer and more rarified Anne. One would have confused her with this very abyss where, remaining awake in the midst of sleep, her spirit free of knowing, without light, bringing nothing to think in her meeting with thought, she prepared to go out so far in front of herself that on con-tact with absolute nakedness, miraculously passing beyond, she could recognize therein her pure, her very own transparency. Gently, armed only with the name Anne which must serve her to return to the sur-face after the dive, she let the tide of the first and crudest absences rise—absence of sound silence, absence of being death—but after this so tepid and facile nothingness which Pascal, though already terrified, inhabited, she was seized by the diamond absences, the absence of si-lence, the absence of death, where she could no longer find any foot-hold except in ineffable notions, indefinable somethings, sphinxes of unheard rumblings, vibrations which burst the ether of the most shattering sounds, and, exceeding their energy, explode the sounds themselves. And she fell among the major circles, analogous to those of Hell, passing, a ray of pure reason, by the critical moment when for a very short instant one must remain in the absurd and, having left behind that which can still be represented, indefinitely add absence to absence and to the absence of absence and to the absence of the absence of absence and, thus, with this vacuum machine, desperately create the void. At this instant the real fall begins, the one which abolishes itself, nothingness incessantly devoured by a purer nothingness. But at this limit Anne became conscious of the madness of her undertaking. Everything she had thought she had suppressed of herself, she was certain she was finding it again, entire. At this moment of supreme absorption, she recognized at the deepest point of her thought a thought, the miserable thought that she was Anne, the living, the blonde, and, oh horror, the intelligent. Images petrified her, gave birth to her, produced her. A body was bestowed on her, a body a thousand times more beautiful than her own, a thousand times more body; she was visible, she radiated from the most unchangeable matter: at the center of nullified thought she was the superior rock, the crumbly earth, without nitrogen, that from which it would not even have been possible to create Adam; she was finally going to avenge herself by hurling herself against the incommunicable with this grossest, ugliest body, this body of mud, with this vulgar idea that she wanted to vomit, that she was vomiting, bearing to the marvelous absence her portion of excrement. It was at that moment that at the heart of the unheard a shattering noise rang out and she began to howl "Anne, Anne" in a furious voice. At the heart of indifference, she burst into flame, a complete torch with all her passion, her hate for Thomas, her love for Thomas. At the heart of nothingness, she intruded as a triumphal presence and hurled herself there, a corpse, an inassimilable nothingness, Anne, who still existed and existed no longer, a supreme mockery to the thought of Thomas.

IX

WHEN SHE CAME AROUND, entirely speechless now, refus-
ing any expression to her eyes as well as her lips, still stretched out on
the ground, the silence showed her so united with silence that she
embraced it furiously like another nature, whose intimacy would have
overwhelmed her with disgust. It seemed as if, during this night, she
had assimilated something imaginary which was a burning thorn to
her and forced her to shove her own existence outside like some foul
excrement. Motionless against the wall, her body had mingled with the
pure void, thighs and belly united to a nothingness with neither sex nor
sexual parts, hands convulsively squeezing an absence of hands, face
drinking in what was neither breath nor mouth, she had transformed
herself into another body whose life—supreme penury and indigence—
had slowly made her become the totality of that which she could not
become. There where her body was, her sleeping head, there too was
body without head, head without body, body of wretchedness. Doubtless nothing had changed about her appearance, but the glance one might
direct toward her which showed her to be like anyone else was utterly
unimportant, and, precisely because it was impossible to identify her, it
was in the perfect resemblance of her features, in the glaze of naturalness and sincerity laid down by the night, that the horror of seeing her
just as she had always been, without the least change, while it was certain that she was completely changed, found its source. Forbidden spectacle. While one might have been able to bear the sight of a monster,
there was no cold-bloodedness that could hold out against the impression created by this face on which, for hours, in an investigation which
came to nothing, the eye sought to distinguish a sign of strangeness or
bizarreness. What one saw, with its familiar naturalness, became, by

the simple fact that manifestly it was not what one should have seen, an enigma which finally not only blinded the eye but made it experience toward this image an actual nausea, an expulsion of detritus of all sorts which the glance forced upon itself in trying to seize in this object something other than what it could see there. In fact, if what was entirely changed in an identical body—the sense of disgust imposed on all the senses forced to consider themselves insensitive—if the ungraspable character of the new person that had devoured the old and left her as she was, if this mystery buried in absence of mystery had not explained the silence which flowed from the sleeping girl, one would have been tempted to search out in such calm some indication of the tragedy of illusions and lies in which the body of Anne had wrapped itself. There was in fact something terribly suspicious about her mutism. That she should not speak, that in her motionlessness she should retain the discretion of someone who remains silent even in the intimacy of her dreams, all this was, finally, natural, and she was not about to betray herself, to expose herself, through this sleep piled upon sleep. But her silence did not even have the right to silence, and through this absolute state were expressed at once the complete unreality of Anne and the unquestionable and indemonstrable presence of this unreal Anne, from whom there emanated, by this silence, a sort of terrible humor which one became uneasily conscious of. As if there had been a crowd of intrigued and moved spectators, she turned to ridicule the possibility that one might see her, and a sense of ridicule came also from this wall against which she had stretched herself out in a way one might have taken (what stupidity) for sleep, and from this room where she was, wrapped in a linen coat, and where the day was beginning to penetrate with the laughable intention of putting an end to the night by giving the password: "Life goes on." Even alone, there was around her a sad and insatiable curiosity, a dumb interrogation which, taking her as object, bore also, vaguely, on everything, so that she existed as a problem capable of producing death, not, like the sphinx, by the difficulty of the enigma, but by the temptation which she offered of resolving the problem in death.

When day had come, as she was waking up, one might have thought she had been drawn from sleep by the day. However, the end of the night did not explain the fact that she had opened her eyes, and her awakening was only a slow exhausting, the final movement toward rest: what made it impossible for her to sleep was the action of a force which, far from being opposed to the night, might just as well have been called nocturnal. She saw that she was alone, but though she could rise only in the world of solitude, this isolation remained foreign to her, and, in the passive state where she remained, it was not important that her solitude should burst in her like something she did not need to feel and which drew her into the eternally removed domain of day. Not even the sadness was any longer felt as present. It wandered about her in a blind form. It came forward within the sphere of resignation, where it was impossible for it to strike or hit. Crossing over betrayed fatality, it came right to the heart of the young woman and touched her with the feeling of letting go, with absence of consciousness into which she leapt with the greatest abandon. From this moment on, not a single desire came to her to elucidate her situation in any way, and love was reduced to the impossibility of expressing and experiencing that love. Thomas came in. But the presence of Thomas no longer had any importance in itself. On the contrary, it was terrible to see to what extent the desire to enjoy this presence, even in the most ordinary way, had faded. Not only was every motive for clear communication destroyed, but to Anne it seemed that the mystery of this being had passed into her own heart, the very place where it could no longer be seized except as an eternally badly formulated question. And he, on the contrary, in the silent indifference of his coming, gave an impression of offensive clarity, without the feeblest, the most reassuring sign of a secret. It was in vain that she looked at him with the troubled looks of her fallen passion. It was as the least obscure man in the world that he came forth from the night, bathed in transparency by the privilege of being above any interrogation, a transfigured but trivial character from whom the problems were now separating themselves, just as she also saw herself turned away from him by this dramatically empty spectacle, turned away upon herself where there was neither richness nor fullness but the oppressiveness of a dreary satiety, the certainty that there should evolve no other drama than the playing out of a day where despair and hope would be drowned, the useless waiting having become, through the suppression of all ends and of time itself, a machine whose mechanism had for its sole function the measurement, by a silent exploration, of the empty movement of its various parts. She went down into the garden and, there, seemed to disengage herself at least in part from the condition into which the events of the night had thrown her. The sight of the trees stunned her. Her eyes clouded over. What was striking now was the extreme weakness she showed. There was no resistance left in her organism, and with her transparent skin, the great pallor of her glances, she seemed to tremble with exhaustion whenever anyone or anything approached her. In fact one might have wondered how she could stand the contact of the air and the cries of the birds. By the way she oriented herself in the garden, one was almost sure that she was in another garden: not that she walked like a somnambulist in the midst of the images of her slumber, but she managed to proceed across the field full of life, resounding and sunlit, to a worn-out field, mournful and extinguished, which was a second version of the reality she traveled through. Just when one saw her stop, out of breath and breathing with difficulty the excessively fresh, cool air which blew against her, she was penetrating a ratified atmosphere in which, to get back her breath, it was enough to stop breathing entirely. While she was walking with difficulty along the path where she had to lift up her body with each step, she was entering, a body without knees, onto a path in every way like the first, but where she alone could go. This landscape relaxed her, and she felt the same consolation there as if, overturning from top to bottom the illusory body whose intimacy oppressed her, she might have been able to exhibit to the sun which threw light on her like a faint star, in the form of her visible chest, her folded legs, her dangling arms, the bitter disgust which was piecing together an absolutely hidden second person deep within her. In this ravaged day, she could confess the revulsion and fright whose vastness could be circumscribed by no image, and she succeeded almost joyously in forcing from her belly the inexpressible feelings (fantastic creatures having in turn the shape of her face, of her skeleton, of her entire body) which had drawn within her the entire world of repulsive and unbearable things, through the horror that world inspired in her. The solitude, for Anne, was immense. All that she saw, all that she felt was the tearing away which separated her from what she saw and what she felt. The baneful clouds, if they covered the garden, nevertheless remained invisible in the huge cloud which enveloped them. The tree, a few steps away, was the tree with reference to which she was absent and distinct from everything. In all the souls which surrounded her like so many clearings, and which she could approach as intimately as her own soul, there was a silent, closed and desolate consciousness (the only light which made them perceptible), and it was solitude that created around her the sweet field of human contacts where, among infinite relationships full of harmony and tenderness, she saw her own mortal pain coming to meet her.

X

WHEN THEY FOUND HER stretched out on a bench in the garden, they thought she had fainted. But she had not fainted; she was sleeping, having entered into sleep by way of a repose deeper yet than sleep. Henceforth, her advance toward unconsciousness was a solemn combat in which she refused to give in to the thrill of drowsiness until she was wounded, dead already, and defended up to the last instant her right to consciousness and her share of clear thoughts. There was no complicity between her and the night. From the time the day started to fade, listening to the mysterious hymn which called her to another existence, she prepared herself for the struggle in which she could be defeated only by the total ruin of life. Her cheeks red, her eyes shining, calm and smiling, she enthusiastically mustered her strength. In vain the dusk brought its guilty song to her ear; in vain was a plot woven against her in favor of darkness. No sweetness penetrated her soul along the path of torpor, no semblance of the holiness which is acquired through the proper acceptance of illness. One felt that she would deliver into death nothing other than Anne, and that, fiercely intact, retaining everything that she was until the very end, she would not consent to save herself by any imaginary death from death itself. The night went on, and never had there been so sweet a night, so perfect to bend a sick person. The silence flowed, and the solitude full of friendship, the night full of hope, pressed upon Anne's stretched-out body. She lay awake, without delirium. There was no narcotic in the shadows, none of those suspicious touchings which permit the darkness to hypnotize those who resist sleep. The night acted nobly with Anne, and it was with the girl's own weapons, purity, confidence and peace, that it agreed to meet her. It was sweet, infinitely sweet in such a moment of great weakness to feel around oneself a world so stripped of artifice and perfidiousness. How beautiful this night was, beautiful and not sweet, a classic night which fear did not render opaque, which put phantoms to flight and likewise wiped away the false beauty of the world. All that which Anne still loved, silence and solitude, were called night. All that which Anne hated, silence and solitude, were also called night. Absolute night where there were no longer any contradictory terms, where those who suffered were happy, where white found a common substance with black. And yet, night without confusion, without monsters, before which, without closing her eyes, she found her personal night, the one which her eyelids habitually created for her as they closed. Fully conscious, full of clarity, she felt her night join the night. She discovered herself in this huge exterior night in the core of her being, no longer needing to pass before a bitter and tormented soul to arrive at peace. She was sick, but how good this sickness was, this sickness which was not her own and which was the health of the world! How pure it was, this sleep which wrapped around her and which was not her own and blended with the supreme consciousness of all things! And Anne slept.

During the days which followed, she entered into a delicious field of peace, where to all eyes she appeared bathed in the intoxication of recovery. Before this magnificent spectacle, she too felt within herself this joy of the universe, but it was an icy joy. And she waited for that which could be neither a night nor a day to begin. Something came to her which was the prelude not to a recovery but to a surprising state of strength. No one understood that she was going to pass through the state of perfect health, through a marvelously balanced point of life, a pendulum swinging from one world to another. Through the clouds which rushed over her head, she alone saw approaching with the speed of a shooting star the moment when, regaining contact with the earth, she would again grasp ordinary existence, would see nothing, feel nothing, when she could live, live finally, and perhaps even die, marvelous episode! She saw her very far away, this well Anne whom she did not know, through whom she was going to flow with a gay heart. Ah! Too dazzling instant! From the heart of shadows a voice told her: Go.

Her real illness began. She no longer saw anyone but occasional friends, and those who still came stopped asking for news. Everyone understood that the treatment was not winning out over the illness.

But Anne recognized in this another sort of scorn, and smiled at it. Whatever her fate might be, there was more life, more strength in her now than ever. Motionless for hours, sleeping with strength, speed, agility in her sleep, she was like an athlete who has remained prone for a long time, and her rest was like the rest of men who excel in running and wrestling. She finally conceived a strange feeling of pride in her body; she took a wonderful pleasure in her being; a serious dream made her feel that she was still alive, completely alive, and that she would have much more the feeling of being alive if she could wipe away the complacencies and the facile hopes. Mysterious moments during which, lacking all courage and incapable of movement, she seemed to be doing nothing, while, accomplishing an infinite task, she was incessantly climbing down to throw overboard the thoughts that belonged to her alive, the thoughts that belonged to her dead, to excavate within herself a refuge of extreme silence. Then the baneful stars appeared and she had to hurry: she gave up her last pleasures, got rid of her last sufferings. What was uncertain was where she would come forth. She was already suffocating. My God, she is well; no, she is; she is perfect from the point of view of being; she has, elevated to the highest degree, the joy of the greatest spirit discovering his most beautiful thought. She is; no, she is well, she is slipping, the thunder of sensations falls upon her, she is smothered, she cries out, she hears herself, she lives. What joy! They give her something to drink, she cries, they console her. It is still night. Yet she could not help realizing it: around her, many things were changing, and a desolate climate surrounded her, as if gloomy spirits sought to draw her toward inhuman feelings. Slowly, by a pitiless protocol, they took from her the tenderness and friendship of the world. If she asked for the flowers she loved, they gave her artificial roses with no scent which, though they were the only beings more mortal than herself, did not reserve her the pleasure of wilting, fading and dying before her eyes. Her room became uninhabitable: given a northern exposure for the first time, with a single window which admitted only the late afternoon sun, deprived, each day of another lovely object, this room gave every evidence of being secretly emptied in order to inspire in her the desire to leave it as soon as possible. The world too was devastated. They had exiled the pleasant seasons, asked the children to cry out in joy elsewhere, called into the street all the anger of cities, and it was an insurmountable wall of shattering sounds that separated her from mankind.

Sometimes she opened her eyes and looked around with surprise: not only were things changing, but the beings most attached to her were changing as well. How could there be any doubt? There was a tragic lessening of tenderness for her. Henceforth her mother, plunged for hours on end in her armchair without a word, her face ashen, carefully deprived of everything which might have made her lovable, no longer revealed anything of her affection but a feeling which made her ugly, at the very moment when Anne, as never before in her life, needed young and beautiful things. What she had once loved in her mother, gaity, laughter and tears, all the expressions of childhood repeated in an adult, all had disappeared from this face which expressed only fatigue, and it was only far away from this place that she could imagine her again capable of crying, of laughing—laughing, what a wonder! no one ever laughed here—a mother to everyone but her daughter. Anne raised her voice and asked her if she had been swimming. "Be quiet," said her mother. "Don't talk, you'll tire yourself." Obviously, there were no confidences to be shared with a person about to die, no possible relationship between her and those who are enjoying themselves, those who are alive. She sighed. And yet her mother resembled her, and what is more every day added a new trait to this resemblance. Contrary to the rule, it was the mother who took her daughter's face as a model, made it old, showed what it would be like at sixty. This obese Anne, whose eyes had turned gray as well as her hair, this was surely Anne if she were foolish enough to escape death. An innocent play: Anne was not duped. In spite of everything, life did not make itself hateful; she continued to love life. She was ready to die, but she was dying still loving flowers, even artificial flowers, feeling herself horribly orphaned in her death, passionately regretting this ugly Anne, this impotent Anne she would never become. Everything that was insidiously proposed to her so that she would not perceive that she was losing a great deal in leaving the world, this complicity of moralists and doctors, the traditional swindle perpetrated by the sun and by men, offering on the last day as a last spectacle the ugliest images and faces in dark corners, where it is obvious that those who die are content to die... all these deceptions failed. Anne intended to pass into death completely alive, evading the intermediate states of disgust with life, refusal to live. Yet, surrounded by hardness, watched by her friends who tested her with an air of innocence, saying, "We can't come tomorrow, excuse us," and who then, after she had answered in true friendship, "That's not important, don't take any trouble," thought, "How insensitive she is becoming; she no longer cares about anything," faced with this sad plot to reduce her to feelings which, before dying, must degrade her and make all regrets superfluous, the time arrived when she saw herself betrayed by her discretion, her shyness, just what she retained of her habitual manner. Soon they would be saying, "She's no longer herself, it would be better if she died," and then: "What a deliverance for her if she died!" A gentle, irresistible pressure, how could one defend oneself against it? What did she have left that she could use to make it known that she had not changed? Just when she should have been throwing herself incessantly on her friends' shoulders, telling her doctor: "Save me, I don't want to die"—on that one condition they might still have considered her part of the world—she was greeting those who entered with a nod, giving them that which was most dear, a glance, a thought, pure impulses which just recently were still signs of true sympathy, but which now seemed the cold reserve of someone at odds with life at the very least. These scenes struck her and she understood that one does not ask restraint and delicacy of a person who is suffering, feelings which belong to healthy civilizations, but rather crudeness and frenzy. Since it was the law, since it was the only way to prove that she had never had so much attachment for all that surrounded her, she was seized by the desire to cry out, ready to make a move to reinforce every bond, ready to see in those near to her beings who were ever nearer. Unfortunately, it was too late: she no longer had the face or the body of her feelings, and she could no longer be gay with gaiety. Now, to all those who came, whoever they might be (that was unimportant, time was short), she expressed by her closed eyes and her pinched lips the greatest passion ever experienced. And, not having enough affection to tell everyone how much she loved them, she had recourse as well to the hardest and coldest impulses of her soul. It was true that everything in her was hardening. Until then, she still had suffering. She suffered to open her eyes, suffered to receive the gentlest words: it was her one manner of being moved, and never had there been more sensitivity than in this glance which won the simple pleasure of seeing at the cost of cruel, tearing pain. But now, she hardly suffered any more at all; her body attained the ideal of egoism which is the ideal of every body: it was hardest at the moment of becoming weakest, a body which no longer cried out beneath the blows, borrowed nothing from the world, made itself, at the price of its beauty, the equivalent of a statue. This hardness weighed terribly on Anne; she felt the absence of all feeling in her as an immense void, and anguish clutched her. Then, in the form of this primordial passion, having now only a silent and dreary soul, a heart empty and dead, she offered her absence of friendship as the truest and purest friendship; she resigned herself, in this dark region where no one touched her, to responding to the ordinary affection of those around her by this supreme doubt concerning her being, by the desperate consciousness of being nothing any longer, by her anguish; she made the sacrifice, full of strangeness, of her certainty that she existed, in order to give a sense to this nothingness of love which she had become. And thus, deep within her, already sealed, already dead, the most profound passion came to be. To those who cried over her, cold and oblivious she returned hundredfold what they had given her, devoting to them the anticipation of her death, her death, the pure feeling, never purer, of her existence in the tortured anticipation of her nonexistence. She drew from herself not the weak emotions, sadness, regret, which were the lot of those around her, meaningless accidents with no chance of making any change in them, but the sole passion capable of threatening her very being, that which cannot be alienated and which would continue to burn when all the lights were put out. For the first time, she raised the words "give oneself" to their true meaning: she gave Anne, she gave much more than the life of Anne, she gave the ultimate gift, the death of Anne; she separated herself from her terribly strong feeling of being Anne, from the terribly anguished feeling of being Anne threatened with dying, and changed it into the yet more anguished feeling of being no longer Anne, but her mother, her mother threatened by death, the entire world on the point of annihilation. Never, within this body, this ideal of marble, monster of egoism, which had made of its unconsciousness the symbol of its estranged consciousness in a last pledge of friendship, never had there been more tenderness, and never within this poor being reduced to less than death, plundered of her most intimate treasure, her death, forced to die not personally but by the intermediary of all the others, had there been more being, more perfection of being. And so she had succeeded: her body was truly the strongest, the happiest; this existence, so impoverished and restrained that it could not even receive its opposite, nonexistence, was just what she was seeking. It was just that which permitted her to be equal, up to the very end, to all the others, in excellent form to disappear, full of strength for the last struggle. During the moments which followed, a strange fortress rose up around Anne. It did not resemble a city. There were no houses, no palace, no constructions of any sort; it was rather an immense sea, though the waters were invisible and the shore had disappeared. In this city, seated far from all things, sad last dream lost among the shadows, while the day faded and sobbing rose gently in the perspective of a strange horizon, Anne, like something which could not be represented, no longer a human being but simply a being, marvelously a being, among the mayflies and the falling suns, with the agonizing atoms, doomed species, wounded illnesses, ascended the course of waters where obscure origins floundered. She alas had no means of knowing where she arrived, but when the prolonged echoes of this enormous night were melting together into a dreary and vague unconsciousness, searching and wailing a wail which was like the tragic destruction of something nonliving, empty entities awoke and, like monsters constantly exchanging their absence of shape for other absences of shape and taming silence by terrible reminiscences of silence, they went out in a mysterious agony. There is no way to express what they were, these shapes, beings, baneful entities—for us, can something which is not the day appear in the midst of the day, something which in an atmosphere of light and clarity would represent the shudder of terror which is the source of the day? But, insidiously, they made themselves recognized on the threshold of the irremediable as the obscure laws summoned to disappear with Anne. What was the result of this revelation? One would have said that everything was destroyed, but that everything was beginning again as well. Time, coming forth from its lakes, rolled her in an immense past, and, though she could not entirely leave space where she still breathed, drew her toward bottomless valleys where the world seemed to have returned to the moment of its creation. Anne's life—and this very word sounded like a defiant challenge in this place where there was no life—participated in the first ray thrown in all of eternity through the midst of indolent notions. Life-giving forces bathed her as if they had suddenly found in her breast, consecrated to death, the vainly sought meaning of the word "life-giving". Caprice, which built up the infinite framework of its combinations to conjure up the void, seized her and if she did not lose all existence at that moment, her discomfort was all the worse, her transformation greater than if, in her tranquil human state, she had actually abandoned life, for there was no absurdity she was allowed to escape, and in the interval of a time simulated by the fusion of eternity and the idea of nothingness, she became all the monsters in which creation tried itself in vain. Suddenly—and never was anything so abrupt—the failures of chance came to an end, and that which could in no way be expected received its success from a mysterious hand. Incredible moment, in which she reappeared in her own form, but accursed instant as well, for this unique combination, perceived in a flash, dissolved in a flash and the unshakable laws which no shipwreck had been able to submerge were broken, giving in to a limitless caprice. An event so serious that no one near her perceived it and, although the atmosphere was heavy and weirdly transformed, no one felt the strangeness. The doctor bent over her and thought that she was dying according to the laws of death, not perceiving that she had already reached that instant when, in her, the laws were dying. She made an imperceptible motion; no one understood that she was floundering in the instant when death, destroying everything, might also destroy the possibility of annihilation. Alone, she saw the moment of the miracle coming, and she received no help. Oh, stupidity of those who are torn by grief! Beside her, as she was much less than dying, as she was dead, no one thought to multiply their absurd gestures, to liberate themselves from all convention and place themselves in the condition of primal creation. No one sought out the false beings, the hypocrites, the equivocal beings, all those who jeer at the idea of reason. No one said in the silence: "Let us hurry and before she is cold let us thrust her into the unknown. Let us create a darkness about her so that the law may abandon itself disloyally to the impossible. And ourselves, let us go away, lose all hope: hope itself must be forgotten."

Now Anne opened her eyes. There was in fact no more hope. This moment of supreme distraction, this trap into which those who have nearly vanquished death fall, ultimate return of Eurydice, in looking one last time toward the visible, Anne had just fallen into it as well. She opened her eyes without the least curiosity, with the lassitude of someone who knows perfectly well in advance what will be offered to her sight. Yes, there is her room, there is her mother, her friend Louise, there is Thomas. My God, that was just what it was. All those she loved were there. Her death must absolutely have the character of a solemn farewell, each one must receive his squeeze of the hand, his smile. And it is true that she squeezed their hands, smiled at them, loved them. She breathed gently. She had her face turned toward them as if she wished to see them up to the very last moment. Everything that had to be done, she did it. Like every dying person, she went away observing the rituals, pardoning her enemies, loving her friends, without admitting the secret which no one admits: that all this was already insignificant. Already she had no more importance. She looked at them with an ever more modest look, a simple look, which for them, for humans, was an empty look. She squeezed their hands ever more gently, with a grip which did not leave a trace, a grip which they could not feel. She did not speak. These last moments must be without any memory. Her face, her shoulders must become invisible, as is proper for something which is fading away. Her mother whined: "Anne, do you recognize me? Answer me, squeeze my hand." Anne heard this voice: what good was it, her mother was no longer anything more than an insignificant being. She also heard Thomas; in fact, she knew now what she had to say to Thomas, she knew exactly the words she had searched for all her life in order to reach him. But she remained silent; she thought: what good is it—and this word was also the word she was seeking—Thomas is insignificant. Let us sleep.

XI

WHEN ANNE HAD DIED, Thomas did not leave the room, and he seemed deeply afflicted. This grief caused great discomfort to all those present, and they had the premonition that what he was saying to himself at that moment was the prelude to a drama the thought of which filled them with consternation. They went away sadly, and he remained alone. One might think that what he was saying to himself could in no way allow itself to be read, but he took care to speak as if his words had a chance of being heard and he left aside the strange truth to which he seemed chained.

"I suspected," he said, "that Anne had premeditated her death. This evening she was peaceful and noble. Without the coquettishness which hides from the dead their true state, without that last cowardice which makes them wait to die by the doctor's hand, she bestowed death upon herself, entirely, in an instant. I approached this perfect corpse. The eyes had closed. The mouth did not smile. There was not a single reflection of life in the face. A body without consolation, she did not hear the voice which asked, 'Is it possible?' and no one dreamed of saying of her what is said of the dead who lack courage, what Christ said of the girl who was not worthy of burial, to humiliate her: she is sleeping. She was not sleeping. She was not changed, either. She had stopped at the point where she resembled only herself, and where her face, having only Anne's expression, was disturbing to look at. I took her hand. I placed my lips on her forehead. I treated her as if she were alive and, because she was unique among the dead in still having a face and a hand, my gestures did not seem insane. Did she appear alive, then? Alas, all that prevented her from being distinguished from a real person was that which verified her annihilation. She was entirely within herself: in death, abounding in life. She seemed more weighty, more in control of herself. No Anne was lacking in the corpse of Anne. All the Annes had been necessary to bring her back to nothing. The jealous, the pensive, the violent, had served only once, to make her completely dead. At her end, she seemed to need more being to be annihilated than to be, and, dead precisely from this excess which permitted her to show herself entirely, she bestowed on death all the reality and all the existence which constituted the proof of her own nothingness. Neither impalpable nor dissolved in the shadows, she imposed herself ever more strongly on the senses. As her death became more real, she grew, she became larger, she hollowed out a deep tomb in her couch. Obliterated as she was, she drew every glance to her. We who remained beside her, we felt ourselves compressed by this huge being. We were suffocating for lack of air. Each of us discovered with anguish what only casket-bearers know, that the dead double in weight, that they are the largest, the most powerful of all beings. Each bore his portion of this manifest dead person. Her mother, seeing her so like a living person, naively lifted up the girl's head and was unable to bear the enormous weight, proof of the destruction of her daughter. And then, I stayed alone with her. She had surely died for that moment when people might think she had defeated me. For dying had been her ruse to deliver a body into nothingness. At the moment everything was being destroyed she had created that which was most difficult: she had not drawn something out of nothing (a meaningless act), but given to nothing, in its form of nothing, the form of something. The act of not seeing had now its integral eye. The silence, the real silence, the one which is not composed of silenced words, of possible thoughts, had a voice. Her face, more beautiful from one instant to the next, was constructing her absence. There was not a single part of her which was still the prop of any sort of reality. It was then, when her story and the story of her death had faded away together and there was no one left in the world to name Anne, that she attained the moment of immortality in nothingness, in which what has ceased to be enters into a thoughtless dream. It was truly night. I was surrounded by stars. The totality of things wrapped about me and I prepared myself for the agony with the exalted consciousness that I was unable to die. But, at that instant, what she alone had perceived up until then appeared manifest to everyone: I revealed to them, in me, the strangeness of their condition and the shame of an endless existence. Of course I could die, but death shone forth perfidiously for me as the death of death, so that, becoming the eternal man taking the place of the moribund, this man without crime, without any reason for dying who is every man who dies, I would die, a dead person so alien to death that I would spend my supreme moment in a time when it was already impossible to die and yet I would live all the hours of my life in the hour in which I could no longer live them. Who more than I was deprived of the last moment full of hope, so totally deprived of the last consolation which memory offers to those who despair, to those who have forgotten happiness and toss themselves from the pinnacle of life in order to recall its joys? And yet I was really a dead person, I was even the only possible dead person, I was the only man who did not give the impression that he died by chance. All my strength, the sense I had, in taking the hemlock, of being not Socrates dying but Socrates increasing himself through Plato, this certainty of being unable to disappear which belongs only to beings afflicted with a terminal illness, this serenity before the scaffold which bestows upon the condemned their true pardon, made of every instant of my life the instant in which I was going to leave life. All my being seemed to mingle with death. As naturally as men believe they are alive, accepting as an inevitable impulse their breathing, the circulation of their blood, so I ceased living. I drew my death from my very existence, and not from the absence of existence. I presented a dead person who did not confine himself to the appearance of a diminished being, and this dead person, filled with passions but insensitive, calling for his thought upon an absence of thought and yet carefully separating out whatever there might be in it of void, of negation in life, in order not to make of his death a metaphor, an even weaker image of normal death, brought to its highest point the paradox and the impossibility of death. What then distinguished me from the living? Just this, that neither night, nor loss of consciousness, nor indifference called me from life. And what distinguished me from the dead, unless it was a personal act in which at every instant, going beyond appearances which are generally sufficient, I had to find the sense and the definitive explanation of my death? People did not want to believe it, but my death was the same thing as death. Before men who know only how to die, who live up until the end, living people touched by the end of their lives as if by a slight accident, I had only death as an anthropometric index. This is in fact what made my destiny inexplicable. Under the name Thomas, in this chosen state in which I might be named and described, I had the appearance of any living person, but since I was real only under the name of death, I let the baneful spirit of the shadows show through, blood mixed with my blood, and the mirror of each of my days reflected the confused images of death and life. And so my fate stupefied the crowd. This Thomas forced me to appear, while I was living, not even the eternal dead person I was and on which no one could fix their glance, but an ordinary dead person, a body without life, an insensitive sensitivity, thought without thought. At the highest point of contradiction, I was this illegitimate dead person. Represented in my feelings by a double for whom each feeling was as absurd as for a dead person, at the pinnacle of passion I attained the pinnacle of estrangement, and I seemed to have been removed from the human condition because I had truly accomplished it. Since, in each human act, I was the dead person that at once renders it possible and impossible and, if I walked, if I thought, I was the one whose complete absence alone makes the step or the thought possible, before the beasts, beings who do not bear within them their dead double, I lost my last reason for existing. There was a tragic distance between us. A man without a trace of animal nature, I ceased to be able to express myself with my voice which no longer sang, no longer even spoke as the voice of a talking bird speaks. I thought, outside of all image and all thought, in an act which consisted of being unthinkable. Every moment, I was this purely human man, supreme individual and unique example, with whom, in dying, each person makes an exchange, and who dies alone in place of all. With me, the species died each time, completely. Whereas, if these composite beings called men had been left to die on their own, they would have been seen to survive miserably in pieces divided up among different things, reconstituted in a mixture of insect, tree and earth, I disappeared without a trace and fulfilled my role as the one, the unique dead person to perfection. I was thus the sole corpse of humanity. In contradiction of those who say that humanity does not die, I proved in every way that only humanity is capable of dying. I appeared in every one of these poor moribunds, ugly as they were, at the instant full of beauty in which, renouncing all their links with the other species, they become, by renouncing not only the world, but the jackal, the ivy, they become uniquely men. These scenes still glow within me like magnificent festivals. I approached them and their anxiety grew. These miserable creatures who were becoming men felt the same terror at feeling themselves men as Isaac on the altar at becoming a lamb. None of them recognized my presence and yet there was in the depths of them, like a fatal ideal, a void which exerted a temptation over them, which they felt as a person of such complete and imposing reality that they had to prefer that person to any other, even at the cost of their existence. Then the gates of agony opened and they flung themselves into their error. They shrunk, forced themselves to be reduced to nothing to correspond to this model of nothingness which they took for the model of life. They loved only life and they struggled against it. They perished from a taste for life so strong that life seemed to them that death whose approach they anticipated, which they thought they were fleeing as they hurled themselves forward to meet it and which they recognized only at the very last moment when, as the voice was saying to them, 'It is too late,' I was already taking their place. What happened then? When the guard who had stepped away returned, he saw someone who resembled no one, a faceless stranger, the very opposite of a being. And the most loving friend, the best son saw their senses altered before this alien shape and cast a look of horror on that which they loved the most, a cold, unrecognizable look as if death had taken not their friend but their feelings, and now they were the ones, they, the living, who were changing so profoundly that it might have been called a death. Even their relations among themselves were altered. If they touched one another it was with a shudder, feeling that they were experiencing contact with a stranger. Each, with reference to the other, in complete solitude, complete intimacy, each became for the other the only dead person, the only survivor. And when he who wept and he who was wept over came to blend together, became one, then there came an outburst of despair, this strangest moment of the mourning, when, in the mortuary chamber, friends and relations add to themselves the one who has left their number, feel themselves of the same substance, as respectable as he, and even consider themselves the authentic dead person, the only one worthy to impose upon their common grief. And everything, then, seems simple to them. They again bestow on the dead person his familiar nature, after having brushed past him as if he were a scandalous reality. They say: 'I never understood my poor husband (my poor father) better.' They imagine they understand him, not only such as he was when living, but dead, having the same knowledge of him that a vigorous tree has of a cut branch, by the sap which still flows. Then, gradually, the living assimilate those who have disappeared completely. Pondering the dead in pondering oneself becomes the formula of appeasement. They are seen entering triumphally into existence. The cemeteries are emptied. The sepulchral absence again becomes invisible. The strange contradictions vanish. And it is in a harmonious world that everyone goes on living, immortal to the end.

"The certainty of dying, the certainty of not dying, there is all that is left, for the crowd, of the reality of death. But those who contemplated me felt that death could also associate with existence and form this decisive word: death exists. They have developed the habit of saying about existence everything they could say of death for me and, rather than murmur, 'I am, I am not,' mix the terms together in a single happy combination and say, 'I am, while I am not,' and likewise, 'I am not, while I am,' without there being the slightest attempt to force contradictory words together, rubbing them one against the other like stones. As voices were called down upon my existence, affirming in succession, with equal passion: 'He exists for always, he does not exist for always,' that existence took on a fatal character in their eyes. It seemed that I was walking comfortably over the abysses and that, complete in myself, not half-phantom half-man, I penetrated my perfect nothingness. A sort of integral ventriloquist, wherever I cried out, that is where I was not, and also just where I was, being in every way the equivalent of silence. My word, as if composed of excessively high vibrations, first devoured silence, then the word. I spoke, I was by that act immediately placed in the center of the intrigue. I threw myself into the pure fire which consumed me at the same time it made me visible. I became transparent before my own sight. Look at men: the pure void summons their eye to call itself blind and a perpetual alibi exchanged between the night outside and the night within permits them to retain the illusion of day throughout their lives. For me, it was this very illusion which by an inexplicable act seemed to have issued from myself. I found myself with two faces, glued one to the other. I was in constant contact with two shores. With one hand showing that I was indeed there, with the other—what am I saying?—

without the other, with this body which, imposed on my real body, depended entirely on a negation of the body, I entered into absolute dispute with myself. Having two eyes, one of which was possessed of extreme visual acuity, it was with the other which was an eye only because of its refusal to see that I saw everything visible. And so on, for all my organs. I had a part of myself submerged, and it was to this part, lost in a constant shipwreck, that I owed my direction, my face, my necessity. I found my proof in this movement toward the nonexistent in which the proof that I existed, rather than becoming degraded, was reinforced to the point of becoming manifestly true. I made a supreme effort to keep outside myself, as near as possible to the place of beginnings. Now, far from achieving as a complete man, as an adolescent, as protoplasm, the state of the possible, I made my way toward something complete, and I caught a glimpse in these depths of the strange face of him who I really was and who had nothing in common with an already dead man or with a man yet to be born: a marvelous companion with whom I wished with all my might to blend myself, yet separate from me, with no path that might lead me to him. How could I reach him? By killing myself: absurd plan. Between this corpse, the same as a living person but without life, and this unnameable, the same as a dead person but without death, I could not see a single line of relationship. No poison might unite me with that which could bear no name, could not be designated by the opposite of its opposite, nor conceived in relationship to anything. Death was a crude metamorphosis beside the indiscernible nullity which I nevertheless coupled with the name Thomas. Was it then a fantasy, this enigma, the creation of a word maliciously formed to destroy all words? But if I advanced within myself, hurrying laboriously toward my precise noon, I yet experienced as a tragic certainty, at the center of the living Thomas, the inaccessible proximity of that Thomas which was nothingness, and the more the shadow of my thought shrunk, the more I conceived of myself in this faultless clarity as the possible, the willing host of this obscure Thomas. In the plentitude of my reality, I believed I was reaching the unreal. O my consciousness, it was not a question of imputing to you—in the form of revery, of fainting away, of hiatus—that which, having been unable to be assimilated to death, should have passed for something worse, your own death. What am I saying? I felt this nothingness bound to your extreme existence as an unexceptionable condition. I felt that between it and you undeniable ratios were being established. All the logical couplings were incapable of expressing this union in which, without *then* or *because,* you came together, both cause and effect at once, unreconcilable and indissoluble. Was it your opposite? No, I said not. But it seemed that if, slightly falsifying the relationships of words, I had sought the opposite of your opposite, having lost my true path I would have arrived, without turning back, proceeding wondrously from you-consciousness (at once existence and life) to you-unconsciousness (at once reality and death), I would have arrived, setting out into the terrible unknown, at an image of my enigma which would have been at once nothingness and existence. And with these two words I would have been able to destroy, incessantly, that which was signified by the one by that which was signified by the other, and by that which the two signified, and at the same time I would have destroyed by their oppositeness that which constituted the oppositeness of these two opposites, and I would have finished, kneading them endlessly to melt that which was untouchable, by reemerging right beside myself, Harpagon suddenly catching his thief and grabbing hold of his own arm. It was then that, deep within a cave, the madness of the taciturn thinker appeared before me and unintelligible words rung in my ears while I wrote on the wall these sweet words: 'I think, therefore I am not.' These words brought me a delicious vision. In the midst of an immense countryside, a flaming lens received the dispersed rays of the sun and, by those fires, became conscious of itself as a monstrous I, not at the points at which it received them, but at the point at which it projected and united them in a single beam. At this focus-point, the center of a terrible heat, it was wondrously active, it illuminated, it burned, it devoured; the entire universe became a flame at the point at which the lens touched it; and the lens did not leave it until it was destroyed. Nevertheless, I perceived that this mirror was like a living animal consumed by its own fire. The earth it set ablaze was its entire body reduced to dust, and, from this unceasing flame, it drew, in a torrent of sulfur and gold, the consequence that it was constantly annihilated. It began to speak and its voice seemed to come from the bottom of my heart. I think, it said, I bring together all that which is light without heat, rays without brilliance, unrefined products; I brew them together and conjugate them, and, in a primary absence of myself, I discover myself as a perfect unity at the point of greatest intensity. I think, it said, I am subject and object of an all-powerful radiation; a sun using all its energy to make itself night, as well as to make itself sun. I think: there at the point where thought joins with me I am able to subtract myself from being, without diminishing, without changing, by means of a metamorphosis which saves me for myself, beyond any point of reference from which I might be seized. It is the property of my thought, not to assure me of existence (as all things do, as a stone does), but to assure me of being in nothingness itself, and to invite me not to be, in order to make me feel my marvelous absence. I think, said Thomas, and this invisible, inexpressible, nonexistent Thomas I became meant that henceforth I was never there where I was, and there was not even anything mysterious about it. My existence became entirely that of an absent person who, in every act I performed, produced the same act and did not perform it. I walked, counting my steps, and my life was that of a man cast in concrete, with no legs, with not even the idea of movement. Beneath the sun, the one man the sun did not illuminate went forward, and this light which hid from itself, this torrid heat which was not heat, nevertheless issued from a real sun. I looked before me: a girl was sitting on a bench, I approached, I sat down beside her. There was only a slight distance between us. Even when she turned her head away, she perceived me entirely. She saw me with my eyes which she exchanged for her own, with my face which was practically her face, with my head which sat easily on her shoulders. She was already joining herself to me. In a single glance, she melted in me and in this intimacy discovered my absence. I felt she was oppressed, trembling. I imagined her hand ready to approach me, to touch me, but the only hand she would have wanted to take was ungraspable. I understood that she was passionately searching out the cause of her discomfort, and when she saw that there was nothing abnormal about me she was seized with terror. I was like her. My strangeness had as its cause all that which made me not seem strange to her. With horror she discovered in everything that was ordinary about her the source of everything that was extraordinary about me. I was her tragic double. If she got up, she knew, watching me get up, that it was an impossible movement, but she also knew that it was a very simple movement for her, and her fright reached a peak of intensity because there was no difference between us. I lifted my hand to my forehead, it was warm,

I smoothed my hair. She looked at me with great pity. She had pity for this man with no head, with no arms, completely absent from the summer and wiping away his perspiration at the cost of unimaginable effort. Then she looked at me again and vertigo seized her. For what was there that was insane in my action? It was something absurd which nothing explained, nothing designated, the absurdity of which destroyed itself, absurdity of being absurd, and in every way like something reasonable. I offered this girl the experience of something absurd, and it was a terrible test. I was absurd, not because of the goat's foot which permitted me to walk with a human pace, but because of my regular anatomy, my complete musculature which permitted me a normal pace, nevertheless an absurd pace, and, normal as it was, more and more absurd. Then, in turn, I looked at her: I brought her the one true mystery, which consisted of the absence of mystery, and which she could therefore do nothing but search for, eternally. Everything was clear in me, everything was simple: there was no other side to the pure enigma. I showed her a face with no secret, indecipherable; she read in my heart as she had never read in any other heart; she knew why I had been born, why I was there, and the more she reduced the element of the unknown in me, the more her discomfort and her fright increased. She was forced to divulge me, she separated me from my last shadows, in the fear of seeing me with no shadow. She pursued this mystery desperately; she destroyed me insatiably. Where was I for her? I had disappeared and I felt her gathering herself up to throw herself into my absence as if into her mirror. There henceforth was her reflection, her exact shape, there was her abyss. She saw herself and desired herself, she obliterated herself and rejected herself, she had ineffable doubts about herself, she gave in to the temptation of meeting herself there where she was not. I saw her giving in. I put my hand on her knees.

"I am sad; the evening is coming. But I also experience the opposite of sadness. I am at that point where it is sufficient to experience a little melancholy to feel hate and joy. I feel that I am tender, not only toward men but toward their passions. I love them, loving the feelings by which one might have loved them. I bring them devotion and life at the second degree: to separate us there is nothing more than that which would have united us, friendship, love. In the depths of myself, at the end of the day, strange emotions are deposited which take me for their object. I love myself with the spirit of revulsion, I calm myself with fear, I taste life in the feeling which separates me from it. All these passions, forced within me, produce nothing other than that which I am and the entire universe exhausts its rage to make me feel something, vaguely, of myself, feel some being which does not feel itself. Now calm comes down with the night. I can no longer name a single feeling. If I were to call my present state impassivity, I could just as well call it fire. What I feel is the source of that which is felt, the origin believed to be without feeling, the indiscernible impulse of enjoyment and revulsion. And, it is true, I feel nothing. I am reaching regions where that which one experiences has no relation with that which is experienced. I go down into the hard block of marble with the sensation of slipping into the sea. I drown myself in mute bronze. Everywhere hardness, diamond, pitiless fire, and yet the sensation is that of foam. Absolute absence of desire. No movement, no phantom of movement, neither anything immobile. It is in such great poverty, such absence, that I recognize all the passions from which I have been withdrawn by an insignificant miracle. Absent from Anne, absent from my love for Anne to the extent that I loved Anne. And absent, doubly, from myself, carried each time by desire beyond desire and destroying even this nonexistent Thomas where I felt I truly existed. Absent from this absence, I back away infinitely. I lose all contact with the horizon I am fleeing. I flee my flight. Where is the end? Already the void seems to me the ultimate in fullness: I understood it, I experienced it, I exhausted it. Now I am like a beast terrified by its own leap. I am falling in horror of my fall. I aspire vertiginously to reject myself from myself. Is it night? Have I come back, another, to the place where I was? Again there is a supreme moment of calm. Silence, refuge of transparency for the soul. I am terrified by this peace. I experience a sweetness which contains me for a moment and consumes me. If I had a body, I would grip my throat with my hands. I would like to suffer. I would like to prepare a simple death for myself, in an agony in which I would tear myself to pieces. What peace! I am ravaged by delights. There is no longer anything of me which does not open itself to this future void as if to a frightful enjoyment. No notion, no image, no feeling sustains me. Whereas just a moment ago I felt nothing, simply experiencing each feeling as a great absence, now in the complete absence of feelings I experience the strongest feeling. I draw my fright from the fright which I do not have. Fright, terror, the metamorphosis passes all thought. I am at grips with a feeling which reveals to me that I cannot experience it, and it is at that moment that I experience it with a force which makes it an inexpressible torment. And that is nothing, for I could experience it as something other than what it is, fright experienced as enjoyment. But the horror is that there emerges within it the consciousness that no feeling is possible, and likewise no thought and no consciousness. And the worst horror is that in apprehending it, far from dissipating it like a phantom by touching it, I cause it to increase beyond measure. I experience it as not experiencing it and as experiencing nothing, being nothing, and this absurdity is its monstrous substance. Something totally absurd serves as my reason. I feel myself dead—no; I feel myself, living, infinitely more dead than dead. I discover my being in the vertiginous abyss where it is not, an absence, an absence where it sets itself like a god. I am not and I endure. An inexorable future stretches forth infinitely for this suppressed being. Hope turns in fear against time which drags it forward. All feelings gush out of themselves and come together, destroyed, abolished, in this feeling which molds me, makes me and unmakes me, causes me to feel, hideously, in a total absence of feeling, my reality in the shape of nothingness. A feeling which has to be given a name and which I call anguish. Here is the night. The darkness hides nothing. My first perception is that this night is not a provisional absence of light. Far from being a possible locus of images, it is composed of all that which is not seen and is not heard, and, listening to it, even a man would know that, if he were not a man, he would hear nothing. In true night, then, the unheard, the invisible are lacking, all those things that make the night habitable. It does not allow anything other than itself to be attributed to it; it is impenetrable. I am truly in the beyond, if the beyond is that which admits of no beyond. Along with the feeling that everything has vanished, this night brings me the feeling that everything is near me. It is the supreme relationship which is sufficient unto itself; it leads me eternally to itself, and an obscure race from the identical to the identical imparts to me the desire of a wonderful progress. In this absolute repetition of the same is born true movement which cannot lead to rest. I feel myself directed by the night toward the night. A sort of being, composed of all that which is excluded from being, presents itself as the goal of my undertaking.

That which is not seen, is not understood, is not, creates right beside me the level of another night, and yet the same, toward which I aspire unspeakably, though I am already mingled with it. Within my reach there is a world—I call it world, as, dead, I would call the earth nothingness. I call it world because there is no other possible world for me. Just as when one moves toward an object, I believe I am making it come closer, but *it* is the one that understands *me*. Invisible and outside of being, it perceives me and sustains me in being. Itself, I perceive it, an unjustifiable chimera if I were not there, I perceive it, not in the vision I have of it, but in the vision and the knowledge it has of me. I am seen. Beneath this glance, I commit myself to a passivity which, rather than diminishing me, makes me real. I seek neither to distinguish it, nor to attain it, nor to suppose it. Perfectly negligent, by my distraction I retain for it the quality of inaccessibility which is appropriate to it. My senses, my imagination, my spirit, all are dead on the side on which it looks at me. I seize it as the sole necessity, that which is not even a hypothesis... as my sole resistance, I who am annihilating myself. I am seen. Porous, identical to the night, which is not seen, I am seen. Being as imperceptible as it is, I know it as it sees me. It is even the last possibility I have of being seen, now that I no longer exist. It is that glance which continues to see me in my absence. It is the eye that my disappearance requires more and more as it becomes more complete, to perpetuate me as an object of vision. In the night we are inseparable. Our intimacy is this very night. Any distance between us is suppressed, but suppressed in order that we may not come closer one to the other. It is a friend to me, a friendship which divides us. It is united with me, a union which distinguishes us. It is myself, I who do not exist for myself. In this instant, I have no existence except for it, which exists only for me. My being subsists only from a supreme point of view which is precisely incompatible with my point of view. The perspective in which I fade away for my eyes restores me as a complete image for the unreal eye to which I deny all images. A complete image with reference to a world devoid of image which imagines me in the absence of any imaginable figure. The being of a nonbeing of which I am the infinitely small negation which it instigates as its profound harmony. In the night shall I become the universe? I feel that in every part of me, invisible and nonexistent, I am supremely, totally visible. Marvelously bound, I offer in a single unique image the expression of the world. Without color, inscribed in no thinkable form, neither the product of a powerful brain, I am the sole necessary image. On the retina of the absolute eye, I am the tiny inverted image of all things. In my scale, I bestow upon it the personal vision not only of the sea, but of the hillside still ringing with the cry of the first man. There, everything is distinct, everything is melted together. To the prism that I am, a perfect unity restores the infinite dissipation which makes it possible to see everything without seeing anything. I renew the crude undertaking of Noah. I enclose within my absence the principle of totality which is real and perceptible only for the absurd being who overflows totality, for that absurd spectator who examines me, loves me and draws me powerfully into his absurdity. To the extent that I contain within me that whole to which I offer (as the water offered Narcissus) the reflection in which it desires itself, I am excluded from the whole and the whole itself is excluded therefrom, and yet more is the prodigious one who is absent excluded, absent from me and from everything, absent for me as well, and yet for whom I work alone at this absurdity which he accepts. All of us are condemned by the same logical proscription, all three of us (a number which is monstrous when one of the three is everything). We are united by the mutual check in which we hold each other, with this difference, that it is only with reference to my contemplator that I am the irrational being, representing everything outside of him, but it is also with reference to him that I cannot be irrational, if he himself represents the reason of this existence outside of everything. Now, in this night, I come forward bearing everything, toward that which infinitely exceeds everything. I progress beyond the totality which I nevertheless tightly embrace. I go on the margins of the universe, boldly walking elsewhere than where I can be, and a little outside of my steps. This slight extravagance, this deviation toward that which cannot be, is not only my own impulse leading me to a personal madness, but the impulse of the reason which I bear with me. With me the laws gravitate outside the laws, the possible outside the possible. O night, now nothing will make me be, nothing will separate me from you. I adhere marvelously to the simplicity to which you invite me. I lean over you, your equal, offering you a mirror for your perfect nothingness, for your shadows which are neither light nor absence of light, for this void which contemplates. To all that which you are, and, for our language, are not, I add a consciousness. I make you experience your supreme identity as a relationship, I name you and define you. You become a delicious passivity. You attain entire possession of yourself in abstention. You give to the infinite the glorious feeling of its limits. O night, I make you taste your ecstasy. I perceive in myself the second night which brings you the consciousness of your barrenness. You bloom into new restrictions. By my mediation, you contemplate yourself eternally. I am with you, as if you were my creation. My creation.... What strange light is this which falls upon me? Could the effort to expel myself from every created thing have made of me the supreme creator? Having stretched all my strength against being, I find myself again at the heart of creation. Myself, working against the act of creating, I have made myself the creator. Here I am, conscious of the absolute as of an object I am creating at the same time I am struggling not to create myself. That which has never had any principle admits me at its eternal beginning, I who am the stubborn refusal of my own beginning. It is I, the origin of that which has no origin. I create that which cannot be created. Through an all-powerful ambiguity, the uncreated is the same word for it and for me. For it, I am the image of what it would be, if it did not exist. Since it is not possible that it should exist, by my absurdity I am its sovereign reason. I force it to exist. O night, I am itself. Here, it has drawn me into the trap of its creation. And now it is the one that forces me to exist. And I am the one who is its eternal prisoner. It creates me for itself alone. It makes me, nothingness that I am, like unto nothingness. In a cowardly way it delivers me to joy."

XII

THOMAS WENT OUT into the country and saw that spring was beginning. In the distance, ponds spread forth their murky waters, the sky was dazzling, life was young and free. When the sun climbed on the horizon, the genera, the races, even the species of the future, represented by individuals with no species, peopled the solitude in a disorder full of splendor. Dragonflies without wing-cases, which should not have flown for ten million years, tried to take flight; blind toads crawled through the mud trying to open their eyes which were capable of vision only in the future. Others, drawing attention to themselves through the transparency of time, forced whoever looked at them to become a visionary by a supreme prophecy of the eye. A dazzling light in which, illuminated, impregnated by the sun, everything was in movement to receive the glint of the new flames. The idea of perishing pushed the chrysalis to become a butterfly; death for the green caterpillar consisted of receiving the dark wings of the sphinx moth, and there was a proud and defiant consciousness in the mayflies which gave the intoxicating impression that life would go on forever. Could the world be more beautiful? The ideal of color spread out across the fields. Across the transparent and empty sky extended the ideal of light. The fruitless trees, the flowerless flowers bore freshness and youth at the tips of their stems. In place of the rose, the rose-bush bore a black flower which could not wilt. The spring enveloped Thomas like a sparkling night and he felt himself called softly by this nature overflowing with joy. For him, an orchard bloomed at the center of the earth, birds flew in the nothingness and an immense sea spread out at his feet. He walked. Was it the new brilliance of the light? It seemed that, through a phenomenon awaited for centuries, the earth now saw him. The primroses allowed themselves to be viewed by his glance which did not see. The cuckoo began its unheard song for his deaf ear. The universe contemplated him. The magpie he awoke was already no more than a universal bird which cried out for the profaned world. A stone rolled, and it slipped through an infinity of metamorphoses the unity of which was that of the world in its splendor. In the midst of these tremblings, solitude burst forth. Against the depths of the sky a radiant and jealous face was seen to rise up, whose eyes absorbed all other faces. A sound began, deep and harmonious, ringing inside the bells like the sound no one can hear. Thomas went forward. The great misfortune which was to come still seemed a gentle and tranquil event. In the valleys, on the hills, his passing spread out like a dream on the shining earth. It was strange to pass through a perfumed spring which held back its scents, to contemplate flowers which, with their dazzling colors, could not be perceived. Birds splashed with color, chosen to be the repertory of shades, rose up, presenting red and black to the void. Drab birds, designated to be the conservatory of music without notes, sang the absence of song. A few mayflies were still seen flying with real wings, because they were going to die, and that was all. Thomas went his way and, suddenly, the world ceased to hear the great cry which crossed the abysses. A lark, heard by no one, tossed forth shrill notes for a sun it did not see and abandoned air and space, not finding in nothingness the pinnacle of its ascent. A rose which bloomed as he passed touched Thomas with the brilliance of its thousand corollas. A nightingale that followed him from tree to tree made its extraordinary mute voice heard, a singer mute for itself and for all others and nevertheless singing the magnificent song. Thomas went forward toward the city. There was no longer sound or silence. The man immersed in the waves piled up by the absence of flood spoke to his horse in a dialogue consisting of a single voice. The city which spoke to itself in a dazzling monologue of a thousand voices rested in the debris of illuminated and transparent images. Where, then, was the city? Thomas, at the heart of the agglomeration, met no one. The enormous buildings with their thousands of inhabitants were deserted, deprived of that primordial inhabitant who is the architect powerfully imprisoned in the stone. Immense unbuilt cities. The buildings were piled one on the other. Clusters of edifices and monuments accumulated at the intersections. Out to the horizon, inaccessible shores of stone were seen

rising slowly, impasses which led to the cadaverous apparition of the
sun. This somber contemplation could not go on. Thousands of men,
nomads in their homes, living nowhere, stretched out to the limits of
the world. They threw themselves, buried themselves in the earth
where, walled between bricks carefully cemented by Thomas, while
the enormous mass of things was smashed beneath a cloud of ashes,
they went forward, dragging the immensity of space beneath their feet.
Mingling with the rough beginnings of creation, for an infinitely small
time they piled up mountains. They rose up as stars, ravaging the universal order with their random course. With their blind hands, they
touched the invisible worlds to destroy them. Suns which no longer
shone bloomed in their orbits. The great day embraced them in vain.
Thomas still went forward. Like a shepherd he led the flock of the
constellations, the tide of star-men toward the first night. Their procession was solemn and noble, but toward what end, and in what form?
They thought they were still captives within a soul whose borders they
wished to cross. Memory seemed to them that desert of ice which a
magnificent sun was melting and in which they seized again, by somber and cold remembering, separated from the heart which had cher-
ished it, the world in which they were trying to live again. Though
they no longer had bodies, they enjoyed having all the images representing a body, and their spirit sustained the infinite procession of
imaginary corpses. But little by little forgetfulness came. Monstrous
memory, in which they rushed about in frightful intrigues, folded upon
them and chased them from this fortress where they still seemed, fee-
bly, to breathe. A second time they lost their bodies. Some who proudly
plunged their glance into the sea, others who clung with determination to their name, lost the memory of speech, while they repeated
Thomas's empty word. Memory was wiped away and, as they became
the accursed fever which vainly flattered their hopes, like prisoners
with only their chains to help them escape, they tried to climb back up
to the life they could not imagine. They were seen leaping desperately
out of their enclosure, floating, secretly slipping forward, but when
they thought they were on the very point of victory, trying to build
out of the absence of thought a stronger thought which would devour
laws, theorems, wisdom... then the guardian of the impossible seized
them, and they were engulfed in the shipwreck. A prolonged, heavy
fall: had they come, as they dreamed, to the confines of the soul they

thought they were traversing? Slowly they came out of this dream and discovered a solitude so great that when the monsters which had terrified them when they were men came near them, they looked on them with indifference, saw nothing, and, leaning over the crypt, remained there in a profound inertia, waiting mysteriously for the tongue whose birth every prophet has felt deep in his throat to come forth from the sea and force the impossible words into their mouths. This waiting was a sinister mist exhaled drop by drop from the summit of a mountain; it seemed it could never end. But when, from the deepest of the shadows there rose up a prolonged cry which was like the end of a dream, they all recognized the ocean, and they perceived a glance whose immensity and sweetness awoke in them unbearable desires. Becoming men again for an instant, they saw in the infinite an image they grasped and, giving in to a last temptation, they stripped themselves voluptuously in the water.

Thomas as well watched this flood of crude images, and then, when it was his turn, he threw himself into it, but sadly, desperately, as if the shame had begun for him.

Death Sentence

◆

These things happened to me in 1938. I feel the greatest uneasiness in speaking of them. I have already tried to put them into writing many times. If I have written books, it has been in the hope that they would put an end to it all. If I have written novels, they have come into being just as the words began to shrink back from the truth. I am not frightened of the truth. I am not afraid to tell a secret. But until now, words have been frailer and more cunning than I would have liked. I know this guile is a warning: it would be nobler to leave the truth in peace. It would be in the best interests of the truth to keep it hidden. But now I hope to be done with it soon. To be done with it is also noble and important.

Still, I must not forget that I once managed to put these things into writing. It was in 1940, during the last weeks of July or the first weeks of August. Inactive, in a state of lethargy, I wrote this story. But once it was written I reread it and destroyed the manuscript. Today I cannot even remember how long it was.

I will write freely, since I am sure that this story concerns no one but myself. It could actually be told in ten words. That is what makes it so awful. There are ten words to say. For nine years I have held out against them. But this morning, which is the 8th of October (I have just noticed to my surprise) and so nearly the anniversary of the first of those days, I am almost sure that the words which should not be written will be written. For many months now, I think, I have been resolved to do it.

There are several witnesses to what happened, although only one, the one in the best position to know, glimpsed the truth. I used to telephone the apartment where these things happened—often in the beginning, and then less often. I once even lived there, at 15, rue—. I think the young woman's sister remained there for some time. What became of her? She lived, as she liked to say, off the kindness of gentlemen. I assume she's dead.

Her sister had all the strength of will and all the force of life. Their family, of middle-class background, had failed rather miserably: the father had been killed in 1916; the mother, left in charge of a tanning factory, went bankrupt without realizing what was happening. She got married again, to a stock-breeder, and one day the two of them abandoned their separate enterprises and bought a winery on a street in the 15th arrondissement. Whatever money they still had must have been lost there. Theoretically, one part of the factory belonged to the two daughters, and there were often very heated arguments about money. It would be fair to say that over the years Mme. B. had spent a small fortune on the health of her older daughter, which she reproached her with in perfect thoughtlessness.

I have kept "living" proof of these events. But without me, this proof can prove nothing, and I hope no one will go near it in my lifetime. Once I am dead, it will represent only the shell of an enigma, and I hope those who love me will have the courage to destroy it, without trying to learn what it means. I will give more details about this later. If these details are not there, I beg them not to plunge unexpectedly into my few secrets, or read my letters if any are found, or look at my photographs if any turn up, or above all open what is closed; I ask them to destroy everything without knowing what they are destroying, in the ignorance and spontaneity of true affection.

Because of something I did, someone had a very vague suspicion of this "proof" towards the end of 1940. Since she knew almost nothing of the story, she was not even able to skim the truth of it. She only guessed that something was shut up in the closet. (I lived in a hotel then.) She saw the closet, and made a move to open it, but at that moment she was overcome by a strange attack. Falling on the bed, she began to tremble incessantly; all night long she trembled without saying anything; at dawn, she began breathing hoarsely. It went on for about an hour, then sleep overpowered her and gave her a chance to recover. (That person, who was still very young, had more good sense than sensitivity. Even she complained about her unfailing calm. But at that moment her rationality deserted her. I should add that although she had never had an attack before, it could have been the effect of an unsuccessful poisoning attempt two or three years earlier; sometimes poison is reawakened, stirred up, like a dream, in a body that has been very badly shaken.)

The principal dates should be found in a little notebook locked in my desk. The only date I can be sure of is the 13th of October—Wednesday, the 13th of October. But that is hardly important. Since September I had been living in Arcachon. It was during the Munich crisis. I knew she was as ill as anyone could be. I had stopped off in Paris at the beginning of September, as I was returning from a trip, and had gone to see her doctor. He gave her three weeks to live. Yet she got up every day; she lived on equal terms with an exhausting fever, she shivered for hours, but in the end she overcame the fever. On the 5th or 6th of October, I think, she was still going for rides in the car with her sister, along the Champs Elysées.

Although she was several months older than I was, she had a very young face which the disease had hardly touched. It is true that she wore make-up, but without make-up she seemed even younger, she was almost too young, so that the main effect of the disease was to give her the features of an adolescent. Only her eyes, which were larger, blacker, and more brilliant than they should have been—and sometimes pushed from their sockets by the fever—had an abnormal fixity. In a photograph taken during September her eyes are so large and so serious that one must fight against their expression in order to see her smile, though her smile is very conspicuous.

After I spoke to the doctor, I told her, "He gives you another month."

"Well, I'll tell that to the queen mother, who doesn't believe I'm really ill."

I don't know whether she wanted to live or die. During the last few months, the disease she had been fighting for ten years had been making her life more limited every day, and now she cursed both the disease and life itself with all the violence she could rouse. Some time before, she had thought seriously of killing herself. One evening I advised her to do it. That same evening, after listening to me, unable to talk because of her shortness of breath, but sitting up at her table like a healthy person, she wrote down several sentences that she wished to keep secret. I got these sentences from her, in the end, and I still have them. They consist of a few words of instruction: she asks her family to make the funeral as simple as possible and expressly forbids anyone to visit her grave; she also makes a small legacy to A., one of her friends, the sister-in-law of a fairly well-known dancer.

No mention of me. I can see how bitter she had felt when she heard me agree to her suicide. When I think it over carefully, as I did afterwards, I realize that this consent was hardly excusable, was even dishonest, since it vaguely rose from the thought that she should have been dead long ago, but not only was she not dead, she had continued to live, love, laugh, run around the city, like someone whom illness could not touch. Her doctor had told me that from 1936 on he had considered her dead. Of course the same doctor, who treated me several times, once told me, too, "Since you should have been dead two years ago, everything that remains of your life is a reprieve." He had just given me six months to live and that was seven years ago. But he had an important reason for wishing me six feet underground. What he said only suggested what he wanted to happen. In J.'s case, though, I think he was telling the truth.

I hardly remember how the scene ended. It seems to me she meant to tear up the piece of paper. But as I gave it back to her I was seized by a great tenderness for her, a great admiration for her courage, for that cold and watchful look in the face of death. I can still see her at her table, silently writing those final and strange words. That tiny will, in keeping with her propertyless, already dispossessed existence, that last thought, from which I was excluded, touched me infinitely. In it I recognized her violence, her secrecy; I saw that she was at liberty to fight even me up to the last second. She cried often and for long stretches. But her tears were never the tears of a coward. During very violent scenes she hit me two or three times, and I should have stopped her, because as soon as she realized what she had done she was upset, almost terrified: terrified at having touched me and also at having done something mean, but even more at having to recognize her ungovernable excitement, against which I offered no defense. She felt punished by it, offended, and endangered. Yet if she had tried to kill me, I would no doubt have warded off her blows. I could not have caused her the sadness of killing me. A year or two earlier, a young woman had shot at me with a revolver, after vainly waiting for me to disarm her. But I did not love that young woman. As it happened, she killed herself some time after that.

So for these reasons I kept that piece of paper, and for the few strange words it contained. Suicide disappeared from her thoughts. The disease left her no more breathing space. In those days her sister did not live with her all the time. Or at least, leading the sort of life she did, she was often absent, and might or might not return home at night. J. had a cleaning woman who came at meal times, but during the holidays she did not come. So J. was often left alone. The concierge, who liked her fairly well, went up to see her. She had only a few friends, although in the past she had gone out frequently. Even A., whom she was glad to see, bored her. But she would have welcomed anyone, because when she was alone she was afraid. She was very brave, but she was afraid. She was always very afraid of the night. When I first met her, in a hotel where I was staying at the time, she was in a little room on the second floor and I was in a fairly large room on the third. I can't say I knew her, since I had only crossed her path and greeted her several times. But one night she wakened with a start and felt the presence of someone she took to be me standing at the foot of her bed; shortly afterwards she heard the door close and footsteps move away down the hall. Then she was suddenly convinced that I was about to die or had just died. She went up to my room, although she didn't know me, and called to me through the door. Without thinking, I answered, "Don't be afraid," but in a strange voice, more frightening than reassuring. She was still so frightened that she thought I really was dead, and pushed the door, which gave way and opened, though it had been locked. I was not at all sick, though perhaps a little worse than sick. Fairly frightened myself, I woke up. I swore to her that I had not been in her room, that I had not left my own. She stretched out on my bed and fell asleep almost immediately. Of course one could laugh at it, but it is in no way laughable, and the impulse which carried her towards an unknown man in the middle of the night, which left her at his mercy, was a noble impulse, and she acted on it in the most true and just manner. I know of only two people capable of doing a thing like that, and even then I can only be sure of one.

Fear and the disease together changed day into night for her. I don't know what she was afraid of: not of dying, but of something more serious. She had the telephone within arm's reach and she could call the concierge without dialing. Her mother also came once or twice a week, but no sooner had she arrived than she would find an excuse for going away again. That behavior annoyed her. She reproached her mother, then reproached herself for having cried, for having worked herself up to the point of crying, over an incident which she found insignificant and over a person she did not like very much. But it seemed strange to her that even though her mother knew she was in near agony she would not give up, for her sake, the chance to go shopping. That is why she had been happy to learn about the doctor's prognosis: she was delighted at the idea of proving something to her mother. Her mother actually did moan and weep, but would not prolong her visit by even one minute. Every minute stolen from solitude and fear was an inestimable boon for J. She fought with all her strength for one single minute: not with supplications, but inwardly, though she did not wish to admit it. Children are that way: silently, with the fervor of hopeless desire, they give orders to the world, and sometimes the world obeys them. The sickness had made a child of J.; but her energy was too great, and she could not dissipate it in small things, but only in great things, the greatest things.

When I left for Arcachon it had been decided that J. would undergo a new treatment invented by a physicist from Lyons, a treatment that was not yet generally accepted and that appeared to be excellent for sick people who were not very sick, but was almost certain to kill anyone in a critical condition. It was because of the treatment that I had gone to see J.'s doctor. He calculated that there was an eighty percent risk that she would die. Without the treatment, the risk would become certainty—death in three weeks. I liked the idea of this treatment; I don't know why. J. liked it just as much. The doctor hesitated, but was in favor of administering it. I realized later that in many ways the doctor lacked good judgment. He had studied Paracelsus fairly seriously and devoted himself to conducting experiments that were sometimes outrageous and sometimes childish. We tried two or three together during the time I visited him, when he was hoping to get rid of me. He called himself a Catholic, he meant a practicing Catholic. The first day, he greeted me with this statement: "I am fortunate enough to have faith, I am a believer. What about you?" On the wall of his office there was an excellent photograph of the Turin Sudario, a photograph in which he saw two images superimposed on one another: one of Christ and one of Veronica; and as a matter of fact I distinctly saw, behind the figure of Christ, the features of a woman's face—extremely beautiful, even magnificent in its strangely proud expression. One last thing about this doctor: he was not without his good qualities; he was, it seems to me, a great deal more reliable in his diagnoses than most.

During the beginning of my stay in Arcachon, J. wrote to me at fairly great length, and her handwriting was still firm and vigorous. She told me the doctor had just had her sign a paper in case an accident should occur. So the treatment, which consisted of a series of shots—one each day, given to her at home—was about to begin. The evening before, she felt a violent, stabbing pain near her heart and had such a severe attack of choking that she telephoned her mother, who then called the doctor. This doctor, like all fairly prominent specialists, was not often willing to go out of his way. But this time he came quite quickly, no doubt because of the treatment he was supposed to begin administering the next day. I don't know what he saw: he never talked to me about it. To her, he said it was nothing, and it is true that the medicine he prescribed for her was insignificant. But even so, he decided to postpone the treatment several days.

The pain near her heart did not go away, but the symptoms died down and she had triumphed once more. The treatment was discussed again: she wanted it very much, either in order to get it over with or because her energy could no longer be satisfied with an uncertain objective—to live, to survive—but needed a firm decision on which she could lean heavily. Then a curious thing happened. I had sent a very beautiful cast of J.'s hands to a young man who was a professional palm reader and astrologer, and I had asked him to establish the greater coordinates of her fate. J.'s hands were small and she didn't like them; but their lines seemed to me altogether unusual—cross hatched, entangled, without the slightest apparent unity. I cannot describe them, although at this very moment I have them under my eyes and they are alive. Moreover, these lines grew blurred sometimes, then vanished, except for one deep central furrow that corresponded, I think, to what they call the line of fate. That line did not become distinct except at the moment when all the others were eclipsed; then, the palm of her hand was absolutely white and smooth, a real ivory palm, while the rest of the time the hatchings and the wrinkles made it seem almost old; but the deep hatchet-stroke still ran through the midst of the other lines, and if that line is indeed called the line of fate, I must say that its appearance made that fate seem tragic.

137

At that time the young man wrote to me: he said nothing about the hands. I think he challenged the exactness of the cast, although the impression had been taken by a sculptor about whom I will perhaps say something more. But in his astrological finding he described J.'s disease very exactly (I had naturally not told him about it) and announced that after a course of treatment she would be almost completely restored to health. His note ended with these words: she will not die. There were also some comments on J.'s character and on the general course of her destiny; that was left fairly vague. On the whole, the work was quite mediocre, and the only things that struck us were the few accurate details about the disease and, especially, the allusion to the treatment and its wonderful results. J. made fun of it. She was only a little superstitious, and only about unimportant things. In her nightly terror, she wasn't superstitious at all; she faced a very great danger, one that was nameless and formless, altogether indeterminate, and when she was alone she faced it all alone, without recourse to any tricks or charms. Sometimes she read her sister's cards. Her sister went the rounds of all the fortunetellers and tried to captivate prosperous-looking men in cafes (having the waiter bring them another drink). She succeeded once or twice.

The day appointed for the first injection of the treatment (which was supposed to bring on a long fainting fit in any case) was one of the darkest before the Munich crisis. Each morning during the preceding days the hotel manager announced to me that yet another guest, sometimes two, had left the hotel. But he was still somewhat hopeful, because a prominent political figure who had been staying at the hotel for a week had not left. But that day the man called for his car and left; dozens of others left after him. Large though it was, the hotel was already a desert. I ought to have left too, if only for the sake of my work, but I did not. Today I try without success to understand why I stayed away from Paris then, when everything was calling me back. The thought of that absence makes me uneasy, yet the reasons for it escape me. Mysterious as were the consequences of those events, it seems to me that my deliberate absence, which allowed them to happen, is even more mysterious. I knew that J. wanted to see me, and at such a time wanted to see no one but me, although she had told me just the opposite in order not to interrupt my peace and quiet. My newspaper paged me that day, twice, but I did not answer. I was waiting for a telephone call from J., or from her sister, but there wasn't one. I received no news the next day. It could be that I thought of going then, but that isn't certain. It is hard to find out the truth.

The day after that, I received a few words in J.'s hand, in her hand rather than her handwriting, since the handwriting was extraordinarily tortured. She told me that one hour before coming for the first injection, the doctor had decided to leave in order to get his children settled in the country; he would be back in a day or two. "Take cover behind your sandbags," the doctor told her on the telephone, making a stupid allusion to the home front's passive defense. "Well," said J.'s note at the end, "I will soon be even safer, six feet underground." That short letter was written in ink, but was, as I said, absolutely tortured. I had the impression that something in her was on the point of breaking, that in some very dark place inside her a battle was being fought that I was afraid of. For the first time I decided to telephone her. It was around noon. She was alone. I could hardly hear her, because after the first word or two she was overwhelmed by a violent fit of coughing and choking. For a few seconds I listened to this ragged, suffocated breathing; then she managed to say to me, "Hang up," and I hung up.

The following day's letter was written in pencil, but it was longer and more tranquil, perhaps too tranquil. As I had feared, the telephone call upset her greatly: she was tormented by not being able to talk and, even more, by allowing me to hear that coughing, which she had not been able to control, and she had made a foolish effort to silence herself and tell me to hang up; after that effort, she must have lost consciousness, and later found herself on the floor, astonished, she said, and convinced that she had become a very young child again. Clearly, the phrase "hang up" had nearly cost her her life. From then on she remained almost constantly in bed. I telephoned her once or twice more and she talked to me peacefully, saying over and over, with a certain insistence, that when she saw me again she would have some very interesting and remarkable things to tell me. This same assurance appears in one of her letters: "When you come here, I hope I will be able to talk; I am saving all my breath for that moment, when I will tell you many important things that I have to tell you."

In the meantime the doctor had come back. The Munich crisis had begun by then. Since she could not reasonably be expected to go out, the doctor went to her. He told her she had too much courage, that the moment had come to dispense with courage. The treatment was no longer discussed. As he left, he called J.'s sister Louise to the stairway and told her it was inhuman to let her sister suffer like this; that there was no more hope and that they would have to resort to drugs. Louise wrote me about that, even though writing was a big production for her; she said also that J. knew nothing about this conversation and that naturally it would make "the little kid," as she called her older sister, happy to see me again. The conversation on the stairway was soon reported to the patient, who mentioned it to me with astonishing satisfaction in one of her last letters: "So now we come to morphine," she said.

The doctor's decision might seem natural and justified. I think it was. For J. the battle took another form and became even more difficult. This was no longer an honest, open struggle against an enemy who frankly wanted to fight. The shots calmed her, but they were also meant to calm something in her that could not be calmed, a violent and rebellious assertion against a force which did not respect it. She had a horror of hypocritically sweet behavior, and the sudden sweetness of the disease took her by surprise, deceived her, to such a degree that while she had been lively and almost normal before, getting up and going outdoors, now, after very few injections—perhaps two or three—she fell into a state of prostration that transformed her into a dying person. The doctor himself was frightened by this, even though he had foreseen it. He discontinued the injections and even—a surprising thing—withdrew his prescription for them. A nurse was spending the nights close to J. now, and soon began spending both the days and the nights there. Though the patient was irritable by nature, and not very likeable, this nurse, who was fairly young, became attached to her; she was drawn by J.'s beauty, which at the time, it seems, had become extraordinary. It is well known that for an instant after dying, people who were once beautiful become young and beautiful again: the disease, the almost absurd sufferings, the unending struggle to breathe, not to breathe too much, to stop the bursts of coughing which at every attack nearly suffocated her, all that extravagant and ugly violence, which should have made her hideous, could do nothing to mar the perfectly beautiful and young (though somewhat hard) expression that illuminated her face. That is certainly strange. I thought her beauty

140

came from the radiance of her eyes, which were tainted by the poison. But her eyes were almost always closed, or if they opened, they opened for a brief instant, with a rapidity that was actually disconcerting, and looked at the world, recognized it, and kept a sharp eye on it, as if taking it by surprise.

Having been denied morphine, the illness did everything in its power to have it given again. J. did not want to live only for the sake of living. She thought it absurd and even ridiculous to suffer, if things could be otherwise. Stoicism did not suit her, and she became furiously angry when the shots were discontinued. Then it was evident that she was not really sicker than she had been before. The doctor was helpless. At first he objected, but after a scene in which J. insulted him, he yielded to her will, which was as strong as his own. During that scene, J. said to him, "If you don't kill me, then you're a murderer." Later I came across a similar phrase, attributed to Kafka. Her sister, who would have been incapable of inventing something like that, reported it to me in that form and the doctor just about confirmed it. (He remembered her as saying, "If you don't kill me, you'll kill me.")

This time the effects of the morphine were altogether different. J. remained calm, or a little calmer, but the passivity, the calm, was only apparent. It was as though, after having been deceived by the hypocritical drug, she had put herself on her guard and, behind the appearance of sleep, in the depths of her repose, had maintained a vigilance, a penetrating gaze that left her enemy no hope of attacking her unawares. It was from this moment on that her face assumed the expression of beauty that was so striking. I think she enjoyed forcing death to greater honesty and greater truth. She condemned it to become noble.

I'm not very sure how those days were spent. I didn't ask very many questions. I could hardly talk about her. The only person who talked to me was the doctor, a person without tact, often ridiculous, and amazed by what he saw. He talked to me more than he should have, and I questioned him. The nurse wanted to confide in me too. (I think she was called Dangerue, or something like that.) Later she said an odd thing to me: "If you ever become very sick yourself, I would be happy to be sent for." I know that "the little kid" sometimes talked to her at night for quite a long time: she asked her to describe some of the suffering she had witnessed as a nurse; and she asked her, "Have you ever seen death?"

"I have seen dead people, Miss."

"No, death!" The nurse shook her head. "Well, soon you will see it."

Her friend A. wrote to me. The first few lines were dictated by J.: according to these words, she was almost well; don't worry about me, she said, don't worry. Then she had felt misgivings; not being strong enough to write, she had found it strange to write to me through a third person, and had asked her friend to abandon the letter, to forget it. But A. wrote me all that, she told me particularly that J. did not want to disturb my peace and quiet but that it was obvious she thought of nothing but my return, that all the other people annoyed her, jarred on her more and more, that soon she would not be able to stand anyone's presence, as long as I was absent. I think in saying that, she was announcing that she was going to die. This time I decided to return to Paris. But I gave myself two more days. I let her know by telephone or by telegram.

My official address in Paris was a hotel in rue d'O. I went there Monday evening (I've thought about that date and now I'm sure of it) on returning, quite tired out, from Arcachon. In the middle of the night, at two or three o'clock, the telephone woke me up. "Come, please come, J. is dying." The voice was Louise's. I didn't have far to go and I don't think I delayed. I was surprised to find the door of the apartment open. The apartment wasn't big, but it had a fairly large front hall, and in order to reach her room it was necessary to walk down a corridor. In the corridor I bumped into the doctor who was pleased to meet me, took me by the arm, with his usual lack of ceremony, and led me outside onto the landing. "My poor man." He nodded his head in a sinister way. I didn't hear anything he said until the shocking vulgarity of one phrase startled me: "It's a blessed release for the poor creatures." Once again he explained certain things which I don't remember very well: I think he tried to justify his decision to abandon the treatment. He also said, "What strength of will!" because barely half an hour before she had called him herself, working herself up to force him to come; he liked that last outburst. So, she had made him come at the last moment, and not me, she had spoken to him, and not to me. I looked at this great vulgar fellow, who was foolishly repeating, "I told you so; three weeks, exactly three weeks."

"It's been five weeks!" I said this rashly, provoked to exasperation by what he had said. But when I saw him so suddenly taken aback, I reconsidered what I had said, and it dawned on me that at a certain moment in the night she must have felt defeated, too weak to live until morning, when I would see her, and that she had asked the doctor's help in order to last a little longer, one minute longer, the one minute which she had so often demanded silently and in vain. This is what that poor fool mistook for anger, and doubtless he had given in to her by coming, but he was already too late: at a time when she could no longer do anything, he could do even less, and his only help had been to cooperate with that sweet and tranquil death he spoke of with such sickening familiarity. My grief began at that moment.

The room was full of strangers. I think her mother was there, her stepfather, and maybe another relative. All these people were strangers to me. The nurse, whom I didn't know, was there too. This gathering of strangers close to her silent body was what she would have found most unbearable. It was something incongruous which she should have been spared and which turned my grief to bitterness and disgust. I remained standing in front of her, but because of all those people I could not see her. I know I looked at her, stared at her, but did not see her. I could only speak to Louise, who was the only one who reminded me of her as she had been when she was alive, or rather Louise talked to me first: I would have liked to understand why, after having resisted so stubbornly for so many interminable years, she had not found the strength to hold out for such a short time longer. Naively, I thought that interval had been a few minutes, and a few minutes was nothing. But for her those few minutes had been a lifetime, more than that eternity of life which they talk about, and hers had been lost then. What Louise said to me when she telephoned—"She is dying"—was true, was the kind of truth you perceive in a flash, she would die, she was almost dead, the wait had not begun at that moment; at that moment it had come to an end; or rather the last wait had gone on nearly the duration of the telephone call: at the beginning she was alive and lucid, watching all of Louise's movements; then still alive, but already sightless and without a sign of acceptance when Louise said, "She is dying"; and the receiver had hardly been hung up when her pulse, the nurse said, scattered like sand.

Louise did not have much presence of mind, nor much heart. But all of a sudden she must have read in my face that something was about to happen that she knew she did not have the right to see, nor anyone else in the world, and instantly she took them all away. I sat down on the edge of the bed, as I had done many times. She was a little more stretched out than I would have imagined; her head lay on a little cushion and because of that she had the stillness of a recumbent effigy and not of a living being. Her face was serious and even severe. Her lips, tightly pressed together, made me think of her violently clenched teeth which had shut at the last moment and even now did not relax. Her eyelids, too, were lowered. Her skin, strikingly white next to the black brilliance of her hair, wrung my heart. She who had been absolutely alive was already no more than a statue. It was then that I looked at her hands. Fortunately they were not joined, but as they lay askew on the sheet, awkwardly clutched in a last contraction which slightly twisted the fingers, they seemed so little to me, so diminished by the clumsiness of their last effort, so much too weak for the immense battle which that great soul had fought, all alone, that for an instant I was overwhelmed by sadness. I leaned over her, I called to her by her first name; and immediately—I can say there wasn't a second's interval—a sort of breath came out of her compressed mouth, a sigh which little by little became a light, weak cry; almost at the same time—I'm sure of this— her arms moved, tried to rise. At that moment, her eyelids were still completely shut. But a second afterwards, perhaps two, they opened abruptly and they opened to reveal something terrible which I will not talk about, the most terrible look which a living being can receive, and I think that if I had shuddered at that instant, and if I had been afraid, everything would have been lost, but my tenderness was so great that I didn't even think about the strangeness of what was happening, which certainly seemed to me altogether natural because of that infinite movement which drew me towards her, and I took her in my arms, while her arms clasped me, and not only was she completely alive from that moment on, but perfectly natural, gay and almost completely recovered.

The first words she spoke, though, were somewhat distressing. In themselves they weren't; and now that I have just written that they were, I can't really understand why. "How long have you been here?" Those were the words she spoke almost immediately. It could be that I had just realized the strangeness of the situation, and something of that strangeness came through her words. But I believe her voice itself was still a little surprising; her voice was always surprising—fairly harsh, lightly veiled, clouded by disease and yet always very gay or very lively.

But I think I was also struck by its uneasy inflection: as she asked me how long I had been there, it seemed to me she was remembering something, or that she was close to remembering it, and that at the same time she felt an apprehension that was linked to me, or my coming too late, or the fact that I had seen and taken by surprise something I shouldn't have seen. All that came to me through her voice. I don't know how I answered. Right away she relaxed and became absolutely human and real again.

Strange as it may seem, I don't think I gave one distinct thought, during that whole day, to the event which had allowed J. to talk to me and laugh with me again. It is simply that in those moments I loved her totally, and nothing else mattered. I only had enough self-control to go find the others and tell them J. had recovered. I don't know how they took the news; perhaps just as naturally as I did. I vaguely remember that they were huddled in the kitchen and in one of the other rooms and that, according to Louise, who reported it to me, they complained that I had treated them like intruders. I certainly didn't want to mistreat them. I had practically forgotten them, that's all. I remember that later I had Louise ask for authorization to have her sister embalmed. These practices were believed to be unhealthy, to say the least. But whatever impression fearfulness induced them to form of me, I can hardly hold it against them. I must even admit that given such unusual circumstances, these people showed admirable reserve, whether through ignorance or dread or for some other reason, and, in the end, behaved perfectly.

I recall few things worth mentioning about that day. J.'s waking took place at dawn, almost with the sunrise, and the dawn light charmed her. In terms of the illness itself—judging it as though it had followed its natural course—I found her much better than I would have imagined after everything that had been written to me, particularly after so many shots, which had been given to her every day. Apparently the morphine had not affected her spirits at all: someone who is saturated with drugs can seem lucid and even profound, but not cheerful; well, she was extremely and naturally cheerful; I remember that she poked fun at her mother in the kindest manner, which was unusual. When I think of all that took place before it and after it, the memory of that gaiety should be enough to kill a man. But at the time, I simply saw that she was gay, and I was gay too.

During that whole day she had almost no attacks, though she talked and laughed enough to bring on twenty. She ate much more than I did—although for many days she had been unable to eat anything—and her greatest worry was that I ate so little. She was somewhat uneasy because the nurse had taken advantage of my presence to spend the day at home. I noticed, then, a certain connivance between them which I had more evidence of later. She made fun of the doctor again and again. I asked her if she remembered telephoning him that night, if she knew he had come. "So he really came last night!" she said with an almost incredible expression of astonishment and discovery, but she did not ask me any questions. I asked her what those interesting things were that she had said she would talk to me about on my return. Then she had a sort of fit of absent-mindedness and distantly answered: "Yes, when you come back I'll talk to you about it." One of her friends came that afternoon, a young woman originally from Constantinople. J. had spent many months with her but hardly saw her any more. The young woman must have learned that she was very sick, and came out of politeness to see how she was. I don't know what the others told her, but thinking that J. was near the end, she said to them that this was the time when the danger of contagion was greatest and that one shouldn't enter the room. Perhaps that is why they left me in peace: I don't know. She herself did not want to come in, and stuck her head through the half-open door, gesturing and making faces. "What's the matter with her?" J. asked me, suddenly irritated. "Do I frighten her? Am I that ugly?" The girl's behavior was all the more ridiculous because she had the same disease and was two steps away from the grave herself. J. asked for a mirror, looked at herself for a long time and said nothing. She was still very beautiful.

Towards evening she was no worse physically, but her mood had changed a little. I became uneasy too. I began to be aware of how exceptional this situation was. When I passed through Paris in September I had bought J. a big lamp, and she liked its lampshade, which was painted white. She had the lamp placed at the foot of the bed, directly in her line of vision, which must have bothered her, but she wanted it that way. Later, in the course of the night, when I saw that her eyes were fixed, riveted on the light, I suggested to her that it should be moved away or hidden; but she squeezed my wrist so tightly, to hold me back, that in the morning my skin was still white there. As soon as evening came she got the idea that I should leave. When I did not leave, when I did not return to my hotel, she worried about how tired I must be, and as the night advanced her worry turned into astonishment, a question about something mysterious and frightening which she did not press but returned to with greater and greater foreboding. At one point she stared at me with a penetration which makes me shiver now. "Why," she said coldly, "are you staying *precisely* tonight?" I suppose she was beginning to know as much as I did about the events of the early morning, but at that moment I was frightened at the thought that she might discover what had happened to her; it seemed to me that would be something absolutely terrifying for anyone to learn who was naturally afraid of the night. Perhaps I was wrong not to believe she had enough courage, just then, to face even the few things she had been afraid of before, because that night I did not see any fear in her, or if she was afraid, it was because she herself had become frightening. Perhaps I did commit a grave error in not telling her what she was waiting for me to tell her. My deviousness put us face to face like two creatures who were lying in wait for one another but who could no longer see one another.

My excuse is that in that hour I exalted her far above any sort of honesty, and the greatest truth mattered less to me than the slightest risk of worrying her. Another excuse is that little by little she seemed to approach a truth compared to which mine lost all interest. Towards eleven o'clock or midnight she began to have troubled dreams. Yet she was still awake, because I spoke to her and she answered me. She saw what she called "a perfect rose" move in the room. During the day I had ordered some flowers for her that were very red but already going to seed, and I'm not sure she liked them very much. She looked at them from time to time in a rather cold way. They had been put in the hall for the night, almost in front of her door, which remained open for some time. Then she saw something move across the room, at a certain height, as it seemed to me, and she called it "a perfect rose." I thought this dream image came to her from the flowers, which were perhaps disturbing her. So I closed the door. At that moment she really dozed off, into an almost calm sleep, and I was watching her live and sleep when all of a sudden she said with great anguish. "Quick, a perfect rose," all the while continuing to sleep but now with a slight rattle. The nurse came and whispered to me that the night before that word had been the last she had pronounced: when she had seemed to be sunk in complete unconsciousness, she had abruptly awakened from her stupor to point to the oxygen balloon and murmur, "A perfect rose," and had immediately sunk again.

This story chilled me. I told myself that what had happened the night before, from which I had been excluded, was beginning all over again, and that J., drawn by some terrifying but perhaps also alluring and tempting thing, was reverting to those last minutes when the long wait for me had been too much for her. I think that was true. I even think that something was happening then that I found completely disheartening, because I took her hand gently, by the wrist (she was sleeping), and scarcely had I touched it when she sat up with her eyes open, looked at me furiously and pushed me away, saying, "Never touch me again." Then immediately she stretched out her arms to me, just as in the morning, and burst into tears. She cried, she sobbed against me in such a transport of grief that she was on the point of suffocating, and since the nurse had left the room in order not to witness this scene, I had to support her by myself without being able to get the oxygen balloon, which was just out of reach. While this was happening, the nurse came back and gave her the oxygen, which helped her to control herself. But after that she did not let me leave her bedside.

She fell asleep again. Her sleep had a strange way of dissolving in an instant, so that behind it she seemed to remain awake and to be grappling with serious matters there, in which I played perhaps a terrifying role. She had fallen asleep, her face wet with tears. Far from being spoiled by it, her youth seemed dazzling: only the very young and healthy can bear such a flood of tears that way; her youth made such an extraordinary impression on me that I completely forgot her illness, her awakening and the danger she was still in. A little later, however, her expression changed. Almost under my eyes, the tears had dried and the tear stains had disappeared; she became severe, and her slightly raised lips showed the contraction of her jaw and her tightly clenched teeth, and gave her a rather mean and suspicious look; her hand moved in mine to free itself, I wanted to release it, but she seized me again right away with a savage quickness in which there was nothing human. When the nurse came to talk to me—in a low voice and about nothing important—J. immediately awoke and said in a cold way, "I have my secrets with her too." She went back to sleep at once.

What the nurse told me was not altogether without importance. She told me that during the day she had telephoned the doctor to let him know about the patient's changed condition. The doctor had cried, "Oh, good heavens!" That is all the nurse ever dared to tell me about it. J. had been given one shot early in the evening. At two or three o'clock, I became convinced that the same terrible thing that had happened the day before was in danger of repeating itself. It is true that J. did not wake up again. The nurse must have dozed off too. As I listened without pause to her slight breathing, faced by the silence of the night, I felt extremely helpless and miserable just because of the miracle that I had brought about. Then, for the first time, I had a thought that came back to me later and in the end won out. While I was still in that state of mind—it must have been about three o'clock—J. woke up without moving at all—that is, she looked at me. That look was very human: I don't mean affectionate or kind, since it was neither; but it wasn't cold or marked by the forces of this night. It seemed to understand me profoundly; that is why I found it friendly, though it was at the same time terribly sad. "Well," she said, "you've made a fine mess of things." She looked at me again without smiling at all, as she might have smiled, as I afterwards hoped she had, but I think my expression did not invite a smile. Besides, that look did not last very long.

Even though her eyelids were lowered, I am convinced that from then on she lay awake; she lay awake because the danger was too great, or for some other reason; but she purposely kept herself at the edge of consciousness, manifesting a calm, and an alertness in that calm, that was very unlike her tension of a short time before. What proved to me that she was not asleep—though she was unaware of what went on around her because something else held her interest— was that a little later she remembered what had happened nearly an hour before: the nurse, not sure whether or not she was asleep, had leaned over her and suggested she have another shot, a suggestion which she did not seem to be at all aware of. But a little later she said to the nurse, "No, no shot this evening," and repeated insistently, "No more shots." Words which I have all the time in the world to remember now. Then she turned slightly towards the nurse and said in a tranquil tone, "Now then, take a good look at death," and pointed her finger at me. She said this in a very tranquil and almost friendly way, but without smiling.

Now I want to pass rapidly over all that happened. I have said more about it than I would have believed, but I am also touching the limit of what I can say. After she spoke about me as I have described, there was nothing extraordinary in her behavior, and the night ended rather quickly. Towards six o'clock she was sleeping deeply and almost like a healthy person. I arranged things with the nurse so that I could return to the hotel, where I stayed about an hour, and when I came back, Louise told me that she was still the same. But I saw right away that her condition had changed a good deal: the death rattle had begun and her face was the face of a dying person; besides that, her mouth was almost open, which had never happened to her at any time before while she was sleeping, and that mouth, open to the noise of agony, did not seem to belong to her, it seemed to be the mouth of someone I didn't know, someone irredeemably condemned, or even dead. The nurse agreed with me that things had gotten worse, but even so she asked my permission to see another patient and stop off at home, to be gone until the beginning of the afternoon. She thought the doctor would come during the morning, she also thought J. might sleep for many hours, during which one could only wait, without doing anything useful; she pointed out that her pulse was steady and holding up well.

The rattling became so loud and so intense that it could be heard outside the apartment with all the doors closed. The comings and goings in the room seemed completely foreign to the unconscious body, itself a stranger to its own agony. Louise exasperated me a great deal, because the noise frightened her, and her mother also began to come in and make remarks, so that I didn't know where I was and began to hate the whole world; I no longer had any real feelings, not even for J., whose body was half dead and half alive. It could be that I drove these people away or that I went out for a moment (on the landing there was an armchair, and I sat down in it, where I could hear the rasping breath of her coma). What I'm sure of is that at one point during the morning, when I came back, I found J. awake again and feeling very bad. "You've come early," she said to me, and I saw that she had forgotten I had been there all night long. She was intensely annoyed because the nurse was not there. She called Louise, who ordinarily amused her but whose presence she could not bear for very long at a time. Extreme impatience rose from her whole being. If at first I was a little hurt by her coldness towards me, that did not last; I sensed too clearly the reason for that impatience, for that fever, for the surging of all her strength; I saw how, by a quicker movement than anything we could do, she kept one step ahead of the blows that were trying to do away with her. We were all very slow creatures and she needed to move like lightning to save her last breath, to escape the final immobility. I never saw her more alive, nor more lucid. Maybe she was in the last instant of her agony, but even though she was incredibly beset by suffering, exhaustion and death, she seemed so alive to me that once again I was convinced that if she didn't want it, and if I didn't want it, nothing would ever get the better of her. While attack followed attack—but there was no more trace of coma nor any fatal symptoms—when the others were out of the room, her hand which was twitching on mine suddenly controlled itself and clasped mine with the greatest impatience and with all the affection and all the tenderness it could. At the same time she smiled at me in a natural way, even with amusement. Immediately afterwards she said to me in a low and rapid voice, "Quick, a shot." (She had not asked for one during the night.) I took a large syringe, in it I mixed two doses of morphine and two of a sedative, four doses altogether of narcotics. The liquid was fairly slow in penetrating, but since she saw what I was doing she remained very calm. She did not move at any moment. Two or three minutes later, her pulse became irregular, it beat violently, stopped, then began to beat again, heavily, only to stop again, this happened many times, finally it became extremely rapid and light, and "scattered like sand."

I have no better way of describing it. I could say that during those moments J. continued to look at me with the same affectionate and willing look and that this look is still there, but unfortunately I'm not sure of that. As for the rest, I don't want to say anything. The difficulties with the doctor became a matter of indifference to me. I myself see nothing important in the fact that this young woman was dead, and returned to life at my bidding, but I see an astounding miracle in her fortitude, in her energy, which was great enough to make death powerless as long as she wanted. One thing must be understood: I have said nothing extraordinary or even surprising. What is extraordinary begins at the moment I stop. But I am no longer able to speak of it.

I will go on with this story, but now I will take some precautions. I am not taking these precautions in order to cast a veil over the truth. The truth will be told, everything of importance that happened will be told. But not everything has yet happened.

After a week of silence I have seen clearly that if I was expressing badly what I was trying to express, there would not only be no end, but I would be glad that there was no end. Even now, I am not sure that I am any more free than I was at the moment when I was not speaking. It may be that I am entirely mistaken. It may be that all these words are a curtain behind which what happened will never stop happening. The unfortunate thing is that after having waited for so many years, during which silence, immobility, and patience carried to the point of inertia did not for one single day stop deceiving me, I had to open my eyes all at once and allow myself to be tempted by a splendid thought, which I am trying in vain to bring to its knees.

Perhaps these precautions will not be precautions. For some time I lived with a person who was obsessed by the idea of my death. I had said to her: "I think that at certain moments you would like to kill me. You shouldn't resist that desire. I'm going to write down on a piece of paper that if you kill me you will be doing what is best." But a thought is not exactly a person, even if it lives and acts like one. A thought demands a loyalty which makes any slyness difficult. Sometimes it is itself false, but behind this lie I still recognize something real, which I cannot betray.

Its uprightness is what actually fascinates me. When this thought appears, memory is no longer present, nor uneasiness, nor weariness, nor foreboding, nor any recalling of yesterday, nor any plan for to-morrow. It appears, and perhaps it has appeared a thousand times, ten thousand times. What, then, could be more familiar to me? But familiarity is just what has disappeared forever between us. I look at it. It lives with me. It is in my house. Sometimes it begins to eat; sometimes, though rarely, it sleeps next to me. And I, a madman, fold my hands and let it eat its own flesh.

After these events, several of which I have recounted —but I am still recounting them now—I was immediately warned (told everything) about what was in store for me. The only difference, and it was a large one, was that I was living in proud intimacy with terror; I was too shallow to see the misery and worthlessness of this intimacy, and I did not understand that it would demand something of me that a man cannot give. My only strong point was my silence. Such a great silence seems incredible to me when I think about it, not a virtue, because it in no way occurred to me to talk, but precisely that the silence never said to itself: be careful, there is something here which you owe me an explanation for, the fact that neither my memory, nor my daily life, nor my work, nor my actions, nor my spoken words, nor the words which come from my fingertips, ever alluded directly or indirectly to the thing which my whole person was physically engrossed in. I cannot understand this reserve, and I who am now speaking turn bitterly towards those silent days, those silent years, as towards an inaccessible, unreal country, closed off from everyone, and most of all from myself, yet where I have lived during a large part of my life, without exertion, without desire, by a mystery which astonishes me now.

I have lost silence, and the regret I feel over that is immeasurable. I cannot describe the pain that invades a man once he has begun to speak. It is a motionless pain, that is itself pledged to muteness; because of it, the unbreathable is the element I breathe. I have shut myself up in a room, alone, there is no one in the house, almost no one outside, but this solitude has itself begun to speak, and I must in turn speak about this speaking solitude, not in derision, but because a greater solitude hovers above it, and above that solitude, another still greater, and each, taking the spoken word in order to smother it and silence it, instead echoes it to infinity, and infinity becomes its echo.

Someone has said to me, with some annoyance, "In your presence, mouths open." That is possible, although it seems to me true of only a few people, because I have heard very few. But as I have listened to those few, my attention has been so great that they have not been able to be angry with me for what they said, nor reproach themselves with it, nor perhaps remember it. And I have always been more closely bound to them by what they have said to me than by what they could have hidden from me. People who are silent do not seem admirable to me because of that, nor yet less friendly. The ones who speak, or at least who speak to me because I have asked them a question, often seem to me the most silent, either because they evoke silence in me, or because, knowingly or unknowingly, they shut themselves up with me in an enclosed place where the person who questions them allies them with answers that their mouths do not hear.

I want to say, then, that "to have lost silence" does not at all mean what one might think. Besides, it hardly matters. I have decided to take this path. I still lived in the hotel in rue d'O. My room was small, and not very agreeable, but it suited me. In the next room lived a young woman who told me one day, when I made the mistake of speaking to her—she was on her balcony and I was on mine—that I annoyed her because I did not make enough noise. I think I actually did annoy her. In any case I did not disturb her very often, since I was rarely at home because of my work and even at night did not always return. This woman was on the point of breaking off relations with a friend of hers, a businessman from the Avenue de l'Opéra, who made her come to Paris two or three times a year, since she lived in the provinces, in Nantes or Rennes, I no longer remember which. She was married, with two children, and on top of that taught in a private girls' school. I do not know how she managed to fulfill all these obligations at once. Maybe that was pure make-believe. I am reporting these details, which do not interest me, as a way of getting started. I am deliberately trying to cast a spell over myself. And anyway, who can say what is important? This woman had a mingling of freedom and constraint in her character. It was clear that she was making a play for me. One evening when I came home, after having worked hard and with my mind on something else, I went to the wrong door and found myself in her room. There was certainly nothing intentional in this absent-mindedness. We both lived on the fifth or sixth floor, and the lights on that floor did not work. It is true that sometimes as I was coming home, the idea would occur to me that I might easily enter the wrong room, but I thought about it without hoping it would happen; I often did not even remember who lived there. For several minutes she reacted quite well to my presence. I suppose that was because she was wearing a beautiful dressing-gown. Even though it was nearly midnight, she was sitting in her armchair looking perfectly neat and presentable. That fact must have made everything else pleasant for her. Since she seemed quite pretty to me that day, I too thought my error meant something, and I did not tell her I had come in by mistake. Later on, she annoyed me very much. She was always wanting to come into my room and I did not want that. But she taught me something that I would not perhaps have discovered until much later if it had not been for her.

That day, something happened. I remember that she showed me her hand and said, "Look at this scar." On the back of her hand there was a rather large, diagonal swelling. Shortly afterwards I noticed that her mood had changed: a sort of cold respectability was mounting in her face, the sort of moral look which makes even the most beautiful face tiresome, and hers was only slightly pretty. I immediately wanted to leave. At that moment I must have told her I had come in by mistake, but she understood me to say I had made a mistake in coming in, which was something slightly different.

I have just been thinking about her. I realize that though I apparently behaved more or less the way anyone else would have, there must have been something absolutely offensive about my behavior that often made me her enemy. I suppose part of what she told me was true. I asked her questions about history, grammar, and botany, and she knew volumes about them. The only happy moments she spent with me were those hours of recitation, when she delivered entire chapters of Larive-et-Fleury and Malet to me. It relaxed me to listen to her. This knowledge, so incredibly old, soared over me croaking a kind of message which was always the same, and which more or less amounted to this: there is a time for learning, a time for being ignorant, a time for understanding, and a time for forgetting.

During these moments her face had a rather delicate expression. But it is certainly true that the other expression, which came over her unexpectedly and made me want to leave, might very well have been provoked by my attitude, since I behaved in a foolish way, and even if she did not see that clearly, the propriety of her distant past told her something about it from time to time and rose into her face again, where it looked out at me. I see it at this moment, that distant and ambiguous past which was certainly something ugly. But I do not know what I could have been or done to make her defend herself with an expression like that.

This scene appears to me now: I was in the metro. I think I was on my way home. By chance, I found myself sitting across from someone I knew. She told me she was married or about to be married. After one or two stops, she got off. This encounter reminded me of my neighbor C(olette). Suddenly I had the extraordinary impression that I had completely forgotten this woman, whom I saw almost every day, and that in order to remember her I had to seek out someone I had only glimpsed ten years before. If it had not been for that recent encounter, I not only would have lost sight of her altogether, but already, where she had been, there was a kind of immense, impersonal, though animate hole, a sort of living gap, which she emerged from only with difficulty. What complicated this impression was that the forgetting did not seem to be that. I saw her very clearly at that moment, and I would have seen her before, too, if I had thought of it. But on the other hand, I had to ask myself this: during the whole evening, yesterday, when she was there, did I notice her?

This ride on the metro left me with the recollection of a great sadness. The sadness had nothing to do with my short memory. But something profoundly sad was happening there in that car, with all those people going home to lunch. Very close to me was a great unhappiness, as silent as a real unhappiness can be, beyond all help, unknown, and which nothing could cause to appear. And I, as I felt this, was like a traveler walking on a road in the middle of nowhere; the road has summoned him and he walks onward, but the road wants to see if the man who is coming is really the one who should be coming: it turns around to see who he is, and in one somersault they both tumble into the ravine. Unhappy is the path that turns around to look at the man walking on it; and how much more profound was this unhappiness, how much more enigmatic and silent. At the hotel I left the concierge instructions not to disturb me, and gave her the key to my room to hang back up on the board, showing that I was not in. At about five o'clock someone entered the room without knocking. No one had ever dared come there before except the hotel employees and sometimes my brother.

Perhaps I could say why I would have walked a great distance when I had to see someone, though I hate to walk, rather than meet that person within the four walls of this hotel. There was nothing secret here. And besides, a few people always came to where I lived, and some of them came very often. There are quite natural reasons for it: the bother, when people come, of having to see them and hear them long after they have left; the need to make the place where one lives a place where nothing happens, which is why one can be at peace there, and also to make it a vacant place, where people who should not meet do not meet; and finally it is a test, because sooner or later a person who has been asked to stay outside will come there or prowl around nearby, so that at that point one discovers if it is a terrible fault or, quite the opposite, an agreeable thing. All these reasons seem good to me, but naturally they have their bad aspects. Yet there was still one other.

I was stretched out on my bed. It must have been very dark already. There was still a little light, I think, but since the curtains were not drawn, that light could have come from the street. The person who had entered was standing in the middle of the room. I was going to write that she was like a statue, because she was motionless and turned towards the window, and she really did have the look of a statue; but stone was not part of her element; rather, her nature was composed of fear—not an insane or monstrous fear, but one expressed by these words: for her, something irremediable had happened. I once saw a squirrel get caught in a cage that hung from a tree: he leaped across the threshold with all the energy of his very happy life, but hardly had he touched the planks inside when the light trigger clapped the door shut, and even though he had not been hurt, even though he was still free, since the cage was enormous, with a little pile of shells inside, his leap broke off abruptly and he remained paralyzed, struck in the back by the certainty that now the trap had caught him.

The strange thing was that she did not look at me or at anything else in the room. I might have thought she was trying to find the dim light from the window, that she had only come in for that last bit of daylight which fascinated her, sustained her, paralyzed her; but it was so faint that it could not have reached her eyes anyway, and once she had entered, inexplicably, she had only just enough strength left to remain standing in that room without dissolving into thin air. I think I was fairly calm. There are many things I could say about the impression I had, but I have the same impression now, as I look at that same person, who is standing several feet away from the window, just in front of the table, with her back to me; it is about the same time of day, she has come in and she is walking forward. (The room is different.) As I see her this way now, when she is no longer a surprise to me, I experience a much greater shock, a feeling of dizziness and confusion that I never had then, but something cold too, a strange pang, so much so that I would like to beg her to go back and stay behind the door, so that I could go out too. But this is the rule, and there is no way to free oneself of it: as soon as the thought has arisen, it must be followed to the very end.

I think I noticed only one thing: that she had a black, tailored suit on and wore no hat (which was more uncommon then than it is now); I could hardly see her hair, which I thought was much longer than people usually wore it, and because she was bowing her head she looked as though she had been struck or was expecting to be struck. What happened next shows how far she had already slipped outside the normal order of things. As she was turning around, she bumped into the table, and it made a noise. She reacted to the noise with a frightened laugh, and fled like an arrow. Then everything becomes confused. I think that after she cried out I grew wild. I saw her lunge toward the free air, and the instinct of the hunter seized me. I caught up with her near the stairway, grabbed her around the waist, and brought her back, dragging her along the floor as far as the bed, where she collapsed. My fit of rage was one of the few I have had since my very angry childhood, and it was uncontrollable. I do not know where this violence came from; I could have done anything at a time like that: broken her arm, crushed her skull, or even driven my own forehead into the wall, since I do not think this furious energy was directed at her in particular. Like the blast of an earthquake, it was an aimless force which shook people and knocked them over. I have been shaken by this blast too, and so have become a tempest which opens mountains and maddens the sea.

When the light was turned on, she did not seem to remember that tempest very clearly. "I must have fallen down," she said, examining her stockings. She was very surprised to see me out of breath and, I think, still wildeyed. But it was the way I looked that little by little reminded her of something, doubtless not of what had happened, but of her own presence there, her footsteps in the street, this room that she was not familiar with, and—then what? Again she was driven toward the door. One of the funny things about this scene was that although she had overcome many obstacles to arrive at this place, she now thought only of leaving, while I was holding her back not only against her will but also against my own. I should make it clear that she regarded me as someone she had apparently never seen before, that she therefore found herself shut up in a gloomy hotel room, completely disheveled, with a wild man who was throwing himself at her to stop her from making the slightest movement. And I was behaving in an entirely instinctual way too, for I had not realized that I did not know her, and was brutally pushing her back into the room not in order to keep her there, but to prevent her from going outside and losing that feeling of terror which she had found there and which obliged her to control herself or disappear.

Though the circumstances surrounding this encounter became easier to explain later, they were never any clearer than they were at that moment. N(athalie)'s character complicated them even further. One day I asked her, "What made you think of coming?" By then, I had met her four or five times in an office. She answered, "I've forgotten," and I think it was true. She was also extremely shy, though capable of unreasonable behavior. For instance she lost her way quite often in Paris, and though her shyness did not stop her from going up to people, it drove what she wanted to ask them from her mind, or, if she remembered, it made her forget the answer they gave her. She could look someone up that she did not know, if she had to, but if she knew him at all, the errand became, more difficult, and if she knew that he found it annoying to have visitors, it became unbelievably difficult. That day was a Saturday, and she did not have to go to work; but she had a little girl, and she ought to have been with her then; and even if the lateness of the hour clearly did not stop her from going into the hotel, there were a thousand chances that she would get lost in the streets, since she saw very poorly at night.

She told me about it long afterwards—and she remained convinced that I never knew who she was, and yet treated her not like a stranger but like someone who was all too familiar. That was why she nearly went crazy herself: she could not face the immense task of making herself known to a man who was looking at her that way—with eyes in which she could not see herself—and saying to him: you met me at such-and-such a place. That seemed impossible to her. But since at the same time I was behaving with a sort of savage intimacy towards her—and not in the least as though she were a stranger—she was forced to believe that something had happened which she had not noticed, and that actually she was perfectly known to me, even if it meant she was someone she herself did not know. She repeated this to me, or to be more exact she told it to me when I insisted, after she had inadvertently begun a sentence which I had great trouble making her finish because I had spoken to her in a familiar way and also because she thought she should not have heard what I said. At one point I had said to her: "You're crazy, why did you go out today?" When she got home she remembered these words and as soon as she took them in she was extraordinarily happy (whereas her adventure had left a nightmarish feeling), but also convinced that she had just performed an act of madness that her inexperience and thoughtlessness made even more terrible. So she wanted to disappear completely, and after that I got nothing more from her.

This is the picture I have of the rest of the evening. After she left, I again began thinking about the girl who had told me, that morning, that she was going to be married. She worked in a bank; I knew where she lived, in a very nearby street, rue M. (Twice afterwards, it happened that I almost lived there.) I went to that building, where a political bi-weekly also had its offices in those days. On the stairway—the house is old and dilapidated, but the stairway is imposing—a cold draft passed over my shoulders, I felt tired, and I cursed the impulse that had brought me there. What was more, I could not remember exactly where the apartment was, I knocked or rang at several doors, and when no one answered I pushed against one of them without meaning to. Well, the door opened, which frightened me a little, and it opened on an unlighted area (the light in the stairwell having just gone out) which frightened me very much, because I thought I was in the wrong apartment. I had only been in that apartment a few times before; it was a single room, without an entryway, divided in two by a large curtain, with one side for the day, the other for the night. I can say now how I had come to know this young woman. She had been married before, and because of a lung disease, her husband had spent several years in a place where I was spending several weeks. I had seen her there. Six years later I saw her again, through a store window. When

someone who has disappeared completely is suddenly there, in front
of you, behind a pane of glass, that person becomes the most powerful
sort of figure (unless it upsets you). For thirty seconds S(imone) D.
gave me great pleasure, pleasure that was in some ways even immoderate and absurd, and because of those thirty seconds I was much friend-
lier to her than I ever would have thought of being. She had many
good qualities, as far as I can judge; she was simple, and courageous,
accepted nothing from her wealthy in-laws, and was firm in a way that
made her a good, healthy person—but she also had a tendency to be so
honest that she was sometimes brutal: otherwise, it seems to me she
behaved in a normal way. The truth is that after I had been fortunate
enough to see her once through a pane of glass, the only thing I wanted,
during the whole time I knew her, was to feel that "great pleasure"
again through her, and also to break the glass. As she came out of the
store, and as soon as she recognized me, the first thing she said was,
"You know, Simon is dead" (their names were almost identical), "don't
ever speak of him to me." She was certainly very attached to him; what
she said was proof of it.

To come at this time of night, without warning, when she might
have gotten married again, was the last thing she could have expected
from me. It is possible that I was about to go back out, but I do not
really think so, and that gloomy and unfamiliar room fascinates me
now; my objective was certainly there, in the dark. When I think about
the strangeness of what I was doing, I can see a reason for it: I too had
opened a door, and was inexplicably entering a place where no one
expected me; at least that reason occurred to me, as I looked at the
darkness. But if I had wanted to know just how the madness of a short
time before was going to start up again, and how a wild man might
throw himself at me and how I myself might become a figure of terror,
I was mistaken. Behind the curtain a small light was turned on. I recognized the room immediately. Shortly afterwards I felt the draft in
the stairway again: I think I went straight back to the hotel.

At first S. had been rather glum, but she had grown more cheerful
when she heard that I was not sure I would not find her married again.
The ridiculous aspect of this situation drove away her bad mood. As I
was leaving, I thought—and I must make it clear that it was a sad
thought—that any man who is by himself can always go into the home
of a young woman who is alone (and the opposite too, of course),

without any difficulty and at any time of night, as long as he does not have too many reasons for going there. But in my room everything was quite different. Besides having the good qualities I described Simone D. was also honest but reserved. Later I understood that my sudden appearance in the night had actually made her extremely uncomfortable: it was obvious that for her this visitor, who should not have been there, evoked someone who belonged there. That is why she grew more cheerful when I told her I had expected to find her married. That showed her I was not too concerned about the past. But she was left with one doubt, and since she was so very honest she came to find me the next day in the restaurant where I ate, and said to me right away: "You don't approve of my marriage. That's why you came to see me last night." She was the sort of person to whom marriage means something, and though I said to her, "But marriage is not very important," she persisted in the idea that by getting married she was doing away with the past, when a dozen love affairs would have left it intact. She explained to me at length all the reasons she had for getting married. When someone starts in on the "reasons," he soon gets tripped up if he is at all honest, because he has too many reasons, and just one would be enough. Also, as I listened to her I discovered how much her marriage really had bothered me, not for my own sake, of course, and not even for the sake of the dead S., whom I did not remember, but because I had had a foreboding that some secret treachery was going to take place, one of those harrowing events which no one knows anything about, which begin in darkness and end in silence, and against which obscure misery has no weapon.

I would like to say something else now. I am talking about things which seem negligible, and I am ignoring public events. These events were very important and they occupied my attention all the time. But now they are rotting away, their story is dead, and the hours and the life which were then mine are dead too. What is eloquent is the passing moment and the moment that will come after it. The shadow of yesterday's world is still pleasant for people who take refuge in it, but it will fade. And the world of the future is already falling in an avalanche on the memory of the past.

In the end, I strongly urged her to get married. "All right," she said, "fine. But I want to make it very clear that we're not going to see each other again." Then she sent me a letter which said, "If you can give me any explanation, no matter what it is, of why you came the other evening, then give it to me (in a letter)." But I did not answer. It was already the middle of winter. I became ill. The room I have been talking about was extremely warm; an enormous, burning hot pipe ran alongside the bed to feed into the radiator, so that when the radiator was turned off the room was no hotter or colder. It is difficult to express how much I needed that heat, which was killing me. When at night the temperature fell to 76 or 77 degrees (in the daytime it rose to 86), I would become uneasy. I really felt the cold, and this cold paralyzed me as it entered my blood. Later, like many other people, I knew the power of cold. But even at the hardest moments, when the only warmth was in ice, I never had the sense of absolute cold which that 76 degrees gave me. Especially at night, the sort of winter that formed around me had a disconcerting effect, because I felt it just as much when I was asleep, and it mingled with my sleep, from which I broke free again and again, frozen and with frost on my lips.

During this illness, the director of one of the publications where I worked came to see me, and I could not tactfully prevent him from coming in. The same events that I am not talking about were driving him crazy. Since he bored me, I did not say a word; he thought I was nearing my end, he telephoned the doctor, who also gave me up for lost every few weeks, and got this opinion from him: "X? My dear sir, it's about time we raised a cross over him." A few days later, the doctor told me this as though it were an excellent joke. I do not want to dwell on these medical complications. To describe them in a few words, it happened that while the doctor was treating me for an ordinary lung disease he caused a change in my blood by injecting me with something he claimed to have invented: my blood became prematurely "atomic," which meant that it fluctuated in the same way it would have under the influence of radiation. I rapidly lost three quarters of my white blood cells and became frighteningly ill. The doctor put me in his clinic; he thought I was dying. But after two days of a peculiar struggle, I pulled through and he quickly took me home again, where my absence had gone unnoticed.

I will add just a few more words: I promised the doctor I would be silent and I am holding to that silence, by and large. He swore that what he had done was done on purpose, and was not the result of a blunder, and he gave me the reasons for it. That is possible. But his vanity was very great and might have induced him to confess to a crime sooner than admit he had made a mistake. In the end, the result was the same—he caused my blood to become mysterious, and so unstable that it was astonishing to analyze.

Either because of my weakness after that experience, or because one does not always think about the things that are important, when I returned home I did not dwell on the suffering of those two days. I was strangely weak, really, and the word strange belongs here. The strangeness lay in the fact that although the shop window experience I have talked about held true for everything, it was most true for people and objects that particularly interested me. For instance, if I read a book that interested me, I read it with vivid pleasure, but my very pleasure was behind a pane of glass and unavailable to me because of that, but also far away and in an eternal past. Yet where unimportant people and things were involved, life regained its ordinary meaning and actuality, so that though I preferred to keep life at a distance, I had to seek it in simple actions and everyday people. That is why I worked, and always seemed more and more alive.

The night after my return home, as I was lying awake (sleep had left me at the same time as my blood), I heard my neighbor Colette crying violently; with occasional pauses the tears lasted for nearly two hours. This sorrow, in someone who did not seem very sensitive, awoke no sympathy in me: from time to time it disturbed me, because it went on for so long; but endless sorrow cannot move anyone. Still, the next day I made the effort to go see her. As soon as I opened the door, I felt there was something unexpected there, I saw disorder, clothes on the floor: well, I thought, this is misery, how strange it is. But the room was empty; I did not recognize the scattered clothes (even though, to tell the truth, I have since then imagined that I did recognize them). Back in my room, I thought with great surprise about the tears of the night before, so powerful, so violent, and about that impersonal sadness, the sadness of the other side of the wall, which I had not for one second hesitated to assume came from a certain person, with the presumption that is born of indifference, and which had not touched me then but which now overwhelmed me: this sadness communicated a feeling to me that was absolutely distressing, that was dispossessed and in some way bereft of itself; the memory of it became inexpressible despair, despair which hides in tears but does not cry, which has no face and changes the face it borrows into a mask. I telephoned the concierge and asked her, "Who on earth lives in the room next to mine?" Then I wrote to Nathalie (at her office) "I would like to see you. If you want to see me too, come to such-and-such a café, in the rue Royale, at such-and-such a time."

The night before, I had been on the point of dying. So it was with great difficulty that I drove there; N. said absolutely nothing, and for my part I looked at her fixedly, with a mean and sick look, without finding in her (though she was very charming) the slightest reason for this meeting. On top of that, she finally made this unfortunate remark: "Haven't you been very sick?" "Just come to the room," I said in the most menacing tone of voice. I imagine she came with me because of the irremediability of things. But once she was in the room again—even though the circumstances were entirely different—she was visibly seized by the same fear, the same confusion that had first struck her, except that this time she no longer even tried to leave. She stood still and I watched her from my bed. Physically she showed a trace of Slavic influence in the shape of her face, which had a certain thickness, and in the peculiarity of her eyes, which were dull, almost passive, but then suddenly of hallucinating brilliance, more than blue, of jewel-like ardor. Since I was as weak as I have described, I saw her from infinitely far away: she was before my eyes, which see everything, but still I asked myself this question: do I notice her at all? She certainly found herself wrestling with strange feelings, in the room. After all, she thought she had committed an evil act by coming here impulsively. But once here, she could not understand what was happening, she had the feeling that in order to understand she would have to be outside, and once outside, things would perhaps have changed radically. I am summarizing what she wrote to me about it, because though she talked very little she found it easy to write.

I think I can state positively that she said only one thing, but that one thing was strangely bold. In the midst of the silence she asked me, "Do you know other women?" "Yes, of course." A fairly clear meaning can be ascribed to this question. That meaning, I am sure, would be ridiculously misleading, or at least so straightforward, so simple that it would represent nothing of the truth which was touched upon there; and even my answer, in its spontaneity, meant something that had nothing to do with life and the course of the world. I have never been frank. I have never thought that just because you happen to meet many people, you are obliged to surrender them to the curiosity or the jealousy of other people: they appear and disappear in an obscurity which they merit. My frankness was therefore a new right, a warning given in the name of a truth which did not require any ordinary proofs and which emerged from hidden things to assert itself proudly in my mouth.

Nathalie was not at all innocent: she too had met people. During her childhood, in a foreign country, she had lived across from a monastery, a majestic building lost in an estate full of trees and surrounded by a high wall. She was completely preoccupied by what went on behind that wall. One day she heard terrifying cries coming from there, loud, solitary and imploring cries, the sort one can imagine hearing in an insane asylum. From then on the monastery became, for her, a prison for madmen, and the idea formed in her mind that as soon as there was any place she could not enter, after having wanted to enter it, then madness or at least painful and miserable things would come out of it to attack her. She was therefore always a little tempted to anticipate her desires, not because they were important to her, but in order to prevent them from becoming important. I write that because she wrote it to me, certainly not in order to endow her with a particular character; I do not know what her character is, I do not know if she has one.

To show that in the most serious situations beginnings do not matter, I will tell why, according to her, she had the idea of coming to my room that day: she was on the point of committing herself to someone. Since she had been married, but had broken up her marriage, and had always led a very free life too, I do not see how this new step necessarily would have driven her towards a place I had disappeared from. But in any case, at that moment she wanted to make up her mind. So she came into this room, and what did she meet up with here? From me, the motions of a madman who did not recognize her; for her, a feeling of dread which had forced her outside with the thought that she had seen something she had no right to see, so that my name was the one she would most happily have banished from her memory. I will add that when she answered the question I asked—"Why have you come?"—by saying, "I've forgotten," that answer was much more exact and more important (in my opinion) than the one this story holds.

At a certain point in my life I struggled stubbornly against a person I did not want to meet. I was persisting resolutely in this struggle, but

I was watching it at the same time. Seeing many hidden motives in this fight, I took responsibility for them in a spirit of clearsightedness and recognized that my feelings were rather ambiguous. But it was there that my weakness lay—not in the fight itself, which sought only one outcome, but in my misguided lucidity, which made me assume that it had a different outcome and denounce its intentions. For example, events would bring us together in the same foreign city. It would only be a matter of good or bad luck. But if I saw in it the least shadow of calculation I immediately made possible the incidents which drew us toward one another in that city, incidents which never would have taken place if I had not disturbed my good faith. What, then, blinded me? My clearsightedness. What misled me? My straightforward spirit. What makes it happen that every time my grave opens, now, I rouse a thought there that is strong enough to bring me back to life? The very derisive laughter of my death. But know this, that where I am going there is neither work, nor wisdom, nor desire, nor struggle; what I am entering, no one enters. That is the meaning of the last fight.

After I said "Yes, of course," something bad happened to N. That overheated room where I was dying of cold suddenly became a freezing place for her, too. She began to tremble, her teeth chattered, and for a moment she shivered so violently that she lost control of her body. It horrified me to see the cold assaulting her. I could do nothing to help her; by approaching her, by talking to her, I was disobeying the law; by touching her, I could have killed her. To struggle alone, to learn, as she struggled, how through the workings of a profound justice the greatest adverse forces console us and upraise us, at the very moment they are tearing us apart: that is what she had to do. But it seems to me that I may have dreaded something horrible: at one moment, that horror was almost there. The needle is moving forward, I thought, after she had gone.

Still unable to sleep, I spent part of the night looking at the armchair, which was quite far from the bed but turned towards me. Neither light nor darkness have ever bothered me. A persistent thought is completely beyond the reach of its conditions. What has sometimes impressed me about this thought is a sort of hardness, the infinite distance between its respect for me and my respect for it; but hardness is not a fair word: the hardness arose from me, from my own person. I can even imagine this: that if I had walked by its side more often in those days, as I do now, if I had granted it the right to sit down at my table, and to lie down next to me, instead of living intimately with it for several seconds during which all its proud powers were revealed, and during which my own powers seized it with an even greater pride, then we would not have lacked familiarity, nor equality in sadness, nor absolute frankness, and perhaps I would have known something about its intentions which even it could never have known, made so cold by my distance that it was put under glass, prey to one obstinate dream.

After I had spent part of that night in a painful state—I was still very sick, and there remained of my poisoning brief bouts of nausea during which there were sort of cold avalanches, a sickening collapse of empty images—I told myself I would not go out of that room anymore, nor would anyone enter it, that it was cowardly of me to open it halfway on the outdoors, that what I had said—"Yes, of course"—was one speech too many and no one would ever hear it again. (The night had not dispelled N.'s perfume: I could still smell it very clearly.) The next day I took a room n another hotel, though I kept this one. I lived that way as long as I had the means to, sometimes in three or four different places. At the beginning of the war, the idea of renting a room in an apartment that other people lived in led me to the home of a woman who gave dancing lessons. This woman had a daughter thirteen or fourteen years old who spent hours spying on me through the transom of a small parlor that adjoined my room. She would climb up on a chair and watch me with a dazed look on her face. In the beginning, when I took her by surprise, she would hide; but soon she chose to remain in sight. This sly behavior of hers did not make me angry. To see her head up there all the time, that head which seemed alone and poised in empty space, gave me a feeling of calm. But one day, as I came in through the little parlor, I saw her on the chair looking into my room even when I was not there. I slapped her and took her to her mother, saying, "Whenever a woman comes to see me this girl gets up on a chair and looks through the window." Her mother was stupefied. After a minute she said, "But you shouldn't be bringing women here." To be precise, I did not "bring" women there; I only wanted to make her understand the kind of indiscretion her daughter had committed by looking into my room when I was not home.

When I think about it carefully, the change which appeared in Nathalie, after what happened to her, was not evident to me at first, because I myself was changing, and that was unfortunate. I talked about this earlier. An empty movement threw me into each instant; it was my blood that was playing this dirty trick on me and giving me, an animal with very cool blood, all the nervous irritation of an animal with feverish blood. On top of this, I was extremely busy. I can say that by getting involved with Nathalie I was hardly getting involved with anyone: that is not meant to belittle her; on the contrary, it is the most serious thing I can say about a person. But at that time, I saw her most of all as someone charming who was just as free as I was. I went to see her in a sort of run-down attic where she lived alone with her little girl. It seems to me it was an immense place, with an infinite number of rooms; except that they were not rooms but closets, nooks, bits of hallway, all of this more or less empty and neglected. I was only allowed to go into one small room, doubtless the only habitable one. Yet in my mind there is the image of a large rotunda, quite beautiful and well kept up, but perhaps in another building. Nathalie worked; she translated writings from all sorts of different languages, at least from German, English, and Russian. That was an aspect of her character which helped to mislead me about her. For me, the fact that she worked in an office, that she dealt with printed papers, that she accomplished her tasks, put her back in that daily life which I had often required to be merely pleasant, without any ulterior motives, as if, at that very time, I had not spent my nights in an open grave. Still, I cannot say that she was only one face among many; she was less than all the others, that was her peculiar quality, and this quality of being less, when I think about it, is a truly strange anomaly, a surprising and distressing phenomenon, which would have told me something if I had been sensitive to it and yet which I sometimes caught sight of, as I thought about that rare person whom I was neglecting for so many other people. Infidelity may be good, or it may be bad; I am not passing judgment on it: but its merit—as far as earthly things are concerned—is to keep the story in reserve, as it prepares a feeling which will burst into view when it has lost all its rights.

I had been anxious to see her after this "accident," and I had gone up to her attic. I think no one was more incapable of coquetry, I mean purposely indecisive behavior and ambivalent talk. When she saw me there, she suddenly suggested of her own accord, very self-conscious and without any secret purpose, that I come live in that immense place.

In some way this offer followed from the bold things she had said in my room. So that someone in her was continuing to act with a strange end in view and in ways likely to deceive me. My answer, much less serious than the first one, since I was becoming blind to things, was a refusal, enveloped in words and slightly insolent. I was protecting myself from her a little, as though I were in the presence of someone who had threatened my freedom. Besides, I clearly saw the innocence of that offer, but I did not see the ambiguous feelings at the heart of this innocence. She made no remark about this refusal and began playing her role of being no one. With her, everything seemed astonishingly easy. I met her at one place or another, we had dinner, I drove her home. One day she caught sight of me from a distance (she was working for the Ministry of Information then) in one of the immense corridors of the building that housed the Ministry: she saw me waiting. But the idea that she was the person I was waiting for did not occur to her, as though we had not been friends at all, and whenever I seemed to be looking at another woman in an intimate way, she always remained less than a person, neither upset, nor angry, nor curious. One time, though, she narrowed her eyes in a peculiar way; I said to her afterwards: "Your eyes aren't always pleased with me." But something truly astounding was that she no more thought of denying this agitation than of getting angry with herself for having revealed it or with me for having caused it by my bad manners. So she seemed incapable of wanting to hide a feeling behind her feelings. She had said to me twice, with the most simple frankness, that she was perfectly happy when I was there. But nothing allowed me to see what happened when I was not there.

At the moment I forget several scenes in which she was completely different. And this forgetting shows how much more I was able to forget them at the time. One of them, as far as I remember, took place towards the beginning. Whenever I went there, her little girl was shut up or else had gone to bed, so I rarely saw her. This little girl got her own way in everything, that was the rule, she could do what she liked; Nathalie's in-laws, who took care of her most of the time, must have given in about this, in spite of the scandalousness of such a crazy upbringing. No doubt little Christiana had her own opinion of this visitor, who was the only one to expose her to such unusual discipline, although properly speaking it was not discipline, since she was only immediately asked to stay away from the little room. Well, it might seem surprising, but Christiana always respected this rule and if she came, it was after having ceremoniously requested an interview by way of her mother, which proves that this upbringing was not so crazy. One evening, however, perhaps because she was afraid, she left her bed and ran to the little room; I was very pleased to see her, but Nathalie's anger was terrible. She ended up giving her a little wound on the lip with her ring. This act was so extraordinary that although I generally asked her questions about everything, I never dared talk to her about it.

A long time after that scene, she went on a trip to take Christiana to the country. It was very difficult to know what she felt about her daughter. Anyone would have thought she adored her: she sacrificed a thousand precious things for her; she spent hours taking care of her; though her eyes would be tired and though she hated to read, she would read book after book out loud to please her. But she said to me over and over again: "I would willingly grow ten years older and give those ten years to Christiana so that she would be old enough to look to someone else." It is strange, too, that for so long she was opposed to teaching her music. She herself had been taught it by a governess who came to her parents' house. Her older brother was having an affair with this governess, a French student who was easily bored by her studies. N. said that she did not like her brother, but liked the governess a great deal more, and the jealousy aroused in her by these meetings, which always took place at the time of the lessons, completely clouded her mind, so that she learned nothing. So that her mother would not suspect anything, she was forced to play the piano without stopping and very loudly during these intervals. The mystery was how, in spite of this, she was able to become a pianist who played well, who played at least certain pieces well, because there were many that she could neither play nor listen to; for example, she detested Mozart with an incomprehensible hatred. As for Christiana, she swore that she had neither ear, nor voice, nor good hands, which was somewhat true, but not entirely true. One would have thought that for some mysterious reason she wanted to keep her away from the piano at all costs. I said to her: "I'm going to try to give her lessons." I gave her a few, and she took over from me.

On the morning of her departure, she telephoned and asked to see me for a few minutes, which for her was a big initiative. The truth was that I could have come, but did not want to very much. So I gave her a rather unkind answer. Her own answer was an impressive silence, a silence which upset me, which put me in the wrong, and finally I asked her: "Where do you want me to meet you?" "Nowhere." This was said in the most agitated tone of voice; it was a sort of frenzied cry which would not have seemed natural to me even coming from the most violent sort of person. Sometimes I brooded over that "Nowhere."

The last incident was quite different. These outbursts were always unusual and were immediately forgotten. She underwent a minor operation on her eye, made necessary partly by her weak vision, vision which was even abnormal, because in the daytime she saw fairly well, while at night, under artificial light, she could hardly see at all. She assured me that the operation was not serious, and it is true that she did not have to stay at the clinic very long. I also thought that she did not want to be seen with a bandage over her eyes. This time my fault had more serious causes. I could not associate illness with her name. Now I see the reasons for that. But even then I understood quite clearly why something jealous arose in me, a dark torment, a resentment, at the thought of that clinic bed and of a free body which was made both important and non-existent by this serious business of illness. So I did not go to see her. The operation came off very well. Once she was home, I did not go there either—a neglect for which there was no excuse, though there was a pretext. It happened that on the evening chosen for our meeting, I had to go to the theater for reasons connected with my work, and could only tell her at the last minute: she gave me a very kind answer. At the theater, during the intermission, I saw her with a young man I did not know. She seemed very beautiful to me. I saw her passing in front of me, walking back and forth in a place that was very near and infinitely separated from me, as if it were behind a window. I was struck by an insane idea. No doubt I could have talked to her, but I did not want to and maybe I actually was not able to. She remained in my presence with the freedom of a thought; she was in this world, but I was encountering her again in this world only because she was my thought; and what tacit understanding was therefore being established between her and my thought, what terrifying complicity. I must add that she looked at me like someone who knew me very well and even regarded me in a friendly way, but it was a recognition from behind the eyes, without a look and without a sign, a recognition of thought, friendly, cold and dead.

Was this a fleeting impression? It seems to me that it tore my life apart, that from that moment on, I had almost nothing left to learn, and yet, if I look at what I did and how I lived, nothing had changed either; with her, I was neither better nor worse, and she always put up with my presence and my absence equally well. Yet I must recall what was happening. It became more and more serious: thinking and living did not go hand in hand anymore. But if at that time I made an effort— which failed—to enter into the conflict in a more real way, I could not swear that the anxiety of the nation had nothing to do with it, but it is much more true that I sought in the madness of blood and arms hope of escaping the inevitable.

Since we happened to be in the street at the moment Paris was bombed, we had to take shelter in the metro. At that time these formalities were not taken seriously. And N. enjoyed anything that allowed her to leave her work. So the two of us were on the steps in the middle of an enormous crowd, the kind of crowd that is urgent and unwieldy, sometimes as motionless as the earth, sometimes rushing down like a torrent. For quite some time I had been talking to her in her mother tongue, which I found all the more moving since I knew very few words of it. As for her, she never actually spoke it, at least not with me, and yet if I began to falter, to string together awkward expressions, to form impossible idioms, she would listen to them with a kind of gaiety, and youth, and in turn would answer me in French, but in a different French from her own, more childish and talkative, as though her speech had become irresponsible, like mine, using an unknown language. And it is true that I too felt irresponsible in this other language, so unfamiliar to me; and this unreal stammering, of expressions that were more or less invented, and whose meaning flitted past, far away from my mind, drew from me things I never would have said, or thought, or even left unsaid in real words: it tempted me to let them be heard, and imparted to me, as I expressed them, a slight drunkenness which was no longer aware of its limits and boldly went farther than it should have. So I made the most friendly declarations to her in this language, which was a habit quite alien to me. I offered to marry her at least twice, which proved how fictitious my words were, since I had an aversion to marriage (and little respect for it), but in her language I married her, and I not only used that language lightly but, more or less inventing it, and with the ingenuity and truth of half-awareness, I expressed in it unknown feelings which shamelessly welled up in the form of that language and fooled even me, as they could have fooled her.

They did not fool her at all; I am sure of that. And perhaps my frivolity, though it made her a little frivolous too, aroused disagreeable thoughts more than anything else, not to speak of one other thought about which I cannot say anything. Even now, when so many things have become clear, it is difficult for me to imagine what the word marriage could have awoken in her. She had once been married, but that business had left her only the memory of the unpleasant details of the divorce. So that marriage was not very important to her either. And yet why was it that the only time, or one of the only times, she answered me in her own language, was after I had proposed marriage to her: the word was a strange one, completely unknown to me, which she never wanted to translate for me, and when I said to her: "All right, then I'm going to translate it," she was seized by real panic at the thought that I might hit on it exactly, so that I had to keep both my translation and my presentiment to myself.

It is possible that the idea of being married to me seemed like a very bad thing to her, a sort of sacrilege, or quite the opposite, a real happiness, or finally, a meaningless joke. Even now, I am almost incapable of choosing among these interpretations. Enough of this. As I said, I was deluding myself much more than I was her with these words, which spoke within me in the language of someone else. I said too much about it to her not to feel what I was saying; inwardly I committed myself to honoring these strange words; the more extreme they were, I mean alien to what might have been expected of me, the more true they seemed to me because they were novel, because they had no precedent; the more I wanted, since they could not be believed, to make them believable, even to myself, especially to myself, putting all my effort into going farther and farther and building, on what might have been a rather narrow foundation, a pyramid so dizzying that its ever growing height dumbfounded even me. Still, I can put this down in writing: it was true; there cannot be any illusions when such great excesses are involved. My mistake in this situation, the temptations of which I see most clearly, was much more the result of the distance I imagined I was maintaining from her by these completely imaginary ways of drawing close to her. Actually, all that, which began with words I did not know and led me to see her much more often, to call her again and again, to want to convince her, to force her to see something other than a language in my language, also urged me to look for her at an infinite distance, and contributed so naturally to her air of absence and strangeness that I thought it was sufficiently explained by this, and that as I was more and more attracted by it, I was less and less aware of its abnormal nature and its terrible source.

No doubt I went extremely far, the day we took shelter in the metro. It seems to me that I was driven by something wild, a truth so violent that I suddenly broke down all the frail supports of that language and began speaking French, using insane words that I had never dreamt of using before and that fell on her with all the power of their madness. Hardly had they touched her when I was physically aware that something was being shattered. Just at that moment she was swept away from me, borne off by the crowd, and as it hurled me far away, the unchained spirit of that crowd struck me, battered me, as if my crime had turned into a mob and was determined to separate us forever.

I had no news of her during the afternoon (the incident had taken place at about two o'clock). I was working, and the hazards of work are excuse enough for any evasion. I said to myself: if I don't know anything by eight o'clock this evening, I will be mortally uneasy; which quieted my uneasiness for a little while. At the Ministry, no one had seen her, but no one saw anyone at the Ministry. At eight o'clock I looked for her in those empty corridors, and in those offices that were full of people and empty. I looked for her in a little restaurant and I was obliged to have dinner there in order to wait for her. At her house, no one had answered the telephone. Nevertheless, I went there, thinking that she was not answering it. That idea reassured me, I was really certain I would find her in that little room: every time I had gone, she had been there. But the door, which was absolutely deaf, was my worst enemy: if it had been open, I would have put up with the deserted apartment; I would have been able to make out the trail she had left in passing through; I would have had a place where I could wait for her, I would have replaced her by my presence and forced her to come by the obstinacy of my waiting for her. How bitterly I thought of my refusal to live there. And I cursed Christiana for being in the country, where she could not stop her mother from getting lost. At that moment, I was lost myself. My madness no longer arose from my uneasiness nor from my concern for Nathalie, but from an impatience which grew with each passing minute and which went beyond any purpose, turning me into a wanderer in search of nothing. I returned to the neighborhood of the Ministry. I was acting on the idea that if she was to be found anywhere, it would be near the river: an idea which appealed to me only because it was unreasonable, since Nathalie was disgusted by suicide. I stayed there for an infinitely long time. I recall nothing about that person who spent so many hours on a bridge. The night, it seems to me, was impenetrable.

At a certain moment, the uneasiness disappeared completely and reason returned to me, at least a fairly cool and lucid feeling which said to me: the time has come, now you have to do what has to be done. I was living in a hotel in the rue S.; I still had the room in the other hotel, but since the landlord had been called up and the hotel was nearly empty, I had nothing there but some books and I almost never went there; I did not go there at night unless it was really necessary. I did not like the hotel in rue S., which was roomy and comfortable. Because of a whim which I do not understand, I had asked N. never to go there; one morning she had called me there and as I talked to her my bad temper had been so intense that even now I hate that place because of what I said. I felt incapable of spending the night there. The strange thing was that I never thought she might be waiting for me there; I did not even look in the lobby, nor in the lounge, where Central European diplomats engaged in endless conversations, heaping up the greatest visions of unhappiness. I went to ask for a room in a rather shady hotel in the next street, but there were no more rooms available there. I crossed rue de la Paix, which was extraordinarily quiet, and without light. How quiet it was, and how tranquil I was, too. I could hear my footsteps. Rue d'O. was not quiet, but gloomy; the elevator was not working and in the stairwell, from the fourth floor on up, a sort of strange musty smell came down to me, a cold smell of earth and stone which I was perfectly familiar with because in the room it was my very life. I always carried the key with me, and as a precaution I carried it in a wallet. Imagine that stairwell plunged in darkness, where I was groping my way up. Two steps from the door I had a shock: the key was no longer there. My fear had always been that I would lose that key. Often, during the day, I would search my wallet for it; it was a little key, a Yale key, I knew every detail of it. This loss brought back all my anxiety in an instant, and it had been augmented by such a powerful certainty of unhappiness that I had that unhappiness in my mouth and the taste of it has remained there ever since. I was not thinking anymore. I was behind that door. This might seem ridiculous, but I think I begged it, entreated it, I think I cursed it, but when it did not respond, I did something which can only be explained by my lack of self-control: I struck it violently with my fist, and it opened immediately.

I will say very little about what happened then: what happened had already happened long ago, or for a long time had been so imminent that not to have revealed it, when I felt it every night of my life, is a sign of my secret understanding with this premonition. I did not have to take another step to know that there was someone in that room. That if I went forward, all of a sudden someone would be there in front of me, pressing up against me, absolutely near me, of a proximity that people are not aware of: I knew that too. Everything about that room, plunged in the most profound darkness, was familiar to me; I had penetrated it, I carried it in me, I gave it life, a life which is not life, but which is stronger than life and which no force in the world could ever overcome. That room does not breathe, there is neither shadow nor memory in it, neither dream nor depth; I listen to it and no one speaks; I look at it and no one lives in it. And yet, the most intense life is there, a life which I touch and which touches me, absolutely similar to others, which clasps my body with its body, marks my mouth with its mouth, whose eyes open, whose eyes are the most alive, the most profound eyes in the world, and whose eyes see me. May the person who does not understand that come and die. Because that life transforms the life which shrinks away from it into a falsehood.

I went in; I closed the door. I sat down on the bed. Blackest space extended before me. I was not in this blackness, but at the edge of it, and I confess that it is terrifying. It is terrifying because there is something in it which scorns man and which man cannot endure without losing himself. But he must lose himself; and whoever resists will founder, and whoever goes forward will become this very blackness, this cold and dead and scornful thing in the very heart of which lives the infinite. This blackness stayed next to me, probably because of my fear: this fear was not the fear people know about, it did not break me, it did not pay any attention to me, but wandered around the room the way human things do. A great deal of patience is required if thought, when it has been driven down into the depths of the horrible, is to rise little by little and recognize us and look at us. But I still dreaded that look. A look is very different from what one might think, it has neither light nor expression nor force nor movement, it is silent, but from the heart of the strangeness its silence crosses worlds and the person who hears that silence is changed. All of a sudden the certainty that someone was there who had come to find me became so intense that I drew back from her, knocked violently into the bed, and immediately saw her distinctly, three or four paces from me, that dead and empty flame in her eyes. I had to stare at her, with all my strength, and she stared at me, but in a strange way, as if I had been in back of myself, and infinitely far back. Perhaps that went on for a very long time, even though my impression is that she had hardly found me before I lost her. At any rate, I remained in that place for a very long time without moving. I was no longer at all afraid for myself, but for her I was extremely afraid, of alarming her, of transforming her, through fear, into a wild thing which would break in my hands. I think I was aware of that fear, and yet it also seems to me that everything was so entirely calm that I could have sworn there was nothing in front of me. It was probably because of that calm that I moved forward a little, I moved forward in the slowest possible way, I brushed against the fireplace, I stopped; I recognized in myself such great patience, such great respect for that solitary night that I made almost no movement; only my hand went forward a little, but with great caution, so as not to frighten. I wanted most of all to go towards the armchair, I saw that armchair in my mind, it was there, I was touching it. In the end I got to my knees so that I would not be too large, and my hand slowly crossed through the dark, brushed against the wooden back of the chair, brushed against some cloth: there had never been a more patient hand, nor one more calm, nor more friendly; that is why it did not tremble when another hand, a cold hand, slowly formed beside it, and that hand, so still and so cold, allowed mine to rest on it without trembling. I did not move, I was still on my knees, all this was taking place at an infinite distance, my own hand on this cold body seemed so far away from me, I saw myself so widely separated from it, and pushed back by it into something desperate which was life, that all my hope seemed to me infinitely far away, in that cold world where my hand rested on this body and loved it and where this body, in its night of stone, welcomed, recognized and loved that hand.

Perhaps this lasted several minutes, perhaps an hour. I put my arms around her, I was completely motionless and she was completely motionless. But a moment came when I saw that she was still mortally cold, and I drew closer and said to her: "Come." I got up and took her by the hand; she got up too and I saw how tall she was. She walked with me, and all her movements had the same docility as mine. I made her lie down; I lay down next to her. I took her head between my hands and said to her, as gently as I could, "Look at me." Her head actually did rise between my hands and immediately I saw her again three or four paces from me, that dead and empty flame in her eyes. With all my strength, I stared at her, and she too seemed to stare at me, but infinitely far behind me. Then something awoke in me, I leaned over her and said, "Now don't be afraid, I'm going to blow on your face." But as I came near her she moved very quickly and drew away (or pushed me back).

I would like to say that the coldness of these bodies is something very strange: in itself, it is not so intense. When I touch a hand, as I am doing now, when my hand lies under this hand, this hand is not as icy as mine is; but this little bit of cold is profound; it is not a slight radiation from the surface, but penetrates, envelopes, one must follow it and with it enter an unlimited thickness, an empty and unreal depth where there is no possible return to contact with the outside. That is what makes it so bitter: it seems to have the cruelty of something that gnaws at you, that catches hold of you and entices you, and it actually does catch hold of you, but that is also its secret, and one who has enough sympathy to abandon himself to this coldness finds in it the kindness, the tenderness, and the freedom of a real life. It must be said, because it would certainly be useless to shrink from it now: the coldness of a hand, the coldness of a body is nothing, and even if the lips draw near it, the bitterness of that cold mouth is only frightening to someone who can be neither more bitter nor more cold, but there is another barrier which separates us: the lifeless material on a silent body, the clothes which must be acknowledged and which clothe nothing, steeped in insensitivity, with their cadaverous folds and their metallic inertness. This is the obstacle which must be overcome.

In the morning, when I saw her in this room again, she was quite cheerful. After looking at her hands and her fingernails, which were always well cared for, she said right away, but with good humor, "Look,

I'm behaving like a child, I think I've been biting my nails." Later she discovered a little cut at the top of her forehead, under her hair. With infinite emotion, I watched her get up and walk around in that room. I was not thinking about anything; I was entirely taken up with the pleasure of watching her, of watching her make the slightest gesture, the slightest movement. I was determined to ignore my work and hers completely, so that, each minute, she would remain before my eyes.

She resisted this idea a little, but only a little. Anyway, she enjoyed not working. As we went out, I felt a pang of uneasiness, and I could not stop myself from saying to her, "I think you have the key." She took that little key out of her purse in the most natural way and when the door had been closed tossed it back into the purse. Why would I have questioned her at that moment? Such an incredible act on her part, the impulse which had made her deliberately take my wallet from me, put her hand in that wallet, and take hold of the key, could have no justification in this world, and in the same way any questions I might ask seemed to me just as indiscreet as anything I could have reproached her for. If bad luck has it that a person whom one sets above everything and whom one loves more than anything else reads a letter which is not meant for him, it is necessary to be ignorant of it, not to forget it, but if one knows about it, never to know about it, and if one suspects it, to make that frightful incident impossible, by an absolute faith in truth and loyalty—and in fact that incident becomes ashamed of itself and soon withers away to nothing.

If I had questioned N., she would have said, "Yes, I took the key." And if I had asked her, Why did you do it, what she would have answered me without hesitating, what I was sure she was always ready to say in answer, was of such a nature that neither she nor I could have gone on living those hours and those days in a natural manner. Well, I no longer wanted anything but this: I wanted to come in here with her, into a certain café, or enter the tedium of a certain movie theater, hear something laugh, in her, which would signify only frivolous vanity; above all, I wanted to keep the name Nathalie forever, even at the price of her bitten nails and her cut forehead.

I do not see why those hours and those days should not have been extremely happy. I acted in such a way, moved by such emotion and such affection, that I did not have time to feel anything else but the truth of that emotion and the strength of that affection. The fact that

N. was often very reserved did not impress itself on me as though I were missing something, but my own lack of reserve grew because of it, and in my own fever and my own passion, which were more and more exacting, I took for a similarly feverish transport her manner of tolerating from a distance my boundless eagerness to spend time together. Besides, it is certain that she was extremely attached to me, and she was becoming more so every day: but what does the word attachment refer to? And the word passion—what does it mean? And the word ecstasy? Who has experienced the most intense feeling? Only I have, and I know that it is the most glacial of all, because it has triumphed over an immense defeat, and is even now triumphing over it, and at each instant, and always, so that time no longer exists for it.

Naturally, what I had to do was live with her, in her apartment: I had to take my revenge on that door. I went everywhere in the immense loft, everywhere I thought she might be. I did not follow her like a shadow, because a shadow disappears at times, but though she was free at every step, doing everything she wanted to, her liberty still went by way of my own, and if she was alone for an instant, she would find me there even more, because of all the endless questions she knew I would ask her about that instant and about all the other instants when she was living alone. Everyone knows that I talk very little. But at certain times I was driven to talk by a force so compelling, I felt determined to transform the most simple details of life into so many insignificant words, that my voice, which was becoming the only space where I allowed her to live, forced her to emerge from her silence too, and gave her a sort of physical certainty, a physical solidity, which she would not have had otherwise. All this may seem childish. It does not matter. This childishness was powerful enough to prolong an illusion that had already been lost, and to force something to be there which was no longer there. It seems to me that in all this incessant talking there was the gravity of one single word, the echo of that "Come" which I had said to her; and she had come, and she would never be able to go away again.

About a week after that day, a friend involved me in something which I will not talk about in detail, since it does not concern me. What I can say about it is that he was going to fight a duel if I did not succeed in persuading his antagonist, who did not know me any better than I knew him, to be a little reasonable, and the questions that had to be cleared up were of the most intimate kind. This business, which seemed all the more insane because of the general confusion, occupied me for nearly a whole day. I went from one person to the other and reported what had been said, misrepresenting it though I had sworn to convey it in the most faithful way; towards the end of the afternoon I went to the girl's home to give her some papers, and in exchange she gave me some objects. At a time like that, these incidents seemed to me like the last grimace of the world. But this friend felt that the affair was extremely serious, and I liked him.

Perhaps it was a mistake to do this—and besides, all these circumstances and my interpretations of them are only a way for me to remain a little longer in the realm of things which can be told and experienced—my mistake, and it was a glaring one, was to act according to other people's standards. I felt pledged to secrecy and I said only a few vague words to N. about this affair, which had kept me away the whole day. I must emphasize that my discretion was not honorable. Such lack of frankness only meant that after a day devoted to what other people conceived of as honor, I was still completely impregnated with the way of life and the attitude of other people, that is to say I was unfaithful to a way of life and an attitude that were much more important. What do I care about that honor, or even that friend, or even his unhappiness? My own is immense, and next to it other people mean nothing.

One should not have faith in dramatic decisions. There was no drama anywhere. In me it had in one second become weaker, slightly distracted, less real. And the most terrible thing is that in those minutes I was aware of the insane price I was going to pay for an instant of distraction, I knew that if I did not immediately again become a man carried away by an unbridled feeling I was in danger of losing both a life and the other side of a life. This idea was clearly present in me, and I had only to overcome a little fatigue, but it was the fatigue which was whispering this idea to me, and while I thought about it I became more and more false and cold.

At about ten o'clock Nathalie said to me:

"I telephoned X., I asked him to make a cast of my head and my hands."

Right away I was seized by a feeling of terror. "What gave you the idea of doing that?" "The card." She showed me a sculptor's card which was usually with the key in my wallet. "It seems to me you don't always behave very sensibly with that wallet." "Why?" That why implied such

forgetfulness of things that my other feelings were consumed by anxiety. "I beg you, give up that idea." She shook her head. "I can't," she
said sadly. "You can't? Why not?" I hung on her answer, but such
great sadness lay in her eyes, something so motionless and so cold, that
my question remained suspended between us and I would have liked
to hold it up, to raise it to her face, so strongly did I feel that she would
no longer accept it. What I had to do was to come out of myself truly,
and with my life give life to these words. But I was weak, what weakness, what miserable impotence. In the face of her muteness I returned
to myself, I who had perhaps talked to her about X., perhaps described
the process: a process which is strange when it is carried out on living
people, sometimes dangerous, surprising, a process which...Abruptly,
anger burned me: "If you don't answer me," I cried, "I'll never speak
to you again." A threat stupid enough to make the walls tremble, but
which seemed to stop short in front of her. She looked at me ponder-
ously, amicably, with a strange immobility. Why, she is meeting my
eyes, I thought: usually she preferred to look at me when I was not
watching her.

As gently as possible, I asked her:

"Are you listening to me?"

"Yes."

"Will you give up your plan or not?"

She looked at me with a look which I thought was almost willing.

"Say yes," and I took her by the hand to encourage her. "Otherwise
I might just lock you up in this room."

"Where is that?"

"Why, here, in the house."

She listened for a minute, then she asked, "With you?" I nodded. I
was still holding her hand, that hand which was alive gave me hope. Of
her own accord she finally spoke:

"What was the word you said?"

I searched her face. My God, I said to myself absurdly, remind me of
that word.

"What word?" I asked with a slight, promising smile.

I felt two things: that she was not smiling at all, but that even so the
idea was still there.

"Just a minute ago," she murmured, her mind apparently fixed on
the moment when my mouth opened to say it.

"Well," I began. But remembering "this room" I stopped short:

yes, that was probably it. She must have been able to read the agitation in my face, because her hand squeezed mine with an encouragement so persuasive and so intelligent that my coolness deserted me. We looked at one another: how much hope I still had; what a treacherous, bad thing hope is. Little by little her look became smooth again. Because of her weak vision, I would often talk to her about her eyes, which were sometimes passive and empty, and sometimes inflamed by a burning of which only the disquieting reflection was visible. "Do your eyes hurt?" Altogether unexpectedly, this question seemed to stagger her; she got up, and passed her hands through her hair, as she always did in moments of great emotion. She was standing, almost against me, I wanted to take her arm, but she was not paying any attention to my person, which had suddenly been flung extremely far away. Yet I made her sit down. Slowly I put my hand on hers; this contact was like a bitter memory, an idea, a cold, implacable truth, and to fight against this truth could only be a shabby thing. At one moment I saw her lips move and was aware that she was talking, but now I, in turn, no longer made an effort to grasp those words: I looked at them. By chance, I heard the word "plan."

"That's the word," she said.

The memory of what she had been searching for returned to me then, but I must say that even though I was awake and attentive again I was no longer in the least interested; all that belonged to another world, in any case it was too late. Only, as often happens, my lack of interest must have brought her back to life and now, perhaps also because she had broken through a barrier, it was she who took the initiative.

"It isn't a plan any longer," she said timidly.

I understood her very well, her tone of voice was exactly like that of a child who has done something rather bad. Since I did not answer, she tried to find out whether I had understood her, and if I had not, how to think of words that were not too serious, to explain everything. She opened her hands in a gesture which, as I remember it, seems to me wonderfully innocent; then she asked in a weak voice:

"Shouldn't I have done it?"

I think meanness—which remains when everything else is gone—made me shrug my shoulders, but the fact is that perhaps I was beginning to suffer again. She looked so human, she was still so close to me, waiting for a sort of absolution for that terrible thing which was certainly not her fault.

"It was probably necessary," I murmured.

She snatched at these words.

"It was necessary, wasn't it?"

It really seemed that my acquiescence reverberated in her, that it had been in some way expected, with an immense expectancy, by an invisible responsibility to which she lent only her voice, and that now a supreme power, sure of itself, and happy—not because of my consent, of course, which was quite useless to it, but because of its victory over life and also because of my loyal understanding, my unlimited abandon—took possession of this young person and gave her an acuity and a masterfulness that dictated my thoughts to me as well as my few words.

"Now," she said in a rather hoarse voice, "isn't it true that you've known about it all along?"

"Yes," I said, "I knew about it."

"And do you know when it happened?"

"I think I have some idea."

But my tone of voice, which must have been rather yielding and submissive, did not seem to satisfy her will to triumph.

"Well, maybe you don't know everything yet," she cried with a touch of defiance. And, really, within her jubilant exaltation there was a lucidity, a burning in the depths of her eyes, a glory which reached me through my distress, and touched me, too, with the same magnificent pride, the same madness of victory.

"Well, what?" I said, getting up too.

"Yes," she cried, "yes, yes!"

"That this took place a week ago?"

She took the words from my lips with frightening eagerness.

"And then?" she cried.

"And that today you went to X.'s to get...that thing?"

"And then!"

"And now that thing is over there, you have uncovered it, you have looked at it, and you have looked into the face of something that will be alive for all eternity, for your eternity and for mine! Yes, I know it, I know it, I've known it all along."

I cannot exactly say whether these words, or others like them, ever reached her ears, nor what mood led me to allow her to hear them: it was a minor matter, just as it was not important to know if things had really happened that way. But I must say that for me it seems that it did happen that way, setting aside the question of dates, since everything could have happened at a much earlier time. But the truth is not contained in these facts. I can imagine suppressing these particular ones. But if they did not happen, others happen in their place, and answering the summons of the all powerful affirmation which is united with me, they take on the same meaning and the story is the same. It could be that N., in talking to me about the "plan," wanted only to tear apart with a vigilant hand the pretences we were living under. It may be that she was tired of seeing me persevere with a kind of faith in my role as man of the "world," and that she used this story to recall me abruptly to my true condition and point out to me where my place was. It may also be that she herself was obeying a mysterious command, which came from me, and which is the voice that is always being reborn in me, and it is vigilant too, the voice of a feeling that cannot disappear. Who can say: this happened because certain events allowed it to happen? This occurred because, at a certain moment, the facts became misleading and because of their strange juxtaposition entitled the truth to take possession of them? As for me, I have not been the unfortunate messenger of a thought stronger than I, nor its plaything, nor its victim, because that *thought*, if it has conquered me, has only conquered through me, and in the end has always been equal to me. I have loved it and I have loved only it, and everything that happened I wanted to happen, and having had regard only for it, wherever it was or wherever I might have been, in absence, in unhappiness, in the inevitability of dead things, in the necessity of living things, in the fatigue of work, in the faces born of my curiosity, in my false words, in my deceitful vows, in silence and in the night, I gave it all my strength and it gave me all its strength, so that this strength is too great, it is incapable of being ruined by anything, and condemns us, perhaps, to immeasurable unhappiness, but if that is so, I take this unhappiness on myself and I am immeasurably glad of it and to that thought I say eternally, "Come," and eternally it is there.

These pages can end here, and nothing that follows what I have just written will make me add anything to it or take anything away from it. This remains, this will remain until the very end. Whoever would obliterate it from me, in exchange for that end which I am searching for in vain, would himself become the beginning of my own story, and he would be my victim. In darkness, he would see me: my word would be his silence, and he would think he was holding sway over the world, but that sovereignty would still be mine, his nothingness mine, and he too would know that there is no end for a man who wants to end alone.

This should therefore be impressed upon anyone who might read these pages thinking they are infused with the thought of unhappiness. And what is more, let him try to imagine the hand that is writing them: if he saw it, then perhaps reading would become a serious task for him.

The Madness
of the Day

◆

I am not learned; I am not ignorant. I have known joys. That is saying too little: I am alive, and this life gives me the greatest pleasure. And what about death? When I die (perhaps any minute now), I will feel immense pleasure. I am not talking about the foretaste of death, which is stale and often disagreeable. Suffering dulls the senses. But this is the remarkable truth, and I am sure of it: I experience boundless pleasure in living, and I will take boundless satisfaction in dying.

I have wandered; I have gone from place to place. I have stayed in one place, lived in a single room. I have been poor, then richer, then poorer than many people. As a child I had great passions, and everything I wanted was given to me. My childhood has disappeared, my youth is behind me. It doesn't matter. I am happy about what has been, I am pleased by what is, and what is to come suits me well enough.

Is my life better than other people's lives? Perhaps. I have a roof over my head and many do not. I do not have leprosy, I am not blind, I see the world—what extraordinary happiness! I see this day, and outside it there is nothing. Who could take that away from me? And when this day fades, I will fade along with it—a thought, a certainty, that enraptures me.

I have loved people, I have lost them. I went mad when that blow struck me, because it is hell. But there was no witness to my madness, my frenzy was not evident; only my innermost being was mad. Sometimes I became enraged. People would say to me, "Why are you so calm?" But I was scorched from head to foot; at night I would run through the streets and howl; during the day I would work calmly.

Shortly afterward, the madness of the world broke out. I was made to stand against the wall like many others. Why? For no reason. The guns did not go off. I said to myself, God, what are you doing? At that point I stopped being insane. The world hesitated, then regained its equilibrium.

As reason returned to me, memory came with it, and I saw that even on the worst days, when I thought I was utterly and completely miserable, I was nevertheless, and nearly all the time, extremely happy. That gave me something to think about. The discovery was not a pleasant one. It seemed to me that I was losing a great deal. I asked myself, wasn't I sad, hadn't I felt my life breaking up? Yes, that had been true; but each minute, when I stayed without moving in a corner of the room, the cool of the night and the stability of the ground made me breathe and rest on gladness.

Men want to escape from death, strange beings that they are. And some of them cry out "Die, die" because they want to escape from life. "What a life. I'll kill myself. I'll give in." This is lamentable and strange; it is a mistake.

Yet I have met people who have never said to life, "Quiet!", who have never said to death, "Go away!" Almost always women, beautiful creatures. Men are assaulted by terror, the night breaks through them, they see their plans annihilated, their work turned to dust. They who were so important, who wanted to create the world, are dumfounded; everything crumbles.

Can I describe my trials? I was not able to walk, or breathe, or eat. My breath was made of stone, my body of water, and yet I was dying of thirst. One day they thrust me into the ground; the doctors covered me with mud. What work went on at the bottom of that earth! Who says it's cold? It's a bed of fire, it's a bramble bush. When I got up I could feel nothing. My sense of touch was floating six feet away from me; if anyone entered my room, I would cry out, but the knife was serenely cutting me up. Yes, I became a skeleton. At night my thinness would rise up before me to terrify me. As it came and went it insulted me, it tired me out; oh, I was certainly very tired.

Am I an egoist? I feel drawn to only a few people, pity no one, rarely wish to please, rarely wish to be pleased, and I, who am almost unfeeling where I myself am concerned, suffer only in them, so that their slightest worry becomes an infinitely great misfortune for me, and even so, if I have to, I deliberately sacrifice them, I deprive them of every feeling of happiness (sometimes I kill them).

I came out of the muddy pit with the strength of maturity. What was I before? I was a bag of water, a lifeless extension, a motionless abyss. (Yet I knew who I was; I lived on, did not fall into nothingness.) People came to see me from far away. Children played near me. Women lay down on the ground to give me their hands. I have been young, too. But the void certainly disappointed me.

I am not timid, I've been knocked around. Someone (a man at his wit's end) took my hand and drove his knife into it. Blood everywhere. Afterward he was trembling. He held out his hand to me so that I could nail it to the table or against a door. Because he had gashed me like that, the man, a lunatic, thought he was now my friend; he pushed his wife into my arms; he followed me through the streets crying, "I am damned, I am the plaything of an immoral delirium, I confess, I confess." A strange sort of lunatic. Meanwhile the blood was dripping on my only suit.

I lived in cities most of the time. For a while I led a public life. I was attracted to the law, I liked crowds. Among other people I was unknown. As nobody, I was sovereign. But one day I grew tired of being the stone that beats solitary men to death. To tempt the law, I called softly to her, "Come here; let me see you face to face." (For a moment I wanted to take her aside.) It was a foolhardy appeal. What would I have done if she had answered?

I must admit I have read many books. When I disappear, all those volumes will change imperceptibly; the margins will become wider, the thought more cowardly. Yes, I have talked to too many people, I am struck by that now; to me, each person was an entire people. That vast other person made me much more than I would have liked. Now my life is surprisingly secure; even fatal diseases find me too tough. I'm sorry, but I must bury a few others before I bury myself.

I was beginning to sink into poverty. Slowly, it was drawing circles around me; the first seemed to leave me everything, the last would leave me only myself. One day, I found myself confined in the city; traveling was no longer more than a fantasy. I could not get through on the telephone. My clothes were wearing out. I was suffering from the cold; springtime, quick. I went to libraries. I had become friends with someone who worked in one, and he took me down to the overheated basement. In order to be useful to him I blissfully galloped along tiny gangways and brought him books which he then sent on to the gloomy spirit of reading. But that spirit hurled against me words that were not very kind; I shrank before its eyes; it saw me for what I was, an insect, a creature with mandibles who had come up from the dark regions of poverty. Who was I? It would have thrown me into great perplexity to answer that question.

Outdoors, I had a brief vision: a few steps away from me, just at the corner of the street I was about to leave, a woman with a baby carriage had stopped, I could not see her very well, she was manoeuvering the carriage to get it through the outer door. At that moment a man whom I had not seen approaching went in through that door. He had already stepped across the sill when he moved backward and came out again. While he stood next to the door, the baby carriage, passing in front of him, lifted slightly to cross the sill, and the young woman, after raising her head to look at him, also disappeared inside.

This brief scene excited me to the point of delirium. I was undoubtedly not able to explain it to myself fully and yet I was sure of it, that I had seized the moment when the day, having stumbled against a real event, would begin hurrying to its end. Here it comes, I said to myself, the end is coming; something is happening, the end is beginning. I was seized by joy.

I went to the house but did not enter. Through the opening I saw the black edge of a courtyard. I leaned against the outer wall; I was really very cold. As the cold wrapped around me from head to foot, I slowly felt my great height take on the dimensions of this boundless cold; it grew tranquilly, according to the laws of its true nature, and I lingered in the joy and perfection of this happiness, for one moment my head as high as the stone of the sky and my feet on the pavement.

All that was real; take note.

I had no enemies. No one bothered me. Sometimes a vast solitude opened in my head and the entire world disappeared inside it, but came out again intact, without a scratch, with nothing missing. I nearly lost my sight, because someone crushed glass in my eyes. That blow unnerved me, I must admit. I had the feeling I was going back into the wall, or straying into a thicket of flint. The worst thing was the sudden, shocking cruelty of the day; I could not look, but I could not help looking. To see was terrifying, and to stop seeing tore me apart from my forehead to my throat. What was more, I heard hyena cries that exposed me to the threat of a wild animal (I think those cries were my own).

Once the glass had been removed, they slipped a thin film under my eyelids and over my eyelids they laid walls of cotton wool. I was not supposed to talk because talking pulled at the anchors of the bandage. "You were asleep," the doctor told me later. I was asleep! I had to hold my own against the light of seven days—a fine conflagration! Yes, seven days at once, the seven deadly lights, become the spark of a single moment, were calling me to account. Who would have imagined that? At times I said to myself. "This is death. In spite of everything, it's really worth it, it's impressive." But often I lay dying without saying anything. In the end, I grew convinced that I was face to face with the madness of the day. That was the truth: the light was going mad, the brightness had lost all reason; it assailed me irrationally, without control, without purpose. That discovery bit straight through my life.

I was asleep! When I woke up I had to listen to a man ask me, "Are you going to sue?" A curious question to ask someone who has just been directly dealing with the day.

Even after I recovered, I doubted that I was well. I could not read or write. I was surrounded by a misty North. But this was what was strange: although I had not forgotten the agonizing contact with the day, I was wasting away from living behind curtains in dark glasses. I wanted to see something in full daylight; I was sated with the pleasure and comfort of the half light; I had the same desire for the daylight as for water and air. And if seeing was fire, I required the plenitude of fire, and if seeing would infect me with madness, I madly wanted that madness.

They gave me a modest position in the institution. I answered the telephone. The doctor ran a pathology laboratory (he was interested in blood), and people would come and drink some kind of drug. Stretched out on small beds, they would fall asleep. One of them used a remarkable stratagem: after drinking the prescribed drug, he took poison and fell into a coma. The doctor called it a rotten trick. He revived him and "brought suit" against him for this fraudulent sleep. Really! It seems to me this sick man deserved better.

Even though my sight had hardly weakened at all, I walked through the streets like a crab, holding tightly onto the walls, and whenever I let go of them dizziness surrounded my steps. I often saw the same poster on these walls; it was a simple poster with rather large letters:

You want this too. Of course I wanted it, and every time I came upon these prominent words, I wanted it.

Yet something in me quickly stopped wanting. Reading was a great weariness for me. Reading tired me no less than speaking, and the slightest true speech I uttered required some kind of strength that I did not have. I was told, "You accept your difficulties very complacently." This astonished me. At the age of twenty, in the same situation, no one would have noticed me. At forty, somewhat poor, I was becoming destitute. And where had this distressing appearance come from? I think I picked it up in the street. The streets did not enrich me, as by all rights they should have. Quite the contrary. As I walked along the sidewalks, plunged into the bright lights of the subways, turned down beautiful avenues where the city radiated superbly, I became extremely dull, modest, and tired. Absorbing an inordinate share of the anonymous ruin, I then attracted all the more attention because this ruin was not meant for me and was making of me something rather vague and formless; for this reason it seemed affected, unashamed. What is irritating about poverty is that it is visible, and anyone who sees it thinks: You see, I'm being accused; who is attacking me? But I did not in the least wish to carry justice around on my clothes.

They said to me (sometimes it was the doctor, sometimes the nurses), "You're an educated man, you have talents; by not using abilities which, if they were divided among ten people who lack them, would allow them to live, you are depriving them of what they don't have, and your poverty, which could be avoided, is an insult to their needs." I asked, "Why these lectures? Am I stealing my own place? Take it back from me." I felt I was surrounded by unjust thoughts and spiteful reasoning. And who were they setting against me? An invisible learning that no one could prove and that I myself searched for without success. I was an educated man! But perhaps not all the time. Talented? Where were these talents that were made to speak like gowned judges sitting on benches, ready to condemn me day and night?

I liked the doctors quite well, and I did not feel belittled by their doubts. The annoying thing was that their authority loomed larger by the hour. One is not aware of it, but these men are kings. Throwing open my rooms, they would say, "Everything here belongs to us." They would fall upon my scraps of thought: "This is ours." They would challenge my story: "Talk," and my story would put itself at their service. In haste, I would rid myself of myself. I distributed my blood, my innermost being among them, lent them the universe, gave them the day. Right before their eyes, though they were not at all startled, I became a drop of water, a spot of ink. I reduced myself to them. The whole of me passed in full view before them, and when at last nothing was present but my perfect nothingness and there was nothing more to see, they ceased to see me too. Very irritated, they stood up and cried out, "All right, where are you? Where are you hiding? Hiding is forbidden, it is an offense," etc.

Behind their backs I saw the silhouette of the law. Not the law everyone knows, which is severe and hardly very agreeable; this law was different. Far from falling prey to her menace, I was the one who seemed to terrify her. According to her, my glance was a bolt of lightning and my hands were motives for perishing. What's more, the law absurdly credited me with all powers; she declared herself, perpetually on her knees before me. But she did not let me ask anything and when she had recognized my right to be everywhere, it meant I had no place anywhere. When she set me above the authorities, it meant, You are not authorized to do anything. If she humbled herself, You don't respect me.

I knew that one of her aims was to make me "see justice done." She would say to me, "Now you are a special case; no one can do anything to you. You can talk, nothing commits you; oaths are no longer binding to you; your acts remain without a consequence. You step all over me, and here I am, your servant forever." Servant? I did not want a servant at any price.

She would say to me, "You love justice." "Yes, I think so." "Why do you let justice be offended in your person, which is so remarkable?" "But my person is not remarkable to me." "If justice becomes weak in you, she will weaken in others, who will suffer because of it." "But this business doesn't concern her." "Everything concerns her." "But as you said, I'm a special case." "Special if you act—never, if you let others act."

She was reduced to saying futile things: "The truth is that we can never be separated again. I will follow you everywhere. I will live under your roof; we will share the same sleep."

I had allowed myself to be locked up. Temporarily, they told me. All right, temporarily. During the outdoor hours, another resident, an old man with a white beard, jumped on my shoulders and gesticulated over my head. I said to him, "Who are you, Tolstoy?" Because of that the doctor thought I was truly crazy. In the end I was walking everyone around on my back, a knot of tightly entwined people, a company of middle-aged men, enticed up there by a vain desire to dominate, an unfortunate childishness, and when I collapsed (because after all I was not a horse) most of my comrades, who had also tumbled down, beat me black and blue. Those were happy times.

The law was sharply critical of my behavior: "You were very different when I knew you before." "Very different?" "People didn't make fun of you with impunity. To see you was worth one's life. To love you meant death. Men dug pits and buried themselves in them to get out of your sight. They would say to each other, 'Has he gone by? Blessed be the earth that hides us.'" "Were they so afraid of me?" "Fear was not enough for you, nor praise from the bottom of the heart, nor an upright life, nor humility in the dust. And above all, let no one question me. Who even dares to think of me?"

She got strangely worked up. She exalted me, but only to raise herself up in her turn. "You are famine, discord, murder, destruction." "Why all that?" "Because I am the angel of discord, murder, and the end." "Well," I said to her, "that's more than enough to get us both locked up." The truth was that I liked her. In these surroundings, overpopulated by men, she was the only feminine element. Once she had made me touch her knee—a strange feeling. I had said as much to her: "I am not the kind of man who is satisfied with a knee!" Her answer: "That would be disgusting!"

This was one of her games. She would show me a part of space, between the top of the window and the ceiling. "You are there," she said. I looked hard at that point. "Are you there?" I looked at it with all my might. "Well?" I felt the scars fly off my eyes, my sight was a wound, my head a hole, a bull disemboweled. Suddenly she cried out, "Oh, I see the day, oh God," etc. I protested that this game was tiring me out enormously, but she was insatiably intent upon my glory.

Who threw glass in your face? That question would reappear in all the other questions. It was not posed more directly than that, but was the crossroads to which all paths led. They had pointed out to me that my answer would not reveal anything, because everything had long since been revealed. "All the more reason not to talk." "Look, you're an educated man; you know that silence attracts attention. Your dumbness is betraying you in the most foolish way." I would answer them, "But my silence is real. If I hid it from you, you would find it again a little farther on. If it betrays me, all the better for you, it helps you, and all the better for me, whom you say you are helping." So they had to move heaven and earth to get to the bottom of it.

I had become involved in their search. We were all like masked hunters. Who was being questioned? Who was answering? One became the other. The words spoke by themselves. The silence entered them, an excellent refuge, since I was the only one who noticed it.

I had been asked: Tell us "*just* exactly" what happened. A story? I began: I am not learned; I am not ignorant. I have known joys. That is saying too little. I told them the whole story and they listened, it seems to me, with interest, at least in the beginning. But the end was a surprise to all of us. "That was the beginning," they said. "Now get down to the facts." How so? The story was over!

I had to acknowledge that I was not capable of forming a story out of these events. I had lost the sense of the story; that happens in a good many illnesses. But this explanation only made them more insistent. Then I noticed for the first time that there were two of them and that this distortion of the traditional method, even though it was explained by the fact that one of them was an eye doctor, the other a specialist in mental illness, constantly gave our conversation the character of an authoritarian interrogation, overseen and controlled by a strict set of rules. Of course neither of them was the chief of police. But because there were two of them, there were three, and this third remained firmly convinced, I am sure, that a writer, a man who speaks and who reasons with distinction, is always capable of recounting facts that he remembers.

A story? No. No stories, never again.

When the Time Comes

✦

Because the friend who lived with her was not there, the door was opened by Judith. I was extremely, inextricably surprised, certainly much more so than if I had met her by chance. My astonishment was such that it expressed itself in me with these words: "God! Still a face I know!" (Maybe my decision to walk right up to this face had been so strong that it made the face impossible.) But there was also the embarrassment of having come to confirm, here and now, the continuity of things. Time had passed, and yet it was not past; that was a truth that I should not have wanted to place in my presence.

I don't know if the surprise felt by this face was the same as mine. Yet there was clearly such an accumulation of events between us, excessive things, torments, incredible thoughts and also such a depth of happy forgetfulness that it was not at all hard for her not to be surprised by me. I found her surprisingly little changed. The small rooms had been transformed, as I saw right away, but even in this new setting, which I was not managing to take in yet and which I didn't like very much, she was completely the same, not only faithful to her features, to her appearance, but also to her age—young in a way that made her strangely resemble herself. I kept looking at her, I said to myself: So this is why I was so surprised. Her face, or rather her expression, which hardly varied at all, remaining halfway between a most cheerful smile and a most chilly reserve, reawakened in me a terribly distant memory, and it was this deeply buried, very ancient memory that she seemed to be copying in order to appear so young. At last I said to her: "You really have changed very little!" At this moment she was next to a piano I had never imagined in that room. Why this piano? "Are you the one who plays the piano?" She shook her head. Quite a long time

203

afterwards, with sudden animation and in a reproachful tone of voice, she said to me: "Claudia's the one who plays! She sings!" She was looking at me in a strange, spontaneous, lively way, and yet out of the corner of her eye. This look—I don't know why—struck me to the very quick. "who is Claudia?" She did not answer, and again I was struck, but this time so much so, as though by some misfortune, that I became uneasy about the look of resemblance she had, which made her so absolutely young. Now I remembered her much better. She had the most delicate sort of face, I mean that her features had a sort of playfulness and extreme fragility, as though they were controlled by a different appearance, one that was more concentrated, interior, as though age could only harden them. But that was just what had not happened, age had been strangely reduced to impotence. After all, why should she have changed? The past was not so far back, it couldn't be such a great misfortune either. And even I—how could I deny it?— now that I could look at her from the depths of my memory, I was uplifted, taken back to another life. Yes, a strange impulse came to me, an unforgotten possibility that cared nothing for the days, that shone out through the darkest night, a blind force against which surprise and grief could do nothing.

The window was open, and she got up to go and shut it. I realized that until then the street had continued to run through the room. I don't know if all that noise bothered her; I think she wasn't paying much attention to it; but when she turned around and saw me I had the sudden feeling that only then was she seeing me for the first time. I admit that this was a remarkable thing, and at the same moment I also felt—still in an unclear way but already acutely—that it was partly my fault: yes, I saw right away that if in some sense I had escaped her no-tice—and that was perhaps odd—I had also not done everything I should have done in order really to let her catch sight of me, and it was much less odd than it was saddening. For one reason or another, but maybe because I myself had been too busy watching her quite com-fortably, something essential that could only happen if I asked it to happen had been forgotten, and for the moment I didn't know what it was, but forgetfulness was as present as it could be, so much so, espe-cially now that the room was shut up, as to allow me to suspect that outside of it there wasn't much here.

This was, I must say, a discovery so disastrous physically that it took complete control of me. As I was thinking that, I was fascinated by my thought, and overshadowed by it. Well, it was an idea! And not just any idea but one that was proportional to me, exactly equal to me, and if it allowed itself to be thought, I had to disappear. After a moment I had to ask for a glass of water. The words "Give me a glass of water" left me with a feeling of terrible coldness. I was in pain, but completely myself again, and more particularly I had no doubt about what had just happened. When I made up my mind to extricate myself, I tried to remember where the kitchen was. In the hallway it was strangely dark, and I realized because of this that I still wasn't very well. On one side there was the bathroom that opened into the room I had just left, and the kitchen and the second room had to be farther on: in my mind everything was clear, but not outside. Blasted hallway, I thought, was it really this long? Now, when I think of how I was behaving, I'm surprised that I could have made all those efforts without realizing why they cost me so much. I'm not sure I even felt anything unpleasant until the point when, after an awkward movement (having perhaps bumped into a wall), I experienced an atrocious pain, the most lively pain possible—it split my head open—but perhaps more lively than alive; it is hard to express how it was at once cruel and insignificant: a horrible violence, an atrocity, all the more intolerable because it seemed to come to me across a fantastic layer of time, burning in its entirety inside me, an immense and unique pain, as though I had not been touched at this moment but centuries ago and for centuries past, and the quality it had of being something finished, something completely dead, could certainly make it easier to bear but also harder, by turning it into a perseverance that was absolutely cold, impersonal, that would not be stopped either by life or by the end of life. Of course I did not fathom all that right away. I was simply penetrated by a feeling of horror, and by these words, which I still believe: "Oh no, is this beginning again? Again! Again!" I was stopped short, in any case. Wherever it came from, the shock had overtaken me so vigorously that there was enough room in the present instant which it opened up for me to forget endlessly to emerge from it. Walk, go forward—I could certainly do that, and I had to, but rather like an ox that has been hit over the head: my steps were the steps of immobility. These were the most difficult moments. And it is really true that they still endure; through everything, I must turn back to them, and say to myself: I'm still there, I stayed there.

The hallway led to the room that was at the other end. Everything seems to indicate that I looked terribly distraught, I went in more or less without knowing it, without any feeling of going from one place to another, filled with a motionless falling, I couldn't see, I was miles from realizing I couldn't see. I probably stopped on the doorsill. After all, there was a passage there, a thickness that had its own laws or requirements. Finally—finally? —the passage became free, I forced the entrance, and I took two or three steps into the room. Fortunately (but maybe this impression was accurate only for me), I walked with a certain discretion. Fortunately too, as soon as I was really inside a little of that reality touched me. The afternoon, in the meantime, had taken a large leap forward, but there was just enough light so that I could tolerate it. At least I had the feeling I could, just as I recognized in the calm, the patience, and the very weakness of the daylight a concern to respect the life in me that was still so weak. What I did not see, what I saw only at the last... but I would like to be able to pass over all that quickly. I often have an immeasurable desire to abbreviate, a desire that is powerless, because to satisfy it would be too easy for me; however lively it might be, it is too weak for the limitless power I have to accomplish it. Oh, how useless it is to desire anything.

As for this young woman who had opened the door for me, to whom I had talked, who had been real enough, from the past to the present, during an inestimable length of time, to remain constantly visible to me—I would like to let nothing be understood about her, ever. My need to name her, to make her appear in circumstances which, however mysterious they may be, are still those of living people, has a violence about it that horrifies me. This is the reason for my desire to abbreviate, at least its nobler aspect. To pass over the essential—that is what the essential asks of me, asks of me through this desire. If it is possible, let it be this way. I beg my decline to come by itself.

I saw certain parts of the room very clearly, and it had already renewed its alliance with me, but I didn't see her. I don't know why. Soon I looked with interest at a large armchair placed at the far end of the bed (so I had taken several steps into the room in order to reach the foot of the bed); in a corner near the window I noticed a little table with a pretty mirror, but the word for this piece of furniture didn't come to me. At that instant I was near the window, I felt almost well, and if it was true that the daylight was waning as fast as it was mounting again in me, what lucidity remained here and there was enough to show me everything without illusion. I can even say that if I was a little disoriented in that room, that disorientation would have been natural during any visit to anybody, in any one of the thousand rooms I could have gone into.

The only vestige of anomaly was that although no one was there— or I saw no one—this didn't in the least disturb the feeling of naturalness. As far as I know, I found the situation perfect, I didn't want to see the door open and the man or woman who normally lived there come in. In fact, I didn't imagine that anyone lived in the room, or in any other room in the world, if there were any others, which didn't occur to me either. I think for me, at that moment, the world was fully represented by this room with its bed in the middle of it, the armchair and its little piece of furniture. Really, where could anyone have come from? It would have been madness to expect the walls to disappear. Besides, I was not conscious of the world.

Well, according to what she told me, she saw me; she was actually standing in front of the armchair and not one of my movements had escaped her. It was true, I had remained next to the door for quite a few minutes, but not at all with that horribly distraught look I thought I had; rather pale, yes, and with an expression that was cold, "fixed," she said, which made it very clear—but this was a little troubling, even so—that my life was taking place somewhere else and that there could be nothing of me there but this endless immobility. It was also true that I had taken a few steps; passing near the armchair, I had gone to the little piece of furniture and looked at it with interest, I was visibly interested in it, in some sense it served as the justification for my having come in. No, she wasn't surprised to see me paying so little attention to the fact that she was present—because at such a moment she wasn't at all anxious, either, to know if she was present, because even though being cast into the shadow involves some sacrifices, she also took infinite satisfaction in watching me in my truthfulness, for I, not seeing her and not seeing anyone, showed myself in all the sincerity of a man who is alone. To contemplate the truth in flesh and blood, even if one must remain invisible, even if one must plunge forever into the discretion of the most desperate cold and the most radical separation— who hasn't wanted that? But who has had that courage? Only one person, I think.

Why didn't I see her? As I said, I don't really know. It's hard to go back over an impossible thing when it has been surmounted, even harder when one isn't sure the impossibility isn't still there. Countless men walk by one another and never meet; no one thinks this is scandalous; who would want to be seen by everyone? But perhaps I was still everyone, perhaps I was the great number and the inexhaustible multitude—who can say? For me this room was the world, and for my little strength and my little interest it had the immensity of the world; who would require a look to cross the universe? What is strange about not seeing something distant when nearby things are still invisible? Yes, what is inexplicable is not my ignorance but the fact that my ignorance gave in. I would find it unfair, though in keeping with the laws, not to have been able to shatter infinity, nor draw from all the hazards the only one that could be called chance. Bitter chance, and heaped with misfortune, but no matter—chance! Well, I had it, and even if it is lost, I still have it, I'll have it forever. This is what should be surprising.

Things appeared to resolve themselves (appeared? that was already a great deal). At the moment I was closest to her, two steps from the armchair, she could not only see me better, my face livid rather than pale, my forehead cruelly swollen, but almost touch me. This feeling of having brushed against me seemed very strange to her and drove away all other reflections: this was something unexpected, even more, a light that she hadn't glimpsed a second before. After that she followed me with different eyes. Did I exist, then? Then perhaps I existed for her too! Life, she said to herself, and suddenly she had the strength, the immense strength to cry out at me, and while I leaned over the objects on the dresser, she actually did utter a cry that seemed to her to be born, to leap out, from the living memory of her name, but—why? —valiant though this cry was, it did not go beyond its boundaries, it did not reach me, and because of that, she herself did not hear it. Maybe she resigned herself to this. As the daylight faded very fast, she saw less and less of what was happening in the room. Of course it was a room, but all the same so little a room; and certainty could not reside within four walls. What certainty? She did not know, something that resembled her and made her resemble the cold and tranquility of transparent things.

Pride also! The wild statement that has no rights, the pact signed with what defies the origin, oh strange and terrible tranquillity. She went mysteriously past, at one remove from the visible lies, more obvious than she could possibly have been, and the terror she must really have felt at getting lost and always starting to get lost again in the unlimited obviousness had apparently not been more remote than the simple fear of a little girl encountering the dark, late one afternoon, in a garden. Life, she repeated to herself, but already this word was no longer being spoken by anyone, was in no way addressed to me. Life was now a sort of bet being conceived nearby, a bet with the memory of that touch—had it happened?—with that stupefying feeling—would it persist?—that not only did not fade but asserted itself—it too—in the wild manner of something that could have no end, that would always make claims, make demands, that had already set itself in motion, wandered and wandered like a blind thing, without any goal and yet more and more greedy, incapable of seeking anything but turning faster and faster in a furious vertigo, without any voice, walled up, a desire, a shiver turned to stone. It may be that I had a presentiment of this (but hadn't I had this presentiment much earlier? Without it would I have gone in?). That she then rose up before me, not as an empty illusion, but as the imminence of a monumental storm, as the infinite thickness of a breath of granite precipitated against my forehead, yes, but this shock was not a new truth either, nor was the cry that came to me new, nor was the one I heard new, only the immense surprise of the calm was new, an abrupt silence that brought everything to a stop. This caused a remarkable gap, but what did it mean: was it the repose after annihilation? The glory of the next to the last day? I hardly had time to ask myself that, just barely time to seize the truth of that touch—I too—take it by surprise and say to her: "What! You were here! Now!"

Claudia came back shortly afterwards. I didn't know her. As I could see, she was a resolute person who wasn't easily swayed, the same age, I think, as Judith, and her friend since childhood, but who backed her up more like an older sister with a strong character. She had no lack of talents. She had performed brilliantly in the theater, the sort of theater where people sang, and she really did have a voice that could be called very beautiful, dazzling and yet austere, an unforgiving voice. I suppose she knew more about me than most of the people who had come close to me. I imagine that in the beginning Judith had talked to her about me: very little, but endlessly, even so—that was the gloomy side of things. (I had said to her: "I want to live in darkness." But the truth spoke in her without her knowing it, and even when she said nothing, she was still speaking; behind her wall, she was asserting something.)

So I have to think that she was expecting me to return. At least, if she remained disconcerted when she saw me—and I'm sure that she drew back, that for an instant she tried to go back the way she had come, as though, confronted with my presence, she had attempted to find a way out that would have given her the possibility of having been there before me, of having been in a position to open the door for me herself and greet me in her own way—yes, I believe this motion of drawing back was an attempt to recapture her absence, and the effect of it for me, which I blindly took advantage of, was to create a refuge for me in my own amazement and my agitation, which was immense—when she appeared, perhaps I was holding the outcome in my hands and then everything was called into question again. Actually, within my distress, I felt a sort of admiration for the way she went about avoiding total shipwreck. Certainly composure was one of her qualities, and not simply presence of mind but a correct feeling for what had to be known and not known, kept and abandoned. Perhaps, when she saw me, when she recognized me, even as she blunted the edge of the first instant with a skill that had to be attributed to her self-control but which was undoubtedly also the backflow of the movement that had carried me forward—perhaps, driven by her fighting instinct, she said to herself: "Now I won't ever let him go again." I have to admit that the promptness with which she contrived to cut off my retreat gave me this impression. It seems to me she seized upon precisely the point from which it was hardly possible for me to do anything else but what she might choose to decide. I could have seen to it that I was taken elsewhere, I could have appealed to someone else? That's true, and I didn't do it. But did I want to leave? I'm not even convinced that she believed I was seriously ill; it was more that the appearance of the illness became the language that allowed her to speak, the guarantee that entitled her to act in a natural way. I really have to admire the way she was able to think alone, the way she remained free and fought actively, with all the resources of a sleepless attention—and did I fight? Can it be called a fight? Not against her, anyway; at a moment like that, I could not carry her into the center of my self, which belonged to someone else: she lived in the outskirts, at the limit, where difficulties turn into active and real things. This doesn't mean that she was without importance. On the contrary, she whispered at me from that borderland where she was free, she whispered preoccupations that paralyzed time. This paralysis was her victory, this inertia became my struggle.

With her ability to organize quickly—actually, perhaps not all that quickly: quick only next to the slowness of the rest of us—she hurried to settle me on a couch across from the piano. She seemed to be impelled by a strange idea—but perhaps it was pure passion, the pure desire to remain the only one in charge of this place—by the need to snatch me from the room as fast as possible. To keep me, but first to keep me out of here. (Naturally—it was their room, nothing could be more normal than such an arrangement; but her haste? her feverishness as long as I wasn't leaving?)

No less striking was the fact that once she had settled me in the studio she didn't leave me there alone but shut us up there together, I mean she went away immediately with a reserve, a discretion, that may have meant she would not impose herself, but which also had another meaning that I understood very well, without being able to pin it down exactly. To give some idea what it was, I could say that the only aspect of the apartment that made it seem roomy was the hallway that divided it into two areas, but at certain moments she turned it into an immense, desert space, in which it seemed not that we were alone, but, what was much more impressive, that she was alone, that she alone was real, that she alone was endowed with the opulence and the perseverance of life. And, at the same time, this reserve seemed to create a special bond between us, as though, in order to confirm an allusion contained or expressed by my presence, she had given me to understand that where she was concerned I didn't have to worry, she wouldn't say one word more than she should.

If I go back over this instant, the first instant in which, because of that reserve, we were in one another's presence again, but this time cruelly trapped facing each other, I feel as though I am in some way bound to a sadness, and an anxiety, that are capable of obscuring everything. After a short time, probably because she was alone with me— she was there, like a sort of image, made possible by the course of things and the good will of the daily order—I saw that she was feeling embarrassed, uneasy, and that she was also moved by a slight, unstable impulse, a cold gaity that made her difficult to grasp: this showed in her breathing, which wasn't as tranquil as it had been, and in her glance, where a rather strange sparkling glimmer shone like the reflection of a distant resentment, and at last her face assumed an expression of astonishment, of questioning. I hadn't the least notion of how deep that look was. I myself was as weak as I could be, and to say that I showed no understanding wouldn't be saying very much: I wasn't able to read her eyes. I was turning back bitterly towards that meeting a hair's breadth from the end, when the alien power had won out, and this sort of memory couldn't make me feel happy again right away. I said to her—I repeated several times rather sharply: "What's the matter with you? Tell me what's the matter!" When the light was out, I recalled this "What's the matter?", and it horrified me. It was a false cry, a clumsy question imbued with a suspicion, a cold, disconcerting thought. After that, she certainly would have been at a loss to know if "something was the matter" with her. But by way of this suspicion it seems to me that I returned to myself, a solitary self, distant and scattered, retreating before time, who didn't say "you" to anyone in an intimate way and in the presence of whom no one could say "me". I realized it was a strange suspicion, the most confusing kind of illusion, and this confusion didn't reflect the infinite vision of perspectives opening one onto the next, but the sterile sadness of chaos, the afflicted uncertainty that closes itself up again and withdraws, shaking itself.

I got up immediately, determined not to let this cry move across the night. I didn't make much noise. Nevertheless, at the other end of the hallway Claudia was already watching me come near. This was really our first contact; until then, what had taken place had been like sword thrusts in the sky. Oh—there wasn't anything friendly about the way she watched me and waited for me. She was polite, because politeness authorized the greatest coldness. But I must say I wasn't getting up at that hour in order to obey the proprieties. I walked clumsily towards her, and she might have thought we were going to run straight into each other: I'm sure she was prepared to attack me, break my bones if she could and in any case stand up to me without yielding. She didn't budge at any moment. She didn't budge when I was close to her, either, close enough to see that she was still breathing, that she still had arteries and blood. But as soon as I said to her—and I said it calmly— "I've come to see your friend," she shuddered, as though she had been able to tolerate everything except for the truth to have a voice, and she ceased to be massive, unassailable. "My friend!" No irony in her voice, it seemed to me. Gravity, unshakable faith, made her extremely firm, but her intonation—a mixture of arrogance, questioning, triumph— was certainly intended to deny me the right to describe her relation- ships and at the same time victoriously seized my words to preserve them as a recognition of her rights. I think she allowed herself to be tempted by this word, because she repeated it, and this time really in order to listen to it herself, with a sort of uncertainty and happy sur- prise. In a sense, I had more allies in her than she wanted to admit and earthly fever was one of those allies. But she quickly freed herself and hurled at me under her breath: "Judith!" I listened to that, and I lis- tened to it without reacting, because, as often happened with her, see- ing her defend not something small but her very life. I couldn't blame her. I only noticed the cunning way she let this name slip out, to make me understand that she was not fooled, and that the advantage I had given her by clumsily calling her her friend—well, I had done this in order to keep that name for myself. Yet her whisper made me uneasy, she had been afraid, she had groped her way towards something which, dauntless though she was, she was afraid to grasp: yes, she had placed her bet, slowly, without taking her eyes off me, as though in order to be able to withdraw it if the risk became too great. Then what was it? I admit that she found me out cruelly in my mistake.

All the more misguided since, an instant later, her attitude changed completely: she was still polite, but this politeness was seductive, unshadowed, capable of aimiably tolerating any amount of horror and impropriety. At this instant, she was perfect; the naturalness of her behavior protected her, and if she had done senseless things—and she must have—it all took place behind appearances that were too correct to invite comment. "I'll call her," she said, her eyes shining softly; she was protecting my behavior, but without intending anything unpleas- ant, simply in order to classify it with everyday truth that could be immediately realized. Well, I said to myself, she is almost beautiful; up till then I hadn't noticed it. What certainly has to be called her desire to conciliate was putting her face to face with a very conciliatory man; graciousness, comfort, were tranquilly enticing me into their game. Nevertheless, I asked her with some impertinence, since I wasn't for- getting the extraordinary, unlikely promptness with which she had taken up her position when I had just barely stood up: "But was I the one who woke you up?" "It's true—it's very late," she said brusquely, after rubbing her wrist under her eyes. "What is it?" she went on. "Are you in pain? You're not sleeping!" She passed quickly in front of me and pushed against a door, saying: "I have an arsenal of sleeping pills in the kitchen." The kitchen? A cry rose up in me; the words "give me a glass of water" immediately came back to me and with them a feeling of terrible coldness. I went in after her, walking heavily as though I were continuing the journey of that afternoon. "Give me a glass of water," I said, quite ungraciously. At that moment she opened a small medicine cabinet, went over to another piece of furniture, took out a glass, wiped it. The kitchen wasn't large, and two people of our size would inevitably brush against each other. "Should I pour out some drops for you?" She was holding the half filled glass up as high as her face. At that instant she had the tone of voice of someone obeying powerful orders but without any authority herself. "No," I said to her, "not today!"

As I drank, I became aware of my thirst. The water was not only hours late in coming, it didn't get along very well with my thirst. I sat down on a stool and glanced at this woman. "It's a little late for water; I need some alcohol." But she gestured to me that there wasn't any. "There used to be!" No doubt this allusion to a time when a young man was in charge here seemed to her to come from a very contemptible place, but one couldn't expect my thirst to be very considerate. The same state of mind started me on a cross-examination that was anything but subtle. However, to my surprise it led off with a declaration of good will:

"So tell me, my dear, is it such a bother for you to have me here now?"

Perhaps I wasn't in a position to watch her carefully, and it seems to me that during this whole time I saw her through my words, in some sense, but I think she blushed—slightly—probably because of that "my dear" which broke the windows between us so strangely. In any case, though she might have been able to allow herself to blush, her answer was steady:

"Why would it be?" she said boldly (though after a sober silence). "This sort of thing was to be expected. And at the moment it isn't much of a bother."

"At the moment! But do you think things are going to stay this way?"
She was quick to retort:

"They can! All they want is to stay this way—unless someone prevents them."

"Things, yes," I agreed, "they prefer that. And of course you would want that too?"

"Want what?" she asked, hesitating.

"Want things to stay this way!"

Emphatic though my question was, she didn't answer it; she seemed to resist expressing to me what she wanted or didn't want. So I clumsily went ahead:

"Really, would you like it, would you like it so much?"

"Yes," she said brusquely, "more than anything else in the world!"

The silence that followed this statement hardly showed how unexpected, how overwhelming it was, coming from her, how shaken I felt, how uneasy at having provoked it, and how from then on I kept at a respectful distance. How could I not comply with such frankness, such a loyal recognition of the truth? I said almost without thinking:

"Well, how are we going to get out of it now?"

"Get out of it?"

She seemed to have plunged—or was it I?—deep into the speech she had uttered; I could see clearly that now she was looking at me with those intense words, that she was affirmed; raised up in them, and now that she in turn was more than anything in the world, what she saw before her appeared to her only to be the shadow, which was doubtless immense, of her own immensity.

"Claudia," I said, and I stood up resolutely, "I'm afraid of being an inconvenience to you, of being more inconvenient than you're willing to admit. But now, neither one of us can ignore it any longer: something has happened."

"Something?"

"Yes. I'm here right now!"

"Certainly," she said with a confident smile. "You're here! Well, more or less."

"That's exactly right, more or less! That leaves you some margin. More or less! You have a right to choose, you know."

"The choice was made long ago," she said, staring at me with penetrating force.

"Really? You mean…"

"But you won't get out of it that way: you're here, you're here!" she added with fierce gaity. "Frankly, do you think it'll do you any good if…" She hesitated, I saw her wince painfully. It seems to me that I cried out to her: "Don't go any farther!" But she finished in a firm voice: "If you're only here for me."

I couldn't help it, I went close to her, close to this defiant speech, with which she was hurting herself just as much as me. Then what was behind this face? Only the desire for things to stay the way they were? The certainty that I was left out, that I was left out too? Strange face, that allowed itself to be looked at from very close, without yielding anything of its own accord; no, it wasn't even a reserved face, since all of it lay before my eyes, this cold image of my failure. At that instant I was struck by an astonishing recollection of things, all the more difficult because something there was escaping me, evading me, as though hastening not to warn me but to ignore me. I stood next to her, my back against the sink—just in front of me, the whitish pane of the medicine cabinet. Without looking at her and with some distress, I finally said:

"We're alone—is that what you want to make me say?"

"Well, more or less!" she said with the same liveliness. "Not really, of course. I suppose you wouldn't resign yourself to the inevitable, and I…" Her voice weakened to a painful tremor, then rose again on the other side of what she seemed to have expressed without bothering to say it. "Otherwise," she continued, "we wouldn't be here together, and this conversation would be out of place."

"It seems to me that you don't have much sympathy for the character you're conversing with?"

"It's true. I could say to you: not yet. But I'm afraid things will stay this way." She remained silent for a moment. "I think it would be better not to leave this hanging: I am ignoring dissipated feelings, and I'm not interested in what goes on in your world."

Still, I was surprised by the stiffness of her explanation.

I simply said to her, "I'm sorry I can't say exactly the same thing to you, but you won't suffer from it, even if I stay. And now, be frank about this too: wouldn't you really like to see me go? Wouldn't you be relieved if all of a sudden I was far away, as far away as possible?"

The question took her by surprise, for a moment she seemed to be dreaming.

"You mean: leave for good?"

"For good!"

"But would you do it?"

"Yes, I'm prepared to do it."

"Would you promise? No," she said, shaking her head, "I don't believe you, all men are deceitful, all men lie. You lie too, I know it."

"Really! How do you know it?"

"I know it, I know it," she said stubbornly. "I would never be convinced that you were gone for good and that you were far way."

"Don't believe me. I won't swear to it, just for you. I'll leave if that's better, and I'll come back if that's better. But whether or not you think my words are deceitful, let me say this: I'll go and you won't hear any more talk about me if that will really straighten things out for you."

"For me?"

"For both of you."

That upset her more seriously than I had thought it would. A sort of flame, a violent, proud and jealous fire rose in her eyes, which became very black:

"I want you to know," she said in her high voice, "that it won't make any difference to me whether you're here or not. My life won't be changed by it except in ways that don't matter to it, and what's important to it won't be changed. I'll see you, if I have to, and not without some enjoyment, because I'll find it pleasant to talk to you, since you didn't come to see me. What I have, I'll always have: you won't take it away from me. What you don't have, what you've lost, you'll never have again. You said it: we're alone, but you're more alone that I am!"

I think that was more or less what she said, but I won't really swear to it because she had hardly finished her tirade—which had something theatrical about it—as in her anger she was prepared to shower me with even more terrible truths—was it anger? or a need, a desperate energy—when an incident occurred that shouldn't have been in the least unexpected and that nevertheless startled me so, and her too, that I threw myself on her arm like a madman and held her as hard as I could, without her trying to free herself. This incident, which followed her spirited outburst, was that the bedroom door opened. We were struck by this, both of us were overwhelmed, as though this were the strangest thing; perhaps because the noise was so slight, so timid, so different from the din of our voices; or perhaps all of a sudden the strangeness of that silent creaking several feet away, out of our sight, engraved upon the reality of the space of the night the undivulged strangeness of what we had been looking for beneath our words and could discuss calmly as long as this was taking place inside us, but that struck us, struck me with surprise and her with a sort of terror, as soon as we were in danger of seeing something appear outside, in the real proximity of the night open behind us, that was also behind our thoughts. I am sure of this, and the fact that we were both startled was evidence: for her and for me, at that moment, what began to move, to open the door so silently, was nothing less terrible than a *thought*, and no doubt it was quite different for each of us, but in that instant we at least had this much in common, that neither of us was capable or worthy of enduring it. After a moment, I gestured to her, I indicated that I was going to go out quietly. She looked at me in a sort of unconscious way; but as soon as I moved she caught me back, she held me close to her with incredible nervous strength. Was it fear? A reawakening of life? Rather—and this came into my thoughts right away—even though the slight creaking was not followed by another noise, she must have seen that just on the other side there was a timid and frightened expectation that my abrupt approach could take by surprise in a dangerous way: she had the finest instinct for all that; she gave the impression of knowing, better than anyone and better than I, what could happen behind a wall, as if, by sheer force of attention, by having, day and night, spied upon and kept watch over what was escaping her, she had succeeded in reconquering a portion of reality. So I stayed there, tightly held by her, my eyes fixed on the kitchen door. I was beginning to feel ill at ease in the grip of this feverish hand, which kept me from continuing to move away. Now it was no longer possible to go over there, calmly and naturally, in broad daylight, as I should have. I fully realized that the silence here might seem very strange on the other side, now that the night had opened, and the longer we let it go on, the more it became difficult to break, the more it became wrong and, in a word, culpable. I had detected that right away, when she had made me take part in her fear, the complicity of her surprise and that impulse towards concealment we both had in the face of something that demanded the gesture of truth. Maybe she had not calculated anything and I was only being confronted with my own dissimulation and the lack of concern I had shown for true things during that conversation; but the result was the same, and she was the only one who benefitted: I had allowed myself to be caught out between those two silences, one of them separate, exiled, lost in a distance without resources, the other avid, jealous, implacable—and the latter, with which I had nothing in common but an instant's agreement, finally imposed itself on me to such an extent that it made me inseparable from it and resembled the profoundness of an inadmissible fault, I saw this clearly when she let go of me and walked forward by herself, without bothering about me and without any fear of being followed, and went quite naturally into the front hall and a little later into the bedroom, closing the door.

If it hadn't been so great, the deception would have been final. I would have left. I, too, would have gone into the front hall, and from there rejoined the tranquil flow of the rue de la Victoire and gone down towards the Opéra, which I liked at that hour, and I would have been happy. I could see very clearly what kind of light shone on the square, I could see the motion of those streets at such a moment, not furtive, as people think, but familiar and full of kindness; these are the most beautiful hours in the world, hours in which anyone would cheerfully tolerate living an endless life. I said to myself: in an instant I will be down there, and I felt a burst of immense pleasure. The day! These instants of the night-time street are the glory of the day, the wood fire that is already burning and in which each person dissipates and burns in the shiver of a day that doesn't yet know itself. I saw that, I was experiencing that, having already experienced it. These hours were within my reach, hours that asked nothing of me and of which I asked nothing except that they go by without touching me and that they ignore me after having known me. And it's true, they went by happily without me; and I too, unknown to them, went joyfully by, ignored, ignoring the eternal: alone? alone! My decline could accommodate everything.

This continued, the old farce: the last moment, so happy it was on the verge of never being the last. I recognized it, still perfectly happy, with its brightness, its freest and most joyful brightness, but now it was joyfully distant behind the pane of glass, caught up again in the flow of the world, without bitterness at having been put at stake like me. What is a night, after all? It shouldn't seem surprising that I arose from these hours with a feeling of inexpressible pleasure. Yes, this motion had crossed the night, it had been born then, of the good faith of the hours, of the fullness of deception, and it was born again of the dark future, of the trickery of time, and above all of the fact that there would never again be such a great deception. Deception was not possible; I tranquilly discovered that in the morning.

As far as I remember—but I recall only that immense calm: it might well be that the new day opened on what I called Claudia's side, the obligation to respond, politely, to the polite help she gave me, the return to the bathroom, the certainty that my presence was terribly "out of place," as she had said, then the impression that from then on I would have to play a role, if only the comic role that, through her (I was her guest, in any case), would be designed by the appearances of a reasonable life, using me as a model. All this, and the sleep that came, and on the other side of the sleep the noises, the fatigue of the footsteps I went on hearing, probably in the bathroom, fugitive faces that approached and receded, the feeling of an indistinct attention of which I was the center and the thing at stake, this was not the hovering of a hostile surveillance, but something worse that resembled, curiously, the memory of that nervous grip by which I had been held back and even now, in all the dangerous slipping of sleep, still continued to be held back, always saved at the last moment by the decision of an implacable energy: even though these impressions, and a thousand others, all close to fever, to truthless chattering, to the sarcastic erosion of time, dropped on me again and again, terrifying to the fruitless work of the sleeper, all of them also dropped into the same calm which, not being repose at all, but something deep and alive, reconciled them in the wildness of its eddies. Even Claudia did not escape this calm, or perhaps it only existed between her and me, showing her to be less tense, less polite too, perhaps more agitated, coming in and going out somewhat at random, like someone who accepts the law of time and no longer prepares to leap beyond necessity. Maybe she was more sure of herself now, more sure of me, for she had been able to gauge my weaknesses, but that wasn't like her, she didn't slacken so easily, she certainly didn't believe she was the winner just because she had prevailed over one night, she heard, better than anyone, with her sharp ears, all the quiet noises attacking the thickness of the night that she had raised between me and her destiny. And there weren't really so many problems.

I can swear that by letting it pass with all its wonted tranquility, by giving it the right to linger indefinitely in the moments it preferred, without provoking it with questions like these—"What's going to happen now? and tomorrow? after that? but shouldn't I..."—this life glided by in the most natural way, and if it had some difficult moments, they were caused by one or the other of us beginning to force it, and trying, since after all one had to get it over with, to make it result in something.

Naturally, this wasn't defensible, and we certainly weren't there in order to help make our little community stay on its feet: on the contrary, each of us was relying on the imminence of the ending—imminence that had nothing to do with duration—but leaned on it with such force that the edifice of an instant, founded on nothing, could also appear extremely solid. No one had produced this state of things, I mean no one turned around to contemplate it. I don't know what people on the outside thought of it: surely nothing, since they saw nothing, but I have to add that those on the inside were also not disposed to look over their shoulders, to give up the depth of their lives, especially at such a moment, for the pleasure of a rigorous judgment. It was all too certain that this judgment prowled around me, a temptation, a trap in which I couldn't let myself be caught at any price, and even now that I have tied it down, I can control only what I say, not what I have seen. From then on, and even though sometimes I was so close to seeing everything that I had to commit myself to a terrible attempt at passivity just so as not to lose myself in this vision of everyone, from that moment on—and this was undoubtedly the result of a long history, but even more the result of something that wasn't my doing and that I think I won't fathom completely until the time comes, until the proper moment comes—I too had won the right to stick firmly to the passion of my look, to that alone, even if my look was sterile and not very happy.

Were we waiting? I don't think so, or if we were, it was in our singularly prudent behavior in regard to time, which mostly consisted of each of us in our own way—and the ways were very different—appeasing it by making each moment a kind of uneasiness that was afterwards ignored. One way things had a chance of lasting was that the only really active person exert herself to let things stay the way they were. For reasons that weren't very clear—this was one of the areas I didn't want to turn towards—as though she had had the idea that we had reached a point where it was no longer possible to go back, at least not directly, and she had to stop everything with a powerful determination, petrify the situation, or else prolong it, isolate it in such a way that nothing could happen to it except under her control and in keeping with her views, or else in the hope that once it was cut off from its source and floating adrift, this situation, so threatening, would end up disintegrating into a mediocrity that had no future: were these her reasons? Mine, really; something was driving her, something I couldn't fathom. But if it wasn't clear to me what she had in mind, I did see clearly how skillfully she had coached appearances—right away, during the very time I was sleeping—and established around us the setting of a solid existence.

Far too shrewd, moreover, to seem to be the one taking action (whether grudgingly or quite voluntarily), just as she never showed that she intended to encompass the future. As for my visit, it seems to me there was no question of making it interminable by foreseeing that it would last. At the very most, things arranged themselves in such a way that the idea of leaving and even the memory of my arrival had no place there, for the moment—but only for the moment, and because this limited the perspective to a very brief time, it gave the moment an extraordinary poise. As far as I can see there were moments, some very agreeable, others more painful, on which I felt myself to be so firmly established, far from any horizon, that if I had been questioned about the reasons for my presence, I would have answered bravely: "Well, things are still continuing!" They did more than just continue, but even in the more precise observations I could formulate to myself about what "exactly" was happening, in these observations of the moment, which were sufficient for me, for the side of myself that looked at the world, I recognized an authority that went far beyond appearances and resulted from their distant glimmer in the past.

I think we were playing games with one another, but with as little trickery as possible. If I wanted to describe to myself the ways in which each of us was behaving, at first I would see only this strange fact: there was understanding among us. Moments that are still present to me and always astonishingly simple and happy. Certainly neither Claudia nor I, who both had afterthoughts, would have been capable of capturing such a correct tone: in spite of everything, she was inclined to keep an eye on me, and I was inclined to evade her. But in

the tapestry work we were composing thread by thread with our gestures—a tapestry well suited to the decor of a museum—our stiffness
and our strained behavior disappeared because of the perfectly natural
life that flowed between us. I must say, though, that in such an apparently false situation, this naturalness really resembled a spell cast by the
memory of the truth on beings who were much less true. Where I was
concerned, I could not be very perceptive either, nor very difficult. I
had decided to say no more about it. And having decided that, what
was left of me seemed to be occupied only with looking at a face, touching a body—and not at all with holding onto it, even less with asking
questions to find out what that face saw of me. On my part, it was the
movement of haste, the liveliness of an instant that no longer bothers
about anything. What was I asking? At certain moments, I could have
found such a face quite reserved, such a contact quite distant, and such
perfect kindness strangely divided. But these moments had no place in
my existence, which was always reduced to a single moment: a unique
moment, marvelously agreeable and important, that made me feel that
all of space, from the remotest point to the nearest, was entirely occupied by the living reality of one face, and opened the world for me to
the immense measure of that face. Anyone who lives elsewhere has
nothing, but elsewhere was not questioning me. One touch, the most
momentary, and through it I fiercely drew to myself the certainty and
the intimacy of a limitless consent—I needed nothing more than that,
and I was nothing more, and surely nothing else continued to exist,
beyond one confine after another, that was as worthy of the name of
universe: I could not be lured into that, at least as long as the energy of
that instant lasted.

It may be that I'm deluding myself about the quality of our understanding, and perhaps under what I call understanding is really the exaltation and ignorance of my own gesture. I can't decide, but that
doesn't change in any way the fact that those moments were moments
of ignorance and not a fight to the death. I recall very clearly that there
was something animated and lively between us. For example, I see this
image: above the piano and opposite me was hanging a portrait of Judith
dating from a period when I didn't yet know her; it was a splendid
work that I was looking at with pleasure (this must have happened at
the end of the morning). The wood was beginning to catch fire somewhere to my right, somewhere, but closer—I could touch it—a live

body, standing, that must have been turned towards the fire; the wood burned boldly with a flame that thickened the daylight. I stretched out my hand toward this body, fell to the level of her hips, and was burned by the dry, vegetable heat (radiating from the fire), which gave me the impression that she was roasting nicely without noticing it. I said this to her. But I was extremely happy that for my sake she had saturated herself with all the logs' fire so as to offer me this single vivifying point, the blazing end of a twig. She loved the fire, she was very capable where anything to do with the life of the fire was concerned, it was one of the tasks reserved for her, and she was going to make something superb of this one, an immense flame, she said as she stood up again, because she had kneeled to look at it more closely. "Look, look!" Unsettled, she showed me the complicity of the piece of wood going up in flames, and for me too, it was unsettling, that shiver of storm.

At which moments, then, had the amiable conventions been overstepped? I can't say exactly, but on this very morning I think they had already disappeared. One of the signs—afterwards this changed—was that we were together most of the time, like people who were indispensable to one another. One can't help admiring this sensible solution. Since necessity had tugged at us dangerously to put us under the same roof, it would have been ridiculous to pretend to escape it by scattering into different corners of an apartment as big as a pocket handkerchief. Discretion, reserve—this was what threatened to throw us at one another, not a frank recognition of the reality. When I discovered that the fact of not being with Claudia expressed itself—not always, it's true—in the various ailments I've mentioned—and I wasn't surprised, I found it natural that, having so completely taken charge of her life in a difficult period, Claudia was still called upon sometimes to help—well, I took the simplest course. I didn't want to start up again with "What's the matter, what's the matter," nor torment with questions a trouble that didn't want to show itself. I also think that at such a moment I wasn't tempted to carry on conversations: too much time was needed for that, too much indifference, a taste for the future, and my desire went through the instant and through ignorance, not through knowledge.

Yes, those moments were singularly charming. The two of them were living there before my eyes, and the naturalness of the one inspired the other with a rare and wonderful kindness. In my memory that liveliness is wedded to the morning light. The sun shone into the studio until two o'clock. We often ate lunch late, and when it was over I was already tense and in a more somber mood. In the afternoon, I heard the sound of Claudia's voice, a voice that was beautiful but without happiness, that was not easy to listen to without having certain reservations. She sang in several languages (she herself was a foreigner), I don't think she sang simply or even always tastefully; if she became excited, which happened when I found the strength to accompany her, she was excessively theatrical. Perhaps in the midst of her successes she had always been this sublime and tiresome singer who didn't know her real talent. Peculiar gifts, revealed by a sudden coldness, a more abstract rendering, like an imperceptible distancing of the voice. The pathos of the deeper registers had nothing to do with this event. I had heard voices harmoniously bound to desolation, to anonymous misery, I had been attentive to them, but this one was indifferent and neutral, hidden away in a vocal region where it stripped itself so completely of all superfluous perfections that it seemed deprived of itself: her voice was true, but in such a way that it reminded one of the sort of justice that has been handed over to all negative hazards. Short instants, perhaps; certainly, nothing touching or interesting; a little thing that didn't bother about the quality of works, that happened behind the music—and yet an instant of the music—and that communicated...well, what? Really, it communicated very little. Her friend said to her: "You're in poor voice" or "Your voice is thin," and other phrases that dated from her days in the theater. I myself didn't notice what the value of that poor voice was. The ceremony of singing tired me (for a long time singing had been a disappointing area for me); I put up with the gaity, the nothingness of the words, but that glorious voice, the royal interment, returned me in a commanding way to a museum existence. Naturally it was possible not to listen to it; I wondered if she was worried about that, being heard; perhaps she missed the theater, off hand her retirement seemed unreasonable, but was she retired? She had mentioned recording sessions, maybe she was rehearsing at that very moment; yes, she must have been working; that explained why she wasn't really singing, but rather looking for something that would be the beginning, the hope of her own singing. At the time I had the impression that she was holding back, the better to decipher a difficult text. This discovery, the feeling of being useless to her singing, since she was studying, the slow progress of the day, which was already almost dark: yielding to these emotions, I think I was struck by something that became a cloud, but a remarkable cloud, remarkably solid and real. As I watched it come forward, I had the impression that I had heard it often before—she was singing a smooth and distant sort of German—and this impression passed before me, for all of us a stronger light that twisted around and illuminated us from underneath. *Es fällt kein Strahl.* At that instant I must have discovered that it wasn't possible for her to need to work on a piece like that, such a classic. Her voice was marvelous, of an extraordinary restraint: it, too, had folded its wings, and its flight, deep inside a rarer element, continued to seek the simple happiness of singing, while she herself impassively expected—and affirmed—that the singing would not begin.

I don't recall having expressed any opinion about this to her, at least not then; she didn't expect it and I didn't expect it of myself either. Usually, and this was one of the happy aspects of that life, she didn't ask anything of me, she avoided challenging me. In the way she spoke in front of me without speaking for me there was a suggestion that I took to be the desire not to impose their life on me any more than I wanted. It seems to me that lasted quite a long time. Part of the morning, when the "dish of tea" had gone back to the kitchen, was spent in joyful carelessness between the bedroom and the bathroom, but she was not at all embarrassed to go into the studio too, with apparently just as much freedom as though this man, who was a stranger to her, didn't have eyes with which to see her, and this freedom was not even characteristic of her friend. What was surprising was not these free ways but the discretion with which all this happened, approached, receded, became an image veiled, unveiled, and yet still veiled by a certain impersonal air; imperceptibly, she had placed a feeling of reserve between us that left her and left me much freer than any wall, because behind a screen my gaze could always have looked for her, but now, when it found her mulling over her clothes, it found nothing but the phrase "It's her," which naturally couldn't be practically naked.

Each of them had her own household duties. "I'll do this." "I'll do that." These duties were just as important as the large projects of the future, they were solemn decisions that referred to another world. "I'll go buy some wood!" "I'll go to the laundry!" "I'll speak to the concierge!" All this flew over their two cups, in the morning, like eternal vows. "The vacuum cleaner!" "The leak!" "The blocked up garbage chute!" And the conclusion, the dismal end of every venture: "Madame Moffat will get rid of all that." The doors slammed, banged. The chilly air, ferreting about, ran behind them wherever they went, busy, idle, with no other role but to wrap their comings and goings in a fringe of cloth. They walked around a lot, both of them had a certain instability. It was like a treasure hunt, with backtrackings, halts, dives into water, whispers through space, a roving pursuit that could have no other object than to obscure the trail and irritate the pursuers. "When will it be found?" It was already found! Here, and here, constantly. Sometimes she came in staring at her hands: "Now what was I looking for!" A handkerchief, a brush, a pin? It didn't matter, every time it was a treasure, enough for those empty hands. "Gently, now," a voice murmured. "Gently?" The awakening, an immense calm.

This occurred to me: that when I woke up, I found someone close to me. This was certainly part of the charm of the first moments. But I couldn't explain to myself why this idea was so worrying.

I must say that something else, something more serious, was worrying me. Can I say what it was? I would have to be able to go back to a true beginning. I asked—in vain—for help at a particular moment, on a particular day. "At a given moment," as they say; but when was the moment given to me?

Yet my confusion became so great that I tried, not to clear it up, but to make it pass into my life. I had no lack of strength, I busied myself with my little jobs, everyone lives that way. I would sometimes stare through the window for a long time at the disfigured facade of the synagogue (one shouldn't forget the bomb)—that black wall, those beams supporting the entrance or closing it off, a merciless image. Certainly the truth does not die easily.

Because we lived together, I also looked at Judith's face. Familiarity did not wear it out in the least. Beautiful? I think it was, but looking at it isn't the same as describing it. (I certainly didn't photograph it. And I'm convinced that I didn't look at it in order to attribute feelings to it.) Nevertheless, I will say something about it: I found her extraordinarily visible. She appeared—and this was a fascinating, inexhaustible pleasure.

What made the situation terrifying was that I—and surely each of us—was at the very limit of happy feelings. We could have gone even farther? But why? For the sake of what? Farther! Farther was exactly where we were. Desire wanted it? Desire also wanted eternity.

I had woken up feeling a terrible shiver, all awakenings are more or less associated with a shiver. But this one was a greater force, fierce and facetious, and I fully realized it. I was infinitely indebted to it. Without it, what would my desire have been? A lonesome mimicry, grimacing. But it had uplifted me, and because it was the day, its trembling was the trembling of the day. To illuminate, to make something appear, yes; to see, an immense pleasure; but to continue desiring right up to the end—only a shiver like that could make me believe this was possible.

I got up and walked a few steps toward the window. Since the fire had been laid, I had had no trouble lighting the wood, but in the bathroom I became disoriented by the cold and a cave-like darkness (there was no electricity that day); the trembling—the shiver was no more than this trembling—stretched out in me with a rather strange slowness, like a heavy layer, not very icy, like a voice softer than mine, which made the invasion hardly disagreeable. And yet I staggered. I had to go back to the other room, I didn't have the impression I was walking, I was drinking space, I was turning it into water; drunk? gorged with emptiness. I peacefully sank down onto the carpet; I half slept; shortly afterwards, I got dressed without mishap, except that if I moved at all briskly I was caught up again by the astounding transport of that shiver, which hadn't left me at all.

The continuation? Unfortunately this isn't a story. When I discovered that I was bound to this avid day, perhaps I had hoped, in my impatience, my excess of patience, that from now on it would manage things. "Let the shiver decide," that's what our fondness for rest leads us to say. But I had an excuse: the capriciousness, the strangeness of its force. It certainly gave me no orders, it didn't forbid me anything—either to involve myself with space, or to do as I liked—but when the time came, at the right moment, it scattered me through one abyss after another, although—and this was what was strange—this did not seem to me to go beyond the truth of a shiver. My strength was betraying me, but what was it being unfaithful to? To its own limits: it was excessive, hopelessly great.

I threw a piece of wood on the fire. I felt very bad now. I was losing strength quickly. Once I had returned to my bed—but I remained beside it, standing, I had in some sense lost the ability to lie down. Now and then I was shaken by convulsive yawns, spasms far too large for a mouth. Did I want air? I would have been better off falling. But instead of that, I was stirred by an astonishing rage, and failing myself, whom I would have wanted to hurl against the door, I seized around the waist a miserable thing, vaguely white, that had been present throughout this whole scene and that was dissipated by the force of the impact. It was blown out like a light. The impression I had—an effect of my stupor—was that there was an empty spot there, but also, which was very depressing, that something was caught in a trap—between heaven and earth, as they say, I thought these words in German, *zwischen Himmel und Erde*. I must have calmly lain down shortly afterwards.

No doubt "calmly" meant that at this point everything could begin again. It is true that I revived an irritation (to call it that) which, lying down as I was, turned me into a violently constricted private place. As I shook my shoulders and surmised that the strange shiver lurking around there seemed already to have become docile and inoffensive, I was moved by fury: already it was yielding—and to me, to the authority that was being exercised in me despite me. A man who needs the wind in order to burn is always allowed to open the window, to throw himself out. But "calmly" made fun of such childishness.

Another irritating impression: it was broad daylight, and that should be understood to mean precisely a day of broad light. I was watching it, since I had nothing else to do; behind the pane, something surprising seemed to be taking place; what? I wasn't in a very good position to realize this, but the anomaly was visible. Fog, I thought—then I saw that it was beginning to snow, an event that gave me no pleasure at all and that even irritated me like a badly timed joke.

I couldn't deceive myself, there was something rather disturbing about this irritation (and hard to endure): a cry, but too violent, an infinite and voiceless vibration. Is this what thought is—this strength choked by weakness? Then I was thinking dangerously. I was extremely cold. The fire had probably gone out. I recalled that fire with a feeling of sympathy—it had allowed itself to be lit so easily a short time before, and during a snowfall. The flakes had been followed by powder, and the powder by an attractive, radiant outdoors, something too manifest, an insistent appearance, almost an apparition—why that? Was the day trying to show itself?

A little later (I think) my feeling of irritation became quite unreasonable; it may be that this feeling and the snow were connected. The monotony of the outdoors was not a violent chaos, as happens during blizzards, and which would have lent its strength to mine, but in the face of such an excessive inconsistency, more and more fruitless and oppressive, my exasperation mounted in a fantastic way, and yet I was calm, I didn't budge: nothing could have been more terrible. Here the phenomenon of the windowpane was playing a strange game. The snow wasn't stopping there, it was really coming into the room, but was it snow? only its perverse side, something insignificant, shameless and deceitful, though alive. The free air! I thought. Of course, I couldn't appeal to the others. The others were coming and going, in their endless happiness. Doors were banging, shutters were opening: "Look at the snow!" The fire sparkled and burned. The cold? The happiness, the warmth of the cold. My pulse was beating joyfully too. And the marvelous whisper: "Snow, like my country..." "Winter, yet again..." Go farther? Here and here, at each instant.

I could have stood up and broken the windowpanes, flown into a rage, as they say—I think I had enough strength for that. Surely, inside this terrible patience that kept me quiet in the midst of a furious desire, there was a temptation to speak, a terrible, dramatic temptation to denounce this calm, to pronounce one word, the final truth of a word; but I did not speak; it seems to me, in spite of what the books say, that I never spoke. Out of weakness? Out of respect for feelings of happiness? I didn't want to slander with the truth what was even truer—and also, I'm not a judge. It wasn't up to me to speak.

I never spoke, but "never" could end at any instant; "never," a very close limit for someone burning with impatience. At a certain moment, as Claudia passed near me "by chance," the same chance induced her to stop and look at me—in a very instructive way, I mean that she was finding out about me, because of me, my nearness, and I was also being taught in my own way, in some sense I was learning something new (this didn't have to relate to her: new, but also in a free state, a luminous, intermittent particle). Question her? Because of the cold—and there was no electric current for the radiator—our tasks were suspended, or turned into amusements: by this one could tell that the day was perverse. I think that certain ways in which they behaved had never been serious, this lack explained why life was so cheerful.

Even if an incident occurred (as Claudia was running a comb through her friend's hair, I had seen her friend dodge away from her with a *sudden motion,* with *an almost wild leap*), this scene—the hair pulled unintentionally, the angry reaction—belonged to the world of the cheerful life: a lovable caprice, without any importance (but when the law of seriousness has ceased to be imposed, everything becomes extremely important); there was nothing about the scene that could turn it into a real difficulty. I watched them running the brush and comb through each other's hair, turn and turn about, a ceremony with a thousand variations, which stretched out indefinitely. What I saw in this image was an antidote to the dissolving eternity of the snow, a remedy, a game in which time was being put at stake. Surely I had to take this sight into consideration. Was I under an enchantment? Yes, a joyous obligation, the obligation to stay here in order to perpetuate what I was seeing: the thousand variations of the ceremony, Claudia joyously tousling her hair, reminding it of how it used to be arranged, though this hair didn't remember its history at all, so that the game didn't go any farther than approximations, fluffy parodies, under which the expression on her face was accentuated, the atavistic look that didn't seem to be really hers but rather mirrored an aspect of the earth, the inexhaustible resource drawn out by these attempts at disguise. A face like that was hardly made to be seen, I was seeing it unlawfully, in a sense, "by chance," even though at such a moment the whole scene seemed to be taking place only for the sake of this apparition. At such a moment? And when did that moment begin? Nevertheless, it was at just such a moment, with a suddenness I was aware of, a suddenness so dazzling that it took all the power away from the phrase "all at once": I found myself seized again, caught up again by the sudden motion, the *almost wild leap* I spoke of and that took the form of a bolt of lightning. Without my being able to understand exactly when it happened, this sudden movement shook me, I was overcome with horror; I think I saw light, a vision difficult to sustain, instantaneous, connected to that movement, as though the fact that the two of them were torn apart, as though this cruel space... but I can't do it, I can't finish the sentence. I had stood up; I almost fell to the floor. Thank God, I was on the point of dying, these words were not a discovery but, as they crossed my fall, they were revealed under a piercing light, as a sort of oracle choking my strength and goading it into this pitilessly ample vibration: "Death! But in order to die, one had to write—The end! And to do that, one had to write up to the end."

I don't know if this shock set off in me what people call a period of remission. To a certain extent, it was the start of a new era, a tragic one in many respects, but since this shock wandered about freely, it seems hard to take it as a reference point for any sort of beginning. I have never hidden it—it was terrible, terrible, because of its powerful impact which, before it touched me, swept time away, and yet I fell into this open well down to the dizzying heart of time, to a pitilessly precise date, and the same date, though it is hard to know if I was coming to it through an effort against my energy or if it was taking hold of me again because in reality time had not passed. This was one of the thoroughly painful aspects of this event, even though there were others I can't speak of directly. Furthermore, what made it a wild motion was that no matter how much it repeated itself, it wasn't really repeating itself; it wasn't really its own life; and besides, up to a certain point it took into account the orientation of the days and of everyday circumstances, even though the latter were quite fascinated by this unexpected power, even as they tried their best to go on playing their part. I make this observation now, because now, when I found myself back at the same point, soaked in sweat—I had dreamed that I was lying in bathwater—I had an attack of profound weakness. In fact, I had felt this moment coming for a long time. I had managed to say no more about it, to stifle the useless questions about what "exactly" happened, because of my inflamed energy. But now, in this bathtub-shaped ditch which I had been lowered into at a certain moment and where I had been abandoned as though inadvertently, I saw the light from so far away, and it was such a narrow light, so irresolute and detached, that I let go of myself, because after all it is inevitable, and what immediately corresponded to this letting go—naturally I barely realized this—was a cold, indifferent lucidity. Yet I remember what extraordinary sadness this moment brought me. I had lost all my impatience. I felt rather well. This was how I answered a question someone asked me: "Oh no, I'm perfectly fine."

Soaked in sweat, I wanted to go back into the bathroom and immerse myself in the water. I had a vague idea that during an earlier attempt I had been deflected and that I had to set out all over again from there. But when I stood up, I discovered that it was still snowing;

I think I let out an amazing cry, almost a howl; I threw myself on Claudia, who also, it seems to me, spoke more than a few words. Even though there was nothing to indicate that the amplitude of my leap had to stop there—it was clearly capable of carrying me much far-ther—she restrained me firmly and I found myself once again tightly held against her. I was left with a striking memory, if a dim one, of this motion, even though it was unfairly cut short. I should add that her presence, which was, for me, intimately included from the very be-ginning in the vision of "it went on snowing," gave me pleasure. I quickly recovered. I wanted to drink and eat, especially drink. Judith was sent to the kitchen to make some tea, a drink I had little taste for, but I put up with it.

While I drank the tea—it was insipid, sweet, bitter, a sad mixture— I returned to a sort of silence (earlier, I think I had thrown myself into a conversation that was barely under control and over which still floated a grandiose satisfaction). What was in this silence? A question, prob-ably. I couldn't get through the cup of tea. Since I was dressed, I gave up on the water and contented myself with taking a few steps toward the window: it was still snowing, a dense, serious snow, but now I hardly bothered very much about this amazing event. Yet I remained there as long as I could, my forehead at the same height as the deep masses of snow, but I couldn't get through it any more than I could the tea.

Question her? But about what? It wasn't possible that the element of uneasiness and tragic difficulty in my presence passed unnoticed. And yet, who was alluding to it? Who was helping me become aware of it? Perhaps I didn't look like a man who doesn't know what to do? I was certainly calm, and no more calm than necessary, at the level of the calm that was the natural element of the world. At length, I had this impression: I had returned to my bed (but I wasn't lying down); Judith, who was standing, continued to look out the window. I expe-rienced a slight feeling of cold, not the overwhelming cold of a shiver, but a calm, silent cold (once again everything was plunged in a special silence). Perhaps this was because Claudia (she came in carrying some wood) stopped and looked at me in her instructive way, but I can't say it any other way: during the whole time she watched me, I understood that I was out there, in the slight, calm, and in no way disagreeable cold of the outdoors, and that I was looking at her from out there, through the transparency of the frost, in the same profound and silent way.

I will be more explicit about this right now: it was only an idea, the truth of a sensation. It would certainly have been simpler for me at that instant to be a face that belonged to the outdoors plunging into the room and looking questioningly at the people who were there, and no doubt I actually had that sensation, I really had it, but the thing is that perhaps this face was all I could grasp then and all the others could tolerate of the truth: this was why it had its chance. I ask myself this today (groping, for there is a time for seeing and a time for knowing). I ask myself why that distant and tranquil face—which I didn't see, but through whose approach a certain view approached me—presented itself, persisted as a permissible allusion to an event that didn't tolerate any allusion. In the darkness of time, it seems to me that this had been decided in me: I knew everything, and now I had perhaps forgotten everything except the terrible certainty that I knew everything. I couldn't ask questions, I don't think I had the slightest idea what a question might be, and yet it was necessary to ask questions, it was an infinitely great need. How could I have avoided this "tragic difficulty"? How could I not have done everything possible to express it and give it life ? And then what was I if not this reflection of a face that didn't speak and that no one spoke to, capable of nothing more, as it rested on the endless tranquillity of the outdoors, than silently questioning the world from the other side of a windowpane ?

This is why I must say something else. I had returned to my bed. Judith, who was standing, looked attentively out the window, and while she was there, staring as I had done at the deep masses of snow, I myself made a discovery too, calm, passionless (everything, as I said, was plunged in a special silence): that she was looking out the window (not at me), and the proof of the intensity, the intimacy of her gaze, was the silence that nothing could disturb any more than she herself could be disturbed from her watching. And what about me, can I say that I saw her? No, not completely, only from the back, her head three quarters turned away, her hair glossy and unkempt on her shoulders. It seems to me it was at that instant that Claudia, who had come in, looked at me in order to "break the spell," and it was also then that, in the slight cold of the outdoors, I in turn stared at her through the transparency of the frost and questioned her silently.

In what spirit did Claudia go along with this change? She must have had her reasons. When she saw her friend looking out the window so attentively (looking out the window being a phrase she used), she probably didn't feel very happy. I imagine that she didn't like this window, but that she respected it as Judith's own truth, and no doubt for her the day was empty, but she certainly didn't care, it was quite enough for her to look at the one who was looking, this was the one she was interested in and not a strange image, kept dreadfully close by the strength of desire but inaccessible all the same. This last circumstance must have played a part in her compliance. I wonder if she was not trying to enclose the truth, represent it in this remarkably ironic situation: I was there in flesh and blood, but Judith continued to look out the window at me in a sterile way.

I must have noticed—but at what moment?—that it was a constant subject of conversation between the two of them. I had always sensed the existence of a secret, of a sort of preestablished language, and the fact that often I didn't have the key to what they were saying hardly mattered to me, because I didn't trouble myself over spoken things. But it is likely that soon after the instant in which I made that dive upwards—that leap, that surprised and joyous leap towards the words "it was still snowing," which Claudia despotically succeeded in restraining—I must also have realized this: that far from coming out of the fog, I had well and truly plunged into a region of the darkest preoccupations, the darkest images and words.

And what about me, was I in on the secret? At the very most, I was the secret, and for that reason quite far removed from having anything to do with it. And this was probably what I had begun to discover: that I was excluded from it.

I stayed in my corner without moving. The snow had turned into a deep gloom again. On her knees, Claudia was waiting for the logs to make up their minds.

"Well," she said, "it hasn't worked yet."

I asked:

"Could I go to the bathroom? Has the electricity come on again?"

"Why," she said, laughing, "go without light!"

"You know, your bathroom is like a cellar."

The weather was turning wet, and the shopping was put off until later.

I said to Claudia, "Don't you have amazing boots that come up to your knees?"

"Completely ordinary boots, the kind all the women there have. The truth is that the North attracts you, you're a man of the North."

"Yes, but I'm afraid of the cold."

It's true, I suffered from the cold. Did I shiver? It was a cold that didn't play around with shivers. I stood up, walked between the two of them.

"Does either one of you have a pencil?"

Claudia stood up, whistling to herself.

"It has several colors," she said, fiddling with her mechanical pencil. "It doesn't work very well." When I put out my hand, she grabbed me by the wrist with a little capricious gesture: "Don't bother with that. You're much better, you know; you're not going to die. Take a good look at her."

She meant her friend.

"You had an argument this morning," I said.

"Oh! You noticed, you're very observant. And naturally you were pleased?"

"No, I don't like it. I'd rather you got along."

"Now, now, you two!" she said with a little sneer.

"Why are you calling me 'tu'?"

"It doesn't matter, today's a holiday! You never call anyone 'tu'!"

"I think people in your country call each other 'tu' very freely."

She gave me an indirect smile.

"You understood that, you're pretty smart." She added a few words in her beautiful language. "Do you know this proverb: One calls her 'tu', the other takes her?"

"Am I really a man of the North?"

"Yes, a beautiful face from the North, but you're afraid of the cold."

It's true that I suffered terribly from the cold. When I got back to my corner, again I had a strong desire to drink something. "I'm thirsty," I said. The weather was so dark (so infinitely, uselessly white) I turned my head away so that this hour could do its work. A little after, I called to Claudia: "You should go to sleep." "No," she said. "I'll stay up." I felt very sad. Because the time was approaching, I turned to her again: "Give up this hour. Don't stay. It makes me sad that you're here." But she went on sitting up. Towards five o'clock—when the hour was more advanced—a slight shiver went through me, I opened my eyes for a brief instant, and again, though they were rather far away, I saw certain parts of her face that pierced through the space between us: her prominent cheekbones, her bulging eyes. "Now," I said, "do what you want."

The snow turned into a tempest, the black element of the wind. As I streamed with water, as she dried my face, I heard her call out: "Look: it wasn't a dream! His sweat has soaked my handkerchief." But a little later she lost interest in my "sweat." Surely the day had fruitlessly closed again on the limitlessness of the day. Something had escaped it, its own transparency, that fascinated whiteness that had become the amazement of a cry, a smooth, icy face, frightening and frightened, scattered at random and recaptured at random by the wind.

The cold was affecting her. She drank some tea, no doubt strong and burning, which irritated her throat. When she saw that I was listening to her cough, she went out. Judith came and said to me: "She swallowed the wrong way." "Listen!" I said. "I've heard a sound like that before." She became attentive. "Is it possible," she said, "that...?" But already I no longer wanted to see her or hear her.

Some time must have gone by—the question of how to evaluate time was very different for each of us, even though it was still our time. I will measure its duration very exactly by saying that she only stayed in the hallway long enough to catch her breath, and perhaps she went to drink a mouthful of water. But when she came back, she realized that a much longer period had gone by. She became upset and left the room. When I saw that I was alone I became upset too. Twice I called my brother, but he didn't come. Then I turned back towards that terrifying sound of rumination that now marked time's narrative. But when time speaks, already it is no longer time that is speaking.

While I was still alone (I mean, I had my eyes closed), the bundle of voices loosened, then abruptly came apart. "Quick, a glass of water," I asked. "But you can't drink right now." "Quick, please." Again she said, from very close by, at the level of my mouth: "But you won't be able to swallow." Having suddenly, inordinately, opened my eyes on her after these words, I noticed that her Slavic look (probably because of her fatigue, the late hour) was much more pronounced. "You swallowed the wrong way," I remarked. Apparently I said this in a light, almost playful tone, but I wasn't in the least cheerful. She threatened me with her fist, an image I captured by closing my eyes again. I thought of turning back to myself again, for the third time, but everything at that level appeared to me perfectly tranquil and, in fact, light, almost playful. I rested when I could. I felt rather good. When someone asked me a question, this was what I answered, I or the careless and forgetful echo of time: "Why, it's just fine."

Once again I entered the world of the cheerful life. Yet I can't deny it: whatever sort of tenderness, whatever wonderful kindness emerged from this moment—and perhaps the expression, to be welcomed with open arms, had lost something of its startling truth—the fact that it was "once again" remained difficult to absorb. I think that even for the others something was there that wasn't going by, and I believe that the instant, too, in its joyful sincerity and under its lovely face, became confused by the fact that it had appeared. As for me, I was almost immediately devastated by an extreme feverishness. That idea, "the day is beginning," was burning me, it was already reduced, through my life, to the eternity of so few instants, it was already that other idea, "the day is dying"; haste which was stripped of its composure, like a muddle of actions, and yet was a completely lucid demand, because through its entire extent I saw the immensity of the history that I had to set in motion. I found myself on the same level as this beautiful instant, but could I grasp it? Will anyone have trouble understanding that with its wild strength, the shiver was already dragging me farther along? And what maddened my impatience was that the beautiful instant wanted to be kept, eternalized, it was a cheerful instant that did not know or only suspected that by lingering near me, it was condemning itself to become a beautiful apparition, a return that would be forever beautiful, but separated from itself and from me by the greatest cruelty.

Perhaps this impatience was not apparent to the eyes of the cheerful world; perhaps I seemed at most preoccupied: smiling, but under the veil of preoccupations. At the moment of this awakening, I think the darkest sort of thing was happening. Certainly, I opened my eyes on Claudia and I was already moving towards her with all the impetus of a man who is moving towards the day. But, whether because she was shaken by fatigue or because one can't put up indefinitely with something intolerable, even though she was firm in her resolution, hardly had she touched my look when she uttered an amazing cry, almost a howl, and no doubt she flinched back, but, with a brutality that didn't consider anything, I leaped on her fiercely and seized her again. I won't try to justify this violence. This is how things are. A person who is afraid inspires horror, and a person who weakens becomes the victim of a pitiless and unfair strength.

I must add (to be fair) that I was not certain of this very dark incident, and my uncertainty made it even darker, since it couldn't be brought into the daylight except through a preoccupied "I think." Yet something happened; even though I was once again capable of answering: "Why it's just fine," this answer had an odd ring to it in this cheerful world, and perhaps it wasn't her fault, but I had this impression: by retreating before the facts, she had imprudently drawn into the day a prologue to the day that should never have broached the awakening, a live gleam before which she continued to retreat and which was reflected, it seemed to me, in the menacing expression of her own look, in that fierce yet troubled way she now had of staring at me—fierce, hostile and yet faltering (she had large, bulging eyes, very intense and very dry in their expression; under the veil of preoccupation, they had grown even larger, but had softened, and that softness was menacing). Another sign of her preoccupation was that she tried—when I asked her, but I hadn't let go of her yet: "Have you been here very long?"—to tell me everything or at least to tell me one thing. As far as I could see, it was like a vast landscape of temptation, a prayer for perpetual happiness, an offer to hand me the keys to the kingdom, which finally was illuminated by this expansive sentence (which had every appearance of being an answer to my useless questions about what "exactly" had happened): "No one here wants to be connected to a story."

This sentence made a deep impression on me. I thought I saw light spring from it, I had touched a spot of surprising brightness. A sentence? Something slipping, a portrait not yet framed, a brightly sparkling motion that shone in quick dazzles, and this wasn't a calm light, but a sumptuous and whimsical chance, brightness's mood.

I stayed in the dazzle of that speech. Really, this was a complete restatement, a wonderful summary that seemed to me to throw back into shadow everything that I myself, at certain instants, had been able to conceive of the situation (maybe I should add in my defense that what was happening was simple: I was thinking; more and more ideas were coming to me; who could resist such magic?). And undoubtedly, no matter how much pleasure I took in considering this spectral light, I was not blind to its dangerous aspect, but my look of amazement must have been evident enough so that Claudia thought I had completely entered into that powerful way of seeing. So that when I asked her, pointing to her friend, "And she doesn't either?" she had no difficulty answering enthusiastically: "She even less than the others!"

I accepted this plain speech as bravely as I could, it had been tossed off so cheerfully (even though "the others" was not the most precise expression); but, in spite of everything, I couldn't share her enthusiasm. Disconcerted, I think I let go of her. But she lost no time catching hold of me again.

"Sometimes she is far away, very far away," she said, making an impressive gesture with her hand.

"In the past?" I asked timidly.

"Oh, much farther away!"

I pondered, trying to discover what could really be farther away than the past. Meanwhile, she seemed all of a sudden afraid that she had thrown me slightly beyond the limits. She squeezed me hard, then she said, hesitantly and in a dejected voice:

"She sees you."

I immediately felt very uneasy. I had to look away from that speech, which was so extraordinarily repugnant (and also contemptuous), and I grew even more uneasy when I heard myself ask her:

"Where?"

"All over, where you are."

I think that as she said that, her voice faltered a little, so that there was a note of tenderness in it that was hardly usual. She allowed my gaze to penetrate hers, which was soft and because of that menacing. Then I noticed how much I liked that menacing gleam, how much it attracted me. I said to her:

"You don't hate me as much as that!"

She pondered this, though she didn't withdraw from my gaze:

"I feel a sort of sympathy for you." She leaned towards me and added in her somber voice: "Sympathy for the enemy is a very strong feeling."

"But I'm not your enemy," I said gaily. "I've just woken up and at this moment I'm touching you. I like that very much. Have you been here very long?"

"Be careful," she said, pushing me away and shivering; "She's frail; she's almost no one."

I felt it too, I felt a cold breath, an icy insinuation that seemed to me to come from the awakening (but afterwards I thought the insinuation was deep inside her words, strangely ill situated, because they had seemed to me to concern her, whereas they clearly applied to her friend much more). The confusion was so great that she quickly went back to a less dangerous path and said, with her admirable composure:

"It's natural, you look at what's in front of you. You go as close as possible." Then she added: "Beyond the Urals, you know, in the old days women weren't accustomed to sitting down very often. Even when they didn't have anything left to do, they stood like pillars in their kitchens. At the theater, too, it was normal to stand up."

I didn't manage to approach what she was saying as fast as she was inviting me to. I was waiting for something from the room, I was discovering great sterile spaces in the room that reminded me, actually, of the motionlessness of those vast plains.

"In any case," I said to her, "you're letting yourself get very tired."

"Oh, yes! Very much so." But when I saw the effect of this cry of pleasure, I told her the reasons for it: "It's that you're more approachable," I said to her.

I don't know what she thought of that. She sank into a secret, motionless observation that seemed to be the corollary of everything we had said. But it was soon clear what she was thinking:

"Why aren't you satisfied with what you have?"

I studied her awkwardly.

"But what I have," I said, "I don't have."

Even though what she had said appeared almost inoffensive, it had nevertheless been enough to make a new perspective come up between us. Certainly she wanted to tell me something, but what she also wanted just as much was to make me say something.

"It's pointless for you to stay up," I insisted. "You really have to admit that in spite of everything, it will happen..."

"What will happen?"

"Sooner or later all this will slip through your fingers."

If I had counted on this brutal behavior to break down her obstinacy, I was quite wrong.

"Then why," she said, "do you want to do that?"

MAURICE BLANCHOT

Why? I laughed at her question.

"But I don't want to," I told her, "I don't want to."

She wasn't very affected.

"Maybe you don't want it in the same way that I can want what I do, but all the same, it's something that is very much wanted: I sense it," she said in a rigid tone of voice.

"Oh, as far as wanting goes, you're very good at that!" I replied agreeably. "Now it's my turn: if 'I want it', why don't you want it?"

But after thinking about it, she betrayed a disturbance, an emotion that surprised me. And she said in her low voice:

"Perhaps I don't want it as much as you think, not as much as before." She stopped for a second. "Sometimes I, too, feel as though I am inside this thing that is wanted."

"You are? Just you?"

"What I want, my will. It doesn't help that I don't let go of anything, that I never lose sight of her—I can't manage it."

Once again her voice had that slight, vibrant faltering that made it so remarkable.

"But it seems to me just the opposite, that so far you've managed it quite well. You've been amazing, you know."

She was hardly listening to me, and yet, through the stream of her thoughts, she really must have discerned the motion of mine, because she alluded to it with an unexpected distress:

"You too, just now, you were so far away..."

"I was far away?"

She made an impressive gesture, then, leaning on herself as though to find her balance, she said with a disconsolate tranquility:

"I don't know if it will last much longer, because this sort of freedom exhausts all one's strength."

I watched her gently for a long time.

"You're a strange woman. So much will, so much courage, such a strong soul, and all that... for nothing."

She gave me a terrible look and, as though she were going on with the awakening, threw herself backwards uttering an amazing cry, a real howl.

A short time after, I spoke to her gaily: "Well, that was a terrible fight!" But she gestured to me with her hand. Nevertheless, she caught her breath again and left, doing several things to relax and

242

soothe her throat, which was hardly meant for such vociferations. I emerged from this scene "preoccupied." I had heard her rinsing her throat, performing ablutions, this was a dark noise, the echo of a presentiment so distant that it seemed to come to me across the interstices of time. Was it possible? That she thought she was alive and yet already her mouth was full of fraud? I think she was sleeping, but not very deeply, because as soon as I tried to stand up, she woke up and touched me with her look, this look that stared at things through the menace with which she felt stricken, and this was why it was so menacing. "I hardly believe in you," she said softly. I wasn't surprised by that. It was in keeping with the atmosphere of uncertainty, indecision, and even her sentence was tainted with it, it seems to me; for that reason it was not spiteful, but rather disquieting and even mildly pleasant—an irresponsible and incompetent truth that one didn't want to drive away.

"But... do I want to make something be believed?"

She didn't answer, and while the time passed, I eventually wondered if what I had taken for a speech was not simply a delaying phrase, leaving room for what was essential. This led me to ask her:

"What are you going to say now?"

"I hardly believe in you."

"But..." I said, "why that sentence?"

And it's true that when I saw her stick to this, when I heard her persist in that whispering, but nuanced, voice, which was her voice now—a sort of iridescent sincerity in which there was sadness, cunning and a distant resentment—I found her singularly less innocent, as though the young irresponsible truth had continued to signal to her from a place I couldn't see, and its reflection was what passed between us again, but since this was again, it was no longer inoffensive, nor transparent.

"Believe," I said with a little bitterness, "why do you want to believe? My existence is precarious, is that what you're thinking?"

She stared at me with a doubtful expression, which might have signified a desire to answer and the difficulty of answering, or perhaps fatigue, but also a much more important doubt. I had the distinct feeling that she wasn't inclined to content herself with such weak concessions, and, to tell the truth, when I saw that she wasn't satisfied, I thought she was about to repeat... her sentence, it seemed to me it was already on her lips, I heard it in the emptiness of the air. At that moment my anxiety was so great that, in order to prevent what would have been intolerable to her, to anyone, almost at random—but I knew that by doing this I was yielding infinitely to her, exaggeratedly—I murmured: "You want to say that..." She nodded. "But can it be? Yet you touch me, you speak to me." She straightened up with extraordinary violence. "I'm talking!" she said in a tone of the harshest irony. "I'm talking!" She hurled this word with such incredible harshness that it tore open the whispering and became an ordinary human word, I mean, uttered with her beautiful intact voice. It was so stripped of meaning that I trembled, and the same shiver ran through her. Both of us, it seems to me, were involved in the same fear.

Her reaction had been so strong, she had straightened up with such anger, such complete forgetfulness of the circumstances, that not only had she not let go of me, she had drawn me with her, she had sprung with me into the heart of an element which was truly dangerous, unstable, the element of her irony, her unreal sarcasm, where there was no reward for seriousness. It was in some sense an infinite leap. Even though she was restraining me—and because of that I became aware of my own momentum, my desire to push her in front of me—I couldn't help feeling that the slightest thing could make her fall down. She was holding herself heavily upright, pressed against herself, and all that could be heard was the distinct sound of something opening and closing, a dark movement at the back of her throat, which she was trying to relax. I must have asked her: "Would you like something?" But she practically wrung my hands. It was dark then. It seemed there was nothing more to do but to follow the rise, then the fall, of the spasm, a light bubble that burst gently, so close to me that it was natural for my fate to be linked to that noise. At last she had a slight attack of coughing, which forced her into a silent struggle, because all she could do was suppress completely the vibrations that were passing through her throat, so that she gave the impression of fighting behind closed doors, in a world already far away, to which she had withdrawn out of discretion but also out of mistrust. I think she was very hot. Through this heat she found my hands, which were completely cold. "You're cold as ice," she said. She grasped my two hands and quickly, no doubt in order to enjoy a colder touch, put them flat against her throat.

Now I have to say this: even though I saw how real it was, this gesture left me feeling uncomfortable, uneasy. Why? This is hard to understand, but it made me think of a truth whose shadow it would be, it made me think of some sort of unique, radiant thing, as though it had tried to condemn to mere likeness an inimitable instant. Bitter suspicion, disconcerting and burdensome thought. I remained there in the background as though on the edge of the morning. I asked her— I was half sitting up on the couch, but she was close to the wall, leaning slightly over my hands, which she held firmly against her: "Things should stay this way, shouldn't they?" I think this question went unanswered, because, shortly after, I spoke to her joyfully: "Well, that was a terrible attack!" But when I tried to come even closer, she flinched in a peculiar way. I couldn't help saying: "What's wrong, what's wrong?"—words which I was amazed to hear. I added: "Why are you so nervous?" "Because you look so cheerful." That answer made me laugh and she laughed a little too. A slight motion, but one that overtaxed her dangerously. I felt a terrible, convulsive storm pass between my arms, and in order to stay with her, I had to respond to the awesome appeal that rose from the depths of the day at this instant, I was filled with rage, I seized her around the waist, and now that I had caught hold of her again in the midst of the unsteadiness, the static falling of our two bodies together, I held her firmly out of reach of what had no limit. Little by little, she was able to breathe again, she recovered a slight, individual life, and as I was letting go of her, she murmured something hastily, but to give chaos its revenge, I stopped her from emerging from that instant.

The strange thing about the situation was that I sensed how much she had been telling the truth: she had become upset because I was in good spirits. And suddenly that upset me too. I saw how powerful it was—this cheerful force, this kind of enticing determination, this disturbing will that had forced her to laugh, taken her breath away and made her shiver; it seemed ready to rise, to spring toward the trembling of a much stronger turbulence, no longer a slight, frivolous sparkling, but already a blazing trail and a jubilant wrath and a fiery and furious derision. A storm? But a sterile one, in which the unleashing of the most frivolous lightness would turn into the vertigo of an avid circle, avid to uncoil to infinity. This avidness crossed through the day, tormented space, attracted it, set it in motion and transformed it into a strange blazing wheel without a center; boundless exaltation, depth of bitterness and cruelty, and yet what was it? The frivolity of the most cheerful image. In the past, I had thrown myself toward the cheerful life of the day, an unsituated, elusive event. If I tried to recall to myself that immense plunge, I also had to recall the moment when the brightness had recoiled before me, and it could be that this terrible earlier element which, under cover of this recoil, had risen from the depths of the awakening, was what was tormenting the light day, perhaps its approach was provoking this trembling response, this quick condensation of the brightness into fire, and of the fire into a Yes, Yes, Yes burning around a cold core. Had I plunged? But as I woke up in this life, perhaps I awoke this life with me, and perhaps this jubilation signified some prodigious and terrifying motion, in which two elements soared to meet one another—a frozen day and a burning day, or I who eternally preceded the origin and I who eternally radiated the end.

I can't say I tried to hide from this motion. I couldn't have, I didn't want to. But it's true that I also wanted to go back to something serious, I couldn't do without what really has to be called a serious truth. At this instant, Claudia seemed like a true affirmation, an extraordinarily opulent affirmation. I think I hadn't imagined that she would still have so much strength, as though no part of her life was at all worn, though I saw her passing through it. I thought: "Why, she is extraordinarily lonely," and I thought she was lonely because she hadn't vanished, along with everything else, into the illusion of a memoryless intimacy. In a sense this was disconcerting. I asked her: "Do you need air?" "Do you?" Her voice seemed more veiled to me than I had expected, she wasn't weak, she still had a sort of fullness, authority, that I imagine she derived from the force of the way she had spoken. "Does it make you tired to talk?" "No, not at this moment, not with you." I still hadn't let go of her, I held her with all the energy the surprise of her own strength had given me. "Well," I said to her joyfully, "talk to me." "Just like that? Talk nonsense? Without stopping?" I noticed that she had turned toward me, and yet not completely; really, as I listened to her I experienced an extraordinary pleasure, because it was so distinct, so full, though under the veil of a whisper. This was why I was induced to answer: "But you have a lot to say to me now." "To you?" "To me," I said gaily, "to me." Yet I felt her withdraw, contract, and I leaned my head forward: "I think a little noise…" This seemed to tempt her. "Noise?" I nodded. We stayed that way, both of us, waiting.

I think she slept, but not very deeply, because as soon as I stood up she was standing up too. I asked her where Judith was. "Who is Judith?" "Your friend. That's the name I gave her." "I don't like that name. She went to bed. She needs her sleep too." "You leave her alone?" As I was going toward the window, she tried to help me walk. "I'm not a drunk." It was raining now, a peaceful rain that signaled the slow decline of winter. I asked her to point out the different streets to me, and she did: Trinité, Boulevard Haussman, Passage de la Bourse. "Do you like this city?" No, she didn't like it. "Does it make you tired to talk?" "A little." "Was it singing that hurt your throat?" "Singing was what started it. People who sing have to expect problems like that." "I don't know if I told you this, I don't like singing very much, but listening to you was a pleasure." She went to look for her mechanical pencil, which I think she used for writing when she couldn't speak, then slowly she came back and sat down on the couch, and because I was near the window I could see how much lighter, how much larger the room had grown. I looked at the immense space, the wall over there, the door farther off, a little closer the depth of a blank spot. I said to her: "Come to the South with me." She shook her head. "It isn't possible." "Come!" She helped me to take a few steps, at first with rather bad grace, then with a tentative good will. When we reached the middle of the room, she left me, opened the door and went into the hall. It was very dark there, but since she was walking just a little ahead of me, I could distinguish her very clearly. As soon as I appeared, she started walking again; she moved off slowly, with a great and melancholy dignity, turning back slightly to see if she was being followed, but still not stopping. At the point where the hall bent, she paused (I had to adjust to the different air); when the gap between us was small enough, she moved away from the wall and plunged into the even darker part that led to the vestibule. Now I found myself at the point where the hall forked. I stayed there a little while. But when the bedroom door opened, I went on too.

Her friend looked at us both, one after the other, I think, and even though she had turned her head slightly in my direction, something incredibly piercing in this look, coming together with the lively movement of her eyes, immobilized us. I don't think I've ever seen a look as avid as that one. Feelings can be read in the eyes—terror, the shock of desire—but this look was avid, I mean it didn't express light: not clear, not cloudy, and really, perhaps because of its fixity, which was made even more provoking by the fact that her eyes darted back and forth (looking at each of us in turn), if it expressed anything it was the shamelessness of hunger, the nocturnal surprise before the prey. It was certainly a wonderful look: avid? but possessing nothing, insignificant but capable of an immense sarcasm—and more than anything, very beautiful.

She didn't seem dazed, as she would have been if she had just woken up, because when Claudia roughly pulled the covers off her she simply watched with the same expression of sarcastic avidness—and now this avidness was also, it seems to me, curiously interested—but without any surprise. This action didn't bother her, in any case; slyly, she too contemplated her nocturnal body, this body that had been tumbled over into the night. She had her arms modestly down by her sides, in the age-old attitude of repose (but her hand was tightly clenched). Then Claudia did this: she touched her arm to raise it (or shift it), and when it didn't yield, she tried to open her hand. What followed was the work of an instant: with amazing spirit, Judith sat up, shouted two words—then sank back on the bed.

A terrible scene, but one that left me with a feeling of joy, of limitless pleasure. That wonderful head that had been uplifted, what could be more true, and if it had then been thrown down lower than the earth, that was just as much part of the exaltation, that was proof of it, the moment when one no longer worshiped the majesty of a piece of debris, but seized it and tore it apart.

I think the vitality of that scene was all the more overwhelming because it was contained in two or three gestures. What had been depicted was inscribed on an infinitely thin film, but behind it rumbled the freedom of a pure caprice in which the taste for blood hadn't yet been awakened. No one could say of such a scene that it had ever taken place before; it had occurred a first time and only once and its exuberance was the energy of the origin, from which nothing springs. Even when I went back over it to "think" about it—and it required that: an intense meditation—it didn't take me anywhere; face to face we held each other, not at a distance, but in the intimacy of a mysterious familiarity, because she was "you" for me, and I was "me" for her.

What could I have said about it? She wasn't for one moment unforgettable, she didn't want to be held sacred: even when she was terrifying, there was something extraordinarily cheerful about her. No doubt this could not be relived, the moment of collapse, the dreadful alteration of life, unable to control itself, was a blow to memory—and afterwards? afterwards, chaos and yet I swear the last instant infinitely surpassed all the others, because it was on me that this dream body had decomposed, I had held it in my arms, I had experienced its strength, the strength of a dream, of a desperate gentleness, defeated and still persevering, such as only a creature with avid eyes could communicate it to me.

I would like to say this: when a man has lived through something unforgettable, he shuts himself up with it to grieve over it, or he sets off to find it again; he thus becomes the ghost of the event. But this face did not concern itself with memory, it was fixed but unstable. Had it happened once? A first time and yet not the first. It had the strangest relations with time, and this was uplifting too: it did not belong to the past, a face and the promise of that face. In some way it had looked at itself and seized itself in one single instant, after which this terrifying contact had occurred, this mad catastrophe, which could certainly be considered its fall into time, but that fall had also crossed time and carved out an immense emptiness, and this pit appeared to be the jubilant celebration of the future: a future that would never again be new, just as the past refused to have taken place once.

Claudia came back shortly after I did. I could add that these words, which, in my eyes, had once ushered in Claudia's life and made her the person who comes after, came back too, and drew me toward the same truth: I didn't know her. In this way, the whole cycle began again. But though I was still deep inside this intense meditation, I could certainly see her coming near, coming from the depths of return, slowly, with her great and melancholy dignity, I could see her pass close to me and, close though she was, stare at me for a brief instant beyond boundary after boundary, and all this had the dark power of "I didn't know her," but all this also signified the exaltation of this return, the fact that it was a monumental event, elevated to its own glory, in a light that proclaimed not an absent and motionless truth, but the blaze of an ultimate meaning. Yes, she came back shortly afterwards and I didn't know her. But no longer in the light of those feeble words, for they had been obliterated, swept away by the terrifying breath of the two words howled by Judith from the depths of her memory, *Nescio vos*, "I don't know who you are," which she had thrown in our faces, and afterwards she had sunk back in my arms.

The greatest and truest utterance, for me, the radiant heart, the expression of the familiarity and the jealousy of night. And it is true that even these words, these words too, were an echo of another time, she had to have learned them from someone (she was ignorant of almost everything), but what I had perhaps let fall as a grammatical fact was being thrown back at me by the immensity, after great labor on the part of the shadows, thrown back into my face as the benediction and malediction of the night.

Claudia came back shortly after I did. Everything was quiet, and I think she rested then. And yet, later, I saw *her* looking at me through the open door of the hall (I was opposite, in the studio). When I saw her again, she was sitting down, and across the whole space she appeared slightly lower than I was, her body half inclined, her head bent towards her knees. It had happened to me in the past, when I lived alone in the South—and I was in the prime of life, during the day my strength was staggering; but there was a moment in the night when everything would stop—hope, possibility, and the night; then I would open the door and I would look tranquilly down at the bottom of the stairway: it was a completely tranquil and intentionless movement, purely nocturnal, as they say. At this instant, across the immense space, she gave me the impression that she too was sitting down at the bottom of a stairway, on the large step where the stairs turn; having opened the door, I looked at her, she was not looking at me, and all the tranquility of this movement, which was so perfectly silent, today had the truth of this body slightly stooped in an attitude that was not one of expectation, nor of resignation, but of a profound and melancholy dignity. For my part, I could do no more than look at this woman with a gaze that expressed all the calm transparency of a last gaze, as she sat near the wall, her head leaning slightly towards her hands. Could I approach her? Could I go down? I didn't want to, and she herself, in her unwarranted presence, was accepting my look, but not asking for it. She never turned towards me and after I had looked at her I never forgot to go away calmly. This instant was never disturbed, or prolonged, or deferred, and maybe she didn't know me, and maybe she was unknown to me, but it didn't matter, because for one and for the other this instant really was the awaited moment, for both of us the time had come.

Now I have to say it: when the face of such a moment shows itself, one mustn't respect it (bind oneself to it by the sense of something amazing). Certainly, it is a supreme apparition, but this supremacy is that of someone who wants to be not only seen but touched—and not only respected but loved—and not feared at all, because terror would become its temptation, and whoever closes his eyes in its presence makes it blind, just as he who respects it encloses it in the futility of a cold and unreal life. When, in the past, in the South, I shut the door again, I knew that this door represented the proud decision that made it possible for distress to manifest itself to me with such extraordinary dignity, to live near me and for me to live near it, and I knew that that instant would have been turned into humiliation and shame, if I had tried to perpetuate it or tried to find it again. During the day, I didn't think about it; and yet, in the midst of this unconcern, there was no day for me except through the strength of my relationship to this single unknown point and through the even more unknown relationship of this point to me: if this relationship was threatened (but what did the word threatened mean, in such a situation? It really had no meaning, that's why I didn't think about it), the day was also jeopardized and the unconcern turned into an irresolute "I don't remember any more" transmitted to one another by every thing and every hour. In any case, this relationship did not make daily life easy. I did not lack strength, and certainly, when the day began, my understanding with this beginning was an understanding with youth, an understanding on the part of what makes a decision and from the outset goes beyond it. I was leading a more or less normal life; I was in good health, as they say; now and then I wrote a few words—these words, to be precise—but what "exactly" was happening? I wouldn't be able to say, beyond making this observation: that even though I wasn't thinking about it at all, I had bound myself to this "point" and I was looking at it with such self-abuse that the strength of even a more capable man probably wouldn't have been enough for it and that in any case mine, the strength of the day, of the day that was mine, was no longer equal to the tasks of daily life, even though, I must confess, this life was often reduced to very little.

But was this really true and was I looking? Not at something, not at a point, not at anything. I would have been horrified at myself if, on the occasion of that image, which was so discreet, I had shown any interest in it or paid any attention to it. Understand, it was in no way a matter of an image: the image or the figure, however quiet, was, in relation to the supreme dignity of the instant, no more than a vestige of uneasiness, the uneasiness remained poised on the instant, that was why it became apparent. What I mean is that the day evidently had a relationship with that instant of the night, a mysterious, dramatic, and in every way exhausting relationship, and since I too loved the day and since I was also alive, I was involved in the most exhausting intrigue, but that still didn't mean that I was really occupied by it.

I burned, but this terrible fire was the shudder of the distance, and no task corresponded to that distance. I grew more silent (and since I was alone, that meant silent towards myself). Extraordinarily idle and yet having little time. To some degree, my life was exuberance, but to some degree it was poverty of breath, and I could no doubt say to myself that because the forces of desire had bound themselves, in me, to the truth of a single instant, I really had to give that truth not only myself, not only everything, but even more (and more, I imagine, meant the scald of being, which eternally denies the end), but such a calming explanation did not explain to me why I was this torch lit in order to illuminate a single instant, and when one burns with impatience, explaining is the sort of baseness never permitted by the day, though it is in the day that the shudder comes to light. Things happened to me, to me and to the story, events that were more and more curtailed (in the sense that, just as I had become no one or almost no one as the traits of my character weakened, the world was also readily merging with its limit), but this sort of penury of time was disclosing above all the exorbitant pressure of "Something is happening," a jealous immensity that could only curtail or suspend the natural progress of the story. The reason for the strangeness was this: that this extraordinary, living pressure was not that of a point foreign to time, but represented as well the pure passion of time, the pure power of the day, and its exigency did not turn away from life but rather consumed it the moment it touched it and appeared unlivable, in exactly the same way that passion is living, even though the creature touched by passion also destroys the possibility that is life. That is why, in certain respects, this "point" was passion in this world, and the passion of the world could only seek this point.

It could be that I lived in the state of anxiety of a man obliged to take upon himself the anxiety and work of the day—a day that had not begun and was not yet shining except in the distant beginning of an image whose calm was distress and whose supremacy was origin and end. At night, when I got up, who got up with me? At that instant, there was no day, no night, no possibility, no expectation, no uneasiness, no repose, but nevertheless a man standing wrapped in the silence of this speech: there is no day and yet it is day, so that this woman sitting down there against the wall, her body half inclined, her head bent toward her knees, was no closer to me than I was near her, and the fact that she was there did not mean that she was there, nor I, but the conflagration of this speech: now it is happening, something is happening, the end is beginning.

When I opened the door, no one would ask me where I was gonig: there was no one to ask me. When I returned, no one asked me where I had been. Now, someone is asking me "Why, when did you go out?" "Just now."

It is true that I'm talking about anxiety, but it is the shiver of joy that I'm talking about—and distress, but the luster of this distress. I may appear to be prey to the limitless torment of an exorbitant constraint that is also incomprehensible, to the point where if I say, if I too say, the day is night for me, I will express something of this torment. And yet, a mild torment, for in front of me is the lightning, behind me the fall, and in me the intimacy of the shock.

I met this woman I called Judith: she was not bound to me by a relationship of friendship or enmity, happiness or distress; she was not a disembodied instant, she was alive. And yet, as far as I can understand, something happened to her that resembled the story of Abraham. When Abraham came back from the country of Moria, he was not accompanied by his child but by the image of a ram, and it was with a ram that he had to live from then on. Others saw the son in Isaac, because they didn't know what had happened on the mountain, but he saw the ram in his son, because he had made a ram for himself out of his child. A devastating story. I think Judith had gone to the mountain, but freely. No one was freer than she was, no one troubled herself less about powers and was less involved with the justified world. She could have said, "It was a God who wanted it," but for her that amounted to saying, "It was I alone who did it." An order? Desire transfixes all orders.

It wasn't true that we understood each other: on the contrary, there was no understanding. She was, in a sense, much more visible than I, and the more time passed, the more the day and the luster of the day allowed her to be seen, but the hour also came when the blazing frontiers had been crossed and to look at her was to deny almost everything. Unstable? She was not less so than I was. And jealous? Certainly. Capable of violence, even a storm; space fled before her. She had bound herself furiously to the infinite; only there could she find a language in which to say, "Even so, I see it!" But the limitless was not enough for her. That was why she was eternally summoning me out of the infinite.

The fact that she was more and more obvious—this was her splendor, a threat directed against herself—proclaimed that she was alive: yes, she was taking flight, the companion of a single moment. And now? Now, the obviousness had been shattered; the broken pillars of time were holding up their own ruins.

"Now"—strange ray. Now—furious force, pure truth deprived of counsel. It was quite true that we understood each other, but in the depth of now, where passion means loving and not being loved. One who loves is the magnificence of the end; one who is loved is miserly care, obedience to the end. She was bound to me because she radiated the joyful power in whose light I loomed up precisely here, precisely now—at her touch—and I was bound to her because I was the day that made me touch her obviousness. But if "this relationship was threatened," she became a sterile "I want it" and I became a cold and distant image.

She had looked at me for a long time, but I did not see her. Days that were supreme in her eyes. That she was in this way unknown was not a misfortune for her; and her gaze was not modest, but avid: as I said, the most avid of all, since it had nothing. Yet she yielded to the shudder; she stared at me from the depths of an extreme past, a wild place, towards an extreme future, a desert place, and because she was not at all contemplative, that look, oddly brazen, was a constant, violent attempt to seize me, a drunken, joyful challenge unconcerned about either possibility or the moment. Because of that, she was ahead of me, and yet her youth had something unreal about it, a prophetic transparency that injured time and made it anxious about itself. Subjugate me? She didn't want that. Let herself be guided? She couldn't. Touch me? Yes; it was this contact that she called the world, world of a single instant, an instant before which time rebels.

So I remained alone, I mean that I went away, then, into the depths, because in order for her to become visible too, no doubt she had to stop seeing me. Hunger, cold—she lived among such elements, but starved as she was, she moved off as soon as her gaze risked awakening mine, and not with the timidity of a weak soul, but because wildness was her dominion. Without a wild movement, what chance would she have had of springing towards me? But to allow her that leap, I too must draw back and draw back again.

At night, in the South, when I get up, I know that it isn't a question of proximity, or of distance, or of an event belonging to me, or of a truth capable of speaking, this is not a scene, or the beginning of something. An image, but a futile one, an instant, but a sterile one, someone for whom I am nothing and who is nothing to me—without bonds, without beginning, without end—a point, and outside this point, nothing, in the world, that is not foreign to me. A face? But one deprived of a name, without a biography, one that is rejected by memory, that does not want to be recounted, that does not want to survive; present, but she is not there; absent, and yet in no way elsewhere, here; true? altogether outside of what is true. If someone says, she is bound to the night, I deny it; the night doesn't know her. If someone asks me, but what are you talking about? I answer, well, there is no one to ask me that. And the day? The day asks nothing of her, it is not involved with her, it owes her neither loyalty nor belief. I myself haven't looked for her, I haven't questioned her, and if I pass near there, I don't stop. What sort of relations do we have? I don't know. Yet I can sense that the day is bound to her in some way. That there is, between them, not an understanding but the envelopment of a mutual temptation, the rustle of reciprocal attractions—this is no doubt what appears when the day, idle in the midst of its tasks, seems to play with a frivolous power that makes it lighter and freer. I can say that I have witnessed this game, if it is a game. But if it is madness, I can see that I participate in it.

I don't think I've ever been unaware of it, I know I'm mixed up in a profound, static intrigue, one that I mustn't look at, or even notice, that I mustn't be occupied by and that nevertheless requires all my strength and all my time. I will say it again, there is no room around me for an anomaly. The anomaly would be diversion reduced to limits, perceptible and pacifying, though disquieting. But diversion is restless, it doesn't stop anywhere. It doesn't appear at one spot or another, it only causes appearances to be brighter, more evident and also more extensive, so that the boundaries themselves have the beautiful tranquility of the surface. A tranquility that is difficult to contain and, I'm convinced, very strange, even though nothing mysterious or reserved is hidden in it; on the contrary, what it portends is that the day is giving up its profound reserve. The day is without depth, I mean without reserve of future, without a bond with the day, it is untrammeled brightness, transparency extolling itself, a festival, a floating festival, a game in which haste, torment, and agitation are lost—and also definite calm and repose.

Maybe this movement was imperceptible, I don't know. I never saw anything in myself or outside myself that marked any change whatsoever. It's true that when there isn't any air, at a certain moment time becomes the air that breathing exhausts. But if my breath doesn't have any time, this isn't because time is limited, for it doesn't seem to have any limits any more, it is only more attenuated and poorer, and because of that unstable and fleeting. I think I can no longer lose my time, and for a peculiar reason, really, which is that it has already lost itself, having fallen below the things one can lose, having become unknowable, alien to the category of lost time. A mysterious impression, since I occupy myself with fewer and fewer things and yet I am always entirely occupied. What is more, I am subjected to a constant, extreme pressure to reduce my tasks even further, though they are already so far reduced. Surprising, instantaneous obviousness.

I think that time goes by, because after all the days go by, slip past, and with a joyful promptness in the heart of their tranquil light. But I see clearly that for me there is only less and less time at the instant where I am, which explains not why nothing happens, but why what happens is like the repetition of one and the same event—and yet not the same: it sinks to a lower and lower level, where it seems to wander rather in the manner of an image, even though it is absolutely present.

I spoke of an intrigue. It is true that this word is intended to fill a hopeless function, but even so, it expresses in its own way the feeling I have: that I am bound, not to a story, but to the fact that, as I am likely to have less and less of a story, this poverty, far from winning me simpler days, attracts what life I have left in a cruelly complex movement of which I know nothing, if not that it excites the impatience of a desire that doesn't want to wait any longer, as though I were supposed to make my way as soon as possible to the place it is urging me to come to, even though it consists precisely in distancing me from every end and forbidding me to go anywhere.

Anyone who wants to live has to rely on the illusion of a story, but this reliance is not permitted to me. I must recall this: such days are not devoted to an unknown misfortune, they don't confirm the distress of a moribund decision; on the contrary, they are traversed by joyful immensity, a radiant authority, luminescence, pure frivolity, too strong for the days, turning them into a pure dissipation and each event into the image of a displaced episode (an episode that is not in its place, a sort of farce of time, belonging to a different age, a lost and baffled fragment of history). I sometimes think: "I believe I'm going to suffocate from such a lack of memory," but forgetfulness has in no way passed over things. On the contrary, recollection is the ponderous form of this lack of memory. A terrible pause in which nothing stops. It may be that where I am, I have too much of a sort of courage (a sort of dread). This courage keeps me on my feet. I am not unaware that what I have searched for is searching for me at this hour. What I have looked at wants to look me in the face. But to remain on one's feet—how can one give that up? This will is mysterious. I also have the feeling that I am not only staying in my place—yes, with a certain absurd obstinacy, in my place, on my feet—but even more: I have become a little unstable, I move from spot to spot. Of course I don't take many steps, but when I go by, doors slam, the light air runs across the space. Anyone who meets me thinks, "So he is there, at present," but, immediately, "Oh! But here, now!" Is it night? The morning burns. I go down the stairs; again there is emptiness, the gaity of emptiness, the joyful shiver of space and no one, really, is there to notice it; it is true that I myself undoubtedly know something about this light and furtive thrust, about this roving air that hardly disturbs the expanse and that leads me here, and here, but it doesn't seem to concern me particularly; this is how the day is, an endless shimmer, footsteps wandering through the rooms, the muffled thumps of work.

Forgetfulness has not passed over things, but I must say this: that in the brightness where they glitter, in this brightness that doesn't destroy their limits, but unites the unlimited with a constant and joyful "I see you," they shine in the intimacy of a new beginning in which nothing else has a place; and as for me, through them I have the immobility and inconstancy of a reflection, an image wandering among images and drawn along with them in the monotony of a movement that appears to have no conclusion just as it had no beginning. Perhaps, when I get up, I have faith in the beginning: who would rise if he didn't know the day was beginning? But, even though I am still capable of taking many steps, which is why doors slam, windows open and, the light coming in once again, all things are also in their places, unalterable, joyful, definitely present, with a presence that is firm and even so definite and so constant that I know they are indelible, immobile in the glittering eternity of their images. But, seeing them there, where they are, slightly distanced from themselves within their presence, and transformed, by this imperceptible withdrawal, into the happy beauty of a reflection, even though I am still capable of taking many steps, I too can do no more than come and go in the tranquil immobility of my own image, bound to the floating festival of an instant that no longer passes. It may seem astonishing that I should descend so far from myself, into a place one could, I think, call the abyss, and that it should only have surrendered me to the joyful space of a festival, the eternal glitter of an image, and I would be surprised by this too, if I had not felt the burden of this indefatigable lightness, the infinite weight of a sky in which what one sees remains there, where the boundaries sprawl out and the distance shines night and day with the radiance of a beautiful surface.

How terrible things are, when they come out of themselves, into a resemblance in which they have neither the time to corrupt themselves nor the origin to find themselves and where, eternally their own likenesses, they do not affirm themselves but rather, beyond the dark flux and reflux of repetition, affirm the absolute power of this resemblance, which is no one's and which has no name and no face. That is why it is terrible to love and we can love only what is most terrible. To bind oneself to a reflection—who would consent to that? But to bind oneself to what has no name and no face and to give that endless, wandering resemblance the depth of a mortal instant, to lock oneself up with it and thrust it along with oneself to the place where all resemblance yields and is shattered—that is what passion wants. I can say that I bound myself to the immobility that passes both through the night and through the day, the calm phosphorescence of an instant that does not know the eclipse of shadows, that is not extinguished, does not illuminate, for it reveals nothing, is the sparkling happiness of a ray, but this immobility also wanders everywhere, and perhaps I would better tolerate an obviousness that I would never have a hope of seeing elsewhere, a monumental column before which one would remain standing, but this perpetual movement, this infinite caprice, this pursuit that leaves me in the same place and yet makes me keep changing place leads me to believe in a true movement, a movement that is alive and seeks life, even if it is enveloped in the power and the immobility of destiny. Each day, or at least certain days, but also each period of time and each movement of the day shows me, through the radiant space, the flight of a free image soaring from a point that I can't see toward another point that I can't see, and for me both no doubt merge, it is a fixed ascension, full of splendor, but also a dark effort, a cold fantasy, always the same and always futile, out of which likeness comes to affirm likeness, without this amazing activity being able to do anything more than give me the strength to follow the image instant by instant, an image myself, projected into the fire of appearances, as if, in expressing ourselves through each other, both of us were pursuing the possibility of giving an empty point the luster and the living value of a real meaning. And certainly, the point remains empty, in the same way that even though this can keep beginning again, the beginning always remains silent and unknown, but—and this is the strange thing—I don't worry about it and I go on seizing the instant again with an incredible avidity, the same instant through which I seem to catch sight of this glimmer: someone is there who is not speaking, who is not looking at me, yet who is capable of an entrancing life and cheerfulness, though that cheerfulness is also the echo of a supreme event reverberating through the infinite lightness of time, where it cannot settle.

I can't say I'm always conscious of it, of this glimmer, I would probably have to recognize that it often leaves me free, but, how shall I put it, this glimmer is freedom in me, a freedom that tears apart all bonds, that abolishes all tasks, that allows me to live in the world, but on condition that I am almost no one there, and if I have actually seen myself reduced to the transparency of a being one doesn't encounter, this is because little by little it has relieved me of myself, of my character, of the serious and active affirmation that my character represented. What am I, for it? Someone living in the world? With whom it agrees? A face? But it can't dwell in the world, and I know—in the depths of an ignorance, I admit, that can't take this into consideration—that it has the strength of a single instant, that it knows me but doesn't recognize me, that it touches me, and the future is not bound to it but unbound from it. A face? Where it sees me there may be a face, but enveloped, enclosed in the eternity of a reflection, if it is true that the shadow of things is the shining resemblance into which they withdraw and which throws them back infinitely from likeness to likeness.

I think that this is the absolutely dark moment of the plot, the point at which it keeps returning to the present, at which I can no longer either forget or remember, at which human events, around a center as unstable and immobile as myself, indefinitely construct their return. I can recall which road I was made to take by this and how I broke with almost everything—and in this sense too I have forgotten everything— why, as far away as I am, I have to draw back and draw back again into the heart of the instant where I wander like an image bound to a day that passes immobile through the day and to a time that at a certain point always disengages itself from time. I can recall that, however long this road may be and whatever may be its detours through the futile repetition of days and of moments, nothing can prevent it from being once again and yet again the hallway that separated the two small rooms and that I happened to enter: a vacillating darkness where I had to endure the greatest pain and yet came upon the truest and most joyful moment, as though what I had stumbled against was not the cold truth, but the truth transformed into the violence and the passion of the end. I can recall all that, and to recall it is no doubt only one more step into that same space, where to go farther is already to bind myself to the return. And yet, even though the circle is already drawing me along, and even if I had to write this eternally, I would write it in order to obliterate eternity: Now, the end.

The One Who Was Standing Apart From Me

✦

I sought, this time, to approach him. I mean I tried to make him understand that, although I was there, still I couldn't go any farther, and that I, in turn, had exhausted my resources. The truth was that for a long time now I had felt I was at the end of my strength.

"But you're not," he pointed out.

About this, I had to admit he was right. For my part, I was not. But the thought that perhaps I did not have "my part" in mind made it a bitter consolation. I tried to put it another way.

"I would like to be." A manner of speaking which he avoided taking seriously; at least, he didn't take it with the seriousness that I wanted to put into it. It probably seemed to him to deserve more than a wish. I continued to reflect on what "I wanted." I had noticed that he was interested in facts, he became more exacting and perhaps more sincere when it was possible to speak to him in the language everyone spoke, and that language certainly seemed to be the language of facts. Yet the obstacle was that—just then—events seemed to have receded extraordinarily. He came to my assistance in his own way.

"It seems to me," I said, "that in a sense I have everything, except..."

"Except?"

I had the impression he was more attentive now, even though that attention was not directed at me, but was, instead, a silent direction, a hope for himself, a sort of daybreak which, finally, revealed nothing more than the word "except." A little more, nevertheless, for I was induced to add:

"Except that I would like to be rid of it."

I believe that, despite everything, I expected from him an invitation to go forward, and perhaps also a risk, an obstacle. I wasn't fighting, but

I wasn't yielding either, yielding would have required more strength than I had. I can't deny that the need to talk to him, and most often to be the first to talk—as though what I had was the initiative, while he had the discretion, the concern to leave me free, though even that might have been only impotence on his part, and consequently impotence on my part too—this need seemed to me so exhausting, so tormenting, that often I didn't even have enough real strength left to make use of it. I didn't have the feeling that talking was in the least necessary to him, or pleasant, or unpleasant either. He always displayed an extreme loyalty; with the greatest firmness he brought me back from a word that was less true to a word that was more true. Sometimes I wondered if he was not trying to restrain me at all cost. I came to believe that he had always barred my way, even though, if he showed any intention, it was, rather, that of helping me to be done with it. According to him—but I must add that he never declared this to me with as much precision as I am doing—I came closest to his help when I made up my mind to write. He had assumed a strange ascendancy over me in all these thing, so that I had allowed myself to be persuaded that to write was the best way of making our relations bearable. I admit that for some time this way was quite good. But one day I noticed that what I was writing concerned him more and more and, though in an indirect manner, seemed to have no other purpose but to reflect him. I was extremely struck by this discovery. In it I saw what might paralyze me the most, not because I would henceforth try to avoid this reflection, but because, on the contrary, I might go to more trouble to make it manifest. It was then that I caught hold of myself. I knew—but I did not exactly know it, I hoped—that the need to say "I" would allow me to have better mastery over my relations with this reflection. I think personal honesty, personal truth, seemed to me to have something specific about them, capable of momentarily giving me the security of a point of view. Nevertheless, the consequences for my life were disastrous. Not only did I have to give up what is called a normal life, but I lost control of my choices. I also became afraid of words and I wrote fewer and fewer of them, even though the pressure exerted inside myself to make me write them soon became dizzying. I speak of fear, but it was a completely different feeling, a sort of erosion of the future, the impression that I had already said more about it than was possible for me, that I had gotten ahead of myself in such a way that the possibility farthest in the future was already there, a future I could no longer go beyond. At the same time, I forced myself into the fiction of a legal life. I don't know if such a concern wasn't a mistake. My intention was to do nothing that could surprise and interest the world to the extent that it was aware of my conduct and my way of being. This compelled me into all sorts of subterfuges and even a general lie on which, I fear, much of my strength was spent and which, in turn, incited me to stiffen myself excessively against the most innocent activities. In addition to these difficulties, which I am rapidly passing over, there was another, and that was that they did not help me in any way to settle my relations with him, relations in view of which, nevertheless—and thinking, perhaps at his suggestion, that writing was the place where I could be the least bothered by his presence—I had little by little put myself in an almost intolerable situation.

In truth, it was possible that for some time he had been giving me considerable help. He had put me to my task by creating a void around that task and probably by letting me believe that the task would be able to limit and circumscribe the void. This was really how it was, in fact, at least apparently, and even though during the same time I had to go through events so terrible that it would be better to say they went through me and they are still, ceaselessly, going through me, I enjoyed a strange illusion that allowed me not to see that already I should no longer be speaking of task, but of life. This illusion represented a diversion, but also a power that I had acquired for myself. Unconcern was the only gift by which I was capable of drawing it with me into the broad daylight. A moment's success, but in no way diminished by that, since success consisted precisely in joining life and moment. Once the moment was past, the unconcern died away, but the face it had illuminated did not die away, or its manner of darkening was that darkness also became its face. There too, it is possible that he helped me by turning me away from responsibility for the world, by wrapping me in an ambiguous silence that depended as much on my refusal to converse with him as on the fact that in truth, without realizing it, I spoke to him constantly through this very refusal. A help which, if it occurred, consisted in turning my attention away from an event, and an image, with which I could never have behaved in a way that was natural and real, reserved and discreet, without a state of half attention and almost of indifference. But if writing turned me into a shadow to make me worthy of the darkness, I must certainly also think that this maneuver succeeded more than it should have, for I pushed reserve and discretion so far, from this point of view, that not only did I do nothing to trouble those moments, but they did not trouble me either, so that my memory of them makes me wander tragically in the void. All this, all these events, which are so difficult to recapture and grow indistinct through their own presence, all these difficulties, these demands, these efforts, and now this immobility, from which my desire has more and more trouble preserving me, this situation, which is so strange but has become so familiar to me that I can almost no longer refuse to understand it—was all this destined to result in that one sentence: "I sought, this time, to approach him"? "This time," I saw clearly how unjustified such a remark seemed. It appeared there because I wanted to be at the end of my strength. But for my part, I was not, and for such a part "this time" was not "this time," but another time, a time that was always another. I can't hide the fact that the desire to approach him could only with great difficulty be reconciled with the idea that this could ever take place "this time." He did nothing to ward off such an event. It may even be that he awaited it with a sort of hope. But I felt that the whole enterprise was entrusted to me alone, and I must say I wasn't managing it, I wasn't managing it.

"You get by well enough," he remarked. "You're astonishing, you know."

Yes, I got by quite well, but this in itself cast a not very engaging light on everything I could imagine doing; I got by all too well, whereas the best that could have happened to me would have been not to get by at all.

He did not fail to encourage me, but in his own way, and that way was strange, discouraging, for it consisted in assuring me that I had all the time in the world. No doubt the sort of decision inaugurated by my desperate and arbitrary recourse to "this time" implied that until now I had never yet approached him in a spirit of preoccupation, intention, not to say inquisition. I retained the memory of not having done so, not out of fear, but because "I didn't have the time" and simply because I didn't concern myself about it. If I now had all the time in the world, it was therefore because I had given up all other interests but him and in fact all interests, for—and this was the ludicrous aspect of the situation—I couldn't interest myself in him, I could only accord him this lack of interest, this sadness of my inattention that made every presence sterile. He accommodated himself to this, of course, but he seemed to doubt it also, even though in expressing his doubt he never went farther than this phrase:

"Oh, it's not such a necessary thing!"

And what he meant by that had this rather edifying sense:

"Oh, I am not so interested in myself!"

It's true that I could derive another, more convincing inference from his mysterious words of encouragement, that on the whole I didn't have to be afraid of the false steps, the itineraries of error; I didn't have just one road, I had them all, and this should, in fact, have encouraged me to start on my way with an exceptional confidence.

"All of them! But on condition that I have all the time in the world, as long as I have all the time in the world."

He didn't deny it, for it was clearly understood that the characteristic of a road was to provide a shortcut through "time"; it was this shortcut I was looking for, with the unreasonable idea that in it I would find, not what would still be a very long tramp, but the shortest interval, the essence of brevity, to the point that, from the first steps, it seemed to me, refusing to go farther, that I had the right to say to myself: "I'm staying here," and that was what I said to him with greater firmness: "I'm staying here, I'm stopping here," to which he happened precisely to respond with a sort of enthusiasm and without my being able to take it the wrong way: "But you have all the time in the world."

From him, I couldn't take anything the wrong way. I didn't know where or how all this was going to end. He had become my travelling companion, but I couldn't assert that we had everything in common, or else that community would have signified that he had everything in common with me and I nothing with him if we had not clearly tended to have nothing, either one of us. I couldn't attribute bad intentions to him, for he was extraordinarily lacking in intentions. I supposed he was helping me, but I should say his help was such that it left me, more than anything else, at a loss, unfit, and indifferent to being helped in any way, and only a sort of obstinacy permitted me to think that this assistance could be called help and even the greatest possible help. True, I did not always recognize this. I had noted with surprise, with a slight feeling of strangeness, but eventually with discomfort and without surprise, that he was probably lacking enough in intentions to deflect my own, to lead them to the point where they would have to identify with this deflection. I could recall, as an intoxicating navigation, the motion that had more than once driven me toward a goal, toward a land that I did not know and was not trying to reach, and I did not complain that in the end there was neither land nor goal, because, in the meantime, by this very motion, I had lost my memory of the land, I had lost it, but I had also gained the possibility of going forward at random, even though, in fact, consigned to this randomness, I had to renounce the hope of ever stopping. The consolation could have been to say to myself: You have renounced foreseeing, not the unforeseeable. But the consolation turned around like a barb: the unforeseeable was none other than the renouncement itself, as though each event, in order to reach me, in that region where we were navigating together, had demanded of me the promise that I would slip out of my story. This, unfortunately, applied to everything and to the most simple things, those with which, at certain moments, I was prepared to be content. I may say that I had the day at my disposal, but on condition that it should not be this day and, even more, that this one should be in part forgotten, should be the sun of forgetfulness.

All else failing, the idea of assigning to him directly the means that he himself had put at my disposal or that had obliged me to have him at my disposal, to make a place for him that I could no longer measure: I would have liked him to give his opinion of such a plan. But to my surprise, he seemed to ignore my question completely. I must point out that, though he rarely spoke about himself, he gave as little impression as possible of neglecting the person speaking to him: he listened in silence, but in such a way that his silences were not inert, though no doubt slightly suffocating, as if they consisted in repeating in a more distant world, repeating exactly, syllable for syllable, everything one was trying to make him understand. At least—and in fact it did happen that his refusal to answer was not a refusal, but contributed to pursuing the conversation, to obliging it to prolong itself beyond all measure, to wear itself down to such a degree, through repetition and obstinacy, that it could only continue and continue on—if he did not answer, he also did not go on to another subject, for in some way he had to content himself with the paths I drew for him, I mean he no doubt felt he had done his duty sufficiently by giving me my cue. For the moment, he did not give it to me; on the contrary, he asked, as though to put me on the wrong track, and after a silence that increased the volume of the question: "Tell me, won't it be winter soon?"

To say that I stumbled over what he had said would not be saying much. I felt I was passing through one world after another. I could have absorbed myself in it for days, and perhaps I would have, if the thought that at no price should the thread be broken had not brought me back to the necessity of answering, unfortunately to question in my turn: "What winter are you talking about?"

"Well, ours, naturally."

"Ours?"

I remained suspended on that fascinating shared season: "Do you mean that I won't have enough time to..."

It was not that I was afraid to give a name to what I wanted to do, but I already saw his answer, the one that came back in the manner of a joyful promise and did not need much to be lured: "Oh, but you have all the time in the world."

But that answer did not come, and the one that came was in every respect astonishing:

"I mean: aren't you expecting company until then?"

Yes, it was astonishing, and this time I could not overcome my astonishment, except to repeat: "Company? People?"—which led him to repeat, also: "People, people!" in a way that dismissed the conversation, that obliged me to consider that it would not resume except from a completely different source that I would now have to look for. I certainly had something to think about. But I had even more to be quiet about, and that was what was important: the possibility of remaining firmly in one spot, without moving.

I would have liked to think he could remain there too, for, even though he spoke of a place that seemed to be the center of the calm and even though he seemed at certain moments terribly restful, he was, in fact, restful in a terrible way. If I left him to himself, I did not forget him, but I soon lacked the strength to think of him, I was left with nothing but thought, and thinking was what could make our relations most sterile.

"Can I reflect on it?"

"Yes, of course. But for how long?"

"Oh, only a moment!"

He certainly didn't oppose it, but the fact that he added: "What shall we do while you're reflecting?" showed that he wanted to keep himself at a distance from "reflection" and that he didn't want to leave me entirely in it. I couldn't suggest to him that to reflect signified his distance, the faculty of interrupting motion by which what I said escaped me, hastened toward a strange point from which I wasn't sure I could make it come back. But the truth was that his distance really did signify reflection, and to hope to draw near him by dint of reflection did not put hope on a very good path. Nevertheless, I didn't abandon this path altogether. I could say where it was leading me: it was stagnation, empty perseverance, and even stupor, but starting from there, I imagined I had acquired enough heaviness to be able to go forward again, even though reflection consisted above all in repeating: You haven't reflected enough yet (you must become heavier). He himself was far from being without logic, he had a sort of fierce singleness of mind which, because it apparently did not want to lead to anything, represented an almost formidable power, a power one couldn't combat except by suspiciously attributing to it goals, aims, and in this way an extraordinary muddle was developing whose approach, whose threat, I had sensed more than once. I could criticize myself severely for having so often, when faced with the sense of that power, sought refuge in reflection, by asking: "Can I reflect on it?"—which could only assure me "a moment," but at least that moment prevented the circle from closing, restrained me from closing it myself.

I didn't stay long in the place where I had arrived. The feeling of possessing something infinitely important went hand in hand with the impression that I wasn't taking advantage of it, and even though with use, the importance was almost surely destined to dissipate, I had no other way of keeping it alive. "Company, people"—I repeated these words, my words, to myself, words followed, with a joyful force, by his: "People, people!" without his ever betraying the desire to go farther. I couldn't hope to wear out his patience. I could wear out my own, I could wander from place to place, from window to window, to draw support from the outside, but this digression was futile, this coming and going took me back to the same point where I found him again, always more firmly anchored. In this I suffered a monstrous

constraint. I may say that if I had little by little broken with everything, in fact this constraint itself signified the rupture, and I saw only
too clearly that it had overcome my resistance, my will, but I had
gained nothing by it, because for me defeat had taken the worst form
by transforming my broken character into a stiffness impossible to
wear out, an "I'm stopping here, I'm staying here" which paralleled,
which confirmed, its own obstinacy. The fact that he had led me to
break with everything, as though with the promise that now the field
would be open to us, certainly represented the type of illusion for
which I could not hold him responsible, but only myself. It is true
that when I associated with company, he seemed to keep himself at a
distance because of the company, and the need to put an end to an
unfortunate duality, to avail myself of a single loyalty, a single truth,
had little by little pushed me gently, ineluctably—where I was. As a
result, company was lacking but the distance remained, even though
there was nothing left to make us feel it, and, what was more, it didn't
even remain, for it was only one of the forms of this open field which
I alone was to roam. The strange thing was that at this very moment I
believed I recalled what his words were alluding to and how they had
to be answered, but this was also what I wanted to avoid, I wanted
something else, I wanted it with a will that was weak, without capacity, without light, a will that was only an agitated flight through the
house. There is a hunger that is unacquainted with hunger, and it was
this that caused my silence, a silence equal to his, avid, a desert, whereas
his seemed to be fullness and balance, but I lived in the desert. I remember a period when I would constantly ask him a question I could
only address to him from the depths of my unconcern:

"Do you know that?"—to which he would respond:

"Yes, it's true, I know it very well," and from these answers I derived a joyful pleasure, a strange cheerfulness, the impression that this
reduplication was not the frame of the memory but the opening of
space. At present, I lacked unconcern, I remained silent. I certainly
wanted him to speak, but not in order to say, as he so often did, almost at random: "Well another day has passed, hasn't it?"—because
for whom had it passed? I could have asked him this, but he couldn't
have answered that it had passed for us: it would pass later, perhaps; as
I waited, I bore the weight of it and I didn't bear the fruit of it. I
couldn't help expressing my reservation:

"Passed? but for whom? I'm asking myself that."

"Ah! One can certainly ask oneself that."

I keenly pushed my advantage: "Why do you repeat that phrase?"

"Do I repeat it?"—and he seemed less surprised than eager to allow me, in turn, to repeat my protest, to lead me to intensify it a shade by saying: "Yes, you repeat it all the time. Yes, I'm tired of it and you ought to stop doing it"—words I kept to myself, and I was rewarded for that, in a way, because he made this remark:

"But it's to help you."

I tried to explain to myself why the word "help" directed such a sharp point at me, as though he had actually said to me:

"You know, I can do nothing for you but repeat that from time to time."

I didn't succeed in emerging from that feeling, and of everything useful I could have pointed out to him on this subject, all that occurred to me was this remark, which circumvented his own:

"That helps me?"

Which he answered right away with a joyful urgency that was also a reminder of his own fate:

"It helps both of us!"

"You too? You mean we're connected?"

He seemed prepared to study the question, but the examination promptly led to these words:

"Well, you know that very well!"—which were addressed to me in a tone that returned me to myself.

In fact, I didn't know it. I knew there was neither understanding nor community of interest nor anything that corresponded to the idea that we were connected. It only seemed to me that I was in control of that idea, and that as a consequence, I was a judge of the reality of those connections: it depended on me, it depended on me so completely that all that could be said about it was "you know that very well," so that it ought to have been easy to arrive at a certainty on this point, if one difficulty had not remained, which was that for my part, in fact, I did not know it. This feeling gave me the strength to ask him:

"It was a long time ago that we met, wasn't it?"

He seemed to want to measure this time, conscientiously, and the result was a long silence, an abnormally long silence, which seemed destined to fulfill my expectation, soothe it, and perhaps make me pronounce other words, but since I said nothing, he answered in a slightly disappointing way:

"It wasn't so very long ago..."

In the meantime, during this silence, I had changed my idea, and I formulated this new idea with real energy: "But everything depends on what is meant by the word 'meet.'"

He immediately agreed: "Yes! Everything depends on that." I went on: "Perhaps it would be better to say that soon we will meet in earnest."

Which he confirmed without hesitation:

"Soon—I think so too."

"But," I continued, "isn't 'soon' 'now'?"

"That's it—now, whenever you like."

A dialogue which I felt was so disappointing, so uselessly closed only through my own fault and also through the fact that my words—and the same was true of his—could only return to their point of departure; why? if I had known that, a great burden would have been lifted from me. I imagined it had to do with time. After all, we were talking, but perhaps everything had been said, and what I went on saying was incapable of consuming any time, also incapable of stopping it, freezing it. But why had everything been said?—between us? This explained his way of being, his patience, and the feeling of distress that seemed to me the mark, the sincerity of our relations. When I alluded to a meeting, I could only be alluding to that "everything has been said" which was the truth of it, and it was quite immaterial, dangerously immaterial, whether it had taken place a long time ago or not so very long ago or even "then," a "then" that compromised the future, since all these words were only one of the forms of our meeting, forms whose choice was given up to me with a "whenever you like" whose cruel transparency I understood. Then I made this remark, which showed how little importance I attached to my "reflections":

"Aren't we too close to each other now?"

But, as though to concede that I was right, he limited himself to asking in turn:

"Too close?"

"Yes," I said, "too close: I'm not thrusting you away, I probably wouldn't have the strength to, I don't have the desire to either. I mean that if this desire exists, it doesn't succeed in making a choice between you and me. Can I make this choice? That's the question I'm asking you."

He appeared astonished by this flood of words, whose disorderly and demanding quality made them seem more like the force of breathing than like words and, in fact—a coincidence I might have reflected upon—I noticed that the wind, as though it had taken over from them or as though I had found in its power the memory of my decision, had at that moment begun to blow, a harsh, cold wind, as often prevailed in those regions of the South. Even he appeared to notice it.

"At least," he said, "at least...."

I can't explain why those two words did me some good, perhaps they reduced my tension, perhaps they expressed to me something about his nature; I didn't linger over them for long, because he added:

"We want to be reasonable, we want to wait," and after a moment that marked something like his hesitation at a threshold:

"Isn't this house pleasant?"

I answered briefly: "Yes, it is."

My dryness didn't stop him from wanting to dig deeper into the ground, and "dig" expressed exactly, I believe, what he wanted: to find out what foundations we were built on:

"It is!" he said. "Would you find it tiresome to describe it to me—yet again?"

I have to confess that even though I understood the extraordinary assistance he was giving me, I was put on my guard by his last words, which almost mechanically forced me to answer.

"I can't do it."

But he didn't allow himself to be discouraged:

"Together we could do it."

"Together?"

"You know," he said with a sort of fervor, "I would like to do something for you, I would like to do everything for you."

"Everything?"

The silence that followed was equal to that "everything": I felt that I should sink into it, but what I also felt was that at the same time I should make everything around me that was still solid slide into it.

I must have remained in the same place for a long time (I was standing at the bottom of the staircase, but I probably sat down on one of the steps a little later). Because of this last cry, something of me had been taken from myself; I touched the outside more, I also touched it less, I looked at the room, which seemed to extend quite far, I couldn't see its limits very clearly, I remembered the space instead, as I remembered myself. I stood up to go to the kitchen for a glass of water, but I must have mistaken the door, I saw below me a dimly lit, disorderly room which I didn't have the strength to go down into (probably the store-room).

I found myself again a little farther on. I heard a door bang, no doubt the one I must not have closed behind me, which the wind was flinging back. But this noise seemed very distant to me. Everything was extraordinarily calm. Looking out through the large bay windows—there were three of them—I saw that someone was standing on the other side; as soon as I noticed him, he turned to the window and, without pausing where I was, stared rapidly, with an intense but rapid gaze, at the whole expanse and depth of the room. I was perhaps in the center of it. I couldn't see clearly the garden that had to be outside, but I recalled it with great vividness, with a force that resembled desire. I could make out what was around it. While I was inside that image, I tried to look again, a little farther, to see if someone was still there, but I didn't succeed, or not altogether. Yet I remembered these words: "People, people," which led me to say, softly:

"I think someone is there."

"Someone? Here?"

"Just now someone was looking through the window."

"Through the window?"

Words spoken in a tone of voice so uncommon, so quiet, that I in turn began to feel a kind of fear. What frightened me was that he seemed to repeat my words without altogether understanding them, and this thought occurred to me: Does he know what a window is?

"Someone who was outside looking into the room."

"Here?"

"Where we are."

He said, again:

"Who was it?"

"I don't know, I didn't see him well enough."

"And did he see you?"

I reflected. I don't know why, but this question caused me some anguish; all I could say to him was:

"Perhaps he didn't see me, perhaps he didn't see anyone."

At that moment I felt a weariness—to use that word—that bore into space, that sought to substitute for it another, thinner space, an empty, rootless air. Yet I heard him go on to say to me:

"You know, we should remain alone, we are alone."

It may be that some time went by, a time that was also airless and rootless. I was still thirsty, I had sat down next to a table, and when I heard him murmur, "This is a moment that will pass," I confused those words with these others: "Another day has passed, hasn't it?"; and that memory made me shiver, something in me broke. I had endured so many struggles, I had been so far—and where was "so far"? Here, next to a table. Perhaps my silence, my immobility, and the feeling that a kind of balance had been established between us, restored some of my strength to me; perhaps, on the contrary, I had gained in weakness; at a certain moment, I found myself in the room again, and beyond the table, in the spot where I had said to myself that the end had to be situated, there was a wall and, I believe, a mirror, at least a lightly shining surface. I tried to recognize this spot— was this where I had just been? was this me? In any case, at present the person who happened to be there was also leaning on a table. Thirst, the need to exhaust the space, made me stand up. Everything was extraordinarily calm. Looking at the large bay windows—there were three of them—I saw that someone was standing on the other side; as soon as I noticed him, he turned to the window and, without pausing where I was, he stared intensely at the expanse and depth of the room. I was still next to the table, I wanted to turn around quickly to face this figure, but I was surprised that I was now very near the windows and yet felt I was still in the middle of the room. This forced me to look strangely at a point that was not given to me, closer than it seemed to me, close in an almost frightening way, for it did not take into account my own distance. While I looked for the figure almost randomly, I noticed, in a flash—a flash that was the shining, tranquil light of summer—that I was holding this figure against my eyes, a few steps away, the few steps that must still have separated me from the bay windows, and the impression was so vivid that it was like a spasm of brightness, a shiver of cold light. I was so struck that I couldn't help murmuring:

"Don't move, I think someone is there."

"Someone? Here?"

"Someone is looking at us through the window."

"Through the window?"

Words which immediately gave me a feeling of dread, horror, as though the emptiness of the window were reflected in them, as though all this had already taken place, and once again, once again. I think I cried out, I slipped or fell against what seemed to me to be the table. Yet I heard him say to me again:

"You know, there is no one there."

I retained a memory of this that resembled the space in which I stood up again a little later. Yet I was rational enough to lean on the table, slowly follow its edge, and in this way I went a little farther. It was now much darker, although the little daylight that remained had an exceptional reality, as if outside me. It was this daylight that held me firmly against the wall, did not allow me to move away from it, as though, according to it, all the danger, which also had the force of a ruinous desire, was situated somewhere more in the middle of the room. The path, a narrow margin, led me—where it wanted, to another spot, where I too, no doubt, wanted to be led, at another moment, but when I reached it, I thought right away that it was the kitchen I had already been looking for. What struck me was a little wall that divided it, a partition over which one's gaze passed joyously: it was like a reserve, an unexpected gaiety of space, an emptiness within an emptiness. The place had the gayest appearance, a brightness poured down into it which, in contrast to the place I had come from, evoked the most certain moment of the day, a midday freed of the seasons and the hours. A silent light, however, which, as I saw, entered through a small kitchen window. What struck me further was that here I recognized all the disorder of a life that was habitual to me: I must have eaten here, at this table, only a few moments before—a glass, a bottle, a pharmaceutical tube. As I recalled my thirst, I wanted to drink, but the bottle was empty.

The strength that had brought me this far deserted me at this moment. I asked him (this happened when I found myself in front of the table, with its disorder intact): "What do you think of this room?"

"It's nice."

"It's strange, isn't it?"

"No, it's nice."

"At the moment, you have two rooms at your disposal."

A remark which he greeted with good humor:

"I certainly expect to have others too."

"And I?"

"Well, you will have them along with me."

I didn't want to raise any objections, what I wanted took an unexpected form:

"Do you know where I was before I came here?"

"Yes," he said, "actually I know very well."

"So you don't think I've always been here?"

I tried to think about my question, which gave me such a breadth of uncertainty, such a depth of sadness and forgetfulness that I had to complete it, shortly afterwards, with this other one:

"Do you mean I've moved away, moved farther and farther away? but why? what could possibly have occurred? what has happened?"

"I wonder."

This phrase, a sort of parenthesis in which time circulated, struck me, even though he often used it, for it suddenly seemed to have a meaning I hadn't seen so clearly until now, and this induced me to add:

"Do you mean it hasn't happened yet?"

But I sensed it, my question came too late, it could only strike—gently—against the foggy presence of that remark, through which he reaffirmed himself, though not without apprehension:

"Yes, I wonder about that."

I tried, in turn, to wonder about it; for a moment I thought I was succeeding—and the place where I arrived was nothing less than that beautiful bright spot, the kitchen, for whose sake I had broken the silence and which I looked at now as though it had been the space open to the one who wondered about it. Was it here?

He didn't answer, but the silence closed on me again as though he had said: there is no "here" for such a pain. I felt it immediately, I was tied to that pain, it too had closed on me again, it had its space, its walls, its tranquil light. Yes, it was a peaceful summer, that pain, and perhaps it had brought me here, but "here," though everything in it seemed as completely motionless as in a place where nothing happens, could not be here. I remained here nevertheless. It seems to me that remaining was also what the pain wanted, and I believe I had the impression it needed me for that; but, at the same time, it drew me powerfully, with a strength I wouldn't be able to describe. I saw the door, slightly open: beyond, the darkness, the half-light, of the room, farther beyond, the center of the room. I must say, now, that I had this thought: that my companion knew more about it than I, it was possible, that he had relations with it that made me believe that with his help I could understand it better, make it even more transparent and myself more transparent in it, it was a diffuse manifestness, a tempting light toward which truth itself drove me, but nevertheless I could not unite them in myself, I couldn't do it; on the contrary, they seemed to me as unknown to each other as I was perhaps close to both of them. This was, in a way, the most terrible thing about it: one can't really disappear when one must die in two separate worlds. What added to the temptation to appeal to him was that since I was talking to him and he was answering me, I was ahead and in any case directed toward him, engaged in the promise he had put at the center of things, in a sense, by declaring to me that he "wanted to do everything for me," a promise by which I was so completely surrounded that it, too, was the space in which I was moving. Eventually I asked him:

"I spoke of you as a companion. Isn't that a thoughtless word?"

"I might be your companion? Whom did you say that to?"

"To myself, while I was reflecting."

"I don't think I'm behind that word, I think you shouldn't use it."

"But don't you remember what you promised me?"

"Do I remember it? Deeply, warmly—I wouldn't forget it so quickly."

I turned toward that reticence, it was not disappointing, but attractive, it was like a kind of timidity, perhaps because it slipped away into memory. It was this—I was not fooled by it—that committed me to going farther, to saying to him:

"Wouldn't it be more convenient if I could name you?"

"You would like to give me a name?"

"Yes, at this moment I would like to." And when he did not answer: "Wouldn't that make things easier? Don't we have to come to that?"

But he still seemed to be dwelling on his question:

"Give me a name? But why?"

"I don't know exactly: maybe to lose my own."

Which, strangely enough, caused him to recover his good humor:

"Oh, you won't get out of it that way!"

A reply which, I understood very well, summoned my own, awaited my own:

"But I don't want to get out of it."

And to avoid that expectation which sought to beguile in me words that had already been spoken, I had to make an effort that resulted in this question:

"Aren't there already many words between us?"

"Yes, certainly, many writings."

Then I remarked with some incoherence:

"You mean there shouldn't be any name between us?'

"Yes, that's it," but he added, with a lack of connection that showed that my own had not escaped him:

"You know, words should not frighten us."

Perhaps I didn't always realize it, since he unfailingly answered me with great good will, but to address him, hear him—and also to maintain our direction toward a goal I couldn't see, that I only sensed— took more strength than I had: a silent strength that assumed I had already freely abandoned my own and yet required of me—or was this a mistake, a trap?—the affirmation, reduced to the tightest transparency, that my presence was still maintained. I wasn't fighting against an adversary, nor was this a fight; I wasn't defending myself and I wasn't attacking anyone, no one was attacking me. If he had made my life an infinite torment and an infinite task, this was perhaps because of the infinite complicity I had constantly found in him, without being aware of it, I could only mention to him the limit I wanted to place in front of me: was this conversation going to stop abruptly yet again? hadn't I already said to him what I now had to answer him once more?

"I am tired of your presence."

"To such a point?"

"Yes to such a point, to such a point, as you hear me say."

He let some time go by. I had the feeling he was preparing to say: "What should I do?"—and I was ready to turn that question around: "What can you do?"

But he skipped ahead oddly:

"Is it at this point that we should become connected in a more real way? You wish for something of that sort, don't you?"

I couldn't deny it, I had wished for it; when? just a short time before; perhaps I no longer wanted it now. But he took no notice of my hesitations:

"And you would like to be connected in order to be able to disconnect yourself too?"

Yes I had also had that thought, but I had had to move away from it because of its form:

"It isn't as clear as that," and he confirmed this right away:

"That would be of little use to us, that would stop us pointlessly."

"Stop us?"

"Yes, but pointlessly."

I was close to admitting this, perhaps too quickly, for, as though to keep me on that slope of agreement, he said to me with an intimacy, an impetuosity, that was almost crazy:

"You have drawn me to you in a powerful way: aren't you speaking, aren't you hearing me? Isn't our element the same? What do you want? To leave this element?"

I could only say to him:

"When you speak that way, I feel closer to you."

"Close to you, close to what is close to you, not to me."

"Not to you? And yet," I said desperately, "you have just pointed it out—I'm speaking to you."

"You're speaking!" he cried brusquely in a tone of incredible scorn that seemed to me to come from a different mouth—oh, from an infinite past. I was tied to the spot.

As far as I could understand, I heard—and no doubt almost immediately—the shock of a muffled sound, the powerful banging of a door. The wind! That thought carried me out of the room in a motion I was only aware of when I found myself in a darker spot. I was seized by an immense need to act. The insistence, the return of the wind exercised an obvious authority over me. This need expressed the empty haste of the outdoors, responded to an appeal, a need to wander that falsified and confused space. It was a sort of rest: far from here, far from here and yet here. I could just as well have believed I was in a deserted place—but there was a difference I tried to perceive; I did not strain at it, I saw it well enough to be fascinated by it: it was that if I moved here and there, if at present I impersonally performed my tasks—I had turned on the lights, I had closed the door to the storeroom—this possibility of wandering, this work meant that somewhere, elsewhere, I had in fact been "tied to the spot." But when? For the moment, I could hardly think about it, I didn't even feel any disturbance, or only a slight impersonal uneasiness, as though, for me, fear was the fear that I risked causing in someone else. Yes, I recalled his reply, the violence of his repudiation, by which he had apparently tried to break me, but I could not "take it badly," I could only acknowledge that he was right, I who alone was still right, and exactly what had happened? Surely, this went farther back; surely, when this had been said, something quite different had come to light through this remark, had sought a way out, something older, dreadfully old, which had perhaps even taken place at all times, and at all times I was tied to the spot. This seemed to me to explain why I could now come and go in this room, doing the things one habitually does—I had opened a cupboard, I ate quickly, then, when I was finished, I went to draw the curtains over the large bay windows. In any case, I had the feeling that I was less mistaken about all these motions, about the person performing them, who, now, was climbing the stairs and, I imagine, going to bed. To see him disappear was not, properly speaking, strange, since it was myself. But I cannot hide the fact that there was nevertheless something anguishing about this disappearance, something I couldn't control: he seemed so impersonal, he seemed to forget with such severity what he left behind him, forbidding himself to know whether, if he now entered that room, a room which opened off the bend in the staircase, in order to go to sleep like everyone else, this really happened because somewhere else he was tied to the spot.

Yet I couldn't sleep. The wind had become the violence, the distress of the wind, but it was not that powerful noise from outdoors that kept me awake, it was, on the contrary, the amazing calm that such a noise left intact. I couldn't be mistaken about this calm: it was like a place reserved within a place, which nevertheless was not situated here, which I thought I would be more likely to find by going backwards, by wandering, but I also couldn't reach it, for if I had the right to speak of the one who had "disappeared" in the third person, it was nevertheless myself, who was here and remained here. I couldn't say that he slept, I felt his reserve, his muteness, which accepted the night and, through the night, riveted space to a single spot, whereas perhaps I could neither stop speaking nor withdraw. I persuaded myself that he was, "for his part," even more inaccessible than I to my companion—the one who did not recognize himself behind that word—more of a stranger and in some sense removed from his element; I persuaded myself of this precisely in feeling his reserve, the fact that even his motions did not speak. A reserve that seemed terrible to me, at that moment, as anguishing as his disappearance, to which it was surely connected, as though he had distanced himself, obliterated himself, in the impersonal existence, in the extreme distress that is not even that of someone, and although the right to speak of myself in the third person seemed to me justified by such an obliteration, I must acknowledge that speaking of him caused me an infinite uneasiness, a frightful sadness, with the feeling that this reserve deserved better, called for a silence that unfortunately resisted, even though it seemed to be the slope that invited me—me too—to slide down to it. This was why, in that night in which I heard only my own thought, to which nothing responded but that reserve which, nevertheless, was none other than myself, I promised myself to keep the secret of that "third person" at least from my companion, even while asking myself if I would have enough strength for it, if the secret did not mean that I lacked this strength.

But what is one night? The next day, I got up as usual. "As usual" was an expression that came to me from outside, a sort of open window in that closed space. All night I had wanted this moment: to get up and for everything to be as usual. I couldn't have expressed exactly what this desire meant: a need to lean on the world? a concern to verify the day? to recognize appearances? I believe I humbly hoped to have the strength to get up. That happened, and more easily than I had hoped, above all more quickly. I had only time to say to myself:

"How fast all this is happening! What, is it day?"

Which was echoed by the old remark:

"Another day has passed, hasn't it?"

I turned around toward him, and something of my sympathy, my gesture of confidence and welcome must have touched him, for when I said to him spontaneously: "Last night was infinitely long," I heard him answer me with a sort of delicacy:

"Wouldn't it be best not to move from here?"

"But I've already moved," I gaily pointed out to him.

"Then let's go," he immediately added, without further specifying the spot we should go to.

I climbed the steps, I went into a small toilet. On the same level, and a little later, opening the door I thought was the door to the stairway—but it must have been contiguous to it—I was in some sense attracted by the surprise, pierced and drawn by that surprise, which resembled the gaiety of the day, the shiver of a light so startling that, as I moved forward in that little room, it made me enter the heart of summer, and was I moving forward? it was the space that was opening, a limitless space, a day without hindrance, free, and that freedom, even though it was not without coldness—for I was immobilized in a feeling of radiant emptiness—was like the floating fantasy of summer. I assuredly recognized that little room where I didn't doubt I had spent a good deal of time and which, at that instant, gave me the impression of a watchtower, open on two sides, but empty (not that it was empty of objects, I now noticed a table), and yet empty to a degree that was exalting and, I fear, difficult to sustain. I think there was also a couch, for it seemed to me that I lay down on it, and when fatigue, the burden of that instant, threw me back against the wall, I continued to see the room in all its expanse, in its empty, uninhabited, and yet very cheerful presence. I can imagine that I kept silent for quite a long time. A little after, I came and sat down at the table. I was certain that I had already sat down there, and perhaps it had been just a short time before, perhaps now: the disturbance I felt came from the fact that in some way I myself was finding myself there again, and the thought that I was there, tied to the spot, immediately seized me again with an overwhelming force, at once more hopeless and more sterile than when it had struck me before. I couldn't help saying to him:

"I have the impression this is where I live."

"Are you sure?"

"I find this room strange."

"No, it's fine."

Certainly it was, and extraordinarily agreeable, as attractive as though all the movement of space were concentrated here in order to make it a burning beginning, the site of an encounter in which there was no one and in which I was not myself. Once again I had to let myself be drawn along by that impression.

A little later, I found myself back on the bed. Nothing was different: I still saw the table, it extended from one window to the other, from west to east, as far as I could tell. What struck me, what I tried to bring out of my musings, was why, in this little room, the impression of life was so strong, a radiant life, not of another age, but of the present moment, and mine—I knew it with a clear, joyful knowledge—and yet that clarity was extraordinarily empty, that summer light gave the greatest feeling of distress and coldness. This is open space, I said to myself, the vast country: here I work. The idea that I lived here—that I worked here—meant, it is true, that at this moment I was only here as an image, the reflection of a solitary instant sliding through the immobility of time. A cold thought I could not break down, that pushed me back, threw me back against the wall, just as "here" changed into "far from here," but that distance immediately became the radiance of the day, the soaring and the happiness of all of space burning, con-suming itself to the transparency of a single point. What a vision! But, alas, only a vision. Yet I felt myself powerfully connected to that in-stant and in some sense under its domination, because of this my mas-ter, in the impression that here a sovereign event was taking place and that to live consisted for me in being eternally here and at the same time in revolving only around here, in an incessant voyage, without discovery, obedient to myself and equal to sovereignty. Yes, this was the highest degree of life and even though, through this life, I had strayed into a deadly calm and a deadly solitude, I could say: it must be, it must be—I draw you to myself in a powerful way.

I can imagine how much time that lasted. I recall that after I left the little room—I left it because in reality I could no longer endure that moment, which meant, as I knew, that that moment could not en-dure me—as I was going away (I was going down the stairs) the feel-ing came to me, touched me, that I had gotten out just in time, but I was not fooled by the freedom I was thus giving myself, even if it resembled this remark: "You should go look downstairs and see if you're there," a remark as light as I myself, and that lightness expressed my aimless steps, the movement that drove me from one room to the other, while the doors banged and the wind slid joyfully behind space, at the level of the calm and the silence.

Downstairs, however—at the bottom of the staircase—I had to stop. Here I had stopped before, and the conviction that now I had to

confront something, perhaps a task, seemed connected to this stopping. I recognized the darker day, although at this moment it was almost bright, the silence too, which was not greater than in the spot I
had come from, but a little different, poorer, more desolate, as though
it lacked something it needed to be a real silence, just as it seemed that
only the presence of someone could transform it into a true solitude.
Little by little I had this presentiment: that here, in relation to this
place, I was burdened with a responsibility I could not turn away from,
that obliged me to remain behind, as though to wipe out footsteps or
begin over again what had not been done; yes, I had to respond to a
role that I did not know, but that I could not disregard, that was more
intimate with me than I myself and the burden of which I accepted as
I momentarily gave it this name: responsibility toward solitude, deliverance to captive images.

I must confess that I would have liked to go on. Why this task? Why
did it fall on me? Why had I come in here? Who was stopping me from
leaving? Who was holding me back? No one, less than I, believed in the
truth of a task, no one who was more alien to a duty, whatever it was.
And can one call by the name of "duty" what is not due to anyone?
"Responsibility" what dissipates in the absence of a response? A task,
but one that can't be grasped, a demand, but empty, gloomy, and devastating, and yet a task, a responsibility, a duty. I could only turn to my
companion, the one who was not accompanying me, and say to him: "I
know what's going to happen, I know exactly. I will describe to you
where I am, I believe I can trust you?"

"Yes, I think so, but on condition that I can also trust you."

"You mean that I should describe things to you as I see them?"

"As I would like to see them, as I would see them," and he added:
"Yes, everything depends on that."

I reflected on that, it opened new horizons to me. I would have liked
to make him understand how much what he was asking of me with
such simplicity went beyond everything, exceeded my means, exceeded
me, but out of fear that he would yield to my reasons and because I felt,
with all the force of what was manifest, that in fact "everything depended on that," I chose to answer him:

"Yes, that's clear, that's what I should do, even if I can't do it. Listen,
at this moment I'm at the bottom of the staircase, almost right up against
the steps, on the other side and quite near me there is an armchair, but

I'm not looking at it, because I'm turned toward the room that lies a little farther on. You see how things are?"

"More or less. It's dark, isn't it?"

"It isn't very dark, it's the day that is dark. You know, everything is extraordinarily calm."

Yes everything was extraordinarily calm. Even he must have sensed that it was already too late, for he said softly:

"Stay where you are, don't move."

I wouldn't have been able to move, but what he was asking of me was no doubt something else: to confine myself to that moment of description, to keep it empty at all costs, to preserve it, prevent it from drifting—toward what could not fail to happen. I think I made a slight motion or tried to shift, but I ran up against my own immobility, and I immediately had the full sensation that in the armchair very near me—it was the proximity that was insane, for my hand, almost without moving, could have brushed against it—someone was sitting, someone I now perceived in a profound, intense way, even though the form was absolutely motionless, slightly bent over, but I didn't see it directly, for it was a little behind me. This lasted for one marvelously tranquil and profound instant, after which I said to him quickly:

"For a moment now, someone has been sitting here, in the armchair."

Right away, I was shaken, pierced, not because I felt the insane proximity of this presence, this intense, living, yet unmoving nearness: I could endure that, it seems to me I had always endured it; but the words themselves, from which I had expected some help to come, at the very least another sort of light, myself and reality stepping back; instead opened me up to the shiver of manifestness that formed the depth of that presence, made it ungovernable—inexplicably, absolutely human and yet absolute. And when he asked me: "Someone? Here?" the fact that I was awaiting his words, the shiver that ran behind them, enveloped them in a fear that he seemed to feel, a fear that drove that instant back toward another sort of time, older, fearfully old—all of this moved forward silently, expressed that image, seemed to take possession of it, then swerved toward this question:

"Who is it?"

"I don't know."

"Have you ever seen him before?"

"I don't think so"—but then this was suddenly torn from me: "Yes, I have seen him before."

It seemed obvious to me that he himself had drawn me there, that he had at least forced me to come to that word, to illuminate the visible side of an instant against which I had stood firm—I mean, with which I had lived side by side silently and in a manly way without its being able to come near. Now everything was said, at least at that second I had the violent, splendid certainty of it, which dissipated almost at the same moment, as soon as he asked me:

"When did you see him?"

I had to move away, for now I saw to my left the whiteness of a door that was sunk in the floor: the door to the storeroom, probably. I think I wanted to reach the table that was much farther on, beyond the center of the room, but as I was going around another armchair I suddenly noticed a bed or a couch, but a remarkably broad and vast one, occupying one whole area of the room. The fact that I had not yet paid any attention to it struck me sharply; with joy I thought: one never sees everything in a room. I remained very surprised by the impression of immense tranquillity given off by that sight, it seemed to me I had never before noticed such a calm surface, such a restful, even, and silent expanse. I imagine I looked at that bed for quite a long time. I can't say the idea of lying down on it didn't occur to me; on the contrary, I felt the liveliest desire to do that, a desire that also took this form: that in that spot, I would have a completely different perspective on the room, a possibility of describing it that cheered me, delighted me infinitely, as though this would have been a friendly trick to play on my old companion. However, I did not lie down on it and I don't believe I really considered doing it. It didn't seem entirely possible to me. Why? I can't say exactly: the thought that I was here, but only by chance, because of a misfortune of time and also because somewhere else I was tied to the spot—and perhaps in the kitchen or upstairs, in the little room, the watchtower, where my musings evoked the image of the watchman, of the one who lives in the day and bears its weight—this thought now disappeared into another, that here I had to confront something, a task, a responsibility, but at this moment, what seized me again with an amazing intensity was the sensation of my immobility of the certainty that once again kept me in that spot. There was no movement I could have made. Where I was, without turning around, I could see the steps, there were six or seven before one reached the sort of vault, rather low and heavy, under which the staircase made a turn. Now, the perception of what I saw brought a response to my companion. The figure was over there, I saw it motionless, almost turned away, as it seemed to me, and I had the feeling that at the moment my eyes were fixed on it, it was preparing to climb the last steps and disappear. This movement which was not carried out, gave that presence a new truth, and the whole distance that separated us, measuring a few steps, made it astonishingly close, closer than a short time before when, as I realized, what made its insane proximity apparent was the distress of its distance. But the strangest thing was that in the space at that confined spot—and the form was, I saw, almost leaning against the wall—even though it couldn't see me and probably knew nothing of me, it was nevertheless stopped and suspended under my gaze, as though the fact that my gaze was riveted to it had, in fact, riveted it to that point. There was something odd, absolutely unhappy about that and I was so shaken by it that the background of strangeness against which this scene was unfolding was transformed. Probably, affected by my disturbance, I must have moved slightly: now I saw the staircase from a steeper perspective, rising abruptly toward the figure I was still staring at, which revealed itself more, so that the impression I had was that of someone larger than I had thought, yes, it was this feeling that struck me then, of someone a little larger than he should have been, and I don't know why this singularity was like a disconcerting summons to my eyes, an insistence that maddened my gaze and prevented its grasping anything. It seems to me that I was prepared to approach even closer, perhaps to bring this moment back to life, to allow it to reconquer itself; but what happened and what I could have foreseen, actually struck me as unexpected—I believe I had never forgotten him to this degree before—and, when he asked me: "Do you see him at this moment?" I, in my surprise and also because of a sort of pain that I felt spring up in me, faced with this speech, which sought to encroach on me and participate in a guarded moment, did not answer, no doubt incapable. Shortly after, from very far away, from the distance that was made of my resistance and my disavowal, I heard him murmur:

"You know, there's no one there."

I don't know if I welcomed the remark at that moment, but at that moment, with extreme emotion, I saw the figure visibly move a little, I saw it slowly climb a step, approach the turn, and enter the area of shadow.

Among all the impressions I had, I think the strongest was this: that the evidence of reality had never been as pressing as in this slip toward disappearance; in this movement, something had been revealed that was an allusion to an event, to its intimacy, as though, for this figure, to disappear was its most human truth and also the truth closest to me. And the other feeling I had was the counterpart of such a certainty: the disheartening but also radiant emptiness expressed for me by this disappearance, an event I was not even tempted to ascribe directly to what my companion had said. I won't say I saw no connection between these two signs, but I sensed a deeper, more imposing interdependence, that of two spheres that didn't know each other, two moments in time perhaps entirely foreign to each other and coming together within their shared foreignness. Which had come before the other? He had now uttered that remark, but "now" had perhaps already happened in the past, was repeating itself, was taking place again—again? but it couldn't take place again, and everything returned to being empty and lifeless. This feeling expressed, at that point, the desperate movement I was making and that perspicacity could only cause to be infinite. Yes, it had already taken place, and the question of knowing just when was a futile one, the certainty of remembering a matter of indifference, for it seemed to me that I belonged, not to the order of things that happen and that one remembers with joy or sadness, but to the element of hunger and emptiness where what does not take place, because of that, begins again and again without any beginning or any respite.

I did not deny that I would have done anything, given up anything, to be able to get out of there, and yet the certainty that I couldn't, despite my desire and despite appearances, was enveloped in this idea: which was that I had to stay there, keep standing there, this was my task, the beginning of a decision I had to sustain by remaining always on my feet, betraying it as little as possible, without ever being relieved of myself, but always confronting a demand that gave me the feeling I myself had also disappeared and, far from thinking I was more free of it, that I was connected by this disappearance, connected ever more closely to it, of being called, sworn to sustain it, make it more real, more true and, at the same time, push it farther, always farther, to a point truth can no longer reach, where possibility ceases. I saw the terrible, deceptive aspect of such a thought, I fought against it, and it did not resist, its lightness left me free, became the transparency I couldn't rip apart without harming a free moment. At certain times, it seemed to me this transparency was the only solid ground that still remained to me and, if I went forward, it was by resting on it, on my own image thus reflected, while this reflection was perpetuated to infinity, indifferent to the ruins of time. A reflection that had no doubt attracted me by its fragility, the assurance that in resting on it I would inevitably fall fast, but the fall was infinite, at each moment of the fall the reflection formed again under my steps, indestructible. I would also sometimes feel, and precisely at that moment, that this task—a word I would have liked to choose to be even more insignificant, emptier, and, because of that, more appropriate to its imperious power—this demand was the bond that joined me to myself, to the one who had lived in the small room, close to the daylight and bearing its weight. Perhaps I was necessary to him, and no doubt such a necessity weighed on me as much as one can be heavy to oneself, but I also sensed that he was placing a certain hope in me, that this task and this burden were related to that expectation. What was he expecting? I did not know. Could it have been that the strange distance established between us, through which, as I clearly saw, entered the infinite torment that was my space and my air and my days, could it have been that this distance, interior and yet measured by the reality of a few moments, yes, the fact that I was a little on this side, a little behind, in this strangely perilous, but strangely attractive region of the reflection—did this immense separation give me a sort of release? But why this suspense, this pause? I couldn't see all this clearly, and this darkness also had the weight of my task and my responsibility, for I too, in my own way, was looking for the daylight, even if I had to be content with an errant, imprisoned gleam, the scintillation of an instant which I sometimes almost preferred to the light of the world. Yes, I said to myself, my part is the best—for my part, I am here, I'm staying here.

Which he did not fail to answer:

"But you have all the time in the world."

I noticed, then, that I had reached the table, whose round surface I saw turning about an empty vase, and even though I had had the impression of having fallen there, I was calmly seated, which did not prevent me from thinking: what a shame I didn't fall on the bed, whose peaceful image remained in my mind. I didn't feel very tired, but rather disoriented, prodigiously without any work to do, and this being without work was also my task, it occupied me: perhaps it represented a dead time, an interval of abandonment and faintness on the part of the watchman, a weakness that obliged me to be alone, myself, but the empty disturbance in which I was moving about had to have another meaning, evoked hunger, evoked a need to wander, to go farther, by asking: "Why did I come in here? am I looking for something?" whereas I was perhaps not looking for anything and "farther" was still here and here, at each instant. This I knew. Knowing formed part of that solitude, formed that solitude, was at work in my being without work, closed the ways out. In my lack of work, I asked him:

"Do you know what happened just now?"

"Yes, I know very well, but do you want us to talk about it? Is that a good thing? We must be reasonable."

"It may not be a very good thing, but I'm not really speaking either. You remember, you pointed that out to me."

"Do I remember? Profoundly, amicably; you were struck by it."

"I didn't take it badly. I, too, think we aren't really talking: one can't call this speech."

Which led him to say to me:

"Is that what you're thinking now?" but he didn't leave me the time to explain it, for without transition he went on to this certainty:

"Oh, we understand each other perfectly!"

As I was reflecting on this assurance, he suddenly asked me with a strange voracity:

"Are you writing? Are you writing at this moment?"

A question that chilled me, as though there had been a lack of taste on his part in this, a dog snuffling at its own smell.

"I don't do it at night, at this time of year. It's already cold."

"And the summer?"

"Yes, in the summer, sometimes."

He firmly continued his inquiry:

"And do you read?"

"Not much, not as much as I should."

"Why don't you read?"

I must admit I was shaken by the seriousness and the passionate interest of his questions: Why wasn't I reading? I asked myself, and from that question sprang an answer I gave him rather joyfully:

"I would rather converse with you," which he, too, accepted joyfully, by repeating:

"Oh, we understand each other perfectly."

But perhaps not as well as he would have liked, for his reply took him back to mine, which he seemed to turn around:

"Yes, we are conversing with each other," and the silence that resulted from this emerged from that dislocated remark, revealed its fault, its cleft, which disturbed me painfully. In myself, I said to myself:

"Now let's see what you're worth," and I thought to prove to myself what I was worth by declaring brusquely to him:

"You know, I trust you, except on one point, because there really was someone here, just now."

"Really?"

"Yes, really, really."

I understood the risk I was running by affirming this reality in front of him like that, but something drove me to maintain it whatever the cost, it seemed to me I owed the credit for it to an event which I should not allow to be obliterated, which I would otherwise never be able to go back to, and which also needed this indefinitely maintained assurance in order to realize itself. I wanted to make him understand that on this point I wouldn't yield, I wouldn't deny my certainty. In fact, my conviction didn't seem to find him alien to it, only disconcerted, and at that moment I leaped at the thought that I had perhaps forgotten certain details, that there was a lacuna through which reality had escaped, that I had, for example, neglected to describe to him the armchair that I could see by lifting my eyes, though it was in the depth of the room, quite far from me, it is true, and even farther from him: a sturdy country chair that sometimes reminded me of Van Gogh's. The fact that someone was sitting there, in that armchair, had a humble truth to it, the truth of this very cramped place, and I could only reflect inexhaustibly on that truth, of which so little remained to me, for it didn't even signify repose, an attitude of repose, but equally well indifference to repose. Perhaps he discerned what he took to be a doubt, though it was, on the contrary, the torment of a certainty reduced to itself alone; he asked me softly:

"Who was it?"

"I don't know." But he didn't forget that I had said more to him, and he made me feel it in his next question:

"Did he see you?"

I thought about it, and I felt the anguish, the sadness, that recalled to me the presence of that figure, riveted to a single point by the fact that I was riveting it with my gaze: it was no longer more than that point, then, an empty, silent point, an empty moment that had become tragically foreign to my gaze at the very moment when my gaze became the error of what rivets and my gaze itself was empty, did not enter that zone, entered it without reaching it, encountered only the emptiness, the closed circle of its own vision. Upon which he insisted:

"What was he like?"

"I don't think I want to describe him to you, at least not now. It seems to me I shouldn't."

"You mean you could?"

"I don't think I should ask it of myself."

"Ah!" he said strangely, "I see, I see, you respect him." And when I did not deny it, he abruptly changed the subject, and this new subject was revealed by these words:

"Aren't you afraid of it? Isn't it a frightening association?"

The word "frightening" startled me, bewildered me. All of a sudden I saw it with a force that, in fact, did not leave me intact: what had been there was frightening, was what I could not associate with, and in this slipping, it seemed to me that I myself could no longer associate with anyone, not even with myself. Was it such a feeling of rupture that caused me to be a stranger to that instant, provoked a fall, a dizziness in which, far from repelling the frightening association, I found myself close to it, joined to it by sympathy, by a desire to recognize it? A movement that made me travel through abysms and yet more abysms, and I could have believed someone was there, because what I felt was so like the shiver of his approach. I was so illuminated by this that he, too, had to believe in his presence, and he quickly asked me:

"Do you see him at this moment?"

But this question showed me that the light I had just traveled through wanted to illuminate something quite different, the very answer I gave him at that moment in all its "light":

"Yes, I have seen him before."

A mad thing to say, and as soon as it slipped out, it seemed the most dismal thing that could happen to me, the cowardly impulse that had caused me to replace the disconcerting with the familiar, and, out of a desire to master the unknown, with the already known. And yet, could I reject such a light? Had I not for an instant, been on intimate terms with that absence, so close to it that to see it would have disrupted the intimacy? But that speech.... We listened to it, of course, both of us, and he didn't allow it to move away:

"You mean you saw him somewhere else, somewhere different from here?"

Under the tension imposed on me by his question, I slid into a remark about him that I could have been tempted to make to myself earlier, if I hadn't been so little tempted to approach him through remarks: which was that I felt bound to be all the more frank the more discreetly he existed—if I didn't want to reduce that errant speech of mine, which I rejoined at certain moments in time and at certain points in space, to the whimsicality of an echo, I could not forget to treat it with an infinite seriousness, equal to its infinite complicity and patience. But while I was building myself a rampart out of my remarks, he did not deviate in any way from his direction, as I had hoped, he even affirmed it still more vigorously by adding:

"You mean you know him?"

This made me realize that it would be best to answer:

"I thought I recognized him, but when you ask me that question, I'm convinced that I don't know him in any way befitting that word." I added: "You know very well what I mean."

Loyally, he acknowledged it: "I know."

But listening to him, it occurred to me that perhaps he didn't know it in the same way I did, even though he drew a surprising answer from it:

"And just now, was it the same each time?"

It did not take me long to understand him; he wanted to take back from me a little more than I had given him, and perhaps he left me my certainty, but on condition that it be insignificant, yes, severely deprived of meaning and truth. I was drawn into a path where I only stopped to ask him:

"You mean I'm not always the same?" Which at last showed me where I was going.

I think I was exhausted with bitterness, my courage failed me. I had endured so many struggles, I had been so far, and where was "so far"? Here, by this table, whose surface, too, I saw turning with the lightness of an empty movement, and the person who happened to be there was perhaps writing, and, as for me, I was leaning on him, on me someone else was leaning, on that person, yet another: at the far end of the chain there was still this room and this table. There was nothing I could lean on in the face of such an infinity, I was without strength in the face of the emptiness the question kept opening and closing, so that I could not even fall into it. Rather, it uplifted me, uplifted me with exhaustion, and I think that when I saw myself standing, that movement, that desperate need to exhaust space caused me to fling at him in response, with a suddenness in which was mustered the resolve I made at that moment:

"I will continue to go in this direction, never in any other."

For me, "in this direction" no doubt indicated where he was, the interminable, the place where the moments led me back to such a point of uncertainty and sterility that what had preceded them was obliterated, that they themselves were obliterated. Infinite moments, which I could not master, and the most terrible thing was that, as a constant pressure, I felt the duty to make myself their master, to orient them, to transmit to them that pressure, which sought to make them slide toward an end to which they could not consent. I could not entirely resist this pressure, this imperious narration, it was inside me like an order, an order that I was giving myself, that unsettled me, dragged me along, obliged me to wander. I could not avoid the thought, then, that this pursuit was not mine alone, my error, but that it was also present around me, in the intimacy of space, in the secrecy of that speech, that called to the emptiness and did not find it, or that wanted to recover itself and could not.

Since I was coming and going—at a distance, certainly, but still here—I could not neglect what was happening here, or I, too, had to live according to the truth of negligence, in which, even while adhering to the transparent vision of the day, I found no less important the emptiness of the reflections surrounding me at every instant, and even more: things happened in such a way that, even while seeing them happen infinitely at a distance and farther from me than I ever could have reached, I felt intimately responsible for them. I think that I will express an aspect of the truth, in the language he chose, by saying we understood each other. This understanding was perhaps infinitely strange to me, but even when it escaped me, when I was still outside it, I did not forget it, I continued to feel directly responsible for it, in my uneasiness, doubt and also foreboding, foreboding that was empty, infinitely without happiness but stubborn, demanding, for, without contact with the instant that I had to sustain, and not immobilize, but leave free, even while going to meet it, I was obliged, in the ignorance of an empty foreboding, to give proof of understanding and creative alliance and yet not be concerned about all this, lest the time of the concern come to dislocate the understanding and miserably torment the emptiness.

I can't express myself any other way. It seems to me that in my disarray, in which I had to fight against the interminable and yet lift it up to the daylight, forbid myself to be anxious, in search of an instant that did not want to be sought and that nevertheless desired it, in that space whose resemblance I had to sustain, I applied all my strength to remaining connected to myself. Perhaps this was a mistake, perhaps what I called faithfulness and seriousness, the will to remain on my feet, was only a narrow aspiration to remain, a prayer addressed to the night asking it to linger a little while longer. Yes, it's possible, but one can't deliberately give up contenting oneself, one can only fight to maintain the rigor of a form and contact with the day. Go up, go down, but even in the shadows and as far as possible, one must fight for transparency.

I didn't forget it, the world is based on itself and the earth alone is the seat of the gods. From this, too, came the heavy feeling of my responsibility, the seriousness with which I had to approach myself, follow myself in the trial that obliged me to live short of myself, in the intimacy of wandering, in that understanding with something I could not entirely understand and which I had to sustain firmly, without removing myself from it, and, insofar as I could, without straying.

I had many proofs that we understood each other, but this one in particular made me reflect: when I ceased to be alone, solitude became intense, infinite. There was nothing strange about that truth, it only made the spot where I was staying prodigiously true, the spot I found to be in all aspects like itself, like the description of it produced at this same spot or sometimes elsewhere—the description of it, of all that happened here and that asserted itself here. This resemblance was prodigious, it did not have the incisiveness, the authority of obviousness, rather it was a prodigy, it seemed gratuitous, unjustified, incontestable, but not sure, of a reality more interior and yet all in appearance, all contained in visible splendor, and to come and go, there, was a delight from which I could remove myself all the less because I had the happiness of seeing things in the gaiety of their solitude, which did not take my presence into account, which played with my absence and, it is true, the word "understanding" also had the cheerfulness of a game about which we understood each other. I think the solitude was best expressed by that gaiety: a light laugh of space, a fund of extraordinary playfulness that did away with every reservation, every alternative, and which resonated like the emptiness of an echo, the renunciation of mystery, the ultimate insignificance of lightness. Perhaps I wouldn't have noticed it if he hadn't suddenly asked me:

"Why are you laughing?"

A question that forced me to reflect, for I was not laughing at all, I was, rather, within the musing that had followed my resolve, hardly in a very happy state of mind. A striking question, posed to me, it seemed, at a decisive moment that did not correspond to my state of mind, that evoked another question, another day, and, what was more, I was startled every time he showed he was capable of coming to me by a path I had not laid out. I could have asked him what the object of his question was, but I found this answer myself:

"Because I'm not alone."

Which he translated in his own way:

"Is it that you're not here?"

I took it cheerfully:

"Do you want to know where I am? I've just drawn back the curtains of the large bay windows, and I'm looking out." There I rediscovered, joyfully preserved, the little garden—hardly a garden, a few feet of earth enclosed within walls—which lay just in front of me, a

little beyond the panes, beyond but within my reach, so that by looking outside, I also had the feeling of touching the depths of a memory,
its last chance, so much did that little area extend me, give me a little
more than I should have received, which, because of that, I received
twice over. Once again I remembered the pleasure it had always
brought me and, even at present, I was startled by this unexpected
possibility, this reserve of space and light toward which I was still allowed to turn. This was not the splendor of limitlessness, such that,
there where I lived and worked, in the little room, brightness gave it
to me to contemplate as the unique moment and sovereign intensity
of the outside. Here, there was nothing but a little fragment, something as joyful as a real shrub planted in the heart of a dream. Which I
saw—but at that instant I had the impression that what I saw was cruelly lacking to him. I was also struck by the loyalty that permitted me to
keep him at a distance, never to think that he could play his game alone.
Which quickly led me back to my answer, over which, I then saw, he
had remained poised, without taking notice of my contemplation, and
I received his own answer once again:

"It's true, you're not alone, but we are alone."

That "we" impressed me, appeared to have a different tone. It seemed
to me that before he spoke he had withdrawn from my vicinity, had
exiled himself, and this exile became the basis of the understanding,
whence, then, like a breath exhaled, the life of the speech, worn, burned,
yet strangely alive, was expressed. The "we" appeared to me to be an
allusion to that exile, to the fascinating need to distance himself under
the pretext of coming close, and it occurred to me that if I had to ex-
pend such strength in these conversations, it was because I first had to
distance him, distance myself from him, and the greater the distance
was, the more profound and true the speech was, like everything that
comes from far away. This was not the tranquil delay, the suspension
that I granted myself so often while "reflecting": it was a silent, powerful struggle, but also scarcely real, a dream movement, in which I had to
deprive myself of life, abstain from myself, so as to make all approaches
useless to him and allow him to give voice to the distance. But was this
how it was? What I have just called exile did not evoke separation, but
return, presence in the shining world of negligence, and perhaps the
effort I was making consisted in opening up, everywhere I happened to
be, an interval that was his dwelling place, in erecting the tent of exile

where I could communicate with him—because he was not there. But was this how it was? I catch myself imagining that if he withdrew from my question, he never withdrew completely and, in this apparently open field, he left a remnant, as the day does in the night, a simulacrum of presence that falsified space and made it into a place of error. Perhaps I should have struggled harder so that he would distance himself more, more sincerely, in a way that was not a piece of trickery, an imposture, the game of understanding and the gaiety of solitude. But for that, didn't he have to be a little more present? Hadn't he said that to me himself? Hadn't he, at a singularly dramatic moment, mentioned the desire to bind me in order to be able to unbind me? Yes, he had revealed himself to me in that thought, and I was still suffering its touch, its glamour. "When you say 'we,' I'm not sure of what you're saying. It doesn't refer either to you or to me, does it?"

"To us!"

Yes, that created an extraordinary opening, which allowed me to say to him:

"I've been doing a lot of thinking lately. I have the impression that you used to remain more hidden. You were perhaps something extraordinary, but I lived with an extraordinary thing without being disturbed by it, without seeing it and without knowing it."

"Do you miss those days?"

"No, I don't miss them."

"An extraordinary thing."

From the way he repeated it, I thought he had not really heard the word. I had noticed that he liked facts, he had a strange curiosity, almost a passion for the simplest events and things, which he carried off "to his side of things" with a surprising, painful voracity, for often I had the impression that he didn't know what was involved, that the words which designated these things remained opaque for him, at least inasmuch as he had not rolled them around inside his sphere for very long. Nevertheless, I must not have spoken entirely for myself, because he continued to attack me on this word:

"Is it as extraordinary as all that?"

I stood firm:

"Yes, it was, extraordinarily so."

He remained silent before saying to me:

"Aren't you using that word just to be agreeable?"

"To give you an idea of what I think."

"Maybe it's not agreeable to me. Are we so extraordinary for each other?"

"Maybe I'm shielding myself behind that word. It must remind me of certain things. I also find it strange, sometimes, to converse with you."

"Yes, we are conversing."

I was struck, as I had been once before, by how that word seemed to open up, reveal a fissure, whence rose a painful silence, a neutral expanse which he was tempted to travel endlessly, without regard to time, adding one step to another without hoping ever to encounter fatigue there, exhaustion: this stood between us, and now that I was returning, after a respite—perhaps under the influence of that image—to the room, I saw better—I thought I saw this—how it merged with its own resemblance, which did not surprise me, but prevented me from grasping it in all its extent, also took away my desire to do that, and what struck me even more was how that presence—slipping and yet preserved within that slipping—was of an ambiguous, strange truth, quite indifferent to all truth, to a certainty on the basis of which I could have roamed through it, closed it on its limits. Even if I could try to believe I was responsible for what happened here, this responsibility only marked the emptiness of the event, the lack of seriousness expressed by "Why are you laughing?," a laugh that I would no doubt have remembered hearing, if it had not been the very scattering of that recollection, a light, colorless laugh, around which it was not possible to fix even an invisible presence. I think I had never felt to such a degree how much I, too, stood between us. I had always suspected that when I said "me" it was to oblige him in his turn to say "I," to come out of that depth, that sordid, sterile neutrality where, in order to be on an equal footing, I would have had to become him for myself. A region I had perhaps approached in an earlier time, without realizing it, so much was I joined to him by the movement of youth and liveliness of heart, and I must have had the thought that I believed I was close enough to say "you" to him and far enough away to hear him say "me," that under the veil of these first persons, shielded by that equality that I had to wrest from him each time by a vehement insistence, I thought, at least momentarily, that I was preserved from the danger of hearing the anonymous, the nameless, speak in him, I must have had that thought, but now I felt it had led me where I wanted to avoid going, for I had perhaps succeeded—by certain ruses—in keeping him shielded from me, but now this contact with me was anonymous, and what resulted from it was nothing other than the lightness of a chattering without truth, the infinite shimmering of joyful reflections and sparkling instants. Nothing extraordinary, as he had said, nothing grave or overwhelming, even though it was impossible to breathe here and dwell here, as though one could only breathe, hope, by means of a little seriousness. This was no doubt why I had to ask him more and more often:

"Can I reflect on it?"—to which he did not fail to answer: "Yes, of course, but for how long?"

When had all this begun? It went on, it did not begin. It did not go on, it was necessarily endless. Why, whatever point I started from, did I necessarily arrive at the same place, the place where I was? And the place where I was, I had to think, was, when we were conversing, the place where he was maintaining his reserve. This reserve was our common space, a "Help yourself yourself," where an unlimited confidence was affirmed that I sometimes thought was reciprocal, but that, for my part, I'm afraid, still hid a desire, the concern to preserve the moment in which we would speak in earnest.

In that space, it was perhaps because I was still trying to hold on to my part—and this was why I was not at the end of my strength, for my part I was not—that I lived in a constant concealment, without knowing where it came from. The simplest thing was to believe that in fact I was concealing something from him, it was easy, he didn't impose himself, he didn't force me in any way. But actually I knew very well that this couldn't be called concealing, and on the contrary, the more I committed myself unreservedly to this space, the more I suffocated at the approach of concealment. He wasn't in the least concerned about what I might think or do. Once, I had been able to live in the world, it didn't bother me and I didn't bother it. But little by little and under the constraint of this concealment, in order to avoid this suffocating element, that I thought I could dissipate this way, I had withdrawn from everything in order not to appear to hide anything from him anymore, so that now, I no longer lived in the world, but in concealment. I tried, behind the shield of this word, to move farther forward. I tried to understand why, in this space, there were still knots and tensions, strong areas in which everything was a demand, others in which everything leveled out, an interlacing of expectation and forgetting that incited one to an uninterrupted agitation. I couldn't get rid of the idea that if I had only struggled harder against certain of his remarks, if, instead of hearing them, taking an interest in them, answering them, I had stoutly laid hold of them, by allowing them to mask out, to follow their own path even to the depth of a slow maelstrom, I would have ceased to wander on the surface this way, in a world of vestiges and half-hopes. Still, this was only an idea. At other times, perhaps when I brought a little composure to my reflection, it was my own words that I was prepared to trust. I didn't mean that they intended what I didn't intend, nor even that their capacity, their loyalty were sufficient; on the contrary, they were heavy, not very malleable, and at the same time immoderate, pedantic, loquacious, but it sometimes happened, and, precisely at the approach of concealment, that they appeared to reflect what was essential, respond to it, and what they had said was perhaps insignificant, didn't help me in any way, rather hindered me by allowing me to believe that it had been conversed in emptiness, but only because I obstinately kept myself at a distance; fear, attachment, lack of strength, forgetfulness—this was what kept me withdrawn, whereas speeches, no longer obedient, for some time now, to these general feelings, echoed what was no doubt only an echo, but in this way took their places next to concealment, occupied its place, took its place.

I tried to offer him this remark. I sensed that I should not have done it. It sometimes occurred to me that what he was expecting from me was a tranquil conversation without gaps, a chatty exchange in the center of which he would have dozed like a slight suspicion. But I could not help saying to him:

"Where we are, everything conceals itself, doesn't it?"

Scarcely was it spoken before this remark sank into the emptiness, reverberated there emptily, awoke the infinitely distended outside, the infinite pain of the affirmation occupying all of space, where what was said kept passing through the same point again, was the same, and, always, at whatever moment, said the same thing and eternally remained lacking. I can't say that in this way I was freed of that speech.

On the contrary, it returned to me constantly, as though it were its own answer, and each time I was done with it, but each time I expressed it again, for it demanded that: to be said and said again.

I must have stayed in the same place for quite a long time. From one moment to the next, I said to myself: now, it will no longer be possible for me to reflect (when I reflected, I did not reflect, properly speaking, it was like a prayer addressed to time, asking it please to do its work). I was standing a few feet away from a vast, excessively wide bed: I was not even sure, in fact, that it was not the ground, and this prevented me from lying down on it, as I would have liked. I did not see objects distinctly, I perceived the room as a whole, I touched it, as it touched me, through the slight relation that caused the scattering of a slight but infinite laugh to pass between us. This laugh ran along the border of space, without crossing it, but also seemed to be that space, and this gaiety, though foreign to me, nevertheless passed by where I thought I was, dispersed me, dispersed my decision about the serious things I nevertheless had to do. I must have headed toward the kitchen. The thought that for a very long time now I had been heading toward that spot, a thought which itself had a stifling aspect and an amusing aspect, though one kept passing into the other, caused it to happen that when I touched a door, recalling that the storeroom where I was in danger of falling was not far from there, I turned away, and what immediately seized me again was the desire to drink, I was thirsty, that thirst led me back the way I had come.

"Give me a glass of water," I said in a low voice. I could barely hear the words. Yet he answered distinctly:

"I can't give it to you. You know I can't do anything."

I listened to that. The words had something extraordinarily attractive about them, they were distinct, accurate—within my reach—and yet it seemed they didn't know me and I, too, didn't know them. Here was a new phenomenon which, I said to myself, I should worry about for the future, but at that moment it was so light, so irresponsible, and at the same time of such amplitude that I couldn't concern myself about controlling it. Perhaps I didn't understand anything, perhaps I was calling "speech" something that was speechless, but here, what was speechless was already a speech, what was not understood was expressed. I should have gone farther, but I realized I was immobilized by sadness, it was so empty; it spoke in the name of a distance so exhausted, so stubborn, it was bound up with such a pain, a pain so obliterated. Was it here?

I didn't expect an answer, but the one that came was in fact the revelation of the danger in which I found myself. As though the word "here" had drawn me elsewhere or as though I myself, because of my inconstancy, had lightly pushed it before me, I passed back over his words, or, in them, as in a healthy core, still visible, I rediscovered my own, that phrase I had had to say, I rediscovered it, but then I perceived the infinitesimal, frightfully slender bond that connected me to it, its strange, impersonal nature, the infinitesimal part of it that allowed me to say it was mine and consequently say it: when I spoke, didn't I have the impression I was already witnessing that speech from very far away? Didn't I have the feeling that it had preceded me long before, and wasn't it through an unexpected movement, an unexpected withdrawal that, having been face to face with it, I had had the strength not to miss it? Yes, I had had that strength, the strength to prevent it from being said, in my place, by someone or by no one, but if I felt that following that withdrawal I could still have uttered it, I felt no less that, all the same and in any case, it had already uttered itself alone.

What was immediately apparent to me was that I had to remain in that place. Perhaps this discovery did not teach me more than I already knew. Perhaps, by showing me the single point by which I was holding myself to something true, it only tightened around me the anxiety of the emptiness, as though, these words being the only ones in which I still dwelled, I had felt them come apart as the last resting place whence I could stop the errant coming and going. Now I understood clearly—it seemed to me I understood—why I had to stay here. But, being here, where was I? Why near him? Why, behind everything I said and everything he answered, was there this remark: "Where we are, everything conceals itself, doesn't it?"—a remark I understood, did not understand, it had no understanding. Everything was extraordinarily calm, but he did not cease to be equal to that calm, and the silence, profound though it was, was still less silent than he, and constantly appeared to be pursued, obliterated; I could only say to myself: now, that's it for the silence. An impression in which I could not find myself again.

It was a little farther on that I found myself again. I must have been closer to the middle of the room, for it appeared to me in a new light:

it was rather low, less broad than long, yet quite large. What stopped me from describing it, from maintaining it firmly in a description, was that I couldn't grasp it. It wasn't a question of remembering, and wasn't I really there, wasn't I in it, really, as he had suggested to me? I did not refuse to believe it, but my belief also lacked reality, so that I didn't really believe it. That this had to do with my relations with him, with the solitude of that "we" in which I had to hold myself, always distancing him so that, in that distance, he could express himself and I could understand him, in which I had to hold myself, but not withdraw: offer myself dangerously to that suffocating element that, when it showed itself, stopped me from concealing myself in it, forced me to wander or dispersed me by holding me open to the power of concealment—this was what I thought; and if I did not understand this thought, at least I rested on it, it was this place, in a certain way, and it was from here that I saw the room where I nevertheless remained. As I looked out through the large bay windows—everything was extraordinarily calm at that moment—and while I saw a strange, dreamy daylight circulate around the curtain of green leaves, a daylight as luminous as I could have imagined, but with a light that was not entirely light, that resembled it, expressed the pleasure of having broken out of the depths to lose itself in the light slipping off the surface, I couldn't help remembering: someone was standing beyond the windows; as soon as I recalled this, he turned toward the window and, without stopping where I was, stared rapidly, with an intense, rapid gaze, at the entire extent, the entire depth of the room. This view vanished almost immediately, but the impression did not vanish, the terrible impression of a return to the same sterile point, at the same indefatigable instant, as though all paths led me back to it, all words at a certain moment passed through this presence whose intensity, whose living force, evoked only the impurity of that moment, the desire in me to find something more to see, to stop there and rest there. This feeling was so strong, so greatly deprived me of the use of myself, that when I heard the murmured words—"Someone is looking at us through the window"; "Through the window?"—I was in some sense delivered, traversed by something happy, and not only because I had yielded to the inevitable, but at that instant something opaque in the word "window" became transparent to me, and what I grasped in that transparency was precisely this light: the moment was approaching when he would no longer understand my words. A presentiment I could not follow through to its end, I lacked the strength, I lacked myself.

I can imagine how long that lasted, for the thought that I had, as I recovered myself, was no doubt the same one I had had as I fell: that, in fact, I was at last falling. But I saw that I had only sat down close to a table, and at the same time I heard the question—it passed through space like an avid shiver—"Are you writing? Are you writing at this moment?" Hearing this, I shivered in turn, I understood that what had awakened me, led me back here, was this voracious murmur that I had not ceased to listen to, for it seemed difficult to escape such an avid continuity, such an uninterrupted insistence, or to set limits to it. It was slightly nauseating, but not without a character of gaiety that invited me to join in with it. Still, I felt a disturbance, an uneasiness that gave me the idea that these words embarrassed me because they followed one another so lightly that I couldn't know if what was involved was a question or only an order, an encouragement. Since I had the impression that these words were not addressed precisely to me, I felt a certain freedom in relation to them, the freedom of being able to answer them lightly myself, if need be. It was this freedom, the impression that I was not being challenged which, without my knowing it, must have driven me to take part. I asked weakly:

"Am I writing?"

This slipped out of me more like a sigh than a speech, but weak as this perturbation was, it was enough to disrupt the equilibrium, and right away, as though attracted by this emptiness, his uninterrupted murmur, which had until now wandered at random, turned around impetuously against me, confronted me, while he asked me with an authority that contrasted ridiculously with the weakness of my resources:

"Are you writing, are you writing at this moment?"

To which I could not help answering him:

"But you know very well that I can no longer write and I am almost not myself any longer."

Words I regretted because of their seriousness, and they were immediately followed, in the furtive manner of a light laugh, though from a little farther away, by his own words:

"Are you writing, are you writing at this moment?"

I didn't allow myself to be deflected from the certainty of being at a turning point that required all my strength, all my attention, by the recollection that I had already, and at almost every instant, been certain I was approaching a turning point from which I then saw that he had only turned me back, led me back. I fully realized where this new assurance came from, this resolution to go farther, yes, in this direction, never in another, a resolution I made at that instant. I could see him: we had stood face to face; at least, I had had this feeling, and before now I had never had it. The fact that nothing happy had resulted from it, that nothing had even resulted at all, wasn't enough to stop me. For this feeling—not the feeling of having my back to the wall, but the desire, faced with this formidable demand that had looked at me, stared at me where I was not dwelling, trying to draw me along into the emptiness of an airless and rootless time—was the desire, faced with such a demand, to come back to something true which, in order to answer him, had spoken in me. Even if he had disregarded this answer, it had still entered his space, I was now establishing myself on it, I had reached it, I had to maintain it even in the midst of the regret from which I also could not entirely separate myself.

This was so much the case that, thinking of what he had often said to me—"Well, another day has passed, hasn't it?"—I welcomed this remark with satisfaction, with gratitude, as though from time immemorial he had been destined to show me this new day. Yes, the old day had passed, and the glow that was illuminating this moment was like that which might have succeeded in announcing to me: "This is the point you have reached, this is what you are." I was still close to the table. I was no less close to the decisive quality of my remark, near which I remained, yet without being able to distinguish them from his, from what I was certainly obliged, if only because I had answered him, to consider to be his question. The question had not been shaken by it, but that only rendered more significant a fact I was gradually becoming aware of: that it had brought my answer with it and that now I scarcely recognized the latter as mine, mingled as it was with that murmur which remained, in the distance, like a promise and a seduction. I considered the thing, at first with the enthusiasm of my confidence in that moment, but gradually with the foreboding, the apprehension, of having pointlessly handed over to him the center of myself, the heart of the citadel—far from having won it away from him—and when he said to me: "But isn't that what writing is?" I did not in the least experience the pleasure, the interest, of a new remark, but a spasm of disgust at rediscovering our two sentences clasped against each other, mingled in a cold intimacy, in the emptiness of their own indifference, and it was as though I had had to fight far away from myself, but also far away from him, where we were neither one nor the other.

It was at this distance, from very far away, that I heard him repeat softly: "I think that's what writing is," no doubt to let me know that if he was recovering the advantage, it was not in an underhand way, but by complying with the truth, by welcoming it more deeply than I, at a depth before which I stopped short. I, too, was tempted to descend to this depth, but I could do no more than reaffirm myself:

"Even where I am with it? At the point where I am with it?"—the purpose of which was mainly to ask him where I was. I expected to hear him answer me by echoing me: "But where are you with it?" and perhaps this remark would have opened a path for me toward myself, but since he said nothing more, I wasn't in control of the silence, I couldn't resist this murmur, which underlay it. I asked him:

"We're connected by writings, aren't we?"

To which he immediately answered: "Yes, that's right," and then added the following, which showed me that he did not forget anything, that nothing was lost:

"But you know there must be no name between us."

I hardly took any notice of this last remark, perhaps because in myself I was no longer back at that moment when I wanted to give him a name, or perhaps because, without my knowing it, staring at that moment, I had lent him one. But above all, I was distanced from this thought by another thought: we were connected, he had recognized this, he had recognized it by a "Yes" of which I grasped the immensity, the immutable, immobile force that also confirmed all our past words, but in which above all reverberated the affirmation of the whole space we had entered, that space from which there was nothing to cut back, nothing to push back, which, even in the emptiness, affirmed, and affirmed again, in such a way that it seemed to warn me that henceforth, whatever might be my refusals, my statements that "I can't do any more," everything would nevertheless be resumed by that monumental "Yes," everything would end in it slowly, solemnly. "Yes, that's right." A calm expanse, yet one I couldn't remain close to; on the contrary, what occurred to me was that I should make use of it and that since we were connected, we were connected starting now and for now. Now, as he had promised me, he was going to "do something for me." I asked him:

"Don't you want to help me now?"

It seemed to me he hesitated, with an infinite hesitation that I filled with the firmness, the exigency of my expectation, of my impatience, too, which closed again when he answered me, from very far away, in a low voice:

"You know I can't help you."

I immediately stood up and, as though my thirst had returned, went to the kitchen. There, I looked for a glass, but for a reason I could not discern, that search came to nothing or something caused me not to go on with it. Coming back to the room, where I was surprised by the darkness, I heard him ask:

"What have you just been doing? Are you in pain?"

"I'm tired, but I feel better already."

"Yes, you'll get your strength back."

Because I was bothered by how little light there was, I said to him:

"I haven't yet spoken with you about this, but very near here there's a large bed, and I'm going to lie down on it."

"A large bed?"

At that moment, I searched my mind to find out whether I had really drunk that glass of water just now. Soon I was almost sure that it had not happened, something had stopped me from doing it. I reflected a little more, Finally, I said to him:

"I've forgotten something, I must go back to the kitchen."

"As you like," he said. "You have plenty of time."

Yet I didn't go back. Now I lacked the strength I had thought I owed to the drink. I sat down on the edge of the bed, no doubt in order to continue reflecting, but soon I also lacked the strength to think all this was important. I only asked myself if someone else had been there in my place, which seemed to explain why I retained such a cold memory of that action. I also thought about his last remark, on which I was now invited to rest. I thought about it with friendliness, even though this rest was a sleepless one, an empty one. But I also desired nothing other than that emptiness and that immobility.

Often before, in moments of great anguish, I had dreamed of breaking all ties, it seems to me I had said this to him, it seems to me it was in order to untie these bonds that I had wanted to tie them, to tie myself to him in such a way that the understanding, having become real, could really be destroyed. Perhaps I had even dreamed further; perhaps I only approached in order to fight him, in a combat that would separate him from himself, even if only by separating me from myself forever. A dream that expressed only my lassitude, the sterility of my lassitude, the point of forgetfulness where I was trying in vain to fool myself about what I knew best, and what I knew was that I could not take anything the wrong way, coming from him. In the most unhappy moments, I think I never revealed a single twinge of regret, of resentment, a single feeling of being at fault—which, in return, no doubt deprived me of hope. It doesn't matter. I never failed to say he was right, I who alone was right, and he never caused me to be guilty with respect to myself. If this is what loses me by preventing me from losing myself, if this is what binds me by ceaselessly pushing back the end, I accept this bond and I will endure this trial through the infinity of time.

Why this confidence? And is it confidence? I do not rely more on him than on myself, only a little more on him because he is less sure than I. A little more on him, because I find a little less in him than in me. Confidence? But at least nothing that might summon up distrust, nothing that ought to incline me to regret this encounter, if it took place. Confidence? Then confidence in the abyss, confidence that the abyss won't fail me, won't betray me.

I've never thought he might reveal anything important to me; I don't expect any revelation from him. This, too, makes us right for each other. And yet, didn't I expect something, didn't I want to ask him, as I do still at this moment: "I can trust you, can't I?"—and I immediately hear him answer me:

"Yes, but on condition that I can trust you."

"You mean I have to talk to you incessantly, without stopping?"

"Talk, describe things."

Which was enough to awaken a spirit of uncertainty.

"Why describe?" I asked him "There's nothing to describe, there's almost nothing left."

Why this voracious hunger for facts that he perhaps didn't understand but that he wanted to have anyway, this blind hunger in him that I immediately felt in myself as the uneasiness of nausea? Was he really looking for something? But he wasn't looking for anything, he couldn't be looking for anything in particular; to believe that would have driven me mad on the spot, and I didn't even think he had a particular relationship with me: not with me, not with me. And yet, I felt the approach of this aimless, patient voracity, that awaited, without ever becoming discouraged, an infinitesimal particle of an insignificant reality—in the form of my own disgust I felt its approach, its groping search, which I had to stop, at least, if not satisfy. What could I give him? A gesture, another step, a sigh, a last sigh? Or his own words, which I would have liked to keep at a distance once and for all, but which he tirelessly seized again, as though in them there was still a vestige of life which he wanted to reduce even more in order to disappropriate me of it, so that I would have nothing left that belonged to me? I said to him with a brusqueness that tore even me apart:

"You want to know where I am? But nothing has changed, we're still in the same spot, we'll always be here; yes, I find it strange to converse with you, strange to come to this, strange to stay here; why does it cost me so much strength? Why must I devote myself to something that costs me so much, without respite, without wanting it, without expecting anything from it? Am I going to continue chatting with you? It exhausts me, it doesn't even exhaust me."

So many words that expressed only the dangerous increase in my strength, as I immediately became aware, and much more so, even, when I heard him ask me:

"You want to see something new?" as though he himself, curiously, was infinitely avid for what might be new. This movement caused my agitation to subside, obliged me to return silently to the truth of that moment:

"Not necessarily new; perhaps nothing that would be new for anyone."

I imagined he was ready to elaborate on this theme, but soon he, in turn, cut it short:

"No, nothing new."

A remark in which I had to steep myself. It was in relation to this remark that I said to him a little later:

"At this moment, I am sitting on the edge of a bed, I will no doubt get up, soon it will be day."

"It's dark, isn't it?"

"It's not very dark, it's the light that's dark."

"Don't you want to stretch out now?"

"Yes, I think I'm going to stretch out, it's a large bed, unmade and disorderly. Do you want me to describe things to you as I see them?"

"Yes, that's it, as we are able to see them, as we will see them."

Nevertheless, I did not lie down. I had in some sense forgotten what was needed in order to do that, and yet, lying down, I would no doubt have been closer to that shared vision into which he was drawing me in defiance of my strength or so as to turn me away from it, destroy it by ignoring it. If I had stretched out, what would have happened? I could at least imagine: nothing was more tempting than that great stretch of space, already uncovered, that immensity where there would have been no respect for my person, where my rest would not be merely like a companion asleep near me in my wakefulness. Why not try it? I dream of that a few moments. During this dream, my hand is somehow invited by the tranquillity of the space, there nothing moves, nothing stable or moving, but a smooth immobility toward which I turn as I lie down on my side, which does not disturb or restrict the expanse of space. It is true that I am only on the edge of the real posture which I recognize a little beyond me in the form of a slight stirring which I feel, with a certain surprise, as a firm, almost solid resistance. Here there is something like a single wrinkle of space, I see it, in some way, and the fact that it should be just there, like a discordant irregularity, ought to warn me, but already unconcerned, I tip myself back lightly, joyously, trusting in space, in its indifference and its inattention. Thus, this latter movement is accomplished with a facility that expresses my own cheerfulness, but scarcely does it assert itself than all the power of the emptiness tightens around me, encloses me, holds me back and pushes me back into the depth of an endless fall, so that the gap into which I fall has the exact dimensions of my body, is my body into which I can't possibly fall and against which I collide at this moment as against a cold, foreign presence that throws me back where I am. This is the beginning, I said to myself, things began this way. Yes, such is the dream, and I have a suspicion of what it would like to show me: that if it is now forbidden for me to stretch out, this is because I am already stretched out at that point where, nevertheless, I am no longer there, but someone is there. What does such a moment want from me? It takes all my strength away from me, it leaves me here, not standing, not lying down, without rights and without repose, not working and yet occupied without respite by this idleness, not ignorant but knowing too much, not immobile but on the edge of an eternal agitation. What does it ask me to do? The fall is endless, it therefore leaves me nothing to do, I can't stop the fall, I don't have the means to do it, I'm not even falling, I'm only sitting on the edge of a bed, while there plunges into the distance the slight derision of a murmur: "Are you writing, are you writing at this moment?"

I can't say I tore myself from such a dream. It's true that in this night—I call it night, and yet it is the brilliant light of summer—I am still bound to a certain effort, to a life that has the appearance of life. I sometimes hear myself thinking: this is perhaps only the beginning. I sometimes also believe that even though nothing is happening, I am drawing near the place where I was hoping to fight. It was here, over there, where I heard him talking from, and it was the fight that was talking to me. Here the decisive fight takes place, everything is ready for the decision, the words themselves are ready, they are even already spoken, the decision is not only ready, it has been made, has everything therefore come to an end? Yes, everything has come to an end; and what was decided? Just this—that there would be no end, so that I continue to hear the fight, I approach the spot where the decision was made, and I say to myself: perhaps this is still merely the beginning, always merely the beginning.

I don't think about the future, I don't give myself a future, and not even a present. The present keeps bending, traversed by that empty gaiety that is only the limitless and empty absence of all present, it does not see itself in the past, nothing in it passes, nothing finishes, and if it becomes so heavy for me to carry, it is because of this burden of lightness, this laughing load I have to hold up in the center of a dreamy day that hides me from myself. It is in such a day that I must decide if he is really inviting me to write. He does not force me to do it, he does not even advise me to do it. But nevertheless, he has put into my mind the thought that if we are bound together, we are bound by writings. This means that I am in control of the reality of this bond;

to make this bond real, I must therefore write, and not once and for all, but all the time, or perhaps one single time, this is not specified, but a time for which I have plenty of time, a time that exhausts all the reality of time. A tempting thought, no doubt empty like a dream, oppressive and nauseating like everything that is empty, but in the middle of which I can dwell all the more lightly because it does not ask either realization or even the dream of that realization.

If he were tempting me only with that thought, I would be able to resist it easily, it would exhaust itself, dissolved within the space that brings it to me. No, he doesn't invite me to write, he doesn't ask it of me, but he seeks to persuade me that I am not doing anything else. And how can I avoid that impression? Against it, I have no defense, it has something necessary about it that goes beyond the conciliatory tranquillity of dreams, it has no need of proofs, it can't be overcome by anything, it collides, as against itself, against the truth of appearance that shows me sitting on the edge of the bed or not sitting, but perhaps lying down, or not even lying down, incapable of doing anything but wandering. I can't refute it, because it leaves me no room in which to move around it, it occupies all of space, it is tied to the affirmation of all of space, it affirms absolutely, and I can't think of breaking this circle, I don't think of it because I belong to this circle, and it is possible, in fact, that I'm not writing, because I can't, and I am almost no longer myself, but that's what it is, to write: at the point where I am, nothing else can be expressed, and this emptiness, this immobility is nothing more, and I can't do, I don't want, anything else.

What makes this situation terrible is that despite everything it demands infinitely, not of me, perhaps, or this demand demands this: that I not be taken into account. It does not consider my resources, these are perhaps very paltry, they are perhaps relatively still infinite, in any case obviously insufficient. Nevertheless, something is asked of me, it is not a duty nor an order—this is not asked of me, it must be accomplished by the fact that I have come to this, and to have come to this means: to go further, further in this direction, never in another.

I must say it, since I am here to say it: it is a frightening ordeal. It has no limits, it knows neither day nor night, it concerns itself with neither events nor desires; what is possible, it pushes away; what cannot be, that alone satisfies it; of him who has nothing it asks; he who

answers its demand doesn't know it and, because of that, doesn't answer. It may be that at one time I thoughtlessly obeyed its call, but
then who doesn't obey? he who is not called? but obeying proves
nothing about the call, the call always takes place, it doesn't need anyone to answer, it never really takes place, that is why it isn't possible
to answer it. But he who does not answer, more than any other, is
enclosed in his answer.

When did I give myself up to this risk? Perhaps while sleeping,
perhaps in the course of a night when, by an unreflecting movement,
by a single word into which I had put all of myself, the decision of
time, having been shaken, caused me to pass into the indecision of
the absence of time, there where the end is always still the unending.
But if that is an imprudence, why mightn't I have committed it? could
I live without committing it? did I regret it? Free not to surrender
myself to this risk, don't I surrender myself to it from one moment to
the next? and at present, is this beginning again? but nevertheless it is
not beginning again, it is an absolutely different moment, without
any parallel, without any tie to the past, without any concern for the
future, and yet it is also beginning again, is the same, is the emptiness
of repetition, the infinite pain that always passes through the same
point again, and always, at whatever moment it may be, this is said,
and eternally I express it.

He doesn't rush me, he isn't an adversary, he doesn't oppose me, this
is why I can't defend myself by fighting, the fight isn't even deferred, he
himself is the incessant deferral of the fight. And in a certain way I am
happy about it, because where I am, reserve obliges me to reserve myself, and his infinite complicity lends itself to this, to the point where I
not only allow myself to turn away from myself, but am entirely this
infinite turning away. When he sought to persuade me that I wasn't
doing anything else, I never opposed this movement in any other way
than by concessions that I allowed myself to wrest away, that I offered
him with the thought that, this way, the moment that had seemed to me
to put us face to face would return, it was this moment that I had in
view, it was this, I'm sure, that after having inspired in me a gesture of
frankness and firmness, drew me along to a place where there was no
longer anything firm. It began when, bringing me back to the phrase
that scarcely was one, that in any case left the field open to all the others—"Am I writing?"—it seemed to me he was inviting me to complete
it, sustain it, which, at a certain moment, caused me to add:

"Yes, at one time; perhaps, at one time." A miserable remark, miserably defective, in which "perhaps" tried to appease "at one time," whereas "at one time" already contains the uncertainty of a "perhaps" and this certainly showed how weak my "Yes" still was, but also how "at one time" was for me a weak defense against the "Yes" I had said. I saw this even before he repeated: "At one time," and when he had repeated it, I saw it even more from the neutral tone that was his, that asked for no clarification, added nothing to the word, only said what was said by the word, which in this nakedness only appeared all the more suspect, deceptive, inconsistent, without frankness, not even doubtful, but having no other form than its own doubt, entirely traversed and formed by the cloud of this doubt, in which all that could be seen was my desire to preserve the present moment. A little after, he asked: "And what were you writing?"—to which, seeing his insistence and in order to try to take back what I had granted to him, I answered:

"Perhaps it wasn't me, but someone else, someone who is merely close to me."

A point of view he immediately adopted:

"Well, then, what was he writing?"

I listen to this. Who is he addressing? who is involved here? who is speaking? who is listening? who could answer such a distance? this comes from so far away and it doesn't even come, why is he ignoring me? why is this ignorance within my reach? why does it make itself understood? A speech? And yet not a speech, barely a murmur, barely a shiver, less than silence, less than the abyss of emptiness: the fullness of emptiness, something one can't silence, occupying all of space, uninterrupted and incessant, a shiver and already a murmur, not a murmur, but a speech, and not just any speech, but distinct, appropriate: within my reach. I summoned up my whole being to answer him:

"He wasn't writing, and he mustn't be involved here."

But as though he had heard only the beginning of my answer or as though my remark itself had wiped out the prohibition against speaking, he asked: "And at present, is he writing?"—which was immediately followed by the slight derision of his words: "Are you writing, are you writing at this moment?"

What is going to happen, then? Did I really have this desire to steal away, to unload myself on someone else? or rather to conceal in me the unknown, not to disturb it, to wipe out its footsteps so that what it has accomplished may be accomplished without leaving any remains, in such a way that it not be accomplished for me who dwells on the edge, outside the event, which no doubt passes by with the brilliance, noise, and dignity of lightning, without my being able to do more than perpetuate its approach, take its indecision by surprise, maintain it, maintain myself in it without yielding. Was this at an earlier time, where I lived and worked, in the little room in the form of a watch-tower, in that place where already, in some sense having disappeared, far from feeling unburdened of myself, I had, on the contrary, the duty to protect that disappearance, to persevere in it in order to push it farther, always farther? Wasn't it there, in the extreme distress that is not even someone's distress, that I had been presented with the right to speak of myself in the third person? Didn't I have to keep the secret concerning "him" even from my companion, even without knowing if I would have the strength, if the secret did not signify lack of strength, withdrawal, the emptiness of the moment? Didn't I have my attention constantly turned to him? I don't mean I was thinking about him: he couldn't have tolerated a thought, he had nothing in him that could have allowed itself to be thought, but surely I would have liked to convince myself that my task was to protect him against the nameless, to keep the nameless by my side and not give anything over to him but myself. A thought that pleased me, because it as-signed me a role and gave me a certain importance, but I nevertheless had enough sense to reject it, for how was I to defend him, I who didn't know him, and from whom would he have had to protect him-self, if not from me? What was more, I knew that to think of him, to claim to protect him, was only a sly way of revealing him, and I also knew this: unmasked, he could no longer be anything else—but me.

At that moment, this was what I sensed: for a long time now, my companion had been trying to attain it, to look at it in me. I was not intentionally betraying it, but I had become too weak, I was almost no one, and to see me was already to see it, to speak to me was no longer to speak of me. What is going to happen, then? Why try to stop it?

I think I have to write. I think all the words we have exchanged are crowded around me and I won't resist their pressure for very long, that probably for a long time now, an infinite time I haven't really been resisting them any longer. It seems to me that if I write, it will be I writing: I will bind my companion to me in such a way that he will approach only me and that what must remain unknown will remain safeguarded. In this way, the space opened by his allusion will close again. In this fissure there is a danger that I don't fully understand, a danger that is not merely mortal, but rather holds death in check, is perhaps death, but held in check. And at the same time, wasn't it strangely attractive? didn't it make what he said firmer, more true, indifferent and true? didn't a whistle pass through that fissure that called to mind the wind of the distance, the freshness of the natural air, and no doubt I had only received it exhausted, more a memory than the force of the wind, but if the fissure had been enlarged, perhaps the open air itself would have seized me and carried me along, perhaps it would have been there that, if I threw out my anchor, instead of hearing it scrape my empty depth of myself, I would rediscover the deeps of the open sea, and not infinity, for which I have no need, but the single moment in which I would tie myself to the end with enough strength for it to become true, for it not to be excluded from the truth and for the truth to light up in it.

An impression that was powerful, pressing, that forced me to go back to the distant period, when I still heard the sound of the wind shaking the house during the autumn storms, to ask myself if, should I truly come to the point of writing, I wouldn't need to be helped in my task by that work and that effort of the wind, and I asked myself why, for so long now, I had been kept away from that help, dwelling in such a calm that I probably wouldn't have had the strength to tolerate even a slight whistle finding its way through the vent, yet I wasn't surprised by this, and if the wind, with the gusts of approaching winter, seemed driven far back by a force infinitely greater than its own, I said to myself that I knew this force and that it was the power of the memory of summer.

In any case, I couldn't assign an exact moment to the answer I would give him, if I ever succeeded in saying to him:

"Yes, at this moment, exactly at this moment." That these last words were the only ones that counted in his sentence was what I discovered with a sort of gratitude, so that this whole sentence, so anguishing for me, regained a youthful face from this, and he himself a more truthful presence. As I reflected on it from this new perspective, I saw that it was an almost innocent murmur, something a little more disturbing than the sound of blood or the beating of an agitated heart, but that circulated through the house joyfully, without respite. If I no longer heard it, I imagined it had gone to another spot, had been called elsewhere by its own gaiety, by the lightness that turned it into a question. Sometimes—and then a certain uneasincss returned—I asked myself if that appearance of caprice, of restless and aimless vagabondage did not conceal a search, an obscure hunt, a stubborn pursuit, and this feeling, though I did not believe it, became an uncontrollable alarm, when it seemed to me that it was approaching a spot I could have situated, for instance the staircase, or that it was flying up and assaulting the little room, the place where I had the impression I had already returned once with my companion. Terrible imprudence. But I must say that just as I had enough confidence in him, in his loyalty, to be assured that he would not play his game alone, even though he was capable of coming to me by unprepared paths, to the same degree I mistrusted certain of his words which I did not distinguish, once they were said, from mine, a mistrust that yielded to a joyful enthusiasm once I recognized their frivolity, their fussiness and futility, but which weighed most of the time with a heavy weight on me, with the weight formed of their own heaviness, their inertia and, coupled with their irresponsibility, the perseverance that made them sterile, unreal and eternal. They sustained a certain life in this house from which I was not very willing to turn away—another source of their danger— a life that held me in a place, where I should not have lingered, and I sometimes asked myself if, in these other rooms where no doubt, because of them, I would stay at certain times, I did not live with a life that was more alert, more carefree, and on terms of equality with the earth. As I heard them talk in that joyful, incessant way, it would only have required of me an effort against myself, a momentary forgetting of the truth, to let myself believe I was talking with beings much more real than I was myself, just then, at least more alive, yes, beings, here, from whom I was only separated because I was not here, or if I was here, I was surrounded by the solitude of that "we are alone" that had opposed me, every time I moved away from myself.

In these moments then, it was the need to pacify those words, suspend for a moment their agitated flight through the house, bring them back, also, to themselves by keeping them away from the feverish earth, that obliged me to ask myself if I shouldn't write—now. It seemed to me that only by writing could I soothe this uneasiness, which, it seemed, could carry them to meet a mouth that was alive, capable of giving them the happiness of breath, and that I could also, in this uneasiness, soothe the image which, at their summons, was crossing through the days and nights. A task concerning which I barely glimpsed what it demanded of me, for I no doubt found it easy to wish to calm the moment, free it of the distress that was making it appear, but if I could hope to succeed in this by bringing the words back to their birthplace, I myself would perhaps have to descend, into another time, pass into a place where it would no longer be a question of appearance or image, but a supreme moment toward which I would have to descend firmly and which I would not be able to seize except by desiring it with all the strength and transport of passion.

In this way I understood better why this was what it was, to write: I understood it, I mean this word became completely other, much more demanding even than I had thought it was. To be sure, it was not to my power that it had made its appeal, nor to myself either, but to "this moment" when I could do nothing—and thus it seemed to me that writing had to consist in drawing near that moment, would not give me power over it, but, by some act unknown to me, would make me a gift of this moment, near which, for an infinite time now, I had dwelled without reaching it—far from here and yet here, I clearly perceived the risk I was going to expose myself to: instead of making the words go back over the frontier they had crossed, the risk, on the contrary, of disturbing them more and more, of tormenting them by driving them mad with an empty, unbridled desire, to the point that at a certain moment, passing through me in their frantic pursuit, they would carry me once again toward a space dangerously open to the illusion of a world to which we would, however, not have access, for the thought that this access might be granted to us, if the assault was conducted with enough vehemence and skill, had not yet come to tempt me, that temptation was only part of the risk, the risk was the pivot around which what was threat turned immediately into hope, and I myself turned around myself, given up to every appeal of this place where all I could do was wander.

To say that I understand these words would not be to explain to myself the dangerous peculiarity of my relations with them. Do I understand them? I do not understand them, properly speaking, and they too who partake of the depth of concealment remain without understanding. But they don't need that understanding in order to be uttered, they do not speak, they are not interior, they are, on the contrary, without intimacy, being altogether outside, and what they designate engages me in this "outside" of all speech, apparently more secret and more interior than the speech of the innermost heart, but, here, the outside is empty, the secret is without depth, what is repeated is the emptiness of repetition, it doesn't speak and yet it has always been said already. I couldn't compare them to an echo, or rather, in this place, the echo repeated in advance: it was prophetic in the absence of time.

The fact that they were deprived of intimacy to this degree was, it seems to me, what associated me, in the course of their wandering, their coming and going, with a feeling of infinite unhappiness, with the chill of the greatest distress I had ever had to endure, a distress that immediately reverberated in an endless gaiety that made him ask me: "Why are you laughing?"—which I could not answer except to say:

"Because I'm not alone," a phrase that, in its turn, flew off dangerously through the house. Perhaps the idea that I must save them from this lack of intimacy also belongs to the project of writing, an idea I could have had at an earlier time, an idea to which, no doubt uselessly, I sacrificed my right to summon another person and say "you" to him. But this is only an idea from an earlier time, I can't hope to give them what I myself have been deprived of, I don't even want to, they often please me extraordinarily this way (which is another aspect of the danger): they beguile me by this busy lack of work, this torment which is a kind of laughter, this presence in which I am never "me" for them nor they "you" for me, a presence that is no doubt disabling, for I'm not able to deal with anything in them, disabling but attractive, an enigma there is no need to elucidate, the key word to the enigma is this enigma, capable not of devouring me, but of associating me with its devouring avidity.

If I question myself seriously, I must recognize that, if not all these words, at least the most brilliant and the most enticing, the ones that uplift me almost outside of myself (and in a certain light each is always the most brilliant), could only steal away or oppose "this moment" in which I ought to write. And I recognize it with all the more apprehension because they sometimes gave me the opposite feeling:

"sometimes" means during certain periods which, to distinguish them from others in which everything seems easier, I call nocturnal, and they themselves appear to me profoundly nocturnal, it is in these moments that they crowd around me, like dreams being dreamt by my side, and I myself am only an image in their dream, I feel the power of their conjuring and how they, too, feel the strength of my dream, feeling the infinite desire to participate in it, to enter into the sphere of that dream, a desire so lively that it is itself the night, that it creates the night in which we find ourselves together again, reunited, but through the ignorance we have in common, through the community of our ignorance which causes it to happen that even when I hear them, I do not hear them, and when I speak them, nothing is said, even though everything may be said in them forever. And no doubt what they may ask of me has no relation to the idea of writing, it is rather they who want to be inscribed in me as though to allow me to read on myself, as on my gravestone, the word of the end, and it is true that, during these nocturnal moments, I have the feeling of being able to read myself that way, read in a dangerous way, well beyond myself, to the point where I am no longer there, but someone is there.

Beautiful hours, profound words which I would like to belong to, but which would, themselves, also like to belong to me, words empty and without connection. I can't question them and they can't answer me. They only remain close to me, as I remain close to them. That is our dialogue. They stand motionless, as though erect in these rooms; at night, they are the concealment of the night; in the day, they have the transparency of the day. Everywhere I go, they are there.

What do they want? We're not familiar to one another, we don't know one another. Words from the empty depth, who has summoned you? Why have you become manifest to me? Why am I occupied with you? I shouldn't occupy myself with you, you shouldn't occupy yourselves with me, I must go farther, I won't unite you to hope or to the life of a breath.

I don't know that they press on me, but I sense it. I see a sign of it in the immobility which, even when they seem to wander, even when I leave them, keeps them crowded around me in a circle whose center I am in spite of myself. And this circle is sometimes larger, sometimes smaller, but for me the distance doesn't change, and the circle is never interrupted, the expectation is never broken, I could call myself a prisoner of that expectation if it were more real, but since it remains silent and uncertain, I am only a prisoner of the uncertainty of the expectation.

Am I their goal, what they are seeking? I will not believe it. But sometimes they stare at me with a power so restrained, a silence so reserved, that this silence points me out to myself; then I have to remain firm, I have to struggle with my refusal to believe, and the more I struggle, in general successfully, the more I see that I owe the strength that gives me this success only to them, to their proximity, to the firmness of their inattention.

I'm not their goal, but why do they remain? why are they turned toward me, even if they are not directed toward me? Why, outside my companion and as though to a certain extent they had a free life, must I look at them without linking them to him, with a gaze that is perhaps connected to the word "write," but that is, in that case, connected to it as the thing that may best turn me away from it? I can ask myself that, I could try to find out at what moment they first attracted my gaze, they turned me in their direction to the point that all things are visible to me through their transparent presence and they hold me in the fixedness of their appearance. When did this happen? A vain question, it has always been happening; but I didn't perceive it, which says a good deal about my blindness, I didn't see them as an obstacle, I didn't see them, whereas now, I am looking at them: as though they have risen from their graves.

I didn't invoke them, I am without power over them, and they have no relations with me. We remain side by side, it's true, but I don't know them; I live close to them, and perhaps I must live because of them, perhaps because of them I am sustained in myself, but I am also somehow separated from that proximity, it is in that separation that we are close, there they remain, there they pass, and they respond to no one.

They don't importune, nor do they attract me; if they attracted me, from that assurance I would also draw the strength to drive them back. But I don't desire that, desire can't penetrate this circle, only forgetfulness penetrates it. It seems to me that here forgetfulness does its work, a forgetfulness of a particular sort, in which I don't forget myself, behind which I shield myself, on the contrary, as behind a borrowed "me," one that allows me always to say "me" with a semblance of authority. I forget nothing, it is in this respect that I belong to forgetfulness.

They're always together. No doubt this means I can only see them together, together even though unconnected, motionless around me though wandering. I see them all, never one in particular, never one single one in the familiarity of an undivided gaze, and if, even so, I try to stare at one of them separately, what I'm looking at then is a terrible, impersonal presence, the frightening affirmation of something I don't understand, don't penetrate, that isn't here and that nevertheless conceals itself in the ignorance and emptiness of my own gaze. But this occurs only when I try to isolate one of them, to maintain in a single one of them what makes them all separate, what keeps them all at a distance.

I mustn't alarm them, nor tame them. I must remain still so that they will remain still. Deal with their presence in a loyal way, and "loyally" means without attributing any law to them, without attributing myself to this presence as to a law—and perhaps not taking them into account. But the fact of once having opened my eyes on them prevents me now from ever closing my eyes again. For one instant, this was visible to me, and now it is this instant in which everything is visible to me that I look at and retain, despite myself, without being able to drive it away. In return, and because, in a way I don't understand, I fascinate them, I have to remain within their fascination. This isn't noticed, doesn't disturb appearances, is nothing but an uncertain expectation. Next to them, I am like a man who has already held himself up in the water too long and who sees, coming to meet him, what appears to be the body of a drowned man: only one? perhaps two, perhaps ten, he can't distinguish them, nothing distinguishes them, and they probably do him no harm, they merely hold themselves motionless around him; if he asks himself: What do they want? he knows very well that this question is without meaning, without reality, just as that meeting is not real. Nevertheless, eventually, and because he is growing more and more tired, he can't help finding this immobility heavy, it presses on him, it clings to him, and he asks himself: what does this immobility want?

Everything has an end, but distress does not, it does not know sleep, it does not know death, from one instant to the next I put this to the test; day doesn't illuminate it, night is its depth, its living memory. The circle they form around me encloses me on the outside and yet always within me still. It is infinite, and because of this I suffocate inside it; one can only suffocate in infinity, but I suffocate slowly here, infinitely. I thought I was only the center of this circle, but I already fill it entirely, that is why everything is motionless and, they themselves being crowded against this immobility, I think I see them, but I am really touching them, they hold me against myself, as I hold them desperately beyond me.

The feeling I am left with: I will not yield, I can't do otherwise.

Strange impression of daylight in this feeling, not that of any sort of hope, but of an accurate direction, of confidence that doesn't alter, of affirmation that persists: I will go in that direction, never in another.

A feeling that is immediately disturbed, for the thought goes through me that if I wanted to, I would receive an increase in strength from them. But this is the strength to which I can't consent; why? I don't know more precisely; nevertheless, I still know that this depends on me, on me at each instant, I know it even in forgetfulness and even when, looking at them, I have the presentiment that it would be enough for me to say to one of them—but only to one—"Come," for it to shout its name, and right away I would emerge from that reserve in which, even if the instant doesn't stand there, I stand in its place, in that spot where, in the confidence that is suitable to the abyss, I await the instant that will say to me: "Now everything is all right, you don't have to talk anymore."

Then this other thought: instead of remaining in that reserve, haven't you already abandoned it? have you even touched it? perhaps you've never been outside, or only in an earlier time, but not now, not again, this can't take place again, everything is empty and lifeless.

What darkened, obliterated those hours, I feel, was that the immobility was still only the agitation, the feverishness that came to me from that presence, the strength their proximity communicated to me, the desire that strength gave me to attribute a goal to them, to free them by an intention: did they really want to come alive? did they want to make themselves free, not with a second-hand freedom, but free with respect to their origin and by obliterating it, by forgetting it, with a forgetfulness deeper than death? A terrible thought, a thought in which forgetfulness is at work.

Escape them? With me they escape, I carry them along without even noticing it, or I think I see them wandering once again through the house, but I'm the one continuing to perform the gestures of life. Sometimes—and this should frighten me, but this doesn't frighten me—it seems to me I look at them in a more familiar way. Especially at night, thinking freely of my past life, I have the impression that they're taking part in it, that they're feeding on it, that they could live it, if I thought about it in a more lively way. Then they close me in tightly, and in this irresolute immobility I can only become their dream, the dream of this night in which they remain close to me, as I remain close to them, in the intimacy of this night which ceaselessly passes through the day, which is the day for me, in which they are standing, looming up all around, forming the empty, infinite circle that is still me, even if already I'm no longer there. In these moments, how can I see them as an obstacle? how can I think they interpose themselves between their origin and me? Instead, I trust in them, I look at them in that trustfulness that addresses neither one nor the other, that doesn't attribute a gaze to them, that doesn't discover a face in them, that leaves them what they are, images without eyes, a closed immobility that silently conceals itself and in which concealment is revealed. We're so close it seems to me I form a circle with them, form a circle around someone whom neither they nor I see, for my eyes are no more open than theirs are. This explains our new familiarity, the different air I breathe, the expectation that is not theirs but mine, an expectation of which I am not the prisoner, but the guardian. We stand around him. We don't know if he is one alone or if he is many. We don't know if he is sleeping, riveted to his rest, or if he is coming down to us, without knowing it and without seeing us. Our task is to maintain the circle, but why? We don't know.

From these moments I return preoccupied. In a certain way, this preoccupation prevents my return, it also prevents me from bringing back with me the part of me that belongs to the circle or, if it comes back, it is foreign to me, not an enemy, but distant as though I had almost nothing more in common with myself. I realized by this sign that, even though I was neither more removed nor more separated from him, it was harder for me to turn toward my companion, perhaps because when I turned toward him, something in me turned away from him, but it was also the opposite: I had to search in vain for a conversation that had been pursued, pushed farther. Formerly, at a period when my unconcern allowed me to find support in things, the thought had come to me to fight him with what was strongest in him: I would raise silent walls around him; I would never question him, and if he passed through the interstices of time I wouldn't answer him. What did I have in view? To control him? to treat him as an equal? Maybe my desire was more obscure, more profoundly tied to him, and this desire is what I recover today, but in the form of a suffocating apprehension, the anxious feeling the word "forgetfulness" brings with it. I think that at certain moments I'm afraid of forgetting him, losing him in forgetfulness and making forgetfulness the only abyss where he could be lost.

A threat, an immobility, against which my head rests, full of distress and pain, and what turns this into a kind of dizziness is that he doesn't seem more distant to me, but on the contrary, too tangibly present, as though the discomfort of forgetfulness were already drawing him to the surface. I turn in his direction with more difficulty, but with the exhausting feeling that he has never been so close and that if, in order to think of him, I were not obliged first to pass through the thought that I am forgetting him, I would hold him in a proximity that would pierce through all reserve. Thinking of him had always been a subterfuge for determining a place for him and distancing myself, for a moment, from that place, but at present I keep hesitating to summon him to where I am for fear of drawing him into a speech already obscured by forgetfulness. Because of this, I have to avoid him, keep on my guard, put him on his guard too, explain to him the danger our relations are putting him in, a danger all the more obsessive because I don't have a clear view of it, because he alone could help me understand it better, understand why he is exposed to it. What I sense is that this danger makes him closer, more tangible, attracts him, attracts him to me, which is where the danger comes from—and how could I imperil him? A thought that belongs to the threat, just as mysterious, just as threatening as it is, a thought which I have never had before, at least not about him, and which I'm not sure I'm still having, a rarefied thought in which it is hard for me to remain, even though everything in it seems to me illuminated with a new, blinding light. When I say he is close, he is only more present, with a presence that is too immediate, that makes him close to me without making me close to him, that distances me from him instead, by keeping me here where I am. It would certainly be a sign of uneasiness, of weakness, if, instead of staying at a distance, he began wandering around very close to appearances, as he has never been tempted to do in his respect for my reason and the calm of his certainty. He lacks something, clearly, but I am incapable of finding out what, incapable of supplying it, just barely capable of acknowledging, of watching over that approach, and of struggling to keep it from being expressed through signs. I can't say I'm lying in wait for him, or if I am it is in my memory, as though the greatest danger were in seeing him appear there. I'm not lying in wait for him, but the feeling that I attract him more than he attracts me—that through my mediation a power is exercised that is already taking him to the frontiers of this world—is in some sense the root of the word "forgetfulness," the source of the disturbance I can't control, for it is a disturbing feeling, it conceals within itself a temptation difficult to overcome, in which I ceaselessly risk showing myself to be strong against myself. It is tempting to attract the unknown to oneself, to want to bind it by a sovereign decision; it is tempting, when one has power over the distance, to stay inside the house, to summon it there and to continue, in that approach, to enjoy the calm and the familiarity of the house. But perhaps I had already summoned it, maybe it was too late: this was the presentiment that made my time a dead time in which it seemed to me I was fighting in vain against something that had already happened, even though, despite everything, I retained this certainty: I will not yield.

Perhaps I wouldn't have felt so assaulted by this change if I hadn't suddenly discovered—a revelation that became wedded to the day, after which there was no more day for me—that I not only was hearing him speak, but that now I could hear how difficult, how impossible it was for him to speak. An overwhelming impression. One moment, and I couldn't doubt it: it didn't speak, it didn't make any noise, and yet it would have liked to speak, it desperately aspired to speak, after infinite efforts it came to the threshold of speech only to collapse on it, perish there, putrefy there in a breath whose last vibration I just barely perceived. How could I endure it? I asked him quickly: "Did you just say something to me?" and he answered me no less promptly: "But didn't you just speak to me?"—which made me glimpse more than I would have liked. I tried, at least, not to show it to him, I couldn't put him directly in the presence of my thought, so I confessed only the easiest thing:

"All these times I have thought there were too many words between us."

"Between us?" He seemed to descend into this question, but I saw clearly that for me this interval, in the form of a ditch, no longer had its depth. Suddenly, he said in a feverish way:

"Yes, we must speak constantly, without stopping."

"Do you want that?"

"It must be! Now! Now!" He said this in a tone so piercing, so bestial, that I became disoriented and in turn nearly shouted:

"Don't talk that way—not now."

Immediately afterwards, near me, there was a quick noise of something falling, a dull falling noise, without depth.

"What happened?" I said in a low voice.

His curiosity was instantly aroused.

"Yes, what happened?"

"It was a noise of falling, as though someone had fallen at my feet, just as I finished speaking to you."

"You had just spoken?"

"I was just saying to you...."

But I didn't linger over that word, I didn't linger over it especially since the same incident that had led to it now took its place: yet not entirely the same, it was closer, it seemed able to cross the threshold, the silence lifted under the effort of which I sensed the gigantic pulsation, a cry, the madness of a cry within which everything would break, more than a cry, a word, but already this had collapsed, the cry had not been delivered, and I, too, had not been delivered from it.

This incident, by good fortune, took place shortly before nightfall. Only the night could contain, could stop the effect of the tear it had made. For a long time I examined the thought that, as long as I was speaking to him, he would find in what I said, however paltry it was, an appeasement that would then allow him to answer me from the depth of his reserve. It is true that the anomaly only seemed to occur when he tried to come to me without my knowing or without waiting for me to clear a path for him. I was not even sure of this, for there were still too few instances, and at least one, the last, appeared to be an exception. Yet I could not detach myself from my remark, it seemed striking to me, just as I had always been struck by that power of initiative he had, which he very rarely made use of and almost always in a lusterless way, but in spite of that, I retained an extraordinary memory of it: every time, I had been surprised, shaken—frightened? a little frightened, as though all of a sudden I had understood that instead of remaining riveted to the chain of words, a chain so long it allowed him to roam all spaces with the appearance of freedom, he kept breaking the chain, and even more, that there was no chain and that chance alone allowed him to emerge precisely where I was and nowhere else. When I talked to him, I felt the weight of the chain, it was tiring but reassuring, the chain was only a fiction, but the weight was real. When he appeared by way of roads that had not been prepared, everything seemed capable of happening, everything that had been acquired through days of effort and struggle seemed to be lost in order to make room for him: I didn't have the feeling of a true freedom, it was something else, I don't know what, a possibility that wasn't a possibility, a simplicity that overcame the imposture, but one from which nothing arose; it was a beginning, not even a beginning, perhaps not much of anything; when I summoned it up in memory, what I called initiative resembled one word too many, one that might have leaped over the series, but, after having distanced all the rest, made a place for itself there and strengthened the imposture. Perhaps, after all, nothing was more disappointing. All that remained was to understand why, within this disappointment, I wasn't disappointed, why, in this moment when I had to think of it as of a lost possibility, I found it so painful to have to renounce it, so distressing to commit myself, once and for all, to preventing him henceforth from coming unexpectedly and, in order to do that, always preparing the way for him, anticipating his initiatives, going before him, talking to him constantly, without stopping, without leaving any emptiness and without ever breaking the chain, so that he would not stray outside himself. A duty I did not want to shirk, but why this task? Why, in the calm of the night, did it appear to me, in the end, prodigiously difficult, but also prodigious, to the point of giving me back, at the moment when I was about to collapse, a superabundance of strength, an impetuousness of movement that didn't concern itself with anything? I understood it when I realized that this task had brought me back, without my knowing it and by an unsuspected path, to the word "write." In the circle of the night, this word suddenly rose up like a radiant intuition, as though it were presenting itself for the first time, with all the youthfulness of an indestructible dream, all the seriousness of a task I might not have the strength to bear, but that would bear me, on condition that for an instant I provide it with a point of support. I wasn't trying to recover all the reasons that had been pushing this word to the forefront for so long: everything, in that moment, was converging on it, everything was igniting in order to make it shine, and in its light the sovereign exaltation of the last day was already rising and setting.

As soon as the feeling that it was necessary brought me to my feet, the poverty of the day was what struck me, however, what made me feel, once again, how close to appearances my companion must be, how thin these appearances were. Yes, it was this that I saw first, the extraordinary thinness of the day, its tenuousness, its superficial brilliance. It was certainly a beautiful day, but terribly worn. I was standing at the table now. I was alone, with a different sort of solitude. I said to myself: "I must forget everything that happened before this night. I have a task to perform, and I also have the strength to perform it, the two fit each other exactly, as a cut fits the knife blade that made it. No doubt my strength is divided up, spread out through the whole of my life, whereas the task is concentrated in a single moment in which it waits, but it waits patiently; I can't fail it; with or without me, it will be accomplished." I was fully aware that what I called "my task" was astonishingly simple, that in truth it was already entirely realized, completed, there before me, and that now I had only to see this, make it apparent to my eyes. But for this, I would have had to relax for a moment, and I couldn't because I was paralyzed by the idea that my relations with my companion had lost all their simplicity. Never before had I spied on him. Never had he given me the feeling he was spying on me. Perhaps I was constantly occupied with him, but in this occupation I was free, all too free. I wasn't watching over him, I wasn't waiting for him, I talked to him and to talk to him required of me a very great effort, but this effort was made as though in my absence, in a spot where, nevertheless, I was so firmly gathered that I couldn't desire anything that wasn't immediately given to me. But now I found before me this thought that we were separated by forgetfulness, that within the forgetfulness he could be imperiled, that my duty consisted in preventing him from emerging from his depth, in pushing him back with my hand, the slightest pressure from which had once been enough to keep him at a distance, whereas now, it

would surely require all my attention, all my strength, all my life, to
preserve in one single point the integrity of the day. This made me
nervous. I would have needed to be able to look at things calmly.
Surely there were still more resources in them than I could suspect. I
said to myself:

"Be patient with yourself; be alone for a moment; abandon everything, abandon even the night." But these words only agitated me,
gave me a feeling of the emptiness that had to be filled up, the real
words that I lacked in order to succeed in that, my desire to return
precisely to the night in which I had approached them and, in my
expectation of that night, I no longer saw anything of the day but its
dreamy lightness, the light that seemed to have lost the edge of its
manifestness and in which I could not make out anything, not even
that the day was not lacking to me. Yet, the strange thing, in the corner where I was, near the table where, however, I wasn't writing—I
couldn't call it writing—was that at no time did I lose the instinct,
the certainty, that here, at least, he would remain himself, that in this
place, as he had promised me, a moment would come when "he would
do everything for me." I kept remembering what he had said, and it
was this memory I presented him with when I asked him:

"Don't you want to help me now?" I waited for his answer with a
faith, a hope, that he must have sensed and that I sensed in turn when
he said quietly, probably after quite some time:

"I can't help you. You know that—I can't do anything."

I was driven from my place by these words, it seemed; I had to go
to another spot, another room, probably the kitchen where for a moment I found the tranquil light of summer again and looked at it with
a shock of pleasure, but I didn't linger there, for I had the feeling time
was pressing. Once I was back in the room, where the darkness of the
day made me hesitate, I heard him ask me, with some anxiety:

"What did you just do?"

"Why, I drank a glass of water."

"Are you in pain?"

"I was tired, but I feel better already."

"Yes, it takes a moment to go away. Don't you want to rest?"

The truth was that I wanted to walk a little more. I felt a certain
dizziness, a strangely solitary fear:

"We're completely alone."

"Yes, we're alone."

I walked, I took a few steps. Having become used to the darkness, I recognized the familiar space of the room, the tranquil openings of the large bay windows, a little closer to me the table, and almost next to me an uncovered and disordered bed.

"I think the best thing for me now would be to lie down."

"Yes, that's right." Almost immediately after, he asked me:

"You're tall, aren't you?"

But I didn't realize where these words were coming from, nor why they enveloped me once again with the impression of naturalness that had always marked our relations. I didn't realize it because I seemed to hear him in the tranquil simplicity of the past, but when I answered him: "Fairly tall," and he added: "Couldn't you describe to me what you're like?" I had such a strong feeling—probably at finding myself once again in the truth of his reserve, at the very moment when I feared I was left out of it—that I could only think of answering:

"Yes, that's easy." As I said this, I thought, in fact, that there was a mirror on the wall on the other side of the table, though I didn't intend to look at myself in it, but the memory of that mirror helped me say to him:

"I believe I look rather young."

"Young? Why?"

I thought for a moment:

"It's because I'm thin."

A remark that didn't seem to reach him, he seemed so occupied with allowing the word "young" to come to him, profoundly, in a disturbing way, repeating it as though he wanted henceforth to confine himself to it, to the point that, understanding that he wouldn't let go of it again of his own accord, I made haste, in order to deflect him from it, to find another reason: "And also because the face is very bright," which did, in fact, attract him strongly, while at the same time inducing him to raise this doubt, which he expressed shortly afterwards:

"But isn't there also something dark about it?"

I stood firm:

"No, it may be too naked, formed in too hasty a manner, but the eyes are bright, they have an astonishing brightness, in fact, a brightness that is cold, then suddenly brilliant, but most of the time very calm."

"How do you know that?"

"I think I've been told that."

But he pursued his advantage:

"Who told you that?"

"People."

"Ah yes, people. People"—a word that seemed to awaken an ominous echo in him, but he did not stop there. He went on:

"Extraordinarily calm?"

"Maybe not always."

"Maybe too calm!"—in a way that would have made me fear once again that I would never see him tear himself away from this word, if he had not abruptly ended by saying joyfully:

"Well, I see, I see," as though really, for him, something like a portrait had emerged from me.

Despite this joyous tone, I couldn't help thinking he wouldn't be satisfied with such an incomplete picture. I would have liked to make it more expressive, bring it close to the truth, which, through my fault, he had not correctly penetrated. I would especially have liked to go back to a trait that seemed essential to me, show him that this face was usually very gay, that this gaiety penetrated even the darkest moments, moments from which, even then, arose the glimmer of a brightness that was joyful, perhaps distant, almost absent, but all the more tangible because of that. I said to him:

"You know, there is a smile on that face."

This immediately pleased him in an extraordinary way; he asked feverishly:

"Where is it? In the eyes?"

"In the eyes, too, I think."

"Even when you're asleep?"

I thought about it: yes, even when I was asleep. While I was trying to imagine how he pictured that smile, he suddenly said to me, with that ferreting, unilluminated sort of eagerness he had:

"People like that, don't they?"

"Yes, they probably liked it." I almost asked him: "And do you like it?" but I didn't do it, I didn't have time to decide to do it, because he added: "I see, I see," and then I had the feeling that this time he had really taken possession of this face, that at least he was going to begin to carry it off toward those regions where it eluded my power of attraction, regions close to which I would try to advance, without yielding, either, to the inclination that attracted me to him. I must have spent a long time reflecting on what I called his sphere, the abrupt lightening of our relations, a lightening which, however, didn't seem to me to correspond to anything new, as though I merely realized, now, that they had never really changed. Then this idea occurred to me—that if our relations were the same, it didn't mean he himself had remained identical; it seemed to me I should have asked him this: "Haven't you changed a little?"—which I already heard him answering with: "But you've changed too!" and wouldn't that have led me to say to him: "You mean you're not still the same?"— a thought that was more like a shiver than a word, but even though this thought was terrible to look at, I stared at it anyway, I let myself descend into it as far as that point from which I did not turn away, even when I had to hear something cry out that had neither form nor limit, something revolting, the mud of the deepest places, the frenetic vitality that did not bother either to recognize me or to let itself be recognized. If I could succeed in doing this, it was because this was still only the reflection of a thought. At least I didn't refuse to do this until the moment when, being still within the powerful meditation that enveloped me, I noticed that my eyes were open on something that I didn't at first grasp, a point, not a point, but a blossoming, a smile of the whole of the space, which expressed, occupied all of the space, in which I then recognized precisely what I had wanted to describe to him, a smile that was free, without hindrance, without a face, that radiated softly out from this absence, illuminated it, gave it a resemblance, a name, a silent name. I looked at this smile without surprise, without disturbing it, without being disturbed by it, as though this calm had gradually been penetrated by the revelation that at this moment the figure was entering the sphere, that there it was being accepted in the form in which it had been described, that the smile now belonged to the distance, that I had really given it to the distance, that in this gift the distance would find nourishment and a temporary safeguard against forgetfulness, which had as a corollary this idea—that right now, in some way, I did not have this smile, this face.

How long this lasted I can't imagine, it wasn't an imaginary time, it also didn't belong to the time of things that happen. After the first contact, I began to look at him with more precautions; I must have been afraid that if I stared at him in too lively a way I would lose or destroy what I had so few guides for grasping. But I felt, on the contrary, how little this view depended on my gaze, how it eluded my gaze without remaining a stranger to it. This was not addressed to me, perhaps it came from me, I could still recall it, but as a picturesque detail, without importance: at present, it was the tranquil smile of no one, intended for no one, and near which one could not dwell near oneself, not an impersonal smile and perhaps not even a smile, the presence of the impersonal, acquiescence to its presence, the evasive, immense, and very close certainty that no one was there and that no one was smiling, which was, however, expressed by an infinite, fascinating smile, so tranquilly fascinating that when the uneasiness in the face of this fixed point returned, I could only look at it calmly, in the calm that radiated from it, and also in a friendly way, for an intimate ray of friendliness came to me from it. Nothing calmer than that, a visible circle of calm—and yet, something that immediately made me see something else, not so calm, a calm not soothed, shivering, as though it hadn't reached the point from which there is no longer any return, as though it wasn't free, yet, from all faces, still desired one, feared being separated from it: sometimes giving me the feeling of wandering desperately around the face, sometimes the hope of drawing near it, the certainty of recapturing it, of having recaptured it, an unforgettable impression of its unity with the face, even though the face itself remained invisible, a marvelous unity, sensed as a happiness, a piece of luck that dispersed shadows, that went beyond the day, something for which one was prepared to sacrifice everything, a thrilling resemblance, the thrill of the unique, the force of a desire that again and again recaptures what it once held—but what is happening? resemblance does not cease to be present behind everything, it even imposes itself, becomes more majestic, I divine it as I have never seen it, it is the moving reflection of all space, and the smile also affirms its immensity, affirms the majesty of this resemblance which is almost too vast, the smile seems to lose itself in the resemblance and through the smile the resemblance seems to become a resemblance that strays, without resemblance. A fissure still infinitesimal: the smile only smiles more mysteriously, as though the lost unity was even closer to the truth of this smile, which, nevertheless, slowly, with infinite patience, has already become once again the pain

337

of an empty smile, the calm smiling of that pain. Oh, endless returns, vicissitudes of a dispiriting slowness! At certain moments, I can't doubt it: what is smiling really is the smile of a face, of a face I don't see but that remains the indestructible certainty of that smile. Then, once again, I can't doubt it, it is ineffably poised on emptiness; in it, the emptiness opens on a smiling allusion torn across by a slight derision.

How long has this lasted? The feeling that I'm the one involved in this must play its part in this absolutely slow movement, this unmoving oscillation, which I would out distance in vain, with which, on the contrary, I must unite even more through my own immobility, and once again it approaches what I believe I still know, it rises, it reveals a possibility of unique joy, which is perhaps no longer mine, but no matter, it is a joy for itself, a happiness in which I don't have to participate, which illuminates in me even the feeling of not being here in order to take part in it, and, once again, it unbinds the unity of that joy, it detaches it, detaches it from itself, as it has detached it from me, but with such patience that the smile of absolute distress always becomes, once again, the smile of absolute peace, and the latter, again, the reflection of the empty depth. Sometimes I say to myself:

"Don't look at that, let it decide between you and him, let the decision leave you, don't go back." But the fact that this no longer depends on me creates a relationship I don't want to avoid. No doubt I have decided it, but to witness the solitary struggle of my decision, its tenacity, which, in the element of hunger and emptiness, makes it find satiety and fullness once again, to feel how it would need to be decided again and again to the point of exhaustion, and nevertheless, in its detachment, to perceive the point of truth that makes it smile— all this, too, belongs to the decision, and I must not free myself of it, nor allow myself to be distracted from it. No doubt I could still do it? Who would not liberate himself from the depth of a reflection? And yet it seems that already it has taken possession of the day, that it insinuates itself into it, fascinates it, alters it, becomes the work of another day. True, this does not spoil its beauty: it is also the smile of the day and this smile is only the more beautiful because of it, as though in this smile its protective envelope begins to dissolve and into this dissolution penetrates a light that is closer to me, more human. Perhaps everything that dies, even the day, comes close to man, asks of man the secret of dying. All this will not last very much longer. Already, I sense in a distant way that I no longer have the right to call out to my companion—and would he still hear me? where is he right now? perhaps very near here? perhaps he is right under my hand? perhaps he is the one my hand is slowly pushing away, distancing once again? No, don't distance him, don't push him away, draw him to you instead, lead him to you, clear the way for him, call him, call him softly by his name. By his name? but I mustn't call him, and at this moment I couldn't. You can't? at this moment? But it is the only moment, it is urgently necessary, you haven't said everything to him, the essential part is missing, the description must be completed, "It must be. Now! Now!" What have I forgotten? why doesn't everything disappear? why is it someone else who is entering the sphere? then, who is the one involved here? wasn't it I who took the drink? was it he? was it everyone? that wasn't possible, there was a misunderstanding, it had to be brought to an end. All the force of the day had to strain toward that end, rise toward it, and perhaps he answered immediately, but when the end came, after the scattering of a few seconds, everything had already disappeared, disappeared with the day.

LITERARY ESSAYS

FROM DREAD TO LANGUAGE

A writer who writes, "I am alone" or, like Rimbaud, "I am really from beyond the grave," can be considered rather comical. It is comical for a man to recognize his solitude by addressing a reader and by using methods that prevent the individual from being alone. The word *alone* is just as general as the word *bread*. To pronounce it is to summon to oneself the presence of everything the word excludes. These aporias in the language are rarely taken seriously. It is enough that the words do their duty and that literature does not cease to appear possible. The writer's "I am alone" has a simple meaning (no one near me) that the use of language contradicts in appearance only.

If we dwell on these difficulties, we risk discovering this: that the writer is under suspicion of a half lie. To Pascal, who complains of being abandoned in the world, Paul Valéry says, "A distress that writes well is not so complete that it hasn't salvaged from the shipwreck..."; but a distress that writes in a mediocre way deserves the same reproach. How can a person be alone if he confides to us that he is alone? He summons us in order to drive us away; he muses on us in order to persuade us that he is not musing on us; he speaks the language of men at the moment when there is no longer, for him, either language or man. It is easy to believe that this person, who ought to be separated from himself by despair, not only retains the thought of some other person but uses this solitude to create an effect that obliterates his solitude.

Is the writer only half sincere? That is really of little importance and it is clear that the reproach is a superficial one. Perhaps Pascal is so unhappy for the very reason that he writes brilliantly. The capacity that he retains of making himself admirable by expressing his misery enters into the horror of his condition as its most painful cause. Some people suffer because they cannot express completely what they feel. They are distressed by the obscurity of their feelings. They think they would be relieved if they could turn the confusion in which they are lost into precise words. But another suffers from being the fortunate interpreter of his misfortune. He suffocates in that intellectual freedom he still has and that allows him to see where he is. He is torn apart by the harmony of his images, by the air of happiness radiating from what he writes. He experiences this contradiction as the unavoidably oppressive aspect of the exaltation that he finds in that writing, an exaltation that crowns his disgust.

The writer could, of course, not write. That is true. Why would man at the farthest reach of solitude write, "I am alone," or, like Kierkegaard, "I am all alone here"? Who forces him into this activity, in a situation where, knowing nothing of himself or of anything else but a crushing absence, he becomes completely passive? Fallen into terror and despair, perhaps he will pace around and around like a hunted animal in a room. One can imagine that he lives deprived of the thought that would make him reflect his unhappiness, of the eyes that would let him perceive the face of that unhappiness, of the voice that would permit him to complain of it. Mad, wildly insane, he lacks the organs he needs to live with others and himself. But these images, however natural they may be, are not convincing. It is to the intelligent witness that the mute animal appears to be a victim of solitude. The person who is alone is not the one who experiences the impression of being alone; this monster of desolation needs the presence of another if his desolation is to have a meaning, another who, with his reason intact and his senses preserved, renders momentarily possible the distress that had until then been impotent.

A writer is not free to be alone without expressing the fact that he is alone. Even if he has reached the point where everything touching the act of writing has become vanity, he is still tied to arrangements of words; in fact, it is in the use of expression that he coincides most completely with the nothingness without expression that he has become. Precisely that which causes language to be destroyed in him also obliges him to use language. He is like a hemiplegic for whom the same illness constitutes both an obligation to walk and a prohibition against walking. He is forced to run ceaselessly in order to prove with each movement that he is deprived of movement. He is all the more paralyzed because of the fact that his limbs obey him. He suffers from the horror that turns his sound legs, his vigorous muscles, and the satisfying exercise he derives from them into the proof and the cause of the impossibility of his progress. In the same way that the distress of any man presupposes at a certain point that to be reasonable would be insane (he would like to lose his reason, but he discovers it in the very loss into which it is sinking), a person who writes is committed to writing by the silence and the privation of language that have stricken him. As long as he is not alone, he either writes or does not write; the hours he passes searching for and weighing words he senses only as something necessary to his calling, his pleasure, or his inspiration; he is deceiving himself when he speaks of an irresistible necessity. But if he lands at the outer limit of solitude, where the external considerations of art, knowledge, and the public disappear, he no longer has the freedom to be anything other than what his situation and the infinite disgust he feels would want absolutely to prevent him from being.

The writer finds himself in this more and more comical condition—of having nothing to write, of having no means of writing it, and of being forced by an extreme necessity to keep writing it. Having nothing to express should be taken in the simplest sense. Whatever he wants to say, it is nothing. The world, things, knowledge, are for him only reference points across the void. And he himself is already reduced to nothing. Nothing is his material. He rejects the forms in which it offers itself to him as being something. He wants to grasp it not in an allusion but in its own truth. He seeks it as the no that is not no to this, to that, to everything, but the pure and simple no. What is more, he does not seek it; it stands apart from all investigation; it cannot be taken as an end; one cannot propose to the will that it adopt as its end something that takes possession of the will by annihilating it: it is not, that is all there is to it; the writer's "I have nothing to say," like that of the accused, contains the whole secret of his solitary condition.

What makes these reflections difficult to pursue is that the word *writer* seems to designate an occupation rather than a human condition. A cobbler in a state of dread could laugh at himself for providing others with the means of walking while he himself is caught in a paralyzing trap. However, it does not occur to anyone to describe his dread as though it were characteristic of a man who repairs shoes. The feeling that produces dread is only accidentally linked to an object, and it reveals precisely that this object—on account of which one is losing oneself in an endless death—is insignificant to the feeling it provokes and to the man it is torturing. One dies at the thought that any object to which one is attached is lost, and in this mortal fear one also feels that this object is nothing, an interchangeable sign, an empty occasion. There is nothing that cannot feed dread, and dread is, more than anything else, this indifference to what creates it, although at the same time it seems to rivet the man to the cause it has chosen.

It sometimes seems, in a strange way, as though dread characterized the writer's function, and, stranger still, as though the fact of writing deepened the dread to the point of attaching it to him rather than to any other sort of man. There comes a moment when the literary man who writes out of loyalty to words writes out of loyalty to dread; he is a writer because this fundamental anxiety has revealed itself to him, and at the same time it reveals itself to him inasmuch as he is a writer; more than that, it seems to exist in the world only because there are, in the world, men who have pushed the art of signs to the point of language, and concern for language to the point of writing, which demands a particular will, a thoughtful consciousness, the protection and retention of the use of the powers of discourse. It is because of this that the case of the writer has something exorbitant and inadmissible about it. It seems comical and miserable that in order to manifest itself, dread, which opens and closes the sky, needs the activity of a man sitting at his table and forming letters on a piece of paper. This may well be shocking, but in the same way that the necessary condition for the solitude of a madman is the presence of a lucid witness. The existence of the writer is proof that within one individual there exist side by side both a man full of dread and one who is cool and calculating, both a madman and a reasonable being, a mute who has lost all words firmly wedded to an orator, master of discourse. The case of the writer is special because he represents the paradox of dread in a special way. Dread challenges all the realities of reason, its methods, its possibilities, its very capacity to exist, its ends, and yet dread forces reason to be there; it summons it to be reason as perfectly as it can; dread itself is only possible because there continues to exist in all its power the faculty that dread renders impossible, that it annihilates.

The sign of his importance is that the writer has nothing to say. This is laughable, too. But this joke has obscure requirements. First of all, it is not so usual for a man to have nothing to say. It may happen that a certain individual temporarily silences all the words that express him, by dismissing discursive knowledge, by seizing a current of silence that emerges from his deep inner life. Then, he says nothing, because the faculty of saying has been broken off; he is in an order where words are no longer in their places, have never existed, do not even propose themselves as a slight erasure of silence; he is entirely absent from what is being said. But for the writer the situation is different. He remains attached to discourse; he departs from reason only in order to be faithful to it; he has authority over language, and he can never completely send it away. Having nothing to say is for him characteristic of someone who always has something to say. In the center of garrulousness he finds the zone of laconicism where he must now remain.

This situation is full of torments and it is ambiguous. It cannot be confused with the sterility that sometimes overwhelms an artist. In fact, it is so different from this sterility that all the noble and rare thoughts he has, the abundance and success of the images, the flow of literary beauty, are what put the writer in a position to attain the emptiness that will be, in his art, the answer to the dread that fills his life. Not only has he not broken with words, but they come to him grander, more brilliant, more successful than they have ever been for him before; he is capable of the most varied works; there is a natural connection between his most exact thoughts and his most seductive writings; it is marvelously easy for him to join number and logic; his whole mind is language. This is the first sign that if he has nothing to say, it is not for lack of means, but because everything he can say is controlled by the nothingness that dread makes appear to him as his own object among the temporary objects that dread gives itself. It is towards this nothingness that all literary powers flow back, as towards the spring that must exhaust them, and this nothingness absorbs them not in an effort to be expressed by them, but rather to consume them with neither aim nor result. This is a singular phenomenon. The writer is called upon by his dread to perform a genuine sacrifice of himself. He must spend, he must consume, the forces that make him a writer. This spending must also be genuine. Either to be content with not writing anymore, or to write a work in which all the values that the mind held in potential reappear in the form of effects, is to prevent the sacrifice from being made or to replace it by an exchange. What is required of the writer is infinitely more difficult. He must be destroyed, in an act that really puts him at stake. The exercise of his power forces him to sacrifice that power. The work he makes signifies that there is no work made. The art he uses is an art in which perfect success and complete failure must appear at the same time, the fullness of means and irremediable debasement, the reality and the nothingness of the result.

When someone composes a work, that work can be destined to serve a certain end—moral, religious, political—that is exterior to it; we say then that art is serving alien values; it is being exchanged in a practical way for certain realities, whose price it raises. But if the book is not useful for anything, it appears as a disruptive phenomenon in the totality of human relations, which are based on the equivalence of the currencies exchanged, on the principle that corresponding to every production of energy there should be a potential energy in a produced object, an energy capable of being thrown back again, in one form or another, into the uninterrupted circuit of forces; the book that art has produced and that cannot produce any other kind of value than that which it represents seems to be an exception to the law that is assumed in the maintenance of all existence; it expresses a disinterested effort; it profits, in a privileged or scandalous way, from an invaluable position; it is reduced to itself; it is art for art's sake. Nevertheless—and the endless discussions about art for art's sake show this—the work of art only appears, to insensitive eyes, to be an exception to the general law of exchanges. It is not useful for anything?—say the critics; but it is useful for something precisely because it is not useful for anything; its usefulness is to express that useless part without which civilization is not possible; or it is useful to art, which is one of man's goals or is a goal in itself or is the image of the absolute, etc.... We could elaborate on this subject in a thousand ways. This is all futile because it is clear that the work of art does not represent a true phenomenon of spending. On the contrary, it signifies an advantageous operation of transformation of energy. The author has produced more than himself; he has carried what he has received to a higher point of efficacy; he has been creative; and what he has created is from now on a source of values whose fecundity goes far beyond the forces spent to bring it into being.

The writer plunged into dread is himself painfully aware that art is not a ruinous operation; he is trying to lose himself (and to lose himself as a writer), and yet sees that by writing he increases the credit of humanity, and thus his own, since he is still a man; he gives art new hopes and riches that return to weigh him down; he transforms into forces of consolation the hopeless orders he receives; he saves with nothingness. This contradiction is so enormous that it seems to him no stratagem can put an end to it. The artist's traditional misfortunes—to live poor and miserable, to die as he completes his work—naturally do not figure in the structure of his future. The hope of the nihilist—to write a work, but a destructive work, representing, because of what it is, an undefined possibility of things that will no longer be—is equally foreign to him. He sees into the intention of the first—who believes he is sacrificing his existence, whereas he is actually putting the whole of it into the work that is to eternalize it—and the naïve scheme of the second, who offers men, in the form of limited upheavals, an infinite vision of renewal. His own path is different. He obeys dread, and dread orders him to lose himself, without that loss being compensated by any positive value.

"I do not want to attain something," the writer says to himself. "On the contrary, I want to prevent that something that I am when I write from resulting, because of the fact that I write, in anything, in any form. It is indispensable to me to be a writer who is infinitely smaller in his work than in himself, and this through the complete and honest use of all his means. I want this possibility of creating, as it becomes creation, not only to express its own destruction along with the destruction of everything it challenges—that is to say everything—but also not to express it. For me it is a question of making a work that does not even have the reality of expressing the absence of reality. What retains the power of expression retains the greatest real value, even if what is expressed has none; but to be inexpressive does not put an end to the ambiguity which still derives from inexpressiveness the result that what is then expressed is the need to express nothing."

This monologue is fictitious, because the writer cannot set for himself as a project, in the form of a considered and coherent plan, that which he is required to hold as the very opposite of a project, with the most obscure and emptiest of constraints. Or, more precisely, his dread is increased by the exigency that forces him to pursue within a methodical task the concern which he cannot realize except through an act of immediate disruption of himself. His will, as the practical power to order what is possible, itself becomes full of dread. His clear reason, still capable of establishing a dialogue with itself, becomes, because it is clear and discursive, the equal of the impenetrable madness that reduces him to silence. Logic identifies with the unhappiness and fright of consciousness. However, this substitution can only be temporary. If the rule is to obey dread and if dread accepts only what increases it, for the time being it is tolerable to try to shift it to the level of a limited plan, because that effort carries it to a higher point of uneasiness, but this cannot last; active reason quickly imposes the stability that is its law; full of dread a moment before, now it turns dread into a reason; it turns anxious seeking into a chance for forgetfulness and repose. Once this usurpation has taken place, and even before it happens, just in the threat of it that is glimpsed even in the most carefully distrustful use of the creative mind, all work becomes impossible. Dread requires the abandonment of what threatens to make it weaker; it requires it, and this abandonment, by signifying the failure of the agreement that had been desired for its very difficulty, increases dread enormously; it even becomes so great that, freed of its means and losing contact with the contradictions in which it is sinking, it moves toward a strange satisfaction; as it reduces itself, it no longer sees more than itself, it is contemplation that veils itself and perception that fragments itself; a sort of sufficiency comes into being along with its insufficiency; the devastating movement that it is draws it toward a definitive splitting apart; it will lose itself in the current that is inducing it to loose everything. But at this new extremity, the kind of dread dissolving into drunkenness that it feels itself becoming impels it towards the outside again. With increased heaviness, dread comes back to the logical expression that makes it feel—in a reasonable way, that is, a way deprived of delights—the contradictions that keep putting it back in the present. Creation is attempted again, all the more somber because it is attempted more violently and all the more meticulous because the memory of failure points to the fact that it is threatened by a new failure. Work is temporarily possible in the impossibility that weighs it down. And this continues to be the case until that very possibility presents itself as real, by destroying the share of impossibility that was its condition.

The writer cannot do without his project, since the depth of his dread is tied to the fact that this dread cannot do without methodic realization. But he is tempted by bizarre projects. For example, he wants to write a book in which the operation of all his forces of meaning will be reabsorbed into the meaningless. (Is the meaningless that which escapes objective intelligibility? These pages composed of a discontinuous series of words, these words that do not presume any language, can always, in the absence of an assignable meaning, and through the harmony or discordance of sounds, produce an effect that represents their justification.) Or else he proposes to himself a work from which the possibility of a reader will be excluded. (Lautréamont seems to have had this dream. How not to be read? One would like to arrange the book to resemble a house that would open easily to visitors; yet as soon as they went into it, they would not only have to get lost there, they would be caught in a treacherous trap; once there they would cease to be what they had been, they would die. What if the writer destroyed his work as soon as he had written it? That happens; it is a childish subterfuge; nothing has been accomplished so long as the structure of the work does not make the reader impossible, that reader being first of all the writer himself. One can imagine a book to which the author, man on the one hand, insect on the other, could have access only in the act of writing it; a book that would destroy him as capacity to read, without abolishing him as reason writing; that would take away from him the sight, the memory, the understanding of what he had composed with all his strength and all his mind.) Or again, he contemplates a work so foreign to his dread that it is its echo, because of the silence it keeps. (But the incognito is never real; any banal sentence attests to the despair that exists in the depths of language.)

It is because of the puerile nature of all these artifices that they are pondered and formulated with such gravity. Childishness anticipates its failure by taking upon itself a mode of being too slight for it to be sanctioned by success or lack of success. These attempts have in common the fact that they are seeking a complete solution to a situation that would be ruined and transformed into its opposite by a complete solution. These attempts do not have to fail, but they must not succeed. Neither do they have to balance success and failure in deliberate pattern, so that ambiguity is left with the responsibility for the decision. All the projects we have mentioned can in fact be reduced to ambiguity and are not even conceivable outside the protection of a multifaceted intention. The writer can get this loss of meaning—the meaning which he requires of a text deprived of all intelligibility—from the most reasonable of texts if the latter seems to advertise its obviousness as a challenge to immediate comprehension. To this he adds the further obscurity, that there is doubt about the nonsense of this sense, that as reason plays its customary tricks on itself, it only dies in the game because it obstinately refuses to play. The ambiguity is such that one cannot take it at its word either as reason or as unreason. Perhaps the page that is absurd because it is sensible really is sensible; perhaps it does not make the slightest sense; how does one decide? Its nature is linked to a change in perspective, and there is nothing in it that allows it to be fixed in a definitive light. (One can always say that its meaning is to admit of both interpretations, to disguise itself sometimes as good sense, sometimes as nonsense, and thereby to be determined as indetermination between these two possibilities; but that in itself betrays the structure of the page, because it is not postulated that the truth of the page is to be sometimes one thing and sometimes another; on the contrary, it is possible that it is uniquely this, uniquely that; it imperiously demands this choice; to the indetermination in which we try to grasp it, it adds the claim that it is also absolutely determined by one or the other of the two terms between which it oscillates.)

Yet ambiguity is not a solution for the writer who is full of dread. It cannot be conceived as a solution. As soon as it is part of a project and appears as the expression of a scheme, it gives up the multiplicity which is its nature, and freezes in the form of an artifice whose exterior complexity is constantly being reduced by the intention that has brought it into being. I can read a poem with a double, triple, or perhaps no meaning, but I do not hesitate over the meaning of these varied meanings and in this I see a determination to reach myself through the enigma. Where the enigma shows itself as such, it vanishes. It is only an enigma when it does not exist in itself, when it hides itself so deeply that it slips away into what causes its nature to be to slip away. The writer who is full of dread encounters his dread as an enigma, but he cannot have recourse to the enigma in order to obey the dread. He cannot believe that by writing under a mask, by borrowing pseudonyms, by making himself unknown, he is putting himself right with the solitude which he is fated to apprehend in the very act of writing. Since he is an enigma himself, an enigma as writer who must write and not write, it is not within his means to use enigma in order to be faithful to his enigmatic nature. He knows himself as torment, but this torment is not enclosed in a particular feeling, it is no more sadness than it is joy, nor is it knowledge experienced in the unknowable that underlies it: it is a torment that uses everything to justify itself and gets rid of everything, that espouses any object at all and escapes, through every object, the absence of object; that appears to be apprehensible in the shiver which binds death to the feeling of being, but that makes death ridiculous in the sight of the void it hollows out; that nevertheless does not allow one to send it away, that on the contrary demands that one submit to it and desire it, and makes deliverance from it into a worse torment, burdened by what makes it lighter. To say of this torment: I obey it by abandoning my written thought to oscillation, by expressing it through a code, would be to represent it as interesting me only in the mystery in which it reveals itself; however, I no more know it as mysterious than as familiar, neither as a key to a world which has no key, nor as an answer to the absence of a question; if it consigns me to enigma, it does so by refusing to link me to enigma; if it tears me apart with obviousness, it does so precisely by tearing me apart; it is there—of that I am certain—but it is there in the dark, and I cannot maintain that certainty except in the collapse of all the conditions of certainty, and first of all in the collapse of what I am when I am certain it is there.

If ambiguity were the essential mode of revelation for the man full of dread, we would have to believe that dread has something to reveal to him that he nevertheless cannot grasp, that it put him in the presence of an object whose dizzying absence is all that he feels, that it conveys to him, through failure and also through the fact that failure does not put an end to anything, a supreme possibility which he must, as a man, renounce, but whose meaning and truth he can at least understand in the existence of dread. Ambiguity presupposes a secret that no doubt expresses itself by vanishing, but that in this vanishing allows itself to be glimpsed as a possible truth. There is a beyond in which, if I reached it, I would perhaps be reaching only myself, but which also has a meaning outside me, and even for me has no other meaning than that of being absolutely outside me. Ambiguity is the language used by a messenger who tries to teach me what I cannot learn and who completes his instruction by warning me that I am learning nothing of what he is teaching me. Such an equivocal belief is not absent from certain moments of dread. But the dread itself can only tear it apart in every positive aspect it still retains. Dread transforms it into a weight that is crushing and that nevertheless amounts to nothing at all. It changes this speaking mouth, this mouth that speaks ably through the confusion of tongues, through silence, through truth, through falsehood, into an organ condemned to speak passionately in order to say nothing. It retains ambiguity, but it takes its task away from it. All that it allows to survive, of this misreading which keeps the mind in suspense through the hope of an unknowable truth, is the labyrinth of multiple meanings in which the mind continues its search without any hope of a possible truth.

Dread has nothing to reveal and is itself indifferent to its own revelation. It is not concerned about whether or not anyone reveals it; it draws anyone who has tied himself to it towards a mode of being in which the need to make oneself the subject of one's speech is already obsolete. Kierkegaard made of the demoniac one of the most profound forms of dread and the demoniac refuses to communicate with the outside, it does not want to make itself manifest; if it wanted to, it would not be able to; it is confined within that which makes it inexpressible; it is filled with dread by solitude and by the fear that this solitude might be broken. But the point is that for Kierkegaard, the mind must reveal itself, dread comes from the fact that, all direct communication being impossible, the only authentic way to go towards the other seems to be to enclose oneself in the most isolated interiority, and this path itself is a dead end unless it insists on being recognized as a dead end. However, even though dread weighs like a stone on the individual, crushing and tearing to shreds what he has in common with men, it does not stop with this tragedy of mutilation, but turns on individuality itself, on the insane, tattered, harrowing aspiration to be only oneself, in order to force it out of its refuge, in which to live is to live sequestered. Dread does not allow the recluse to be alone. It deprives him of the means by which he could have some relation to another, making him more alien to his reality as a man than if he had suddenly been changed into some sort of vermin; but once he has been stripped in this way, and is about to bury himself in his monstrous particularity, dread throws him back out of himself and, in a new torment that he experiences as a suffocating irradiation, it confounds him with what he is not, turning his solitude into an expression of his communication and this communication into the meaning assumed by his solitude and drawing from this synonymy a new reason to be dread added to dread.

The writer does not write in order to express the concern that is his law. He writes without a goal, in an act that nevertheless has all the characteristics of a deliberate composition, and his concern for it craves realization at each instant. He is not trying to express his self full of dread any more than he is trying to express his self lost to itself; he has no use for this anxiety that wants to manifest itself as though by manifesting itself it dreamed it was saving itself; he is not its spokesman or the spokesman of some inaccessible truth within it; he is responding to a demand, and the response he makes public has nothing to do with that demand. Is there a vertigo in dread that prevents it from being communicated? In a sense yes, since it appears unfathomable; man cannot describe his torment, his torment escapes him; he believes that he will not be able to express what it is all about; he says to himself: I will never convey this suffering faithfully. But the point is that he imagines there is something to convey; he conceives his situation on the model of all other human situations; he wants to formulate its content; he pursues its meaning. In reality, dread has no mysterious underside; it exists completely in the obviousness that makes us feel it is there; it is entirely revealed as soon as one says: I am full of dread. One can write volumes to express what it is not, one can describe it in its most remarkable psychological forms, one can relate it to fundamental metaphysical notions; there will be nothing more in all this rubbish than there is in the words *I am full of dread,* and these words themselves signify that there exists nothing else but dread.

Why should dread feel reluctant to be summoned outside? It is just as much the outside as the inside. The man to whom it has revealed itself (which does not mean that it has shown him the depths of its nature, since it has no depths), the man it has grasped in a profound way allows himself to be seen in the various expressions in which dread attracts him; he does not show himself complacently and he does not hide himself scrupulously; he is not jealous of his privacy, he neither flees nor seeks what shatters it; he cannot attach definitive importance to his solitude or to his union with another; full of dread when he withholds himself; full of dread even more when he gives himself, he feels he is bound to a necessity that cannot be altered by the yes or no of reality. Now it must be admitted that the writer who perceives the whole paradox of his task in the passion that is constantly hidden and that he constantly wants to lay bare, is realizing his torture, making a thing out of it, presenting it to himself as an object to be represented, one that is undoubtedly inaccessible, but nevertheless analogous to all the objects that it is the role of art to express. Why should the unhappiness of his condition be that he has to represent that condition—with the consequence that if he succeeds in representing it, his unhappiness will be changed into joy, his destiny fulfilled? He is not a writer because of his unhappiness, and his unhappiness does not come from the fact that he is a writer, but placed before the necessity of writing, he can no longer escape it, once he submits to it as an unrealizable task, unrealizable no matter what its form, and yet possible in that impossibility.

I have nothing to say about my dread, and it is not because it is seeking to be expressed that it stalks me as soon as I let myself fall silent. But dread also causes me to have nothing to say about anything, and it stalks me no less when I try to justify my task by giving it an end. However, I am not permitted to write just anything at all. The feeling that what I am doing is useless is connected to that other feeling, that nothing is more serious. It is not as the result of an order declaring to me: everything is permitted, do what you want, that I find myself before the expiration of the anything at all; it is as a limit to a situation that turns everything important to me into the equivalent of an anything at all and refuses me this anything at all precisely when it has become nothing to me. I can play my destiny in a game of dice, as long as I play it as chance exterior to me and accept it as a destiny absolutely tied to me; but if the dice are there in order to change into a whim the too burdensome fatality that I am no longer able to want, it is now in my interest to play and because of that interest in the game, I become a gambler who makes the game impossible (it is no longer a game). In the same way, if the writer wants to draw lots for what he writes, he can only do it if this operation represents the same necessity of reflection, the same search for language, the same cumbersome and useless effort as the act of writing. This is to say that for him, drawing lots is writing, writing while making both his mind and the use of his gifts the equivalent of pure chance.

It will always be harder for man to use his reason rigorously and adhere to it as to a coincidence of fortuitous events than to force it to imitate the effects of chance. It is relatively easy to elaborate a text with any letters at all taken at random. It is more difficult to compose that text while feeling the necessity of it. But it is extremely arduous to produce the most conscious and the most balanced sort of work while at each instant comparing the forces of reason that produce it to an actual game of caprice. It is in this sense that the rules defining the art of writing, the constraints placed upon it, the fixed forms that transform it into a necessary system—insurmountable obstacles to the throw of the dice— are all the more important for the writer because they make more exhausting the act of consciousness by which reason, following these very rules, must identify itself with an absence of rules. The writer who frees himself of precepts to rely on chance is failing to meet the requirement that commands him to experience chance only in the form of a mind subject to precepts. He tries to escape his creative intelligence, experienced as chance, by surrendering himself directly to chance. He appeals to the dice of the unconscious because he cannot play dice with extreme consciousness. He limits chance to chance. This is the basis of his quest for texts ravaged by randomness and his attempt to come to terms with negligence. It seems to him that by doing this he is closer to his nocturnal passion. But the point is that for him, the day is still there next to the night, and he needs to betray himself through fidelity to the norms of clarity, for the sake of what is without form and without law.

FROM DREAD TO LANGUAGE

Acceptance of the rules has this limit: that when they have been obliterated and have become habits, they retain almost nothing of their form as constraints and have the spontaneity of that which is fortuitous. Most of the time, to give oneself to language is to abandon oneself. One allows oneself to be carried away by a mechanism that takes upon itself all the responsibility of the act of writing. True automatic writing is the habitual form of writing, writing that has used the mind's deliberate efforts and its erasures to create automatisms. The opposite of automatic writing is a dread-filled desire to transform the gifts of chance into deliberate initiatives, and, more specifically, the concern to take upon oneself, as a power in every way similar to chance, the consciousness that adheres to rules or invents them. The instinct that leads us, in dread, to flee from the rules—if it is not itself flight from dread—comes, then, from the need to pursue these rules as true rules, as an exacting kind of coherence, and no longer as the conventions and means of a traditional commodity. I try to give myself a new law, and I do not seek it because it is new or it will be mine—this consideration of novelty or originality would be ridiculous in my position—but because its novelty is the guarantee that it is really a law, for me, a law that imposes itself with a rigor I am aware of and that impresses more heavily upon me the feeling that it has no more meaning than a toss of the dice.

Words give to the person who writes them the impression of being dictated to him by usage, and he receives them with the uneasy feeling of finding in them an immense reservoir of fluency and fully staged effects—staged without his power having had any part in it. This uneasiness can lead him to reject completely the words that belong to practical life, to break off the familiar voice he listens to so nonchalantly, less absorbed by what he writes under its influence than by the gestures and instructions of the croupier at the gaming table. It then seems to him necessary to resume responsibility for words, and, by sacrificing them in their servile capacity—precisely in their fitness to be of service to him—to recover, with their revolt, the power he has to be master of them. The object of the ideal of "words set free" is not to release words from all rules, but to free them from a rule one no longer submits to, in order to subject them to a law one really feels. There is an effort to make the act of writing the cause of a storm of order and a paroxysm of consciousness all the more filled with dread because this consciousness of a faultless organization is also the consciousness of an absolute failure of order. Regarded in this light, it quickly becomes clear that to invent new rules is no more legitimate than to reinvent the old rules; on the contrary, it is harder to give usage back its value as a constraint, to awaken in ordinary language the order that has been effaced from it, to adhere to habit as to the summons of reflection itself. To give a purer meaning to the words of the tribe can be to give words a new meaning, but it is also to give words their old meaning, to grant them the meaning they have, by reviving them as they have not ceased to be.

If I read, language, whether logical or completely musical (non-discursive), makes me adhere to a common meaning which, because it is not directly connected to what I am, interposes itself between my dread and me. But if I write, I am the one who is making the common meaning adhere to language, and in this act of signification I carry my forces, as much as I can, to their highest point of effectiveness, which is to give a meaning. Everything in my mind, therefore, strives to be a necessary connection and a tested value; everything in my memory strives to be the recollection of a language that has not yet been invented and the invention of a language that one recollects; to each operation there corresponds a meaning, and to these operations as a group, there corresponds that other meaning that there is no distinct meaning for each of them; words have their meaning as the substitute for an idea, but also as a composition of sounds and as a physical reality; images signify themselves as images, and thoughts affirm the twofold necessity that associates them with certain expressions and makes them thoughts of other thoughts. It is then that one can say that everything written has, for the one who writes it, the greatest meaning possible, but has also this meaning, that it is a meaning bound to chance, that it is nonmeaning . Naturally, since esthetic consciousness is only conscious of a part of what it does, the effort to attain absolute necessity and through it absolute futility is itself always futile. It cannot succeed, and it is this impossibility of succeeding, of reaching the end, where it would be as though it had never succeeded, that makes it constantly possible. It retains a little meaning from the fact that it never receives all its meaning, and it is filled with dread because it cannot be pure dread. The unknown masterpiece always allows one to see in the corner the tip of a charming foot, and this delicious foot prevents the work from being finished, but also prevents the painter from facing the emptiness of his canvas and saying, with the greatest feeling of repose: "Nothing, nothing! At last, there is nothing."

LITERATURE
AND THE RIGHT TO DEATH

One can certainly write without asking why one writes. As a writer watches his pen form the letters, does he even have a right to lift it and say to it: "Stop! What do you know about yourself? Why are you moving forward? Why can't you see that your ink isn't making any marks, that although you may be moving ahead freely, you're moving through a void, that the reason you never encounter any obstacles is that you never left your starting place? And yet you write—you write on and on, disclosing to me what I dictate to you, revealing to me what I know; as others read, they enrich you with what they take from you and give you what you teach them. Now you have done what you did not do; what you did not write has been written: you are condemned to be indelible."

Let us suppose that literature begins at the moment when literature becomes a question. This question is not the same as a writer's doubts or scruples. If he happens to ask himself questions as he writes, that is his concern; if he is absorbed by what he is writing and indifferent to the possibility of writing it, if he is not even thinking about anything, that is his right and his good luck. But one thing is still true: as soon as the page has been written, the question which kept interrogating the writer while he was writing—though he may not have been aware of it—is now present on the page; and now the same question lies silent within the work, waiting for a reader to approach—any kind of reader, shallow or profound; this question is addressed to language, behind the person who is writing and the person who is reading, by language which has become literature.

This concern that literature has with itself may be condemned as an infatuation. It is useless for this concern to speak to literature about its nothingness, its lack of seriousness, its bad faith; this is the very abuse of which it is accused. Literature professes to be important while at the same time considering itself an object of doubt. It confirms itself as it disparages itself. It seeks itself: this is more than it has a right to do, because literature may be one of those things which deserve to be found but not to be sought.

Perhaps literature has no right to consider itself illegitimate. But the question it contains has properly speaking nothing to do with its value or its rights. The reason the meaning of this question is so difficult to discover is that the question tends to turn into a prosecution of art and art's capacities and goals. Literature is built on top of its own ruins: this paradox has become a cliché to us. But we must still ask whether the challenge brought against art by the most illustrious works of art in the last thirty years is not based on the redirection, the displacement, of a force laboring in the secrecy of works and loath to emerge into broad daylight, a force the thrust of which was originally quite distinct from any deprecation of literary activity or the literary Thing.

We should point out that as its own negation, literature has never signified the simple denunciation of art or the artist as mystification or deception. Yes, literature is unquestionably illegitimate, there is an underlying deceitfulness in it. But certain people have discovered something beyond this: literature is not only illegitimate, it is also null, and as long as this nullity is isolated in a state of purity it may constitute an extraordinary force, a marvelous force. To make literature become the exposure of this emptiness inside, to make it open up completely to its nothingness, realize its own unreality—this is one of the tasks undertaken by surrealism. Thus we are correct when we recognize surrealism as a powerful negative movement, but no less correct when we attribute to it the greatest creative ambition, because if literature coincides with nothing for just an instant, it is immediately everything, and this everything begins to exist: what a miracle!

It is not a question of abusing literature, but rather of trying to understand it and to see why we can only understand it by disparaging it. It has been noted with amazement that the question "What is literature?" has received only meaningless answers. But what is even stranger is that something about the very form of such a question takes away all its seriousness. People can and do ask "What is poetry?", "What is art?", and even "What is the novel?" But the literature which is both poem and novel seems to be the element of emptiness present in all these serious things, and to which reflection, with its own gravity cannot direct itself without losing its seriousness. If reflection, imposing as it is, approaches literature, literature becomes a caustic force, capable of destroying the very capacity in itself and in reflection to be imposing. If reflection withdraws, then literature once again becomes something important, essential, more important than the philosophy, the religion or the life of the world which it embraces. But if reflection, shocked by this vast power, returns to this force and asks it what is it, it is immediately penetrated by a corrosive, volatile element and can only scorn a Thing so vain, so vague, and so impure, and in this scorn and this vanity be consumed in turn, as the story of Monsieur Teste has so clearly shown us.

It would be a mistake to say that the powerful negative contemporary movements are responsible for this volatizing and volatile force which literature seems to have become. About one hundred fifty years ago, a man who had the highest idea of art that anyone can have—because he saw how art can become religion and religion art—this man (called Hegel[1]) described all the ways in which someone who has chosen to be a man of letters condemns himself to belong to the "animal kingdom of the mind." From his very first step, Hegel virtually says, a person who wishes to write is stopped by a contradiction: in order to write, he must have the talent to write. But gifts, in themselves, are nothing. As long as he has not yet sat down at his table and written a work, the writer is not a writer and does not know if he has the capacity to become one. He has no talent until he has written, but he needs talent in order to write.

This difficulty illuminates, from the outset, the anomaly which is the essence of literary activity and which the writer both must and must not overcome. A writer is not an idealistic dreamer, he does not contemplate himself in the intimacy of his beautiful soul, he does not submerse himself in the inner certainty of his talents. He puts his talents to work; that is, he needs the work he produces in order to be conscious of his talents and of himself. The writer only finds himself, only realizes himself, through his work; before his work exists, not only does he not know who he is, but he is nothing. He only exists as a function of the work; but then how can the work exist? "An individual," says Hegel, "cannot know what he [really] is until he has made himself a reality through action. However, this seems to imply that he cannot determine the *End* of his action until he has carried it out; but

---

[1] In this argument, Hegel is considering human work in general. It should be understood that the remarks which follow are quite remote from the text of the *Phenomenology* and make no attempt to illuminate it. The text can be read in Jean Hippolyte's translation and pursued further through his important book, *Genèse et structure de la Phénoménologie de l'esprit de Hegel*.

at the same time, since he is a *conscious* individual, he must have the action in front of him beforehand as *entirely his* own, i.e. as an *End*."[2] Now, the same is true for each new work, because everything begins again from nothing. And the same is also true when he creates a work part by part: if he does not see his work before him as a project already completely formed, how can he make it the conscious end of his conscious acts? But if the work is already present in its entirety in his mind and if this presence is the essence of the work (taking the words for the time being to be inessential), why would he realize it any further? Either: as an interior project it is everything it ever will be, and from that moment the writer knows everything about it that he can learn, and so will leave it to lie there in its twilight, without translating it into words, without writing it—but then he won't ever write: and he won't be a writer. Or: realizing that the work cannot be planned, but only carried out, that it has value, truth and reality only through the words which unfold it in time and inscribe it in space, he will begin to write, but starting from nothing and with nothing in mind—like a nothingness working in nothingness, to borrow an expression of Hegel's.

In fact, this problem could never be overcome if the person writing expected its solution to give him the right to begin writing. "For that very reason," Hegel remarks, "he has to start immediately, and, whatever the circumstances, without further scruples about beginning, means, or End, proceed to action."[3] This way, he can break the circle, because in his eyes the circumstances under which he begins to write become the same thing as his talent, and the interest he takes in writing, and the movement which carries him forward, induce him to recognize these circumstances as his own, to see his own goal in them. Valéry often reminded us that his best works were created for a chance commission and were not born of personal necessity. But what did he find so remarkable about that? If he had set to work on *Eupalinos* of his own accord, what reasons would he have had for doing it? That he had held a piece of shell in his hand? Or that opening a dictionary one morning he happened to read the name Eupalinos in *La Grande*

---

[2] Hegel, *Phenomenology of Spirit*, trans. A.W. Miller, p. 240, Oxford University Press, 1977; Chapter V, Section la, "The spiritual animal kingdom and deceit or the 'matter in hand' itself."—*Tr.*

[3] *idem.*—*Tr.*

Encyclopédie? Or that he wanted to try dialogue as a form and happened to have on hand a piece of paper that lent itself to that form? One can imagine the most trivial circumstance as the starting point of a great work; nothing is compromised by that triviality: the act by which the author makes it into a crucial circumstance is enough to incorporate it into his genius and his work. In this sense, the publication *Architectures* which commissioned *Eupalinos* from Valéry was really the form in which he originally had the talent to write it: that commission was the beginning of that talent, was that talent itself, but we must also add that that commission only became real, only became a true project through Valéry's existence, his talent, his conversations in the world and the interest he had already shown in this sort of subject. Every work is an occasional work: this simply means that each work has a beginning, that it begins at a certain moment in time and that that moment in time is part of the work, since without it the work would have been only an insurmountable problem, nothing more than the impossibility of writing it.

Let us suppose that the work has been written: with it the writer is born. Before, there was no one to write it; starting from the book, an author exists and merges with his book. When Kafka chances to write the sentence, "He was looking out the window," he is —as he says— in a state of inspiration such that the sentence is already perfect. The point is that he is the author of it—or rather that because of it, he is an author: it is the source of his existence, he has made it and it makes him, it is himself and he is completely what it is. This is the reason for his joy, his pure and perfect joy. Whatever he might write, "the sentence is already perfect." This is the reason for his joy, his pure and perfect joy. This is the strange and profound certainty which art makes into a goal for itself. What is written is neither well nor badly written, neither important nor frivolous, memorable nor forgettable: it is the perfect act through which what was nothing when it was inside emerges into the monumental reality of the outside as something which is necessarily true, as a translation which is necessarily faithful, since the person it translates exists only through it and in it. One could say that this certainty is in some sense the writer's inner paradise and that *automatic writing* has only been one way of making this golden age real— what Hegel calls the pure joy of passing from the night of possibility into the daytime of presence—or again, the certainty that what bursts into the light is none other than what was sleeping in the night. But what is the result of this? The writer who is completely gathered up and enclosed in the sentence "He was looking out the window" apparently cannot be asked to justify this sentence, since for him nothing else exists. But at least the sentence exists, and if it really exists to the point of making the person who wrote it a writer, this is because it is not just his sentence, but a sentence that belongs to other people, people who can read it—it is a universal sentence.

At this point, a disconcerting ordeal begins. The author sees other people taking an interest in his work, but the interest they take in it is different from the interest that made it a pure expression of himself, and that different interest changes the work, transforms it into something different, something in which he does not recognize the original perfection. For him the work has disappeared, it has become a work belonging to other people, a work which includes them and does not include him, a book which derives its value from other books, which is original if it does not resemble them, which is understood because it is a reflection of them. Now the writer cannot disregard this new stage. As we have seen, he exists only in his work, but the work exists only when it has become this public, alien reality, made and unmade by colliding with other realities. So he really is inside the work, but the work itself is disappearing. This is a particularly critical moment in the experiment. All sorts of interpretations come into play in getting beyond it. The writer, for example, would like to protect the perfection of the written Thing by keeping it as far away from life outside as possible. The work is what he created, not the book that is being bought, read, ground up and praised or demolished in the marketplace of the world. But then where does the work begin, where does it end? At what moment does it come into existence? Why make it public if the splendor of the pure self must be preserved in the work, why take it outside, why realize it in words which belong to everyone? Why not withdraw into an enclosed and secret intimacy without producing anything but an empty object and dying echo? Another solution—the writer himself agrees to do away with himself: the only one who matters in the work is the person who reads it. The reader makes the work; as he reads it, he creates it; he is its real author, he is the consciousness and the living substance of the written thing; and so the author now has only one goal, to write for that reader and to merge with him. A hopeless endeavor. Because the reader has no use for a work written for him, what he wants is precisely an alien work in which he can discover something unknown, a different reality, a separate mind capable of transforming him and which he can transform into himself. An author who is writing specifically for a public is not really writing: it is the public that is writing, and for this reason the public can no longer be a reader; reading only appears to exist, actually it is nothing. This is why works created to be read are meaningless: no one reads them. This is why it is dangerous to write for other people, in order to evoke the speech of others and reveal them to themselves: the fact is that other people do not want to hear their own voices; they want to hear someone else's voice, a voice that is real, profound, troubling like the truth.

A writer cannot withdraw into himself, for he would then have to give up writing. As he writes, he cannot sacrifice the pure night of his own possibilities, because his work is alive only if that night—and no other—becomes day, if what is most singular about him and farthest removed from existence as already revealed now reveals itself within shared existence. It is true that the writer can try to justify himself by setting himself the task of writing—the simple operation of writing, made conscious of itself quite independently of its results. As we know, this was Valéry's way of saving himself. Let us accept this. Let us accept that a writer may concern himself with art as pure technique, with technique as nothing more than the search for the means by which what was previously not written comes to be written. But if the experiment is to be a valid one, it cannot separate the operation from its results, and the results are never stable or definitive, but infinitely varied and meshed with a future which cannot be grasped. A writer who claims he is only concerned with how the work comes into being sees his concern get sucked into the world, lose itself in the whole of history; because the work is also made outside of him, and all the rigor he put into the consciousness of his deliberate actions, his careful rhetoric, is soon absorbed into the workings of a vital contingency which he cannot control or even observe. Yet his experiment is not worthless: in writing, he has put himself to the test a nothingness at work, and after having written he puts his work to the test as something in the act of disappearing. The work disappears, but the fact of disappearing remains and appears as the essential thing, the movement which allows the work to be realized as it enters the stream of history, to be realized as it disappears. In this experiment, the writer's real goal is no longer the ephemeral work, but something beyond that work: the truth of the work, where the individual who writes—a force of creative negation—seems to join with the work in motion through which this force of negation and surpassing asserts itself.

This new notion, which Hegel calls the Thing Itself, plays a vital role in the literary undertaking. No matter that it has so many different meanings: it is the art which is above the work, the ideal that the work seeks to represent, the World as it is sketched out in the work, the values at stake in the creative effort, the authenticity of this effort; it is everything which, above the work that is constantly being dissolved in things, maintains the model, the essence and the spiritual truth of that work just as the writer's freedom wanted to manifest it and can recognize it as its own. The goal is not what the writer makes, but the truth of what he makes. As far as this goes, he deserves to be called an honest, disinterested conscience—*l'honnête homme*. But here we run into trouble: as soon as honesty comes into play in literature, imposture is already present. Here bad faith is truth, and the greater the pretension to morality and seriousness, the more surely will mystification and deceit triumph. Yes, literature is undoubtedly the world of values, since above the mediocrity of the finished works everything they lack keeps appearing as their own truth. But what is the result of this? A perpetual enticement, an extraordinary game of hide-and-seek in which the writer claims as an excuse that what he has in mind is not the ephemeral work but the spirit of that work and of every work—no matter what he does, no matter what he has not been able to do, he adapts himself to it, and his honest conscience derives knowledge and glory from it. Let us listen to that honest conscience; we are familiar with it because it is working in all of us. When the work has failed, this conscience is not troubled: it says to itself, "Now it has been fully completed, for failure is its essence; its disappearance constitutes its realization," and the conscience is happy with this; lack of success delights it. But what if the book does not even manage to be born, what if it remains a pure nothing? Well, this is still better: silence and nothingness are the essence of literature, "the Thing Itself." It is true: the writer is willing to put the highest value on the meaning his work has for him alone. Then it does not matter whether the work is good or bad, famous or forgotten. If circumstances neglect it, he congratulates himself, since he only wrote it to negate circumstances. But when a book that comes into being by chance, produced in a moment of idleness and lassitude, without value or significance, is suddenly made into a masterpiece by circumstantial events, what author is not going to take credit for the glory himself, in his heart of hearts, what author is not going to see his own worth in that glory, and his own work in that gift of fortune, the working of his mind in providential harmony with his time?

A writer is his own first dupe, and at the very moment he fools other people he is also fooling himself. Listen to him again: now he states that his function is to write for others, that as he writes he has nothing in mind but the reader's interest. He says this and he believes it. But it is not true at all. Because if he were not attentive first and foremost to what *he* is doing, if he were not concerned with literature as his own action, he could not even write: he would not be the one who was writing—the one writing would be no one. This is why it is futile for him to take the seriousness of an ideal as his guarantee, futile for him to claim to have stable values: this seriousness is not his own seriousness and can never settle definitively where he thinks he is. For example: he writes novels, and these novels imply certain political statements, so that he seems to side with a certain Cause. Other people, people who directly support the Cause, are then inclined to recognize him as one of themselves, to see his work as proof that the Cause is really his cause, but as soon as they make this claim, as soon as they try to become involved in this activity and take it over, they realize that the writer is not on their side, that he is only on his own side, that what interests him about the Cause is the operation he himself has carried out—and they are puzzled. It is easy to understand why men who have committed themselves to a party, who have made a decision, distrust writers who share their views; because these writers have also committed themselves to literature, and in the final analysis literature, by its very activity, denies the substance of what it represents. This is its law and its truth. If it renounces this in order to attach itself permanently to a truth outside itself, it ceases to be a literature and the writer who still claims he is a writer enters into another aspect of bad faith. Then must a writer refuse to take an interest in anything, must he turn his face to the wall? The problem is that if he does this, his equivocation is just as great. First of all, looking at the wall is also turning towards the world; one is making the wall into the world. When a writer sinks into the pure intimacy of a work which is no one's business but his own, it may seem to other people—other writers and people involved in other activities—that at least they have been left at peace in their Thing and their own work. But not at all. The work created by this solitary person and enclosed in solitude contains within itself a point of view which concerns everyone, implicitly passing judgment on other works, on the problems of the times, becoming the accomplice of whatever it neglects, the enemy of whatever it abandons, and its indifference mingles hypocritically with everyone's passion.

What is striking is that in literature, deceit and mystification are not only inevitable but constitute the writer's honesty, whatever hope and truth are in him. Nowadays people often talk about the sickness of words, and we even become irritated with those who talk about it, and suspect them of making words sick so they can talk about it. This could be the case. The trouble is that this sickness is also the words' health. They may be torn apart by equivocation, but this equivocation is a good thing—without it there would be no dialogue. They may be falsified by misunderstanding—but this misunderstanding is the possibility of our understanding. They may be imbued with emptiness—but this emptiness is their very meaning. Naturally, a writer can always make it his ideal to call a cat a cat. But what he cannot manage to do is then believe that he is on the way to health and sincerity. On the contrary, he is causing more mystification than ever, because the cat is not a cat, and anyone who claims that it is has nothing in mind but this hypocritical violence: Rolet is a rascal.[4]

There are many reasons for this imposture. We have just been discussing the first reason: literature is made up of different stages which are distinct from one another and in opposition to one another. Honesty, which is analytical because it tries to see clearly, separates these stages. Under the eyes of honesty pass in succession the author, the work, and the reader; in succession the art of writing, the thing written, and the truth of that thing or the Thing Itself; still in succession, the writer without a name, pure absence of himself, pure idleness,

---

[4] Blanchot is referring to a remark made by Nicolas Boileau (1637-1711) in his first *Satire*: "J'appelle un chat un chat et Rolet un fripon" ("I call a cat a cat and Rolet a rascal"). Rolet was a notorious figure of the time.—*Tr.*

then the writer who is work, who is the action of a creation indifferent to what it is creating, then the writer who is the result of this work and is worth something because of this result and not because of the work, as real as the created thing is real; then the writer who is no longer affirmed by this result but denied by it, who saves the ephemeral work by saving its ideal, the truth of the work, etc. The writer is not simply one of these stages to the exclusion of the others, nor is he even all of them put together in their unimportant succession, but the action which brings them together and unifies them. As a result, when the honest conscience judges the writer by immobilizing him in one of these forms, when, for instance, it attempts to condemn the work because it is a failure, the writer's other honesty protests in the name of the other stages, in the name of the purity of art, which sees its own triumph in the failure—and likewise, every time a writer is challenged under one of his aspects he has no choice but to present himself as someone else, and when addressed as the author of a beautiful work, disown that work, and when admired as an inspiration and a genius, see in himself only application and hard work, and when read by everyone, say: "Who can read me? I haven't written anything." This shifting on the part of the writer makes him into someone who is perpetually absent, an irresponsible character without a conscience, but this shifting also forms the extent of his presence, of his risks and his responsibility.

The trouble is that the writer is not only several people in one, but each stage of himself denies all the others, demands everything for itself alone and does not tolerate any conciliation or compromise. The writer must respond to several absolute and absolutely different commands at once, and his morality is made up of the confrontation and opposition of implacably hostile rules.

One rule says to him: "You will not write, you will remain nothingness, you will keep silent, you will not know words."

The other rule says: "Know nothing but words."

"Write to say nothing."

"Write to say something."

"No works; rather, the experience of yourself, the knowledge of what is unknown to you."

"A work! A real work, recognized by other people and important to other people."

"Obliterate the reader."

"Obliterate yourself before the reader."

"Write in order to be true."

"Write for the sake of truth."

"Then be a lie, because to write with truth in mind is to write what is not yet true and perhaps never will be true."

"It doesn't matter, write in order to act."

"Write—you who are afraid to act."

"Let freedom speak in you."

"Oh! do not let freedom become a word in you."

Which law should be obeyed? Which voice should be listened to? But the writer must listen to them all! What confusion! Isn't clarity his law? Yes, clarity too. He must therefore oppose himself, deny himself even as he affirms himself, look for the deepness of the night in the facility of the day, looking in the shadows which never begin, to find the sure light which cannot end. He must save the world and be the abyss, justify existence and allow what does not exist to speak; he must be at the end of all eras in the universal plenitude, and he is the origin, the birth of what does nothing but come into being. Is he all that? Literature is all that, in him. But isn't all that what literature would *like* to be, what in reality it is not? In that case, literature is nothing. But is it nothing?

Literature is not nothing. People who are contemptuous of literature are mistaken in thinking they are condemning it by saying it is nothing. "All that is only literature." This is how people create an opposition between action, which is a concrete initiative in the world, and the written word, which is supposed to be a passive expression on the surface of the world; people who are in favor of action reject literature, which does not act, and those in search of passion become writers so as not to act. But this is to condemn and to love in an abusive way. If we see work as the force of history, the force that transforms man while it transforms the world, then a writer's activity must be recognized as the highest form of work. When a man works, what does he do? He produces an object. That object is the realization of a plan which was unreal before then: it is the affirmation of a reality different from the elements which constitute it and it is the future of new objects, to the extent that it becomes a tool capable of creating other objects. For example, my project might be to get warm. As long as this project is only a desire, I can turn it over every possible way and still it will not make me warm. But now I build a stove: the stove transforms the empty ideal which was my desire into something real; it affirms the presence in the world of something which was not there before, and in so doing, denies something which was there before; before, I had in front of me stones and cast iron; now I no longer have either stones or cast iron, but instead the product of the transformation of these elements—that is, their denial and destruction—by work. Because of this object, the world is now different. All the more different because this stove will allow me to make other objects, which will in turn deny the former condition of the world and prepare its future. These objects, which I have produced by changing the state of things, will in turn change me. The idea of heat is nothing, but actual heat will make my life a different kind of life, and every new thing I am able to do from now on because of this heat will also make me someone different. Thus is history formed, say Hegel and Marx—by work which realizes being in denying it, and reveals it at the end of the negation.[5]

But what is a writer doing when he writes? Everything a man does when he works, but to an outstanding degree. The writer, too, produces something—a work in the highest sense of the word. He produces this work by transforming natural and human realities. When he writes, his starting point is a certain state of language, a certain form of culture, certain books, and also certain objective elements—ink, paper, printing presses. In order to write, he must destroy language in its present form and create it in another form, denying books as he forms a book out of what other books are not. This new book is certainly a reality: it can be seen, touched, even read. In any case, it is not nothing. Before I wrote it, I had an idea of it, at least I had the project of writing it, but I believe there is the same difference between that idea and the volume in which it is realized as between the desire for heat and the stove which makes me warm. For me, the written volume is an extraordinary, unforeseeable innovation—such that it is impossible for me to conceive what it is capable of being without writing it. This is why it seems to me to be an experiment whose effects I

---

[5] Alexandre Kojève offers this interpretation of Hegel in his *Introduction à la lecture de Hegel* (Leçons sur *La Phénomenologie de l'Esprit*, selected and published by Raymond Queneau).

371

cannot grasp, no matter how consciously they were produced, and in the face of which I shall be unable to remain the same, for this reason: in the presence of something other, I become other. But there is an even more decisive reason: this other thing—the book—of which I had only an idea and which I could not possibly have known in advance, is precisely myself become other.

The book, the written thing, enters the world and carries out its work of transformation and negation. It, too, is the future of many other things, and not only books: by the projects which it can give rise to, by the undertakings it encourages, by the totality of the world of which it is a modified reflection, it is an infinite source of new realities, and because of these new realities existence will be something it was not before.

So is the book nothing? Then why should the act of building a stove pass for the sort of work which forms and produces history, and why should the act of writing seem like pure passivity which remains in the margins of history and which history produces in spite of itself? The question seems unreasonable, and yet it weighs on the writer and its weight is crushing. At first sight one has the impression that the formative power of written works is incomparably great; one has the impression that the writer is endowed with more power to act than anyone else since his actions are immeasurable, limitless: we know (or we like to believe) that one single work can change the course of the world. But this is precisely what makes us think twice. The influence authors exert is very great, it goes infinitely far beyond their actions, to such an extent that what is real in their actions does not carry over into their influence and that tiny bit of reality does not contain the real substance that the extent of their influence would require. What is an author capable of? Everything—first of all, everything: he is fettered, he is enslaved, but as long as he can find a few moments of freedom in which to write, he is *free* to create a world without slaves, a world in which the slaves become the masters and formulate a new law; thus, by writing, the chained man immediately obtains freedom for himself and for the world; he denies everything he is, in order to become everything he is not. In this sense, his work is a prodigious act, the greatest and most important there is. But let us examine this more closely. Insofar as he *immediately* gives himself the freedom he does not have, he is negating the actual conditions for his emancipation, he is neglecting to do the real thing that must be done so that the abstract idea of freedom can be realized. His negation is *global*. It not only negates his situation as a man who has been walled into prison but bypasses time that will open holes in these walls; it negates the negation of time, it negates the negation of limits. This is why this negation negates nothing, in the end, why the work in which it is realized is not a truly negative, destructive act of transformation, but rather the realization of the inability to negate anything, the refusal to take part in the world; it transforms the freedom which would have to be embodied in things in the process of time into an ideal above time, empty and inaccessible.

A writer's influence is linked to this privilege of being master of everything. But he is only master of everything, he possesses only the infinite; he lacks the finite, limit escapes him. Now, one cannot act in the infinite, one cannot accomplish anything in the unlimited, so that if a writer acts in quite a real way as he produces this real thing which is called a book, he is also discrediting all action by this action, because he is substituting for the world of determined things and defined work a world in which *everything* is *instantly* given and there is nothing left to do but read it and enjoy it.

In general, the writer seems to be subjected to a state of inactivity because he is the master of the imaginary, and those who follow him into the realm of the imaginary lose sight of the problems of their true lives. But the danger he represents is much more serious. The truth is that he ruins action, not because he deals with what is unreal but because he makes *all* of reality available to us. Unreality begins with the whole. The realm of the imaginary is not a strange region situated beyond the world, it is the world itself, but the world as entire, manifold, the world as a whole. That is why it is not in the world, because it is the world, grasped and realized in its entirety by the global negation of all the individual realities contained in it, by their disqualification, their absence, by the realization of that absence itself, which is how literary creation begins, for when literary creation goes back over each thing and each being, it cherishes the illusion that it is creating them, because now it is seeing and naming them from the starting point of *everything*, from the starting point of the *absence* of everything, that is, from nothing.

Certainly that literature which is said to be "purely imaginative" has its dangers. First of all, it is not pure imagination. It believes that it stands apart from everyday realities and actual events, but the truth is that it has stepped aside from them; it is that distance, that remove from the everyday which necessarily takes the everyday into consideration and describes it as separateness, as pure strangeness. What is more, it makes this distance into an absolute value, and then this separateness seems to be a source of general understanding, the capacity to grasp everything and attain everything immediately, for those who submit to its enchantment enough to emerge from both their life, which is nothing but limited understanding, and time, which is nothing but a narrow perspective. All this is the lie of a fiction. But this kind of literature has on its side the fact that it is not trying to deceive us: it presents itself as imaginary; it only puts to sleep those who want to go to sleep.

What is far more deceitful is the literature of action. It calls on people to do something. But if it wants to remain authentic literature, it must base its representation of this "something to do," this predetermined and specific goal, on a world where such an action turns back into the unreality of an abstract and absolute value. "Something to do," as it may be expressed in a work of literature, is never more than "everything remains to be done," whether it presents itself as this "everything," that is, as an absolute value, or whether it needs this "everything," into which it vanishes, to justify itself and prove that it has merit. The language of a writer, even if he is a revolutionary, is not the language of command. It does not command; it presents; and it does not present by causing whatever it portrays to be present, but by portraying it behind everything, as the meaning and the absence of this everything. The result is either that the appeal of the author to the reader is only an empty appeal, and expresses only the effort which a man cut off from the world makes to reenter the world, as he stands discreetly at its periphery—or that the "something to do," which can only be recovered by starting from absolute values, appears to the reader precisely as that which cannot be done or as that which requires neither work nor action in order to be done.

As we know, a writer's main temptations are called stoicism, skepticism, and the unhappy consciousness. These are all ways of thinking that a writer adopts for reasons he believes he has thought out carefully, but which only literature has thought out in him. A stoic: he is the man of the universe, which itself exists only on paper, and, a prisoner or a poor man, he endures his condition stoically because he can write and because the one minute of freedom in which he writes is enough to make him powerful and free, is enough to give him not his own freedom, which he derides, but universal freedom. A nihilist, because he does not simply negate this and that by methodical work which slowly transforms each thing: he negates everything at once, and he is obliged to negate everything, since he only deals with everything. The unhappy consciousness! It is only too evident that this unhappiness is his most profound talent, since he is a writer only by virtue of his fragmented consciousness divided into irreconcilable moments called: inspiration— which negates all work; work—which negates the nothingness of genius; the ephemeral work—in which he creates himself by negating himself; the work as everything—in which he takes back from himself and from other people everything which he seems to give to himself and to them. But there is one other temptation.

Let us acknowledge that in a writer there is a movement which proceeds without pause, and almost without transition, from nothing to everything. Let us see in him that negation that is not satisfied with the unreality in which it exists, because it wishes to realize itself and can only do so by negating something real, more real than words, more true than the isolated individual in control: it therefore keeps urging him towards a worldly life and a public existence in order to induce him to conceive how, even as he writes, he can become that very existence. It is at this point that he encounters those decisive moments in history when everything seems put in question, when law, faith, the State, the world above, the world of the past—everything sinks effortlessly, without work, into nothingness. The man knows he has not stepped out of history, but history is now the void, the void in the process of realization; it is *absolute* freedom which has become an event. Such periods are given the name Revolution. At this moment, freedom which aspires to be realized in the *immediate* form of *everything* is possible, everything can be done. A fabulous moment—and no one who has experienced it can completely recover from it, since he has experienced history as his own history and his own freedom as universal freedom. These moments are, in fact, fabulous moments: in them, fable speaks; in them, the speech of fable becomes action. That the writer should be tempted by them is completely appropriate. Revolutionary action is in every respect analogous to action as embodied in literature: the passage from nothing to everything, the affirmation of the absolute as event and of every event as absolute. Revolutionary action explodes with the same force and the same facility as the writer who has only to set down a few words side by side in order to change the world. Revolutionary action also has the same demand for purity, and the certainty that everything it does has absolute value, that it is not just any action performed to bring about some desirable and respectable goal, but that it is itself the ultimate goal, the Last Act. This last act is freedom, and the only choice left is between freedom and nothing. This is why, at that point, the only tolerable slogan is: *freedom or death*. Thus the Reign of Terror comes into being. People cease to be individuals working at specific tasks, acting here and only now: each person is universal freedom, and universal freedom knows nothing about elsewhere or tomorrow, or work or a work accomplished. At such times there is nothing left for anyone to do, because everything has been done. No one has a right to a private life any longer, everything is public, and the most guilty person is the suspect—the person who has a secret, who keeps a thought, an intimacy to himself. And in the end no one has a right to his life any longer, to his actually separate and physically distinct existence. This is the meaning of the Reign of Terror. Every citizen has a right to death, so to speak: death is not a sentence passed on him, it is his most essential right; he is not suppressed as a guilty person—he needs death so that he can proclaim himself a citizen and it is in the disappearance of death that freedom causes him to be born. Where this is concerned, the French Revolution has a clearer meaning than any other revolution. Death in the Reign of Terror is not simply a way of punishing seditionaries; rather, since it becomes the unavoidable, in some sense the desired lot of everyone, it appears as the very operation of freedom in free men. When the blade falls on Saint-Just and Robespierre, in a sense it executes no one. Robespierre's virtue, Saint-Just's relentlessness, are simply their existences already suppressed, the anticipated presence of their deaths, the decision to allow freedom to assert itself completely in them and through its universality negate the particular reality of their lives. Granted, perhaps they caused the Reign of Terror to take place. But the Terror they personify does not come from the death they inflict on others but from the death they inflict on themselves. They bear its features, they do their thinking and make their decisions with death sitting on their shoulders, and this is why their thinking is cold, implacable; it has the freedom of a decapitated head. The terrorists are those who desire absolute freedom and are fully conscious that this constitutes a desire for their own death, they are conscious of the freedom they affirm, as they are conscious of their death which they realize, and consequently they behave during their lifetimes not like people living among other living people, but like beings deprived of being, like universal thoughts, pure abstractions beyond history, judging and deciding in the name of all of history.

Death as an event no longer has any importance. During the Reign of Terror individuals die and it means nothing. In the famous words of Hegel, "It is thus the coldest and meanest of all deaths, with no more significance than cutting off a head of cabbage or swallowing a mouthful of water."[6] Why? Isn't death the achievement of freedom—that is, the richest moment of meaning? But it is also only the empty point in that freedom, a manifestation of the fact that such a freedom is still abstract, ideal (literary), that it is only poverty and platitude. Each person dies, but everyone is alive, and that really also means everyone is dead. But "is dead" is the positive side of freedom which has become the world: here, being is revealed as absolute. "Dying," on the other hand, is pure insignificance, an event without concrete reality, one which has lost all value as a personal and interior drama, because there is no longer any interior. It is the moment when I *die* signifies to me as I die a banality which there is no way to take into consideration: in the liberated world and in these moments when freedom is an absolute apparition, dying is unimportant and death has no depth. The Reign of Terror and revolution—not war—have taught us this.

The writer sees himself in the Revolution. It attracts him because it is the time during which literature becomes history. It is his truth. Any writer who is not induced by the very fact of writing to think, "I am the revolution, only freedom allows me to write," is not really writing. In 1793 there is a man who identifies himself completely with revolution and the Reign of Terror. He is an aristocrat clinging

---

[6] Hegel, *op. cit.*, p. 360.—*Tr.*

to the battlements of his medieval castle, a tolerant man, rather shy and obsequiously polite: but he writes, all he does is write, and it doesn't matter that freedom puts him back into the Bastille after having brought him out, he is the one who understands freedom the best, because he understands that it is a time when the most insane passions can turn into political realities, a time when they have a right to be seen, and are the law. He is also the man for whom death is the greatest passion and the ultimate platitude, who cuts off people's heads the way you cut a head of cabbage, with such great indifference that nothing is more unreal than the death he inflicts, and yet no one has been more acutely aware that death is sovereign, that freedom is death. Sade is the writer *par excellence,* he combines all the writer's contradictions. Alone: of all men he is the most alone, and yet at the same time a public figure and an important political personage; forever locked up and yet absolutely free, theoretician and symbol of absolute freedom. He writes a vast body of work, and that work exists for no one. Unknown: but what he portrays has an immediate significance for everyone. He is nothing more than a writer, and he depicts life raised to the level of a passion, a passion which has become cruelty and madness. He turns the most bizarre, most hidden, the most unreasonable kind of feeling into a universal affirmation, the reality of a public statement which is consigned to history to become a legitimate explanation of a man's general condition. He is, finally, negation itself: his *oeuvre* is nothing but the work of negation, his experience the action of furious negation, driven to blood, denying other people, denying God, denying nature and, within this circle in which it runs endlessly, reveling in itself as absolute sovereignty.

Literature contemplates itself in revolution, it finds its justification in revolution, and if it has been called the Reign of Terror, this is because its ideal is indeed that moment in history, that moment when "life endures death and maintains itself in it" in order to gain from death the possibility of speaking and the truth of speech. This is the "question" that seeks to pose itself in literature, the "question" that is its essence. Literature is bound to language. Language is reassuring and disquieting at the same time. When we speak, we gain control over things with satisfying ease. I say, "This woman," and she is immediately available to me, I push her away, I bring her close, she is everything I want her to be, she becomes the place in which the most surprising sorts of transformations occur and actions unfold: speech is life's ease and security. We can't do anything with an object that has no name. Primitive man knows that the possession of words gives him mastery over things, but for him the relationship between words and the world is so close that the manipulation of language is as difficult and as fraught with peril as contact with living beings: the name has not emerged from the thing, it is the inside of the thing which has been dangerously brought out into the open and yet it is still the hidden depths of the thing; the thing has therefore not yet been named. The more closely man becomes attached to a civilization, the more he can manipulate words with innocence and composure. Is it that words have lost all relation to what they designate? But this absence of relation is not a defect, and if it is a defect, this defect is the only thing that gives language its full value, so that of all languages the most perfect is the language of mathematics, which is spoken in a rigorous way and to which no entity corresponds.

I say, "This woman." Hölderlin, Mallarmé, and all poets whose theme is the essence of poetry have felt that the act of naming is disquieting and marvelous. A word may give me its meaning, but first it suppresses it. For me to be able to say, "This woman" I must somehow take her flesh and blood reality away from her, cause her to be absent, annihilate her. The word gives me the being, but it gives it to me deprived of being. The word is the absence of that being, its nothingness, what is left of it when it has lost being—the very fact that it does not exist. Considered in this light, speaking is a curious right. In a text dating from before *The Phenomenology*, Hegel, here the friend and kindred spirit of Hölderlin, writes: "Adam's first act, which made him master of the animals, was to give them names, that is, he annihilated them in their existence (as existing creatures)."[7] Hegel means that from that moment on the cat ceased to be a uniquely real cat and became an idea as well. The meaning of speech, then, requires that before any word is spoken there must be a sort of immense hecatomb, a preliminary flood plunging all of creation into a total sea. God had created living things, but man had to annihilate them. Not until then did they take on meaning for him, and he in turn created them out of the death into which they had disappeared; only

---

[7] From a collection of essays entitled *System of 1803-1804*. A. Kojève, in his *Introduction à la lecture de Hegel*, interpreting a passage from *The Phenomenology*, demonstrates in a remarkable way how for Hegel comprehension was equivalent to murder.

instead of beings (*êtres*) and, as we say, existants (*existants*), there remained only being (*l'être*), and man was condemned not to be able to approach anything or experience anything except through the meaning he had to create. He saw that he was enclosed in daylight, and he knew this day could not end, because the end itself was light, since it was from the end of beings that their meaning—which is being—had come.

Of course my language does not kill anyone. And yet: when I say, "This woman," real death has been announced and is already present in my language; my language means that this person, who is here right now, can be detached from herself, removed from her existence and her presence and suddenly plunged into a nothingness in which there is no existence or presence; my language essentially signifies the possibility of this destruction; it is a constant, bold allusion to such an event. My language does not kill anyone. But if this woman were not really capable of dying, if she were not threatened by death at every moment of her life, bound and joined to death by an essential bond, I would not be able to carry out that ideal negation, that deferred assassination which is what my language is.

Therefore it is accurate to say that when I speak: death speaks in me. My speech is a warning that at this very moment death is loose in the world, that it has suddenly appeared between me, as I speak, and the being I address: it is there between us as the distance that separates us, but this distance is also what prevents us from being separated, because it contains the condition for all understanding. Death alone allows me to grasp what I want to attain; it exists in words as the only way they can have meaning. Without death, everything would sink into absurdity and nothingness.

This situation has various consequences. Clearly, in me, the power to speak is also linked to my absence from being. I say my name, and it is as though I were chanting my own dirge: I separate myself from myself, I am no longer either my presence or my reality, but an objective, impersonal presence, the presence of my name, which goes beyond me and whose stone-like immobility performs exactly the same function for me as a tombstone weighing on the void. When I speak, I deny the existence of what I am saying, but I also deny the existence of the person who is saying it: if my speech reveals being in its nonexistence, it also affirms that this revelation is made on the basis of the nonexistence of the person making it, out of his power to remove himself from himself, to be other than his being. This is why, if true language is to begin, the life that will carry this language must have experienced its nothingness, must have "trembled in the depths; and everything in it that was fixed and stable must have been shaken." Language can only begin with the void; no fullness, no certainty can ever speak; something essential is lacking in anyone who expresses himself. Negation is tied to language. When I first begin, I do not speak in order to say something, rather a nothing demands to speak, nothing speaks, nothing finds its being in speech and the being of speech is nothing. This formulation explains why literature's ideal has been the following: to say nothing, to speak in order to say nothing. That is not the musing of a high-class kind of nihilism. Language perceives that its meaning derives not from what exists, but from its own retreat before existence, and it is tempted to proceed no further than this retreat, to try to attain negation in itself and to make everything of nothing. If one is not to talk about things except to say what makes them nothing, well then, to say nothing is really the only hope of saying everything about them.

A hope which is naturally problematic. Everyday language calls a cat a cat, as if the living cat and its name were identical, as if it were not true that when we name the cat we retain nothing of it but its absence, what it is not. Yet for a moment everyday language is right, in that even if the word excludes the existence of what it designates, it still refers to it through the thing's nonexistence, which has become its essence. To name the cat is, if you like, to make it into a non-cat, a cat that has ceased to exist, has ceased to be a living cat, but this does not mean one is making it into a dog, or even a non-dog. That is the primary difference between common language and literary language. The first accepts that once the nonexistence of the cat has passed into the word, the cat itself comes to life again fully and certainly in the form of its idea (its being) and its meaning: on the level of being (idea), the word restores to the cat all the certainty it had on the level of existence. And in fact that certainty is even much greater: things can change if they have to, sometimes they stop being what they are—they remain hostile, unavailable, inaccessible; but the being of these things, their idea, does not change: the idea is definitive, it is sure, we even call it eternal. Let us hold on to words, then, and not revert back to things, let us not let go of words, not believe they are sick. Then we'll be at peace.

Common language is probably right, this is the price we pay for our peace. But literary language is made of uneasiness; it is also made of contradictions. Its position is not very stable or secure. On the one hand, its only interest in a thing is in the meaning of the thing, its absence, and it would like to attain this absence absolutely in itself and for itself, to grasp in its entirety the infinite movement of comprehension. What is more, it observes that the word cat is not only the nonexistence of the cat, but a nonexistence made *word*, that is, a completely determined and objective reality. It sees that there is a difficulty and even a lie in this. How can it hope to have achieved what it set out to do, since it has transposed the unreality of the thing into the reality of language? How could the infinite absence of comprehension consent to be confused with the limited, restricted presence of a single word? And isn't everyday language mistaken when it tries to persuade us of this? In fact, it is deceiving itself and it is deceiving us, too. Speech is not sufficient for the truth it contains. Take the trouble to listen to a single word: in that word, nothingness is struggling and toiling away, it digs tirelessly, doing its utmost to find a way out, nullifying what encloses it—it is infinite disquiet, formless and nameless vigilance. Already the seal which held this nothingness within the limits of the word and within the guise of its meaning has been broken; now there is access to other names, names which are less fixed, still vague, more capable of adapting to the savage freedom of the negative essence—they are unstable groups, no longer terms, but the movement of terms, an endless sliding of "turns of phrase" which do not lead anywhere. Thus is born the image that does not directly designate the thing, but rather, what the thing is not; it speaks of a dog instead of a cat. This is how the pursuit begins in which all of language, in motion, is asked to give in to the uneasy demands of one single thing that has been deprived of being and that, after having wavered between each word, tries to lay hold of them all again in order to negate them all at once, so that they will designate the void as they sink down into it—this void which they can neither fill nor represent.

Even if literature stopped here, it would have a strange and embarrassing job to do. But it does not stop here. It recalls the first name which would be the murder Hegel speaks of. The "existant" was called out of its existence by the word and it became being. This *Lazare, veni foras* summoned the dark cadaverous reality from its primordial depths and in exchange gave it only the life of the mind. Language knows that its kingdom is day and not the intimacy of the unrevealed; it knows that in order for the day to begin, for the day to be that Orient which Hölderlin glimpsed—not light that has become the repose of noon, but the terrible force that draws beings into the world and illuminates them—something must be left out. Negation cannot be created out of anything but the reality of what it is negating; language derives its value and its pride from the fact that it is the achievement of this negation; but in the beginning, what was lost? The torment of language is what it lacks because of the necessity that it be the lack of precisely this. It cannot even name it.

Whoever sees God dies. In speech what dies is what gives life to speech; speech is the life of that death, it is "the life that endures death and maintains itself in it." What wonderful power. But something was there and is no longer there. Something has disappeared. How can I recover it, how can I turn around and look at what exists *before*, if all my power consists of making it into what exists *after*? The language of literature is a search for this moment which precedes literature. Literature usually calls it existence; it wants the cat as it exists, the pebble *taking the side of things,* not man, but the pebble, and in this pebble what man rejects by saying it, what is the foundation of speech and what speech excludes in speaking, the abyss, Lazarus in the tomb and not Lazarus brought back into the daylight, the one who already smells bad, who is Evil, Lazarus lost and not Lazarus saved and brought back to life. *I say a flower!* But in the absence where I mention it, through the oblivion to which I relegate the image it gives me, in the depths of this heavy word, itself looming up like an unknown thing, I passionately summon the darkness of this flower, I summon this perfume that passes through me though I do not breathe it, this dust that impregnates me though I do not see it, this color which is a trace and not light. Then what hope do I have of attaining the thing I push away? My hope lies in the materiality of language, in the fact that words are things, too, are a kind of nature—this is given to me and gives me more than I can understand. Just now the reality of words was an obstacle. Now, it is my only chance. A name ceases to be the ephemeral passing of nonexistence and becomes a concrete ball, a solid mass of existence; language, abandoning the sense, the meaning which was all it wanted to be, tries to become senseless. Everything physical takes precedence: rhythm, weight, mass, shape, and then the paper on which one writes, the trail of the ink, the book. Yes, happily language is a thing: it is a written thing, a bit of bark, a sliver of rock, a fragment of clay in which the reality of the earth continues to exist. The word acts not as an ideal force but as an obscure power, as an incantation that coerces things, makes them *really* present outside of themselves. It is an element, a piece barely detached from its subterranean surroundings: it is no longer a name, but rather one moment in the universal anonymity, a bald statement, the stupor of a confrontation in the depths of obscurity. And in this way language insists on playing its own game without man, who created it. Literature now dispenses with the writer: it is no longer this inspiration at work, this negation asserting itself, this idea inscribed in the world as though it were the absolute perspective of the world in its totality. It is not beyond the world, but neither is it the world itself: it is the presence of things before the *world* exists, their perseverance after the world has disappeared, the stubbornness of what remains when everything vanishes and the dumbfoundedness of what appears when nothing exists. That is why it cannot be confused with consciousness, which illuminates things and makes decisions; it is *my* consciousness *without me*, the radiant passivity of mineral substances, the lucidity of the depths of torpor. It is not the night; it is the obsession of the night; it is not the night, but the consciousness of the night, which lies awake watching for a chance to surprise itself and because of that is constantly being dissipated. It is not the day, it is the side of the day that day has rejected in order to become light. And it is not death either, because it manifests existence without being, existence which remains below existence, like an inexorable affirmation, without beginning or end—death as the impossibility of dying.

By turning itself into an inability to reveal anything, literature is attempting to become the revelation of what revelation destroys. This is a tragic endeavor. Literature says: "I no longer represent, I am; I do not signify, I present." But this wish to be a thing, this refusal to mean anything, a refusal immersed in words turned to salt; in short, this destiny which literature becomes as it becomes the language of no one, the writing of no writer, the light of a consciousness deprived of self, this insane effort to bury itself in itself, to hide itself behind the fact that it is visible—all this is what literature now manifests, what literature now shows. If it were to become as mute as a stone, as passive as the corpse enclosed behind that stone, its decision to lose the capacity for speech would still be legible on the stone and would be enough to wake that bogus corpse.

Literature learns that it cannot go beyond itself towards its own end: it hides, it does not give itself away. It knows it is the movement through which whatever disappears keeps appearing. When it names something, whatever it designates is abolished; but whatever is abolished is also sustained, and the thing has found a refuge (in the being which is the word) rather than a threat. When literature refuses to name anything, when it turns a name into something obscure and meaningless, witness to the primordial obscurity, what has disappeared in this case—the meaning of the name—is really destroyed, but signification in general has appeared in its place, the meaning of the meaninglessness embedded in the word as expression of the obscurity of existence, so that although the precise meaning of the terms has faded, what asserts itself now is the very possibility of signifying, the empty power of bestowing meaning—a strange impersonal light.

By negating the day, literature recreates day in the form of fatality; by affirming the night, it finds the night as the impossibility of the night. This is its discovery. When day is the light of the world, it illuminates what it lets us see: it is the capacity to grasp, to live, it is the answer "understood" in every question. But if we call the day to account, if we reach a point where we push it away in order to find out what is prior to the day, under it, we discover that the day is already present, and that what is prior to the day is still the day, but in the form of an inability to disappear, not a capacity to make something appear: the darkness of necessity, not the light of freedom. The nature, then, of what is prior to the day, of prediurnal existence, is the dark side of the day, and that dark side is not the undisclosed mystery of its beginning, but its inevitable presence—the statement "There is no day," which merges with "There is already day," its appearance coinciding with the moment when it has not yet appeared. In the course of the day, the day allows us to escape from things, it lets us comprehend them, and as it lets us comprehend them, it makes them transparent and as if null—but what we cannot escape from is the day: within it we are free, but it, itself, is fatality, and day in the form of fatality is the being of what is prior to the day, the existence we must turn away from in order to speak and comprehend.

If one looks at it in a certain way, literature has two slopes. One side of literature is turned toward the movement of negation by which things are separated from themselves and destroyed in order to be known, subjugated, communicated. Literature is not content to accept only the fragmentary, successive results of this movement of negation: it wants to grasp the movement itself and it wants to comprehend the results in their totality. If negation is assumed to have gotten control of everything, then real things, taken one by one, all refer back to that unreal whole which they form together, to the world which is their meaning as a group, and this is the point of view that literature has adopted—it looks at things from the point of view of this still *imaginary* whole which they would *really* constitute if negation could be achieved. Hence its non-realism—the shadow which is its prey. Hence its distrust of words, its need to apply the movement of negation to language itself and to exhaust it by realizing it as that totality on the basis of which each term would be nothing.

But there is another side to literature. Literature is a concern for the reality of things, for their unknown, free, and silent existence; literature is their innocence and their forbidden presence, it is the being which protests against revelation, it is the defiance of what does not want to take place outside. In this way, it sympathizes with darkness, with aimless passion, with lawless violence, with everything in the world that seems to perpetuate the refusal to come into the world. In this way, too, it allies itself with the reality of language, it makes language into matter without contour, content without form, a force that is capricious and impersonal and says nothing, reveals nothing, simply announces—through its refusal to say anything—that it comes from night and will return to night. In itself, this metamorphosis is not unsuccessful. It is certainly true that words are transformed. They no longer *signify* shadow, earth, they no longer represent the absence of shadow and earth which is meaning, which is the shadow's light, which is the transparency of the earth: opacity is their answer; the flutter of closing wings is their speech; in them, physical weight is present as the stifling density of an accumulation of syllables that has lost all meaning. The metamorphosis has taken place. But beyond the change that has solidified, petrified, and stupefied words two things reappear in this metamorphosis: the meaning of this metamorphosis, which illuminates the words, and the meaning the words contain by virtue of their apparition as things or, if it should happen this way, as vague, indeterminate, elusive existences in which nothing appears, the heart of depth without appearance. Literature has certainly triumphed over the meaning of words, but what it has found in words considered apart from their meaning is meaning that has become thing: and thus it is meaning detached from its conditions, separated from its moments, wandering like an empty power, a power no one can do anything with, a power without power, the simple inability to cease to be, but which, because of that, appears to be the proper determination of indeterminate and meaningless existence. In this endeavor, literature does not confine itself to rediscovering in the interior what it tried to leave behind on the threshold. Because what it finds, as the interior, is the outside which has been changed from the outlet it once was into the impossibility of going out—and what it finds as the darkness of existence is the being of day which has been changed from explicatory light, creative of meaning, into the aggravation of what one cannot prevent oneself from understanding and the stifling obsession of a reason without any principle, without any beginning, which one cannot account for. Literature is that experience through which the consciousness discovers its being in its inability to lose consciousness, in the movement whereby, as it disappears, as it tears itself away from the meticulousness of an I, it is recreated beyond unconsciousness as an impersonal spontaneity, the desperate eagerness of a haggard knowledge which knows nothing, which no one knows, and which ignorance always discovers behind itself as its own shadow changed into a gaze.

One can, then, accuse language of having become an interminable resifting of words, instead of the silence it wanted to achieve. Or one can complain that it has immersed itself in the conventions of literature when what it wanted was to be absorbed into existence. That is true. But this endless resifting of words without content, this continuousness of speech through an immense pillage of words, is precisely the profound nature of a silence that talks even in its dumbness, a silence that is speech empty of words, an echo speaking on and on in the midst of silence. And in the same way literature, a blind vigilance which in its attempt to escape from itself plunges deeper and deeper into its own obsession, is the only rendering of the obsession of existence, if this itself is the very impossibility of emerging from existence, if it is being which is always flung back into being, that which in the bottomless depth is already at the bottom of the abyss, a recourse against which there is no recourse.[8]

Literature is divided between these two slopes. The problem is that even though they are apparently incompatible they do not lead toward distinctly different works or goals, and that an art which purports to follow one slope is already on the other. The first slope is meaningful prose. Its goal is to express things in a language that designates things according to what they mean. This is the way everyone speaks; and many people write the way we speak. But still on this side of language, there comes a moment when art realizes that everyday speech is dishonest and abandons it. What is art's complaint about everyday speech? It says it lacks meaning: art feels it is madness to think that in each word some thing is completely present through the absence that determines it, and so art sets off in quest of a language that can recapture this absence itself and represent the endless movement of comprehension. We do not need to discuss this position again, we have described it at length already. But what can be said about this kind of art? That it is a search for a pure form, that it is a vain preoccupation with empty words? Quite the contrary: its only concern it true meaning; its only preoccupation is to safeguard the movement by which this meaning becomes truth. To be fair, we must consider it more significant than any ordinary prose, which only subsists on false meanings: it represents the world for us, it teaches us to discover the total being of the world, it is the work of the negative in the world and for the world. How can we help admiring it as preeminently active, lively and lucid art? Of course we must. But then we must appreciate the same qualities in Mallarmé, who is the master of this art.

Mallarmé is on the other slope of literature, too. In some sense all the people we call poets come together on that slope. Why? Because they are interested in the reality of language, because they are not interested in the world, but in what things and beings would be if there were no world; because they devote themselves to literature as

---

[8] In his book *De l'existence à l'existant*, Emmanuel Lévinas uses the term *il y a* ["there is"] to throw some "light" on this anonymous and impersonal flow of being that precedes all being, being that is already present in the heart of disappearance, that in the depths of annihilation still returns to being, being as the fatality of being, nothingness as existence: when there is nothing, *il y a* being. See also *Deucalion I. [Existence and Existents*, tr. A. Lingis, Kluwer, Boston, 1978.—*Tr.*]

to an impersonal power that only wants to be engulfed and submerged. If this is what poetry is like, at least we will know why it must be withdrawn from history, where it produces a strange insect-like buzzing in the margins, and we will also know that no work which allows itself to slip down this slope towards the chasm can be called a work of prose. Well, what is it then? Everyone understands that literature cannot be divided up and that if you choose exactly where your place in it is, if you convince yourself that you really are where you wanted to be, you risk becoming very confused, because literature has already insidiously caused you to pass from one slope to the other and changed you into something you were not before. This is its treachery; this is also its cunning version of the truth. A novelist writes in the most transparent kind of prose, he describes men we could have met ourselves and actions we could have performed; he says his aim is to express the reality of a human world the way Flaubert did. In the end, though, his work really has only one subject. What is it? The horror of existence deprived of the world, the process through which whatever ceases to be continues to be, whatever is forgotten is always answerable to memory, whatever dies encounters only the impossibility of dying, whatever seeks to attain the beyond is always still here. This *process* is day which has become fatality, consciousness whose light is no longer the lucidity of the vigil but the stupor of lack of sleep, it is existence without being, as poetry tries to recapture it behind the meaning of words, which reject it.

Now here is a man who does more observing than writing: he walks in a pine forest, looks at a wasp, picks up a stone. He is a sort of scholar, but this scholar fades away in the face of what he knows, sometimes in the face of what he wants to know; he is a man who learns for the sake of other men: he has gone over to the side of objects, sometimes he is water, sometimes a pebble, sometimes a tree, and when he observes things, he does it for the sake of things, and when he describes something, it is the thing itself that describes itself. Now, this is the surprising aspect of the transformation, because no doubt it is possible to become a tree, and is there any writer who could not succeed in making a tree talk? But Francis Ponge's tree is a tree that has observed Francis Ponge and that describes itself as it imagines Ponge might describe it. These are strange descriptions. Certain traits make them seem completely human: the fact is that the tree knows the weakness of men who only speak about what they know; but all these metaphors borrowed from the picturesque human world, these images which form an image, really represent the way things regard man, they really represent the singularity of human speech animated by the life of the cosmos and the power of seeds; this is why other things slip in among these images, among certain objective notions—because the tree knows that science is a common ground of understanding between the two worlds: what slip in are vague recollections rising from deep down in the earth, expressions that are in the process of metamorphosing, words in which a thick fluidity of vegetable growth insinuates itself under the clear meaning. Doesn't everyone think he understands these descriptions, written in perfectly meaningful prose? Doesn't everyone think they belong to the clear and human side of literature? And yet they do not belong to the world but to the underside of the world; they do not attest to form but to lack of form, and they are only clear to a person who does not penetrate them, the opposite of the oracular words of the tree of Dodona—another tree—which were obscure but concealed a meaning: these are clear only because they hide their lack of meaning. Indeed, Ponge's descriptions begin at that hypothetical moment after the world has been achieved, history completed, nature almost made human, when speech advances to meet the thing and the thing learns to speak. Ponge captures this touching moment when existence, which is still mute, encounters speech at the edge of the world, speech which as we know is the murderer of existence. From the depths of dumbness, he hears the striving of an antediluvian language and he recognizes the profound work of the elements in the clear speech of the concept. In this way he becomes the will that mediates between that which is rising slowly to speech and speech which is descending slowly to the earth, expressing not existence as it was before the day, but existence as it is after the day: the world of the end of the world.

Where in a work lies the beginning of the moment when the words become stronger than their meaning and the meaning more physical than the word? When does Lautréamont's prose lose the name of prose? Isn't each sentence understandable? Isn't each group of sentences logical? And don't the words say what they mean? At what moment, in this labyrinth of order, in this maze of clarity, did meaning stray from the path? At what turning did reason become aware that it had stopped "following," that something else was continuing, progressing, concluding in its place, something like it in every way, something reason thought it recognized as itself, until the moment it woke up and discovered this other that had taken its place? But if reason now retraces its steps in order to denounce the intruder, the illusion immediately vanishes into thin air, reason finds only itself there, the prose is prose again, so that reason starts off again and loses its way again, allowing a sickening physical substance to replace it, something like a walking staircase, a corridor that unfolds ahead—a kind of reason whose infallibility excludes all reasoners, a logic that has become the "logic of things." Then where is the work? Each moment has the clarity of a beautiful language being spoken, but the work as a whole has the opaque meaning of a thing that is being eaten and that is also eating, that is devouring, being swallowed up and recreating itself in a vain effort to change itself into nothing.

Lautréamont is not a true writer of prose? But what is Sade's style, if it isn't prose? And does anyone write more clearly than he does? Is there anyone less familiar than he—who grew up in the least poetic century—with the preoccupations of a literature in search of obscurity? And yet in what other work do we hear such an impersonal, inhuman sound, such a "gigantic and haunting murmur" (as Jean Paulhan says)? But this is simply a defect! The weakness of a writer who cannot be brief! It is certainly a serious defect—literature is the first to accuse him of it. But what it condemns on one side becomes a merit on the other; what it denounces in the name of the work it admires as an experience; what seems unreadable is really the only thing worth being written. And at the end of everything is fame; beyond, there is oblivion; farther beyond, anonymous survival as part of a dead culture; even farther beyond perseverance in the eternity of the elements. Where is the end? Where is that death which is the hope of language? But language is the *life that endures death and maintains itself in it.*

If we want to restore literature to the movement which allows all its ambiguities to be grasped, that movement is here: literature, like ordinary speech, *begins* with the *end*, which is the only thing that allows us to understand. If we are to speak, we must see death, we must see it behind us. When we speak, we are leaning on a tomb, and the void of that tomb is what makes language true, but at the same time void is reality and death becomes being. There is being—that is to say, a logical and expressible truth—and there is a world, because we can destroy things and suspend existence. This is why we can say that there is being because there is nothingness: death is man's possibility, his chance, it is through death that the future of a finished world is still there for us; death is man's greatest hope, his only hope of being man. This is why existence is his only real dread, as Emmanuel Lévinas has clearly shown,[9] existence frightens him, not because of death which could put an end to it, but because it excludes death, because it is still there underneath death, a presence in the depths of absence, an inexorable day in which all days rise and set. And there is no question that we are preoccupied by dying. But why? It is because when we die, we leave behind not only the world but also death. That is the paradox of the last hour. Death works with us in the world; it is a power that humanizes nature, that raises existence to being, and it is within each one of us as our most human quality; it is death only in the world—man only knows death because he is man, and he is only man because he is death in the process of becoming. But to die is to shatter the world; it is the loss of the person, the annihilation of the being; and so it is also the loss of death, the loss of what in it and for me made it death. As long as I live, I am a mortal man, but when I die, by ceasing to be a man I also cease to be mortal, I am no longer capable of dying, and my impending death horrifies me because I see it as it is: no longer death, but the impossibility of dying.

Certain religions have taken the impossibility of death and called it immortality. That is, they have tried to "humanize" the very event which signifies: "I cease to be a man." But it is only the opposite thrust that makes death impossible: through death I lose the advantage of being mortal, because I lose the possibility of being man; to be man beyond death could only have this strange meaning—to be, in spite of death, still capable of dying, to go on as though nothing had happened, with death as a horizon and the same hope—death which would have no outcome beyond a "go on as though nothing had happened," etc. This is what other religions have called the curse

---

[9] He writes, "Isn't dread in the face of being—horror of being—just as primordial as dread in the face of death? Isn't fear of being just as primordial as fear for one's being? Even more primordial, because one could account for the latter by means of the former." (*De l'existence á l'existant*)

of being reborn: you die, but you die badly because you have lived badly, you are condemned to live again, and you live again until, having become a man completely, in dying you become a truly blessed man—a man who is really dead. Kafka inherited this idea from the Kabbalah and Eastern traditions. A man enters the night, but the night ends in awakening, and there he is, an insect. Or else the man dies, but he is actually alive; he goes from city to city, carried along by rivers, recognized by some people, helped by no one, the mistake made by old death snickering at his bedside; his is a strange condition, he has forgotten to die. But another man thinks he is alive, the fact is he has forgotten his death, and yet another, knowing he is dead, struggles in vain to die; death is over there, the great unattainable castle, and life was over there, the native land he left in answer to a false summons; now there is nothing to do but to struggle, to work at dying completely, but if you struggle you are still alive; and everything that brings the goal closer also makes the goal inaccessible.

Kafka did not make this theme the expression of a drama about the next world, but he did try to use it to capture the present fact of our condition. He saw in literature the best way of trying to find a way out for this condition, not only of describing it. This is high praise, but does literature deserve it? It is true that there is powerful trickery in literature, a mysterious bad faith that allows it to play everything both ways and gives the most honest people an unreasonable hope of losing and yet winning at the same time. First of all, literature, too, is working towards the advent of the world; literature is civilization and culture. In this way, it is already uniting two contradictory movements. It is negation, because it drives the inhuman, indeterminate side of things back into nothingness; it defines them, makes them finite, and this is the sense in which literature is really the work of death in the world. But at the same time, after having denied things in their existence, it preserves them in their being; it causes things to have a meaning, and the negation which is death at work is also the advent of meaning, the activity of comprehension. Besides this, literature has a certain privilege: it goes beyond the immediate place and moment, and situates itself at the edge of the world and as if at the end of time, and it is from this position that it speaks about things and concerns itself with men. From this new power, literature apparently gains a superior authority. By revealing to each moment the whole of which it is a part, literature helps it to be aware of the whole that it is not and to become another moment that will be a moment within another whole, and so forth; because of this, literature can be called the greatest ferment in history. But there is one inconvenient consequence: this whole which literature represents is not simply an idea, since it is *realized* and not formulated abstractly—but it is not realized in an objective way, because what is real in it is not the whole but the particular language of a particular work, which is itself immersed in history: what is more, the whole does not present itself as real, but as fictional, that is, precisely as whole, as everything: perspective of the world, grasp of that *imaginary* point where the world can be seen in its entirety. What we are talking about, then, is a view of the world which realizes itself as unreal using language's peculiar reality. Now, what is the consequence of this? As for the task which is the world, literature is now regarded more as a bother than as a serious help; it is not the result of any true work, since it is not reality but the realization of a point of view which remains unreal; it is foreign to any true culture, because culture is the work of a person changing himself little by little over a period of time, and not the immediate enjoyment of a fictional transformation which dispenses with both time and work.

Spurned by history, literature plays a different game. If it is not really in the world, working to make the world, this is because its lack of being (of intelligible reality) causes it to refer to an existence that is still inhuman. Yes, it recognizes that this is so, that in its nature there is a strange slipping back and forth between being and not being, presence and absence, reality and nonreality. What is a work? Real words and an imaginary story, a world in which everything that happens is borrowed from reality, and this world is inaccessible; characters who are portrayed as living—but we know that their life consists of not living (of remaining a fiction); pure nothingness, then? But the book is there and we can touch it, we read the words and we can't change them; is it the nothingness of an idea, then, of something which exists only when understood? But the fiction is not understood, it is experienced through the words with which it is realized, and for me, as I read it or write it, it is more real than many real events, because it is impregnated with all the reality of language and it substitutes itself for my life simply by existing. Literature does not act: but what it does

is plunge into this depth of existence which is neither being nor nothingness and where the hope of doing anything is completely eliminated. It is not explanation, and it is not pure comprehension, because
the inexplicable emerges in it. And it expresses without expressing, it
offers its language to what is murmured in the absence of speech. So
literature seems to be allied with the strangeness of that existence which
being has rejected and which does not fit into any category. The writer
senses that he is in the grasp of an impersonal power that does not let
him either live or die: the irresponsibility he cannot surmount becomes the expression of that death without death which awaits him at
the edge of nothingness; literary immortality is the very movement by
which the nausea of a survival which is not a survival, a death which
does not end anything, insinuates itself into the world, a world sapped
by crude existence. The writer who writes a work eliminates himself
as he writes that work and at the same time affirms himself in it. If he
has written it to get rid of himself, it turns out that the work engages
him and recalls him to himself, and if he writes it to reveal himself and
live in it, he sees that what he has done is nothing, that the greatest
work is not as valuable as the most insignificant act, and that his work
condemns him to an existence that is not his own existence and to a
life that has nothing to do with life. Or again he has written because in
the depths of language he heard the work of death as it prepared living
beings for the truth of their name: he worked for this nothingness and
he himself was a nothingness at work. But as one realizes the void, one
creates a work, and the work, born of fidelity to death, is in the end no
longer capable of dying; and all it brings to the person who was trying
to prepare an unstoried death for himself is the mockery of immortality.

Then where is literature's power? It plays at working in the world,
and the world regards its work as a worthless or dangerous game. It
opens a path for itself towards the obscurity of existence and does
not succeed in pronouncing the "Never more" which would suspend its curse. Then where is its force? Why would a man like Kafka
decide that if he had to fall short of his destiny, being a writer was the
only way to fall short of it truthfully. Perhaps this is an unintelligible
enigma, but if it is, the source of the mystery is literature's right to
affix a negative or positive sign indiscriminately to each of its moments
and each of its results. A strange right—one linked to the question of

ambiguity in general. Why is there ambiguity in the world? Ambiguity is its own answer. We can't answer it except by rediscovering it in the ambiguity of our answer, and an ambiguous answer is a question about ambiguity. One of the ways it reduces us is by making us want to clear it up, a struggle that is like the struggle against evil Kafka talks about, which ends in evil, "like the struggle with women, which ends in bed."

Literature is language turning into ambiguity. Ordinary language is not necessarily clear, it does not always say what it says; misunderstanding is also one of its paths. This is inevitable. Every time we speak we make words into monsters with two faces, one being reality, physical presence, and the other meaning, ideal absence. But ordinary language limits equivocation. It solidly encloses the absence in a presence, it puts *a term* to understanding, to the indefinite movement of comprehension; understanding is limited, but misunderstanding is limited, too. In literature, ambiguity is in some sense abandoned to its excesses by the opportunities it finds and exhausted by the extent of the abuses it can commit. It is as though there were a hidden trap here to force ambiguity to reveal its own traps, and as though in surrendering unreservedly to ambiguity literature were attempting to keep it—out of sight of the world and out of the thought of the world—in a place where it fulfills itself without endangering anything. Here ambiguity struggles with itself. It is not just that each moment of language can become ambiguous and say something different from what it is saying, but that the general meaning of language is unclear: we don't know if it is expressing or representing, if it is a thing or means that thing, if it is there to be forgotten or if it only makes us forget it so that we will see it; if it is transparent because what it says has so little meaning or clear because of the exactness with which it says it, obscure because it says too much, opaque because it says nothing. There is ambiguity everywhere: in its trivial exterior—but what is most frivolous may be the mask of the serious; in its disinterestedness—but behind this disinterestedness lie the forces of the world and it connives with them without knowing them, or again, ambiguity uses this disinterestedness to safeguard the absolute nature of the values without which action would stop or become mortal; its unreality is therefore both a principle of action and the incapacity to act: in the same way that the fiction in itself is truth and also indifference to truth; in the same way that if it allies itself with morality, it corrupts itself, and if it rejects morality, it still perverts itself; in the same way that it is nothing if it is not its own end, but it cannot have its end in itself, because it is without end, it ends outside itself, in history, etc.

All these reversals from *pro* to *contra*—and those described here—undoubtedly have very different causes. We have seen that literature assigns itself irreconcilable tasks. We have seen that in moving from the writer to the reader, from the labor to the finished work, it passes through contradictory moments and can only place itself in the affirmation of all the opposing moments. But all these contradictions, these hostile demands, these divisions and oppositions, so different in origin, kind, and meaning, refer back to an ultimate ambiguity whose strange effect is to attract literature to an unstable point where it can indiscriminately change both its meaning and its sign.

This ultimate vicissitude keeps the work in suspense in such a way that it can choose whether to take on a positive or negative value and, as though it were pivoting invisibly around an invisible axis, enter the daylight of affirmations or the back-light of negations, without its style, genre, or subject being accountable for the radical transformation. Neither the content of the words nor their form is involved here. Whether the work is obscure or clear, poetry or prose, insignificant, important, whether it speaks of a pebble or of God, there is something in it that does not depend on its qualities and that deep within itself is always in the process of changing the work from the ground up. It is as though in the very heart of literature and language, beyond the visible movements that transform them, a point of instability were reserved, a power to work substantial metamorphoses, a power capable of changing everything about it without changing anything. This instability can appear to be the effect of a disintegrating force, since it can cause the strongest, most forceful work to become a work of unhappiness and ruin, but this disintegration is also a form of construction, if it suddenly causes distress to turn into hope and destruction into an element of the indestructible. How can such imminence of change, present in the depths of language quite apart from the meaning that affects it and the reality of that language, nevertheless be present in that meaning and in that reality? Could it be that the meaning of a word introduces something else into the word along with it, something which, although it protects the precise signification of the word and does not threaten that signification, is capable of completely modifying the meaning and modifying the material value of the word? Could there be a force at once friendly and hostile hidden in the intimacy of speech, a weapon intended to build and to destroy, which would act behind signification rather than upon signification? Do we have to suppose a meaning for the meaning of words that, while determining that meaning, also surrounds this determination with an ambiguous indeterminacy that wavers between yes and no?

But we can't suppose anything: we have questioned this meaning of the meaning of words at length, this meaning which is as much the movement of a word towards its truth as it is its return through the reality of language to the obscure depths of existence; we have questioned this absence by which the thing is annihilated, destroyed in order to become being and idea. It is *that life which supports death and maintains itself in it*—death, the amazing power of the negative, or freedom, through whose work existence is detached from itself and made significant. Now, nothing can prevent this power—at the very moment it is trying to understand things and, in language, to specify words—nothing can prevent it from continuing to assert itself as continually differing possibility, and nothing can stop it from perpetuating an irreducible *double meaning*, a choice whose terms are covered over with an ambiguity that makes them identical to one another even as it makes them opposite.

If we call this power negation or unreality or death, then presently death, negation, and unreality, at work in the depths of language, will signify the advent of truth in the world, the construction of intelligible being, the formation of meaning. But just as suddenly, the sign changes: meaning no longer represents the marvel of comprehension, but instead refers us to the nothingness of death, and intelligible being signifies only the rejection of existence, and the absolute concern for truth is expressed by an incapacity to act in a real way. Or else death is perceived as a civilizing power which results in a comprehension of being. But at the same time, a death that results in being represents an absurd insanity, the curse of existence—which contains within itself both death and being and is neither being nor death. Death ends in being: this is man's hope and his task, because nothingness itself helps to make the world, nothingness is the creator of the world in man as he works and understands. Death ends in being: this is man's laceration, the source of his unhappy fate, since by man death comes to being and by man meaning rests on nothingness; the only way we can comprehend is by denying ourselves existence, by making death *possible,* by contaminating what we comprehend with the nothingness of death, so that if we emerge from being, we fall outside the possibility of death, so that if we emerge from being, we fall outside the possibility of death, and the way out becomes the disappearance of every way out.

This original double meaning, which lies deep inside every word like a condemnation that is still unknown and a happiness that is still invisible, is the source of literature, because literature is the form this double meaning has chosen in which to show itself behind the meaning and value of words, and the question it asks is the question asked by literature.

THE ESSENTIAL SOLITUDE

It seems we have learned something about art when we experience what the word solitude designates. This word has been tossed around much too freely. Yet what does it mean to "be alone"? When is one alone? As we ask ourselves this question, we should not simply return to thoughts that we find moving. Solitude on the level of the world is a wound we do not need to comment on here.

Nor do we have in mind the solitude of the artist, the solitude which he is said to need if he is to practice his art. When Rilke writes to the Comtesse de Solms-Laubach (August 3, 1907): "Except for two short interruptions, I have not pronounced a single word for weeks; at last my solitude has closed in and I am in my work like a pit in its fruit," the solitude he speaks of is not essentially solitude: it is self-communion.

The solitude of the work.

In the solitude of the work—the work of art, the literary work—we see a more essential solitude. It excludes the self-satisfied isolation of individualism, it is unacquainted with the search for difference; it is not dissipated by the fact of sustaining a virile relationship in a task that covers the mastered extent of the day. The person who is writing the work is thrust to one side, the person who has written the work is dismissed. What is more, the person who is dismissed does not know it. This ignorance saves him, diverts him and allows him to go on. The writer never knows if the work is done. What he has finished in one book, he begins again or destroys in another. Valéry, who celebrates this privilege of the infinite in the work, still sees only its easiest aspect: the fact that the work is infinite means (to him) that although the artist is not capable of ending it, he is nevertheless capable of turning it into the enclosed space of an endless task whose incompleteness develops mastery of the spirit, expresses that mastery, expresses it by developing it in the form of power. At a certain point, circumstances—that is history—in the form of an editor, financial demands, social duties, pronounce the missing end and the artist, freed by a purely compulsory outcome, pursues the incomplete elsewhere.

According to this point of view, the infinity of the work is simply the infinity of the spirit. The spirit tries to accomplish itself in a single work, instead of realizing itself in the infinity of works and the movement of history. But Valéry was in no way a hero. He chose to talk about everything, to write about everything: thus, the scattered whole of the world diverted him from the rigor of the unique whole of the work—he amiably allowed himself to be turned away from it. The *etc.* was hiding behind the diversity of thoughts, of subjects.

Nevertheless, the work—the work of art, the literary work—is neither finished nor unfinished: it is. What it says is exclusively that: that it is—and nothing more. Outside of that, it is nothing. Anyone who tries to make it express more finds nothing, finds that it expresses nothing. Anyone who lives in dependence on the work, whether because he is writing it or reading it, belongs to the solitude of something that expresses only the word *being*: a word that the language protects by hiding it or that the language causes to appear by disappearing into the silent void of the work.

The first framework of the solitude of the work is this absence of need which never permits it to be called finished or unfinished. The work can have no proof, just as it can have no use. It cannot be verified—truth can lay hold of it, renown illuminate it: this existence concerns it not at all, this obviousness makes it neither certain nor real, nor does it make it manifest.

The work is solitary: that does not mean that it remains incommunicable, that it lacks a reader. But the person who reads it enters into that affirmation of the solitude of the work, just as the one who writes it belongs to the risk of that solitude.

The work, the book.

If we want to examine more closely what such statements suggest, perhaps we should look for their source. The writer writes a book, but the book is not yet the work, the work is not a work until the word *being* is pronounced in it, in the violence of a beginning which is its own; this event occurs when the work is the innermost part of someone writing it and of someone reading it. We can therefore ask ourselves this: if solitude is the writer's risk, doesn't it express the fact that he is turned, oriented towards the open violence of the work, never grasping more than its substitute, its approach, and its illusion in the form of the book? The writer belongs to the work, but what belongs to him is only a book, a mute accumulation of sterile words, the most meaningless thing in the world. The writer who experiences this void simply believes that the work is unfinished, and he believes that with a little more effort and the luck of some favorable moments, he—and only he—will be able to finish it. And so he sets back to work. But what he wants to finish, by himself, remains something interminable, it ties him to an illusory labor. And in the end, the work ignores him, it closes on his absence, in the impersonal, anonymous statement that it is—and nothing more. Which we express by remarking that the artist, who only finishes his work at the moment he dies, never knows his work. And we may have to reverse that remark, because isn't the writer dead as soon as the work exists, as he himself sometimes forsees, when he experiences a very strange kind of worklessness.[1]

"Noli me legere."

The same situation can also be described this way: a writer never reads his work. For him, it is the unreadable, a secret, and he cannot remain face to face with it. A secret, because he is separated from it. Yet this impossibility of reading is not a purely negative movement, rather it is the only real approach the author can have to what we call a work. Where there is still only a book, the abrupt *Noli me legere*

---

[1] This is not the situation of the man who works and accomplishes his task and whose task escapes him by transforming itself in the world. What this man makes is transformed, but in the world, and he recaptures it through the world, at least if he can recapture it, if alienation is not immobilized, if it is not diverted to the advantage of a few, but continues until the completion of the world. On the contrary, what the writer has in view is the work, and what he writes is a book. The book, as such, can become an active event in the world (an action, however, that is always reserved and insufficient), but it is not action the artist has in view, but the work, and what makes the book a substitute for the work is enough to make it a thing that, like the work, does not arise from the truth of the world; and it is an almost frivolous thing, if it has neither the reality of the work nor the seriousness of real labor in the world.

already causes the horizon of another power to appear. An experience that is fleeting, though immediate. It does not have the force of a prohibition, it is a statement that emerges from the play and the meaning of the words—the insistent, harsh and poignant statement that what is there, in the inclusive presence of a definitive text, still rejects—is the rude and caustic emptiness of rejection—or else excludes, with the authority of indifference, the person who has written it and now wants to recapture it by reading it. The impossibility of reading is the discovery that now, in the space opened by creation, there is no more room for creation—and no other possibility for the writer than to keep on writing the same work. No one who has written the work can live near it, dwell near it. This is the very decision that dismisses him, that cuts him off, that turns him into the survivor, the workless, unemployed, inert person on whom art does not depend.

The writer cannot dwell near the work: he can only write it, and once it is written he can only discern the approach to it in the abrupt *Noli me legere* that distances him, that moves him away or forces him to return to that "remove" where he first came in, to become the understanding of what he had to write. So that now he finds himself back again, in some sense at the beginning of his task, and he rediscovers the neighborhood of the outside, the errant intimacy of the outside, which he was not able to make into a dwelling.

Perhaps this ordeal points us in the direction of what we are looking for. The writer's solitude, then, this condition that is his risk, arises from the fact that in the work he belongs to what is always before the work. Through him the work arrives, is the firmness of a beginning, but he himself belongs to a time dominated by the indecision of beginning again. The obsession that ties him to a privileged theme, that makes him repeat what he has already said, sometimes with the power of enriched talent, but sometimes with the prolixity of an extraordinarily impoverishing repetition, less and less forcefully, more and more monotonously, illustrates his apparent need to come back to the same point, to retrace the same paths, to persevere and begin again what, for him, never really begins, to belong to the shadow of events instead of the object, to what allows the words themselves to become images, appearances—instead of signs, values, the power of truth.

Persecutive prehension.

It occurs that a man who is holding a pencil may want very much to let go of it, but his hand will not let go: quite the opposite—it tightens, it has no intention of opening. The other hand intervenes with more success, but then we see the hand that we may call sick slowly gesturing, trying to recapture the object that is moving away. What is strange is the slowness of this gesture. The hand moves through a time that is hardly human, that is neither the time of viable action nor the time of hope, but rather the shadow of time which is itself the shadow of a hand slipping in an unreal way towards an object that has become its shadow. At certain moments, this hand feels a very great need to grasp: it must take the pencil, this is necessary, this is an order, an imperious requirement. The phenomenon is known as "persecutive prehension."

The writer seems to be master of his pen, he can become capable of great mastery over words, over what he wants to make them express. But this mastery only manages to put him in contact, keep him in contact, with a fundamental passivity in which the word, no longer anything beyond its own appearance, the shadow of a word, can never be mastered or even grasped; it remains impossible to grasp, impossible to relinquish, the unsettled moment of fascination.

The writer's mastery does not lie in the hand that writes, the "sick" hand that never lets go of the pencil, that cannot let it go because it does not really hold what it is holding; what it holds belongs to shadow, and the hand itself is a shadow. Mastery is always the achievement of the other hand, the one that does not write, the one that can intervene just when it has to, grasp the pencil and take it away. Mastery, then, consists of the power to stop writing, to interrupt what is being written, giving its rights and its exclusive cutting edge back to the instant.

We must resume our questions. We have said: the writer belongs to the work, but what belongs to him—what he finishes alone—is only a book. The restriction of "only" responds to the expression "alone." The writer never stands before the work, and where there is a work, he does not know it, or more exactly, he is ignorant of his very ignorance, it is only present in the impossibility of reading, an ambiguous experience that sends him back to work.

The writer sets back to work. Why doesn't he stop writing? If he breaks with the work, as Rimbaud did, why does that break strike us as a mysterious impossibility? Is it simply that he wants a perfect work, and if he keeps on working at it, is this only because the perfection is never perfect enough? Does he even write for the sake of a work? Is he preoccupied by it as the thing that will put an end to his task, as a goal worthy of all his efforts? Not at all. And the work is never that for the sake of which one is able to write (that for the sake of which one might relate to what is written as to the exercise of a power).

The fact that the writer's task comes to an end when he dies is what hides the fact that because of this task his life slips into the unhappiness of infinity.

The interminable, the incessant.

The solitude that comes to the writer through the work of literature is revealed by this: the act of writing is now interminable, incessant. The writer no longer belongs to the authoritative realm where expressing oneself means expressing the exactness and certainty of things and of values depending on the meaning of their limits. What is written consigns the person who must write to a statement over which he has no authority, a statement that is itself without consistency, that states nothing, that is not the repose, the dignity of silence, because it is what is still speaking when everything has been said, what does not precede speech because it instead prevents it from being a beginning of speech, just as it withdraws from speech the right and the power to interrupt itself. To write is to break the bond uniting the speech to myself, to break the relationship that makes me talk towards "you" and gives me speech within the understanding that this speech receives from you, because it addresses you, it is the address that begins in me because it ends in you. To write is to break this link. What is more, it withdraws language from the course of the world, it deprives it of what makes it a power such that when I speak, it is the world that is spoken, it is the day that is built by work, action and time.

The act of writing is interminable, incessant. The writer, they say, stops saying "I." Kafka observes with surprise, with enchantment and delight, that as soon as he was able to substitute "he" for "I" he entered literature. This is true, but the transformation is much more profound.

The writer belongs to a language no one speaks, a language that is not addressed to anyone, that has no center, that reveals nothing. He can believe he is asserting himself in this language, but what he is asserting is completely without a self. To the extent that, as a writer, he accedes to what is written, he can never again express himself and he cannot appeal to you either, nor yet let anyone else speak. Where he is, only being speaks, which means that speech no longer speaks, but simply is—dedicates itself to the pure passivity of being.

When to write means to consign oneself to the interminable, the writer who agrees to sustain its essence loses the power to say "I." He then loses the power to make others say "I." Thus it is impossible for him to give life to characters whose freedom would be guaranteed by his creative force. The idea of a character, like the traditional form of the novel, is only one of the compromises that a writer—drawn out of himself by literature in search of its essence—uses to try to save his relations with the world and with himself.

To write is to make oneself the echo of what cannot stop talking—and because of this, in order to become its echo, I must to a certain extent impose silence on it. To this incessant speech I bring the decisiveness, the authority of my own silence. Through my silent mediation, I make perceptible the uninterrupted affirmation, the giant murmur in which language, by opening, becomes image, becomes imaginary, an eloquent depth, an indistinct fullness that is empty. The source of this silence is the self-effacement to which the person who writes is invited. Or, this silence is the resource of his mastery, the right to intervene maintained by the hand that does not write—the part of himself that can always say no, and, when necessary, appeals to time, restores the future.

When we admire the tone of a work, responding to the tone as what is most authentic about it, what are we referring to? Not the style, and not the interest and the quality of the language, but precisely the silence, the virile force through which the person who writes, having deprived himself of himself, having renounced himself, has nevertheless maintained within his effacement the authority of a power, the decision to be silent, so that in this silence what speaks without beginning or end can take on form, coherence and meaning.

Tone is not the voice of the writer, but the intimacy of the silence he imposes on speech, which makes this silence still *his own,* what remains of himself in the discretion that sets him to one side. Tone makes the great writers, but perhaps the work is not concerned about what makes them great.

In the effacement to which he is invited, the "great writer" still restrains himself: what speaks is no longer himself, but it is not the pure slipping of the speech of no one. Of the effaced "I," it retains the authoritarian, though silent affirmation. It retains the cutting edge, the violent rapidity of active time, of the instant. This is how he is preserved inside the work, is contained where there is no more restraint. But because of this the work, too, retains a content; it is not completely interior to itself.

The writer we call classic—at least in France—sacrifices the speech that is his own within him, but in order to give voice to the universal. The calm of a form governed by rules, the certainty of a speech freed from caprice, in which impersonal generality speaks, assures him a relationship with truth. Truth that is beyond person and would like to be beyond time. Literature then has the glorious solitude of reason, that ratified life at the heart of the whole that would require resolution and courage—if that reason were not in fact the equilibrium of an orderly aristocratic society, that is, the noble contentment of a section of society that concentrates the whole in itself, by isolating itself and maintaining itself above what permits it to live.

When to write is to discover the interminable, the writer who enters this region does not go beyond himself towards the universal. He does not go towards a world that is more sure, more beautiful, better justified, where everything is arranged in the light of a just day. He does not discover the beautiful language that speaks honorably for everyone. What speaks in him is the fact that in one way or another he is no longer himself, he is already no longer anyone. The "he" that is substituted for "I"—this is the solitude that comes to the writer through the work. "He" does not indicate objective disinterest, creative detachment. "He" does not glorify the consciousness of someone other than me, the soaring of a human life that, within the imaginary space of the work of art, keeps its freedom to say "I." "He" is myself having become no one, someone else having become the other; it is the fact that there, where I am, I can no longer address myself to myself, and that the person who addresses himself to me does not say "I," is not himself.

Recourse to the "Journal."

It is perhaps striking that the moment the work becomes the pursuit of art, becomes literature, the writer feels a growing need to preserve a relationship with himself. He feels an extreme reluctance to relinquish himself in favor of that neutral power, formless, without a destiny, which lies behind everything that is written, and his reluctance and apprehension are revealed by the concern, common to so many authors, to keep what he calls his *Journal*. This is quite unlike the so-called romantic complacencies. The Journal is not essentially a confession, a story about oneself. It is a Memorial. What does the writer have to remember? Himself, who he is when he is not writing, when he is living his daily life, when he is alive and real, and not dying and without truth. But the strange thing is that the means he uses to recall himself to himself is the very element of forgetfulness: the act of writing. Yet this is why the truth of the Journal does not lie in the interesting and literary remarks to be found in it, but in the insignificant details that tie it to everyday reality. The Journal represents the series of reference points that a writer establishes as a way of recognizing himself, when he anticipates the dangerous metamorphosis he is vulnerable to. It is a path that is still viable, a sort of parapet walk that runs alongside the other path, overlooks it and sometimes coincides with it, the other being the one where the endless task is wandering. Here, real things are still spoken of. Here, the one who speaks retains his name and speaks in his name, and the date inscribed belongs to a common time in which what happens really happens. The Journal—this book that is apparently completely solitary—is often written out of fear and dread in the face of the solitude that comes to the writer through the work.

Recourse to the Journal indicates that the person writing does not want to break with the happiness, the decorum of days that are really days and that really follow one another. The Journal roots the movement of writing in time, in the humbleness of the everyday, dated and preserved by its date. Perhaps what is written there is already only insincerity, perhaps it is said without concern for what is true, but it is said under the safeguard of the event, it belongs to the affairs, the incidents, the commerce of the world, to an active present, to a stretch of time that is perhaps completely worthless and insignificant, but that at least cannot turn back; it is the work of something that goes beyond itself, goes towards the future, goes there definitively.

The Journal shows that already the person writing is no longer capable of belonging to time through ordinary firmness of action, through the community created by work, by profession, through the simplicity of intimate speech, the force of thoughtlessness. Already he does not really belong to history anymore, but he does not want to lose time either, and since he no longer knows how to do anything but write, at least he writes at the demand of his day-to-day story and in keeping with his everyday preoccupations. Often writers who keep journals are the most literary of all writers, but perhaps this is precisely because in doing so they avoid the extreme of literature, if literature is in fact the fascinating domain of the absence of time.

The fascination of the absence of time.

To write is to surrender oneself to the fascination of the absence of time. Here we are undoubtedly approaching the essence of solitude. The absence of time is not a purely negative mode. It is the time in which nothing begins, in which initiative is not possible, where before the affirmation there is already the recurrence of the affirmation. Rather than a purely negative mode, it is a time without negation, without decision, when *here* is also *nowhere*, when each thing withdraws into its image and the "I" that we are recognizes itself as it sinks into the neutrality of a faceless "he." The time of the absence of time is without a present, without a presence. This "without a present," however, does not refer to a past. *Formerly* had the dignity and the active force of *now*; memory still bears witness to this active force, memory which frees me from what would otherwise recall me, frees me from it by giving me the means to summon it freely, to dispose of it according to my present intention. Memory is the freedom from the past. But what is without a present does not accept the present of a memory either. Memory says of an event: that was, once, and now never again. The irremediable nature of what is without a present, of what is not even there as having been, says: that has never occurred, never a single first time, and yet it is resuming, again, again, infinitely. It is without end, without beginning. It is without a future.

The time of the absence of time is not dialectical. What appears in it is the fact that nothing appears, the being that lies deep within the absence of being, the being that is when there is nothing, that is no longer when there is something—as though there were beings only through the loss of being, when being is lacking. The reversal that constantly refers us back, in the absence of time, to the presence of absence, but to this presence as absence, to absence as affirmation of itself, affirmation in which nothing is affirmed, in which nothing ceases to be affirmed, in the aggravation of the indefinite—this movement is not dialectical. Contradictions do not exclude one another there, nor are they reconciled there; only time, for which negation becomes our power, can be the "unity of incompatible things." In the absence of time, what is new does not renew anything; what is present is not contemporary; what is present presents nothing, represents itself, belongs now and henceforth and at all times to recurrence. This is not, but comes back, comes as already and always past, so that I do not know it, but I recognize it, and this recognition destroys the power in me to know, the right to grasp, makes what cannot be grasped into something that cannot be relinquished, the inaccessible that I cannot cease attaining, what I cannot take but can only take back—and never give up.

This time is not the ideal immobility that is glorified under the name of the eternal. In the region we are trying to approach, here is submerged in nowhere, but nowhere is nevertheless here, and dead time is a real time in which death is present, in which it arrives but does not stop arriving, as though by arriving it rendered sterile the time that permits it to arrive. The dead present is the impossibility of realizing a presence—an impossibility that is present, that is there as that which doubles every present, the shadow of the present, which the present carries and hides in itself. When I am alone, in this present, I am not alone, but am already returning to myself in the form of Someone. Someone is there, where I am alone. The fact of being alone is that I belong to this dead time that is not my time, nor yours, nor common time, but the time of Someone. Someone is what is still present when no one is there. In the place where I am alone, I am not there, there is no one there, but the impersonal is there: the outside as what anticipates, precedes, dissolves all possibility of personal relationship. Someone is the faceless He, the One of which one is a part, but who is a part of it? No one is part of the One. "One" belongs to a region that cannot be brought into the light—not because it conceals a secret alien to all revelation, not even because it is radically dark, but because it transforms everything that has access to it, even light, into anonymous, impersonal being, the Not-true, the Not-real and yet always there. In this sense, the "One" is what appears closest to one when one dies.[2]

Where I am alone, day is no longer anything but the loss of an abode, it is an intimacy with the outside, the outside that is placeless and without repose. The act of coming here causes the one who comes to be part of the dispersal, the fissure in which the exterior is a stifling intrusion, the nakedness and cold of that in which one remains exposed, where space is the dizziness of being spaced. Then fascination reigns.

The image.

Why fascination? Seeing implies distance, the decision that causes separation, the power not to be in contact and to avoid the confusion of contact. Seeing means that this separation has nevertheless become an encounter. But what happens when what you see, even though from a distance, seems to touch you with a grasping contact, when the manner of seeing is a sort of touch, when seeing is a *contact* at a distance? What happens when what is seen imposes itself on your gaze, as though the gaze had been seized, touched, put in contact with appearance? Not an active contact, not the initiative and action that might still remain in a true touch; rather, the gaze is drawn, absorbed into an immobile movement and a depth without depth. What is given to us by contact at a distance is the image, and fascination is passion for the image.

What fascinates us, takes away our power to give it a meaning, abandons its "perceptible" nature, abandons the world, withdraws to the

---

[2] When I am alone, I am not the one who is here and you are not the one I am far away from, nor other people, nor the world. At this point we begin to ponder the idea of "essential solitude and solitude in the world." [See Blanchot's four pages entitled "La solitude essentielle et la solitude dans le monde" in the appendix to *L'Espace litteraire* (Gallimard, 1955)—Tr.]

near side of the world and attracts us there, no longer reveals itself to us and yet asserts itself in a presence alien to the present in time and to presence in space. The split, which had been the possibility of seeing, solidifies, right inside the gaze, into impossibility. In this way, in the very thing that makes it possible, the gaze finds the power that neutralizes it—that does not suspend it or arrest it, but on the contrary prevents it from ever finishing, cuts it off from all beginning, makes it into a neutral, wandering glimmer that is not extinguished, that does not illuminate: the circle of the gaze, closed on itself. Here we have an immediate expression of the inversion that is the essence of solitude. Fascination is the gaze of solitude, the gaze of what is incessant and interminable, in which blindness is still vision, vision that is no longer the possibility of seeing, but the impossibility of not seeing, impossibility that turns into seeing, that perseveres—always and always—in a vision that does not end: a dead gaze, a gaze that has become the ghost of an eternal vision.

It can be said that a person who is fascinated does not perceive any real object, any real form, because what he sees does not belong to the world of reality, but to the indeterminate realm of fascination. A realm that is so to speak absolute. Distance is not excluded from it, but it is excessive, being the unlimited depth that lies behind the image, a depth that is not alive, not tractable, absolutely present though not provided, where objects sink when they become separated from their meaning, when they subside into their image. This realm of fascination, where what we see seizes our vision and makes it interminable, where our gaze solidifies into light, where light is the absolute sheen of an eye that we do not see, that we nevertheless do not leave off seeing because it is the mirror image of our own gaze, this realm is supremely attractive, fascinating: light that is also the abyss, horrifying and alluring, light in which we sink.

Our childhood fascinates us because it is the moment of fascination, it is fascinated itself, and this golden age seems bathed in a light that is splendid because it is unrevealed, but the fact is that this light is alien to revelation, has nothing to reveal, is pure reflection, a ray that is still only the radiance of an image. Perhaps the power of the maternal figure derives its brilliance from the very power of fascination, and one could say that if the Mother exerts this fascinating attraction, it is because she appears when the child lives completely under the gaze of fascination, and so concentrates in herself all the powers of enchantment. It is because the child is fascinated that the mother is fascinating, and this is also why all the impressions of our earliest years have a fixed quality that arises from fascination.

When someone who is fascinated sees something, he does not see it, properly speaking, but it touches him in his immediate proximity, it seizes him and monopolizes him, even though it leaves him absolutely at a distance. Fascination is tied in a fundamental way to the neutral, impersonal presence, the indeterminate One, the immense and faceless Someone. It is the relationship—one that is itself neutral and impersonal—that the gaze maintains with the depths that have no gaze and no contour, the absence that one sees because it is blinding.

The act of writing.

To write is to enter into the affirmation of solitude where fascination threatens. It is to yield to the risk of the absence of time, where eternal recommencement holds sway. It is to pass from the I to the He, so that what happens to me happens to no one, is anonymous because of the fact that it is my business, repeats itself in an infinite dispersal. To write is to arrange language under fascination and, through language, in language, remain in contact with the absolute milieu, where the thing becomes an image again, where the image, which had been allusion to a figure, becomes an allusion to what is without figure, and having been a form sketched on absence, becomes the unformed presence of that absence, the opaque and empty opening on what is when there is no more world, when there is no world yet.

Why this? Why should the act of writing have anything to do with this essential solitude, the essence of which is that in it, concealment appears?[3]

---

[3] We will not try to answer this question directly here. We will simply ask: just as a statue glorifies marble—and if all art tries to draw out into the daylight the elemental depths that the world denies and drives back as it asserts itself—isn't language in the poem, in literature, related to ordinary language in the same way that the image is related to the thing? We are apt to think that poetry is a language which, more than any other, does justice to images. Probably this is an allusion to a much more essential transformation:

the poem is not a poem because it includes a certain number of figures, metaphors, comparisons. On the contrary, what is special about a poem is that nothing in it strikes a vivid image. We must therefore express what we are looking for in another way: in literature, doesn't language itself become entirely image, not a language containing images or putting reality into figures, but its own image, the image of language—and not a language full of imagery—or an imaginary language, a language no one speaks—that is to say, spoken from its own absence—in the same way that the image appears on the absence of the thing, a language that is also addressed to the shadow of events, not to their reality, because of the fact that the words that express them are not signs, but images, images of words and words in which things become images?

What are we trying to describe by saying this? Aren't we headed in a direction that will force us to return to opinions we were happy to relinquish, opinions similar to the old idea that art was an imitation, a copy of the real? If the language in a poem becomes its own image, doesn't that mean that poetic speech is always second, secondary? According to the customary analysis, an image exists after an object: it follows from it; we see, then we imagine. After the object comes the image. "After" seems to indicate a subordinate relationship. We speak in a real way, then we speak in an imaginary way, or we imagine ourselves speaking. Isn't poetic speech nothing more than a tracing, a weakened shadow, the transposition of the unique speaking language into a space where the requirements for effectivenesss are attenuated? But perhaps the customary analysis is wrong. Perhaps, before we go any further, we should ask ourselves: but what is the image? (See the essay entitled "The Two Versions of the Imaginary.")

Two Versions of the Imaginary

But what is the image? When there is nothing, that is where the image finds its condition, but disappears into it. The image requires the neutrality and the effacement of the world, it wants everything to return to the indifferent depth where nothing is affirmed, it inclines towards the intimacy of what still continues to exist in the void; its truth lies there. But this truth exceeds it; what makes it possible is the limit where it ceases. Hence its dramatic aspect, the ambiguity it evinces, and the brilliant lie with which it is reproached. A superb power, says Pascal, which makes eternity into nothingness and nothingness into an eternity.

The image speaks to us, and it seems to speak intimately to us about ourselves. But intimately is to say too little; intimately then designates that level where the intimacy of the person breaks off, and in that motion points to the menacing nearness of a vague and empty outside that is the sordid background against which the image continues to affirm things in their disappearance. In this way, in connection with each thing, it speaks to us of less than the thing, but of us, and in connection with us, of less than us, of that less than nothing which remains when there is nothing.

The fortunate thing about the image is that it is a limit next to the indefinite. A thin ring, but one which does not keep us at such a remove from things that it saves us from the blind pressure of that remove. Through it, that remove is available to us. Through what there is of inflexibility in a reflection, we believe ourselves to be masters of the absence that has become an interval, and the dense void itself seems to open to the radiation of another day.

In this way the image fills one of its functions, which is to pacify, to humanize the unformed nothingness pushed towards us by the residue of being that cannot be eliminated. It cleans it up, appropriates it, makes it pleasant and pure and allows us to believe, in the heart of the happy dream which art too often permits, that at a distance from the real, and immediately behind it, we are finding, as a pure happiness and a superb satisfaction, the transparent eternity of the unreal.

"For," says Hamlet, "in that sleep of death what dreams may come, when we have shuffl'd off this mortal coil..." The image, present behind

each thing and in some sense the dissolution of that thing and its con-
tinuance in its dissolution, also has, behind it, that heavy sleep of death
in which dreams might come to us. When it wakes or when we wake it,
it can very well represent an object to us in a luminous *formal* halo; it has
sided with the *depth,* with elemental materiality, the still undetermined
absence of form (the world that oscillates between the adjective and the
substantive), before sinking into the unformed prolixity of indetermination. This is the reason for its characteristic passivity: a passivity that
makes us submit to it, even when we are summoning it, and causes its
fleeting transparency to arise from the obscurity of destiny returned to
its essence, which is that of a shadow.

But when we confront things themselves, if we stare at a face, a corner of a room, doesn't it also sometimes happen that we abandon ourselves to what we see, that we are at its mercy, powerless before this
presence that is suddenly strangely mute and passive? This is true, but
what has happened is that the thing we are staring at has sunk into its
image, that the image has returned to that depth of impotence into which
everything falls back. The "real" is that with which our relationship is
always alive and which always leaves us the initiative, addressing that
power we have to begin, that free communication with the beginning
that is ourselves; and to the extent that we are in the day, the day is still
contemporary with its awakening.

According to the usual analysis, the image exists after the object: the
image follows from it; we see, then we imagine. After the object comes
the image. "After" means that first the thing must move away in order
to allow itself to be grasped again. But that distancing is not the simple
change of place of a moving object, which nevertheless remains the same.
Here the distancing is at the heart of the thing. The thing was there, we
grasped it in the living motion of a comprehensive action—and once it
has become an image it instantly becomes ungraspable, noncontemporary,
impassive, not the same thing distanced, but that thing as distancing, the
present thing in its absence, the thing graspable because ungraspable,
appearing as something that has disappeared, the return of what does
not come back, the strange heart of the distance as the life and unique
heart of the thing.

In the image, the object again touches something it had mastered in
order to be an object, something against which it had built and defined
itself, but now that its value, its signification, is suspended, now that the

world is abandoning it to worklessness and putting it to one side, the truth in it withdraws, the elemental claims it, which is the impoverishment, the enrichment that consecrates it as image.

Nevertheless: doesn't the reflection always seem more spiritual than the object reflected? Isn't it the ideal expression of that object, its presence freed of existence, its form without matter? And artists who exile themselves in the illusion of images, isn't their task to idealize beings, to elevate them to their disembodied resemblance?

The image, the mortal remains.

At first sight, the image does not resemble a cadaver, but it could be that the strangeness of a cadaver is also the strangeness of the image. What we call the mortal remains evades the usual categories: something is there before us that is neither the living person himself nor any sort of reality, neither the same as the one who was alive, nor another, nor another thing. What is there, in the absolute calm of what has found its place, nevertheless does not realize the truth of being fully here. Death suspends relations with the place, even though the dead person relies heavily on it as the only base left to him. Yes, the fact is that that base is lacking, place is missing, the cadaver is not in its place. Where is it? It is not here and yet it is not elsewhere; nowhere? but the fact is that then nowhere is here. The cadaverous presence establishes a relation between here and nowhere. First of all, in the mortuary chamber and on the death bed, the repose that must be maintained shows how fragile the ultimate position is. Here is the cadaver, but here, in turn, becomes a cadaver: "here below," speaking absolutely, with no "up there" exalting itself any longer. The place where one dies is not just any place at all. One does not willingly transport these remains from one spot to another: death jealously secures its place and unites with it to the very bottom, in such a way that the indifference of that place, the fact that it is nevertheless just any place at all, becomes the depth of its presence as death becomes the support of indifference, the yawning intimacy of a nowhere without difference, yet one that must be situated here.

Remaining is not accessible to the one who dies. The deceased, we say, is no longer of this world, he has left it behind him, but what is left behind is precisely this cadaver, which is not of this world either—even

419

though it is here—which is, rather, behind the world, something the living person (and not the deceased) has left behind him and which now affirms, on the basis of this, the possibility of a world-behind, a return backwards, an indefinite survival, indeterminate, indifferent, about which we only know that human reality, when it comes to an end, reconstitutes its presence and proximity. This is an impression we can call common: someone who has just died is first of all very close to the condition of a thing—a familiar thing that we handle and approach, that does not keep us at a distance and whose soft passivity reveals only its sad impotence. Of course dying is a unique event, and someone who dies "in your arms" is in some sense your fellow creature forever, but he is dead, now. Everyone knows that action must be taken quickly, not so much because the stiffness of the cadaver will make it more difficult, but because human action will very soon be "displaced." Very soon there will be—undisplaceable, untouchable, riveted to here by the strangest kind of embrace and yet drifting with it, dragging it farther below—no longer an inanimate object but Someone, the insupportable image and the figure of the unique becoming anything at all.

The resemblance of cadavers.

The striking thing, when this moment comes, is that though the remains appear in the strangeness of their solitude, as something disdainfully withdrawn from us, just when the sense of an interhuman relationship is broken, when our mourning, our care and the prerogative of our former passions, no longer able to know their object, fall back on us, come back towards us—at this moment, when the presence of the cadaver before us is the presence of the unknown, it is also now that the lamented dead person begins to *resemble himself*.

Himself: isn't that an incorrect expression? Shouldn't we say: the person he was, when he was alive? Himself is nevertheless the right word. Himself designates the impersonal, distant and inaccessible being that resemblance, in order to be able to be resemblance to someone, also draws towards the day. Yes, it is really he, the dear living one; but all the same it is more than him, he is more beautiful, more imposing, already monumental and so absolutely himself that he is in some sense *doubled* by himself, united to the solemn impersonality of himself by resemblance and by image. This large-scale being, important and superb, who impresses the living as the apparition of the original—until then unknown—sentence of the last Judgment inscribed in the depths of the being and triumphantly expressing itself with the help of the distance: he may recall, because of his sovereign appearance, the great images of classic art. If this connection is valid, the question of the idealism of this art will seem rather vain; and the fact that in the end idealism should have no guarantee but a cadaver—this can be retained in order to show how much the apparent spirituality, the pure formal virginity of the image is fundamentally linked to the elemental strangeness and to the shapeless heaviness of the being that is present in absence.

If we look at him again, this splendid being who radiates beauty: he is, I can see, perfectly like himself; he resembles *himself*. The cadaver is its own image. He no longer has any relations with this world, in which he still appears, except those of an image, an obscure possibility, a shadow which is constantly present behind the living form and which now, far from separating itself from that form, completely transforms itself into a shadow. The cadaver is reflection making itself master of the reflected life, absorbing it, substantially identifying itself with it by making it lose its value in terms of use and truth and change into something incredible—unusual and neutral. And if the cadaver resembles to such a degree, that is because it is, at a certain moment, preeminently resemblance, and it is also nothing more. It is the equal, equal to an absolute, overwhelming and marvelous degree. But what does it resemble? Nothing.

This is why each living man, really, does not yet have any resemblance. Each man, in the rare moments when he shows a similarity to himself, seems to be only more distant, close to a dangerous neutral region, *astray* in *himself*, and in some sense his own ghost, already having no other life than that of the return.

By analogy, we can also recall that a utensil, once it has been damaged, becomes its own *image* (and sometimes an esthetic object: "those outmoded, fragmented, unusable, almost incomprehensible, perverse objects" that André Breton loved). In this case, the utensil, no longer disappearing in its use, *appears*. This appearance of the object is that of resemblance and reflection: one might say it is its double. The category of art is linked to this possibility objects have of "appearing," that is, of abandoning themselves to pure and simple resemblance behind which there is nothing—except being. Only what has surrendered itself to the image appears, and everything that appears is, in this sense, imaginary.

The resemblance of cadavers is a haunting obsession, but the act of haunting is not the unreal visitation of the ideal: what haunts is the inaccessible which one cannot rid oneself of, what one does not find and what, because of that, does not allow one to avoid it. The ungraspable is what one does not escape. The fixed image is without repose, especially in the sense that it does not pose anything, does not establish anything. Its fixity, like that of the mortal remains, is the position of that which remains because it lacks a place (the fixed idea is not a point of departure, a position from which one could move away and progress, it is not a beginning, but a beginning again). We know that in spite of its so tranquil and firm immobility the cadaver we have dressed, have brought as close as possible to a normal appearance by obliterating the disgrace of its illness, is not resting. The spot it occupies is dragged along by it, sinks with it, and in this dissolution assails—even for us, the others who remain—the possibility of a sojourn. We know that at "a certain moment," the power of death causes it to leave the fine place that has been assigned to it. Even though the cadaver is tranquilly lying in state on its bier, it is also everywhere in the room, in the house. At any moment, it can be elsewhere than where it is, where we are without it, where there is nothing, an invading presence, an obscure and vain fullness. The belief that at a certain moment the dead person begins to wander, must be ascribed to the intuition of that *error* he now represents.

Finally, an end must be put to what is endless: one does not live with dead people under penalty of seeing *here* sink into an unfathomable *nowhere,* a fall that is illustrated by the fall of the House of Usher. The dear departed, then, is conveyed to another place, and undoubtedly the site is only symbolically at a distance, in no way unlocatable, but it is nevertheless true that the *here* of *here lies*, full of names, of solid construction, or affirmations of identity, is preeminently the anonymous and impersonal place, as though, within the limits drawn for it and in the vain guise of a pretension capable of surviving everything, the monotony of an infinite erosion were at work obliterating the living truth that characterizes every place, and making it equal to the absolute neutrality of death.

(This slow disappearance, this infinite attrition of the end, may illuminate the very remarkable passion of certain women who become poisoners: their pleasure does not lie in causing suffering nor even in killing slowly, bit by bit, or by stifling, but rather it lies in reaching the indefiniteness that is death by poisoning time, by transforming it into an imperceptible consumption; in this way they brush with horror, they live furtively below all life, in a pure decomposition which nothing divulges, and the poison is the white substance of that eternity. Feuerbach tells of one poisoner for whom poison was a lover, a companion to whom she felt passionately drawn; when, after she had been in prison for several months, she was presented with a small bag of arsenic that belonged to her and was asked to identify it, she trembled with joy, she experienced a moment of ecstasy.)

The image and signification.

Man is made in his own image: this is what we learn from the strangeness of the resemblance of cadavers. But this formula should first of all be understood this way: *man is unmade according to his image.* The image has nothing to do with signification, meaning, as implied by the existence of the world, the effort of truth, the law and the brightness of the day. Not only is the *image* of an object not the *meaning* of that object and of no help in comprehending it, but it tends to withdraw it from its meaning by maintaining it in the immobility of a resemblance that has nothing to resemble.

Certainly we can always recapture the image and make it serve the truth of the world; but then we would be reversing the relationship that characterizes it: in this case, the image becomes the follower of the object, what comes after it, what remains of it and allows us to have it still available to us when nothing is left of it, a great resource, a fecund and judicious power. Practical life and the accomplishment of real tasks demand this reversal. Classical art, at least in theory, implied it too, glorying in bringing back resemblance to a figure and the image to a body, in reincorporating it: the image became vitalizing negation, the ideal labor through which man, capable of denying nature, raised it to a higher meaning, either in order to know it, or to take pleasure in it through admiration. In this way, art was both ideal and true, faithful to the figure and faithful to the truth that is without figure. Impersonality, in the end, verified the works. But impersonality was also the troubling site of encounter where the noble ideal, concerned for values, and the anonymous, blind and impersonal resemblance exchanged places and passed for each other in a mutual deception. "How vain is painting, that excites admiration through its resemblance to things whose originals one does not admire at all!" Nothing more striking, then, than this strong distrust of Pascal's for resemblance, as he felt that it surrendered things to the sovereignty of the void and to the most vain kind of persistence, an eternity which, as he said, is nothingness, nothingness which is eternity.

The two versions.

Thus there are two possibilities for the image, two versions of the imaginary, and this duplicity comes from the initial double meaning produced by the power of the negative and the fact that death is sometimes the work of truth in the world, sometimes the perpetuity of something that does not tolerate either a beginning or an end.

It is therefore really true that in man, as contemporary philosophies have it, comprehension and knowledge are connected to what we call finitude, but where is the end in this finitude? It is certainly contained in the possibility that is death, but it is also "taken up again" by it, if in death the possibility that is death dissolves too. And it still seems, even though all of human history signifies the hope of overcoming that ambiguity, that to settle it or to go beyond it always involves in one sense or in the other the greatest dangers: as though the choice between death as possibility of comprehension and death as horror of the impossibility also had to be the choice between sterile truth and the prolixity of the not-true, as though scarcity were tied to comprehension and fecundity to horror. This is why ambiguity, though it alone makes choice possible, always remains present in choice itself.

But in this case, how does *ambiguity* manifest itself? What is happening, for example, when one sees an event as image?

To experience an event as image is not to free oneself of that event, to dissociate oneself from it, as is asserted by the esthetic version of the image and the serene ideal of classical art, but neither is it to engage oneself with it through a free decision: it is to let oneself be taken by it, to go from the region of the real, where we hold ourselves at a distance from things the better to use them, to that other region where distance hoids us, this distance which is now unliving, unavailable depth, an inappreciable remoteness become in some sense the sovereign and last power of things. This movement implies infinite degrees. Thus psychoanalysis says that the image, far from leaving us outside of things and making us live in the mode of gratuitous fantasy, seems to surrender us profoundly to ourselves. The image is intimate, because it makes our intimacy an exterior power that we passively submit to: outside of us, in the backward motion of the world that the image provokes, the depth of our passion trails along, astray and brilliant.

Magic takes its power from this transformation. Through a methodical technique, it induces things to awaken as reflection, and consciousness to thicken into a thing. From the moment we are outside ourselves—in that ecstasy that which is the image—the "real" enters an equivocal realm where there is no longer any limit, nor any interval, nor moments, and where each thing, absorbed in the void of its reflection, draws near the consciousness, which has allowed itself to be filled up by an anonymous fullness. Thus the universal unity seems recreated. Thus, behind things, the soul of each thing obeys the spells now possessed by the ecstatic man who has abandoned himself to the "universe." The paradox of magic is certainly obvious: it claims to be initiative and free domination, whereas in order to create itself, it accepts the reign of passivity, that reign in which there are no ends. But its intention remains instructive: what it wants is to act on the world (manoeuver it), beginning with being which precedes the world, the eternal this-side where action is impossible. This is why it would rather turn towards the strangeness of the cadaver, and its only serious name is black magic.

To experience an event as image is not to have an image of that event, nor is it to give it the gratuitousness of the imaginary. The event, in this case, really takes place, and yet does it "really" take place? What happens seizes us, as the image would seize us, that is, it deprives us, of it and of ourselves, keeps us outside, makes this outside a presence where "I" does not recognize "itself." A movement that involves infinite degrees. What we have called the two versions of the imaginary, this fact that the image can certainly help us to recapture the thing in an ideal way, being, then, its vitalizing negation, but also, on the level we are drawn to by its own weight, constantly threatening to send us back, no longer to the absent thing, but to absence as presence, to the neutral double of the object, in which belonging to the world has vanished: this duplicity is not such that one can pacify it with an "either, or else," capable of permitting a choice and of taking away from choice the ambiguity that makes it possible. This duplicity itself refers to a double meaning that is ever more primary.

The levels of ambiguity.

If thought could, for a moment, maintain ambiguity, it would be tempted to say that there are three levels on which it occurs. On the level of the world, ambiguity is the possibility of understanding; meaning always escapes into another meaning; misunderstanding is useful to comprehension, it expresses the truth of the understanding that one is never understood once and for all.

Another level is that expressed by the two versions of the imaginary. Here, there is no longer a question of a perpetual double meaning, of the misunderstanding that helps or deceives understanding. Here, what speaks in the name of the image "sometimes" still speaks of the world, "sometimes" introduces us into the indeterminate region of fascination, "sometimes" gives us the power to use things in their absence and through fiction, thus keeping us within a horizon rich in meaning, "sometimes" makes us slip into the place where things are perhaps present, but in their image, and where the image is the moment of passivity, having no value either significative or affective, being the passion of indifference. Nevertheless, what we distinguish by saying "sometimes, sometimes" ambiguity says by saying always, to a certain extent, the one and the other; it expresses, moreover, the significant image in the heart of fascination, but already fascinates us through the clarity of the most pure, the most formed image. Here, *meaning* does not escape into another meaning, but into the *other* of all meaning and, because of ambiguity, nothing has meaning, but everything *seems* to have infinitely much meaning: meaning is no longer anything more than a semblance; the semblance causes the meaning to become infinitely rich, causes this infinitude of meaning to have no need of being developed, to be immediate, that is, also to be incapable of being developed, to be simply immediately empty.[1]

---

[1] Can one go farther? Ambiguity expresses being as dissimulated; it says that being is, insofar as it is dissimulated. For being to accomplish its work, it must be dissimulated: it works by dissimulating itself, it is always reserved and preserved by dissimulation, but also subjected to it; dissimulation then tends to become the purity of negation. But at the same time, ambiguity, when everything is dissimulated, says (and this saying is ambiguity itself): all being *is* through dissimulation, being is essentially being in the heart of dissimulation.

Ambiguity, then, no longer consists only of the incessant movement through which being returns to nothingness and nothingness refers back to being. Ambiguity is no longer the primordial Yes and No in which being and nothingness are pure identity. Essential ambiguity lies rather in the fact that—before the beginning—nothingness is not equal to being, is only the *appearance* of the dissimulation of being, or else that dissimulation is more "original" than negation. So that one could say: *ambiguity is essential in inverse proportion to the capacity of dissimulation to recapture itself in negation.*

READING

Reading: we are not surprised to find admissions like this in a writer's travel diary: "Always such dread at the moment of writing…" and when Lomazzo talks about the horror that seized Leonardo every time he tried to paint, we can understand this, too, we feel we could understand it.

But if a person confided to us, "I am always anxious at the moment of reading," or another could not read except at rare, special times, or another would disrupt his whole life, renounce the world, forego work and happiness in the world, in order to open the way for himself to a few moments of reading, we would undoubtedly place him alongside Pierre Janet's patient who was reluctant to read because, she said, "when a book is read it becomes dirty."

The person who enjoys simply listening to music becomes a musician as he listens, and the same kind of thing happens when someone looks at paintings. The world of music and the world of painting can be entered by anyone who has the key to them. That key is the "gift," and the gift is the enchantment and understanding of a certain taste. Lovers of music and lovers of painting are people who openly display their preference like a delectable ailment that isolates them and makes them proud. The others modestly recognize the fact that they have no ear. One must be gifted to hear and to see. This gift is a closed space—the concert hall, the museum—with which one surrounds oneself in order to enjoy a clandestine pleasure. People who do not have the gift remain outside, people who have it go in and out as they please. Naturally, music is loved only on Sunday; this god is no more demanding than the other.

Reading does not even require any gift, and it refutes that recourse to a natural privilege. No one is gifted—not the author, not the reader—and anyone who feels he is gifted primarily feels he is not gifted, feels that he is infinitely unequipped, that he lacks the power attributed to him, and just as being an "artist" means not knowing there is already an art, not knowing there is already a world, so reading, seeing, and hearing works of art demands more ignorance than knowledge, it demands a knowledge filled with immense ignorance, and a gift that is not given beforehand, a gift that is received, secured and lost each time in self-forgetfulness. Each picture, each piece of music presents us with the organ we need in order to receive it, "gives" us the eye and the ear we need in order to see it and hear it. Nonmusicians are people who decide in the very beginning to reject the possibility of hearing, they hide from it as though suspiciously closing themselves off from a threat or an irritation. André Breton repudiates music, because he wants to preserve within himself his right to hear the discordant essence of language, its nonmusical music, and Kafka, who constantly recognizes that he is more closed to music than anyone else in the world, manages to regard this defect as one of his strong points: "I am really strong, I have one particular strength, and that is—to characterize it in a brief and unclear manner—my nonmusical being."

Usually someone who does not like music cannot tolerate it at all, just as a man who finds a Picasso painting repellent excludes it with a violent hatred, as though he felt directly threatened by it. The fact that he hasn't even looked at the picture says nothing against his good faith. It is not in his power to look at it. Not looking at it does not put him in the wrong, it is a form of his sincerity, his correct presentiment of the force that is closing his eyes. "I refuse to look at that." "I could not live with that before my eyes." These formulations define the hidden reality of the work of art—its absolute intolerance—more powerfully than the art lover's suspect complacencies. It is quite true that one cannot live with a picture before one's eyes.

The plastic work of art has a certain advantage over the verbal work of art in that it renders more manifest the exclusive void within which the work apparently wants to remain, far from everyone's gaze. Rodin's "The Kiss" allows itself to be looked at and even thrives on being looked at; his "Balzac" is without gaze, a closed and sleeping thing, absorbed in itself to such a degree that it disappears. This decisive separation, which sculpture takes as its element and which sets out another, rebellious space in the center of space—sets out a space that is at once hidden, visible, and shielded, perhaps immutable, perhaps without repose—this protected violence, before which we always feel out of place, does not seem to be present in books. The statue that is unearthed and displayed for everyone's admiration does not expect anything, does not receive anything, seems rather to have been torn from its place. But isn't it true that the book that has been exhumed, the manuscript that is taken out of a jar and enters the broad daylight of reading, is born all over again through an impressive piece of luck? What is a book that no one reads? Something that has not yet been written. Reading, then, is not writing the book again but causing the book to write itself or *be* written—this time without the writer as intermediary, without anyone writing it. The reader does not add himself to the book, but his tendency is first to unburden it of any author, and something very hasty in his approach, the very futile shadow that passes across the pages and leaves them intact, everything that makes the reading appear superfluous, and even the reader's lack of attention, the slightness of his interest, all his infinite lightness affirms the book's new lightness: the book has become a book without an author, without the seriousness, the labor, the heavy pangs, the weight of a whole life that has been poured into it—an experience that is sometimes terrible, always dangerous, an experience the reader effaces and, because of his providential lightness, considers to be nothing.

Although he does not know it, the reader is involved in a profound struggle with the author: no matter how much intimacy remains today between the book and the writer, no matter how directly the author's figure, presence, and history are illuminated by the circumstances of publication—circumstances that are not accidental but that may be already slightly anachronistic—in spite of this, every reading in which consideration of the writer seems to play such a large role is an impeachment that obliterates him in order to give the work back to itself, to its anonymous presence, to the violent, impersonal affirmation that it is. The reader himself is always fundamentally anonymous, he is any reader, unique but transparent. Instead of adding his name to the book (as our fathers did in the past), he rather erases all names by his nameless presence, by that modest, passive, interchangeable, insignificant gaze under whose gentle pressure the book appears written, at one remove from everything and everyone.

Reading transforms a book the same way the sea and the wind transform the works of men: the result is a smoother stone, a fragment that has fallen from heaven, without any past, without any future, and that we do not wonder about as we look at it. Reading endows the book with the kind of sudden existence that the statue "seems" to take from the chisel alone: the isolation that hides it from eyes that see it, the proud remoteness, the orphan wisdom that drives off the sculptor just as much as it does the look that tries to sculpt it again. In some sense the book needs the reader in order to become a statue, it needs the reader in order to assert itself as a thing without an author and also without a reader.

What reading brings to it is not first of all a more human truth; but neither does it make the book into something inhuman, an "object," a pure compact presence, fruit from the depths unripened by our sun. It simply "makes" the book—the work—become a work beyond the person who produced it, beyond the experience expressed in it and even beyond all the artistic resources that various traditions have made available. The nature of reading, its singularity, illuminates the singular meaning of the verb "to make" in the expression "it makes the work become a work." Here the word "make" does not indicate a productive activity: reading does not make anything, does not add anything; it lets be what is; it is freedom—not the kind of freedom that gives being or takes it away, but a liberty that receives, consents, says yes, can only say yes, and in the space opened by this yes, allows the work's amazing decision to be affirmed: that it is—and nothing more.

"Lazare, veni foras."

Reading that accepts the work for what it is and in so doing unburdens it of its author, does not consist of replacing the author by a reader, a fully existent person, who has a history, a profession, a religion, and is even well read, someone who, on the basis of all that, would begin a dialogue with the other person, the one who wrote the book. Reading is not a conversation, it does not discuss, it does not question. It never asks the book—and certainly not the author—"What exactly did you mean? Well, what truth are you offering me?" True reading never challenges the true book: but it is not a form of submission to the "text" either. Only the nonliterary book is presented as a stoutly woven web of determined significations, as an entity made up of real affirmations: before it is read by anyone, the nonliterary book has already been read by everyone, and it is this preliminary reading that guarantees it a secure existence. But the book whose source is art has no guarantee in the world, and when it is read, it has never been read before; it only attains its presence as a work in the space opened by this unique reading, each time the first reading and each time the only reading.

This is the source of the strange freedom exemplified by reading, literary reading. It is free movement, if it is not subject to anything, if it does not depend on anything already present. The book is undoubtedly there—not only in its reality as paper and print, but also in its nature as a book, this fabric of stable significations, this affirmation that it owes to a preestablished language, and also this precinct formed around it by the community of all readers, which already includes me even though I have not read it, and also made up of all other books, which, like angels with interlaced wings, watch closely over the unknown volume, because if even one book is threatened, a dangerous breach is opened in the world's library. And so the book is there, but the work is still hidden, perhaps radically absent, in any case disguised, obscured by the obviousness of the book behind which it awaits the liberating decision, the *Lazare, veni foras*.

The mission of reading seems to be to cause this stone to fall: to make it transparent, to dissolve it with the penetration of a gaze which enthusiastically goes beyond it. There is something dizzying about reading, or at least about the outset of reading, that resembles the irrational impulse by which we try to open eyes that are already closed, open them to life; this impulse is connected to desire, which is a leap, an infinite leap, just as inspiration is a leap: I want to *read* what has nevertheless not been written. But there is more, and what makes the "miracle" of reading—which perhaps enlightens us concerning the meaning of all thaumaturgy—even more singular is that here the stone and the tomb not only contain a cadaverous emptiness that must be animated, but they also constitute the presence—hidden though it is—of what must appear. To roll the stone, to move it away, is certainly something marvelous, but we accomplish it each instant in our everyday language, and we converse each instant with this Lazarus, who has been dead for three days, or perhaps forever, and who, beneath his tightly woven bandages, is sustained by the most elegant conventions, and answers us and talks to us in our very hearts. But what responds to the appeal of literary reading is not a door falling or becoming transparent or even becoming a little thinner; rather, it is a rougher kind of stone, more tightly sealed, crushing—a vast deluge of stone that shakes the earth and the sky.

Such is the particular nature of this "opening," which is what reading is made up of: only what is more tightly closed opens; only what has been borne as an oppressive nothingness without consistency can be admitted into the lightness of a free and happy Yes. And this does not tie the poetic work to the search for an obscurity that would confound everyday understanding. It merely establishes a violent rupture between the book that is there and the work that is never there beforehand, between the book that is the concealed work and the work that cannot affirm itself except in the thickness—thickness made present—of this concealment: it establishes a violent rupture, and the passage from a world in which everything has some degree of meaning, in which there is darkness and light, to a space where nothing has any meaning yet, properly speaking, but to which, even so, everything that has meaning returns as to its own origin.

But these remarks would also risk deceiving us, if they seemed to say that reading was the work of clearing a way from one language to another, or a bold step requiring initiative, effort, and the conquest of obstacles. The approach to reading may be a difficult kind of happiness, but reading is the easiest thing in the world, it is freedom without work, a pure Yes blossoming in the immediate.

The light, innocent Yes of reading.

Reading, in the sense of literary reading, is not even a pure movement of comprehension, the kind of understanding that tries to sustain meaning by setting it in motion again. Reading is situated beyond comprehension or short of comprehension. Nor is reading exactly an appeal that the unique work that should disclose itself in reading reveal itself behind the appearance of common speech, behind the book that belongs to everyone. No doubt there is some sort of appeal, but it can only come from the work itself, it is a silent appeal that imposes silence in the midst of the general noise, an appeal the reader hears only as he responds to it, that deflects the reader from his habitual relations and turns him towards the space near which reading bides and becomes an approach, a delighted reception of the generosity of the work, a reception that raises the book to the work that it is, through the same rapture that raises the work to being and turns the reception into a ravishment, the ravishment in which the work is articulated. Reading is this abode and it has the simplicity of the light and transparent Yes that is this abode. Even if it demands that the reader enter a zone in which he has no air and the ground is hidden from him, even if, beyond these stormy approaches, reading seems to be a kind of participation in the open violence that is the work, in itself reading is a tranquil and silent presence, the pacified center of excess, the silent Yes that lies at the heart of every storm.

The freedom of this Yes—which is present, ravished, and transparent—is the essence of reading. Because of this, reading stands in contrast to that aspect of the work which, through the experience of creation, approaches absence, the torments of the infinite, the empty depths of something that never begins or ends—a movement that exposes the creator to the threat of essential solitude, that delivers him to the interminable.

In this sense, reading is more positive than creation, more creative, although it does not produce anything. It shares in the decision, it has the lightness, the irresponsibility, the innocence of the decision. It does nothing and everything is accomplished. For Kafka there was dread, there were unfinished stories, the torment of a wasted life, of a mission betrayed, every day turned into an exile, every night exiled from sleep, and finally, there was the certainty that "*The Metamorphosis* is unreadable, radically flawed." But for Kafka's reader, the dread turns into ease and happiness, the torment over faults is transfigured into innocence, and in each scrap of text there is delight in fullness, certainty of completion, a revelation of the unique, inevitable unpredictable work. This is the essence of reading, of the light Yes which—far more effectively than the creator's dark struggle with chaos, in which he seeks to disappear so as to master it—evokes the divine share of creation.

This is why an author's grievances against the reader often seem misplaced. Montesquieu writes, "I am asking a favor that I am afraid no one will grant me: and that is not to judge twenty years' work in a moment's reading; to approve or condemn the entire book and not just a few sentences," and he is asking something that artists are often sorry they do not have, as they think with bitterness how their works are the victims of a casual reading, a distracted glance, a careless ear: such effort, such sacrifice, such care, such calculation, a life of solitude, centuries of meditation and seeking—all this is appraised, judged and annihilated by the ignorant decision of the first person to come along, by a chance mood. And when Valéry worries about today's uncultivated reader who demands that facility accompany his reading, this worry may be justified, but the culture of an attentive reader, the scruples of a reading filled with devotion, an almost religious reading, one that has become a sort of cult, would not change anything; it would create even more serious dangers, because although the lightness of a casual reader, dancing quickly around the text, may not be true lightness, it has no consequences and holds a certain promise: it proclaims the happiness and innocence of reading, which may in fact be a dance with an invisible partner in a separate space, a joyful, wild dance with the "tomb." Lightness from which we must not hope for the impulse of a graver concern, because where we have lightness, gravity is not lacking.

THE GAZE OF ORPHEUS

When Orpheus descends to Eurydice, art is the power that causes the night to open. Because of the power of art, the night welcomes him; it becomes the welcoming intimacy, the understanding and the harmony of the first night. But Orpheus has gone down to Eurydice: for him, Eurydice is the limit of what art can attain; concealed behind a name and covered by a veil, she is the profoundly dark point towards which art, desire, death, and the night all seem to lead. She is the instant in which the essence of the night approaches as the *other* night.

Yet Orpheus' work does not consist of securing the approach of this "point" by descending into the depths. His *work* is to bring it back into the daylight and in the daylight give it form, figure and reality. Orpheus can do anything except look this "point" in the face, look at the center of the night in the night. He can descend to it, he can draw it to him—an even stronger power—and he can draw it upwards, but only by keeping his back turned to it. This turning away is the only way he can approach it: this is the meaning of the concealment revealed in the night. But in the impulse of his migration Orpheus forgets the work he has to accomplish, and he has to forget it, because the ultimate requirement of his impulse is not that there should be a work, but that someone should stand and face this "point" and grasp its essence where this essence appears, where it is essential and essentially appearance: in the heart of the night.

The Greek myth says: one cannot create a work unless the enormous experience of the depths—an experience which the Greeks recognized as necessary to the work, an experience in which the work is put to the test by that enormousness—is not pursued for its own sake. The depth does not surrender itself face to face; it only reveals itself by concealing itself in the work. A fundamental, inexorable answer. But the myth also shows Orpheus' destiny is not to submit to that law—and it is certainly true that by turning around to look at Eurydice, Orpheus ruins the work, the work immediately falls apart, and Eurydice returns to the shadows; under his gaze, the essence of the night reveals itself to be inessential. He thus betrays the work and Eurydice and the night. But if he did not turn around to look at Eurydice, he still would be betraying, being disloyal to, the boundless and imprudent force of his impulse, which does not demand Eurydice in her diurnal truth and her everyday charm, but in her nocturnal darkness, in her distance, her body closed, her face sealed, which wants to see her not when she is visible, but when she is invisible, and not as the intimacy of a familiar life, but as the strangeness of that which excludes all intimacy; it does not want to make her live, but to have the fullness of her death living in her.

It is only this that he has come to look for in Hell. The whole glory of his work, the whole power of his art and even the desire for a happy life in the beautiful light of day are sacrificed to this one concern: to look into the night at what the night is concealing—the *other* night, concealment which becomes visible.

This is an infinitely problematical impulse which the day condemns as an unjustifiable act of madness or as the expiation of excess. For the day, this descent into Hell, this impulse toward the empty depths, is already excessive. It is inevitable that Orpheus defy the law forbidding him to "turn around," because he has already violated it the moment he takes his first step towards the shadows. This observation makes us sense that Orpheus has actually been turned towards Eurydice all along: he saw her when she was invisible and he touched her intact, in her absence as a shade, in that veiled presence which did not conceal her absence, which was the presence of her infinite absence. If he had not looked at her, he would not have drawn her to him, and no doubt she is not there, but he himself is absent in this glance, he is no less dead than she was, not dead with the tranquil death of the world, the kind of death which is repose, silence, and ending, but with that other death which is endless death, proof of the absence of ending.

Passing judgment on what Orpheus undertakes to do, the day also reproaches him for having shown impatience. Orpheus' mistake, then, would seem to lie in the desire which leads him to see Eurydice and to possess her, while he is destined only to sing about her. He is only Orpheus in his song, he could have no relationship with Eurydice except within the hymn, he has life and actuality only after the poem and through the poem, and Eurydice represents nothing more than that magical dependence which makes him into a shade when he is not singing and only allows him to be free, alive, and powerful within the space of the Orphic measure. Yes, this much is true: only in the song does Orpheus have power over Eurydice, but in the song Eurydice is also already lost and Orpheus himself is the scattered Orpheus, the "infinitely dead" Orpheus into which the power of the song transforms him from then on. He loses Eurydice because he desires her beyond the measured limits of the song, and he loses himself too, but this desire, and Eurydice lost, and Orpheus scattered are necessary to the song, just as the ordeal of eternal worklessness is necessary to the work.

Orpheus is guilty of impatience. His error is that he wants to exhaust the infinite, that he puts an end to what is unending, that he does not endlessly sustain the very impulse of his error. Impatience is the mistake made by a person who wishes to escape the absence of time; patience is the trick that tries to master this absence of time by turning it into another kind of time, measured in a different way. But true patience does not exclude impatience; it is the heart of impatience, it is impatience endlessly suffered and endured. Orpheus' impatience is therefore also a correct impulse: it is the source of what will become his own passion, his highest patience, his infinite sojourn in death.

Inspiration.

Although the world may judge Orpheus, the work does not judge him, does not point out his faults. The work says nothing. And everything happens as if, by disobeying the law, by looking at Eurydice, Orpheus was only yielding to the profound demands of the work, as though, through this inspired gesture, he really had carried the dark shades out of Hell, as though he had unknowingly brought it back into the broad daylight of the work.

To look at Eurydice without concern for the song, in the impatience and imprudence of a desire which forgets the law—this is *inspiration*. Does this mean that inspiration changes the beauty of the night into the unreality of the void, makes Eurydice into a shade and Orpheus into someone infinitely dead? Does it mean that inspiration is therefore that problematic moment when the essence of the night becomes something inessential and the welcoming intimacy of the first night becomes the deceptive trap of the *other* night? This is exactly the way it is. All we can sense of inspiration is its failure, all we can recognize of it is its misguided violence. But if inspiration means that Orpheus fails and Eurydice is lost twice over, if it means the insignificance and void of the night, it

also turns Orpheus towards that failure and that insignificance and coerces him, by an irresistible impulse, as though giving up failure were
much more serious than giving up success, as though what we call the
insignificant, the inessential, the mistaken, could reveal itself—to someone who accepted the risk and freely gave himself up to it—as the source
of all authenticity.

His inspired and forbidden gaze dooms Orpheus to lose everything—not only himself, not only the gravity of the day, but also the
essence of the night: this much is certain, inevitable. Inspiration means
the ruin of Orpheus and the certainty of his ruin, and it does not promise the success of the work as compensation, anymore than in the work
it affirms Orpheus' ideal triumph or Eurydice's survival. The work is
just as much compromised by inspiration as Orpheus is threatened by
it. In that instant it reaches its extreme point of uncertainty. This is
why it so often and so strongly resists what inspires it. This is also why
it protects itself by saying to Orpheus: "You will only be able to keep
me if you do not look at *her*." But this forbidden act is precisely the
one Orpheus must perform in order to take the work beyond what
guarantees it, and which he can perform only by forgetting the work,
carried away by a desire coming out of the night and bound to the
night as its origin. In this respect, the work is lost. This is the only
moment when it is absolutely lost, when something more important
than the work, more stripped of importance than the work, is proclaimed and asserted. The work is everything to Orpheus, everything
except that desired gaze in which the work is lost, so that it is also only
in this gaze that the work can go beyond itself, unite with its origin
and establish itself in impossibility.

Orpheus' gaze is Orpheus' ultimate gift to the work, a gift in which
he rejects the work, in which he sacrifices it by moving towards its
origin in the boundless impulse of desire, and in which he unknowingly still moves towards the work, towards the origin of the work.

For Orpheus, then, everything sinks into the certainty of failure,
where the only remaining compensation is the uncertainty of the
work—for does the work ever exist? As we look at the most certain
masterpiece, whose beginning dazzles us with its brilliance and decisiveness, we find that we are also faced with something which is fading
away, a work that has suddenly become invisible again, is no longer
there, and has never been there. This sudden eclipse is the distant

memory of Orpheus' gaze, it is a nostalgic return to the uncertainty of the origin.

Gift and sacrifice.

If forced to stress what such a moment seems to reveal about inspiration, we would have to say: it connects inspiration with *desire*.

It introduces into the concern for the work the gesture of *unconcern* in which the work is sacrificed: the last law of the work has been transgressed, the work has been betrayed for the sake of Eurydice, the shade. This unconcern is the movement of sacrifice, a sacrifice which can only be unconcerned, thoughtless, which is perhaps a failing, is immediately atoned for as though it were a failing, but whose substance is thoughtlessness, unconcern, innocence: an unceremonious sacrifice in which the unconcerned gaze which is not even a sacrilege, which has none of the heaviness or gravity of an act of profanation, returned the sacred itself—night in its unapproachable depth—to the inessential, which is not the profane but rather does not fall within these categories.

The essential night which follows Orpheus—before the careless look—the sacred night which he holds enthralled in the fascination of his song and which is at that point kept within the limits and the measured space of the song, is certainly richer, more august, than the empty futility which it becomes after Orpheus looks back. The sacred night encloses Eurydice, encloses within the song something which went beyond the song. But it is also enclosed itself: it is bound, it is the attendant, it is the sacred mastered by the power of ritual—that word which means order, rectitude, law, the way of Tao and the axis of Dharma. Orpheus' gaze unties it, destroys its limits, breaks the law which contains, which retains the essence. Thus Orpheus' gaze is the extreme moment of freedom, the moment in which he frees himself of himself and—what is more important—frees the work of his concern, frees the sacred contained in the work, *gives* the sacred to itself, to the freedom of its essence, to its essence which is freedom (for this reason, inspiration is the greatest gift). So everything is at stake in the decision of the gaze. In this decision, the origin is approached by the force of the gaze, which sets free the essence of the night, removes concern, interrupts the incessant by revealing it: a moment of desire, unconcern, and authority.

Inspiration is bound to *desire* by Orpheus' gaze. Desire is bound to *unconcern* by *impatience*. A person who is not impatient will never reach the point of being unconcerned—that moment when concern merges with its own transparency; but a person who does not get beyond impatience will never be capable of Orpheus' unconcerned, thoughtless gaze. This is why impatience must be the heart of deep patience, the pure bolt of lightning which leaps out of the breast of patience because of its infinite waiting, its silence, and its reserve, not only as a spark lit by extreme tension, but also like the glittering point which has eluded that waiting: the happy chance of unconcern.

The leap.

The act of writing begins with Orpheus' gaze, and that gaze is the impulse of desire which shatters the song's destiny and concern, and in that inspired and unconcerned decision reaches the origin, consecrates the song. But Orpheus already needed the power of art in order to descend to that instant. This means: one can only write if one arrives at the instant towards which one can only move through space opened up by the movement of writing. In order to write one must already be writing. The essence of writing, the difficulty of experience and the leap of inspiration also lie within this contradiction.

THE SONG OF THE SIRENS
Encountering the Imaginary

The Sirens: evidently they really sang, but in a way that was not satisfying, that only implied in which direction lay the true sources of the song, the true happiness of the song. Nevertheless, through their imperfect song, songs which were only a song still to come, they guided the sailor towards that space where singing would really begin. They were therefore not deceiving him; they were really leading him to his goal. But what happened when he reached that place? What was that place? It was a place where the only thing left was to disappear, because in this region of source and origin, music itself had disappeared more completely than in any other place in the world; it was like a sea into which the living would sink with their ears closed and where the Sirens, too, even they, as proof of their good will, would one day have to disappear.

What sort of song was the Sirens' song? What was its defect? Why did this defect make it so powerful? The answer some people have always given is that it was an inhuman song—no doubt a natural noise (what other kind is there?), but one that remained in the margins of nature; in any case, it was foreign to man, and very low, awakening in him that extreme delight in falling which he cannot satisfy in the normal conditions of his life. But, others say, there was something even stranger in the enchantment: it caused the Sirens merely to reproduce the ordinary singing of mankind, and because the Sirens, who were only animals— very beautiful animals because they reflected womanly beauty—could sing the way men sing, their song became so extraordinary that it created in anyone who heard it a suspicion that all human singing was really inhuman. Was it despair, then, that killed men moved to passion by their own singing? That despair verged upon rapture. There was something marvelous about the song: it actually existed, it was ordinary and at the same time secret, a simple, everyday song which they were suddenly forced to recognize, sung in an unreal way by strange powers, powers which were, in a word, imaginary; it was a song from the abyss and once heard it opened an abyss in every utterance and powerfully enticed whoever heard it to disappear into that abyss.

Remember that this song was sung to sailors, men prepared to take risks and fearless in their impulses, and it was a form of navigation too: it was a distance, and what it revealed was the possibility of traveling that distance, of making the song into a movement towards the song and of making this movement into the expression of the greatest desire. Strange navigation, and what was its goal? It has always been possible to believe that those who approached it were not able to do more than approach it, that they died from impatience, from having said too soon: "Here it is; here is where I will drop anchor." Others have claimed that, on the contrary, it was too late: the goal had always been overshot; the enchantment held out an enigmatic promise and through this promise exposed men to the danger of being unfaithful to themselves, unfaithful to their human song and even to the essence of song, by awakening in them hope and the desire for a marvelous beyond, and that beyond was only a desert, as though the region where music originated was the only place completely without music, a sterile dry place where silence, like noise, burned all access to the song in anyone who had once had command of it. Does this mean that there was something evil in the invitation which issued from the depths? Were the Sirens nothing more than unreal voices, as custom would have us believe, unreal voices which were not supposed to be heard, a deception intended to seduce, and which could only be resisted by disloyal or cunning people?

Men have always made a rather ignoble effort to discredit the Sirens by accusing them flatly of lying: they were liars when they sang, frauds when they sighed, fictions when they were touched—nonexistent in every way; and the good sense of Ulysses was enough to do away with this puerile nonexistence.

It is true, Ulysses did overcome them, but how did he do it? Ulysses— the stubbornness and caution of Ulysses, the treachery by which he took pleasure in the spectacle of the Sirens without risking anything and without accepting the consequences; this cowardly, mediocre and tranquil pleasure, this moderate pleasure, appropriate to a Greek of the period of decadence who never deserved to be the hero of the *Iliad*; this happy and confident cowardice, rooted in a privilege which set him apart from the common condition, the others having no right to such elite happiness but only to the pleasure of seeing their leader writhe ludicrously, grimacing with ecstasy in empty space, but also a right to the satisfaction of gaining mastery over their master (no doubt this was the lesson they learned, this was for them the true Song of the Sirens): Ulysses' attitude, the amazing deafness of a man who is deaf because he can hear, was enough to fill the Sirens with a despair which until then had been felt only by men, and this despair turned them into real and beautiful girls, just this once real and worthy of their promise, and therefore capable of vanishing into the truth and depth of their song.

Even once the Sirens had been overcome by the power of technology, which will always claim to trifle in safety with unreal (inspired) powers, Ulysses was still not free of them. They enticed him to a place which he did not want to fall into and, hidden in the heart of *The Odyssey*, which had become their tomb, they drew him—and many others—into that happy, unhappy voyage which is the voyage of the tale—of a song which is no longer immediate, but is narrated, and because of this made to seem harmless, an ode which has turned into an episode.

The secret law of the tale.

This is not an allegory. A very obscure struggle takes place between every tale and the encounter with the Sirens, that enigmatic song which is powerful because of its insufficiency. A struggle in which Ulysses' prudence—whatever degree he has of truth, of mystification, of obstinate ability not to play the game of the gods—has always been exercised and perfected. What we call the novel was born of this struggle. What lies in the foreground of the novel is the previous voyage, the voyage which takes Ulysses to the moment of the encounter. This voyage is a completely human story, it takes place within the framework of human time, it is bound up with men's passions; it actually takes place and is rich enough and varied enough to consume all the narrators' strength and attention. Once the tale has become a novel, far from appearing poorer it takes on all the richness and breadth of an exploration, one which sometimes embraces the immensity of the voyage and sometimes confines itself to a small patch of space on the deck and occasionally descends into the depths of the ship where no one ever knew what the hope of the sea was. The rule the sailors must obey is this: no allusion can be made to a goal or a destination. And with good reason, surely. No one can sail away with the deliberate intention of reaching the Isle of

Capri, no one can set his course for it, and if anyone decides to go there he will still proceed only by chance, by some chance to which he is linked by an understanding difficult to penetrate. The rule is therefore silence, discretion, forgetfulness.

We must recognize that a certain preordained modesty, a desire not to have any pretensions and not to lead to anything, would be enough to make many novels irreproachable books and to make the genre of the novel the most attractive of genres, the one which, in its discretion and its cheerful nothingness, takes upon itself the task of forgetting what others degrade by calling it the essential. Diversion is its profound song. To keep changing direction, to move on in an apparently random way, avoiding all goals, with an uneasy motion that is transformed into a happy sort of distraction—this has been its primary and most secure justification. It is no small thing to make a game of human time and out of that game to create a free occupation, one stripped of all immediate interest and usefulness, essentially superficial and yet in its surface movement capable of absorbing all being. But clearly, if the novel fails to play this role today, it is because technics has transformed men's time and their ways of amusing themselves.

The tale begins at a point where the novel does not go, though in its refusals and its rich neglect it is leading towards it. Heroically, pretentiously, the tale is the tale of one single episode, that in which Ulysses encounters the inadequate and enticing song of the Sirens. Except for this great, naive pretension, apparently nothing has changed, and because of its form the tale seems to continue to fulfill its ordinary vocation as a narrative. For example, *Aurélia* is presented as the simple account of a meeting, and so is *Une saison en Enfer*, and so is *Nadja*. Something has happened, something which someone has experienced who tells about it afterwards, in the same way that Ulysses needed to experience the event and survive it in order to become Homer, who told about it. Of course the tale is usually about an exceptional event, one which eludes the forms of everyday time and the world of the usual sort of truth, perhaps any truth. This is why it so insistently rejects everything which could connect it with the frivolity of a fiction (the novel, on the other hand, contains only what is believable and familiar and yet is very anxious to pass for fiction). In the *Gorgias*, Plato says "Listen to a beautiful tale. Now you will think it is a fable, but I believe it is a tale. I will tell you what I am going to tell you as a true thing." What he told was the story of the Last Judgment.

Yet if we regard the tale as the true telling of an exceptional event which has taken place and which someone is trying to report, then we have not even come close to sensing the true nature of the tale. The tale is not the narration of an event, but that event itself, the approach to that event, the place where that event is made to happen—an event which is yet to come and through whose power of attraction the tale can hope to come into being, too.

This is a very delicate relationship, undoubtedly a kind of extravagance, but it is the secret law of the tale. The tale is a movement towards a point, a point which is not only unknown, obscure, foreign, but such that apart from this movement it does not seem to have any sort of real prior existence, and yet it is so imperious that the tale derives its power of attraction only from this point, so that it cannot even "begin" before reaching it— and yet only the tale and the unpredictable movement of the tale create the space where the point becomes real, powerful, and alluring.

When Ulysses becomes Homer.

What would happen if instead of being two distinct people Ulysses and Homer comfortably shared their roles, and were one and the same presence? If the tale Homer told were simply Ulysses' movement within the space opened up for him by the Song of the Sirens? If Homer's capacity to narrate were limited by how far he went as Ulysses—a Ulysses free of all impediments, though tied down—towards the place where the power to speak and to narrate was apparently promised to him as long as he disappeared there?

This is one of the strange things about the tale, or shall we say one of its pretensions. It only "narrates" itself, and in the same moment that this narration comes into being it creates what it is narrating; it cannot exist as a narration unless it creates what is happening in that narration, because then it contains the point or the plane where the reality "described" by the story can keep uniting with its reality as a tale, can secure this reality and be secured by it.

But isn't this a rather naive madness? In one sense, yes. That is why there are no tales, and that is why there is no lack of tales.

To listen to the Song of the Sirens is to cease to be Ulysses and become Homer, but only in Homer's story does the real encounter take place, where Ulysses becomes the one who enters into a relationship with the force of the elements and the voice of the abyss.

This seems obscure, it is like the embarrassment the first man would have felt if, in order to be created, he himself had had to pronounce in a completely human way the divine *Fiat lux* that would actually cause his eyes to open.

Actually, this way of presenting things simplifies them a great deal—which is why it produces these artificial or theoretical complications. Of course it is true that only in Melville's book does Ahab meet Moby Dick; yet it is also true that only this encounter allows Melville to write the book, it is such an imposing encounter, so enormous, so special that it goes beyond all the levels on which it takes place, all the moments in time where we attempt to situate it, and seems to be happening long before the book begins, but it is of such a nature that it also could not happen more than once, in the future of the work and in that sea which is what the work will be, having become an ocean on its own scale.

Ahab and the whale are engaged in a drama, what we can call a metaphysical drama, using the word loosely, and the Sirens and Ulysses are engaged in the same struggle. Each wants to be everything, wants to be the absolute world, which would make it impossible for him to coexist with the other absolute world, and yet the greatest desire of each is for this coexistence and this encounter. To bring Ahab and the whale, the Sirens and Ulysses together in one space—this is the secret wish which turns Ulysses into Homer and Ahab into Melville, and makes the world that results from this union into the greatest, most terrible, and most beautiful of all possible worlds: a book, alas, only a book.

Of Ahab and Ulysses, the one with the greater will to power is not the more liberated. Ulysses has the kind of deliberate stubbornness which leads to universal domination: his trick is to seem to limit his power; in a cold and calculating way he finds out what he can still do, faced with the other power. He will be everything, if he can maintain a limit, if he can preserve that interval between the real and the imaginary which is just what the Song of the Sirens invites him to cross. The result is a sort of victory for him, a dark disaster for Ahab. We cannot deny that Ulysses understood something of what Ahab saw, but he stood fast within that understanding, while Ahab became lost in the image. In other words, one resisted the metamorphosis while the other entered it and disappeared inside it. After the test, Ulysses is just as he had been before, and the world is poorer, perhaps, but firmer and more sure. Ahab is no longer, and for Melville himself the world keeps threatening to sink into that

worldless space towards which the fascination of one single image draws
him.

The metamorphosis.

The tale is bound up with the metamorphosis alluded to by Ulysses
and Ahab. The action that the tale causes to take place in the present is
that of metamorphosis on all the levels it can attain. If for the sake of
convenience—because this statement cannot be exact—we say that what
makes the novel move forward is everyday, collective or personal time,
or more precisely, the desire to urge time to speak, then the tale moves
forward through that *other* time, it makes that other voyage, which is
the passage from the real song to the imaginary song, the movement
which causes the real song to become imaginary little by little, though
all at once (and this "little by little, though all at once" is the very time
of the metamorphosis), to become an enigmatic song always at a distance, designating this distance as a space to be crossed and designating the
place to which it leads as the point where singing will cease to be a lure.

The tale wants to cross this space, and what moves it is the transformation demanded by the empty fullness of this space, a transformation which
takes place in all directions and no doubt powerfully transforms the writer
but transforms the tale itself no less and everything at stake in the tale,
where in a sense nothing happens except this very crossing. And yet what
was more important for Melville than the encounter with Moby Dick, an
encounter which is taking place now and is "at the same time" always
imminent, so that he keeps moving towards it in a stubborn and disorderly quest, but since this encounter is just as closely related to the source,
it also seems to be sending him back into the depths of the past—Proust
lived under the fascination of this experience and in part succeeded in
writing under it.

People will object, saying: but the events they are talking about belong
primarily to the "lives" of Melville, Nerval, Proust. It is because they have
already met Aurélia, because they have tripped over the uneven paving
stones, seen the three church towers, that they can begin to form, an
image, a story, or words—that will let us share a vision close to their
own vision. Unfortunately, things are not that simple. All the ambiguity
arises from the ambiguity of time which comes into place here and which

allows us to say and to feel that the fascinating image of the experience is present at a certain moment, even though this presence does not belong to any present, and even destroys the present which it seems to enter. It is true, Ulysses was really sailing, and one day, on a certain date, he encountered the enigmatic song. And so he can say: now—this is happening now. But what happened now? The presence of a song which was still to be sung. And what did he touch in the presence? Not the occurrence of an encounter which had become present, but the overture of the infinite movement which is the encounter itself, always at a distance, from the place where it asserts itself and the moment when it asserts itself, because it is this very distance, this imaginary distance, in which absence is realized, and only at the end of this distance does the event begin to take place, at a point where the proper truth of the encounter comes into being and where, in any case, the words which speak it would originate.

Always still to come, always in the past already, always present—beginning so abruptly that it takes your breath away—and yet unfurling itself like the eternal return and renewal—*"Ah,"* says Goethe, *"in another age you were my sister or my wife"*—this is the nature of the event for which the tale is the approach. This event upsets relations in time, and yet affirms time, the particular way time happens, the tale's own time which enters the narrator's duration in such a way as to transform it, and the time of the metamorphoses where the different temporal ecstasies coincide in an imaginary simultaneity and in the form of the space which art is trying to create.

The Power and the Glory

I would like to make a few brief and simple statements that may help us to situate literature and the writer.

There was a time when a writer, like an artist, had some relation to glory. Glorification was his work, glory was the gift he gave and received. Glory in the ancient sense is the radiance of a presence (sacred or royal). And Rilke, too, says that to glorify does not mean to make known; glory is the manifestation of being as it advances in its magnificence as being, free of what conceals it, secure in the truth of its exposed presence.

Glory is followed by renown. Renown applies more exactly to the name. The power of naming, the force of what denominates, the dangerous assurance of the name (there is danger in being named) become the privilege of the person who can name and make what he names be understood. Understanding is subject to notoriety. Speech eternalized in writing promises immortality. The writer has thrown in his lot with what triumphs over death; he knows nothing of what is temporary; he is the friend of the soul, a man of the spirit, guarantor of what is eternal. Even today, many critics seem to believe sincerely that the vocation of art and literature is to eternalize man.

Renown is succeeded by reputation, just as the truth is succeeded by opinion. The fact of publishing—publication—becomes the essential thing. This can be taken in a superficial sense: the writer is known to the public, he has a large reputation, he wants to become prominent, highly valued, because he needs value—which is money. But value is procured by the public, and what excites the public? Publicity. Publicity becomes an art in itself, it is the art of all the arts, it is what is most important, since it determines the power that gives determination to everything else.

Here we are beginning to deal with considerations of a sort that we must not simplify in our polemical enthusiasm. The writer publishes. To publish is to make public; but to make public is not just to bring about a simple displacement, causing something to pass from the private state to the public state, as though from one place—the innermost heart, the closed room—to another place—the outside, the street. Nor is it a matter of revealing a piece of news or a secret to one person in particular.

The "public" is not made up of a large or small number of readers, each reading for himself. Writers like to say that they write their books intending them for a single friend. A resolution that is certain to be disappointed. There is no place in the public for a friend. There is no place for a particular person; any more than there is for particular social structures—families, groups, classes, nations. No one is part of the public and yet the whole world belongs to it, and not only the human world but all worlds, all things and no thing: the others. Because of this, no matter what severe censorship is imposed, no matter how faithfully the orders are obeyed, for authority there is always something suspect and displeasing about the act of publishing. This is because it causes the public to exist, and the public, always indeterminate, eludes the firmest political determinations.

To publish is not to cause oneself to be read, and it is not to give anything to be read. What is public is precisely what does not need to be read; it is always known already, in advance, with a kind of knowledge that knows everything and does not want to know anything. The public's interest, which is always excited, insatiable, and yet satisfied, which finds everything interesting but at the same time takes no interest in anything, is a movement that has been very wrongly described in a disparaging way. Here we see the same impersonal power, though in a relaxed and stabilized form, that lies at the origin of the literary effort as both obstacle and resource. The author speaks against an undefined and incessant speech, a speech without beginning or end—against it but also with its help. The reader eventually reads against the public's interest, against that distracted, unstable, versatile and omniscient curiosity, and he emerges with difficulty from that first reading which has already read before it reads: reading against it but even so through it. The reader, participating in a neutral kind of understanding, and the author, participating in a neutral kind of speech, would like to suspend these for a moment to allow room for a clearer form of expression.

Take the institution of literary prizes. It is easily explained by the structure of modern publishing and the social and economic organization of intellectual life. But when we think about the satisfaction that a writer, with rare exceptions, inevitably feels as he receives a prize that often represents nothing, we must explain it not in terms of the fact that his vanity has been flattered, but of his strong need for that communication before communication which is public understanding, in terms of the appeal of the profound and superficial clamor, in which everything appears, disappears, but remains, within a vague presence, a sort of River Styx that flows in broad daylight through our streets and irresistibly draws the living as though they were already shades, eager to become memorable so as to be better forgotten.

Nor is it a question of influence. It is not even a question of the pleasure of being seen by the blind crowd, or of being known by unknown people, a pleasure that implies the transformation of an indeterminate presence into a specific public, already defined, that is, the degeneration of an impalpable movement into a perfectly manipulable and accessible reality. On a slightly lower level, we will find all the political frivolities of the spectacle. But the writer will never win at this game. The most famous writer is not as well known as a daily radio announcer. And if he is eager to have intellectual power, he knows that he is wasting it in this insignificant notoriety. I believe the writer does not want anything for himself or for his work. But the need to be published—that is, to achieve outside existence, to attain that opening onto the outside, that divulgence-dissolution that takes place in our large cities—belongs to the work, like the memory of the impulse it grew out of, an impulse it must keep prolonging even though it wants to overcome it absolutely, an impulse it terminates for an instant, in effect, every time it is a work.

This reign of the "public," by which we mean the "outside" (the attractive force of a presence that is always there—not close, not distant, not familiar, not strange, it has no center, it is a kind of space that assimilates everything and retains nothing) has changed the writer's destination. Just as he has become a stranger to glory, just as he prefers anonymous groping to renown, and has lost all desire for immortality, so is he gradually—although at first glance this may seem less certain—abandoning the kind of pursuit of power that Barrès on the one hand and Monsieur Teste on the other—one by exerting an influence and the other by refusing to exert that influence—incarnated as two very characteristic types. You will say: "But never before have people who write been so involved in politics. Look at the petitions they sign, the interest they show, look how readily they believe they are authorized to judge everything simply because they write." It is true: when two writers meet, they never talk about literature (fortunately); their first remarks are always about politics. I want to suggest that in general writers are quite without any desire to play a role or assert power or hold a magistracy, rather, they

are surprisingly modest even in their fame, and very far removed from
the cult of personality (actually, this trait is a consistent way to distinguish which of two contemporary writers is a modern writer and which
an old-fashioned writer); the fact is that they are the more drawn to
politics the more they stand shivering in the outside, at the edge of the
public's uneasiness, seeking that communication before communication whose attraction they feel constantly invited to respect.

This can have the worst kind of result. It produces "these omniscient
observers, these omniscient *chatterboxes,* these omniscient *pedants,* who
know everything about everything and settle everything right away, who
are quick to make final judgments about things that have just happened,
so that soon it will be impossible for us to learn anything: we already
know everything," whom Dionys Mascolo describes in his essay "on
France's intellectual poverty."[1] Mascolo adds: "People here are informed,
intelligent and acquisitive. They understand everything. They understand each thing so quickly that they do not take the time to think about
anything. They do not understand anything... Just try forcing people
who have already understood everything to admit that something *new*
has happened!" Exactly these characteristics—though in this description they are slightly exaggerated and pointed, even degenerative—belong to public existence: neutral comprehension, infinite opening, in-
tuitive and presentient understanding in which everyone is always up to
date on recent events and has already decided about everything, meanwhile ruining every true value judgment. And so this apparently has the
worst sort of result. But it also creates a new kind of situation in which
the writer, in some sense losing his own existence and his individual
certainty, and experiencing a kind of communication that is still indeterminate and as powerful as it is impotent, as full as it is empty, sees
himself, as Mascolo remarks so justly, "reduced to impotence," "but
reduced also to simplicity."

We might say that when the writer becomes involved in politics today, with an energy the experts do not like, he is still not involved in
politics but rather in the new, scarcely perceived relationship that the
literary work and literary language are seeking to arouse through contact with the public presence. This is why, when he talks about politics,

---

[1] Dionys Mascolo, *Lettre polonaise sur la misère intellectuelle en France (Polish Letter on France's
Intellectual Poverty).*

he is already talking about something else—ethics; and talking about ethics, he is talking about ontology; talking about ontology, he is talking about poetry; when he talks, finally, about literature, "his only passion," it is only to revert to politics, "his only passion." This mobility is deceptive and can, once again, result in the worst kind of thing: those futile discussions that publicly active men unfailingly call "byzantine" or "intellectual" (qualifiers that are themselves, naturally, a part of that empty loquaciousness, when they do not serve to hide the irritable weakness of powerful men). All we can say about such mobility—whose difficulties and facilities, whose requirements and risks, have been shown us by Surrealism, which Mascolo correctly describes and defines[2]—is that it is never mobile enough, never faithful enough to that anguishing and extremely fatiguing instability that keeps growing and cultivates in all speech the refusal to abide by any definitive statement.

I must add that even though, because of this mobility, the writer is dissuaded from being any kind of expert, incapable even of being an expert in literature, much less in a particular literary genre, he nevertheless does not strive for the universality which the *honnête homme* of the seventeenth century, then Goethean man, and finally man in the classless society—not to speak of man in the conception of Father Teilhard, who is yet further removed—propose to us as a fantasy and a goal. Just as public understanding has always understood everything already, in advance, but obstructs all true understanding; just as the public clamor is absence and void of all firm and decided speech, always saying something other than what is said (producing a perpetual and formidable mix-up that Ionesco allows us to laugh at); just as the public is indetermination that destroys every group and every class; so the writer, coming under the fascination of what is at stake when he "publishes," and, seeking a reader in the public as Orpheus did Eurydice in Hell, turns to a kind of speech that is the speech of no one and that no one will understand, because it is always addressed to someone else, always awakening another person in the person who hears it, always arousing the

---

[2] "I must emphasize the extreme importance of Surrealism, the only intellectual movement in France in the first half of the twentieth century.... With a rigorousness that can in no way be called outmoded, Surrealism alone, between the two World Wars, was able to issue demands that were at once the demands of pure thought and the direct demands of men. Only Surrealism, with untiring tenacity, was able to recall that *revolution and poetry are the same thing.*"

expectation of something different. This speech is not universal, not something that would make literature a Promethean or divine power, having rights over everything, but rather the movement of a speech that is dispossessed and rootless, that prefers to say nothing rather than to claim to say everything, and each time it says something, only designates the level beneath which one must still descend if one wants to begin speaking. In our "intellectual poverty," then, there is also the wealth of thought, there is the indigence that gives us the presentiment that to think is always to learn to think less than we think, to think the absence which is also thought, and when we speak, to preserve this absence by bringing it to speech, if only—as is happening today—through an excess of repetitions and prolixity.

Nevertheless, when a writer rushes so eagerly into a concern for the anonymous and neutral existence that is public existence, when he seems to have no other interest, no other horizon, isn't he becoming involved in something that should never occupy him, or at least only indirectly? When Orpheus descends into hell in search of the work, he confronts a completely different Styx: a nocturnal separation that he must enchant with a look, but a look that does not freeze it. This is the essential experience, the only experience in which he must engage himself completely. Once he has returned to daylight, his only role in relation to the exterior powers is to disappear, quickly torn to pieces by their delegates, the Maenads, while the diurnal Styx, the river of public clamor in which his body has been scattered, carries within itself the work, singing, and not only carries it but wants to transform itself into song within it, maintain in the work its own fluid reality, its infinitely murmuring flux, stranger to all shores.

If the writer today, thinking he is descending into Hell, is satisfied with descending as far as the street, this is because the two rivers, the two great movements of primary communication, flow into one another and tend to mingle. This is because the profound primordial clamor—in which something is said but without speech, or something is silent but without silence—is not unlike the speech that does not speak, the understanding that is misunderstood and always listening, that is the public "mind" and "way." The result of this is that very often the work seeks to be published before it exists, it seeks its realization not in the space that is its own but through exterior animation, that life which appears sumptuous but which is dangerously inconsistent as soon as one tries to appropriate it.

Such confusion is not accidental. This extraordinary muddle, which results in the writer publishing before he has written, the public forming and transmitting what it does not understand, the critic judging and defining what he does not read, and lastly the reader being forced to read what has not yet been written—this movement, which confuses all the different moments in the formation of the work by anticipating them each time, also brings them together in a quest for a new unity. Whence the richness and the poverty, the pride and the humility, the extreme disclosure and the extreme solitude of our literary effort, which at least has the merit of desiring neither power nor glory.

THE NARRATIVE VOICE
(the "he," the neuter)

I write (I pronounce) this sentence: "The life forces are sufficient only up to a certain point." As I pronounce it, I have something very simple in mind: the sensation of weariness that constantly makes us feel that life is limited; you take a few steps down the street, eight or nine, then you fall. The limit set by weariness limits life. The meaning of life is in turn limited by this limit: a limited meaning of a limited life. But a reversal occurs, a reversal that can be discovered in various different ways. Language alters the situation. The sentence I pronounce tends to draw into the very inside of life the limit that was only supposed to mark it on the outside. Life is called limited. The limit does not disappear, but it takes from language the perhaps not unlimited meaning that it claims to limit: the meaning of the limit, by affirming it, contradicts the limitation of meaning or at least displaces it; but because of this there is a risk of losing the knowledge of the limit understood as limitation of meaning. Then how are we to speak of this limit (convey its meaning), without allowing the meaning to un-limit it? Here, we must enter another kind of language, and in the meantime realize that the sentence "The life forces..." is not, as such, entirely possible.

✦

Nevertheless, let us adhere to it. Let us write a tale in which it has a place as an achievement of the tale itself. What is the difference between these two identical sentence? There is certainly a very great difference. I can describe it roughly this way: the tale is like a circle that neutralizes life, which is not to say that it has no relationship to it but that its relationship to it is a neutral one. Within this circle, the meaning of what is, and of what is said, is definitely still given, but from a withdrawn position, from a distance where all meaning and all lack of meaning is neutralized beforehand. A reserve that exceeds every meaning already signified, without being considered a richness or a pure and simple privation. It is like speech that does not illuminate and does not obscure.

Often, in a bad tale—assuming that there are bad tales, which is not altogether certain—we have the impression that someone is speaking in the background and prompting the characters or even the events with what they have to say: an indiscreet and clumsy intrusion; it is said to be the author talking, an authoritarian and complacent "I" still anchored in life and barging in without any restraint. It is true, this is indiscreet—and this is how the circle is wiped out. But it is also true that the impression that someone is talking "in the background" is really part of the singularity of narrative and the truth of the circle: as though the center of the circle lay outside the circle, in back and infinitely far back, as though the *outside* were precisely this center, which could only be the absence of all center. Now, isn't this outside, this "in back"—which is in no way a dominating or lofty space from which one could grasp everything in a single glance and command the events (of the circle)—isn't this the very distance that language receives, as its limit, from its own deficiency, a distance that is certainly altogether exterior, but that inhabits language and in some sense constitutes it, an infinite distance such that to stay within language is always to be already outside, a distance such that, if it were possible to accept it, to "relate" it in the sense appropriate to it, one could then speak of the limit, that is, bring to the point of speech an experience of limits and the limit-experience? Regarded from this point of view, then, the tale is the hazardous space where the sentence "The life forces..." can be asserted in its truth, but where, in turn, all sentences, even the most innocent ones, risk assuming the same ambiguous status that language assumes at its limit. A limit that is perhaps the neuter.

I will not hark back to the subject of "the use of personal pronouns in the novel," which has given rise to so many noteworthy studies.[1] I think I should go farther back. If, as has been shown (in *L'Espace littéraire),* to write is to pass from "I" to "he," but if "he" when substituted for "I" does not simply designate another me, any more than it does esthetic disinterestedness—that impure contemplative enjoyment that allows the reader and the spectator to participate in the tragedy as a distraction—what remains to be discovered is what is at stake when

---

[1] I am referring to Michel Butor's *Répertoire II* (Éditions De Minuit).

writing responds to the demands of this uncharacterizable "he." In the narrative form, we hear—and always as though in addition to other things—something indeterminate speaking, something that the evolution of this form outlines, isolates, so that it gradually becomes manifest, though in a deceptive way. The "he" is the unlighted occurrence of what takes place when one tells a story. The distant epic narrator recounts exploits that happened and that he seems to be reproducing, whether or not he witnessed them. But the narrator is not a historian. His song is the domain where the event that takes place there comes to speech, in the presence of a memory; memory—muse and mother of muses—contains within it truth, that is, the reality of what takes place; it is in his song that Orpheus really descends to the underworld—which we express by adding that he descends to it through the power of his singing; but this song, already instrumental, signifies an alteration in the institution of narration. To tell a story is a mysterious thing. The mysterious "he" of the epic institution very quickly divides: the "he" becomes the impersonal coherence of a *story* (in the full and rather magical meaning of this word); the *story* stands by itself, preformed in the thought of a demiurge, and since it exists on its own, there is nothing left to do but tell it. But the *story* soon becomes disenchanted. The experience of the disenchanted world introduced into literature by Don Quixote is the experience that dissipates the *story* by contrasting it to the banality of the real—this is how realism seizes on the form of the novel, for a long time to come, and this form becomes the most effective genre for the developing bourgeoisie. The "he" is here uneventful everyday life, what happens when nothing happens, the course of the world as it is unnoticed, the passing of time, routine and monotonous life. At the same time—and in a more visible way—the "he" marks the intrusion of a character: the novelist is a person who refuses to say "I" but delegates that power to other people; the novel is filled with little "egos"—tormented, ambitious, unhappy, though always satisfied in their unhappiness; the individual asserts himself in his subjective richness, his inner freedom, his psychology; the novelistic narration, that of individuality—not taking into consideration the content itself—is already marked by an ideology to the extent that it assumes that the individual, with all his particular characteristics and his limits, is enough to express the world, that is to say, it assumes that the course of the world remains that of the individual.

As we can see, then, the "he" has split in two: on the one hand, there is something to tell, and that is the *objective* reality as it is immediately present to the interested gaze, and on the other hand, this reality is reduced to a constellation of individual lives, *subjectivities,* a multiple and personalized "he," a manifest "ego" under the veil of an apparent "he." In the interval of the tale, the voice of the narrator can be heard with more or less appropriateness, sometimes fictive, sometimes without any mask.

What has surrendered in this remarkable construction? Almost everything. I will not dwell on it.

There is something else that should be said. Let us draw a comparison—while remaining aware of the clumsiness of such a procedure, since it is unduly simplistic—between the impersonality of the novel as it is rightly or wrongly attributed to Flaubert and the impersonality of a novel by Kafka. The impersonality of the impersonal novel is the impersonality of esthetic distance. The rule is imperious: the novelist must not intervene. The author—even if *Madame Bovary* is *myself*—does away with all direct relations between himself and the novel; reflection, commentary, moralizing intrusion, still brilliantly legitimate in Stendhal or Balzac, become mortal sins. Why? For two reasons that are different but that almost merge. The first: what is told has an esthetic value to the extent that the interest one takes in it is interest from a distance; disinterestedness—an essential category in the judgment of taste since Kant and even since Aristotle—means that an esthetic act should not be based on an interest, if it wants to create a legitimate interest. A disinterested interest. Thus the author must heroically move away and keep his distance so that the reader or the spectator can also remain at a distance. The ideal is still the performance of classical theater: the narrator is there only to raise the curtain; the play is really performed from time immemorial and in some sense without him; he does not tell—he shows; and the reader does not read—he looks, attending, taking part without participating. The other reason is almost the same, though it is completely different: the author must not intervene, because the novel is a work of art and the work of art exists all by itself, an unreal thing, in the world outside the world, it must be left free, the props must be removed, the moorings cut, so that it can be sustained in its status as an imaginary object (but here Mallarmé, that is, an entirely different requirement, is already on the horizon).

Let us talk about Thomas Mann for a moment. His is an interesting case, because he does not respect the rule of nonintervention: he constantly involves himself in what he is telling, sometimes through interposed persons, but also in the most direct kind of way. What about this unwarranted intrusion? It is not moralizing—a stand taken against a certain character—it does not consist of illuminating things from outside— the thrust of the creator's thumb as he shapes his figures the way he wants them. It represents the intervention of the narrator challenging the very possibility of narration—an intervention that is, consequently, an essentially critical one, but in the manner of a game, of a malicious irony. Flaubert's kind of impersonality, contracted and difficult, still affirmed the validity of the narrative mode: to tell was to show, to allow to be or to make exist, without there being any reason—despite the great doubts one could already entertain—to question oneself about the limits and the shapes of the narrative form. Thomas Mann knows very well that we have lost our naivety. He therefore tries to restore it, not by ignoring illusion, but on the contrary, by creating it, making it so visible that he plays with it, just as he plays with the reader and by doing so draws him into the game. With his great sense of the narrative feast, Thomas Mann thus succeeds in restoring it as a feast of the narrative illusion, giving us back a second degree ingenuousness, that of the absence of ingenuousness. One could therefore say that if esthetic distance is denounced in his work, it is also proclaimed, affirmed by a narrative awareness that adopts itself as theme, whereas in the more traditional impersonal novel, it disappeared, putting itself between parentheses. Storytelling was a matter of course.

Storytelling is not a matter of course. As we know, the narrative act is generally taken in charge by a certain character, not that this character tells the story directly, or makes himself the narrator of a story that has already been experienced or that is in the process of being experienced, but because he constitutes the center around which the perspective of the tale is organized: everything is seen from this point of view. There is, therefore, a privileged "I," if only that of a character discussed in the third person, who takes great pains not to exceed the possibilities of his knowledge and the limits of his position: this is the realm of

James's ambassadors, and it is also the realm of the subjectivist formulae, in which the authenticity of the narrative depends on the existence of a free subject—formulae that are correct insofar as they represent the decision to stick to a certain prejudice (obstinacy and even obsession constitute one of the rules that seem to be imposed when writing is involved—form is obstinate, that is its danger), correct but in no way definitive, because on the one hand they wrongly assert that there might be some kind of equivalency between the narrative act and the transparency of a consciousness (as though to tell were simply to be conscious, to project, to reveal, to cover up by revealing), and on the other hand they maintain the primacy of the individual consciousness, which they say is only secondly and even secondarily an articulate consciousness.

In the meantime, Kafka wrote. Kafka admires Flaubert. The novels he writes are marked by an austerity that would permit a distracted reader to place them in the line of Flaubert. Yet everything is different. One of these differences is essential to the subject we are discussing. Distance—creative disinterestedness (so evident in Flaubert to the extent that he has to struggle to maintain it)—the distance that was the writer's and the reader's distance from the work and permitted the pleasure of contemplation, now enters into the very sphere of the work in the guise of an irreducible strangeness. No longer challenged, reestablished as something denounced, as in Thomas Mann (or Gide), it is the environment of the novelistic world, the space in which the narrative experience unfolds in unique simplicity—the experience one does not recount but that is involved when one recounts. A distance that is not simply lived as such by the central character, always at a distance from himself, just as he is at a distance from the events he experiences or the people he encounters (that would still be only the manifestation of a singular I); a distance that distances even him, removing him from the center, since it constantly decenters the work, in a way that is not measurable and not discernible, at the same time as it introduces into the most rigorous narration the alteration of another kind of speech or of the other as speech (as writing).

The consequences of this sort of change will often be misinterpreted. One consequence, immediately evident, is noteworthy. As soon as the alien distant becomes the stake and seems the substance of the story, the reader, who until then has been identifying, though from afar, with the story in progress (living it, for his part, in the mode of contemplative irresponsibility), can no longer be disinterested in it, that is, enjoy it with disinterestedness. What is happening? What new demand is being made on him? It is not that this concerns him: on the contrary, it does not concern him at all, and perhaps it does not concern anyone; it is in some way the *nonconcerning,* but in turn, the reader can no longer comfortably keep his distance from it, since there is no way that he can situate himself correctly in relation to what does not even present itself as unsituatable. Then how is he to remove himself from the absolute distance that has in some sense taken all removal back into itself? Without any support, deprived of the interest of reading, he is no longer allowed to look at things from far away, to keep that distance between them and himself that is the distance of the gaze, because the distant in its nonpresent presence, is not available either close up or far away and cannot be the object of a gaze. From now on, it is no longer a question of vision. Narration ceases to be what is presented to be seen, through a chosen actor-spectator as intermediary and from his viewpoint. The realm of the circumspect consciousness—of narrative circumspection (of the "I" that looks at everything around it and stands fast under its gaze)—has been subtly shaken, without of course coming to an end.

What Kafka teaches us—even if this expression cannot be directly attributed to him—is that storytelling brings the neuter into play. Narration governed by the neuter is kept in the custody of the "he," the third person that is neither a third person, nor the simple cloak of impersonality. The "he" of narration in which the neuter speaks is not content to take the place usually occupied by the subject, whether the latter is a stated or implied "I" or whether it is the event as it takes place in its impersonal signification.[2] The narrative "he" dismisses all

---

[2] The "he" does not simply take the place traditionally occupied by a subject; as a moving fragmentation, it changes what we mean by place: a fixed spot, unique or determined by its placement. Here we should say once again (confusedly): the "he," scattering after the fashion of a defect in the simultaneous plurality—the repetition—of a moving and diversely unoccupied place, designates "his" place as both the place from which he will always be lacking and which will thus remain empty, and also as a surplus of place, a place that is always too much: hypertopy.

subjects, just as it removes every transitive action or every objective possibility. It does this in two forms: 1) the speech of the tale always lets us feel that what is being told is not being told by anyone: it speaks in the neuter; 2) in the neuter space of the tale, the bearers of speech, the subjects of the action—who used to take the place of characters—fall into a relationship of nonidentification with themselves: something happens to them, something they cannot recapture except by relinquishing their power to say "I" and what happens to them has always happened already: they can only account for it indirectly, as self-forgetfulness, the forgetfulness that introduces them into the present without memory that is the present of narrating speech.

Of course this does not mean that the tale necessarily relates a forgotten occurrence or the occurrence of the forgetfulness that dominates lives and societies which, separated from what they are—alienated, as we say—move as though in their sleep to try to recapture themselves. It is the tale—independently of its content—that is forgetfulness, so that to tell a story is to put oneself to the test of this first forgetfulness that precedes, initiates, and destroys all memory. In this sense, telling is the torment of language, the incessant search for its infinity. And the tale is nothing else but an allusion to the initial deviation that writing brings, that carries writing away and that causes us, as we write, to yield to a sort of perpetual turning away.

The act of writing—that deflected relationship to life through which what is of no concern is asserted.

The narrative "he," whether it is absent or present, whether it asserts itself or conceals itself, whether or not it changes the conventions of writing—linearity, continuity, readability—in this way marks the intrusion of the other—understood as neuter—in its irreducible strangeness, in its wily perversity. The other speaks. But when the other speaks, no one is speaking, because the other—which we must refrain from honoring with a capital letter that would establish it in a majestic substantive, as though it had some substantial, even unique, presence—is never precisely simply the other, rather it is neither one thing nor the other, and the neuter that indicates it withdraws it from both, as from the unity, always establishing it outside the term, the act, or the subject where it claims to exist. The narrative (I do not say narrating) voice derives its aphony from this. It is a voice that has no place in the work but does not hang over it either, far from falling out of some sky under the guarantee of a superior Transcendence: the "he" is not the "encompassing"of Jaspers, but rather a kind of void in the work—the absence-word that Marguerite Duras describes in one of her tales: "a hole-word, hollowed out in its center by a hole, by the hole in which all the other words should have been buried," and the text goes on: "One could not have spoken it, but one could have made it resound—immense, endless, an empty gong..."[3] It is the narrative voice, a neuter voice that speaks the work from that place-less place in which the work is silent.

The narrative voice is neuter. Let us take a quick look at what traits characterize it at first approach. For one thing, it says nothing, not only because it adds nothing to what there is to say (it does not know anything), but because it underlies this nothing—the "to silence," and the "to keep silent"—in which speech is here and now already engaged; thus it is not heard, first of all, and everything that gives it a distinct reality begins to betray it. Then again, being without its own existence, speaking from nowhere, suspended in the tale as a whole, it is not dissipated there either, as light is, which, though invisible itself, makes things visible: it is radically exterior, it comes from exteriority itself, the outside that is the special enigma of language in writing. But let us consider still other traits, traits that are actually the same. The narrative voice that is inside only insofar as it is outside, at a distance without any distance, cannot be embodied: even though it can borrow the voice of a judiciously chosen character or even create the hybrid position of mediator (this voice which destroys all mediation), it is always different from what utters it, it is the indifferent-difference that alters the personal voice. Let us say (on a whim) that it is spectral, ghost-like. Not that it comes from beyond the grave and not even because it might represent once and for all some essential absence, but because it always tends to absent itself in its bearer and also to efface him as center, thus being neuter in the decisive sense that it cannot be

---

[3] *Le Ravissement de Lol V. Stein* (Gallimard) [*The Ravishing of Lol V. Stein*, trans. by Richaid Seaver, Grove Press, 1966, p.38]

central, does not create a center, does not speak from a center, but on the contrary, at the limit would prevent the work from having a center, withdrawing from it all special focus of interest, even that of afocality, and also not allowing it to exist as a completed whole, once and forever accomplished.

Tacit, it attracts language obliquely, indirectly and within this attraction—that of oblique speech—allows the neuter to speak. What does that indicate? The narrative voice carries the neuter. It carries the neuter in that: 1) to speak in the neuter is to speak at a distance, preserving that distance, without *mediation* or *community,* and even experiencing the infinite distancing of distance, its irreciprocity, its irrectitude or its asymmetry—because the greatest distance dominated by asymmetry, without one or another of its boundaries being privileged, is precisely the neuter (one cannot neutralize the neuter); 2) the neuter speech neither reveals nor conceals. This is not to say that it signifies nothing (by claiming to renounce sense in the form of nonsense), it means it does not signify in the same way the visible-invisible signifies, but that it opens another power in the language, one alien to the power of illumination (or of darkening), of comprehension (or of misapprehension). It does not signify in the optical manner; it remains outside the light-shadow reference that seems to be the ultimate reference of all knowledge and communication to the point of making us forget that it has only the value of a venerable, that is to say, inveterate, metaphor; 3) the demand of the neuter tends to suspend the attributive structure of the language, that relationship to being, implicit or explicit, that is immediately posed in our languages as soon as something is said. It has often been remarked—by philosophers, linguists, political commentators—that nothing can be denied that has not already been posed beforehand. To put it another way, all language begins by articulating, and in articulating it affirms. But it could be that telling (writing) is drawing language into a possibility of saying that would say without saying being and still without denying it either—or, more clearly, too clearly, that it is establishing the center of gravity of speech elsewhere, where speaking is not a matter of affirming being nor of needing negation in order to suspend the work of being, the work that ordinarily occurs in every form of expression. In this respect, the narrative voice is the most critical one that can communicate unheard. That is why we tend, as we listen to it, to confuse it with the oblique voice of unhappiness or the oblique voice of madness.[4]

---

[4] This voice—the narrative voice—is the one I hear, perhaps rashly, perhaps rightly, in the tale by Marguerite Duras that I mentioned a short while ago. The night forever without any dawn—that ballroom in which the indescribable event occurred that cannot be recalled and cannot be forgotten, but that one's forgetting retains—the nocturnal desire to turn around in order to see what belongs neither to the visible nor to the invisible, that is, to stay for a moment, through one's gaze, as close as possible to strangeness, where the rhythm of reveal-oneself-conceal-oneself has lost its guiding force—then, the need (the eternal human desire) to bring about acceptance in another person, to live once again in another person, a third person, the dual relationship, fascinated, indifferent, irreducible to any mediation: a neuter relationship, even if it implies the infinite void of desire—finally, the imminent certainty that what has happened once will always begin again, will always betray itself and reject itself: these really are, it seems to me, the "coordinates" of narrative space, that circle where, as we enter it, we incessantly enter the outside. But who is telling the story here? Not the reporter, the one who formally—and also a little shamefacedly—does the speaking, and actually takes over, so much so that he seems to us to be an intruder, but rather that which cannot tell a story because it bears—this is its wisdom, this is its madness—the torment of impossible narration, knowing (with a closed knowledge anterior to the reason-unreason split) that it is the measure of this outside, where, as we reach it, we are in danger of falling under the attraction of a completely exterior speech: pure extravagance.

The Absence of the Book

Let us try to question ourselves, that is, admit in the form of a question something that cannot reach the point of questioning.

1. *"This insane game of writing."* With these words, simple as they are, Mallarmé opens up writing to writing. The words are very simple, but their nature is also such that we will need a great deal of time—a great variety of experiments, the work of the world, countless misunderstandings, works lost and scattered, the movement of knowledge, and finally the turning point of an infinite crisis—if we are to begin to understand what decision is being prepared on the basis of this end of writing that is foretold by its coming.

2. Apparently we only read because the writing is already there, laid out before our eyes. Apparently. But the first person who ever wrote, who cut into stone and wood under ancient skies, was far from responding to the demands of a view that required a reference point and gave it meaning, changed all relations between seeing and the visible. What he left behind him was not something more, something added to other things; it was not even something less—a subtraction of matter, a hollow in the relation to the relief. Then what was it? A hole in the universe: nothing that was visible, nothing that was invisible. I suppose the first reader was engulfed by that non-absent absence, but without knowing anything about it, and there was no second reader because reading, from then on understood to be the vision of an immediately visible—that is, intelligible—presence, was affirmed for the very purpose of making this disappearance into *the absence of the book* impossible.

3. Culture is linked to the book. The book as repository and receptacle of knowledge is identified with knowledge. The book is not only the book that sits in libraries—that labyrinth in which all combinations of forms, words and letters are rolled up in volumes. The book is the Book. Still to be read, still to be written, always already written, always already paralyzed by reading, the book constitutes the condition for every possibility of reading and writing.

471

The book admits of three distinct investigations. There is the empirical book; the book acts as vehicle of knowledge; a given determinate book receives and gathers a given determinate form of knowledge. But the book as book is never simply empirical. The book is the *a priori* of knowledge. We would know nothing if there did not always exist in advance the impersonal memory of the book and, more importantly, the prior inclination to write and read contained in every book and affirming itself only in the book. The absolute of the book, then, is the isolation of a possibility that claims not to have originated in any other anteriority. An absolute that will later tend to assert itself in the Romantics (Novalis), then more rigorously in Hegel, then more radically— though in a different way—in Mallarmé, as the totality of relations (absolute knowledge or the Work), in which would be achieved either consciousness, which knows itself and returns to itself after having been exteriorized in all its dialectically linked figures, or language, closed around its own statement and already dispersed.

Let us recapitulate: the empirical book; the book: condition for all reading and all writing; the book: totality or Work. But with increasing refinement and truth these forms all assume that the book contains knowledge as the presence of something virtually present and always immediately accessible, if only with the help of mediations and relays. Something is there which the book presents in presenting itself and which reading animates, which reading reestablishes—through its animation—in the life of a presence. Something that is, on the lowest level, the presence of a content or of a signified thing; then, on a higher level, the presence of a form, of a signifying thing or of an operation; and, on a higher level still, the development of a system of relations that is always there already, if only as a future possibility. The book rolls up time, unrolls time, and contains this unrolling as the continuity of a presence in which present, past, and future become actual.

4. *The absence of the book* revokes all continuity of presence, just as it evades the questioning conveyed by the book. It is not the interiority of the book, nor its continuously evaded Meaning. Rather it is outside the book, though it is enclosed in it, not so much its exterior as a reference to an outside that does not concern the book.

The more the Work assumes meaning and acquires ambition, retaining in itself not only all works, but all the forms of discourse and all

the powers of discourse, the more the absence of the work seems about
to propose itself, though without ever allowing itself to be designated.
This happens with Mallarmé. With Mallarmé, the Work becomes aware
of itself and so knows itself as something coinciding with the absence of
the work, the latter then deflecting it from ever coinciding with itself,
and dooming it to impossibility. A deviation in which the work disappears into the absence of the work, but in which the absence of the work
always escapes the more it reduces itself to being nothing but the Work
that has always disappeared already.

5. The act of writing is related to the absence of the work, but is
invested in the Work as book. The insanity of writing—*the insane game*—
is the relationship of writing, a relationship established not between
writing and the production of the book, but, through the production of
the book, between the act of writing and the absence of the work.

To write is to produce absence of the work (worklessness). Or: writing is the absence of the work as it *produces itself* through the work and
throughout the work. Writing as worklessness (in the active sense of the
word) is the insane game, the indeterminacy that lies between reason
and unreason.

What happens to the book during this "game," in which worklessness is set loose during the operation of writing? The book: the passage
of an infinite movement, a movement that goes from writing as an operation to writing as worklessness; a passage that immediately impedes.
Writing passes through the book, but the book is not that to which it is
destined (its destiny). Writing passes through the book, completing itself there even as it disappears in the book; and yet, we do not write for
the book. The book: a ruse by which writing goes towards *the absence of
the book.*

6. Let us try to gain a clearer understanding of the relation of the
book to *the absence of the book.*

a) The book plays a dialectical role. In some sense it is there so that
not only the dialectic of discourse can take place, but also discourse as
dialectic. The book is the work language performs on itself: as though
the book were necessary in order for language to become aware of language, for it to know itself and complete itself in its incompleteness.

b) Yet the book that has become a work—the whole literary process, whether it asserts itself as a long succession of books or is manifested in one unique book or in the space that takes the place of that book—is both more of a book than the others and already beyond the book, outside its category and outside its dialectic. *More* a book: a book of knowledge scarcely exists as a book, as a developed volume; the work, on the other hand, makes a claim to be singular: unique, irreplaceable, it is almost a person; this is why there is a dangerous tendency for the work to promote itself into a masterpiece, and also to make itself essential, that is, to designate itself by a signature (it is not only signed by the author, but also somehow by itself, which is more serious). And yet it is already outside the book process: as though the work only indicated the opening—the interruption—through which the neutrality of writing passes, as though the work were oscillating suspended between itself (the totality of language) and an affirmation that had not yet been made.

What is more, in the work, language is already changing direction— or place: place of direction—no longer the logos that participates in a dialectic and knows itself, rather, it is engaged in a different relationship. So that one can say the work hesitates between the book, vehicle of knowledge and fleeting moment of language, and the Book, raised to the Capital Letter, Idea, and Absolute of the book—and then between the work as presence and the absence of the work that is constantly escaping and in which time as time is disturbed.

7. The end of the act of writing does not lie in the book or in the work. As we write the work, we are drawn by the absence of the work. We necessarily fall short of the work, but this does not mean that because of this deficiency we fall under the necessity of the absence of the work.

8. The book: a ruse by which the energy of writing, relying on discourse and allowing itself to be carried along by the vast continuity of discourse, separating itself from it at the limit, is also the use of discourse, restoring to culture that alteration which threatens it and opens it to the absence of the book. Or the book is a labor through which writing, changing the givens of a culture, of "experience," of knowledge. that is to say of discourse, obtains another product that will constitute a new modality of discourse as a whole and will integrate itself with it even as it claims to disintegrate it.

The absence of the book: reader, you would like to be its author, and then you would be nothing more than the plural reader of the Work.

How long will it last—this lack that is sustained by the book and that expels the book from itself as book? Produce the book, then, so that it will detach itself, disengage itself as it scatters: this will not mean that you have produced *the absence of the book*.

9. The book (the civilization of the book) declares: there is a memory that transmits things, there is a system of relations that arranges things; time becomes entangled in the book, where the void still belongs to a structure. But the absence of the book is not based on writing that leaves a mark and determines a directed movement, whether this movement develops linearly from a beginning toward an end, or is deployed from a center toward the surface of a sphere. The absence of the book makes an appeal to writing that does not commit itself, that does not settle out, is not satisfied with disavowing itself, nor with going back over its tracks to erase them.

What summons us to write, when the time of the book determined by the beginning-end relation, and the space of the book determined by deployment from a center, cease to impose themselves? The attraction of (pure) exteriority.

The time of the book, determined by the beginning-end (past-future) relation based on a presence. The space of the book determined by deployment from a center, itself conceived as the search for a source.

Everywhere that there is a system of relations that arranges, a memory that transmits, everywhere that writing gathers in the substance of a mark that reading regards in the light of a meaning (tracing it back to an origin whose sign it is), when emptiness itself belongs to a structure and allows itself to be adjusted, then there is the book: the *law* of the book.

As we write, we always write in the name of the exteriority of writing and against the exteriority of the law, and always the law uses what is written as a resource.

The attraction of (pure) exteriority—the place where, since the outside "precedes" any interior, writing does not deposit itself in the manner of a spiritual or ideal presence subsequently inscribing itself and then leaving a mark, a mark or a sedimentary deposit that would allow one to track it down, in other words to restore it—on the basis of that mark as deficiency—to its ideal presence or ideality, its fullness, its integrity as presence.

Writing marks but leaves no mark; it does not allow us to work our way back from some vestige or sign to anything more than itself as (pure) exteriority and, as such, never given as either forming itself, or being gathered in a unifying relationship with a presence (to be seen, to be heard), or with the whole of presence or the Unique, present-absence.

When we begin to write, either we are not beginning or we are not writing: writing does not accompany beginning.

10. In the book, the uneasiness of writing—the energy—tries to come to rest in the favor of the work (*ergon*), but the absence of the work always summons it immediately to respond to the deflection of the outside, where what is affirmed no longer finds its measure in a relationship of unity.

We have no "idea" of the absence of the work, certainly not as a presence, but also not as the destruction of the thing that would prevent this absence, if only in the form of absence itself. To destroy the work, which itself is not, to destroy at least the affirmation of the work and the dream of the work, to destroy the indestructible, to destroy nothing so that an idea that is out of place here will not impose itself—the idea that to destroy would be enough. The negative can no longer be operative where an affirmation has been made that affirms the work. And in no case can the negative lead to the absence of the work.

Reading would be reading in the book the absence of the book, and as a consequence producing this absence where there is no question of the book being absent or present (defined by an absence or a presence).

The absence of the book: never contemporaneous with the book, not because it emerges from another time, but because it is the source of noncontemporaneity from which it, too, comes. The absence of the book: always diverging, always lacking a present relationship with itself, so that it is never received in its fragmentary plurality by a single reader in the present of his reading, unless, at the limit, with the present torn apart, dissuaded—

The attraction of (pure) exteriority or the vertigo of space as distance, fragmentation that only drives us back to the fragmentary.

The absence of the book: the prior deterioration of the book, the game of dissidence it plays with reference to the space in which it is inscribed; the preliminary dying of the book. Writing, the relation to every book's *other*, to what is de-scription in the book, a scripturary demand beyond discourse, beyond language. The act of writing at the edge of the book, outside the book.

Writing outside language, writing which would be in some sense originally language making it impossible for there to be any object (present or absent) of language. Then writing would never be man's writing, which is to say it would never be God's writing either; at most it would be the writing of the other, of dying itself.

11. The book begins with the Bible, in which the logos is inscribed as law. Here the book achieves its unsurpassable meaning, including what extends beyond it everywhere and cannot be surpassed. The Bible takes language back to its origin: whether this language is written or spoken, it is always the theological era that opens with this language and lasts as long as biblical space and time. The Bible not only offers us the highest model of a book, the specimen that will never be superceded; the Bible also encompasses all books, no matter how alien they are to biblical revelation, knowledge, poetry, prophecy, proverbs, because it contains the spirit of the book; the books that follow it are always contemporaneous with the Bible: the Bible certainly grows, expands with itself in an infinite growth that leaves it identical, permanently sanctioned by the relationship of Unity, just as the ten Laws set forth and contain the monologos, the One Law, the law of Unity that cannot be transgressed and never can be denied by negation alone.

The Bible: a testamentary book in which the alliance is declared, that is to say, the destiny of speech bound to the one who bestows language, and in which he consents to remain through this gift that is the gift of his name, that is to say, also the destiny of this relationship of speech to language, which is dialectic. It is not because the Bible is a sacred book that the books which spring from it—the whole literary process—are marked with the theological sign and cause us to belong to the realm of the theological. It is just the opposite: it was because the testament—the alliance of speech—was rolled up in a book, took the form and structure of a book, that the "sacred" (what is separated from writing) found its place in theology. The book is in essence theological. This is why the first manifestation of the theological (and the only one that continues to unfold and to develop) could only have been in the form of a book. In some sense God does not remain God (does not become divine) except as He speaks through the book.

Mallarmé, confronting the Bible in which God is God, establishes a work in *which the insane game of writing* sets to work and already disowns itself, encountering indeterminacy with its double game: necessity, accident. The Work, the absolute of the voice and of writing, is unworked even before it has been accomplished, before it ruins the possibility of accomplishment by being accomplished. The Work still belongs to the book, and because of this it helps sustain the biblical aspect of every Work, and yet designates the disjunction of a time and a space that are *something other*, precisely that which can no longer assert that it is in a relationship of unity. The Work as book leads Mallarmé outside his name. The Work in which the absence of the work is in effect leads the man who is no longer called Mallarmé to madness: let us understand, if we can, that this *to* means the limit which would be decisive madness if it were crossed; and this obliges us to conclude that the limit—"the edge of madness"—if conceived as indecision that cannot decide, or as nonmadness, is more essentially mad: would be abyss, not the abyss, but the edge of the abyss.

Suicide: what is written as necessity in the book is denounced as chance in the absence of the book. What one says, the other repeats, and this statement that reiterates, by virtue of this reiteration encompasses death—the death of self.

12. The anonymity of the book is such that in order to sustain the book it calls for the dignity of a name. The name is that of a temporary particularity that supports reason and that reason authorizes by raising it to itself. The relationship of the Book and the name is always contained in the historical relationship that linked absolute knowledge of system with Hegel's name: this relationship of the Book and of Hegel, identifying the latter with the book, carrying him along in its development, made Hegel into post-Hegel. Hegel-Marx, and then Marx radically estranged from Hegel, who continues to write, to correct, to know, to assert the absolute law of written discourse.

Just as the Book takes the name of Hegel, the work, in its more essential (more uncertain) anonymity, takes the name of Mallarmé, with the difference that Mallarmé not only recognizes the anonymity of the Work as his own trait and the indication of his own place, not only withdraws into this manner of being anonymous, but does not call himself the author of the Work, suggesting at the very most, hyperbolically, that he is the capacity—never a unique or a unifiable capacity—to read the nonpresent Work, that is, the capacity to respond, by his absence, to the work that continues to be absent (but the absent work is not *the absence of the work*, is even separated from it by a radical break).

In this sense, there is already a decisive distance between Hegel's book and Mallarmé's work, a difference evidenced by their different ways of being anonymous in the naming and signing of their works. Hegel does not die, even if he disavows himself in the displacement or reversal of the System: every system still names him, Hegel is never altogether without a name. Mallarmé and the work have no relationship, and this lack of relationship is played out in the Work, establishing the work as what would be forbidden to this particular Mallarmé as to anyone else with a name, and ultimately forbidden to the work when conceived as capable of completing itself by and through itself. The Work is not freed of the name because it could be produced without someone producing it, but because anonymity affirms that it is constantly already beyond whatever could name it. The book is the whole, whatever the form of that totality, whether or not the structure of that totality is completely different from that which a belated reading assigns to Hegel. The Work is not everything, it is already outside everything, but, in its resignation, it is still designated as absolute. The Work is not bound up with success (with completion) as the book is, but with disaster: but this disaster is yet another affirmation of the absolute.

Let us say briefly that the book can always be signed, it remains indifferent to who signs it; the work—Festivity as disaster—requires resignation, requires that whoever claims to write it renounce himself and cease to designate himself.

Then why do we sign our books? Out of modesty, as a way of saying: these are still only books, indifferent to signatures.

13. The "absence of the book"—which the written thing provokes as the future of writing, a future that has never come to pass—does not form a concept anymore than the word "outside" does, or the word "fragment," or the word "neuter," but it helps conceptualize the word "book." It is not some contemporary expositor who gives Hegel's philosophy its coherence and conceives of it as a book, thus conceiving of the book as the finality of absolute Knowledge; beginning at the end of the 19th century, it is Mallarmé. But Mallarmé, through the very force of his experience, immediately pierces through the book to designate (dangerously) the Work whose center of attraction—a center that is always off center—would be writing. The act of writing, *the insane game*. But the act of writing has a relationship, a relationship of otherness, with the absence of the Work, and it is precisely because he senses this radical alteration that comes to writing and through writing with the absence of the Work that Mallarmé is able to name the Book, naming it as the thing that gives meaning to becoming by suggesting a place and a time for it: first and last concept. But Mallarmé does not yet name the absence of the book or he only recognizes it as a way of thinking the Work, the Work as failure or impossibility.

14. *The absence of the book* is not the book coming apart, even though in some sense coming apart lies at the origin of the book and is its opposing principle. The fact that the book is always coming apart (disordering itself) still only leads to another book or to a possibility other than the book, but not to the absence of the book. Let us admit that what obsesses the book (what haunts it) would be the absence of the book that it always lacks, contenting itself with containing it (holding it at a distance) without containing it (transforming it into content). Let us also admit the opposite, that the book encloses the absence of the book that excludes it, but that the absence of the book is never conceived only on the basis of the book and only as its negation. Let us admit that if the book carries meaning, the absence of the book is so alien to meaning that nonmeaning does not concern it either.

It is very striking that within a certain tradition of the book (the one derived from the kabbalists' formulation, although there it is a question of sanctioning the mystical signification of the literal presence), what is called the "written Torah" preceded the "oral Torah," the latter then giving rise to the edited version that alone constitutes the Book. Here, thought is confronted with an enigmatic proposition: Nothing precedes writing. Yet the writing on the first tablets does not become readable until after they are broken and because they are broken—after and because of the resumption of the oral decision, which brings us to the second writing, the one we know, rich in meaning, capable of issuing commandments, always equal to the law it transmits.

Let us try to examine this surprising proposition by relating it to what might be a future experiment of writing. There are two kinds of writing, one white, the other black; one makes the invisibility of a colorless flame invisible, the other is made accessible in the form of letters, characters, and articulations by the power of the black fire. Between the two there is orality, which, however, is not independent, but always involved with the second kind of writing, because it is the black fire itself, the measured darkness that limits, defines all light, makes all light visible. Thus, what we call oral is designation in a temporal present and a presence of space, but also, at first, development or mediation as it is guaranteed by a discourse that explains, welcomes and defines the neutrality of the initial inarticulation. The "oral Torah" is therefore no less written, but is called oral in the sense that as discourse it alone allows there to be communication, otherwise known as *commentary,* speech that both teaches and declares, authorizes and justifies: as though language (discourse) were necessary for writing to give rise to common legibility and perhaps also to the Law understood as prohibition and limit; and also as though the first writing, in its configuration of invisibility, had to be considered *outside speech* and directed only towards the *outside*, an absence or a fracture so primordial that it will have to be broken to escape the savagery of what Hölderlin calls the aorgic.

15. Writing is absent from the Book, being the nonabsent absence on the basis of which the Book, having absented itself from this absence, makes itself readable (on both its levels—the oral and the written, the Law and its exegesis, the forbidden and the thought of the forbidden) and comments on itself by enclosing history: the closing of the book, the severity of the letter, the authority of knowledge. What we can say about this writing, which is absent from the book and yet stands in a relationship of otherness with it, is that it remains alien to

readability, that it is unreadable insofar as to read is necessarily to enter through one's gaze into a relationship of meaning or nonmeaning with a presence. There would, therefore, be a writing exterior to the kind of knowledge that is gained through reading, and also exterior to the form and the requirements of the Law. Writing, (pure) exteriority, alien to every relationship of presence, and to all legality.

The moment the exteriority of writing *slackens*, that is, responds to the appeal of the oral force, agreeing to be informed in language giving rise to the book—the written discourse—this exteriority tends to appear as the exteriority of the Law, on the highest level, and on the lowest level as the interiority of meaning. The Law is writing itself which has renounced the exteriority of interlocution to designate the place of the interdicted. The illegitimacy of writing, always rebellious towards the Law, hides the asymmetrical illegitimacy of the Law in relation to writing.

Writing: exteriority. Perhaps there is a "pure" exteriority of writing, but this is only a postulate, a postulate that is already disloyal to the neutrality of writing. In the book that signs our alliance with every Book, exteriority does not succeed in authorizing itself on its own, and as it writes down its name, it does so under the space of the Law. The exteriority of writing, spreading itself out in layers in the book, becomes exteriority as law. The Book speaks as Law. Reading it, we read in it that everything which is, is either forbidden or allowed. But isn't this structure of permission and prohibition a result of our level of reading? Isn't there perhaps another reading of the Book in which the book's other would cease to be proclaimed in precepts? And if we were to read this way, would we read yet another book? Wouldn't we be about to read *the absence of the book?*

The initial exteriority: perhaps we should assume that its nature is such that we would not be able to tolerate it except under the sanction of the Law. What would happen if the system of prohibition and limitation stopped protecting it? Or might it simply be there, at the limit of possibility, just to make the limit possible? Is this exteriority nothing more than a requirement of limit? Is limit itself conceived only through a definition that is necessary at the approach of the unlimited and that would disappear if it was ever passed—for that reason impassable, yet always passed because it is impassable?

16. Writing contains exteriority. The exteriority that becomes Law falls henceforth under the protection of the Law—which, in turn, is written; that is, once again under the protection of writing. We must assume that this reduplication of writing, which immediately designates it as difference, only affirms, through this duplicity, the quality of exteriority itself, which is always developing, always exterior to itself, in a relationship of discontinuity. There is a "first" writing, but since this writing is the first writing, it is already distinct from itself, separated because of what marks it, being at the same time nothing but that mark and also different from it, if the mark is made there, and broken, outdistanced, and denounced to such a degree—in that outside, that disjunction where it is revealed—that a new rupture will be necessary, a break that is violent but human (and, in this sense, defined and delimited), so that, having become an explosive text—and the initial fragmentation having been replaced by a determined act of rupture— the law may, under the mask of the forbidden, redeem a promise of unity.

In other words, the breaking of the first tablets is not a break with an original state of undivided harmony; on the contrary, what it initiates is the substitution of a limited exteriority (in which the possibility of a limit is intimated) for an exteriority without limitation, the substitution of a lack for an absence, of a break for a gap, of an infraction for the pure-impure fraction of the fragmentary, the fraction that falls short of the sacred separation, crowding into the scission of the neuter (which is the neuter). To put it yet another way, we must break with the first exteriority so that language, henceforth regularly divided, in a reciprocal bond of mastery with itself, grammatically constructed, will engage us in mediate and immediate relationships with the second exteriority, in which the logos is law and the law logos—relationships that guarantee discourse and then dialectic, where the law in turn will dissolve.

The "first" writing, far from being more immediate than the second, is alien to all these categories. It does not bestow its gifts generously through some ecstatic participation in which the law that protects the One merges with it and ensures confusion with it. The first writing is otherness itself, a severity and austerity that never grant authority, the burning of a parching breeze, infinitely more rigorous than any law. The law is what saves us from writing by forcing writing to act indirectly through the rupture—the transitiveness—of speech. A salvation that introduces us to knowledge and, through our desire for knowledge, even to the Book, where knowledge maintains desire by hiding it from itself.

17. The nature of the Law: it is infringed upon even before it has been stated; from that time on, certainly, it is promulgated in a high place, at a distance and in the name of what is distant, but without any relationship of direct knowledge with those for whom it is destined. From this we could conclude that the law, as it is transmitted, tolerates transmission, becomes a law of transmission, is only constituted as a law by the decision to fail to do so: there would be no limit if the limit were not passed, revealed as impassable by being passed.

Yet doesn't the law precede all knowledge (including knowledge of the law), knowledge which it alone opens, preparing it for its conditions by a preliminary "it must be," even if only from the Book in which the law attests to itself through the order—the structure—that it looms over as it establishes it?

Always anterior to the law, neither founded in nor determined by the necessity of being brought to knowledge, never endangered by someone's misunderstanding, always essentially affirmed by the infraction that implies reference to it, attracting in its trial the authority that submits itself to it, and all the more firm because it is open to easy transgression: the law.

The law's "it must be" is not primarily a "thou shalt." "It must be" applies to no one or, more deliberately, applies only to no one. The nonapplicability of the law is not only a sign of its abstract force, of its inexhaustible authority, of the reserve it maintains. Incapable of saying *thou,* the law is never directed at anyone in particular: not because it is universal, but because it separates in the name of unity, being separation itself that prescribes for the sake of what is unique. This is perhaps the law's august lie: itself having "legalized" the outside in order to make it possible (or real), it frees itself of all determination and all content in order to preserve itself as pure inapplicable form, pure exigency to which no presence is able to respond, yet immediately particularized in multiple norms and, through the code of alliance, in ritual forms so as to allow for the discreet inferiority of a return to self, where the infrangible intimacy of the "thou shalt" will be affirmed.

18. The ten laws are only laws with reference to Unity. God—the name that cannot be spoken in vain because no language can contain it—is only God so that He can carry the Unity and designate its sovereign finality. No one will try to attack the One. And then the Other bears witness, bears witness for none other than the Unique, a reference that unites all thought to what is *unthought*, keeping it turned towards the One as towards something upon which thought cannot infringe. It is therefore important to say: not the unique God, but Unity is necessarily God, transcendence itself.

The exteriority of the law finds its measure in responsibility towards the One, it is an alliance of the One and the many that thrusts aside as impious the primordiality of difference. Yet in the law itself there is still a clause that retains some memory of the exteriority of writing, when it is said: thou shalt make no images, thou shalt not represent, thou shalt reject presence in the form of resemblance, sign, and mark. What does that mean? First, and almost too clearly, the prohibition of the sign as mode of presence. The act of writing—if that act is relating oneself to the image and naming the idol—makes its mark outside the exteriority proper to it, an exteriority that writing then repels in its effort to overwhelm it, both by the void of words and by the pure signification of the sign. "Thou shalt make no idol" is thus, in the form of the law, not a statement about the law, but about the exigency of writing that precedes any law.

19. Let us admit that the law is obsessed by exteriority, that this obsession haunts it and that it separates itself from this obsession, in the name of the very separation that establishes it as a form, in the movement in which this obsession formulates it as law. Let us admit that exteriority as writing, a relation always without relation, can be called exteriority that *slackens* into law, precisely when it is *more tense,* when it has the tension of a gathering form. We need to know that as soon as the law exists (finds its place), everything changes, and it is the so-called "initial" exteriority that—in the name of a law that from now on cannot be denounced— presented as slackness, as undemanding neutrality, in the same way that writing outside the law, outside the book, seems at that point to be nothing more than the return to a spontaneity without rules, an automatism of ignorance, an irresponsible gesture, an immoral game. To put it another way, one cannot climb back up from exteriority

as law to exteriority as writing; going back up, in this context, would be going down. That is to say: one cannot "go back up" save by accepting the fall—though one is incapable of consenting to it—an essentially indeterminate fall into inessential chance (what the law disdainfully calls a game—a game in which everything is risked each time, and everything is lost: the necessity of law, the chance of writing). The law is the summit, there is no other. Writing remains outside the arbitration between high and low.[1]

---

[1] I dedicate (*and disavow*) these uncertain pages to the books in which the absence of the book is already being produced by being promised; these books were written by_____, but will only be designated here by the lack of a name, for the sake of friendship.

AFTER THE FACT*

Mallarmé to an unpublished author who had asked him to write an introduction or prefatory note to his work: "I abhor prefaces that come from the author himself, but those that come from someone else I find even more distasteful. My friend, a real book needs no introduction; it's a bolt from the blue, and it behaves like a woman with her lover, needing no help from a third party, the husband..."

In a completely different context I have written: "*Noli me legere.*" A prohibition against reading that tells the author he has been disposed of. "You will not read me." "I do not remain as a text to be read except through the process that slowly devours you while writing." "You will never know what you have written, even if you have written only to find this out."

Prior to the work, the work of art, the work of writing, the work of words, there is no artist—neither a writer nor a speaking subject— since it is the production that produces the producer, bringing him to life or making him appear in the act of substantiating him (which, in a simplified manner, is the teaching of Hegel and even the Talmud: do- ing takes precedence over being, which does not create itself except in creating—what? Perhaps anything: how this anything is judged de- pends on time, on what happens, on what does not happen: what we call historical factors, history, without however looking to history for the last judgment). But if the written work produces and substantiates the writer, once created it bears witness only to his dissolution, his disappearance, his defection and, to express it more brutally, his death, which itself can never be definitely verified: for it is a death that can never produce any verification.

Thus, before the work, the writer does not yet exist; after the work, he is no longer there: which means that his existence is open to ques- tion—and we call him an "author!" It would be more correct to call him an "actor," the ephemeral character who is born and dies each

---

* Editor's Note: This text was first published in English at the end of *Vicious Circles: Two Fictions and "After the Fact"* (1985), based on the *Après Coup précédé par Le ressassement éternel* (Editions de Minuit: Paris, 1983), which itself expanded the edition of *Le Ressassement éternel* (1951) by adding this essay.

487

evening in order to make himself extravagantly seen, killed by the performance that makes him visible—that is, without anything of his own or hiding anything in some secret place.

From the "not yet" to the "no longer"—this is the path of what we call the writer, not only his time, which is always suspended, but what brings him to life through an interrupted becoming.

Has anyone noticed that Valéry, in imagining the utopia of Monsieur Teste, was the most romantic of men without knowing it? In his notes he writes innocently: "*Ego*—I dreamed of a being who had the greatest gifts—not to do anything with them, having assured himself [how?] that he had them. I told Mallarmé about it one Sunday on the quai d'Orsay." Now, what is this being—a musician, a philosopher, a writer, an artist, a Sovereign—who *can* do everything and yet does nothing? None other than the romantic genius, an I so superior to itself and its creation that it proudly forbids itself to be shown, a God then who refuses to be a demiurge, the infinite All Powerful One who will not condescend to be limited by a work, no matter how sublime (cf. Duchamp). Or else, it is in the most ordinary things that the extraordinary ones must be felt: no masterpiece (what poverty, what mediocrity in this master; to accept nothing less than being the greatest, the highest); but if Teste betrays himself, it is through the mystery of banality, through what makes him *appear* as someone unperceived. (I do not intend to diminish Valéry by revealing the adolescent naiveté of his central project, and even less so because on top of this there is the demand of extreme modesty: the "genius" can only hide himself, efface himself; he cannot leave behind any marks, cannot do anything that could show him to be superior in what he does and even in what he is; the divine incognito, the hidden God, who does not hide himself in order to make the one who finally finds him more praiseworthy, but because he is ashamed of being God or knowing himself to be God—or, furthermore, God must remain unknown to himself, or else we would give him a Self, a self in our own image. I don't know if Freud, the unbeliever, thought that he had made the unconscious his God.)

After this parenthesis, I return to the problem. If the written word, which is always impersonal, changes, dismisses, and abolishes the writer as writer, if not the man or the writing subject (others will say that it enriches him, that it makes him more than he was before, that he is created by it—from which comes the traditional notion of the author—or else that it has no other end except to allow him to use his mind—Valéry again), yes, if the work, in its operation, no matter how slight it is, is so destructive as to engage the operator in the equivalent of suicide, then how can he turn back (ah, the guilty Orpheus) to what he believes he is leading into the light—to judge it, to consider it, to recognize himself in it and, in the end, to make himself the privileged reader of it, the principle commentator or simply the zealous helper who gives or imposes his version, resolves the enigma, reveals the secret and authoritatively interrupts (we are, after all, talking about the author) the hermeneutic chain, since he claims to be the adequate interpreter, the first or the last?

Noli me legere. Does this impossibility have an aesthetic, ethical, or ontological value? We would have to look at it more closely. It is a polite appeal, a strange warning, a prohibition that has always let itself be violated already. "Please do not…" If the work is comparable to Eurydice, the request—the very humble request—not to turn around to look at it (or to read it) is just as anguishing for it, the one who knows that the "law" will make it disappear (or at least illuminate it to such a degree that it will dissolve in the light) that it is a temptation for the enchanter whose whole desire is to persuade himself that there is someone beautiful following him, rather than a futile simulacrum or a void wrapped in vain words. Even Mallarmé, the most secretive and discrete of poets, gives some hints as to the manner in which the *Coup de dés* should be read. Even Kafka read his stories to his sisters, sometimes even to a public audience, which, finally, does not mean that he read them for himself as pieces of writing—an affirmation of writing—but dangerously agreed to lend them his voice, to substitute for the legend (the enigma of what must be read) the living and speaking evidence of a diction and a presence that imposed its own meaning—or at least a meaning.

Such a temptation is necessary. To give in to it is perhaps inevitable. I remember the story, *Madame Edwarda.* I was surely one of the first to read it and to be convinced (overwhelmed to the point of silence) of what was unique about this work (only several pages long) and what set it above all literature, and in such a way that there could never be any word of commentary attached to it. I exchanged a few emotional words with Georges Bataille, not in the way you talk to an author about a book of his you admire, but in order to make him understand that such an encounter was enough for my entire life, just as the fact of having written the book should have been enough for his. All this happened during the worst days of the Occupation. This small book—the most minimal of books, published under a pseudonym and read by just a few people—was destined to sink clandestinely into the probable ruin of each of us (author, reader)—with no traces left of this remarkable event. As we know, things turned out differently.

Even so, without overstepping the bounds of tact, I would like to add something. Later, when the war was over and Georges Bataille's life had also changed, he was asked to republish the book—or, more accurately, to allow it to be given a real publication. To my great horror, he told me one day that he wanted to write a sequel to *Madame Edwarda* and asked my advice. I felt as though someone had just punched me; I blurted out: "It's impossible. I beg of you, don't touch it." The matter was then dropped, at least between the two of us. It will be remembered that he could not prevent himself from writing a preface under his own name, chiefly to introduce his name, so that he could take responsibility (indirectly) for a piece of writing that was still considered scandalous. But this preface, no matter how important it was, did not in the least undermine the absolute nature of *Madame Edwarda*—nor have the full-scale commentaries it has inspired (particularly the one by Lucette Finas and, more recently, the one by Pierre-Phillipe Jandin). All that can be said, all that I can say myself, is that the reading of this book has probably changed. Admiration, reflection, comparison with other works—the things that perpetuate a book are the very things that flatten it or equalize it; if the book raises up literature, literature reduces it to its own level, no matter what importance we might give it. What remains is the nakedness of the word "writing," a word no less powerful than the feverish revelation of what for one night, and forever after that, was "Madame Edwarda."

Vicious Circles. I have been asked—someone inside me has asked—to communicate with myself, as a way of introducing these two old stories, so old (nearly fifty years old) that, without even taking into account the difficulties I have just expressed, it is not possible for me to know who wrote them, how they were written, and to what unknown urgency they were responding. I remember (it is only a memory and perhaps false) that I was astonishingly cut off from the literature of the time and knew about nothing except what is called classical literature, with nevertheless some inkling of Valéry,

Göethe, and Jean-Paul. Nothing that could have prepared me to write these innocent stories that resound with murderous echoes of the future. There have been commentaries, profound commentaries that I will take care not to comment on myself, about "The Last Word" (1935). This piece was not written for publication. Nevertheless, it did finally appear twelve years later in the series "L'age d'or" edited by Henri Parisot. But, as it happened, this was the last work in the series—which had run out of funds and was about to disappear—and the book was not even sold anywhere (if I am not mistaken). This was a way of remaining faithful to the title. Undoubtedly, to begin writing only to come so quickly to the end (which was the encounter with the last word), meant at least that there was the hope of not making a career, of finding the quickest way to have done with it right at the start (it would be dishonest to forget that, at the same time or in the meantime, I was writing *Thomas the Obscure,* which was perhaps about the same thing, but precisely did not have done with it and, on the contrary, encountered in the search for annihilation (absence) the impossibility of escaping being (presence)—which was not even a contradiction in fact, but the demand of an endlessness that is unhappy even in dying). In this sense, the story was an attempt to short circuit the other book that was being written, in order to overcome that endlessness and reach a silent decision, reach it through a more linear narrative that was nevertheless painfully complex: which is perhaps why (I don't know) there is the sudden convocation of language, the strange resolution to deprive language of its support, the *watchword* (no more restraining or affirmative language, that is to say, no more language—but no: there is still a speech with which to say this and not to say this), the renunciation of the roles of Teacher and Judge—a renunciation that is itself futile—, the Apocalypse finally, the discovery of nothing other than universal ruin, which is completed with the fall of the last Tower, which is no doubt the Tower of Babel, while at the same time the owner is silently thrown outside (the being who has always assured himself of the meaning of the word "own"—apparently God, even though he is a beast), the narrator who has maintained the privilege of the ego, and the simple and marvelous girl, who probably knows everything, in the humblest kind of way.

This kind of synopsis or outline—the paradox of such a story—is chiefly distinguished by recounting the absolute disaster as having taken place, so that the story itself could not have survived either, which makes it impossible or absurd, unless it claims to be a prophetic work, announcing to the past a future that has already arrived or saying what there still is when there is nothing: *there is*, which holds nothingness and blocks annihilation so that it cannot escape its interminable process whose end is repetition and eternity—the vicious circle.

Prophetic also, but for me (today) in a way that is even more inexplicable, since I can only interpret it in the light of the events that came afterwards and were not known until much later, in such a way that this later knowledge does not illuminate but withdraws understanding from the story that seems to have been named—by antiphrasis?—"The Idyll," or the torment of the happy idea (1936). The theme that I recognize first of all, because Camus made it "familiar" several years later—that is, made it the opposite of what he meant—is indicated in the first words: "the stranger." Who is the stranger? There is no adequate definition here. He comes from somewhere else. He is well received, but received according to rules he cannot submit to and which in any event put him to the test—take him to death's door. He himself draws the "moral" from this and explains it to one of the newcomers: "You'll learn that in this house it's hard to be a stranger. You'll also learn that it's not easy to stop being one. If you miss your country, every day you'll find more reasons to miss it. But if you manage to forget it and begin to love your new place, you'll be sent home, and then, uprooted once more, you'll begin a new exile." Exile is neither psychological nor ontological. The exile cannot accommodate himself to his condition, nor to renouncing it, nor to turning exile into a mode of residence. The immigrant is tempted to naturalize himself, through marriage for example, but he continues to be a migrant. In a place where there is no way out, to escape is the demand that restores the call of the outside. Is it a vain attempt? The prison is not a prison. The guards have their weaknesses, unless their negligence does not belong to the make-believe freedom that would be a temptation and an illusion. Likewise, the extreme politeness, even sincere cordiality of those who regretfully apply the law, does not resemble the tranquil and inflexible "correction" which, several years later, caught willing slaves in the trap of their false humanity, slaves who were incapable of recognizing the masked barbarity that temporarily allowed them to live in a reassuring order.

And yet it is difficult not to think about all this after the fact. Impossible not to think of the ridiculous work carried out in the concentration camps, where the condemned transported mountains of stones from one spot to another and then back to the starting place—not for the glory of some pyramid, but to destroy work itself, along with the sad workers. This happened at Auschwitz, this happened at the Gulag. Which would tend to show that if the imaginary runs the risk of one day becoming real, it is because it has its own rather strict limits and that it can easily foresee the worst because the worst is always the simplest and it always repeats itself.

But I don't think that "The Idyll" can be interpreted as the reading of an already menacing future. History does not withhold meaning, no more than meaning, which is always ambiguous—plural—can be reduced to its historical realization, even the most tragic and the most enormous. That is because the story does not explain itself. If it is the tension of a secret around which it seems to elaborate itself and which immediately declares itself without being elucidated, it only announces its own movement, which can lay the groundwork for the game of deciphering and interpretation, but it remains a *stranger* to itself. From this, it seems to me, and even though it seems to open up the unhappy possibilities of a life without hope, the story as such remains light, untroubled, and of a clarity that neither weighs down nor obscures the pretension of a hidden or serious meaning. The questioning it would imply, I am told, could, in conjunction with the title, be expressed in different forms, all of them necessarily naive and simplistic: for example, why in such a world is the question of the masters' happiness so important and in the end still unresolved? There are appearances, there are only appearances, and how to believe in them, how to call them anything but what they are? Or, is a society which admits that the most unhappy episodes come from itself—either because of this or in spite of this—at heart idyllic? These are some questions, but they are too general to call forth answers, or not to remain questions in spite of the answers they are given. The story contains them perhaps, but on condition that it not be reduced through them to a content, to anything that can be expressed in any other way.

In all respects, it is an unhappy story. But, precisely, as a story, which says all it has to say in saying it, or, better, which announces itself as the clarity that comes both before and as a condition of the serious or ambiguous meaning it also transcribes, it itself is the idyll, the little idol that is unjust and injurious to the very thing it utters, happy in the misfortune it portends and that it endlessly threatens to turn into a lure. This is the law of the story, its happiness and, because of it, its unhappiness, not because, as Valéry reproached Pascal, a beautiful form would necessarily destroy the horror of every tragic truth and make it bearable, even delicious (catharsis). But, before all distinctions between form and content, between signifier and signified, even before the division between utterance and the uttered, there is the unqualifiable Saying, the glory of a "narrative voice" that speaks clearly, without ever being obscured by the opacity or the enigma or the terrible horror of what it communicates.

That is why, in my opinion—and in a way different from the one that led Adorno to decide with absolute correctness—I will say there can be no fiction-story about Auschwitz (I am alluding to *Sophie's Choice*). The need to bear witness is the obligation of a testimony that can only be given—and given only in the singularity of each individual—by the impossible witnesses—the witnesses of the impossible—; some have survived, but their survival is no longer life, it is the break from living affirmation, the attestation that the good that is life (not narcissistic life, but life for others) has undergone the decisive blow that leaves nothing intact. From this it would seem that all narration, even all poetry, has lost the foundation on which another language could be raised—through the extinction of the happiness of speaking that lurks in even the most mediocre silence. Forgetfulness no doubt does its work and allows for works to be made again. But to this forgetfulness, the forgetting of an event in which every possibility was drowned, there is an answer from a failing memory without memories, and the immemorial haunts this memory in vain. Humanity as a whole had to die through the trial of some of its members, (those who incarnate life itself, almost an entire people, a people that has been promised an eternal presence). This death still endures. And from this comes the obligation never again to die only once, without however allowing repetition to inure us to the always essential ending.

I return to "The Idyll," a story from before Auschwitz, a story nevertheless of a wandering that does not end with death and which that death cannot darken, since it ends with the affirmation of the "the superb and victorious sky," a stranger in a strange country, saying that no matter what happens, the light of what is said, even if it is in the unhappiest of words, does not stop shining, in the same way that light and airy radiance always transform the dark night, the night without stars. As if the darkness had become—is this a boon, is this a curse?—yes, had become the shining of the interminable day, the light of the first day.

A story from before Auschwitz. No matter when it is written, every story from now on will be from before Auschwitz. Perhaps life continues. Let us remember the end of *The Metamorphosis*. Right after Gregor Samsa has died in agony and solitude, everything is reborn, and his sister, even though she was the most compassionate of all, gives herself up to the hope of renewal that her young body promises her. Kafka himself thought he threw a shadow on the sun and that once he was gone his family would be happier. So he died, and then what happened? There was only a short time left; almost everyone he loved died in those camps which, no matter what their names, all had the same name: Auschwitz.

I cannot hope for "The Idyll" or "The Last Word" to be read from this perspective (this non-perspective). And yet, even wordless death remains something to be thought about—perhaps endlessly, to the very end. "A voice comes from the other shore. A voice interrupts the words of what has already been said." (Emmanuel Levinas).

Translators' Notes

NOTE ON *THOMAS THE OBSCURE*
(David Lewis Edition)

This translation presents the second version of *Thomas l'obscur* (the only version available at this time). The original work was designated as a novel (*roman*), the revision as a *récit*. Three-quarters of the bulk of the original disappeared in the process.

It is tempting, in this context, to give away some of the secrets of the complex rhetoric of this rich work, to analyze them,* to beg the reader to realize the fact that much of the discomfort he will experience in confronting this work is due to other factors than the translator's failure to iron out difficult points. Suffice it to say that the translator's energies and abilities have been taxed principally to respect and retain the author's level of difficulty, of challenge to the reader, to translate at once the clarity and the opacity of the original.

Robert Lamberton

✦

NOTE ON *THOMAS THE OBSCURE*
(Station Hill Edition)

Thomas and the Possibility of Translation

Still, one must translate (because one must): at the very least one must begin by searching out in the context of *what* tradition of language, in *what sort* of discourse the invention of a form that is new is situated—a form that is eternally characterized by newness and nevertheless necessarily participates in a relationship of connectedness or of rupture with other manners of speaking. There scholarship intervenes, but it bears less on the nearly unrecoverable and always malleable facts of culture than on the texts themselves, witnesses that do not lie if one decides to remain faithful to them.

L'Entretien infini, 119-120

Blanchot is writing here of the difficulty of approaching the language of Heraclitus. The pretext of his observations on translation is the principle developed by Clémence Ramnoux that Heraclitus' language remains largely untranslatable because of the subsequent formation (completed in the age of Plato and Aristotle) of a basic vocabulary of abstractions that constitute fundamental building blocks of our language and thought.[1] Heraclitus, no less than Homer, speaks a language which is foreign to our own on the levels of vocabulary, of semantic fields, of the relationship of the word to that which it designates.

By the Fourth Century BC we (Europeans) had become linguistic dualists. *Signifiant* and *signifié* were forever divorced, the arbitrariness of their association exposed.[2] Nevertheless, from before the moment of Socrates—in the age which lies in his enormous shadow (since we see him invariably illuminated from a proximal source, himself a myth projected back into the Fifth Century by Plato and Xenophon and constituting the brightness that creates the darkness around and beyond him)—from before Socrates we have a few precious verbal artifacts expressing, manifesting the state of language before the *felix lapsus* of the Greek enlightenment.

Subsequent texts are susceptible to translation. The languages in which they originally became manifest constitute arbitrary wrappings applied to a core of ideas. The situation recalls a science fiction film of the Forties in which substantial, corporeal, but utterly transparent (and therefore invisible) monsters were throwing the world into disorder. Once captured and subdued they revealed their form when coated with *papier mâché*. Any other plastic medium would have served the same expressive function: fly paper, clay, perhaps even spray-paint. These interchangeable media would have expressed the same fortuitously imperceptible outline: the bug eyes, the claws, the saber-toothed-tiger fangs.

The truest Platonist among translators, Thomas Taylor, expressed the relationship with characteristic clarity and good conscience in 1787:

> That words, indeed, are no otherwise valuable than as subservient to things, must surely be acknowledged by every

---

[1] These ideas are probably more familiar to English readers in the form they take in the work of Eric Havelock, who explored the problems posed by the language of Homer and the Presocratics in his *Preface to Plato*.

[2] The Neoplatonists and the Middle Ages may have forgotten that this was the case, but this quasi-mythic formulation of our intellectual history still retains its basic truth.

liberal mind, and will alone be disputed by him who has spent the prime of his life, and consumed the vigour of his understanding, in verbal criticisms and grammatical trifles. And, if this is the case, every lover of truth will only study a language for the purpose of procuring the wisdom it contains; and will doubtless wish to make his native language the vehicle of it to others. For, since all truth is eternal, its nature can never be altered by transposition, though, by this means, its dress may be varied, and become less elegant and refined. Perhaps even this inconvenience may be remedied by sedulous cultivation…. [*Concerning the Beautiful*, Introduction]

Maurice Blanchot has not, to my knowledge, addressed himself publicly to the problem of translating Maurice Blanchot. I have inevitably wondered what he would think of my efforts, though I have respectfully refrained from entering into a dialogue with him.[3] In the absence of any concrete evidence, I imagine the author of the works of Maurice Blanchot responding to the idea, the fact of the translation of his work (whether mine or another) with that "Nietzschean hilarity" Jeffrey Mehlman sees as characteristic of him—the dialectical twin of the austerity of his prose—and that this imaginary confrontation might be summed up in a phrase from *Celui qui ne m'accompagnait pas* equally evoked by Mehlman: "This gaiety passed into the space I thought I occupied and dispersed me" ("Orphée scripteur," *Poétique* 20 [1974]).

To do justice to the problem of translating Blanchot, to provide a theoretical substructure to lend credibility to the enterprise, would require the formulation of a methodology antithetical to (but not exclusive of) that of Thomas Taylor. This second position would insist upon the absolute opacity of language, on the impossibility of translation, on the incorporeality of the bug-eyed monsters and the absurdity of the effort to reclothe them in some new plastic medium. It would emphasize the integrity of each word, each phrase, each volume of the original text and the necessary triviality of the effort to create some equivalent for it. It would, finally, rush between the legs of the Socratic colossus and take refuge in the absolute refusal of the duality of language, planting itself firmly beyond the fall, beyond the radiance.

---

[3] This is, however, not impossible. Lydia Davis corresponded with Blanchot regarding her beautiful translation of *L'Arrêt de mort* (Station Hill Press, 1978). She has told me that—not surprisingly—he insisted on the importance of her contribution and on the fact that *Death Sentence* was, finally, her book.

This methodology would, of course, be no methodology at all. It would not open up a possible mode of action, but humbly, insistently, it would join hands with the viable methodology of Thomas Taylor to undermine and redeem the good conscience of that methodology. On the level of application, it would illuminate (but not solve) the major problem that confronts the translator of Blanchot (and not uniquely of Blanchot: one is tempted to say of any text since Joyce, since Mallarmé, since Nietzsche). This is the problem of the *unit* to be translated. Word, phrase, sentence, paragraph, work: all demand to be rendered as unities, one enclosed within the other without the sacrifice of their integrity. And then there is the bug-eyed monster—Thomas Taylor would call it the eternal thought. Whether or not it exists, it makes its demands, it disrupts the world.

This is the point I have reached in the understanding of my task. Blanchot is not Heraclitus but *Thomas l'Obscur* is more than coincidentally related to Héraclite l'obscur—*ho skoteinos, obscurus*, an epithet used in antiquity to separate *this* Heraclitus from others of the same name, such as the allegorical commentator on Homer. Both epithets are probably developments from *ainiktes*, "the riddler," applied to the Ephesian philosopher by the third century satirist Timon of Phlius (so Geoffrey Kirk). Blanchot himself insists on the epithet and its force which extends beyond the satirist's trivial slur to indicate the fundamental impulse to "make the obscurity of language respond to the clarity of things" (*L'Entretien infini*, 122). As he goes on to project the heritage of Heraclitus' mode of discourse, expressed in the figure of Socrates himself, Blanchot (as so often in his critical writings) illuminates the method of his own fiction: "...Heraclitus then becomes the direct predecessor and as if the first incarnation of the inspired *bavard,* inopportunely and prosaically divine, whose merit, as Plato claims—and surely it is a merit of the first order—consisted in the circularity of his undertakings, which 'by thousands of revolutions and without advancing a step would always return to the same point'" (*L'Entretien infini*, 125). Surely this is the same *bavard* whose austere, gay tone is heard in the belated incarnation of the narrative voice of *Thomas l'obscur.*

What other mysteries does that infuriating title hide? A reviewer of the first edition of this translation pointed to Cocteau's *Thomas l'imposteur* (Naomi Greene in *Novel* 8 [1975]). Perhaps she was correct. While working on the translation I considered every Thomas from the magical evangelist to the master of all the Schoolmen and the unfortunate Archbishop of Canterbury. I find it hard to believe that the second element of the title does not deliberately echo Thomas Hardy's title, and beyond that that the gravedigger scene of the fifth chapter of *Thomas l'obscur* does not echo the arrested burial of Jude's children, and specifically this tableau:

> A man with a shovel in his hands was attempting to earth in the
> common grave of the three children, but his arm was held back
> by an expostulating woman who stood in the half-filled hole.

But the very ambiguity of the status of these "references" constitutes an element of Blanchot's deliberate smokescreen to foil the efforts of both reader and translator, both condemned to try to determine "in the context of *what* tradition of language, of *what sort* of discourse" his own invention is situated.

The reviewer mentioned above was kind enough to describe this translation as "a labor of love." I am deeply grateful to her for that description. For this new edition I have attempted to articulate some of the presuppositions of that labor, from the cooler perspective of eight years' distance. I hope that, in the spirit of Blanchot's essay on Heraclitus, I have remained faithful to *the text itself* and maintained its integrity as a witness.

Robert Lamberton
February, 1981

NOTE ON *DEATH SENTENCE*

This translation follows the first edition of *L'Arrêt de Mort* (1948). In the Second edition (1971), the brief final section was deleted by the author.

Lydia Davis

✦

NOTE ON *WHEN THE TIME COMES*

Like other works of Maurice Blanchot, this novel is rife with syntactical and semantic difficulties. Often, however, in translating his work, to clarify is to simplify and to betray. The challenge for the translator, then, is to write the book in English with an equivalent of Blanchot's limpid obscurity.

I would like to thank P. Adams Sitney and Paul Auster for taking the time to read over this translation and point out the moments when the prose became either too limpid or too obscure.

Lydia Davis

NOTE ON *THE GAZE OF ORPHEUS*

The challenge of translating Blanchot's work follows inevitably from the brilliance and complexity of his thought and style: the translator, a lonely sort of acrobat, becomes confused in a labyrinth of paradox, or climbs a pyramid of dependent clauses and has to invent a way down from it in his own language. The challenge, though, is not only to the translator, but also to the text: now it undergoes the closest of examinations, and every word is ferreted for its meaning. In some sense the text and the translator are locked in struggle—"I attacked that sentence, it resisted me, I attacked another, it eluded me"—a struggle in which, curiously, when the translator wins, the text wins too, and when the translator loses, what wins is the demon inhabiting the space between languages, champion of the inviolability of each language. And the demon says, in Blanchot's words, "The translator is guilty of a greater impiety. Enemy of God, he intends to rebuild the Tower of Babel."

The translator: "He lives on nothing but alms" (Valery Larbaud). Peculiar outcast, ghost in the world of literature, recreating in another form something already created, creating and not creating, writing words that are his own and not his own, writing a work not original to him, composing with utmost pains and without recognition of his pains or the fact that the composition really is his own. "A writer of singular originality precisely where he seems to have no claim to any. He is the secret master of the difference between languages..." (Blanchot). And courageous, for he must have the courage to destroy if he is to create.

The act of translation: the "idea" takes off in wild flight, and the translator pursues it every way he can, though even once it is caught, it may slip away again as he tries to bend it into another language: the soul of the text crossing from one body to another, expelled by a sneeze for one dangerous moment... Often what is contained between the first capital letter of a sentence and the final period is a complex problem, an entire project. Then the period comes to represent for the translator a moment during which he cannot be assaulted. He enters the next sentence, and he is entering another hazardous territory.

The translated work: curiously unlocated, an odd non-being. This is not an American work, and not a French work, but a version in

English of a French work. The language here approximating another language, the words here in some sense pieced together—since *these* words and this thought were not born together, since these words have been imposed on this thought. And there are problems special to Blanchot's thought, among them: *récit* ("narrative," "account") as Blanchot uses it has a meaning deliberately distinct from that of *histoire* ("story," "narrative")—perhaps in its greater emphasis on the telling, the recital of events true or false—and here that distinction is preserved in the differentiation between "tale" and "story"; and Blanchot's *neutre* could be, almost equally, "neuter" or "neutral"—but "neuter" is closer to what seems to be a specifically grammatical reference.

And part of the idea is lost when it loses its own words: a word such as *manque* in French—both "lack" and "defect"—becomes in English either "lack" or "defect". The word *ouverture*—"opening" and "overture"—becomes one or the other. *Etre* is both "being" and "to be," as *écrire* is "to write" and "the act of writing" in general, though *écriture,* too, is "writing": "the act of writing" and "the thing written." The same problem in the opposite direction: a word like "work," which must stand in for both *oeuvre,* "work of art or literature," and *travail,* "labor."

When the French was particularly rich in meaning, the English had to be poorer, though often the correspondence was direct enough so that perhaps little was lost. Beyond the problems common to all translations of layered and much-meditated works, however, Blanchot's work contains its own extraordinary ambiguities—some that have baffled everyone called in to help, though reasonable solutions were eventually found. Among the meticulously critical readers of the book in manuscript were P. Adams Sitney, its Editor, who took it to heart as much as the translator did, and Michael Coffey, who voluntarily dedicated his time and skill as copyeditor to giving the book its finishing touches. Paul Auster deserves special thanks for his constant encouragement and thoughtful advice, and for first pointing the way to the works of Maurice Blanchot. Finally, warmest appreciation goes to Robert Lamberton, himself an experienced translator of Blanchot, for the hard and patient work he did on the manuscript. Checking each essay sentence by sentence against the French, he questioned everything he found unclear or believed to be wrong, suggested alternatives which were most often adopted, caught several omissions of a phrase or a whole sentence, and occasionally rewrote an extremely difficult and complex sentence so that it came closer to the coherence of the original. He was the book's essential critic.

Lydia Davis
February, 1981

Afterword

Publishing Blanchot in America
A Metapoetic View

After two decades of publishing the writing of Maurice Blanchot, we find ourselves still standing at the threshold. Slowly—very slowly—we may be learning the meanings of our own commitments. The decision to publish Blanchot has seemed at times fully conscious, perhaps willful, and yet curiously receptive, something unforeseeable, indeed inseparable from (our sense of) the nature of the work itself, its precarious adventure *on the edge*. In many ways publishing this most mysterious of writers is hardly different from reading him: one is always at the beginning of knowing what it is one is doing. This is not a matter of doubting the importance—the "literary value"—of the work; quite the contrary, we only grow more certain that this is work of the first order. To read it is to be changed by it—each time one reads it. It makes little difference in this regard whether one is reading the same book over again or an entirely new work—"this unique reading, each time the first reading and each time the only reading" (to quote Blanchot's "Reading"). This work challenges, alters, opens the meaning of reading itself, and therefore of publishing, proclaiming, defining…. In this way it stands with the great transformative works of any tradition—we might choose the "Prophetic Books" of William Blake as our exemplar here—which are also *beyond* tradition, indeed, subversive of traditional force itself while carrying forward its vital current.

To see ourselves thus at the threshold—the *limen*—has encouraged us these twenty years to discover a certain humility before a grand task, the presentation of work that chastens the very thinking it inspires, and indeed frustrates any form of aggrandizement. It has, frankly, taken us these two decades to discover how to read it—a confession we may have to make yearly, and each decade, such is the textual vista one enjoys at its threshold. In short, to know this work as publisher/reader is to wish to serve it, appropriately. To perform the function of Guardians of the Portal of an authentic Mystery translates more simply as custodians of the door—at a minimum, offering unfettered access, keeping the door swinging open (it closes automatically and too easily). Our position at the *limen* earns us no special rights; and we are not specialists or advocates, certainly not scholars or critics, but, frankly, poets, readers, accepting the responsibility to maintain access. So we may be forgiven for advancing the prejudice of our perspective—a penchant for reporting the *liminal*. In celebrating two decades of publishing Blanchot with this combined edition, we wish to suggest that our angle of viewing may have a truth in it that coincides with something true about the work of Maurice Blanchot—its threshold nature, its liminality. And this "truth" leaves us—publishers and readers alike—standing on the same verge, book in hand.

And a very large book it is.[1] Of Station Hill's eight Blanchot books, it contains six complete and most of a seventh, in English translations here by Lydia Davis, Paul Auster and Robert Lamberton, all extraordinary writers in their own right. When we published the first book, *Death Sentence*, no one at the trade book level was publishing him and very few Americans were reading him in any depth.[2] Although occasionally bookstores reported strong interest—the St. Marks Bookstore exulted over an avid "cult following" of *Death Sentence* on the Lower East Side of Manhattan—a Blanchot readership took its own time in developing. No small number have wondered with Geoffrey Hartman "why it took so long to introduce him to the English-speaking world," particularly given Blanchot's enormous influence on the Continent, expressed in Hartman's "extravagant claim" in the 1981 Preface to *The Gaze of Orpheus and Other Literary Essays*:

> When we come to write the history of criticism for the 1940 to 1980 period, it will be found that Blanchot, together with Sartre, made French "discourse" possible, both in its relentlessness and its acuity. That "discourse," like many French things, is not to everyone's taste, yet it could prove more powerful and persistent than the notion of taste itself.

Certainly getting beyond limitations of "taste," as well as many species of "interpretation" and "deconstruction," is fundamental to an appropriately open reading of Blanchot. The more one reads him, the more evident is his impact on European writing and on the relatively small number of American writers sensitive to European discourse. Many wonder if such a writer could ever truly take root, so to speak, in the American literary terrain. Blanchot's work seems a far cry from concerns "in the American grain" (to borrow William Carlos Williams' defining phrase)—and yet, the issue is by no means either simple or clear. No doubt his fortunes in American readership owe a lot to certain waves of current interest in the thought of Heidegger, Lévinas, Bataille, Derrida and a complex and elusive range of writers in one way or another sympathetic to the project of Deconstruction. In general Blanchot's readers owe an undeniable debt to this rich and endlessly problematic lineage, which is (necessarily) so uneasy with itself. It is of course mind-bendingly difficult to say anything in this matter that is neither simplistic nor reductive. Yet we are here writing from a viewpoint of American readership, itself unsettled, often at odds within its numerous and nuanced crosscurrents, and ever in the midst of a struggle between one or another brand of Protectionism and Free Trade advocacy. The question we wish to pose is, literary/philosophical politics aside, can we move toward a radically new view of a "possible Blanchot" specific to America—a practice of writing/reading somehow *in the American grain*? Such a question might well be most useful left as a question—i.e., an invitation.

This is, after all, an American book. And that declaration is meant as an act of clearing in the spirit of generosity Blanchot indeed has urged us toward. More than one of his translators has gotten the message that the work they do in the name of translation is *now their work.* This freeing message also has a bite: the translator's responsibility to American reading. This is hardly a matter of trying to please anyone or meet a standard. What it has been a matter of—for which we are grateful—is the exercise of "native" powers belonging to these particular writers, mysteriously appropriate to Blanchot's work, now somehow also *their* work, which has stood the test of time. For all the difficulties of meeting the astonishing range of resonance in the French text— notorious instances include reverberations of a word over many pages, such as *oeuvre,* unfolding its nuances and nuanced contrary, *désoeuvrement*—the simple truth is Blanchot *reads* in English.

Translated text of this order takes root in an*other* native ground in many ways—adoption into curricula, acceptance as "literary classic" by educated readers generally, influence on writers and artists.... Perhaps the most elusive—yet deepest—kind of "rooting" is the *further life* a work receives through the work of other writers and artists. This is hard to track, but when a work comes to further life by showing up inside a new work, its own direct power can be illuminated. For instance, a text like *Thomas the Obscure* freshly reappears, revealing certain un-charted dimensions, in the work of artist Gary Hill, particularly his veritable invocation of the *récit* (including the physical pages of the book) in the single-channel video *Incidence of Catastrophe* as well as in multimedia installations like *Beacon (Two Versions of the Imaginary)*. This *sui generis* "reading" of Blanchot is but one instance of his incursion into North American arts, and certainly there is a complex trail to follow through poetry, fiction and a range of discursive modalities.

Yet there are deeper issues not fully embraced in thinking about transplantation of a work or the related matter of its influence. Amongst the many ports of entry into Blanchot's work, perhaps most important for us, from an American perspective, has been a gradually emerging sense of his contribution to what one might call the *possibility of writing beyond*—that is, writing that goes beyond models, genres, contexts, and any limiting concept of what writing is. It is not entirely satisfying to assign such an issue to a conventional intellectual domain, although the closest is perhaps *poetics* in the broadest sense; yet, in the interest of granting inquiry a further scope and scale, we resort to a notional in-novation under the name *metapoetics*, the principles by which writing is beyond itself, the practice of the unknown, the poetics of (im)possibility. (We retain in *meta-* the double root of "beyond" and "middle," the poetics of what goes beyond and yet is always in the very middle.)[3] We are thinking here of a characteristic operative prin-ciple in the innermost workings of the Blanchot text that bears a deep (but not necessarily a surface) kinship with innovative American writ-ing—especially poetry and especially of the second half of this century. This is a matter of the greatest importance and difficulty, concerning the very transformative force at the center of writing itself. Blanchot's own invocation of this transformative force is embedded in specific con-texts and subtle processes of distinction. To attempt here to characterize (and inevitably simplify) this "operative principle" is of course to risk reducing it to literary method, procedure, technique, or style or to over-state one aspect of this complex writer, when what one wishes is to attend the imageless vision at the heart of an infinite conversation.

Our experience of American poetry over the past few decades—the necessary context of our observations here—has pointed us toward a metapoetic possibility in the limitless ways that poetry redefines it-self—redefines, that is, language, the very possibility of language, and

everything that we reflexively know and are through language, with
the implication that being itself is at stake. Within this metapoetic view,
poetry's tendency toward radical self-redefinition can be tracked in
any number of ways, yet in some essential sense these ways lead back
to something like a root poetic impulse, showing up in the way a poem
turns upon its occasion. This meaning of "verse" says that in its specific
turning a poem performs most essentially what it is.

Among the many sources of inspiration for this view is the poet
Charles Olson,[4] not only his famous poetic principle of "projective
verse" or "composition by field," with its call for energetic integrity
in writing,[5] but his special use of the eighth century Chinese alchemi-
cal text translated as *The Secret of the Golden Flower:* "That which exists
through itself is what is called Meaning." For Olson this is a fundamental principle of poetics. Accordingly, we might say that a poem is a
"meaningful" projection of a certain force turning upon its occasion,
wherein it exists through itself. The emphasis is on an always immedi-
ate/mediate self-defining torsion, a middle zone that is instantly yet
radically (in-standingly yet rootedly) *open*, the instance of itself beyond any particular definition of itself. It is as though a vertical *axis*
moves within any "point instance" of the text *and* any moment of true
reading. The turning upon the occasion—a self-composing field linked,
for Olson, with a projection through and to an actual environment,
moving energetically toward the reader—is a turning upon an invisible axis in the poem, in language at its most intensely alive.[6]

This sense of axiality, as the principle of certain texts that remain
radically open, can be illuminating to consider in relation to the works
of a range of American poets[7] and, to an impressive degree, to Blanchot's
work from *Thomas the Obscure* on. Axiality, in our view, is at work in
the unfolding of texts that might not otherwise seem related—at work,
that is, from the perspective of the text's emergence, the experience of
its reader, or the internal dynamics of the text itself. Metapoetically,
the axial implicitly involves the granting of a certain permission and
the acceptance of a certain responsibility to allow each event of language or step in thought to reconfigure the work at large, even as it
takes its place within it. The thinker/poet/writer allows himself to be
startled, pause, and respond to the not yet drawn-out significance of the
very thought he has just articulated. Axiality is metapoetically instrumental in transgressing established, time-honored boundaries, including not

only the boundaries of poetic conventions, genres (poetry, fiction, philosophical discourse) or even the concrete poetics of a specific work, but the very distinction between writer and reader. In a work of high axial intensity, reader, in some measure, metamorphoses into poet, faced with orientational choice at any moment, required to define and declare the very context of choice. The identities of writer/reader/text have become liminal to each other. The poet/reader's journey is direct but never straight, called again and again to turn on a dime as a condition of moving "forward."

The force of the axial is to drive reading into the open center of attention, into the intensive "presentness" of itself, as if the text, through being read, were present to itself, facing (into, back around to) itself, in touch with something as enigmatic and as raw as its own source.[8] The axial destabilizes thinking, disorients it, but in such a way as to bring attention to thinking as the process of orientation itself, which allows it to become self-orienting. One reads it with the whole of one's living awareness, including the body, as if what one sees is on a verge, precarious, never separate from its own falling, one's own falling. The axial embodies the instant reversibility of anything thinkable, and when a space of stillness awakens in the axial moment like the eye of the storm, it is the storm that sees, as a reader, the possibility of reading, the space of liminality. This seeing is reorienting—a *radial* orientation, extending in all textual directions at once, so that through the axial the text, possible language, is continually revisioned. In an intensely axial moment—of proprioceptive disorientation—the whole of a text undergoes reorientation, as does the body of the writer's work at large and, indeed, the entire scope of its intentionality.

In one of the episodes of *Thomas the Obscure*, the relationship of reader to text literally inverts: text reads reader. Under the pressure of a liminality that binds reader to what he reads, Thomas' reading psyche mutates until it begins to manifest the enigmatic properties that it finds in the book he is reading—like a language with no bottom, rooted in the absolute, a spontaneous cabala opening in the words on the page *intensively read*. The strange reciprocity brought on by entrainment to the Other—something like Blake's principle that we become what we behold—is carried in *Thomas* to a transmogrifying extreme worthy of Blake himself. Thomas lost in the outside void that is infinitely deep inside the word, a kind of demonic encounter, is also like Blake's evocation of self-loss in non-entity ("There is a Void, outside of existence, which if entered into/Englobes itself & becomes a Womb, such was Albion's Couch...").[9] Thomas the reader, on the verge and beyond, is one possible result of an encounter with the liminal.

So an axial art is an art of torsion and pause, of self-interruption, a site of catastrophe. In the space of pause there is turbulence at the center of which is attentive stillness, an axis of attention, evoked by T.S. Eliot as "the still point of the turning world" (*Four Quartets*). When reading/awareness turning upon that center (the experience may be turmoil or dizzying momentum or something quite unknown) turns back to itself, it may induce a still point within reading in which the nature of reading is radically available to itself, open beyond characterization. Here is Blanchot's sense of the axial in "Literature and the Right to Death," a defining moment for his own work and for that of a great many others. Blanchot refers to

> an *ultimate ambiguity* whose strange effect is to attract literature to *an unstable point where it can indiscriminately change both its meaning and its sign.*
>
> This ultimate vicissitude keeps the work in suspense in such a way that it can choose whether to take on a positive or a negative value and, as though it were *pivoting invisibly around an invisible axis*, enter the daylight of affirmations or the back-light of negations, without its style, genre, or subject being accountable for the *radical transformation*. Neither the content of the words nor their form is involved here. Whether the work is obscure or clear, poetry or prose, insignificant, important, whether it speaks of a pebble or of God, there is something in it that does not depend on its qualities and that deep within itself is always *in the process of changing the work from the ground up*. It is as though in the very heart of literature and language, beyond the visible movements that transform them, a point of instability were reserved, *a power to work substantial metamorphoses*, a power capable of changing everything about it without changing anything. [*Emphasis added.*]

The sense of "ultimate vicissitude [that] keeps the work in suspense" could point to Keats' "Negative Capability" or the terrifying openness wrought by "poetic torsion" in Blake's "prophetic" books.[10] Charles Olson's "Projective Verse" and his own *Maximus Poems* or Robert Duncan's *Passages* display this axial turning, this pivoting about in place, where the force of one's own emergent utterance strikes one as it appears. And for the reader of Blanchot, the expression of the movement of thought itself —one's own thought, or the text's—often shimmers with an energy born of the mind's alertness and capacity to be conditioned by its own act. Blanchot speculates on the sources of this energy as perhaps deriving from a deeply situated property of language itself:

> Could it be that the meaning of a word introduces something else into the word along with it, something which, although it protects the precise signification of the word and does not threaten that signification, is capable of completely modifying the meaning and modifying the material value of the word? Could there be *a force at once friendly and hostile hidden in the intimacy of speech*, a weapon intended to build and to destroy, which would *act behind signification rather than upon signification*? Do we have to suppose a meaning for the meaning of words that, while determining that meaning, also surrounds this determination with *an ambiguous indeterminacy that wavers between yes and no*? [*Emphasis added.*]

What is the nature of the (re)orientation the axial makes possible? This all-important question is also ultimately difficult, and we must stretch our language to account for it. The potential for axial reorientation is intrinsic to any given text, as it particularly "exists through itself," and thus the sense of reorientation is unique to each instance. Its realization, furthermore, is "animated" (Blanchot's word) through an actual reading. Orientation—in the axial sense always reorientation—implies a certain way of reading, a reading open to the axial, and, speculatively, we would need a "poetics of reading" that might then define something like "reading by field."[11] For orienting does occur in an activated field, larger than the text, and so it is also, and simultaneously, somehow outside the text. Yet this outside remains within the context that is the text in its virtual field, its power to reverberate outward. It is as though the torsional force draws its orientational power up from an "undertime," a time that is always already not time, a still point waiting to (not) happen.

A poetics of reading would help us inquire into the consequences of axiality, including how it initiates us into "other" ways of reading, how, indeed, Blanchot changes reading. The way Blanchot's text instructs in reading is quite different from the way Robert Duncan's or John Cage's instructs, yet the transformations of any one of them may initiate us into the transformational reading that goes beyond all models. At the heart of such reading is always somehow the issue of orientation. In passing through a certain passage we may feel we see anew, as if reading refocuses us, like opening eyes in the back of our head or in our ears. John Cage has spoken of a necessary "unfocus." Axial orientation awakens a state of liminal attention or awareness in liminality—"an ambiguous indeterminacy that wavers between yes and no." Another name for the "space of literature"—*l'espace littéraire*—may indeed be *liminality,* a space that calls a reader beyond ordinary orientation—the bilateral, the binary, the dual—and towards radical orientation—the radial, the plural, the mediate. Does *liminal orientation*—wherein the identity of what is being oriented is, through reading, brought into question—imply *another thinking* peculiar to liminal space? An awkward question gesturing towards a *poetics of thinking.*

The "standing" of Blanchot's work is liminal to all the likely categories. Obviously he has all along favored writers whose works challenge inherited domains—Lautréamont, Sade, Artaud, Kafka, Bataille. And for the most part his lineage of thinkers consists preeminently of those for whom poetics is somehow at the heart of thinking—Nietzsche, Heidegger. He shares with the latter a discovery of thinking *through* the reading of poets whose work embodies ontological orientation—Hölderlin, Rilke. Blanchot's reading of these poets displays a transformation within reading. This reading is not other than his thinking. At its most relentlessly rigorous this thinking eludes paraphrase and summation, as though serious engagement with thinking recalls one all the way to the torsional matrix of its questions. To say to oneself what it is Blanchot thinks on a certain point, one must always return to a site in language and work one's way outward. Recalling a certain thought calls up the trace of something as particular as the climate of a place, the weather of a particular day, an element of the time of the saying, as though thought turned upon its occasion.[12] To think the thought one has to get situated in it.

In Blanchot the poetics overtakes the thinking. This is not the same thing as taking it over, which would imply that somehow thinking is given up in favor of poetry. Obviously this is not so. Rather, an essential poetics, an axiality, may be said to *wed* thinking so as to carry it beyond itself.[13] Among the permissions of the axial are the disjunctive, the paratactic and the fragmentary, which allow a complete movement of thought, small or large, to stand both alone and beside a next thought, each freely turning upon its occasion and at its own non-cumulative rate. There is a silence, a zero point in the voice of thought, on either side. And in place of a totalizing progression, there is a frequent return to beginnings and endings, a rhythm of gaps, silences, spaces, and still points, each moment a withdrawal from time and a return to "under-time." A pulsation of emptiness/emergence—of *begin here, begin now*—replaces both rhythmic and logical expectation. The impulse toward totalization and system-building is frustrated by the sheer freshness of discursive arising. In the history of the intentional fragmentary, power is reabsorbed in the originarity of utterance. Pascal, Nietzsche, Blanchot.

In the mysterious dialogue of the ontological recital, *The One Who Was Standing Apart from Me*, the axial shows up not only in the fragmentary narrative—the identities of the speaker and his "companion," including the latter's "reality status," are richly and ambiguously woven in the telling—but also in the musical force of thinking that manifests in its verbal reverberations. Key words ("companion," "writing," "work," etc.) and phrases ("reflect on it") appear, mutate and thread through fields of thought—*thinking fields*, as it were, in which the thinking is twistingly *ambi-valent* as to its agency and location and seems to embody a radial process of orientation. Questions, speculations, and a range of tentative verbal gestures spread out in radiant ecologies of attention and thoughtful definition. As in Blake's later "Prophetic" books, the text is relentless—no rest, no resolution, no reduction to subjectivity, and no transcendence in any repeatable or referentially constant sense. Holes in the historical, the social, and the psychological are mirrored in time-warps in the syntactical. Here as elsewhere in both the "fiction" and "discourse," it is the *field* that thinks and speaks. Reading entrains to the state of the field, as if "meaning" is what rises up from beneath the text and between the words, sentences and thoughts that hold attention. This attention is provisional, only held until the axial moment cuts it loose and returns it to the field in an*other* state of receptivity. In these ontological "tellings," the poetics of reading and of thinking become a single discipline.

When the field of reading is thus aroused, it becomes a very particular "energy construct"[14] at work "behind signification," overriding genre and other categorical distinctions. For instance, Blanchot's way of axially/musically reverberating key words in the *récit*, mentioned above, is linked to a processual opening of, as it were, concept words employed in rigorous thinking. For the most part these are really ordinary words seeming to do the big work of philosophical terminology by slowly, continuously gathering (working) and dispelling (unworking) a charge. The word becomes a torsional matrix of meanings that unfold from the incessant, recurrent (un)work. The integrity of the continuous *opening of the word inside writing* retains it *outside the language-space* wherein affirmation and negation reside. These—what to call them?— "dissipative" words, "mind-degradable" terms?—include, for example, "death," "space," and "literature" in the works presented here and in, especially, *The Space of Literature*,[15] but also "patience," "waiting," "attention," "passivity," and others that become fully thematical in works such as *The Writing of Disaster*.[16] In each case a signifier puts before us a signification that stands outside the ordinary meaning paired with a contrary; thus, "death" as organic termination of life becomes an impossibility, while death as dying characterizes all life; "literature" no longer contrasts with mere writing and arches beyond any valorized sense of cultural production; "patience" is not exclusive of impatience; "passivity" may be operative within both passivity and action; "waiting" is not waiting *for* anything; and "attention" exceeds what attention pays attention to. These "transcendent" terms recall, in their relationless relation to the ordinary words that they both "ruin" and extend, expressions from negative theologies and mystical or esoteric studies that similarly attempt to express what the oppositions of ordinary language render ineffable: the "Unground" of Meister Eckhart, the "Gateless Gate" of Zen Buddhism, the "rootless root" of Dzogchen,[17] and so forth.

Blanchot has devoted many careful studies to writers on mystical, theological, and theophanic topics, and a fair reading of them will show him by no means unsympathetic and, even, as he says in relation to Simone Weil, a "friend" of the work. Beyond this direct interest, the *récits* sometimes deliver dramatic and phenomenologically vivid narrations of initiatic journeys (the first two chapters of *Thomas the Obscure*), epiphanies of timeless states (*When the Time Comes*), returns from the dead (*Death Sentence*), and reports of detachment and ecstasy (*The Madness of the Day*). It would be strange not to inquire into the relation between these persistent, explicit concerns and the esoteric teachings which they so strikingly parallel, indeed offering so many astonishing insights.

An "occult reading" of Blanchot is undeniably possible, even impossible to deny, and, indeed, despite the probability that it would not be taken seriously by most current students of Blanchot, it is probably inevitable, given the sense of Mystery that pervades the *récits*. Yet to see Blanchot in such texts as liminal to the esoteric in fact deepens the free space of the work and allows it what is certainly one of its unexplored truths—that it is more mysterious than the Occult, because it remains free of that defining context while retaining the spirit of inquiry of serious esoteric writing.

Of course much of Blanchot's writing takes pains to distance itself from any suggestion of affinity with practices of, say, "mystical fusion," favoring, in this regard, the thought of Emmanuel Lévinas and Franz Rosenzweig, which sees in the difficult distance of prosaic conversation (as opposed to poetic rapture or any form of communion) the possibility of ethical life. Yet often Blanchot's writing is uncommonly sensitive to the nuances of awareness and "altered states"[18] and seems to articulate, with a precision rarely equaled by mystical thinkers themselves, the very heart of the mystical. Consider this passage from Blanchot's piece on Simone Weil:

> Attention is waiting: not the effort, the tension, or the mobilization of knowledge around something with which one might concern oneself. Attention waits. It waits without precipitation, leaving empty what is empty and keeping our haste, our impatient desire, and, even more, our horror of emptiness from prematurely filling it up. Attention is the emptiness of thought oriented by a gentle force and maintained in an accord with the empty intimacy of time.
>
> Attention is impersonal. It is not the self that is attentive in attention; rather, with an extreme delicacy and through insensible, constant contacts, attention has always already detached me from myself, freeing me for the attention that I for an instant become.[19]

Attention, emptiness, and detachment—familiar concerns, of course, in the nuanced philosophical texts of Mahayana Buddhism, and it might not be difficult to convince even the most sophisticated practitioner of Buddhist meditation that the above text offered commentary on the Teachings.[20] It renders articulate the most intimate reaches of both compassional and contemplative experience, territories that Blanchot knows must be shielded, through a kind of reserve, from the necessary violence of speech, and yet, because the emptiness here is precisely that of a *thinking*, there is a demand that language, also with "gentle force" and "in accord with the empty intimacy of time," not abandon its role.

Whether in the literature of esotericism or in the work of Blanchot, what stands outside the totality of speech still submits to a kind of *unknowing knowing*—as if mind and language were destined to provide an intimacy with their own outside. It's an uncanny intimacy without fusion, enigmatically made possible by the very distance that keeps that outside apart. This same enigma, Blanchot will tell us, resides at the origin of language itself.

In the West, the Gnostic writings of the early Christian centuries, quickly declared heretical for (we conjecture) little more than the radical independence and pluck of their textuality, offers a body of thought that curiously "twins" that of Blanchot—an intimacy with the most distant, bearing witness to a knowing that destroys the knowledge sustaining all worldly power. We have found no discussion of Gnosticism in Blanchot, but *Thomas the Obscure* has long seemed to us to echo in some impossible way *The Gospel of Thomas*: "These are the *obscure words* that the living Jesus spoke and Didymos Jude Thomas wrote down."[21] Is there a secret affinity held in reserve? A source of secret wonder and ecstasy under the mad transformations of *Thomas the Obscure*, an undisclosed concern belonging to "the hand that does not write," whose "right to intervene" governs not the content and not the style but the very tonality and resonance, the *rhythmus* and the *undertime* of the writing? Is it neurosis, psychosis, or something between unknown and profoundly known, a "lognosis"? Can we not say of Blanchot's work what he writes of Heraclitus', that it delivers

a language that speaks through enigma, the enigmatic Difference, but without complacency and without appeasing it: on the contrary, making it speak, and, even before it be word, already declaring it as *logos*, that highly singular name in which is reserved the nonspeaking origin of that which summons to speech and at its highest level, there where everything is silence, *"neither speaks nor conceals, but gives a sign.*[22]

George Quasha and *Charles Stein*
Barrytown, New York

[1] The title, *The Station Hill Blanchot Reader*, replaces our original projected title, *A Blanchot Reader*, mainly for three reasons. First, Michael Holland's excellent and essential *The Blanchot Reader* (Blackwell Publishers, Ltd.: Oxford, 1995) was published in the meantime, offering a sense of "reader" that is at the other end of a spectrum from the present volume. He presents a "Blanchot" in the perspective of history, politics, and the writer's development over time, through a poignant choice of texts—many in English for the first time—and rich, informative and careful commentary indicating four stages of an evolving body of work. It is a book with a thesis that will always remain a part of how we read Blanchot.

Second, Christopher Fynsk helped us see that our book has no comparable organizing principle, certainly no thesis, but only the fact that Station Hill published these particular books, mostly "fiction"—the *récits*—and a relatively small collection of "essays" originally intended to be representative, in an introductory way (1981), of Blanchot's discourse. The texts are divided into two major sections represented by the inadequate (but perhaps not significantly misleading) names, "fiction" and "essays." But, although organized chronologically, in neither case is development or evolution emphasized. There is no claim that these works are Blanchot's most important or representative, only that they are, in and of themselves, of great value. Our concern is to allow them their own nature, their difference, their particular power. This "reader" standing as it does in such sharp contrast to Michael Holland's "reader" says that there in no "Reader" but only "readers"; given that the two neutralize each other, there is a potentially unlimited number, embodying any number of principles. A single reader could only distort the very possibility of knowing Blanchot's work "for oneself." Not one, not two, but plural: the open reader.

Third, the name *Station Hill* bespeaks a complex context of publishing literary and non-literary works from an underlying perspective of *metapoetics* in an even broader sense than the one discussed here. The title, then, marks the site of the distinction "publisher" in order to ensure that Blanchot's work, which has inspired no small part of our "publishing program," remain free of any confusion with that program.

Note that not everyone has reacted favorably to our title: indeed, Robert Kelly made the interesting suggestion that we name this book, *The American Blanchot Reader.*

[2] Writers such as Susan Sontag tried for years without success to interest American publishers in Blanchot. The critic P. Adams Sitney was instrumental in our first Blanchot publications. In 1977 at the Arnolfini Arts Center which we (Susan Quasha and George Quasha) had recently founded in conjunction with Station Hill Press in Rhinebeck, New York, Sitney suggested Blanchot as a high priority among major unpublished writers. The poet Robert Kelly directed us to two writers, living locally, who had a connection to Blanchot's work: Lydia Davis, who had published sections of her translation of *Death Sentence* in literary magazines, and Paul Auster, who subsequently worked as managing editor of Station Hill Press and later translated Blanchot's *Le Ressassement éternal* (published as *Vicious Circles*). Lydia Davis would go on to translate other books by Blanchot, including the essays contained in *The Gaze of Orpheus and Other Essays,* selected by P. Adams Sitney, who himself contributed an important critical statement as Afterword. Stan Lewis, who happened to run the Parnassus Bookstore across the street from Station Hill Press in Rhinebeck, had already in 1973 (under the name David Lewis, Inc.) published *Thomas the Obscure* in a beautifully designed hardback edition of Robert

Lamberton's translation. Later, Station Hill would issue the first trade paperback edition. Stan Lewis thus had made the first serious attempt to bring Blanchot to the trade book world in America, although his publication, extraordinary in every way, received little distribution and attention.

[3] The range of meanings of Greek "meta-" includes "between, with, beside, after," in Pokorny 2. me- 702: *The American Heritage Dictionary*.

[4] Charles Olson, along with certain others who taught at the innovative and influential Black Mountain College in the late 1940s and early 1950s (notably John Cage and Robert Duncan), may be seen as part of the same historical "axis" as Blanchot in a redefining period for writing on both sides of the Atlantic. Olson's most influential statement, though only one of many important efforts to define a new poetics, is "Projective Verse," in *Collected Prose*, eds. Donald Allen and Benjamin Friedlander, Introduction by Robert Creeley, University of California Press: Berkeley, 1997. Station Hill is currently publishing Olson's *The Special View of History* (ed. Ann Charters), which bears upon the questions we are raising here.

[5] In Olson's definition of a poem as "composition by field," "the poem must, at all points, be a high-energy construct and, at all points, an energy-discharge." (*Collected Prose,* p.240.) Blanchot, speaking of energy in "The Limit-Experience," says: "Let us not immediately evoke Nietzsche, but Blake: 'Energy is the only life. Energy is Eternal delight" and even Van Gogh: 'There is good in every energetic movement,' for energy is thought (intensity, density, the sweetness of thought pushed to the limit.)" (*The Infinite Conversation,* translated by Susan Hanson, University of Minnesota Press: Minneapolis, 1993, p.453, n.7.)

[6] Blanchot himself sometimes comes close to stating a metapoetic principle of axiality:

"The image is the duplicity of revelation. The image is what veils by revealing; it is the veil that reveals by reveiling in all the ambiguous indecision of the word reveal. The image is image by means of this duplicity, being not the object's double, but the initial division that then permits the thing to be figured; still further back than this doubling it is a folding, a turn of the turning, the 'version' that is always in the process of inverting itself and that in itself bears the back and forth of a divergence. The speech of which we are trying to speak is a return to this first turning—a noun that must be heard as a verb, as the movement of a turning, a vertigo wherein rest the whirlwind, the leap and the fall. Note that the names chosen for the two directions of our literary language accept the idea of this turning; poetry, rightly enough alludes to it most directly with the word 'verse,' while 'prose' goes right along its path by way of a detour that continually straightens itself out… but the turning must already be given for speech to turn about in the torsion of verse. The first turn, the original structure of turning (which later slackens in a back and forth linear movement) is poetry." (*The Infinite Conversation*, p. 30.)

[7] Such a list would be long, but it's worth pointing to a few of the many works that we think embody the "axial" at various levels of working poetics: Louis Zukofsky's *A* and *80 Flowers*, Charles Olson's *Maximus Poems*, Robert Duncan's *Passages*, Jack Spicer's *Language*, Robin Blaser's *The Holy Forest*, Edward Dorn's *Gunslinger*, John Cage's *Empty Words*, Robert Creeley's *Pieces*, Jackson Mac Low's *Bloomsday*, Robert Kelly's *Axon Dendron Tree* or *Sentence*, David Antin's *Talking*, Kenneth Irby's *Orexis*, Armand Schwerner's *The Tablets*, John Clark's *The End of This Side*, Nathaniel Mackey's *Lute of Gassire*, Clark

Coolidge's *The Crystal Text,* Franz Kamin's *Scribble Death,* Chris Mann's *Working Hypothesis,* Susan Howe's *Pythagorean Silence,* Larry Eigner's *Waters/Places/A Time,* Anne Lauterbach's *On a Stair....* We hasten to note that there are many apparent differences in thinking among these poets and between any one of them and Blanchot, but this would be a study in itself and hardly within our scope here. We are simply entertaining the notion of a linking principle.

[8] In anticipation of a well-intentioned retreat to Blanchot's inevitable contrary of "presence," avoiding reification, we acknowledge the difficulty and point the reader to Blanchot's meditation on reading in the essay of that name below (from *The Space of Literature*), particularly the last two pages, "The light, innocent Yes of reading."

[9] From the opening of Blake's *Jerusalem: The Emanation of the Giant Albion* (1804).

[10] Keats' Negative Capability has defined the center for apparently opposing poetics, that of T.S. Eliot and Charles Olson. Blake is probably the first to realize the transformative power of torsional/axial poetics in virtually all of the senses intended here. See "Orc as a Fiery Paradigm of Poetic Torsion," George Quasha, in *Blake's Visionary Forms Dramatic*, ed. David V. Erdman and John E. Grant, Princeton: 1970.

[11] "Reading by field" would seem to be the discipline implied by what Olson has called "composition by field." See above, "Projective Verse."

[12] The poetic principle we are applying here to thinking in language—that at every point it has a certain "torque"—is expressed in Olson's "thinking poem": "whatever is born or done this moment of time, has/ the qualities of/ this moment of/ time." ("Against Wisdom as Such," *Collected Prose*, p. 263.) "An American," says Olson, "is a complex of occasions." ("*Maximus to Gloucester, Letter 27* [withheld]," *The Maximus Poems*, ed. George F. Butterick, University of California Press: Berkeley, 1983, p. 185.) In other words, for an American, according to Olson, order, identity, and meaning itself are rooted in locality and occasion, not traditional categories. For Blanchot, whose thinking might seem to be without location (except, for instance, in specific political writing) and where the effacement of optical presence is a matter of principle, the axial renders thinking itself concrete and actual, immediate and even "site-specific" *within the text*, within *reading*. Paradoxically, in both Olson and Blanchot, *axial* is *actual*. Here, for us, is where reading "in the American grain" opens to Blanchot's *writing beyond*.

[13] For this to be so, could it be that, at the deepest level, the poetic is a possibility within the very nature of thinking, the realization of which carries thinking beyond limitation? If the axial as the root of both poetry and thinking would disclose their common subversive nature, what do we make of thought's wish to stand apart from the poetic, from Plato to Lévinas?

Perhaps seeing Blanchot's thinking as axial also attends its intrinsic response to Heidegger's "Most thought-provoking in our thought-provoking time is that we are still not thinking."

[14] See note 5 above.

[15] Translated by Ann Smock, University of Nebraska Press: Lincoln, 1982.

[16] Translated by Ann Smock, University of Nebraska Press: Lincoln, 1986, 1995.

[17] See Herbert Guenther, *The Matrix of Mystery: Scientific and Humanistic Aspects of rDzogs-chen Thought* (Shambhala Publications: Boulder, 1984): "Experience-as-such, having no

root,/Is the root of all that is./Experience-as-such is gnosemic language;/Gnosemic language is the Wish-Fulfilling Gem Cloud."

[18] An unfortunate term, of course, which *The One Who Was Standing Apart from Me* would be enough to annihilate. This *récit* is a sort of Klein Bottle of "consciousness"— what alters? And toward what? Or is there only the *ever-altering*, and affliction is the fantasy of a *normal*?

[19] "Affirmation (desire, affliction)," *The Infinite Conversation*, p.121.

[20] To be sure, serious Western students and practitioners of Eastern religions, concerned to bring to their experience of non-Western possibilities the finest instruments of Western thought, can do no better than study Maurice Blanchot.

[21] In "Didymos Jude (or Judas)"—meaning "Jude the Twin" (taken in the Syrian church as the twin of Jesus)—perhaps we hear a twinning principle by which *Thomas the Obscure* twins *Jude the Obscure* (Thomas Hardy) as well as the *words obscure* of the *Gospel*, the one Gospel that is not a narrative but a *récit* of the often enigmatic sayings of Jesus (by way of his Twin); a principle, too, that matures in the mysterious dialogical twin of *The One Who Was Standing Apart from Me*.

[22] "Heraclitus," *The Infinite Conversation*, p.92.

Biographical Notes

Maurice Blanchot, born in 1907, is the author of some thirty-five books of fiction and literary and philosophical discourse, the majority of which are now available in English (listed below). His enormous importance for contemporary literature and thought is finally being recognized outside France, and critical studies abound in English as in French. The recent extensive "biographical essay" by Christoph Bident, *Partenaire invisible* (Editions Champ Vallon, 1998) gives a new perspective on the work in view of the life. It includes a full-scale bibliography of works in French. A chronology of his works in French and lists of his works and secondary literature in English may be found on the World Wide Web: http://lists.village.virginia.edu/~spoons/blanchot/blanchot_mainpage.htm.

Lydia Davis is the translator of works by Michel Butor, Michel Leiris, Justine Levy and other French writers, and is the author of books of fiction including *Break It Down*, *Almost No Memory*, and *The End of the Story*. She is on the faculty of the MFA program at Bard College.

Paul Auster is the author of numerous works—poetry, fiction, criticism, and screenplays—including *Hand to Mouth: A Chronicle of Early Failure*, *The New York Trilogy*, the films *Smoke* and *Lulu on the Bridge*, which he also directed. He has translated many poets and is the editor of *The Random House Book of Twentieth-Century French Poetry*.

Robert Lamberton is the author of *Essay on the Life and Poetry of Homer*, *Homer the Theologian: Neoplatonist Allegorical Reading and the Growth of the Epic Tradition*, *Homer's Theology*, and *Hesiod*. His translations include the Greek Neoplatonic commentators on Homer (e.g., *Porphyry on the Cave of the Nymphs*) and he is co-editor of *Homer's Ancient Readers: The Hermeneutics of Greek Epic's Earliest Exegetes*. His subjects range from the classics to film and contemporary literature, and he is Associate Professor of Classics at Washington University in St. Louis.

Christopher Fynsk is Professor of Comparative Literature and Philosophy at The State University of New York at Binghamton, is the author of *Heidegger: Thought and Historicity*, *Language and Relation:…that there is language* and *Infant Figures*.

George Quasha, publisher of Station Hill Press/Barrytown, Ltd., is co-editor of *Open Poetry* and *America a Prophecy* and author of several volumes of poetry including *Somapoetics*, *Giving the Lily Back Her Hands* and *Ainu Dreams* and, with Charles Stein, a series of books on video-installation artist Gary Hill: *Hand Heard/Liminal Objects*, *Tall Ships*, and *Viewer*.

Charles Stein, associate publisher of Station Hill Press/Barrytown, Ltd., is editor of *Being=Space x Action*, author of several volumes of poetry including *Parts and Other Parts*, *Horse Sacrifice* and *The Hat Rack Tree*, and a critical study of Charles Olson, *The Secret of the Black Chrysanthemum*.

OTHER BOOKS IN ENGLISH
BY MAURICE BLANCHOT

Thomas the Obscure (New Version), tr. Robert Lamberton, first in English: New York: David Lewis, 1973; new edition: Barrytown, NY: Station Hill Press, 1988.

Death Sentence, tr. Lydia Davis, Barrytown, NY: Station Hill Press, 1978.

The Gaze of Orpheus and other Literary Essays, ed. P. Adams Sitney, tr. Lydia Davis, pref. Geoffrey Hartman, Barrytown: Station Hill Press, 1981.

The Madness of the Day, tr. Lydia Davis, Barrytown: Station Hill Press, 1981.

The Sirens' Song: Selected Essays, ed. Gabriel Josipovici, tr. Sacha Rabinovitch, Bloomington: Indiana University Press, 1982.

The Space of Literature, tr. Ann Smock, Lincoln and London: University of Nebraska Press, 1982.

The Step Not Beyond, tr. Lycette Nelson, Albany: State University of New York Press, 1982

When the Time Comes, tr. Lydia Davis, Barrytown: Station Hill Press, 1985.

Vicious Circles: Two Fictions & "After the Fact," tr. Paul Auster, Barrytown, NY: Station Hill Press, 1985.

The Writing of the Disaster, tr. Ann Smock Lincoln: University of Nebraska Press, 1986.

The Last Man, tr. Lydia Davis, New York: Columbia University Press, 1987. "Michel Foucault as I Imagine Him," tr. Jeffrey Mehlman, in *Foucault / Blanchot,* New York: Zone Books, 1987.

The Unavowable Community, tr. Pierre Joris, Barrytown: Station Hill Press, 1988.

The One Who Was Standing Apart From Me, tr. Lydia Davis, Barrytown, NY: Station Hill Press: 1992.

The Infinite Conversation, tr. Susan Hanson, Minneapolis and London: University of Minnesota Press, 1993.

The Work of Fire, tr. Charlotte Mandell, Stanford: Stanford University Press, 1995.

The Blanchot Reader, ed. Michael Holland, Oxford: Blackwell, 1995. Contents;

The Most High, tr. Allan Stoekl, Lincoln: University of Nebraska Press, 1996.

Awaiting Oblivion, tr. John Gregg, Lincoln: University of Nebraska Press, 1997.

Friendship, tr. Elizabeth Rottenberg, Stanford: Stanford University Press, 1997.